Praise for Margaret Atwood's
MaddAddam

"What a joy it is to see Margaret Atwood taking such delicious pleasure in the end of the world. . . . Atwood's prose miraculously balances humor, outrage, and beauty. . . . By the moving end of *MaddAddam*, we understand how language and writing produced the beautiful fiction that described our beginnings."
—*The New York Times Book Review*

"[Atwood's] vision of global disaster in the not-too-distant future is thrilling, funny, touching and, yes, horrific."
—*The Washington Post*

"Fiction master Margaret Atwood wields a mighty pen."
—*O, The Oprah Magazine*

"The most profound [book] of the trilogy. . . . An adventure story and a philosophical meditation on humanity's predilection for carnage and creation."
—*The Economist*

"Sardonically funny. . . . [Atwood] certainly has the tone exactly right, both for the linguistic hypocrisy that can disguise any kind of catastrophe, and for the contemptuous dismissal of those who point to disaster. . . . *MaddAddam* is at once a pre- and a post-apocalypse story."
—*The Wall Street Journal*

"The culmination of a satirical dystopian saga a decade in the making. . . . Full of adventure and intrigue." —*San Francisco Chronicle*

MARGARET ATWOOD

MaddAddam

Margaret Atwood, whose work has been published in thirty-five countries, is the author of more than forty books of fiction, poetry, and critical essays. In addition to *The Handmaid's Tale*, her novels include *Cat's Eye*, shortlisted for the 1989 Booker Prize; *Alias Grace*, which won the Giller Prize in Canada and the Premio Mondello in Italy; *The Blind Assassin*, winner of the 2000 Booker Prize; *Oryx and Crake*, shortlisted for the 2003 Man Booker Prize; and *The Year of the Flood*. She is the recipient of the *Los Angeles Times* Innovator's Award, and lives in Toronto with the writer Graeme Gibson.

www.margaretatwood.ca

ALSO BY MARGARET ATWOOD

...

FICTION

POETRY

Double Persephone
The Circle Game
The Animals in That Country
The Journals of Susanna Moodie
Procedures for Underground
Power Politics
You Are Happy
Selected Poems: 1965–1975
Two-Headed Poems
True Stories
Interlunar
Selected Poems II: Poems Selected and New, 1976–1986
Morning in the Burned House
Eating Fire: Selected Poetry, 1965–1995
The Door

NONFICTION

Survival: A Thematic Guide to Canadian Literature
Days of the Rebels, 1815–1840
Second Words
Strange Things: The Malevolent North in Canadian Literature
Two Solicitudes: Conversations (with Victor-Lévy Beaulieu)
Negotiating with the Dead: A Writer on Writing
Moving Targets: Writing with Intent, 1982–2004
Curious Pursuits: Occasional Writing
Writing with Intent: Essays, Reviews, Personal Prose, 1983–2005
Payback: Debt and the Shadow Side of Wealth
In Other Worlds: SF and the Human Imagination

MaddAddam

A NOVEL

MARGARET ATWOOD

Anchor Books
A Division of Random House LLC
New York

FIRST ANCHOR BOOKS EDITION, AUGUST 2014

Earlier versions of some chapters in this book have appeared in *ARC Magazine* (U.K.) and in a very limited edition called *Bearlift*, produced for fund-raising purposes.

The Library of Congress has cataloged the Nan A. Talese/Doubleday edition as follows:
Atwood, Margaret.
Maddaddam : a novel / Margaret Atwood. — First American Edition.
pages cm
1. Science fiction. I. Title.
PR9199.3.A8M34 2013 813'.54—dc23 2013018715

Anchor Trade Paperback ISBN: 978-0-307-45548-2
eBook ISBN: 978-0-385-53783-4

Book design by Pei Loi Koay

www.anchorbooks.com

Printed in the United States of America
10 9 8

For my family

and for Larry Gaynor (1939–2010)

Contents

SCARS

ZEB IN THE DARK

SNOWMAN'S PROGRESS

BLACKLIGHT HEADLAMP

BONE CAVE

The MaddAddam Trilogy: The Story So Far

The first two books in the MaddAddam trilogy are Oryx and Crake *and* The Year of the Flood. MaddAddam *is the third book.*

1. Oryx and Crake

As the story begins, Snowman is living in a tree by the seashore. He believes he is the last true human being left alive after a lethal pandemic has swept the planet. Nearby live the Children of Crake, a gentle humanoid species bioengineered by the brilliant Crake, Snowman's one-time best friend and rival for his beloved, the beautiful and enigmatic Oryx.

The Crakers are free from sexual jealousy, greed, clothing, and the need for insect repellent and animal protein — all the factors Crake believed had caused not only the misery of the human race but also the degradation of the planet. The Crakers mate seasonally, when parts of them turn blue. Crake tried to rid them of symbolic thinking and music, but they have an eerie singing style all their own and have developed a religion, with Crake as their creator, Oryx as mistress of the animals, and Snowman as their reluctant prophet. It is he who has led them out of the high-tech Paradice dome where they were made to their present home beside the ocean.

In his pre-plague life, Snowman was Jimmy. His world was divided into the Compounds — fortified Corporations containing the technocrat elite that controlled society through their collective security arm, the CorpSeCorps — and the pleeblands outside Compound walls, where the rest of society lived, shopped, and scammed, in their slums, their suburbs, and their malls.

Jimmy's early childhood was spent at OrganInc Farms, where his father was working on the pigoons — transgenic pigs with human material designed for transplants, including kidneys and brain tissue. Later, his father was transferred to HelthWyzer, a health-and-wellness Corp. It was at the HelthWyzer high school that adolescent Jimmy first met Crake, then known as Glenn. They bonded over internet porn and complex online games. Among these was Extinctathon, run by the cryptic identity MaddAddam: *Adam named the living animals, Madd-Addam names the dead ones.* They learned to access MaddAddam via a chatroom accessible only to trusted Grandmasters of the game.

Crake and Jimmy lost touch when Crake was accepted at the well-funded Watson-Crick Institute, while word-guy Jimmy had to make do with the run-down Martha Graham liberal arts academy. Oddly, both Crake's mother and stepfather died of a mysterious illness that caused them to dissolve. Then a bioterrorist group with the code-name MaddAddam began using genetically engineered animals and microbes to attack the CorpSeCorps and the ruling infrastructure.

When Jimmy and Crake reconnected years later, Crake was in charge of the Paradice dome, where he was gene-splicing the Crakers. At the same time, he was developing the BlyssPluss pill, which promised sexual ecstasy, birth control, and prolonged youth. Jimmy was surprised to discover that the names of the scientists at Paradice were identical to the user names in the Extinctathon game. In fact, they were the MaddAddamite bioterrorists, traced by Crake via the chatroom, then promised immunity in exchange for their input at Paradice. But the BlyssPluss pill contained a hidden ingredient, and its launch coincided with the onset of the pandemic that erased humanity. In the chaos that resulted, Oryx and Crake both perished, leaving Jimmy alone with the Crakers.

Now, haunted by his memories of dead Oryx and of treacherous Crake, and despairing of his own prospects for survival, an ailing and guilt-ridden Snowman hikes to the Paradice dome in search of the weapons and supplies he knows are there. En route, he's stalked by escaped gen-mod animals, among them the vicious wolvogs and the giant pigoons, made crafty by their human brain tissue.

Oryx and Crake ends with Snowman's discovery of three others who have survived the plague. Should he join them, abandoning the Crakers? Or, knowing the destructive tendencies of his own species, should he kill them? *Oryx and Crake* ends while Snowman is deciding.

2. The Year of the Flood

The Year of the Flood takes place during the same years as *Oryx and Crake*, but is set in the pleeblands outside Compound walls. The story follows the God's Gardeners, a green religion founded by Adam One. Its leaders, the Adams and the Eves, teach the convergence of Nature and Scripture, the love of all creatures, the dangers of technology, the wickedness of the Corps, the avoidance of violence, and the tending of vegetables and bees on pleebland slum rooftops.

The story begins in the present, in Gardener Year Twenty-five – the year of the Waterless Flood, as the Gardeners call the plague. Toby, armed with an archaic rifle, is holed up in the AnooYoo Spa, watching for other survivors – especially Zeb, the streetwise ex-Gardener whom she secretly loves. Violating Gardener codes, she shoots one of the pigoons that have been attacking her kitchen garden. One day she sees a procession of naked people in the distance, headed by a ragged, bearded man. Knowing nothing about Snowman and the Crakers, she believes she is hallucinating.

Meanwhile, young Ren is locked inside the quarantine room of Scales and Tails, the strip club where she's been working. Just before the plague, the club was wrecked by Painballers – dehumanized prisoners of the Corps who have ruthlessly eliminated the other combatants in the Painball arena. Ren knows she will starve to death unless her childhood friend, Amanda, can arrive to unlock the door.

Long before, Toby had been rescued from the abusive Painballer, Blanco, her boss at the unpleasant SecretBurgers stand, by the God's Gardeners. She became an Eve, specializing in mushrooms, bees, and potions. Her teacher, old Pilar – who, like many Gardeners, is a bioscience refugee from the Corps – is secretly still in touch with informants there, including the adolescent Crake.

Ren was one of Toby's Gardener pupils, along with Amanda, a

tough but charismatic pleebrat. Ren's mother, Lucerne, had run away from the HelthWyzer Compound with Zeb, but angered by his failure to commit, she fled the Gardeners and returned to HelthWyzer when Ren was thirteen. Teenaged Jimmy seduced Ren but then discarded her. Eventually she chose to earn her living by dancing at Scales and Tails, the best option available to her.

Disagreeing about tactics, Zeb and his supporters split from Adam One's pacifist Gardeners to engage in active bioterrorist opposition to the Corps, using the MaddAddam chatroom as a rendezvous. The remaining Gardeners, forced into hiding by the CorpSeCorps, continued to prepare for the Waterless Flood.

In the present – Year Twenty-five – Amanda reaches Scales and manages to free Ren. As they celebrate, three of their Gardener friends – Shackleton, Crozier, and Oates – arrive, pursued by Blanco and two other Painballers. The five young people flee, but along the way Ren and Amanda are raped, Amanda is kidnapped, and Oates is murdered.

Ren struggles to the AnooYoo Spa, where Toby nurses her back to health. Then they set out to recover Amanda. After dodging feral pigoons and dealing with vicious Blanco, they find a group of survivors living in a parkette cobb house. Zeb is there, with his group of MaddAddamites; so are a few former Gardeners. They all believe that Adam One must have survived, and are searching for him.

Toby and Ren leave on a risky mission to recover Amanda from her Painballer captors. At the seashore they stumble upon an encampment of strange, partly blue people who have seen two human men and a woman. Guessing these must be Amanda and her Painball kidnappers, Toby and Ren discover them just as Snowman – infected and hallucinating – is about to shoot them with his Paradice spraygun.

The Year of the Flood ends with the Painballers tied to a tree while Ren tends to the battered Amanda and the feverish Snowman. As Toby observes the Gardener forgiveness feast of Saint Julian by serving soup to everyone, the blue-hued Children of Crake approach along the shore, singing their eerie music.

MaddAddam

Egg

The Story of the Egg, and of Oryx and Crake, and how they made People and Animals; and of the Chaos; and of Snowman-the-Jimmy; and of the Smelly Bone and the coming of the Two Bad Men

In the beginning, you lived inside the Egg. That is where Crake made you.

Yes, good, kind Crake. Please stop singing or I can't go on with the story.

The Egg was big and round and white, like half a bubble, and there were trees inside it with leaves and grass and berries. All the things you like to eat.

Yes, it rained inside the Egg.

No, there was not any thunder.

Because Crake did not want any thunder inside the Egg.

And all around the Egg was the chaos, with many, many people who were not like you.

Because they had an extra skin. That skin is called *clothes*. Yes, like mine.

And many of them were bad people who did cruel and hurtful things to one another, and also to the animals. Such as . . . We don't need to talk about those things right now.

And Oryx was very sad about that, because the animals were her Children. And Crake was sad because Oryx was sad.

And the chaos was everywhere outside the Egg. But inside the Egg there was no chaos. It was peaceful there.

And Oryx came every day to teach you. She taught you what to eat, she taught you to make fire, she taught you about the animals, her Children. She taught you to purr if a person is hurt. And Crake watched over you.

Yes, good, kind Crake. Please stop singing. You don't have to sing every time. I'm sure Crake likes it, but he also likes this story and he wants to hear the rest.

Then one day Crake got rid of the chaos and the hurtful people, to make Oryx happy, and to clear a safe place for you to live in.

Yes, that did make things smell very bad for a while.

And then Crake went to his own place, up in the sky, and Oryx went with him.

I don't know why they went. It must have been a good reason. And they left Snowman-the-Jimmy to take care of you, and he brought you to the seashore. And on Fish Days you caught a fish for him, and he ate it.

I know you would never eat a fish, but Snowman-the-Jimmy is different.

Because he has to eat a fish or he would get very sick.

Because that is the way he is made.

Then one day Snowman-the-Jimmy went to see Crake. And when he came back, there was a hurt on his foot. And you purred on it, but it did not get better.

And then the two bad men came. They were left over from the chaos.

I don't know why Crake didn't clear them away. Maybe they were hiding under a bush, so he didn't see them. But they'd caught Amanda, and they were doing cruel and hurtful things to her.

We don't need to talk about those things right now.

And Snowman-the-Jimmy tried to stop them. And then I came, and Ren, and we caught the two bad men and tied them to a tree with a rope. Then we sat around the fire and ate soup. Snowman-the-Jimmy ate the soup, and Ren, and Amanda. Even the two bad men ate the soup.

Yes, there was a bone in the soup. Yes, it was a smelly bone.

I know you do not eat a smelly bone. But many of the Children of Oryx like to eat such bones. Bobkittens eat them, and rakunks, and pigoons, and liobams. They all eat smelly bones. And bears eat them.

I will tell you what a bear is later.

We don't need to talk any more about smelly bones right now.

And as they were all eating the soup, you came with your torches, because you wanted to help Snowman-the-Jimmy, because of his hurt foot. And because you could tell there were some women who were blue, so you wanted to mate with them.

You didn't understand about the bad men, and about why they had a rope on them. It is not your fault they ran away into the forest. Don't cry.

Yes, Crake must be very angry with the bad men. Perhaps he will send some thunder.

Yes, good, kind Crake.

Please stop singing.

Rope

Rope

About the events of that evening — the events that set human malice loose in the world again — Toby later made two stories. The first story was the one she told out loud, to the Children of Crake; it had a happy outcome, or as happy as she could manage. The second, for herself alone, was not so cheerful. It was partly about her own idiocy, her failure to pay attention, but also it was about speed. Everything had happened so quickly.

She'd been tired, of course; she must have been suffering from an adrenalin plunge. After all, she'd been going strong for two days with a lot of stress and not much to eat.

The day before, she and Ren had left the safety of the MaddAddam cobb-house enclave that sheltered the few survivors from the global pandemic that had wiped out humanity. They'd been tracking Ren's best friend, Amanda, and they'd found her just in time because the two Painballers who'd been using her had almost used her up. Toby was familiar with the ways of such men: she'd been almost killed by one of them before she'd become a God's Gardener. Anyone who'd survived Painball more than once had been reduced to the reptilian brain. Sex until you were worn to a fingernail was their mode; after that, you were dinner. They liked the kidneys.

Toby and Ren had crouched in the shrubbery while the Painballers argued over the rakunk they were eating, and whether to attack the Crakers, and what to do next with Amanda. Ren had been scared silly; Toby hoped she wouldn't faint, but she couldn't worry about that because she was nerving herself to fire. Which to shoot first, the bearded one or the shorthair? Would the other have time to grab their spraygun? Amanda wouldn't be able to help, or even run: they had a rope around her neck, with the other end tied to the leg of the bearded one. A wrong move by Toby, and Amanda would be dead.

Then a strange man had shambled out of the bushes, sunburnt and scabby and naked and clutching a spraygun, and had almost shot everyone in sight, Amanda included. But Ren had screamed and run into the clearing, and that had been enough of a distraction. Toby had stepped out, rifle aimed; Amanda had torn free; and the Painballers had been subdued with the aid of some groin kicks and a rock, and tied up with their own rope and with strips torn from the pink AnooYoo Spa top-to-toe sun coverup that Toby had been wearing.

Ren had then busied herself with Amanda, who was possibly in shock, and also with the scabby naked man, whom she called Jimmy. She'd wrapped him up in the rest of the top-to-toe, talking to him softly; it seemed he was a long-ago boyfriend of hers.

Now that things were tidier, Toby had felt she could relax. She'd steadied herself with a Gardener breathing exercise, timing it to the soothing rhythm of the nearby waves – *wish-wash, wish-wash* – until her heart had slowed to normal. Then she'd cooked a soup.

And then the moon had risen.

The rising moon signalled the beginning of the God's Gardeners Feast of Saint Julian and All Souls: a celebration of God's tenderness and compassion for all creatures. *The universe is held in the hollow of His hand, as Saint Julian of Norwich taught us in her mystic vision so long ago. Forgiveness must be offered, loving kindness must be practised, circles must be unbroken. All souls means all, no matter what they may have done. At least from moonrise to moonset.*

Once the Gardener Adams and Eves taught you something, you stayed taught. It would have been next to impossible for her to kill the Painballers on that particular night – butcher them in cold blood, since by that time the two of them were firmly roped to a tree.

Amanda and Ren had done the roping. They'd been to Gardener school together where they'd done a lot of crafts with recycled materials, so they were proficient at knotwork. Those guys looked like macramé.

On that blessed Saint Julian's evening, Toby had set the weaponry to one side — her own antiquated rifle and the Painballers' spraygun, and Jimmy's spraygun as well. Then she'd played the kindly godmother, ladling out the soup, dividing up the nutrients for all to share.

She must have been mesmerized by the spectacle of her own nobility and kindness. Getting everyone to sit in a circle around the cozy evening fire and drink soup together — even Amanda, who was so traumatized she was almost catatonic; even Jimmy, who was shivering with fever and talking to a dead woman who was standing in the flames. Even the two Painballers: did she really think they would have a conversion experience and start hugging bunnies? It's a wonder she didn't sermonize as she doled out the bone soup. *Some for you, and some for you, and some for you! Shed the hatred and viciousness! Come into the circle of light!*

But hatred and viciousness are addictive. You can get high on them. Once you've had a little, you start shaking if you don't get more.

As they were eating the soup, they'd heard voices approaching through the shoreline trees. It was the Children of Crake, the Crakers — the strange gene-spliced quasi-humans who lived by the sea. They were filing through the trees, carrying pitch-pine torches and singing their crystalline songs.

Toby had seen these people only briefly, and in daytime. Gleaming in the moonlight and the torchlight, they were even more beautiful. They were all colours — brown, yellow, black, white — and all heights, but each was perfect. The women were smiling serenely; the men were in full courtship mode, holding out bunches of flowers, their naked bodies like a fourteen-year-old's comic-book rendition of how bodies ought to be, each muscle and ripple defined and glistening. Their bright blue and unnaturally large penises were wagging from side to side like the tails of friendly dogs.

...

Afterwards, Toby could never quite remember the sequence of events, if you could call it a sequence. It had been more like a pleebland street brawl: rapid action, tangled bodies, a cacophony of voices.

Where is the blue? We can smell the blue! Look, there is Snowman! He is thin! He is very sick!

Ren: *Oh shit, it's the Crakers. What if they want... Look at their... Crap!*

The Craker women, spotting Jimmy: *Let us help Snowman! He needs us to purr!*

The Craker men, sniffing Amanda: *She is the blue one! She smells blue! She wants to mate with us! Give her the flowers! She will be happy!*

Amanda, scared: *Stay away! I don't... Ren, help me!* Four large, beautiful, flower-toting naked men close in on her. *Toby! Get them away from me! Shoot them!*

The Craker women: *She is sick. First we have to purr on her. To make her better. And give her a fish?*

The Craker men: *She is blue! She is blue! We are happy! Sing to her! The other one is blue also.*

That fish is for Snowman. We must keep that fish.

Ren: *Amanda, maybe just take the flowers, or they might get mad or something...*

Toby, her voice thin and ineffectual: *Please, listen, stand back, you're frightening...*

What is this? Is this a bone? Several of the women, peering into the soup pot: *Are you eating this bone? It smells bad.*

We do not eat bones. Snowman does not eat bones, he eats a fish. Why do you eat a smelly bone?

It is Snowman's foot that is smelling like a bone. A bone left by vultures. Oh Snowman, we must purr on your foot!

Jimmy, feverish: *Who are you? Oryx? But you're dead. Everyone's dead. Everyone in the whole world, they're all dead...* He starts crying.

Do not be sad, Oh Snowman. We have come to help.

Toby: *Maybe you shouldn't touch... that's infected... he needs...*

Jimmy: *Ow! Fuck!*

Oh Snowman, do not kick. It will hurt your foot. Several of them begin to purr, making a noise like a kitchen mixer.

Ren, calling for help: *Toby! Toby! Hey! Let go of her!*

Toby looks over, across the fire: Amanda has disappeared in a flickering thicket of naked male limbs and backs. Ren throws herself into the sprawl and is quickly submerged.

Toby: *Wait! Don't... Stop that!* What should she do? This is a major cultural misunderstanding. If only she had a pail of cold water!

Muffled cries. Toby rushes to help, but then:

One of the Painballers: *Hey you! Over here!*

These ones smell very bad. They smell like dirty blood. Where is the blood?

What is this? This is a rope. Why are they tied up with a rope?

Snowman showed us rope *before, when he lived in a tree.* Rope *is for making his house. Oh Snowman, why is the rope tied to these men?*

This rope is hurting these ones. We must take it away.

A Painballer: *Yeah, that's right. We're in fucking agony.* (Groans.)

Toby: *Don't touch them, they'll...*

The second Painballer: *Fucking hurry up, Blueballs, before that old bitch...*

Toby: *No! Don't untie... Those men will...*

But it was already too late. Who knew the Crakers could be so quick with knots?

Procession

The two men were gone into the darkness, leaving behind them a snarl of rope and a scattering of embers. Idiot, Toby thought. You should have been merciless. Bashed their heads in with a rock, slit their throats with your knife, not even wasted any bullets on them. You were a dimwit, and your failure to act verges on criminal negligence.

It was hard to see – the fire was fading – but she made a quick inventory: at least her rifle was still there, a small mercy. But the Painballer spraygun was missing. Pinhead, she told herself. So much for your Saint Julian and the loving kindness of the universe.

Amanda and Ren were clinging to each other and crying, with several of the beautiful Craker women stroking them anxiously. Jimmy had toppled over and was talking to a bed of coals. The sooner they could all get back to the MaddAddam cobb house, the better, because they were sitting ducks out here in the dark. The Painballers might come back for the remaining weapons, and if that happened it was already clear to Toby that these Crakers would be no help. *Why did you hit me? Crake will be angry! He will send a thunder!* If she downed a Painballer, the Crakers would throw themselves between her and the finishing shot. *Oh, you have made bang, a man fell down, there is a hole in him, blood is coming out! He is hurt, we must help him!*

But even if the Painballers held off for the moment, there were other predators in the forest. The bobkittens, the wolvogs, the liobams; worse, the enormous feral pigs. And now, with the people gone from the cities and roads, who knew how soon the bears would begin to come down from the north?

· · ·

"We need to go now," she told the Crakers. Several heads turned, several sets of green eyes were looking at her. "Snowman must come with us."

The Crakers all started talking at once. "Snowman must stay with us! We must put Snowman back into his tree." "That is what he likes, he likes a tree." "Yes, only he can talk with Crake." "Only he can tell the words of Crake, about the Egg." "About the chaos." "About Oryx, who made the animals." "About how Crake made the chaos go away." "Good, kind Crake." They began singing.

"We need to get medicine," said Toby desperately. "Otherwise, Jimmy — otherwise, Snowman might die." Blank stares. Did they even understand what dying was?

"What is a *Jimmy*?" Puzzled frowns.

She'd made an error: wrong name. "Jimmy is another name for Snowman."

"Why?" "Why is it another name?" "What does a *Jimmy* mean?" This seemed to interest them much more than death. "Is it the pink skin on Snowman?" "I want a Jimmy too!" This last from a small boy.

How to explain? "Jimmy is a name. Snowman has two names."

"His name is Snowman-the-Jimmy?"

"Yes," said Toby, because it was now.

"Snowman-the-Jimmy, Snowman-the-Jimmy," they repeated to one another.

"Why are there two?" one asked, but the others had switched their attention to the next bewildering word. "What is *medicine*?"

"Medicine is something to help Snowman-the-Jimmy get better," she ventured. Smiles: they liked that idea.

"Then we will come too," said the one who seemed in charge — a tall, brownish-yellow man with a Roman nose. "We will carry Snowman-the-Jimmy."

Two of the Craker men lifted Jimmy easily. Toby was alarmed by his eyes: by the thin slits of white shining between his lids. "Flying," he said as the Crakers swung him into the air.

Toby found Jimmy's spraygun and gave it to Ren to carry, clicking the safety on first: the girl didn't know how to use the thing — why would she? — but it would be sure to come in handy later on.

She'd assumed that only the two Craker volunteers would come back to the cobb house, but the whole crowd tagged along, children included. They all wished to be close to Snowman. The men took turns carrying him; the rest held their torches high, singing from time to time in their eerie waterglass voices.

Four of the women walked with Ren and Amanda, patting them and touching their arms or hands. "Oryx will take care of you," they said to Amanda.

"Don't let any of those blue dicks fucking touch her again," said Ren to them fiercely.

"What is *blue dicks*?" they asked, bewildered. "What is *fucking touch*?"

"Just don't, or else," said Ren. "Or it's trouble!"

"Oryx will make her happy," said the women, though they sounded unsure. "What is *trouble*?"

"I'm okay," said Amanda faintly to Ren. "What about you?"

"You are not fucking okay! Let's just get you back to where the MaddAddams are," said Ren. "They've got beds, and a water pump, and everything. We can clean you up. Jimmy too."

"Jimmy?" said Amanda. "That's Jimmy? I thought he'd be dead, like everyone else."

"Yeah, so did I. But a lot of people aren't. Well, some people. Zeb's not, and Rebecca, and you and me, and Toby, and . . ."

"Where did those two guys go?" said Amanda. "The Painballers. I should've brained them when I had the chance." She laughed a little, blowing off pain in her old pleebrat way. "How far is it?" she said.

"They can carry you," said Ren.

"No. I'm fine."

Moths fluttered around the torches, overhead leaves riffled in the night breeze. How long did they walk? To Toby it seemed like hours, but time is unclear in moonlight. They were heading west, through the Heritage Park; behind them the sound of the waves receded. Though there was a path, she was unsure of the way, but the Crakers appeared to know where they were going.

She listened for sounds, off among the trees – a footfall, a stick cracking, a grunt – keeping herself to the rear of the procession, her rifle at the ready. There was a croaking, a chirp or two: some amphibian, a night bird stirring. She was conscious of the darkness at her back: her shadow stretched huge, blending with the deeper shadows behind.

Poppy

Finally they reached the cobb-house enclave. A single light bulb was burning in the yard; behind the barrier fence, Crozier and Manatee and Tamaraw were standing sentry with their sprayguns, wearing battery-run headlamps gleaned from a bike shop.

Ren ran forward. "It's us!" she called. "It's okay! We found Amanda!"

Crozier's headlamp bobbed as he opened the gate. "Way to go!" he shouted.

"Great! I'll tell the others!" said Tamaraw. She hurried off to the main building.

"Croze! We did it!" Ren said. She threw her arms around him, dropping the spraygun she'd been carrying, and he lifted her, twirled her around, and kissed her. Then he set her down.

"Hey, where'd you get the spraygun?" he said. Ren started crying.

"I thought they'd kill us!" she said. "Them, the two ... But you should've seen Toby! She was so badass! She had her old gun, and then we hit them with rocks, and then we tied them up, but then ..."

"Wow," said Manatee, surveying the Crakers who were crowding in through the gate, talking among themselves. "It's the Paradice dome circus."

"So these are them, right?" said Crozier. "The creepo naked people Crake made? The ones who live down by the shore?"

"I don't think you should call them creepo," said Ren. "They can hear you."

"It wasn't only Crake," said Manatee. "All of us worked on them at the Paradice Project. Me, Swift Fox, Ivory Bill ..."

"Why'd they come with you?" said Crozier. "What do they want?"

"They're only trying to help," said Toby. Suddenly she was very tired; all she wanted to do was stumble into her cubicle and conk out. "Has anyone else been here?" Zeb had left the cobb house at the same time she did, on a search for Adam One and any of the God's Gardeners who might have survived. She wanted to know if he'd returned, but she didn't want to be obvious about it: pining was whining, as the Gardeners used to say, and she'd never worn her heart anywhere near her sleeve.

"Only those pigs again," said Crozier. "Trying to dig under the garden fence. We shone the lights on them and they ran off. They know what a spraygun is."

"Ever since we turned a couple of them into bacon," said Manatee. "Frankenbacon, considering they're splices. I still feel kind of weird about eating them. They've got human neocortex tissue."

"I hope Crake's Frankenpeople aren't moving in with us," said a blond woman who'd come out of the main cobb building with Tamaraw. Toby recognized her from the brief time she'd spent at the cobb house before her search for Amanda: Swift Fox. She must have been over thirty, but she was wearing what looked like a twelve-year-old's ruffle-edged nightie. Now where had she picked that up? Toby wondered. Some looted HottTottsTogs or Hundred-Dollar Store?

"You must be exhausted," Tamaraw said to Toby.

"I don't know why you brought them with you," said Swift Fox. "There's too many of them. We can't feed them."

"We won't have to," said Manatee. "They eat leaves, remember? That's how Crake designed them. So they'd never need agriculture."

"Right," said Swift Fox. "You worked on that module. Me, I did the brains. The frontal lobes, the sensory-input modifications. I tried to make them less boring, but Crake wanted no aggression, no jokes even. They're walking potatoes."

"They're really nice," said Ren. "Anyway, the women are."

"I suppose the males wanted to mate with you; they'll do that. Just don't make me *talk* to them," said Swift Fox. "I'm going back to bed. Night all, have fun with the vegetables." She yawned and stretched, then sauntered slowly away.

"Why's she so crabby?" said Manatee. "She's been like that all day."

"Hormones is my guess," said Crozier. "Check out the nightie, though."

"Too small on her," said Manatee.

"You noticed," said Crozier.

"Maybe she has other reasons for being crabby," said Ren. "Women sometimes do, you know."

"Sorry," said Crozier, putting his arm around her.

Four of the Craker men detached themselves from the group and began to follow Swift Fox, blue penises waving back and forth. Somewhere they'd picked more flowers; they were starting to sing.

"No!" said Toby sharply, as if to dogs. "Stay here! With Snowman-the-Jimmy!" How to make it clear to them that, even with the aid of floral display and serenading and penis-wagging, they couldn't just pile on to any young non-Craker woman who smelled available to them? But they'd already disappeared around the corner of the main house.

The two Craker carriers lowered Jimmy down. He slumped limply against their knees. "Where will Snowman-the-Jimmy be?" they asked. "Where can we purr for him?"

"He'll need to be in a room by himself," said Toby. "We'll find a bed for him, and then I'll get the medicine."

"We will come with you," they said. "We will purr." They picked Jimmy up again, making a chair for him with their arms. The others crowded around.

"Not all of you," said Toby. "He needs to be quiet."

"He can have Croze's room," said Ren. "Can't he, Croze?"

"Who's that?" said Crozier, peering at Jimmy, whose head was lolling to one side, who was drooling into his beard, who was scratching fitfully at himself with one filthy hand through the pink fabric of the top-to-toe, and who noticeably stank. "Where'd you drag *him* in from? Why's he wearing pink? He looks like a fucking ballerina!"

"It's Jimmy," said Ren. "Remember, I told you? My old boyfriend?"

"The one who messed you over? From high school? That child molester?"

"Don't be like that," said Ren. "I wasn't really a child. He's got a fever."

"Don't go, don't go," said Jimmy. "Come back to the tree!"

"You're sticking up for him? After how he dumped you?"

"Yeah, right, but he's kind of a hero now," said Ren. "He helped save Amanda. He almost, you know, died."

"Amanda," said Croze. "I don't see her. Where is she?"

"She's over here," said Ren, pointing to the group of Craker women surrounding Amanda, stroking her and purring gently. They moved aside to let Ren into their circle.

"That's Amanda?" said Crozier. "No shit! She looks like . . ."

"Don't say it," said Ren, putting her arms around Amanda. "She'll look a lot better tomorrow. Or next week, anyway." Amanda started to cry.

"She's gone," said Jimmy. "She flew away. Pigoons."

"Cripes," said Crozier. "This is fucking weird."

"Croze, *everything* is fucking weird," said Ren.

"Okay, right, I'm sorry. I'm almost off sentry. Let's . . ."

"I think I should help Toby," said Ren. "At this moment."

"Looks like I sleep on the ground, since that fuckwit's tagged my bed," Croze said to Manatee.

"Please grow up," said Ren.

That's all we need, thought Toby. Love's young squabbles.

They carried Jimmy into Croze's cubicle and laid him down on the bed. Toby asked two Craker women and Ren to aim the flashlights she'd got from the kitchen. Then she found her medical materials, on the shelf where she'd left them before setting off to find Amanda.

She did all she could for Jimmy: a sponge bath to get off the worst of the dirt; honey applied to the superficial cuts; mushroom elixir for the infection. Then Poppy and Willow, for the pain and for a restful sleep. And the small grey maggots, applied to the foot wound to nibble off the infected flesh. Judging from the smell, the maggots were just in time.

"What are those?" said one of the two Craker women, the tall one. "Why do you put those little animals on Snowman-the-Jimmy? Are they eating him?"

"It tickles," said Jimmy. His eyes were half open; the Poppy was taking effect.

"Oryx sent them," said Toby. That seemed to be a good answer, because they smiled. "They are called *maggots*," she continued. "They are eating the pain."

"What does the pain taste like, Oh Toby?"

"Should we eat the pain too?"

"If we ate the pain, that would help Snowman-the-Jimmy."

"The pain smells very bad. Does it taste good?"

She should avoid metaphors. "The pain tastes good only to the maggots," she said. "No. You should not eat the pain."

"Will he be okay?" Ren said. "Has he got gangrene?"

"I hope not," said Toby. The two Craker women placed their hands on him and began to purr.

"Falling," said Jimmy. "Butterfly. She's gone."

Ren bent over him, brushed his hair back from his forehead. "Go to sleep, Jimmy," she said. "We love you."

Cobb
House

Morning

Toby dreams that she's in her little single bed, at home. Her stuffed lion is on the pillow beside her, and her big shaggy bear that plays a tune. Her antique piggy bank is on her desk, and the tablet she uses for her homework, and her felt-tip crayons, and her daisy-skinned cellphone. From the kitchen comes the sound of her mother's voice, calling; her father, answering; the smell of eggs frying.

Inside this dream, she's dreaming of animals. One is a pig, though six-legged; another is cat-like, with compound eyes like a fly. There's a bear as well, but it has hooves. These animals are neither hostile nor friendly. Now the city outside is on fire, she can smell it; fear fills the air. *Gone, gone,* says a voice, like a bell tolling. One by one the animals come towards her and begin to lick her with their warm, raspy tongues.

At the edge of sleep, she gropes towards the retreating dream: the burning city, the messengers sent to warn her. That the world has been changed utterly; that the familiar is long dead; that everything she used to love has been swept away.

As Adam One used to say, *The fate of Sodom is fast approaching. Suppress regret. Avoid the pillar of salt. Don't look back.*

She wakes to find a Mo'Hair licking her leg: a red-head, its long human hair braided into pigtails, each with a string bow: some sentimentalist among the MaddAddamites has been at work. It must have got out of the pen where they're keeping them.

"Move it," she says to it, shoving it gently with her foot. It gives her a look of addled reproach — they're none too bright, the Mo'Hairs — and clatters out through the doorway. We could use some doors around here, she thinks.

The morning light is filtering in through the piece of cloth that's been hung over the window in a futile attempt to keep out the mosquitoes. If only they could find some screens! But they'd have to install window frames because the cobb house wasn't built to be lived in: it had been a parkette staging pavilion for fairs and parties, and they're squatting in it now because it's safe. It's away from the urban rubble — the deserted streets and random electrical fires and the buried rivers that are welling up now that the pumps have failed. No collapsing building can fall down on it, and as it's only one storey high, it's unlikely to fall down on itself.

She untwists herself from the damp morning sheet and stretches her arms, feeling for sprains and tightness. She's almost too tired to get up. Too tired, too discouraged, too angry with herself over last night's fireside fiasco. What will she tell Zeb when he gets back? Supposing he does get back. Zeb is resourceful, but he's not invulnerable.

She can only hope that he's been more successful with his quest than she has been with hers. There's a chance that some of the God's Gardeners have survived because if anyone would know how to wait out the pandemic that killed almost everyone else, it would be them. During all the years that she spent with them, first as their guest, then as an apprentice, and finally as a high-ranking Eve, they'd planned for catastrophe. They'd built hidden places of refuge and stocked them with supplies: honey, dried soybeans and mushrooms, rose hips, elderberry compote, preserves of various kinds. Seeds to plant in the new, cleansed world they believed would come. Perhaps they'd waited the plague out in one of these refuges — one of their sheltering Ararats, where they hoped they'd be safe while riding out what they termed the Waterless Flood. God had promised after the Noah incident that he'd never use the water method again, but considering the wickedness of the world he was bound to do something: that was their reasoning. But where will Zeb look for them, out there among the ruins of the city? Where to even begin?

Visualize your strongest desire, the Gardeners used to say, *and it will manifest;* which doesn't always work, or not as intended. Her strongest desire is to have Zeb come back safe, but if he does, she'll have to face up once again to the fact that she's neutral territory as far as he's concerned. Nothing emotional, no sexiness there, no frills. A trusted comrade and foot soldier: reliable Toby, so competent. That's about it.

And she'll have to admit her failure to him. *I was a cretin. It was Saint Julian's, I couldn't kill them. They got away. They took a spray-gun.* She won't snivel, she won't cry, she won't give excuses. He won't say much, but he'll be disappointed in her.

Don't be too harsh on yourself, Adam One used to say in his patient blue-eyed way. We all make mistakes. True, she replies to him now, but some mistakes are more lethal than others. If Zeb gets killed by one of the Painballers, it will be her fault. *Stupid, stupid, stupid.* She feels like whacking her head against the cobb-house wall.

She can only hope the Painballers were spooked enough to run very far away. But will they stay away? They'll need food. They might scavenge some quasi-food in the deserted houses and shops from whatever hasn't mouldered or been eaten by rats or looted months ago. They may even blast a few animals – a rakunk, a green rabbit, a liobam – but after they use up their cellpack ammunition, they'll need more.

And they know the MaddAddam cobb house will have some. Sooner or later they'll be tempted to attack at the weakest link: they'll grab a Craker child and offer to swap, as they tried to swap Amanda earlier. It will be sprayguns and cellpacks they'll want, with a young woman or two thrown in – Ren or Lotis Blue or White Sedge or Swift Fox – not Amanda, they've already expended her. Or a Craker female in heat, why not? It would be a novelty for them, a woman with a bright blue abdomen; not the best conversationalists, those Crakers, but the Painballers won't care about that. They'll demand Toby's rifle too.

The Crakers would think it was just a matter of sharing. *They want the stick thing? It would make them happy? Why are you not giving it to them, Oh Toby?* How to explain that you can't hand over a murder weapon to a murderer? The Crakers wouldn't understand murder because they're so trusting. They'd never imagine that anyone would rape them – *What is rape?* Or slit their throats – *Oh Toby, why?* Or slash them open and eat their kidneys – *But Oryx would not allow it!*

Suppose the Crakers hadn't untied those knots. What had she intended to do? Would she have marched the Painballers back to the cobb house, then kept them penned up until Zeb got back and took over and did the necessary thing?

He'd have held some sort of perfunctory discussion. Then there would have been a double hanging. Or maybe he'd have skipped the preliminaries and just hit them with a shovel, saying, Why dirty a rope? The end result would be the same as if she'd snuffed the two of them immediately, right then and there at the campfire.

Enough of such dour stocktaking. It's morning. She has to cut out these daydreams in which Zeb performs decisive leadership acts that she ought to have performed herself. She needs to get up, go outside, join the others. Repair what can't be repaired, mend what can't be mended, shoot what needs to be shot. Hold the fort.

Breakfast

She swings her legs off the bed, sets her feet on the floor, stands. Her muscles hurt, her skin feels like sandpaper, but it's not so bad once you're up.

She chooses a bedsheet — lavender with blue dots — from the selection on her shelf. There's a pile of sheets in every cubicle, like towels in a hotel of old. Her pink top-to-toe from the AnooYoo Spa is in rags and may be infected with whatever it is Jimmy might have: she'll need to burn it. When she gets the time she'll sew a few of the sheets together, with arms and a hood, but meanwhile she drapes the lavender sheet around herself toga-style.

There's no shortage of bedsheets. The MaddAddamites have gleaned enough of them from the city's deserted buildings to last a while, and they also have a stash of pants and T-shirts for heavy work. But the sheets are cooler and one-size-fits-all, so they're the MaddAddamite attire of choice. When the bedsheets are used up they'll have to think of something else, but that won't happen for years. Decades. If they live that long.

A mirror is what she needs. Hard to know how much of a wreck she is without one. Maybe she'll be able to get mirrors onto the next gleaning list. Those, and toothbrushes.

She slings her knapsack with her health-care items over one shoulder: the maggots, the honey, the mushroom elixir, the Willow and Poppy. She'll tend to Jimmy first thing, supposing he's still alive. But only after she's had some breakfast: she can't face the day, much less Jimmy's festering foot, on an empty stomach. Then she picks up her rifle and steps out into the full glare of morning.

Although it's still early, the sun's already burning white. She hoists one end of her bedsheet over her head for protection, checks out the cobb-house yard. The red-headed Mo'Hair, still at large, is eyeing the vegetables through the kitchen-garden fence while chewing on some kudzu. Its friends in the Mo'Hair pen are bleating at it: silver Mo'Hairs, blue ones, green ones and pink ones, brunettes and blondes: the full range of colours. *Hair Today, Mo'Hair Tomorrow* went the ad when the creatures had first been launched.

Toby's present-day hair is a Mo'Hair transplant: she didn't use to be so raven-hued. Maybe that was why the Mo'Hair had come into her cubicle to lick her on the leg. It wasn't the salt, it was the faint smell of lanolin. It thought she was a relative.

Just so long as I don't get jumped by one of the rams, she thinks. She'll have to watch herself for signs of sheepishness. Rebecca must be up by now, dealing with breakfast issues over at the cooking shack; maybe she's got some floral-scented shampoo tucked away in her supply room.

Over near the garden, Ren and Lotis Blue are sitting in the shade, deep in conversation. Amanda is sitting with them, staring off into the distance. Fallow state, the Gardeners would say. They used that diagnosis for a wide range of conditions, from depression to post-traumatic stress to being permanently stoned. The theory was that while in a Fallow state you were gathering and conserving strength, nourishing yourself through meditation, sending invisible rootlets out into the universe. Toby really hopes this is true of Amanda. She'd been such a lively child in Toby's class at the Gardener school, back there on the Edencliff Rooftop Garden. When was that? Ten, fifteen years ago? Amazing how quickly the past becomes idyllic.

Ivory Bill and Manatee and Tamaraw are fortifying the boundary fence. In daylight it looks flimsy, permeable. Onto the skeleton of the old ornamental ironwork paling they've attached an assortment of materials: lengths of wire fencing interwoven with duct tape, a mixture of poles, a row of pointed sticks with their ends set in the ground and the points facing out. Manatee is adding more sticks; Ivory Bill and Tamaraw are on the other side of the fence, with shovels. They appear to be filling in a hole.

"Morning," says Toby.

"Take a look at this," says Manatee. "Something was trying to tunnel under. Last night. Sentries didn't see them, they were chasing those pigs off at the front."

"Any tracks?" said Toby.

"We think it was maybe more of those pigs," Tamaraw says. "Smart — distracting attention, then trying a sneaky dig. Anyway, they didn't get in."

Beyond the boundary fence there's a semicircle of male Crakers, evenly spaced, facing outward, peeing in unison. A man in a striped bedsheet who looks like Crozier — in fact, it is Crozier — is standing with them, joining in the group pee-in.

What next? Is Crozier going native? Will he shed his clothes, take up a cappella singing, grow a huge penis that turns blue in season? If the first two items were the price of entry for the third, he'd do it in a shot. Soon every single human male among the MaddAddamites will be yearning for one of those. And once that starts, how long before the rivalries and wars break out, with clubs and sticks and stones, and then . . .

Get a grip, Toby, she tells herself. Don't borrow trouble. You really, really, really need some coffee. Any kind of coffee. Dandelion root. Happicuppa. Black mud, if that's all there is.

And if there were any booze, she'd drink that too.

A long dining room table has been set up beside the cooking shack. There's a shade sail deployed above it, gleaned from some deserted backyard. All the patios must be derelict now, the swimming pools cracked and empty or clogged with weeds, the broken kitchen windows invaded by the probing green snoutlets of vines. Inside the houses, nests in the corners made from chewed-up carpets, wriggling and squeaking with hairless baby rats. Termites mining through the rafters. Bats hawking for moths in the stairwells.

"Once the tree roots get in," Adam One had been fond of saying to the Gardener inner circle, "once they really take hold, no human-built structure stands a chance. They'll tear a paved road apart in a year. They'll block the drainage culverts, and once the pumping systems fail, the foundations will be eaten away, and no force on earth will be able to stop that kind of water, and then, when the generating stations catch fire or short out, not to mention the nuclear . . ."

"Then you can kiss your morning toast goodbye," Zeb had once added to this litany. He'd just blown in from one of his mysterious courier missions; he looked battered, and his black pleather jacket was ripped. Urban Bloodshed Limitation was one of the subjects he taught the Gardener kids, but he didn't always practise it. "Yeah, yeah, we know, we're doomed. Any hope of some elderberry pie around here? I'm starving." Zeb did not always show a proper reverence towards Adam One.

Speculations about what the world would be like after human control of it ended had been – long ago, briefly – a queasy form of popular entertainment. There had even been online TV shows about it: computer-generated landscape pictures with deer grazing in Times Square, serves-us-right finger-wagging, earnest experts lecturing about all the wrong turns taken by the human race.

There was only so much of that people could stand, judging from the ratings, which spiked and then plummeted as viewers voted with their thumbs, switching from imminent wipeout to real-time contests about hotdog-swallowing if they liked nostalgia, or to sassy-best-girlfriends comedies if they liked stuffed animals, or to Mixed Martial Arts Felony Fights if they liked bitten-off ears, or to Nitee-Nite live-streamed suicides or HottTotts kiddy porn or Hedsoff real-time executions if they were truly jaded. All of it so much more palatable than the truth.

"You know I've always sought the truth," said Adam One that time, in the aggrieved tone he sometimes adopted with Zeb. He didn't use this tone with anyone else.

"Yeah, right, I do know that," said Zeb. "Seek and ye shall find, eventually. And you found. You're right, I don't dispute that. Sorry. Chewing with my mind full. Stuff comes out my mouth." And that tone said, This is the way I am. You know that. Suck it up.

. . .

If only Zeb were here, thinks Toby. She has a quick flash of him disappearing under a cascade of glass shards and chunks of cement as another burnt-out high-rise crashes down, or howling as a chasm opens under his feet and he plummets into an underground torrent no longer controlled by pumps and sewers, or humming carelessly as from behind him appears an arm, a hand, a face, a rock, a knife . . .

But it's too early in the morning to think like that. Also it's no use. So she tries to stop.

Around the table is a collection of random chairs: kitchen, plastic, upholstered, swivel. On the tablecloth — a rosebud-and-bluebird motif — are plates and glasses, some already used, and cups, and cutlery. It's like a surrealist painting from the twentieth century: every object ultrasolid, crisp, hard-edged, except that none of them should be here.

But why not? thinks Toby. Why shouldn't they be here? Nothing in the material world died when the people did. Once, there were too many people and not enough stuff; now it's the other way around. But physical objects have shucked their tethers — Mine, Yours, His, Hers — and have gone wandering off on their own. It's like the aftermath of those riots they used to show in documentaries of the early twenty-first century, when kids would join phone-swarms and then break windows and mob shops and grab stuff, and what you could have was limited only by what you could carry.

And so it is now, she thinks. We have laid claim to these chairs, these cups and glasses, we've lugged them here. Now that history is over, we're living in luxury, as far as goods and chattels go.

The plates look antique, or at least expensive. But now she could break the whole set and it wouldn't cause a ripple anywhere but in her own mind.

Rebecca emerges from the kitchen cooking shack with a platter.

"Sweetheart!" she says. "You made it back! And they told me you found Amanda too! Five stars!"

"She's not in the best shape," says Toby. "Those two Painballers almost killed her, and then, last night . . . I'd say she's in shock. Fallow state." Rebecca's old Gardener, so she'll understand *Fallow*.

"She's tough," says Rebecca. "She'll mend."

"Maybe," says Toby. "Let's hope she's disease-free, and no internal injuries. I guess you heard the Painballers got away. They took a spray-gun too. I really messed up on that."

"Win some, lose some," says Rebecca. "I can't tell you how cheered up I am that you're not dead. I thought those two scumbags would kill you for sure, and Ren too. I was worried sick. But here you are, though I have to say you look like shit."

"Thanks," says Toby. "Nice china."

"Dig in, sweetie. Pig in three forms: bacon, ham, and chops." It hadn't taken them long to backslide on the Gardener Vegivows, thinks Toby. Even Jelack Rebecca is having no problems with the pork. "Burdock root. Dandelion greens. Dog ribs on the side. If I keep it up with the animal protein I'm going to get even fatter than I am."

"You're not fat," says Toby. Though Rebecca has always been solid, even back when they'd worked together slinging meat at Secret-Burgers, before they turned Gardener.

"I love you too," says Rebecca. "Okay, I'm not fat. Those glasses are real crystal, I'm enjoying it. Cost a mint, this stuff did once. Remember at the Gardeners? Vanity kills, Adam One used to tell us, so it was earthenware or die. Though I can see the day coming when we're not gonna be bothered with dishes anymore, we'll just eat with our hands."

"There is a place in even the purest and most dedicated life for simple elegance," says Toby. "As Adam One also used to tell us."

"Yeah, but sometimes that place is the trash can," says Rebecca. "I've got a whole stack of lap-sized linen table napkins, and I can't iron them because there's no iron, and that really bugs me!" She sits down, forks a piece of meat onto her plate.

"I'm glad you're not dead too," says Toby. "Any coffee?"

"Yeah, if you can ignore the burnt twigs and roots and crap. There's no caffeine in it, but I'm counting on the placebo effect. I see you brought a whole mob back with you last night. Those — what would you call them, anyway?"

"They're people," says Toby. Or I think they're people, she adds to herself. "They're Crakers. That's what the MaddAddam bunch calls them, and I guess they should know."

"They're definitely not like us," says Rebecca. "No way close. That little pisher Crake. Talk about fouling up the sandbox."

"They want to be near Jimmy," says Toby. "They carried him back here."

"Yeah, I heard that part," says Rebecca. "Tamaraw enlightened me. They should go back to — to wherever they live."

"They say they need to purr on him," says Toby. "On Jimmy."

"Excuse me? Do what on him?" says Rebecca with a small snort of laughter. "Is that one of their weird sex things?"

Toby sighs. "It's hard to explain," she says. "You have to see it."

Hammock

After breakfast Toby goes over to take a look at Jimmy. He's suspended between two trees in a makeshift hammock fashioned from duct tape and rope. Over his legs is a child's comforter with a pattern of cats playing fiddles, laughing puppies, dishes with faces on them holding hands with grinning spoons, and cows with bells around their necks jumping over moons that are leering at their udders. Just what you need when you're hallucinating, thinks Toby.

Three Crakers – two women and a man – are sitting beside Jimmy's hammock on chairs that may once have belonged with the dining table: dark wood, with retro lyre backs and yellow-and-brown-striped satiny upholstery. The Crakers look wrong on these chairs, but they also look pleased with themselves, as if they're doing something quietly adventurous. Their bodies gleam like gold-threaded spandex; huge pink kudzu moths are fluttering around their heads in living halos.

They're preternaturally beautiful, thinks Toby. Unlike us. We must seem subhuman to them, with our flapping extra skins, our aging faces, our warped bodies, too thin, too fat, too hairy, too knobbly. Perfection exacts a price, but it's the imperfect who pay it.

Each of the Crakers has one hand on Jimmy. They're purring; the hum gets louder as Toby walks over to them.

"Greetings, Oh Toby," says the taller of the two women. How do they know her name? They must have listened more carefully than she'd thought last night. And how should she reply? What are their own names, and is it polite to ask?

"Greetings," she says. "How is Snowman-the-Jimmy today?"

"He is growing stronger, Oh Toby," says the shorter woman. The others smile.

Jimmy does look somewhat better. He's pinker, he's cooler, and he's sound asleep. They've fixed him up: tidied his hair, cleaned his beard. On his head is a battered red baseball cap, on his wrist a round watch with a blank face. A pair of sunglasses with one eye missing is perched awkwardly on his nose.

"Maybe he'd be more comfortable without those things on him," says Toby, indicating the hat and the sunglasses.

"He must have those things," says the man. "Those are the things of Snowman-the-Jimmy."

"He needs them," says the shorter woman. "Crake says he must have them. See, here is the thing for listening to Crake." She lifts the arm with the watch on it.

"And he sees Crake with this," says the man, pointing to the sunglasses. "Only he." Toby wants to ask what the hat is for, but she refrains.

"Why have you moved him outside?" she asks.

"He did not like it in that dark place," says the man. "In there." He nods towards the house.

"Snowman-the-Jimmy can travel better out here," says the taller woman.

"He's travelling?" says Toby. "While he's asleep?" Could they be describing some dream they imagine Jimmy is dreaming?

"Yes," says the man. "He is travelling to here."

"He is running, sometimes fast and sometimes slow. Sometimes walking, because he is tired. Sometimes the Pig Ones are chasing him, because they do not understand. Sometimes he is climbing into a tree," says the shorter woman.

"When he gets to here, he will wake up," says the man.

"Where was he when he started this travelling?" says Toby cautiously. She doesn't want to convey disbelief.

"He was in the Egg," says the taller woman. "Where we were, in the beginning. He was with Crake, and with Oryx. They came out of the sky to meet with him in the Egg, and to tell him more of the stories, so he can tell them to us."

"That is where the stories come from," says the man. "But the Egg is too dark now. Crake and Oryx can be there, but Snowman-the-Jimmy cannot be there any more." The three of them smile warmly at Toby, as if certain she's understood every word they've said.

"May I look at Snowman-the-Jimmy's hurt foot?" she asks politely. They have no objection, though they keep their hands in place and continue with their purring.

Toby checks the maggots underneath the cloth she wrapped around Jimmy's foot the night before. They're busily at work, cleaning up the dead flesh; the swelling and oozing are diminishing. This batch of maggots is nearing maturity: she'll have to get hold of some rotting meat tomorrow, leave it in the sun, attract flies, create new maggots.

"Snowman-the-Jimmy is coming closer to us," says the short woman. "Then he will tell us the stories of Crake, as he always did when he was living in his tree. But today you must tell them to us."

"Me?" says Toby. "But I don't know the stories of Crake!"

"You will learn them," says the man. "It will happen. Because Snowman-the-Jimmy is the helper of Crake, and you are the helper of Snowman-the-Jimmy. That is why."

"You must put on this red thing," says the shorter woman. "It is called a *hat*."

"Yes, a *hat*," says the tall woman. "In the evening, when it is moth time. You will put this hat of Snowman-the-Jimmy on your head, and listen to this shiny round thing that you put on your arm."

"Yes," says the other woman, nodding. "And then the words of Crake will come out of your mouth. That is how Snowman-the-Jimmy would do it."

"See?" says the man. He points to the lettering on the hat: *Red Sox*. "Crake made this. He will help you. Oryx will help too, if the story has an animal in it."

"We will bring a fish, when it is getting dark. Snowman-the-Jimmy always eats a fish, because Crake says he must eat it. Then you will put on the hat and listen to this Crake thing, and say the stories of Crake."

"Yes, how Crake made us in the Egg, and cleared away the chaos of bad men. How we left the Egg and walked here with Snowman-the-Jimmy, because there were more leaves for us to eat."

"You will eat the fish, and then you will say the stories of Crake, as Snowman-the-Jimmy always did," says the shorter woman. They look at her with their uncanny green eyes and smile reassuringly. They seem entirely confident of her abilities.

What are my choices? thinks Toby. I can't say no. They may get disappointed, and go away by themselves, back to the beach, where the Painballers can grab them. They'd be easy prey, especially the children. How can I let that happen?

"All right," she says. "I will come in the evening. I will put on the hat of Jimmy, I mean Snowman-the-Jimmy, and tell you the stories of Crake."

"And listen to the shiny thing," says the man. "And eat the fish." It seems to be a ritual.

"Yes, all of that," says Toby.

Shit, she thinks. I hope they cook the fish.

Story

While gathering up the breakfast dishes, Rebecca thought she saw a grim hatchet-face looking at her from under the trees. It seems to have been a false alarm, thinks Toby: no Painballers appeared, and, even better, no spraygun holes opened in Rebecca and no Craker child was yanked screaming into the shrubbery. Still, everyone's tense.

Toby asks the Craker mothers to move closer to the cobb house. When they look puzzled, she tells them it's a message from Oryx.

The day unscrolls without incident. No travellers return: no Shackleton, no Black Rhino or Katuro. No Zeb. Toby spends the rest of the morning in the kitchen garden, digging and weeding: a mindless exercise that calms her and fills the time. There are some chickenpeas beginning to sprout, and spinach leaves thrusting up, and the feathery tops of carrots. Her rifle is propped nearby.

Crozier and Zunzuncito herd the Mo'Hairs out of their paddock so they can graze. Both carry sprayguns: in a Painballer confrontation they'd have the advantage — two weapons against one — unless they were taken by surprise. Toby hopes they'll remember to check above their heads if there are trees nearby: that must have been how the Painballers caught Amanda and Ren, by dropping down from above.

Why is war so much like a practical joke? she thinks. Hiding behind bushes, leaping out, with not much difference between *Boo!* and *Bang!* except the blood. The loser falls over with a scream, followed with a foolish expression, mouth agape, eyes akimbo. Those old biblical kings, setting their feet on conquered necks, stringing up rival kings on trees, rejoicing in piles of heads — there was an element of childish glee in all of that.

Maybe it's what drove Crake on, thinks Toby. Maybe he wanted to end it. Cut that part out of us: the grinning, elemental malice. Begin us anew.

She eats her lunch early, in solitude, because she's tagged for sentry with her rifle during the regular lunchtime. The food is cold pork and burdock root, with an Oreo cookie from a package gleaned from a pharmacy: a rare treat, carefully rationed. She opens her cookie and licks the white sweet filling before eating the two chocolatey halves: a guilty luxury.

Before the afternoon thunderstorm, five of the Crakers carry Jimmy into the cobb house, along with his Hey-Diddle-Diddle quilt. Toby sits with him while it rains, checks his wound, manages to raise his head so he drinks some of the mushroom elixir, even though he's still unconscious. Her supply is running low, but she doesn't know where to find the right mushrooms for a fresh brew.

A single Craker remains in the room with them, to purr: the others go away. They don't like houses; they'd rather be wet than cooped up. Once the rain stops, four other Crakers appear to carry Jimmy outside again.

The clouds part, the sun comes out. Crozier and Zunzuncito return with the flock of Mo'Hairs. Nothing has happened, they say; or nothing you can put your finger on. The Mo'Hairs were jumpy; it was hard to keep them together. And the crows were making a racket, but what does that tell you? Crows are always making a racket about something.

"Jumpy, how?" says Toby. "What sort of racket?" But they can't be more specific.

Tamaraw, with a denim shirt over her hunched shoulders and a canvas sunhat, attempts to milk the one Mo'Hair that's producing. The milking doesn't go smoothly: there's kicking and bleating, and the pail tips and spills.

Crozier shows the Crakers how to work the hand pump: a retro decoration once but now the source of their drinking water. God knows what's in it, thinks Toby: it's groundwater, and every toxic spill for miles around may have leaked into it. She'll push for rainwater, at least for drinking; though with faraway fires and maybe nuclear meltdowns sending dirty particulate into the stratosphere, God knows what's in that as well.

The Crakers are delighted with the pump; the children scamper over and clamour to have water pumped onto them. After that, Crozier demonstrates the one piece of solar the MaddAddamites have managed to get running; it's connected to a couple of light bulbs, one in the cooking shack and one in the yard. He tries to explain why the lights go on, but they're puzzled. It's obvious to them that the light bulbs are like lumiroses, or the green rabbits that come out at dusk: they glow because Oryx made them that way.

Supper takes place at the long table. White Sedge in an apron with bluebirds on it and Rebecca with a mauve bath towel tied around her middle with yellow satin ribbon dish out the food from the pots, then sit down. Ren and Lotis Blue are at the far end, coaxing Amanda to eat. The MaddAddamites not on sentry duty filter in from their chores.

"Greetings, Inaccessible Rail," says Ivory Bill. He takes pleasure in calling Toby by her old MaddAddam codename. He has a tulip-sprinkled bedsheet draped around his sparse form and a turban-like object made from a matching pillowcase on his head. His angular nose juts out from his leathery face like a beak. It was odd, thinks Toby, how the MaddAddamites chose codenames that mirrored parts of themselves.

"How's he doing?" says Manatee. He's wearing a broad-brimmed straw hat that makes him look like a chubby plantation owner. "Our star patient."

"He's not dead," says Toby. "But he's not what you'd call conscious."

"If he ever was," says Ivory Bill. "We used to call him Thickney. That was his MaddAddam name, back in the early days."

"He was Crake's jackal at the Paradice Project," says Tamaraw. "Once he wakes up, there's a lot he needs to tell us. Before I trample him to death." She snorts to indicate that she's joking.

"Thickney by name, Thickney by nature," says Manatee. "I don't think he had the least freaking idea. He was just a dupe."

"Naturally we wouldn't have had a high opinion of him, to be fair," says Ivory Bill. "He was at the Project by choice. Unlike ourselves." He sticks his fork into a chunk of meat. "Dear lady," he says to White Sedge, "could you possibly identify this substance for me?"

"Ahc-tually," says White Sedge with her British accent, "actually, not."

"We were the brain slaves," says Manatee, spearing another chop. "The captive science brainiacs, working the evolution machines for Crake. What a power-tripper, thought he could perfect humanity. Not that he wasn't brilliant."

"He wasn't alone there," says slender Zunzuncito. "It was big business, the BioCorps were backing it. People were paying through the ceiling for those gene-splices. They were customizing their kids, ordering up the DNA like pizza toppings." He's wearing bifocals. Once we run out of optical products, Toby thinks, it really will be back to the Stone Age.

"Just, Crake was better at it," says Manatee. "He put some accessories into these guys nobody else even thought of. The built-in insect repellent: genius."

"And the women who can't say no. That colour-coded hormonal thing, you have to admire it," says Zunzuncito.

"As a meat-computer set of problems to be solved, it was an intriguing challenge," says Ivory Bill, turning his attention to Toby. "Let me elucidate." He's talking as if they're all at a graduate seminar, while cutting his greens into small, even squares. "For instance, the rabbit gizzard, and the baboon platform for certain chromatic features of the reproductive system —"

"The part where they turn blue," says Zunzuncito helpfully to Toby.

"I was doing the chemical composition of the urine," says Tamaraw. "The carnivore-deterrent element. Hard to test at the Paradice Project — we didn't have any carnivores."

"I was working on the voice box: now that was complex," says Manatee.

"Too bad you didn't code in a Cancel button for the singing," says Ivory Bill. "It gets on the nerves."

"The singing was not my idea," says Manatee sulkily. "We couldn't erase it without turning them into zucchinis."

"I have a question," says Toby. They turn and look at her, as if surprised that she's spoken.

"Yes, dear lady?" says Ivory Bill.

"They want me to tell them a story," says Toby. "About being made by Crake. But who do they think Crake was, and how do they think he made them? What were they told about that, back in the Paradice dome?"

"They think Crake is some sort of a god," says Crozier. "But they don't know what he looks like."

"How do you know that?" says Ivory Bill. "You weren't in Paradice with us."

"Because they fucking told me," says Crozier. "I'm their pal now. I even get to piss with them. It's, like, an honour."

"Good thing they can't ever meet Crake," says Tamaraw.

"No shit," says Swift Fox, who has now joined them. "They'd take one look at their lunatic of a creator and jump off a skyscraper. If there were still any skyscrapers to jump off," she adds morosely. She makes a show of yawning, stretching her arms up and behind her head, thrusting her breasts up and out. Her straw-coloured hair is pulled into a high ponytail, held in place by a powder-blue crocheted scrunchie. Her bedsheet has a dainty border of daisies and butterflies, cinched at the waist with a wide red belt. It's a startling touch: angel cloud meets butcher's cleaver.

"No point in repining, fair lady," says Ivory Bill, switching his gaze from Toby to Swift Fox. He'll be even more pompous, thinks Toby, once the beard he's working on grows in. "Carpe diem. Take every moment as it comes. Gather ye rosebuds." He smiles, a demi-leer; his eyes move down to the red belt. Swift Fox stares at him blankly.

"Tell them a happy story," says Manatee. "Vague on the details. Crake's girlfriend, Oryx, used to do that sort of thing in Paradice, it kept them placid. I just hope that fucker Crake doesn't start performing miracles from beyond the grave."

"Like turning everything to diarrhea," says Swift Fox. "Oh, excuse me, he's already done that. Is there any coffee?"

"Alas," says Ivory Bill, "we are bereft of coffee, dear lady."

"Rebecca says she has to roast some kind of root," says Manatee.

"And there won't be any real cream for it when we do get it," says Swift Fox. "Only sheep goo. It's enough to make you ice-pick your own temples."

The light is fading now, the moths are flying, dusky pink, dusky grey, dusky blue. The Crakers have gathered around Jimmy's hammock. This is where they want Toby to tell the story about Crake and how they came out of the Egg.

Snowman-the-Jimmy wants to listen to the story too, they say. Never mind that he's unconscious: they're convinced he can hear it.

They already know the story, but the important thing seems to be that Toby must tell it. She must make a show of eating the fish they've brought, charred on the outside and wrapped in leaves. She must put on Jimmy's ratty red baseball cap and his faceless watch and raise the watch to her ear. She must begin at the beginning, she must preside over the creation, she must make it rain. She must clear away the chaos, she must lead them out of the Egg and shepherd them down to the seashore.

At the end, they want to hear about the two bad men, and the campfire in the forest, and the soup with a smelly bone in it: they're obsessed by that bone. Then she must tell about how they themselves untied the men, and how the two bad men ran away into the forest, and how they may come back at any time and do more bad things. That part makes them sad, but they insist on hearing it anyway.

Once Toby has made her way through the story, they urge her to tell it again, then again. They prompt, they interrupt, they fill in the parts she's missed. What they want from her is a seamless performance, as well as more information than she either knows or can invent. She's a poor substitute for Snowman-the-Jimmy, but they're doing what they can to polish her up.

She's just at the part where Crake is clearing away the chaos for the third time when their heads all turn at once. They sniff the air. "Men are coming, Oh Toby," they say.

"Men?" she says. "The two men who ran away? Where?"

"No, not the ones who smell of blood."

"Other men. More than two. We must greet them." They all stand up.

Toby looks where they're looking. There are four — four silhouettes, coming nearer along the cluttered street that borders the cobb-house parkette. Their headlamps are on. Four dark outlines, each bringing a shining light.

Toby feels her body unclench, feels air flowing into her in a long, soundless breath. Can a heart leap? Can a person be dizzy with relief?

"Oh Toby, are you crying?"

Homecoming

It's Zeb. Her wish come true. Larger and shaggier than she remembers, and — although it's only been days since Toby last saw him — older. More bowed down. What's happened?

Black Rhino and Shackleton and Katuro are with him. Now that she's closer she can see how tired they are. They're setting down their packs, and the others are crowding around: Rebecca, Ivory Bill, Swift Fox, Beluga; Manatee, Tamaraw, Zunzuncito, White Sedge; Crozier and Ren and Lotis Blue; even Amanda, hanging back from the group.

Everyone's talking; or all the human people are. The Crakers stay on the sidelines, clustered together, eyes big, watching. Ren is crying and hugging Zeb, which is in order: he is, after all, her stepfather. When they were at the Gardeners, Zeb had lived for a time with Ren's luscious mother, Lucerne, who hadn't appreciated him, thinks Toby.

"It's okay," Zeb tells Ren. "Look! You got Amanda back!" He extends an arm; Amanda lets herself be touched.

"It was Toby," says Ren. "She had her gun."

Toby waits, then moves forward. "Good work, sharpshooter," Zeb says to her, even though she didn't shoot anyone.

"You didn't find them?" Toby asks. "Adam One and ..."

Zeb gives her a sombre look. "Not Adam One," he says. "But we found Philo."

The others lean in to listen. "Philo?" says Swift Fox.

"Old Gardener," says Rebecca. "He smoked a lot of ... he liked the Vision Quests. He stayed with Adam One, back when the Gardeners split up. Where was he?" They all understand from Zeb's face that Philo was not alive.

"There were a bunch of vultures on top of a parking garage, so we went up to take a look," says Shackleton. "Near the old Wellness Clinic."

"Where we used to go to school?" says Ren.

"Quite fresh," says Black Rhino. Which means, thinks Toby, that at least some of the missing Gardeners survived the first wave of the plague.

"None of the others?" she says. "Nobody else? Was it the . . . was he sick?"

"No sign of them," says Zeb. "But I'm guessing they're still out there. Adam could be. Food handy? I could eat a bear." Which means he doesn't want to answer Toby right now.

"He eats a bear!" the Crakers say to one another. "Yes! It is as Crozier told us!" "Zeb eats a bear!"

Zeb nods towards the Crakers, who are gazing at him uncertainly. "I see we've got company."

"This is Zeb," Toby tells the Crakers. "He is our friend."

"We are pleased, Oh Zeb. Greetings."

"He is the one, he is the one! Crozier told us." "He eats a bear!" "Yes. We are pleased." Tentative smiles. "What is a *bear*, Oh Zeb – this bear you eat?" "Is it a fish?" "Does it have a smelly bone?"

"They came with us," says Toby. "From the shore. We couldn't stop them, they wanted to be with Jimmy. With Snowman. That's what they call Jimmy."

"Crake's buddy?" says Zeb. "From the Paradice Project?"

"Long story," says Toby. "You should eat."

There's some leftover stew; Manatee goes to get it. The Crakers withdraw to a safe distance; they don't like to be too close to the odours of carnivore cookery. Shackleton wolfs down his stew and moves off to sit with Ren and Amanda and Crozier and Lotis Blue. Black Rhino has two helpings, then goes to take a shower. Katuro says he'll help Rebecca sort out the contents of the packs: they've gleaned more soydines and some duct tape, and a few packs of freeze-dried ChickieNobs, and some Joltbars, and another package of Oreo cookies. A miracle, says Rebecca. It's hard to find any packaged cookies unchewed by rodents.

"Let's check out the garden," Zeb says to Toby. Toby's heart sinks: there must be bad news he wants to break privately.

The fireflies are coming out. The lavender and thyme are in bloom, releasing their airborne flavours. A few self-seeded lumiroses glimmer along the edges of the fence; several of the shimmering green rabbits are nibbling at their bottom leaves. Giant grey moths drift like blown ash.

"It wasn't the plague that killed Philo," says Zeb. "Someone cut his throat."

"Oh," says Toby. "I see."

"Then we saw the Painballers," says Zeb. "The same ones that grabbed Amanda. They were gutting one of those giant pigs. We took a few shots, but they ran off. So we stopped looking for Adam and got back here as fast as we could, because they might be anywhere around here."

"I'm sorry," says Toby.

"About what?" says Zeb.

"We caught them, night before last," she says. "We tied them to a tree. But I didn't kill them. It was Saint Julian's, I just couldn't. They got away, they took their spraygun."

She's crying now. This is pathetic, like baby mice, blind and pink and whimpering. It's not what she does. But she's doing it.

"Hey," says Zeb. "It'll be fine."

"No," says Toby. "It won't be fine." She turns away to leave: if she's going to snivel, she should do it alone. Alone is how she feels, alone is how she'll always be. You're used to solitude, she tells herself. Be a stoic.

Then she's enfolded.

She'd waited so long, she'd given up waiting. She'd longed for this, and denied it was possible. But now how easy it is, like coming home must have been once, for those who'd had homes. Walking through the doorway into the familiar, the place that knows you, opens to you, allows you in. Tells you the stories you've needed to hear. Stories of the hands as well, and of the mouth.

I've missed you. Who said that?

A shape against the night window, glint of an eye. Dark heartbeat.

Yes. At last. It's you.

Bearlift

∷∷∷∷∷

The Story of when Zeb was lost in the Mountains, and ate the Bear

And so Crake poured away the chaos, to make a safe place where you could live. And then . . .

We know the story of Crake. We know it many times. Now tell us the story of Zeb, Oh Toby.

The story of how Zeb ate a bear!

Yes! Ate a bear! A bear! What is a *bear*?

We want to hear the story of Zeb. And the bear. The bear he ate.

Crake wants us to hear it. If Snowman-the-Jimmy was awake, he would tell us that story.

Well then. Let me listen to the shiny thing of Snowman-the-Jimmy. Then I can hear the words.

I am listening very hard. It doesn't help me to listen when you are singing.

So. This is the story of Zeb and the bear. Only Zeb is in the story at first. He is all alone. The bear comes later. Maybe tomorrow the bear will come. For bears to come, you must be patient.

Zeb was lost. He sat down under a tree. The tree was in a big open space, wide and flat, like the beach except there was no sand and no sea, only some chilly pools and a lot of moss. All around but quite far away, there were mountains.

How did he get there? He flew there, in a . . . never mind. That part is in a different story. No, he cannot fly like a bird. Not any more.

Mountains? Mountains are very large and high rocks. No, those are not mountains, those are buildings. Buildings fall down, and then they make a crash. Mountains fall down too, but they do it very slowly. No, the mountains did not fall down on Zeb.

So Zeb looked at the mountains that were all around him but quite far away, and he thought, How will I get through these mountains? They are so large and high.

He needed to get through the mountains because the people were on the other side. He wanted to be with the people. He didn't want to be all alone. Nobody wants to be all alone, do they?

No, they were not people like you. They had clothes on. A lot of clothes, because it was cold there. Yes, it was in the time of the chaos, before Crake poured it all away.

So Zeb looked at the mountains and the pools and the moss, and he thought, What will I eat? And then he thought, Those mountains have a lot of bears living in them.

A bear is a very big, fur-covered animal with big claws and many sharp teeth. Bigger than a bobkitten. Bigger than a wolvog. Bigger than a pigoon. This big.

It speaks with a growl. It gets very hungry. It tears things apart.

Yes, bears are the Children of Oryx. I don't know why she made them so big, with very sharp teeth.

Yes, we must be kind to them. The best way of being kind to bears is not to be very close to them.

I don't think there are any bears very close to us right now.

And Zeb thought, Maybe a bear has smelled me, and maybe it is coming right now, because it is hungry, it is starving, and it wants to eat me. And I will have to fight the bear, and all I have is this quite small knife, and this stick that can make holes in things. And I will have to win the fight, and kill the bear, and then I will have to eat it.

The bear will come into the story quite soon.

Yes, Zeb will win the fight. Zeb always wins the fight. Because that's what happens.

Yes, he knew Oryx would be sad. Zeb felt sorry for the bear. He didn't want to hurt it. But he didn't want to be eaten by it. You don't want to be eaten by a bear, do you? Neither do I.

Because bears can't eat only leaves. Because it would make them sick.

Anyway, if Zeb didn't eat the bear he would have died, and then he wouldn't be here with us right now. And that would be a sad thing too, wouldn't it?

If you don't stop crying I can't go on with the story.

The Fur Trade

There's the story, then there's the real story, then there's the story of how the story came to be told. Then there's what you leave out of the story. Which is part of the story too.

In the story of Zeb and the bear, Toby has left out the dead man, whose name was Chuck. He, too, was lost among the pools and moss and mountains and bears. He, too, did not know the way out. It's unfair to deny him a mention, erase him from time, but putting him into the story would cause more knots and tangles than Toby is prepared to deal with. For instance, she doesn't yet know how this dead man wormed his way into the story in the first place.

"Too bad the fucker died," says Zeb. "I'd have twisted it out of him."

"It?"

"Who hired him. What they wanted. Where he would have taken me."

"*Died* is a euphemism, I take it. He didn't have a heart attack," says Toby.

"Don't be harsh. You know what I mean."

Zeb was lost. He sat down under a tree.

Or not lost completely. He did have a rough idea of where he was: he was somewhere on the Mackenzie Mountain Barrens, hundreds of miles from anywhere with fast food. And not under a tree, more like beside, and not a tree exactly, more like a shrub; though not bushy, more like spindly. A spindly kind of spruce. He noticed the details of the trunk, the small dead underbranches, the grey lichen on it, frilly and intricate and see-through, like whores' underpants.

"What do you know about whore's underpants?" says Toby.

"More than you want me to," says Zeb. "So. When you focus on details like that – close up, really clear, totally useless – you know you're in shock."

The AOH 'thopter was still smouldering. Lucky he got clear before it burst, or before the blimp component did, and thank shit the digital release on the seatbelts had still been working: otherwise he'd have been dead.

Chuck was lying belly down on the tundra, his head at a sick angle, peering over his own shoulder one-eighty degrees, like an owl. Not looking at Zeb, though. Looking up at the sky. No angels there, or none had showed up yet.

Blood was coming from somewhere on the top of Zeb's head, he could feel the warmth trickling down. Scalp wound. Not dangerous, but they bleed a lot. Your head's the most shallow part of you, his sociopath of a father had been in the habit of saying. Except for your brain. And your soul, supposing you've been blessed with one, which I doubt. The Rev had been a big cheerleader for souls, in addition to which he thought he was the boss of them.

Now Zeb found himself wondering if Chuck had a soul, and if it was still hovering over his body like a feeble smell. "Chuck, you stupid fuck," Zeb said out loud. If he'd been given a brief to kidnap himself on behalf of the brainscrapers, he'd have done a way better job of it than Chuck had, the fuckwit.

Too bad Chuck was dead, in a way – he must've had some good sides to him, maybe he liked puppies – but now there was one less asshole in the world, and wasn't that a plus? A checkmark in the column of the forces of light. Or darkness, depending on who was doing the double-entry moral accounting.

Though Chuck hadn't been an ordinary asshole; not grouchy, not aggressive, not like Zeb himself on his asshole setting. Too much the other way. Too friendly, too eager to be on message, man is obsolete, dooming ourselves to extinction, restore the balance of nature and babble babble, he overdid it so much that he sounded preposterous, and in an outfit like Bearlift, with its full quota of preposterous green-hued furfuckers, that took some effort.

They weren't all furfuckers, however: some claimed to be along for the challenge. Adventurous, devil-may-care, no strings on me, tattoo-upholstered, with greasy ponytails like bikers in old movies — boundary-pushing muscle-flexers, boot soles a little too hot for ordinary strolling. That was how Zeb had positioned himself: bulked up on natural steroids, do what had to be done, could take the pace, wings on the ankles, needed the money, liked the shadowy rimlands where nobody official could stick their tentacles into your back pocket, within which the contents of other people's hacked bank accounts might be bashfully lurking.

The card-carrying furfuckers looked down their narrow green true-believer noses at Zeb and his edgy like, but they didn't push that my-shit-don't-stink agenda too hard. They needed the manpower because not everyone on the planet thought it was a great idea to aero/orno/helithopter numerous dumpsterloads of rancid biotrash around the far north so a bunch of mangy Ursidae could gobble it free of charge.

"This was before the oil shortage really kicked in?" says Toby. "And the carbon garboil business took off. Otherwise, they'd never have let you waste such valuable primary material on bears."

"It was before a lot of things," says Zeb. "Though the oil prices were already getting pretty steep."

Bearlift had four old-model 'thopters they'd bought on the grey market. The Flying Pufferfish was their nickname. 'Thopters claimed to use biodesign: they had a helium/hydrogen gas-filled blimp with a skin that sucked in or exhaled molecules like a fish's swim bladder that contracted and expanded and allowed them to lift heavy weights. Plus, they had stabilizing ventral fins, a couple of heli-blades for hovering, and four bird-like flapping wings for manoeuvrability at slow speeds. The upside being minimum fuel consumption, ultra-high freight weight, and the ability to fly low and slow; the downside being that a 'thopter flight took forever, the software on the things failed

regularly, and few among them knew how to fix the brutes. Questionable digimechanics had to be called in, or rather smuggled in from
Brazil, where the digital darkside flourished.

They'd hack you as soon as look at you down there. Roaring business in politicians' medical records and sordid affairs, celebrities' plastic surgeries — that was the small end. At the big end it was one Corp
hacking another. Hacking a powerful Corp was the kind of thing that
could get you into the real crapola, even if you were firewalled by
being on the blackbox payroll of another powerful Corp.

"So I suppose you did it," says Toby. "The kind of thing with the
real crapola."

"Yeah, I'd been down there, just making a living," says Zeb. "That
was one reason I was taking a breather at Bearlift: it was ultra far from
Brazil."

Bearlift was a scam, or partly a scam. It didn't take anyone with half
a brain too long to figure that one out. Unlike many scams it was well
meaning, but it was a scam nonetheless. It lived off the good intentions of city types with disposable emotions who liked to think they
were saving something — some rag from their primordial authentic
ancestral past, a tiny shred of their collective soul dressed up in a cute
bear suit. The concept was simple: the polar bears are starving because
the ice is almost gone and they can't catch seals any more, so let's feed
them our leftovers until they learn to adapt, "*adapt* being the buzz-
word of those days, if you'll recall, though I doubt you're old enough;
you must still have been in playskirts. Learning to wiggle your little
mantrap."

"Stop flirting," said Toby.

"Why? You like it."

"I remember *adapt*," says Toby. "It was another way of saying
tough luck. To people you weren't going to help out."

"You got it," said Zeb. "Anyway, feeding trash to the bears didn't
help them adapt, it just taught them that food falls out of the sky.
They'd start slavering every time they heard the sound of a 'thopter,
they had their very own cargo cult.

"But here's the scammiest part. Yes, the ice had mostly melted;

yes, some polar bears had starved, but the rest of them were drifting southwards, mating up with the grizzlies, from which they'd separated themselves a mere two hundred thousand years ago. So you'd get bears that were white with brown patches or bears that were brown with white patches, or all brown or all white, but whatever was on the outside was no predictor of temperament: the pizzlies would avoid you most of the time, like grizzlies; the grolars would attack you most of the time, like polar bears. You never knew which kind any given bear might be. What you did know was that you didn't want your 'thopter to fall out of the air over bear country."

As Zeb's had just done.

"You stupid fuck," he said again to Chuck. "And whoever hired you is a double stupid fuck," he added, not that they were listening. Or — he had a sudden nasty thought — maybe they were.

Crash

Everything was going fine at Bearlift until Chuck turned up. Zeb was in some trouble at that time, true enough . . .

"Unlike at any other time," says Toby.

"You laughing at me? Victim of a confused youth due to parental abuse? Plus, I grew too fast?"

"Would I laugh?"

"Matter of fact, you would," says Zeb. "Heart like shale. What you need is a good fracking."

Zeb was in some trouble at that time, true enough, but nobody at Bearlift Central seemed to know or care: half of them were in trouble themselves, so it was Don't ask, Don't tell.

The chores were straightforward: load up the edible refuse, in Whitehorse or Yellowknife, sometimes maybe Tuk, where the Beaufort Sea offshore oilrig tankers dumped their garbage when they weren't tipping it illegally. The oilrigs still produced a lot of real-animal-protein leftovers in those days because nothing was too good for the tanker crews. Pork — they ate a lot of pork byproducts — and chicken, or something next door to it. When it was labmeat it was top grade, camouflaged in sausages or meatloaf so you really couldn't tell.

You'd pack the postmeal slops into the 'thopter, then grab a beer, then fly the 'thopter to the Bearlift drop locations, hover while dumping off the loads, fly back. Nothing to it except mind-numbing boredom unless there was bad weather or mechanical failure. In that case you'd have to set the 'thopter down while trying to give the mountainsides a miss, then wait out the weather or kick your heels until Repair showed up. Then repeat. Pretty routine. The worst of it was listening to the green-nosed furfucker sermonizing that went on in the Bearlifttown bars when you were trying to get spongefaced on the crapulous booze they hauled in there and dispensed by the vatful.

Apart from that, it was eat, sleep, and on a good day have a tussle with one or another of the girl staff, though Zeb had to be careful about that because some of them were snarly and others were taken, and he tried to stay out of brawls, never having seen any percentage in rolling around under bar stools with some enraged moron who considered he'd staked eternal twat rights because of his pre-eminent cock and his dimples, and who might have a knife. Unlikely a handgun any more because it was around that time that the CorpSeCorps was confiscating those, having raised the spurious banner of civic safety and thus effectively securing a monopoly for themselves on killing at a distance. Some guys hid their Glocks and other name brands, dug them in under stones in case of dire need, but for the same reason they were unlikely to be carrying. Though not every law and declaration was respected up there in the boonies. Things in the north were always a little fuzzy around the edges, law-wise. So you never knew.

Anyway, the girls. If there was a Back Off sign on a little or big or medium-sized set of cheeks, he always backed off. But if someone crept into his dorm room under cover of darkness, who was he to whimper? He'd been told since a child that he had the morals of a sowbug, and he hated to defeat expectations, in addition to which rejecting a girl's overture would be hurtful to her self-esteem. Some of those wouldn't have stood up too well under the light, but one of them had an amazing floppy ass, and another one had a set of boobs like two bowling balls in a string bag, and . . .

"Too much information," says Toby.

"Don't be jealous," says Zeb. "They're dead now. You can't be jealous of a bunch of dead women."

Toby says nothing. The lush corpse of Zeb's one-time lover, Lucerne, floats in the air between them, unseen, unmentioned, and certainly unburied as far as Toby is concerned.

"Alive is better than dead," says Zeb.

"No contest there," says Toby. "But on second thought you never know till you've tried."

Zeb laughs. "You have an amazing ass too," he says. "Not floppy, though. Compact."

"Tell about Chuck," says Toby.

Chuck entered Bearlift Central as though tiptoeing into a forbidden room while pretending he had a right to be there. Furtive but asser-tive. To Zeb's mind, his clothes were too new. They looked as if Chuck had just come from one of those crispy outfitter shops, zippers and Velcro and flaps all over, like some kind of kinky video puzzle game. Undo this man, find the leprechaun, win a prize. Never trust a man with new clothes.

"But clothes have to be new sometimes," says Toby. "Or they did back then. They weren't created old."

"Real men know how to dirty up their clothes in about one sec-ond," says Zeb. "They writhe around in mud. Apart from the clothes, his teeth were too big and white. When I see those kinds of teeth, I always want to give them a gentle tap with a bottle. See if they're fake, watch them shatter. My dad, the Rev, had teeth like that. He used whitener on them. The teeth plus his tan made him look like some kind of light-up deep-sea devilfish or else a long-dead horse's head in a desert. It was worse when he smiled than when he didn't."

"Back off on the childhood," says Toby. "You'll get woeful."

"Woe, your foe? Say no to woe? Don't preach at me, babe."

"It works for me. Backing off woe."

"You sure about that?"

"So, Chuck."

"So. There was something about his eyes. Chuck's eyes. Laminated eyes. Hard and shiny. They had a sort of transparent lid over them."

The first time Chuck appeared at the canteen table with his tray and said, "Mind if I join you?" he scanned Zeb, an overall back-and-forth of those laminated eyes. Like scanning a barcode.

Zeb glanced up at him. He didn't say yes, he didn't say no. He gave an all-purpose grunt and continued work on his rubbery conundrum of a sausage. You'd have expected Chuck to start with personal questions — where you from, how'd you get here, and so forth — but he didn't. His opening ploy was Bearlift. He said what a great org it was, but since that got no nodding and yupping from Zeb, he intimated that he was only there because he'd hit a bad patch in his life and was, you know, keeping quiet for a while, until things blew over.

"What'd you do, pick your nose?" said Zeb, and Chuck gave a dead-horse-teeth laugh. He said that he guessed Bearlift was for guys who, you know, sort of like the Foreign Legion, and Zeb said the foreign what, and that was the end of that one.

Not that he could shake the guy by being rude. Chuck backed off, but he still managed to be ever-present. Zeb would be at the bar labouring away at the next morning's hangover and all of a sudden there would be Chuck, buddying up, offering to get the next round. Go to the can, take a leak, and there would be Chuck, materializing like ectoplasm, taking a leak two stalls down; or Zeb would be sliding round the corner in the seedier part of Whitehorse and, guess what, Chuck would be sliding round the next corner over. He most likely went through Zeb's stuff in Zeb's broom closet of a room when Zeb wasn't in it.

"He was welcome to it," says Zeb. "Nothing in my dirty laundry but dirty laundry because the real dirty laundry was in my head."

But what was his game? Because it was obvious he had one. At first Zeb thought Chuck was gay and was about to start some trouser nuzzling, but it wasn't that.

Over the next few weeks Chuck and Zeb had flown a couple of lifts together. There were always two in a Pufferfish; you'd take turns dozing. Zeb tried to avoid partnering with Chuck, who by this time was giving him the nape prickles, but on the first occasion the guy Zeb was supposed to have flown with was called away by an aunt's funeral and Chuck had inserted himself into the slot, and the second time the other guy got food poisoning. Zeb wondered if Chuck had paid the two of them off to go missing. Or strangled the aunt, or put *E. coli* in the pizza, to make it convincing.

He waited for Chuck to pop the question while they were in mid-air. Maybe he knew about some of Zeb's earlier capers and was hiring for a hitherto-unknown bunch of darksiders who wanted Zeb to tackle a bolus of seriously forbidden hackery; or maybe it was an extortion outfit after some plutocrat, or a hireling connected with IP thieves who needed a skein of professional trackwork to further their kidnapping of a Corp brainiac.

Or maybe it was a sting – Chuck would propose some flagrantly illegal jest, record Zeb agreeing to do it, and then the giant lobster claws of what passed for the justice system would descend and clench; or maybe there'd be some goofy blackmail demand, as if you could get shit from a stone.

But nothing abnormal happened on these two runs. They must've been soothers, to set Zeb at ease. Signal that Chuck was harmless. Was his dinkiness a deep cover?

It almost worked. Zeb started thinking he himself was paranoid. Twitching at shadows. Worrying about a slithery nobody like Chuck.

That morning – the morning of the crash – had started out as usual. Breakfast, some anonymous bunwich with mysterious ingredients, couple of mugs of caffeine substitute, slice of toasted sawdust. Bearlift got its supplies on the cheap: It considered its cause to be so noble and worthy you were supposed to be humble, eat food stand-ins, save the good stuff for the bears.

Then loading up the offal, biodegradable sacks of it forklifted into the belly of the Puffer. Zeb's scheduled flying partner had been scratched off that day's list – cut his foot dancing barefoot on broken glass to show how tough he was in one of the local knocking shops while higher than the ionosphere on some cretinous pharmaceutical, it was said – and Zeb was supposed to be doubling with an okay guy called Rodge. But when he went to get in, there was Chuck, all togged up with his crispy zippers and Velcro flaps, smiling with his enormous white horse teeth but not with his laminated eyes.

"Rodge get a phone call?" said Zeb. "Grandmother died?"

"Father, in fact," said Chuck. "Nice day. Hey, I brought you a beer." He had one for himself too, just to show he was a regular guy.

Zeb grunted, took the beer, twisted off the top. "Need to take a leak," he said. In the can he poured the beer down the hole. Top seemed to be sealed on, but you could fake those things, you could fake just about anything. He didn't want to swill or munch any item that had been in Chuck's hands.

The Puffers were always complex while taking off: the helicopter blades and the helium/hydrogen blimp provided lift, but the trick was to get high enough before you started the wings flapping, and to cut the heli-blades at exactly the right time, or the whole thing could tip and spiral.

But there was no problem that day. The flight was standard, threading the valleys through and around the Pelly Mountains, pausing to bombard the landscape a few times with bear yummies; then over to the high-altitude Barrens with the Mackenzies all around, postcard snow on the tops, with a couple more drops; then crossing the remains of the Old Canol Trail, still marked by the occasional World War Two telephone pole.

The 'thopter responded well. It stopped flapping and started hovering right over the dump spots, the hatch opened as it was supposed to, and the biotrash tumbled out. At the last feeding station, two bears — one mostly white, one mostly brown — were already cantering towards their personal garbage dump as the 'thopter approached; Zeb could see their fur rippling like a shag rug being shaken. Being that close was always a bit of a thrill.

Zeb turned the 'thopter and headed southwest, back towards Whitehorse. Then he handed over to Chuck because the clock said it was Zeb's turn to catch some zizz. He lay back and blew up the neck pillow and closed his eyes, but he didn't allow himself to drift off because Chuck had been far too alert during the entire flight. You don't get that geared up over a non-event.

They were about two-thirds of the way to the first narrow mountain valley when Chuck made his move. Through his almost-closed eyes, Zeb saw the one hand moving stealthily over towards his thigh, holding a thread of glitter. He sat up fast and whacked Chuck across the windpipe. Not hard enough, though, because although Chuck gasped — not a gasp, hard to describe it — although he made that sound and dropped whatever he'd been holding, he grabbed at Zeb's neck with both hands and Zeb whacked him again, and of course nobody was flying the controls at that point, and in the thrashing around something must've been hit by a leg or a hand or an elbow, and that's when the 'thopter folded two of its four wings and tipped sideways and went down.

And Zeb found himself sitting under a tree, staring at the tree trunk. Astonishing, how clear the frilly edges were, of the lichen; light grey with a tinge of green, and an edge that was darker, so intricate . . .

Stand up, he ordered himself. You need to get moving. But his body didn't hear.

Supplies

A long time later — it seemed like a long time, he felt as if he was wading through transparent sludge — Zeb rolled to one side, put his hands on the ground, pushed himself to his feet beside the spindly kind of spruce. Then he threw up. He hadn't noticed feeling sick right before: he just suddenly puked.

"A lot of animals will do that," he says. "Under stress. Means you don't have to put the energy into digesting. Lightens the load."

"Were you cold?" says Toby.

Zeb's teeth were chattering, he was shivering. He took Chuck's down vest, added it to his own. It wasn't ripped much. He checked the pockets, found Chuck's cellphone, mashed it with a rock to destroy any GPS and eavesdropping functions. It started ringing just before he did the mashing; it took everything not to answer it and pretend he was Chuck. Maybe he should've answered, though, and said that Zeb was dead. He might've learned something. A couple of minutes later his own phone rang; he waited until it stopped, then mashed it as well.

Chuck had a few more toys, though nothing Zeb didn't have himself. Pocketknife, bear spray, bug spray, folded-up tinfoil space-age survival blanket, those things. By great good luck the bear gun they always carried with them in case of groundings and attacks had been tossed out along with Chuck. Bear guns were the exception to the new no-guns rules because even the dickwad CorpSeCorps bureaucrats knew you needed a bear gun up there. The Corps didn't like Bearlift, but they didn't try to shut it down either, though they could have done that with one finger. It served a function for them, sounded a note of hope, distracted folks from the real action, which was bulldozing the planet flat and grabbing anything of value. They had no objection to the standard Bearlift ad, with a smiling green furfucker telling everyone what a sterling lot of good Bearlift was doing, and please send more cash or you'll be guilty of bearicide. The Corps even put some of the cash in themselves. "That was back when they were still massaging their trust-me images," says Zeb. "Once they got a hammerlock on power, they didn't have to bother so much."

Zeb almost stopped shivering when he saw the bear gun. He could've hugged it: at least now he might have half a chance. He didn't find the needle, though, the one Chuck was going to stick into him; too bad about that, he would've liked to have known what was in it. Knockout potion, most likely. Freeze-frame his waking self, then fly him to some seedy rendezvous where the brainscrapers hired by who-knows-who would be waiting to strip-mine his neural data, suck out everything he'd ever hacked and everyone he'd ever hacked for, then leave him a pithed and shrivelled husk, staggering around with induced amnesia in a far-distant ravaged swamp until the local inhabitants stole his trousers and recycled his organs for the transplant biz.

But even if he'd managed to get hold of the needle, what then? Test it out on himself? Stick it in a lemming? "Still, I could have kept it in reserve, for emergencies," says Zeb.

"Emergencies?" says Toby, smiling in the dark. "This wasn't an emergency?"

"No, a real emergency," says Zeb. "Like running into some other person out there. That would be an emergency. Stands to reason it would be a madman."

"Was there any string?" says Toby. "In the pockets. You never know when string will come in handy. Or some rope."

"String. Yeah, now that you mention it. And a roll of fishing line, we always carried that, with a few hooks. Fire-lighter. Mini-binocs. Compass. Bearlift gave us all that Boy Scout stuff, survival basics. I didn't take Chuck's compass though, I already had one. You don't need two compasses."

"Candy bar?" says Toby. "Energy rations?"

"Yeah, couple of shitty little Joltbars, faux nuts. Package of cough drops. I took those. Plus." He pauses.

"Plus what?" says Toby. "Go on."

"Okay, warning: this is gross. I took some of Chuck. Hacked it off with the pocketknife, kind of sawed it. Chuck had a fold-up waterproof jacket, so I wrapped it in that. Not much to eat up there in the Barrens, we all knew that, we'd had the Bearlift course. Rabbits, ground squirrels, mushrooms, but I wouldn't have time to hunt for any of that. Anyway, you can die of eating nothing but rabbits. Rabbit starvation, they called it. No fat on those things. It's like that whatchamacallit diet – the all-protein one. You start to dissolve your own muscles. Your heart gets very thin."

"What part of Chuck did you take?" says Toby. She's surprised she doesn't feel squeamish; she might have, once, back when *squeamish* was an option.

"The fattest part," says Zeb. "The boneless part. The part you'd have taken. Or any sane person."

"Did you feel bad about it?" says Toby. "Stop patting my bum."

"Why?" says Zeb. "Nah, I didn't feel too bad. He'd have done the same. Maybe a stroking action, like this?"

"I'm too skinny," says Toby.

"Yeah, you could use a little more padding. I'll bring you a box of chocolates, if I can find any. Fatten you up."

"Add some flowers," says Toby. "Roll out the full courtship ritual. I bet you never did that in your life."

"You'd be surprised," says Zeb. "I've presented bouquets in my day. Of a kind."

"Go on," says Toby, who doesn't want to think about Zeb's bouquets or what kind they were, or who he may have given them to. "There you are. Mountains in the distance, part of Chuck lying on the ground and the rest in your pocket. What time was it?"

"Maybe three in the afternoon, maybe five, shit, maybe even eight, it would still have been light then," says Zeb. "I'd lost track. It was mid-July, did I say that? Sun hardly sets at all then, up there. Just sort of dips below the horizon, makes a pretty red rim. Then in a few hours up it comes again. That place isn't above the Arctic Circle, but it's up so high it's tundra: two-hundred-year-old willows like horizontal vines, and the wildflowers all bloom at once because the summer's only a couple of weeks long. Not that I was noticing any wildflowers right then."

He thought maybe he should get Chuck out of sight. He put Chuck's pants back on and stuffed him under one of the 'thopter wings. Changed boots with him − Chuck's were better anyway, and they more or less fit − and left a foot sticking out so anyone looking from a distance would think it was Zeb. He figured he might be safer dead, at least in the short-term.

When Bearlift Central saw they'd lost communication, they were bound to send somebody. Most likely it would be Repair. Once they discovered there was nothing left to repair and that nobody was sitting around setting off little flares and waving a white hanky, they'd go away. That was the ethos: don't waste fuel on dead bodies. Let nature recycle them. The bears would take care of it, the wolves, the wolverines, the ravens, and so forth.

But the Bearlifters might not be the only ones who would come to have a look. For his brain-snatch caper, Chuck clearly wasn't working with the Bearlifters: if he had been, he wouldn't have hesitated to try something right at the base, and he would've had help. Zeb would already be a lobotomized shell parked in some zombie town, ex-mining, ex-oil, with a fake passport and no fingerprints. Not that they'd even bother going that far because who would ever miss him?

Chuck's bosses had to be elsewhere, then: they were wherever it was they'd phoned from. But how close was that? Norman Wells, Whitehorse? Anywhere with an airstrip. Zeb needed to move away from the crash as fast as possible, find a place with cover. Which was not so easy on the next-to-bare-naked tundra.

Grolars and pizzlies could do it, though, and they were bigger. But also more experienced.

Bunkie

Zeb started hiking. The 'thopter had come down on a gentle hillside sloping to the west, and west was the direction he took. He had a rough map of the whole area in his head. Too bad he didn't have the paper map, the one they always kept open on their knees when flying up there in case of digital failure.

The tundra was hard walking. Spongy, waterlogged, with hidden pools and slippery moss and treacherous mounds of tussock grass. There were parts of old airplanes sticking out of the peat – a strut here, a blade there, detritus from rash twentieth-century bush pilots caught by fog or sudden winds, long ago. He saw a mushroom, left it alone: he knew little about mushrooms, but some were hallucinogenic. That's all he'd need, an encounter with the 'shroom god while green and purple teddybears skimmed towards him on tiny wings, grinning pinkly. The day had been surreal enough already.

The bear gun was loaded, and he kept the spray ready. If you surprised a bear it would charge. The spray was no good unless you could see the reds of its eyes, so you had a narrow time window – spray and then shoot. If it was a pizzly, that's how things would go. But a grolar would stalk you, and come up from behind.

In a wet patch of sand he found a print, left front paw, and, farther on, some fresh scat. They were most likely watching him right now. They knew he had a packet of blood and muscle, no matter how tidily wrapped: they could smell it. They could smell his fear.

His feet were already drenched, despite Chuck's superior boots. Those boots didn't fit as well as he'd assumed they would. He pictured his feet turning to pallid, blistery dough inside his socks. To take his mind off them – and off the bears, and off dead Chuck, off everything – and to make some noise to warn the pizzlies so neither he nor they would be surprised, he sang a song. It was a habit left over from his so-called youth, when he'd whistle in the dark, whatever dark he'd been locked into. In the dark, in the darkness, in the darkness that was there even when it was light.

Dad's a sadist, Mom's a creep,
Close your eyes and go to sleep.

No, not sleep, even though he was so tired now. He needed to keep going. Forced march.

Idiotic, idiotic, idiotic, idiotic,
Maybe I'm a really bad, a really bad, a bad psychotic.

There was a line of thicker green downhill that signalled a creek. He headed towards it, over the hillocks and the moss and the bare gravelly spots where pebbles had boiled to the surface during the deep frost of the winters. It wasn't particularly cold on that day, it was in fact hot in the sun, but he was still shivering in fits, like a wet dog shaking. He hugged Chuck's vest around himself, on top of his own.

When he was almost to the creek – it was more of a river, it had a swift current – he thought, What if it's bugged? The vest. What if there's a tiny transmitter sewn into it somewhere? They'll think Chuck is alive and moving, though mysteriously not answering his phone. They'll send someone to pick him up.

He took the vest off, waded across the creek to where the flow was the strongest, held the vest underwater. It puffed with trapped air, it wasn't going to sink. He could put stones in the pockets; but better, he let it float away, away from him. He watched it sail downstream like some odd bloated jellyfish, thinking, That was possibly not very fucking bright. I am not focusing.

He scooped cold water into his mouth – Don't drink too much, you'll waterlog – wondering if he'd just swallowed a pisspotful of beaver fever. But surely there were no beavers up here. What could you catch from wolves? Rabies but not from drinking. Dissolved moose poop — would that have tiny worms in it that would suck and tunnel? Some kind of liver fluke?

Why are you standing in the water talking out loud? he asked. In plain view. Go along the creek valley, he ordered. Keep to the shrubbery, out of sight. He was counting in his head: how long would it take from the moment Chuck hadn't answered his phone? Maybe two hours, if you factored in the what-went-wrong panic, the meeting they'd call, by remote or otherwise, the messaging, the wheel-spinning and buck-passing and veiled recriminations. All that crap.

Shoulder-high willows here, sheltered from the wind; grasses, bushes. Flies, blackflies, mosquitoes. Drove the caribou mad sometimes, it was said. You'd see them floating across the muskeg on their wide snowshoe feet, running to nowhere. He used some of the bug spray: not too much, he needed to ration it. Worked his way west, towards where he remembered — he thought he remembered — that he would hit the remnants of the Canol Road. Nothing much left of that road now, but as he recalled from his overhead flights, there were a few buildings along here. An old bunkie, a shed or two.

He aimed for a leaning telegraph pole, an archaic wooden one. There was a tangle of wire beside it, and a caribou skeleton, the antlers snarled; farther on, an oil drum, then two oil drums, then a red truck, in almost pristine condition but no tires. Local hunters most likely took them, carted them away on their four-by-fours, back when they could afford the fuel to come in this far for game. They'd have had some use for tires like those. The truck was that rounded silhouette, streamlined, from the 1940s, which was when the road was built. Some bureauscheme to transport oil inland through a pipeline during World War Two, to keep it from being blown up by coastal submarines. They'd brought a whole bunch of soldiers up from the South to build the system, black guys, a lot of them. They'd never been in subzero cold and five-day blizzards and twenty-four-hour darkness; they must've thought they were in hell. Local legend had it a third of them went crazy. He could see going crazy here, even without the blizzards.

· · ·

One foot sore now, must be a blister, but he couldn't stop to look. He hopped along the crumbled ribbon of the road, shrubs taller and nearby, one eye on the sky, and there was the bunkie. Long low building, wood, no door, but still a roof on it.

Quick, into the shadow. Then he waited. It was so quiet.

Plates of junkyard metal, scraps of wood, rusted wire. Beds must have been over there. Armchair ripped apart. Radio shell, must have been once; the rounded breadloaf shape of that decade. A knob on it still. Spoon. Remains of a stove. Smell of tar. Sunlight through ceiling crack, sifting through dust. Wisps of long-gone desolation, bleached-out grief.

The waiting was worse than the walking. Parts of him throbbed: feet, heart. His breath was so raucous.

Then he wondered if he himself was bugged; if Chuck had done that, just in case — slipped a mini-transmitter into his back pocket when he wasn't looking. If so, he was barbecue: they could be hearing him breathing right now. They'd even have heard him singing. They'd pinpoint him, shoot a mini-rocket at him, and poof.

Nothing to be done.

After — what? an hour? — he saw the ornodrone coming in low. Yes, from the northeast: Norman Wells. It went straight to the crash and made a couple of passes, transmitting visuals. Whoever was controlling it back at its base made a decision. It fired at the broken wing where Chuck lay concealed, couple of thuds. Then it blew up whatever was left of the 'thopter. It was as if Zeb could hear the voices: *Nobody left alive. You sure? Couldn't be. Both of them? Has to be. Anyway, made sure, scorched earth now.*

He held his breath, but the drone didn't follow the trail of the floating vest, and it ignored the derelict Canol bunkie; it merely turned and headed back to where it came from. They'd have wanted to get there first and mop up, then disappear fast before Bearlift Repair showed up.

Which it did, in its usual leisurely fashion. Get a move on, Zeb thought. I'm hungry. Repair hovered over the wreckage, Oh-my-Godding, no doubt, Poor-bastarding, Never-had-a-chancing. Then it, too, departed, back towards Whitehorse.

As the red twilight settled in and the mist gathered and the temperature fell, Zeb made a small fire on top of a slab of metal so he wouldn't burn the place down, inside the building so the smoke would hit the ceiling and disperse. No telltale column. He got himself a little warmer that way. Then he did some cooking. Then he ate.

"Just like that?" says Toby. "Wasn't it a little abrupt?"

"What?"

"Well, it was . . . I mean . . ."

"You mean it was meat? You pulling a vegetarian?"

"Don't be wicked."

"You wanted me to say a prayer? Thank you, God, for making Chuck such a fuckwit and having him provide for me in this unselfish though truly unintentional dumbass manner?"

"You're making fun."

"Then don't go all old Gardener on me."

"Hey! You're old Gardener yourself! You were Adam One's right-hand man, you were a pillar of . . ."

"Well, I wasn't then. A fucking pillar. Anyway, that's a whole other story."

It wasn't that easy, of course. Zeb cut small chunks and used a rusted-wire skewer, and also gave a lecture to himself – *This is Nutrition, capital N! You think you'll make it out of here without Nutrition?* Nonetheless, there were some swallowing issues. Luckily he'd had a lot of practise in distancing himself from things that went into his mouth, most recently the grub at Bearlift – some of which probably *was* grub, a popular protein-enhancer in dried and ground form.

But his first tests of that nature had come earlier, one of the Rev's instructive punishments being that those with potty-mouths should be forced to eat the contents of said potty. How not to smell, how not to taste, how not to think: it was like the See No Evil, Hear No Evil, Speak No Evil blind, deaf, and mute monkeys who sat on the miniature oil drum on his mother's dressing table with their paws clamped over their upper orifices, providing a role model for her that she was happy to follow. *Have you been sick? What's that on your chin?* He said, You're a dog, eat your own vomit. He pushed my head into the ... *Now, Zebulon, don't make up stories. You know your father wouldn't have done such a thing! He loves you!*

Slam the trapdoor on that one, roll a boulder. More to the point was how to stay warm. There was some crumbling tarpaper in the corner, not much use but some. He spread it on the floor, hoping it would act as a heat-retaining vapour barrier. Dry socks would have helped; he made a little teepee of sticks, draped the damp socks over it near the dying embers of his fire, hoping they wouldn't scorch. Then he heated several medium-sized stones in the coals. He bundled his cold feet inside the down vest, unfolded the two space-age reflecting survival blankets, his own and Chuck's, scrunched himself up inside them, added the hot stones underneath. Keep the core warm, that was Lesson One. Keep the feet from dropping off, always a good plan going forward. Remember that hands without fingers are not much use for tasks requiring small-muscle skills, such as doing up your bootlaces.

Was there grunting outside the bunkie in the dim hours, was there scratching? No door on the place, anything could walk right in. Wolverine, wolf, bear. Maybe the smoke kept them off. Did he sleep? He must have. It got light soon enough.

He woke up singing.

Roamin' here, roamin' there, roamin' in my underwear,
I got a sweetie covered in hair,
She's all pussy everywhere...

Some hoarse, twisted stagtime bellowing event. Energizing, though. Instant man-cave bonding. "Shut up," he told himself. "You want to die frivolously?" "Don't much matter, nobody's looking," he riposted.

His socks weren't dry, but they were drier. What a fool, he should've taken Chuck's socks from his gone but not forgotten fishbelly feet. He put the socks on, folded up the survival blankets, and stuffed them into his pockets – damn things would never go back into their little envelopes once you took them out – packed up his Practical Pig toolguy trinkets and the remains of his picnic, then took a cautious look out the door.

Mist everywhere. Grey as an emphysema cough. Just as well because now the flying visibility would be low, a good deterrent for airborne snoopers. Though not so good for Zeb himself because now he wouldn't know where he was going, as such. But surely it was a case of follow the yellow brick road, minus the bricks and with no Emerald City at the end.

There were only two possible directions: northeast to Norman Wells, rough going on a decaying track jumbled with glacier-dumped boulders; or southwest to Whitehorse, through the chilly, misty mountain valleys. Both of those destinations were far, far away, and if he were making odds he wouldn't have bet on himself. But the Whitehorse route hooked up on the Yukon side with a real road, one that could handle motorized vehicles. More chance of a hitchhike pickup there. Or something. Or other.

He set off through the mist, keeping to the degraded gravel surface. If this were a movie he'd be fading to white, then gone, and the credits would be rolling up over him. But not so fast, not so fast, he was still alive. "Enjoy the moment," he urged himself.

I love to go a-wandering, along the bums of sluts,
And as I go I love to sing, although they drive me nuts.
Fuckeree, fuckera, fuckeree, fucker ah hah hah hah hah ha...

"You are not taking this seriously," he scolded. "Oh shut up," he replied. "I've heard that a lot." Talking to yourself, not so positive. Doing it out loud, even worse. Delirium had not set in, however; though how could he be sure?

The mist burnt off at eleven a.m. or so; the sky turned blue; a wind began to blow. Two ravens were shadowing him, high in the air, dipping to eyeball him, passing rude remarks about him back and forth. They were waiting for something to begin eating him so they could pitch in and grab a snack: not so deft at making the first incisions, ravens, they always hunted with hunters. He ate a Joltbar, he came to a stream with a washed-out bridge, he had to choose: wet boots or crippled bare feet? He chose the boots, removing his socks first. The water was cold, with an X for Xtra. "This freezing sucks," he said, and it did.

Then he had to choose between putting the socks back on and getting them wet or the dubious delight of hiking in boots only, sure to accentuate the blister he already had. The boots themselves would soon be borderline useless.

"You get the picture," he says. "On and on. It was that kind of thing all day, with the wind blowing and the sun shining."

"How far had you gone?" says Toby.

"How to measure? Out there, miles don't count. Let's just say not far enough," he says. "And by then I was running on empty."

He spent the night hunkered down between two boulders, shivering like a timber despite the two crackly metal survival blankets and the fire he'd made from dead willow and creekside mini-birch.

By the time the next pink sunset had come round he'd run out of food. He'd stopped worrying about bears; in fact, he was longing to meet one, a big fat one he could sink his teeth into. He dreamed of little globules of fat sifting down through the air like snow, the pellet-shaped kind of snow, not the flakes; he dreamed of it settling down on him, into his bodily creases and crannies, plumping him up. The brain was 100 per cent cholesterol, so he needed the boost, he hungered for it. He could visualize the inside of his body, the ribs encasing a hollow, a hollow lined with teeth. If he stuck out his tongue in such a fatfall the air would taste like chicken soup.

In the gloaming there was a caribou. It looked at him, he looked at it. Too far away for him to shoot, too fast for him to chase. Those things could skim over the top of the muskeg as if on skis.

The next day was bright and almost hot; things in the distance were wobbly at the edges, like a mirage. Was he hungry any more? Hard to tell. He could sense words rising from him, burning away in the sun. Soon he'd be wordless, and then would he still be able to think? No and yes, yes and no. He'd be up against it, up against everything that filled the space he was moving through, with no glass pane of language coming between him and not-him. Not-him was seeping into him through his defences, through his edges, eating away at form, sending its rootlets into his head like reverse hairs. Soon he'd be overgrown, one with the moss. He needed to keep moving, preserve his outlines, define himself by his own shockwaves, the wake he left in the air. To keep alert, to stay attuned to the, to the what? To whatever might come at him and stop him dead.

At the next washed-out bridge a bear congealed from the low shrubs flanking the river. It was not there and then it was there, and it reared up, startled, offering itself. Was there growling, a roar, a stench?

No doubt, but Zeb can't remember. He must have sprayed its eyes with the bear spray and shot it point-blank, but there's no photo record.

Next thing he knew he was butchering it, hacking away at it with his inadequate knife. Blood up to the wrists, then bonanza: the meat, the fur. The two ravens stood at a distance, making R noises, waiting their turn: gobbets for him, followed by pickings for them.

"Not too much," he told himself, chewing, recalling the dangers of stuffing yourself on an empty stomach, especially on something so rich and supersaturated. "Little at a time." His voice came to him muffled, as if he was telephoning himself from underground. What did this taste like? Who cared? Having eaten the heart, could he now speak the language of bears?

Picture him the next day or the next or sometime, halfway there, wherever there is, though he retains the belief that it is in fact somewhere. He's got new footgear — wraps of hide, fur side in, tied with crisscross strips like a fashion item in a cave-man comic. He's got a fur cape, he's got a fur hat, and all of it doubles as sleeping gear, heavy and stinky. He's porting a meat cargo and a big wad of fat. If he had the time he'd render the fat into grease and smear it on himself, but as it is he injects it into his mouth like bite-sized fuel. And it is fuel, he's burning it; he can feel the heat of it travelling through his veins.

"Goodbye to care," he sings. The ravens are sticking with him, shadowing him. Now there are four of them: he's the Pied Piper of ravens. "*There's a bluebird on my windowsill,*" he sings to them. His mother went in for cheerful, upbeat retro crap. That, and perky hymns.

And now, coming towards him along the relatively smooth stretch of road ahead, far in the distance, there's a cyclist. Some rugged mountain bike adventurer out of his mind on endorphins. They pass through Whitehorse from time to time, augment their kits at the outfitter stores, head for the hills to test their endurance mettle on the Old Canol Trail. They pedal as far as the bunkie — that's their usual trajectory. Then they pedal back, thinner, stringier, madder. Some bring tales of alien abductions, some of talking foxes, some of human voices on the tundra at night. Or semi-human voices. Trying to lure them.

No, two cyclists. One quite a bit ahead. Lovers' tiff, he speculates. The normal thing would be to stick together.

Useful things, mountain bikes. Also pannier packs and whatever might be in them.

Zeb hides in the creekside shrubbery, waits for the first one to go past. A woman, blond, sporting the thighs of a stainless-steel nutcracker goddess in her shiny skintight cyclewear. Under her streamlined helmet she's squinting into the wind, frowning fit to kill with her skimpy eyebrows over her trendy little wind/sun goggles. Away she goes, bumpity-bump, ass taut as an implanted tit, and now here comes the guy, keeping his distance, morose, mouth down at the corners. He's pissed her off, he's feeling the whip. He's burdened with a misery Zeb can alleviate.

"Arrgh," Zeb yells, or words to that effect.

"Arrgh?" says Toby, laughing.

"You know what I mean," says Zeb.

Short form: he leaps out of the bushes and onto the guy, making a growly noise, in his bear-fur coverings. There's a strangled yelp from the target, then a metallic toppling. No need to bash the poor sucker, he's out cold anyway. Just take the cycle with its twin saddle packs and make off.

When he looks behind, the girl has stopped. He can picture her recently clamped mouth an open O, the O of woe. Now she'll be sorry she tongue-lashed the sad bugger. She'll thunder-thigh back, kneel and minister, rock and cradle, dab at scrapes, shed tears. The lad will come to and gaze into her ungoggled eyes, the simp, and all will be forgiven, whatever it was. Then they will use her cellphone to call for aid.

What will they say? He can imagine.

When he's out of sight, down a hill, and around a corner, he goes through the saddlebags. What a trove: a poker hand of Joltbars, some sort of quasi-cheese product, an extra windcheater, a mini-stove with fuel cylinder, a pair of dry socks, spare boots with thick soles – too small, but he'll cut out the toes. A cellphone. Best of all, an identity:

he can use some of that. He mashes the cellphone and hides it under a rock, then makes his way sideways over the tundra, squish squish, bike and all.

Luckily there's a palsa that's been ripped open, no doubt by an enraged grolar in search of evasive ground squirrels. Zeb digs himself and the bike into the moist black earth, leaving a vantage point between clods. After a long damp wait, here comes the 'thopter. It hovers over where the two young cyclists must be hugging and shivering and thanking their lucky stars, and down goes the ladder, and, after a time, up go the lovers, and then they're carried away in the slow, low 'thopter, flippity-flop, blimpity-blimp. What a story they will have to tell.

And they tell it. Once in Whitehorse, having shed his bearskin wrappings some time back and sunk them in a pond, having changed into the fresh gear provided by Fortune, having grabbed a hitchhike, having freshened up considerably and altered his hairstyle, having hacked certain features of the cyclist's identity and run some cash through a backdoor known to him by memory, and having swiftly topped up his own cash flow thereby, he reads all about it.

Sasquatches are real after all, and they've migrated to the Mackenzie Mountain Barrens. No, it couldn't have been a bear because bears can't ride mountain bikes. Anyway, this thing was seven feet tall with eyes almost like a man's, and it smelled terrible, and it showed signs of almost-human intelligence. There's even a picture, taken on the girl's cellphone: a brown blob, with a red circle around it to signal which of the many brown blobs in the picture is the significant one.

Within a week, Bigfoot-believers from around the world have formed a posse and mounted an expedition to the site of the discovery, and are combing the area for footprints and tufts of hair and piles of dung. Soon, says their leader, they will have a batch of definitive DNA, and then the scoffers will be shown up for the corrupt, fossilized, obsolete truth-deniers that they are.

Very soon.

The Story of Zeb and Thank You and Good Night

Thank you for bringing me this fish.

Thank you means . . . *Thank you* means you did something good for me. Or something you thought was good. And that good thing was giving me a fish. So that made me happy, but the part that really made me happy was that you wanted me to be happy. That's what *Thank you* means.

No, you don't need to give me another fish. I am happy enough for now.

Don't you want to hear about Zeb?

Then you must listen.

After Zeb came back from the high and tall mountains with snow on top, and after he had taken off the skin of the bear and put it on himself, he said Thank You to the bear. To the spirit of the bear.

Because the bear didn't eat him, but allowed him to eat it instead, and also because it gave him its fur skin to put on.

A *spirit* is the part of you that doesn't die when your body dies.

Dies is . . . it's what the fish do when they are caught and then cooked.

No, it is not only fish that die. People do it as well.

Yes. Everyone.

Yes, you as well. Sometime. Not yet. Not for a long time.

I don't know why. Crake made it that way.

Because . . .

Because if nothing ever died, but everything had more and more babies, the world would get too full and there wouldn't be any room.

No, you will not be cooked on a fire when you die.

Because you are not a fish.

No, the bear was not a fish either. And it died in a bear way. Not in a fish way. So it was not cooked on a fire.

Yes, maybe Zeb said Thank You to Oryx too. As well as to the bear.

Because Oryx let Zeb eat one of her Children. Oryx knows that some of her Children eat other ones; that is the way they are made. The ones with sharp teeth. So she knew that Zeb could eat one of her Children too, because he was very hungry.

I don't know whether Zeb said Thank You to Crake. Maybe you could ask Zeb that, the next time you see him. Anyway, Crake is not in charge of bears. Oryx is in charge of bears.

Zeb put on the bear's fur to keep warm.

Because he was very cold. Because it was colder there. Because of the mountains all around, with snow on the top.

Snow is water that is frozen into little pieces called snowflakes. *Frozen* is when water becomes hard like rock.

No, snowflakes have nothing to do with Snowman-the-Jimmy. I don't know why part of his name is almost the same as a snowflake.

I am doing this thing with my hands on my forehead because I have a headache. A headache is when there is a pain in your head.

Thank you. I am sure purring would help. But it would also help if you would stop asking so many questions.

Yes, I think Amanda must have a headache too. Or some sort of ache. Perhaps you could do some purring for her.

I think that's enough of the story of Zeb for tonight. Look, the moon is rising. It's your bedtime.

I know you don't have beds. But I have a bed. So it is my bedtime now. Good night.

Good night means that I hope you will sleep well, and wake up safely in the morning, and that nothing bad will happen to you.

Well, such as . . . I can't think what sort of bad things might happen to you.

Good night.

Scars

Scars

She's tried to be discreet, sneaking off alone every night after she's told the Crakers their story, then joining Zeb once out of eyesight. But she's not fooling anyone, or anyone among the humans.

Naturally, they see it as funny. Or the younger ones do – Swift Fox, Lotis Blue, Croze and Shackie, Zunzuncito. Even Ren, probably. Even Amanda. Romance among the chronologically challenged is giggle fodder. For the youthful, lovelorn and wrinkly don't blend, or not without farce. There's a moment past which the luscious and melting becomes the crusty and wizened, the fertile sea becomes the barren sand, and they must feel she's passed that moment. Brewing herbs, gathering mushrooms, applying maggots, tending bees, removing warts – beldam's roles. Those are her proper vocations.

As for Zeb, he's probably less comic to them than puzzling. From their socio-bio vantage point, he should be doing what alpha males do best: jumping the swooning nubiles that are his by right, knocking them up, passing his genes along via females who can actually parturiate, unlike her. So why is he wasting his precious sperm packet? they must wonder. Instead of, for instance, investing it wisely in the ovarian offerings of Swift Fox. Which is almost certainly that girl's take on things, judging from the body language: the eyelash play, the tit thrusts, the hair-tuft flinging, the armpit display. She might as well be flashing a blue bottom, like the Crakers. Baboons in spate.

Stop that, Toby, she tells herself. This is how it starts, among the closed circles of the marooned, the shipwrecked, the besieged: jealousy, dissention, a breach in the groupthink walls. Then the entry of the foe, the murderer, the shadow slipping in through the door we forgot to lock because we were distracted by our darker selves: nursing our minor hatreds, indulging our petty resentments, yelling at one another, tossing the crockery.

Beleaguered groups are prone to such festering: such backbiting, such infighting. At the Gardeners, they'd held Deep Mindfulness sessions about this very subject.

Ever since they've been lovers, Toby has been dreaming that Zeb is gone. In real life he is in fact gone while she dreams, as there isn't enough room for both of them on Toby's single-bed-sized slab in her broom closet of a room. So in the middle of each night Zeb sneaks off like someone in an ancient English country-house farce, groping in the darkness back to his own cramped cubicle.

But in the dreams he really is gone – gone far away, nobody knows where – and Toby is standing outside the cobb-house fence, looking down the road, now overgrown with kudzu vines and choked with parts of broken houses and smashed-up vehicles. There's a soft bleating sound, or is it weeping? "He won't be back," says a watercolour voice. "He won't ever be back."

It's a woman's voice: is it Ren, is it Amanda, is it Toby herself? The scenario is sweetly sentimental, like a pastel greeting card – awake, she'd be annoyed by it, but in dreams there is no irony. She cries so much that her clothes are damp with tears, luminous tears that flicker like blue-green gasfire in what is now becoming the darkness, or is she in a cave? But then a large cat-like animal comes to console her. It rubs up against her, purring like the wind.

She wakes to find a small Craker boy in the room with her. He's lifted the edge of the damp sheet that entwists her and is gently stroking her leg. He smells of oranges, and of something else. Citrus air freshener. They all smell like this, but the young ones more.

"What are you doing?" she asks as calmly as she can. My toenails are so dirty, she thinks. Dirty and jagged. Nail scissors: put them on the gleaning list. Her skin is coarse beside the pristine skin on the hand of this child. Is he glowing from within, or is his skin so fine-grained it reflects the light?

"Oh Toby, you have legs underneath," says the boy. "Like us."

"Yes," she says. "I do."

"Do you have breasts, Oh Toby?"

"Yes, I have those as well," she says, smiling.

"Are there two? Two breasts?"

"Yes," she says, resisting the urge to add, "so far." Is he expecting one breast, or three, or maybe four or six, like a dog? Has he ever seen a dog up close?

"Will a baby come out from between your legs, Oh Toby? After you turn blue?"

What is he asking? Whether non-Craker people like her can have babies, or whether she herself might have one? "If I were younger, then a baby might come out," she says. "But not now." Though her age isn't the deciding factor. If her whole life had been different. If she hadn't needed the money. If she'd lived in another universe.

"Oh Toby," says the Craker boy, "what sickness do you have? Are you hurt?" He puts up his beautiful arms to hug her. Are those tears in his strange green eyes?

"It's all right," she says. "I'm not hurt any more." She'd sold some of her eggs to pay the rent, back in her pleebland days, before the God's Gardeners had taken her in. There'd been infection: all her future children, precluded. Surely she'd buried that particular sadness many years ago. If not, she ought to bury it. In view of the total situation — the situation of what used to be thought of as the human race — such emotions ought to be dismissed as meaningless.

She's about to add, "I have scars, inside me," but she stops herself. *What is a scar, Oh Toby?* That would be the next question. Then she'd have to explain what a scar is. *A scar is like writing on your body. It tells about something that once happened to you, such as a cut on your skin where blood came out. What is writing, Oh Toby? Writing is when you make marks on a piece of paper — on a stone — on a flat surface, like the sand on the beach, and each of the marks means a sound, and the sounds joined together mean a word, and the words joined together mean... How do you make this writing, Oh Toby? You make it with a keyboard, or no — once you made it with a pen or a pencil, a pencil is a . . . Or you make it with a stick. Oh Toby, I do not understand. You make a mark with a stick on your skin, you cut your skin open and then it is a scar, and that scar turns into a voice? It speaks, it tells us things? Oh Toby, can we hear what the scar says? Show us how to make these scars that talk!*

No, she should stay away from the whole scar business. Otherwise she might inspire the Crakers to start carving themselves up to see if they can let out the voices.

"What's your name?" she says to the little boy.

"My name is Blackbeard," says the child gravely. Blackbeard, the notorious murdering pirate? This sweet child? A child who will never have a beard when he grows up because Crake did away with body hair in his new species. A lot of the Crakers have odd names. According to Zeb, Crake named them — Crake, with his warped sense of humour. Though why shouldn't their names be odd, to go with their general oddity?

"I am very happy to meet you, Oh Blackbeard," she says.

"Do you eat your droppings, Oh Toby?" says Blackbeard. "As we do? To digest our leaves better?"

What droppings? Edible poo? No one warned her about this! "It is time to go and see your mother, Oh Blackbeard," says Toby. "She must be worried about you."

"No, Oh Toby. She knows I am with you. She says you are good and kind." He smiles, showing perfect little teeth: enchantment. They are all so attractive — like airbrushed cosmetic ads. "You are good like Crake. You are kind like Oryx. Do you have wings, Oh Toby?" He cranes his neck, trying to see behind her. Maybe the earlier hug was only a stealthy way of feeling her back for the feathered stubs that might be sprouting there.

"No," says Toby. "No wings."

"I will mate with you when I am bigger," says Blackbeard. He offers this heroically. "Even if you are . . . even if you are only a little blue. Then you will have a baby! It will grow in your bone cave! You will be happy!"

Only a little blue. It must mean that he recognizes her comparative age, though *old* is not something the Crakers have a word for. "Thank you, Oh Blackbeard," says Toby. "Now run along. I have to eat my breakfast. And I must go and visit Jimmy — I must visit Snowman-the-Jimmy, to see if his sickness is better." She sits up and plants her feet squarely on the floor, a sign for the boy to leave.

Though not a sign he understands. "What is *breakfast*, Oh Toby?" he says. She forgot: these people don't have meals as such. They graze, like herbivores.

He eyes her binoculars, pokes her stack of bedsheets. Now he's stroking her rifle, where it stands in the corner. It's something a normal human child might do: idle fiddling, curious handling. "Is this your breakfast?"

"Don't touch that," she says a little sharply. "That is not breakfast, that is a special thing for . . . Breakfast is what we eat in the morning — the people like me, with extra skins."

"Is it a fish?" says the boy. "This breakfast?"

"Sometimes," says Toby. "But for breakfast today, I will eat part of an animal. An animal with fur. Perhaps I will eat its leg. There will be a smelly bone inside. You wouldn't want to see such a smelly bone, would you?" she says. That will surely get rid of him.

"No," says the child dubiously. He wrinkles his nose. He seems intrigued, however: who wouldn't want to peek from behind the curtain at the trolls' revolting feasts?

"Then you should go away," says Toby.

Still he lingers. "Snowman-the-Jimmy says the bad people in the chaos ate the Children of Oryx," he says. "They killed them and killed them, and ate them and ate them. They were always eating them."

"Yes, they were," says Toby, "but they were eating them in the wrong way."

"Were the two bad men eating them in the wrong way too? The ones who ran away?"

"Yes," says Toby. "They were."

"How are you eating them, Oh Toby? The legs of the Children?" His huge eyes are fixed on her as if she's about to sprout fangs and pounce on him.

"The right way," she says, hoping he won't ask what the right way is.

"I saw a smelly bone. It was behind the kitchen. Is it breakfast? Do the bad men eat such bones?" says Blackbeard.

"Yes," says Toby. "But they do other bad things too. Many bad things. Much worse things. We must all be very careful, and not go into the forest by ourselves. If you see those bad men or anyone like them, you must come and tell me right away. Or tell Crozier, or Rebecca, or Ren, or Ivory Bill. Any of us." She's gone over this point several times with all of the Crakers, the adults too, but she's not sure they've taken it in. They gaze at her and nod, chewing slowly as if thinking, but they don't seem frightened. It's worrying, their lack of fear.

"Not Snowman-the-Jimmy or Amanda," the boy says. "We can't tell them. Because they are sick." At least he's grasped that much. He pauses as if considering. "But Zeb will make the bad men go away. Then everything will be safe."

"Yes," says Toby. "Then everything will be safe." Already the Crakers have constructed a formidable set of beliefs about Zeb. Soon he'll be all-potent and able to fix every ill; and that could be troublesome, because of course he can't. Not even for me, thinks Toby.

But the name of Zeb is reassuring to Blackbeard. He smiles again, lifts his hand, gives a little wave, like a president of old, like a queen in a cavalcade, like a movie star. Where has he picked up that gesture? Now he's sidling backwards through the doorway. He doesn't take his eyes off Toby until he's around the corner.

Did I scare him? she thinks. Will he go back to the others and tell them disgusting marvels, as real children — as children do?

Violet Biolet

Outside the main house the day is underway. The others must already have had their breakfasts, though Swift Fox and Ivory Bill are still at the table, engaged no doubt in some kind of arcane flirtation, she for practise, he in pathetic earnest.

Toby looks around for Zeb, but he is nowhere to be seen; maybe he's taking a shower. Crozier is just setting off with the Mo'Hair flock; Zunzuncito is with him, toting a spraygun, covering his back. Jimmy's hammock is under the tree, watched over by a trio of Crakers.

Lotis Blue and Ren are working on an addition to the cobb house. The MaddAddamites have voted to expand the number of sleeping cubicles; they'll make the new ones roomier, more like a real house. The core structure was built as a demonstration of olden-day ways: ersatz antiquity, like a dinosaur made of cement. The Tree of Life Natural Materials Exchange used to be held in this space; Toby remembers coming here with the God's Gardeners to peddle their recycled soap and their vinegar and honey and mushrooms and roof-top vegetables, back when there had still been buying and people to buy things, selling and people to sell them.

I ought to look around for some bees, she thinks. There must be escapees, living in the trees. It would be calming as well as useful to tend a few hives.

The cobb-house construction has to be done in stages. This morning Ren and Lotis Blue are mixing up the mud, straw, and sand in a plastic wading pool decorated with Mickey Mice. The wood frame is in place, the layers of cobb are being added day by day. Drying each layer is a problem in view of the afternoon thunderstorms, but luckily they've been able to glean some plastic sheeting for coverups.

Amanda sits near the two of them, hands in her lap, doing nothing. She does nothing a lot. Maybe it's slow healing, Toby thinks, like slow cooking. Maybe the end result will be better that way. But at least she's gained some weight. She has been making some effort over the past few days: pulling out a weed or two, culling the odd slug or snail. In the old Edencliff Rooftop Garden days, they'd have relocated Our Fellow Vegetable Eaters by throwing them down onto the street — slugs, too, had a right to live, went the mantra, though not in inappropriate locations such as salad bowls, where they might be harmed by chewing. But now their numbers are too overwhelming — every plant seems to generate slugs and snails as if spontaneously — so by common though unspoken agreement they're being dropped into salt water.

Amanda seems to enjoy that slightly, despite the writhing and frothing. But the cobb-house building work is too much for her. She used to be so strong: nothing used to frighten her. She'd been a tough pleebrat, she'd lived by her wits, she could handle anything. Of the two of them, Ren was the weaker, the more timid. Whatever has happened to Amanda — whatever was done to her by the Painballers — must have been extreme.

Several Craker kids are watching the mud mixing. No doubt they're asking questions. *Why are you doing that? Are you making a chaos? What are those, with the round black things on their heads? What is a* mickeymouse? *But they do not look like mice, we have seen mice, mice do not have big white hands*, and so forth. Every new thing they discover in the territory of the MaddAddamites is a source of wonder for them. Yesterday Crozier managed to glean a package of cigarettes during his shepherding stroll, and the Crakers have not got over it. *He set fire to a white stick! He put it in his mouth! He breathed in the smoke! Why did you do that, Oh Crozier? Smoke is not for breathing, smoke is for cooking a fish*, and so on.

"Just tell them it's a Crake thing," said Toby, so Crozier did. The Crake gambit was one-size-fits-all.

Some of the Crakers — a number of the women, several of the smaller kids — are over in the erstwhile playground outside the cobb-house boundary fence, munching away at the kudzu vines draping the swing set. Kudzu is one of their favourite plants, which shows foresight on the part of Crake because there won't be a shortage of kudzu any time soon. They've got the red plastic slide almost uncovered, and the children are stroking it as if it's alive. Who remembered the swing set was under there, before they started gnawing?

Toby heads for the violet biolet, not only because she needs to but also because she doesn't want to arrive at the breakfast table before Swift Fox leaves it. She consciously suppresses the word *slut*: a woman should not use that word about another woman, especially with no exact cause.

Really? says her inner slut-uttering voice. You've seen the way she looks at Zeb. Eyelashes like Venus flytraps, and that sideways leer of the irises, like some outdated cut-rate prostibot commercial: Bacteria-Resistant Fibres, 100% Fluid-Flushing, Lifelike Moans, ClenchOMeter for Optimal Satisfaction.

She takes a breath, calls on her Gardener meditation training. She visualizes her anger pushing out through her skin like a snail horn, then lets the small bud of fury wither and fall away. She smiles gently in the direction of Swift Fox, thinking, All you want is a quick jump, you want to snag him just to show you can. Nail him up on your trophy wall. You know nothing about him, you can't truly value him, he isn't yours, you don't know how long I waited . . .

Which counts for nothing. Nobody cares. There's no fairness, there's no ownership. She has no claims. If Zeb tumbles into bed with Swift Fox — even if he tiptoes into that bed, even if he oozes into it — what she is entitled to say about that is exactly nothing. For all she knows he's double-dipping already, leaving her in affectionate sleepy-time mode — though maybe a little too much like best pals, with a little too much camaraderie between them, no? — but all the time secretly still hungry; then ducking outside, then inside through a different doorway to slide himself voraciously into the voracious Swift Fox.

It doesn't bear thinking about, so she won't think about it. *Will not* think. Wills herself *not*.

The violet biolets are part of the original park installation: three stalls for men, three for women. Their solar cells are still operating, running the ultraviolet LEDs and the small aerating-fan motors. As long as the biolets are still functioning, the MaddAddamites won't have to dig outhouse pits. Luckily there's lots of toilet paper to be gleaned in the nearby streets, as it wasn't an item heavily looted during the pillaging phase of the plague. What would you do with a skid of toilet paper? You couldn't get drunk on it.

The walls inside the biolet are still covered with pleebland inscriptions: several generations of them, one layer on top of another. There'd been a time when those still devoted to some norm of propriety had tried to paint the words over, but a few kids bent on self-expressive anarchy could destroy in an hour a white surface it had taken a crew three days to blandify.

To Daryn, Im ur bitch, ur my King,
I <3 you more than anything
Fk the Corps
Loris a stuck up cunt
I hope ur raped by 100000 pit bulls

People who write on washroom walls, Shld roll their shit in little balls, And those who read these words of wit, Shld have to eat those balls of shit

Call me/ Best for ur $/ Ull scream 24/7 & die in a pond of Cum
STAY OUT MY WAY A hat OR ILL KNIFE U

And shyly, unfinished: *Try love the World needs*

What to eat, where to shit, how to take shelter, who and what to kill: are these the basics? thinks Toby. Is this what we've come to, or come down to; or else come back to?

And who do you love? And who loves you? And who loves you not? And, come to think of it, who seriously hates you.

Blink

Under the trees Jimmy is still slumbering. Toby checks his pulse — calmer; changes his maggots — the wound on his foot has stopped festering; and pours some mushroom elixir into him, mixed with a little Poppy.

An oval of chairs is arranged around the hammock, as if Jimmy is the central offering at a feast: a giant salmon, a boar on a platter. Three Crakers are purring over him, taking turns: two men and a woman, gold, ivory, ebony. It's a different three every few hours. Do they have only so much purring quotient, are they like batteries that have to be recharged? Naturally they need time off to graze and water themselves, but does the purring itself have a sort of electrical frequency?

We'll never know, thinks Toby, holding Jimmy's nose to make him open his mouth: no way of wiring up their brains for scientific studies, not any more. Which is lucky for them. In the olden days they'd have been kidnapped from the Paradice Project dome by some rival Corp, then injected and jolted and probed and sliced apart to see how they were put together. What made them tick, what made them purr, what made them click. What, if anything, made them sick. They'd have ended up as slabs of DNA in a freezer.

Jimmy swallows, sighs; his left hand twitches. "How has he been today?" Toby asks the three Crakers. "Has he been awake at all?"

"No, Oh Toby," says the gold-coloured man. "He is travelling." This one has bright red hair, long slender limbs; despite the skin colour, he looks like something from a children's storybook. An Irish folktale.

"But now he has stopped," says the ebony man. "He has climbed into a tree."

"Not his real tree," says the ivory woman. "Not the tree he lives in."

"He has gone to sleep in this tree," says the ebony man.

"You mean, he's sleeping inside his sleep?" says Toby. This seems wrong: it shouldn't be possible. "In the tree in his dream?"

"Yes, Oh Toby," says the ivory woman. All three of them gaze at her with their lambent green eyes, as if she's twirling a piece of string and they are bored cats.

"Perhaps he will sleep for a long time," says the golden man. "He is stuck there, in the tree. If he will not wake up and travel to here, he will not wake up at all."

"But he's getting better!" says Toby.

"He is afraid," says the ivory woman in a matter-of-fact voice. "He is afraid of what is in this world. He is afraid of the bad men, he is afraid of the Pig Ones. He doesn't want to be awake."

"Can you talk to him?" says Toby. "Can you tell him it's better to be awake?" No harm in trying: maybe they have some form of inaudible communication that might reach Jimmy, wherever he is. A wavelength, a vibration.

But now they aren't looking at her. They're looking at Ren and Lotis Blue, who are walking over with Amanda in tow, sheltering behind them.

The three of them sit down on the empty chairs, Amanda hesitantly. Ren and Lotis Blue are muddy from their building activities, but Amanda is pristine. The other two give her a shower every morning, choose a fresh bedsheet for her, braid her hair.

"We thought we'd take a break from the house," says Ren. "See how Jimmy — see how Snowman-the-Jimmy is doing."

The ivory woman smiles widely at them, the two men smile less widely: the Craker men are nervous around the younger cobb-house women now. Ever since they've learned that rambunctious group copulation is not acceptable, they don't know what's expected of them. They begin conferring together in low voices, leaving the ivory woman as the sole purrer.

Is she blue? One is blue. Two others were blue, we joined our blue to their blue but we did not make them happy. They are not like our women, they are not happy, they are broken. Did Crake make them? Why did he make them that way, so they are not happy? Oryx will take care of them. Will Oryx take care of them, if they are not like our women? When Snowman-the-Jimmy wakes up, we will ask him these things.

I'd like to be a fly on the wall, thinks Toby. Listening to Jimmy justifying the ways of Crake towards men, or semi-men.

"Will Jimmy – will Snowman-the-Jimmy be okay?" asks Lotis Blue.

"I think so," says Toby. "It will depend on his . . ." She doesn't want to say "immune system" because the Crakers will hear. (*What is an* immune system? *It is something you have inside yourself that helps you and makes you strong. Where can we find an immune system? Is it from Crake, will he send us an immune system?*, and so on.) "It depends on his dreaming." No comment from the Crakers: so far, so good. "But I'm sure he'll wake up soon."

"He needs to eat," says Lotis Blue. "He's so thin! He can't live on nothing."

"You can go a long time without food," says Ren. "They did fasts, at the Gardeners? You can go for days. Weeks." She leans over and reaches out, smoothing back Jimmy's hair. "I wish we could give him a shampoo," she says. "He's getting rank."

"I think he just said something," says Lotis Blue.

"It was only a mumble. We could sponge him off," says Ren. "Like, a sponge bath." She leans closer. "He looks a bit shrivelled. Poor Jimmy. I hope he doesn't die."

"I'm hydrating him," says Toby. "And there's the honey, I'm feeding him that." Why is she sounding like a head nurse? "We do wash him," she says defensively. "We do it every day."

"Well anyway, he's not so feverish," says Lotis Blue. "He's cooling down. Don't you think?"

Ren feels Jimmy's forehead. "I don't know," she says. "Jimmy, can you hear me?" They all watch: Jimmy doesn't twitch. "I'd say he's warm. Amanda? See what you think." She's trying to involve her, thinks Toby. Get her interested in something. Ren was always a kindly child.

If she is blue, the Lotis one, should we mate with her? No, we should not. Do not sing to them, do not pick flowers for them, do not wag your penis at them. These women scream with fright, they do not choose us even if we give them a flower, they do not like a wagging penis. We do not make them happy, we do not know why they scream. But sometimes they do not scream with fright, sometimes they . . .

"I need to lie down," says Amanda. She stands up, walks unsteadily away towards the cobb house.

"I'm really worried about her," says Ren. "She threw up this morning, she couldn't eat any breakfast. That's extreme Fallow."

"Maybe it's a bug," says Lotis Blue. "Something she ate. We really need a better way of washing the dishes, I don't think the water is . . ."

"Look," says Ren. "He blinked."

"He is hearing you," says the ivory woman. "He is hearing your voice, and now he is walking. He is happy, he wants to be with you."

"With me?" says Ren. "Really?"

"Yes. Look, he is smiling." There is indeed a smile, or the trace of a smile, thinks Toby. Though maybe it's only gas, as with babies.

The ivory woman waves away a mosquito that has settled on Jimmy's mouth. "Soon he will be awake," she says.

Zeb
in the
Dark

Zeb in the Dark

It's evening. Toby has dodged her storytime session with the Crakers. Those stories take a lot out of her. Not only does she have to put on the absurd red hat and eat the ritual fish, which isn't always what you'd call cooked, but there's so much she needs to invent. She doesn't like to tell lies, not deliberately, not lies as such, but she skirts the darker and more tangled corners of reality. It's like trying to keep toast from burning while still having it transform into toast.

"I'll come tomorrow," she told them. "Tonight I must do an important thing for Zeb."

"What is the important thing you must do, Oh Toby? We would like to be your helpers." At least they didn't ask what *important* means. They seem to have put together an idea of it: somewhere between dangerous and delicious.

"Thank you," she said. "But it is a thing that only I can do."

"Is it about the bad men?" asked little Blackbeard.

"No," Toby said. "We have not seen the bad men for many days. Maybe they have gone far away. But we must still be careful, and tell others if we see them."

One of the Mo'Hairs has gone missing, Crozier has told her privately – the red-headed one with the braids – but it may simply have strayed off while grazing. Or else a liobam got it.

Or something worse, thinks Toby: something human.

The day has been stifling. Even the afternoon thunderstorm hasn't cleared away the humidity. Under normal conditions – but what is *normal?* – lust should have been drained of its supercharge by this weather;

muffled, as if under a damp mattress. She and Zeb should have been limp, enervated, exhausted. But instead they'd snuck away from the others even earlier than usual, slippery with longing, every pore avid, every capillary suffused, and thrashed around like newts in a puddle.

Now it's deep twilight. Purple darkness wells up from the earth, bats flit past like leathery butterflies, night flowers open, musking the air. They're sitting outside in the kitchen garden for the evening breeze, what there is of it. Their fingers are loosely entwined; Toby can feel, still, a small current of electricity moving between them. Tiny iridescent moths are shimmering around their heads. What do we smell like to them? she wonders. Like mushrooms? Like crushed petals? Like dew?

"Help me out here," says Toby. "I need more to go on, for the Crakers. They're insatiable on the subject of you."

"Like what?"

"You're their hero. They want your life story. Your miraculous origins, your supernatural deeds, your favourite recipes. You're like royalty to them."

"Why me?" says Zeb. "I thought Crake did away with all that. They aren't supposed to be interested."

"Well, they are. They're obsessed with you. You're their rock star."

"Lord fuck a dog. Can't you just make up some piece of crap?"

"They cross-examine like lawyers," says Toby. "At the very least I need the basics. The raw material." Does she want to know about Zeb for the sake of the Crakers, or for herself? Both. But mostly for herself.

"I'm an open book," says Zeb.

"Don't be evasive."

Zeb sighs. "I hate going back to all that. I had to live it, I don't like reliving it. Who cares?"

"I do," says Toby. And so do you, she thinks. You still do care. "I'm listening."

"Persistent, aren't you?"

"I've got all night. So, you were born . . ."

"Yeah, admitted." Another sigh. "Okay. First you need to understand: we got the wrong mothers."

"Wrong, how?" she says to the face she can barely see. A plane of cheekbone, a shadow, a glint of eye.

The Story of the Birth of Zeb

I have put on the red hat of Snowman. I have eaten the fish. I have listened to the shiny thing. Now I will tell the story of the birth of Zeb.

You don't have to sing.

Zeb did not come from Crake, not like Snowman. And he wasn't made by Oryx, not like rabbits. He was born, the same way you are born. He grew in a bone cave, just like you, and came out through a bone tunnel, just like you.

Because underneath our clothing skins, we are the same as you. Almost the same.

No, we do not turn blue. Though we might smell blue sometimes. But our bone cave is the same.

I don't think we need to discuss blue penises right now.

I know they are bigger. Thank you for pointing that out.

Yes, we do have breasts. The women do.

Yes, two.

Yes, on the front.

No, I will not show them to you right now.

Because this story is not about breasts. This story is about Zeb.

A very long time ago, in the days of the chaos — before Crake cleared it all away — Zeb lived in the bone cave of his mother. And Oryx took care of him there, as she takes care of all those who live in the bone caves. And then he travelled into this world through the bone tunnel. And then he was a baby, and then he grew.

And he had an older brother whose name was Adam. But Adam's mother was not the same mother as the mother of Zeb.

Because when Adam was very young, Adam's mother ran away from Adam's father.

Running away means she went very quickly to a different place. Though she may not have done any running as such. Perhaps she walked, or drove in a . . . So Adam never saw her any more.

Yes, I'm sure it was sad for him.

Because she wanted to mate with more than one male, not only with Zeb's father. Or that is what Zeb's father told him.

Yes, it was a good thing to want, and she would have been happy if she could be living with you. She could mate with four males at once, like you. She would be very happy then!

But Zeb's father did not see it that way.

Because he had done a thing with her called *marriage*, and with marriage there was supposed to be one male for each female and one female for each male. Although sometimes there were more. But there were not supposed to be.

Because it was the chaos. It was a thing of the chaos. That is why you can't understand it.

Marriage is gone now. Crake cleared it away because he thought it was stupid.

Stupid means things Crake didn't like. There were a lot of things Crake thought were stupid.

Yes, good, kind Crake. I will stop telling this story if you sing.

Because it makes me forget what I am telling.

Thank you.

So then Adam's father found a new woman to have marriage with, and Zeb was born. Now little Adam was not lonely, because he had a brother. And Adam and Zeb helped each other. But Zeb's father was sometimes hurtful to them.

I don't know why. He thought pain was good for children.

No, he was not as bad as the two bad men who were hurtful to Amanda. But he was not a kind person.

I don't know why some people then were not kind. It was a thing of the chaos.

And Zeb's mother was often taking a nap, or doing other things that interested her. She was not very interested in small children. And she said, "You will be the death of me."

Death of me is hard to explain. It meant she was displeased with the things they were doing.

No, Zeb did not kill his mother. *Death of me* is just a thing she said. She said it a lot.

Why did she say it if it wasn't true? It was . . . those people talked that way. It wasn't true or not true. It was in between. It was a way of telling about a feeling you might have. It was a manner of speaking. A *manner of speaking* means . . .

You are right. Zeb's mother was not a kind person either. Sometimes she helped Zeb's father lock Zeb up in a closet.

Lock up means . . . *closet* means . . . It was a very small room and it was dark in there, and Zeb couldn't get out. Or they thought he couldn't get out. But soon Zeb learned a lot about opening closed doors.

No. His mother couldn't sing. Not like your mothers. And your fathers. And you.

But Zeb could sing. That is one of the things he did when he was locked inside the closet. He sang.

The PetrOleum Brats

Zeb's mother, Trudy, was the goody-goody, and Adam's mother, Fenella, was the shag-anything trashbunny. Or that was the story told by Trudy and the Rev. Since the two of them claimed that Zeb was so freaking useless and they were so righteous, naturally he thought he'd been adopted, since he couldn't possibly have come from two such pristine sources of DNA as them.

He used to daydream that he'd been left behind by Fenella, who must have been his real, worthless mother. She'd been forced to flee in a hurry, and hadn't been able to tote him along when she was running away — she'd dropped him on the doorstep in a cardboard box, to be taken in and trodden underfoot by this Trudy person, who was unrelated to him and lying about it. Fenella — wherever she was — deeply regretted her abandonment of him, and was planning to come back and get him once she could manage it. Then they would go far, far away together, and do absolutely everything on the long list of things that were frowned upon by the Rev. He saw them sitting on a park bench together, eating licorice twists and happily picking their noses. Just for instance.

But that was when he was little. Once he figured out genetics, he decided that Trudy must've secretly had it off with some fix-it guy with a wrench who doubled as a housebreaker and petty thief. Or else a gardener: she used to snaffle illegal Tex-Mex guys with black hair, like Zeb's. She'd pay them not enough to wheelbarrow soil around, dig up shrubs, dump more rocks on her rock garden, which was the only thing that really held her attention in the way of nurturing and tending, as far as Zeb could tell. She was always out there with one of those little fork-tongued weeders or messing up ant nests with hot vinegar.

" 'Course I could have inherited the criminality from the Rev, he had the chromosomes for it," says Zeb. "He just tarted up his misdemeanours and made them look respectable, whereas I was the real raw deal. He was furtive and sly, I was right in the face."

"Don't be too down on yourself," says Toby.

"You don't get it, babe," says Zeb. "I'm bragging."

The Rev had his very own cult. That was the way to go in those days if you wanted to coin the megabucks and you had a facility for ranting and bullying, plus golden-tongued whip-'em-up preaching, and you lacked some other grey-area but highly marketable skill, such as derivatives trading. Tell people what they want to hear, call yourself a religion, put the squeeze on for contributions, run your own media outlets and use them for robocalls and slick online campaigns, befriend or threaten politicians, evade taxes. You had to give the guy some credit. He was twisted as a pretzel, he was a tinfoil-halo shit-nosed frogstomping king rat asshole, but he wasn't stupid.

As witness his success. By the time Zeb came along, the Rev had a megachurch, all glass slabbery and pretend oak pews and faux granite, out on the rolling plains. The Church of PetrOleum, affiliated with the somewhat more mainstream Petrobaptists. They were riding high for a while, about the time accessible oil became scarce and the price shot up and desperation among the pleebs set in. A lot of top Corps guys would turn up at the church as guest speakers. They'd thank the Almighty for blessing the world with fumes and toxins, cast their eyes upwards as if gasoline came from heaven, look pious as hell.

"Pious as hell," says Zeb. "I've always liked that phrase. In my humble view, pious and hell are the flip sides of the same coin."

"Humble view?" says Toby. "Since when?"

"Since I met you," says Zeb. "Just one glance at your fine ass, one of the miracles of creation, and I realize what a shoddy construction I am by comparison. Next you'll have me scrubbing the floor with my tongue. Give a guy a break or I might get shy."

"Okay, I'll allow one humble view," says Toby. "Tell on."

"Can I kiss your clavicle?"

"In a minute," says Toby. "After you get to the point." She's new to flirting, but she's enjoying it.

"You want my point? You talking dirty?"

"Rain check. You can't stop now," says Toby.

"Okay, deal."

The Rev had nailed together a theology to help him rake in the cash. Naturally he had a scriptural foundation for it. Matthew, Chapter 16, Verse 18: "Thou art Peter, and upon this rock I will build my church."

"It didn't take a rocket-science genius, the Rev would say, to figure out that *Peter* is the Latin word for rock, and therefore the real, true meaning of 'Peter' refers to petroleum, or oil that comes from rock. 'So this verse, dear friends, is not only about Saint Peter: it is a prophecy, a vision of the Age of Oil, and the proof, dear friends, is right before your eyes, because look! What is more valued by us today than oil?' You have to give it to the rancid bugger."

"He really preached that?" says Toby. Is she supposed to laugh or not? From Zeb's tone she can't tell.

"Don't forget the Oleum part. It was even more important than the Peter half. The Rev could rave on about the Oleum for hours. 'My friends, as we all know, *oleum* is the Latin word for oil. And indeed, oil is holy throughout the Bible! What else is used for the anointing of priests and prophets and kings? Oil! It's the sign of special election, the consecrated chrism! What more proof do we need of the holiness of our very own oil, put in the earth by God for the special use of the faithful to multiply His works? His Oleum-extraction devices abound on this planet of our Dominion, and he spreads his Oleum bounty among us! Does it not say in the Bible that you should forbear to hide your light under a bushel? And what else can so reliably make the lights go on as oil? That's right! Oil, my friends! The Holy Oleum must not be hidden under a bushel – in other words, left underneath the rocks – for to do so is to flout the Word! Lift up your voices in song, and let the Oleum gush forth in ever stronger and all-blessed streams!'"

"That's an imitation?" says Toby.

"Fuckin' right. I could do the whole spiel standing on my head, I had to listen to it enough. Me and Adam both."

"You're good at it," says Toby.

"Adam was better. In the Rev's church — and around the Rev's dinner table too — we didn't pray for forgiveness or even for rain, though God knows we could have used some of each. We prayed for oil. Oh, and natural gas too — the Rev included that in his list of divine gifts for the chosen. Every time we said grace before meals the Rev would point out that it was oil that put the food on the table because it ran the tractors that plowed the fields and fuelled the trucks that delivered the food to the stores, and also the car our devoted mother, Trudy, drove to the store in to buy the food, and the power that made the heat that cooked the food. We might as well be eating and drinking oil — which was true in a way — so fall on your knees!

"Around this point in the speech Adam and me would start kicking each other under the table. The idea was to kick the other one so hard he would yelp or flinch, but not to give any sign yourself, because whoever made a noise would get whacked or have to drink piss. Or worse. But Adam was never a yelper. I admired him for that."

"Not literally?" says Toby. "The piss?"

"Cross my heart," says Zeb. "Now where'd I put that stone-cold heart thing of mine?"

"I thought you liked each other," says Toby. "You and Adam."

"We did. Kicking under the table is a guy thing."

"You were how old?"

"Too old," says Zeb. "Though Adam was older. Only a couple of years older, but he was what the Gardeners would call an old soul. He was wise, I was foolish. It was always like that."

Adam was a skinny little squirt. Though older, he wasn't nearly as strong as Zeb, once Zeb made it past the age of five. Adam was methodical: he contemplated, he thought things through. Zeb was impulsive: he shot from the hip, he let rage take him over. It got him into trouble and got him out of it in about equal measure.

But in combination the two of them were pretty effective. They were joined at the head: Zeb was the bad one who was good at bad things, Adam was the good one who was bad at good things. Or who used good things as a front for his bad things. Adam and Zebulon: bookends, as in the alphabet. That cute A–Z name symmetry was the Rev's idea: he liked to theme-park everything.

Adam was always being held up as an example. Why couldn't Zeb behave well, the way his brother did? Sit up straight, don't squirm, eat properly, your hand is not a fork, don't wipe your face on your shirt, do what your father says, say yes sir and no sir, and so on. That was how Trudy would talk, almost begging; all she wanted was peace and quiet, she didn't really enjoy the consequences of Zeb's pushbacks and sulkiness – the welts and bruises and scars. She wasn't a sadist as such, not like the Rev. But she was the centre of her own universe, big-time. She wanted the perks, and the Rev was the ever-flowing source of the cash that paid for them.

After telling Zeb what a model kid Adam was, she would go on to say that Adam's line-toeing was all the more special, all the more praiseworthy, considering . . . then she would trail off because Adam's mother, Fenella, was never mentioned at length if Trudy and the Rev could help it. You'd think they'd have used her and her scandalous douchebag behaviour as a stick to beat Adam with – disparage his genetic inheritance – but they never did. He was too good at inno-cence, or the show of it, with his big blue eyes and his thin, saintly looking face.

Zeb got hold of some old photos of Fenella – they were on a thumb-drive, at the bottom of a storage box in the closet, the one he was fre-quently locked into. He'd hidden a mini-light in there so he could see in the dark. He found the drive, then nicked it and plugged it into the Rev's computer to see what would happen. The thing still worked: there were about thirty pics of Fenella, some with tiny Adam, a few with the Rev, none of them smiling much. The thumbdrive must've been an oversight because there were no other pictures of Fenella in the house. She didn't look in any way slutty; she had the same thin, truthful, big-eyed look that Adam had.

Zeb had quite a crush on her: if only he could talk to her and tell her what was going on she would be on his side, she'd despise the whole setup as much as he did. She must have done, because hadn't she run away? Though she didn't look like the running-away type, she didn't look strong enough.

Sometimes he felt jealous of Adam, because he'd once had Fenella for his mother, and all Zeb had was Trudy. Then he'd let resentment of Adam's failsafe punishment evasion system get the better of him, and he'd mess with Adam in private: turd in the bed, dead mouse in the sink, switch the hot and cold taps in their shower – he'd figured out plumbing by then – or just apple-pie his sheets. Boy meanies. The Rev had done well out of his oil stocks, in addition to the gushing wells of his parishioners' savings, and they lived in a big house, with Trudy and the Rev at the opposite end to Adam and Zeb. So if Adam yelped they wouldn't hear him. Though he never did yelp; he just beamed out the reproachful I-forgive-you gaze that was ten times more annoying.

Sometimes Zeb would tease Adam about Fenella. He'd say she must have tattoos all over, tits and all; he'd say she was a cokehead; he'd say she went off with a biker, no, a dozen bikers, did them all, one after the other; he'd say she was peddling it on the street in Vegas to deranged addicts and syphilitic pimps. Why was he saying those gross and repugnant things about the woman he considered his other self, his fairy-dust spirit helper, next door to a marble goddess? Who knows?

The strange thing was, Adam didn't talk back. He'd just smile in an eerie way, as if he knew something Zeb didn't.

Adam never ratted about Zeb's juvenile pranks. Even then he was a secretive little bugger. Anyway, the two of them mostly worked as a team. At school – CapRock Prep, a private school funded by one of the OilCorps, boys only – they were known as the Holy PetrOleum Brats because of their dad's position, but nobody picked on them openly, not once Zeb was big enough. Adam alone would have been a sitting duck, he was so stringy and transparent; but if anyone lifted a finger in his direction, Zeb would beat the crap out of them. He only had to do that twice. Word got around.

Schillizzi's Hands

In face of the brainwashing team of Trudy and the Rev, Adam and
Zeb took joint evasive action. What were they evading, apart from
punishment? Anything that might lead in the direction of the path of
righteousness, the Holy PetrOleum Path, the path the Rev and Trudy
were forever urging them to tread.

In Adam's case, this action took the form of blue-eyed lying – he
could make just about anyone except Zeb think he was innocent as
an egg unlaid – whereas Zeb had the instincts of a sneak thief. Time
spent in the punishment closet had its upside, hairpins had their uses,
and it was not long before he had the secret run of the house, tiptoeing through the bureau drawers and emails of his elders while they
believed him securely imprisoned among the winter coats and outdated consumer electronics. Lockpicking became his hobby, and soon
enough, with the aid of clandestine sessions on the school's digital
facilities and free time at the public library, hacking became his voca-
tion. In his fantasy world no code could keep him out, no door could
shut him in, and fantasy merged into reality the older and more practised he became.

At first he stuck to porno peepsites and pirated acid rock and freakshow music – all forbidden by the Church, needless to say: it went in
for buttoned-up collars and public chastity vows, and its music sucked
like a thousand Monster Leeches from Outer Space. So Zeb would
earphone the Luminescent Corpses or the Pancreatic Cancers or the
Bipolar Albino Hookworms while trolling onscreen for ever-new
and cunningly deployed girl body parts. No harm in it really: they'd
already made the videos, so what he was doing was just a form of time
travel. He wasn't *causing* anything.

Then, once he felt ready, he decided to up the ante and really test his powers.

The Church of PetrOleum was high-tech enabled, with a dozen sophisticated online social media and donation sites skimming the cash from the faithful 24/7. The security on those sites was supposed to be as foolproof as such things got, with two layers of coding knitware any potential klepto would have to penetrate before making off with the debit accounts. And the system did keep out such kleptos; but it had no defence against an insider job, such as the one Zeb managed to pull off so spectacularly when he was barely sixteen.

The Rev's weak point was his belief in his own invulnerability, so he was careless; and as he had no head for number-letter combos, he wrote down passwords. Then he hid them in places so obvious even the Easter Bunny would scoff. The cufflink box? The toes of the Sunday shoes? Retro-cretin, sighed Zeb, extracting the wafers of paper, memorizing their cryptic scribblings, then replacing box or shoe in its exact previous location.

Once possessed of the keys to the kingdom, Zeb diverted the river of donations – not all of it, a mere .09 per cent, margin of error, he wasn't lobotomized – into several accounts of his own devising, making sure that the donors got the standard grovelling thank-you and guilt-inducing pep-talk message from the church, plus a hate slogan or two directed at the Enemies of God's Holy Oil: "Solar Panels Are Satan's Work," "Eco Equals FreakO," "The Devil Wants You to Freeze in the Dark," "Serial Killers Believe in Global Warming."

For his stash-the-cash hideaways he used an identity pieced together from fragments he'd appropriated by stealth attacks on fuzzily fenced targets, such as 3-D avatar gaming destinations, AdoptAFish and similar bioweepy charities, and Feel-iT-enabled porno installations in suburban malls. ("Haptic feedback gives you true, stimulating flesh-on-flesh sensations! Say goodbye to faked screams and groans, this is the real thing! Warning: Do Not Expose Your Electronic Device to Moisture. Do Not Place Terminals in Your Mouth or Other Mucous Membrane Regions. Severe Burns May Result.")

No surprise, really, for Zeb to discover during one of his trolling expeditions that the Rev himself was a frequent visitor to the haptic wanksites, though he indulged himself at home – he couldn't afford to be caught in a mall – and hid the feedback terminals in his golf club bag. He favoured those sites involving whips, penetration with bottles, and nipple-burning. He was also a big fan of the historical re-enactment beheading sites, which were relatively expensive, maybe because of the props and costumes – "Mary, Queen of Scots: Feel This Hot Red-Head Spurt," "Anne Boleyn: Royal Slut! Did It with Her Brother, She'll Do It with You, Then You Get to Slice Her Dirty Little Neck," "Katherine Howard: Turn This Stone Cold Fox Stone Cold with One Whack of Your Powerful Blade," "Lady Jane Grey: Make This Elite Virgin Pay the Price of Snootiness, Blindfold Optional." These gave you the sensation, right in your own hands, of what it felt like to decapitate a woman with an axe. ("Fun! Historic! Educational!")

For extra payment you could decapitate them without their clothes on, which was more exciting. Zeb took a few turns at it himself – courtesy of the Rev's account, which he cooked accordingly – so he had grounds for the clothes versus naked comparison. A naked woman on her knees, about to lose her head – why was this riveting? Was he callous or a psychopath or something? No, psychopaths had a brain chip missing, according to Adam, who read up on these things. They couldn't feel empathy; screaming and tears were just annoying noises as far as they were concerned. So they couldn't feel shitty and/or pervy about what they were doing, not like Zeb.

He thought about hacking in and recoding the program so that when the axe came down you got the sensation not in your hands but in your own neck. What would it feel like to have your head chopped off? Would it hurt, or would the shock cancel that out? Or would you get a rush of empathy? But too much empathy could be dangerous. Your heart might stop.

Were those naked, kneeling, and shortly to be headless women real or not? He guessed not because reality online was different from the everyday kind of reality, where things hurt your body. And they wouldn't be allowed to murder real women right onscreen: surely that was illegal. But the effects were so amazing and 3-D that you ducked the gush of blood.

Adam didn't see the attraction of these activities once he found out about them, which he did because Zeb couldn't resist the urge to share his knowledge about the Rev's secret life. Which was now also, to some extent, his own.

"That is depraved," was Adam's comment.

"Right! That's the *point*! What are you, gay?" Zeb said, but Adam only smiled.

The Rev's frustrated kink urges must have been in need of an outlet: Zeb was now too large and surly to take a chance on as a sado-subject. He might hit back, and the Rev was at heart a coward, so the belting and piss-drinking and imprisonment were now in the past. Nor was Trudy an option for the warped bastard, since – despite her stand-by-your-mealticket subservience – she would never put up with leather halters and nipple piercing and flagellation with a cane, or eating her own excrement. Information is power, so Zeb thanked his lucky stars for the online haptic-feedback sites, and made a record of the number of times the Rev had used them, and took care to store away this Santa's packsack of red velvet information for future use. Though the Rev might manage to electrocute himself via his own dick in the meantime – blow himself up like an overboiled hotdog – and Zeb would sure like to be an eye at the keyhole for that hilarious little fiasco. He briefly considered rewiring the haptic terminals to achieve this very effect, but was unsure of the voltage it would take. A Rev just badly scorched rather than no-refunds dead could mean big trouble: he'd figure out who did it, for sure.

By this time Zeb had magic fingers: he could play code the way Mozart played the piano, he could warble in cuneiform, he could waltz through firewalls like a tiger of old leaping through a flaming circus hoop without singeing a whisker. He could slip into the PetrOleum Church accounting – both sets of books, the official set and the actual one – in a few swift moves, and he did, on a regular basis. This went on for a couple of years, as the .09 per cents piled up, and Zeb grew taller and sprouted more body hair, and worked out in the gym at Cap-Rock Prep, where he took care to keep in the middle of the bell curve gradeswise, especially in IT, so that his extraterrestrial hacking talents would not be suspected.

In six months he would graduate, and what then? He had some

notions, but so did his parental overseers. The Rev had made it known that through his connections he could get Zeb a coveted job in the northern oil desert, driving one of the humungous machines that wrangled oil-rich bituminous gravel. It would make a man of Zeb, he said, leaving the possible definition of *man* floating in the air between them. (Child torturer? Religious fraudster? Online girl decapitator?) Also, the money was good. Then, when he'd done that for a while, Zeb could decide on what calling he wished to pursue.

There were three subtexts to this: 1) The Rev wanted Zeb to go very far away because he was beginning to be afraid of him, and rightly so. 2) With any luck, Zeb would get lung cancer, or a third eye, or scales like an armadillo: the air up there was so toxic you mutated in about a week.

And 3) Zeb was not brilliant. Not like Adam, who − in the hopes that he would carry on in the old man's fraudchurch biz − had been sent to Spindletop U. and had majored in PetrTheology, Homiletics, and PetrBiology; this last, as far as Zeb could see, required you to learn biology in order to disprove it. That took a certain kind of intellectual adroitness, a kind − it was implied − that Zeb lacked. Galley slave would be more his level.

"I think that's a wonderful idea," said Trudy. "You should be so grateful to your father for taking all that trouble. Not every boy has a father like yours."

Smile, Zeb ordered himself. "I know," he said. The word *smile* meant "carving knife" in Greek. He'd found that on the web, when he wasn't decapitating historical figures.

Zeb missed Adam when he wasn't there, and he suspected it was mutual. Who else could they talk to about the improbable sublayers of their lives? Who else could do a hilarious word-for-word imitation of the Rev's Prayer to Saint Lucic-Lucas, to whom God had revealed the Holy Oil?

When they were apart they avoided text messages, phone calls, or anything else with an electronic signal: the internet, as was well known, leaked like a prostate cancer patient, and the Rev was most likely snooping, if not on Adam, at least on Zeb. But when Adam would come back for vacations it was old-home week. Zeb would welcome him with an amphibian in the shoe or an arthropod in the cuff-link box or a burr or two artfully stuck onto the inside of his Y-fronts, though they were getting too old for this kind of japery, so it was more of a nostalgia thing.

Then they'd go out onto the tennis court and pretend to play a game, and murmur together in brief snatches across the net, comparing notes. Zeb would want to know if Adam had got laid yet, a question that was skilfully evaded. Adam would want to know how much money Zeb had skimmed off from the Church and sequestered in his secret stowaway accounts, since it was their firm plan to disappear from the Rev's charmed circle once they had sufficient funds.

It was Adam's last vacation before graduating. Zeb was sitting at the Rev's home office desk monitor with a pair of medical latex gloves on, humming under his breath, while Adam stood watch at the window in case the Rev's gas-guzzling tycoon car or Trudy's Hummerette drove up.

"You've got Schillizzi's hands," Adam said to him in that neutral way he had. Was it admiration or merely observation?

"Schillizzi?" said Zeb. "Hot crap, the botulistic old bugger's embezzling again, only this is a lot more! Look at this!"

"I wish you wouldn't swear," said Adam in his mildest voice.

"Stuff yourself," said Zeb cheerfully. "And he's stashing it in a bank account in Grand Cayman!"

"Schillizzi was a well-known white-hat twentieth-century safe-cracker," said Adam, who was interested in history, unlike Zeb. "He never used explosives, only his hands. He was legendary."

"I bet the old fart's planning a jump," said Zeb. "Here today, then zap, and the next morning he's sucking up martinis on a tropical beach and renting lick-your-cleft bimbettes, leaving the fuckin' faithful out in the cold with their pants down."

"Not in Grand Cayman, he won't," said Adam. "They're mostly underwater. But those banks have relocated to the Canaries; there are more mountains there. Only they've kept the Grand Cayman corporate names. Preserving a tradition, I suppose."

"Wonder if he'll take Trusty Fusty Trudy with him?" said Zeb. Adam's knowledge of banking surprised him, but then Adam's knowledge of a lot of things surprised him. It was hard to know what Adam knew.

"He won't take Trudy," said Adam. "She's becoming too financially demanding. She suspects what he's up to."

"You know this how?"

"An educated guess," said Adam. "The body language. She's giving him the narrow eyes at breakfast, when he's not looking. She's nagging him about vacations, and when are they going to take one. Also she's feeling held back in her interior decoration ambitions: note her on-show collection of wallpaper samples and paint chips. She's tired of playing the angel wife for the benefit of the congregation. She feels she's helped to create the domestic surplus, and she wants more scope."

"Like Fenella," said Zeb. "She wanted more scope too. At least she got out early."

"Fenella didn't get out," said Adam in his neutral voice. "She's under the rock garden."

Zeb turned in the Rev's ergonomic swivel chair. "She's what?"

"Here they come," said Adam. "Both at once, it's a convoy. Power down."

Mute and Theft

"Say that again," said Zeb once they were on the tennis court and safely out of hearing. Neither of them was much good at tennis, but they pretended to practise. They stood side by side, serving balls over the net or, more often, into it. Their rooms were bugged – Zeb had discovered that years ago, and enjoyed feeding misinformation into his desk lamp and then looping it back to himself via the Rev's computer – but it was best to play dumb by leaving the bugs where they were.

"Under the rock garden," said Adam. "That's where Fenella is."

"You're sure?"

"I watched them burying her," said Adam. "From the window. They didn't see me."

"This wasn't a ... you didn't dream it?" said Zeb. "You must've been fucking fetal!" Adam gave him the fisheye: not only did he not approve of obscenity, he never seemed to get used to it. "I mean, really young," Zeb amended. "Kids make stuff up." For once he was shaken: he could barely think straight.

If Adam's story was true – and why would he invent this? – it changed Zeb's whole view of himself. Fenella had shaped his story about his past, and also the one about his future, but suddenly Fenella was a skeleton: she'd been dead all along. So, no secret helper waiting out there: he'd never had one. There was no understanding family member he would someday locate, once he'd found the Exit sign and unlocked the invisible locks and cut his way out of the Rev's chicken-hawk-wired coop. He was flying a wing-damaged solo, all alone except for his joined-at-the-head-wound brother, who could well turn pious on him for real, he had the talent. Then Zeb himself would be drifting in Voidsville, out in the cold and dark, like a torn-loose astronaut in one of those old five-tomato space flics. He slammed a ball into the net.

"I was almost four," Adam said in his I-have-spoken-and-therefore-it-is-so voice that was too much like the Rev's for comfort. "I have clear memories of that time."

"You never told me," Zeb said. He was offended: Adam had not deemed him trustworthy. That hurt. They were supposed to be a team.

"You would have let it slip," said Adam. "Then who knows what they would've done?" He tossed his ball up, tapped it lightly over the net. "You could've ended up under the rock garden as well. Not to mention me."

"Wait," said Zeb. "They? You mean fucking Trudy was in on this too?"

"I already told you," said Adam. "There is no need to swear."

"Sorry, it just fucking slipped out," said Zeb. No way he was going to let Adam tell him how to talk. "Trudy the Good?"

"Must've been something in it for her," said Adam in his I-am-loftily-overlooking-your-provocation voice. "If only blackmail material. Or maybe she wanted Fenella out of the way, to clear her path. My guess is she was already pregnant with you. The Church of PetrOleum doesn't sanction divorce, what with the Holy Oil at the marriage ceremony. As we know."

So now it was Zeb's fault, the death of Fenella. For having the bad taste to get himself conceived. Shit. "How did they do it?" he said. "The two of them? Did they slip arsenic into her tea, or . . ." Not a decapitation, he thought, ashamed of himself. They wouldn't have gone that far.

"I don't know. I was only four. I just saw the burial."

"So all that about her being whore-pill trash, deserting her baby and so forth, that was just . . ."

"It's what the congregation wanted to believe," said Adam. "And they did believe it. Bad mothers are always a good story, for them."

"Maybe we should call the CorpSeCorps," said Zeb. "Tell them to bring shovels."

"I wouldn't risk it," said Adam. "There's quite a few Petrobaptists on the force, and there are a number of OilCorps heavies on the Church board. There's a lot of overlap because of the benefits to both parties. They're agreed on the need to crush dissent. So the OilCorps would cover up for the Rev over a pure and simple wife murder that didn't per se threaten its holdings, since they'd know there'd be much credibility lost through a scandal. They'd accuse the two of us of mental instability. Shut us away, use the heavy drugs. Or, as I said – dig a couple of new holes in the rock garden."

"But we're his kids!" said Zeb, sounding about two years old even to himself.

"You think that would stop him?" said Adam. "Blood is thinner than money. He'd hear a convenient voice from God, suggesting a son sacrifice for the greater good. Remember Isaac. He'd slit our throats and set fire to us, because this time God wouldn't send a sheep."

Which was about as dark as Zeb could remember Adam ever being. "So," he said. He was out of breath, although they'd barely been moving. "Why are you telling me about this now?"

"Because if what you've said about your successful cash-diverting activities is true, we have accumulated enough money," said Adam. "Also the Church might catch you doing the diverting. Time to go, while we still can. Before they send you off to die in the tar pits," he added. "It would be called an accident. Of course."

Zeb was touched. Adam was looking out for him. He always thought further ahead than Zeb did.

They waited until the next day, when the Rev had a board meeting and Trudy was heading up the Ladies' Prayer Circle. Then they took a solarcab to the bullet train station, exchanging fake info for the benefit of the driver's flapping ears. Most of those guys were snoops, formal or informal. The script was that Adam was on his way back to Spindletop and Zeb was seeing him off. Nothing unusual in that.

From a net café at the station, Zeb cleaned out the Rev's Grand Cayman hidey-hole account while Adam acted nonchalant and scanned for anyone who looked too interested. Once the Rev's funds were secured and transferred, Zeb sent the infected gonad a couple of messages, using a lilypad pathway to delay potential cyberhounds as long as possible. He hacked into a men's underarm deodorant video ad, clicked on the gleaming, depilatoried stud's belly button – he'd gone through that pixel wormhole before – then skipped to a home and garden site, appropriate under the circumstances, and chose a trowel. From it he launched his messages.

The first message said, "We know who's under the rocks. Don't follow us." The second contained the details of the Rev's thefts from the Church of PetrOleum's charity initiative funds, and another warning: "Don't leave town or this goes public. Stay put and await instructions." That would give the mildewed old bugger the idea that they'd be back in touch soon for blackmail purposes, which must be their motive, and he could lie in wait for them.

"That should do it," said Adam, but Zeb couldn't resist adding a third message: a copy of the details of the Rev's Feel-iT haptic site transactions. Lady Jane Grey had been his favourite: he must have decapitated her at least fifteen times.

"Wish I could watch," said Zeb, once they were on the train. "When he opens his mail. And even better, when he finds out his Cayman bank stash is gone."

"Gloating is a character flaw," said Adam.

"Up yours," said Zeb.

He spent the trip looking out the window at the passing scenery: gated communities like the one they'd just fled, fields of soybeans, frackware installations, windfarms, piles of gigantic truck tires, heaps of gravel, pyramids of discarded ceramic toilets. Mountains of garbage with dozens of people picking through it; pleebland shanty towns, the shacks made of discarded everything. Kids standing on the shack roofs, on the piles of garbage, on the piles of tires, waving flags made of colourful plastic bags or flying rudimentary kites, or giving Zeb the finger. The odd camera drone drifted overhead, purporting to be scanning traffic, logging the comings and goings of who-knew-who. Those things were bad news if they were hunting for you specifically: he'd gathered that much from web gossip.

But the Rev wouldn't be searching for them yet. He'd still be at the board lunch, gobbling down the labmeat hors d'oeuvres and the farmed tilapia.

Hackety-hack, railroad track,
Momma's in the garden, so don't look back,

Zeb hummed. He hoped Fenella's death had been sudden, with none of the Rev's more puke-making obsessions involved.

Beside him Adam was asleep, looking even whiter and thinner than he did when awake, and more like an idealistic statue of some annoying allegorical figure: Prudence. Sincerity. Faith.

Zeb was too high for sleep. Also jittery, despite himself: they'd crossed a big thick barbed-wire line, they'd robbed the ogre, they'd made off with his treasure. There would be fury. So he kept watch.

Who killed Fenella?
A really evil fella.
Hit her on the head,
Gave her quite a whack,
Everything went black,
Now she's fuckin' dead.

Something was running down his face. He used his sleeve to wipe. No snivelling, he told himself. Don't give him the satisfaction.

Once in San Francisco, Adam and Zeb decided to separate. "He won't sit still for this," Adam said. "He's got a lot of contacts. He'll put out a red alert, use his OilCorps networks. We're overly noticeable together."

True enough: they were too disparate. Dark and light, hefty and frail; anomalies like that were memorable. And the Rev's description would be of the two of them, not one at a time.

Mutt and Jeff, Zeb hummed to himself. Mute and Theft. Cute and Deft.

"Don't make that pseudo-musical noise," said Adam. "It draws attention to us. Anyway you're flat." He did have a point. Two points.

In a pleebland grey-market hourly-rental morph-your-backstory kitshop, Zeb crafted identities for them – cardboard, wouldn't stand up to scrutiny, time-sensitive, but good for the next stage of the trip. Adam went north, Zeb went south, each heading for camouflage.

He and Adam had agreed on a dropbox in space. It was the topmost rose being strewn by the zephyrs in a print of Botticelli's *The Birth of Venus*, posted on a much-visited Italian tourism site. Zeb opted for the left tit nipple of Venus, but Adam overruled him: too obvious, he said. It would also be too obvious for them to attempt to contact each other for at least six months, he added: the Rev was vindictive, and by now he'd also be frightened.

Zeb pondered the likely consequences of this vindictiveness and fright. What would he himself do if two young wiseass descendants of his that he'd never liked anyway had made off with his foul secrets? The rage. The betrayal. After all he'd done for Adam. And for Zeb, because weren't his physical chastisements in the best interests of the lad's spiritual development? He was probably still deceiving himself with righteous barf like that.

Among other things, he'd hire some DORCS: digital online rapid capture specialists. They charged a lot but were said to produce results. They'd set up a search algorithm geared to detect likely profile matches online. So it was necessary to stay away from digital as much as possible. No surfing. No purchasing. No socializing. No wisecracking. No porn.

"Just don't act like yourself," was Adam's parting advice.

Deeper into the Pleeblands

Zeb cut his hair in San Fran. He was growing a moustache, and he'd bought some coolish contact lenses on the dark-grey market that not only changed your eye colour but also gave you astigmatism and spurious iris features. But though these might get him through a casual scan, he didn't want to risk closer scrutiny, and the Fickle Fingers of Fake fingerprint distorters he'd also bought were laughable in any professional sense, so it was better not to chance the bullet train again. Also, most of those riding it still believed in the legality of law and the orderliness of order, and might report anything suspicious, as they were constantly being nagged to do.

So he chanced the highways. He hitched south as far as San Jose, working the Truck-A-Pillar convoy stops for rides and trying to look older than he was. Some of the drivers hinted at blowjob payment, but he was too big for them to force it.

The other hazard was the quick-trick pros working the roadside bars. But the only sex he'd had so far had been online, via the haptic-feedback sites; he wasn't ready for actual flesh on flesh. Plus, he was wary of making connections with other people, however brief: who knew how many of them might be trading information on the side? Some of those hustlers were suspiciously well dressed and did not look hungry.

Then there were the diseases. The last thing he needed was to be stuck in a hospital — supposing his ID passed inspection — or enduring a working over from some HospitalCorps security thug, supposing it didn't pass, which was likely. Once the truth of who he was had been vise-gripped out of him, there would be a call to the Rev. Then disposal orders would be issued, or he'd be shipped back in plasticuffs to face the self-righteous music. *I'll teach you to respect me, I have been set in authority over you, God hates you, you are morally worthless, repent on your knees, drink what's in the bucket, flat on the floor, hand me the two-by-four, you want it harder, I'll make you howl,* and so forth and so on, the familiar religio-sado heavy-metal perv litany. Pre-bedtime amusements.

When the Rev had finished with Zeb's neurologically trashed, defenceless, quivering body, it would be into the rock garden with it, eventually; but not before he'd been scorched and zapped into betraying the digital pathway leading to Adam, and had been forced to plant some online lures and instructions for him, including the necessity of not going public with the Rev's fiscal and sexual misdoings and the urgent need for a physical meetup at which all would be explained. Zeb had no illusions about his ability to withstand the kind of implementation the Rev and his helpers would be more than willing to inflict.

So that was the hospital option, supposing he caught pube rot. The alternative to the hospital route didn't appeal either. Dick fester, stiffie shrivel, penis putrefaction: the internet scare sites on that subject were the greeny-yellowy stuff of nightmares. More than enough reason to avoid the beckoning sirens of the Truck-A-Pillar stops, no matter how plump and firm the thighs extending from their red leatherette hot pants, how high their fake-lizard platform shoes, how boldly engraved their dragon and skull tattoos, or how bimplanted the half-melons emerging from their black satin halter tops like rising dough. Not that he'd ever seen rising dough, up close. But he'd seen videos of it. Once-upon-a-time mommy retros that, to tell the truth, made him feel kind of weepy. Had dead Fenella ever done any dough-baking? Because Trudy sure as hell hadn't.

So when the smudgy-mouthed, crack-eyed, jelly-bummed beauties said, "Hey, big boy, how about a quickie, out behind the doughnut stand?" he did not say, *Coming* and he did not say, *Meet you in heaven when I'm dead* and he did not say, *Are you out of your fuckin' mind?* He said nothing.

In addition to the disease factor, he did not yet know how to navigate the dark and darker pathways of the pleeblands: he didn't want to hook up with a total stranger and then wander blind-eyed into some alley or sleazy motel or dubious knocking-shop washroom and come out on a stretcher or in a body bag, if that. More likely was, they'd toss him into a vacant lot and let the rats and vultures take care of him. Now that more and more of the once-public security services were privatized, there was no margin in the proper burial of a drifter like him, or in the apprehension – they liked to use that word, *apprehension* – of whatever scoundrels might have knifed him for pocket change.

His height and his budding 'stache were scant protection. He was green wood, an easy target; they'd get that at one glance, they'd bee-line for him. The pleeblands were far from the school playgrounds of his youth, in which size really did matter. "The bigger they are, the harder they fall," the scrappy little bantams – more than one of them – had said to him then. "Yeah," he'd replied. "But the smaller they are, the more often they fall." Then a swift whack, not even a punch, and down they'd go.

But in the darkest pleeblands, there wouldn't be any verbal foreplay. No rattlesnake-warning quips and banter, just a rapid stab or slice or even a bullet from some obsolete, illegal firearm. The Linthead gang was especially vicious, according to the net. And the Blackened Redfish. And the Asian Fusions. And the Tex-Mexes with their drug-war tricks – the stacks of heads, the legless bodies strung up from old movieland marquees. He figured there must be a lot of Tex-Mexers controlling the Truck-A-Pillar highway heading south, it was close to their territory.

Despite these reservations, or, to be more honest, despite these cowardly fears, he knew that his best hope of cover in the short-term was in the worst part of town. Spending too much money would attract jackals; he was streetwise enough to know that. So once in San Jose he kept a low profile, stayed out of bars, and blended himself into the underclass that swirled around in the lowest pleebs like rats in a dump bin, scrabbling for whatever they could pick up.

For a while he slung quasi-meat products at SecretBurgers. It was ten hours and less than minimum, he had to wear the company T-shirt and a dorkwit cap, but SecretBurgers wasn't fussy about identities. And they had protection against the street gangs for their booth workers, and bought off both official nosies and non-official ones, so nobody hassled him. He felt sorry for the female workers: they were paid less than the guys, and they had to wear tight Ts and fend off customers and management alike. They should have been issued hard plastic visors for their tits.

But his sorrow didn't stop him from finally acquiring in-the-flesh carnal knowledge with one of the SecretBurgers meatbunnies called Wynette, a brownette with big, dark-ringed, starved-looking eyes. In addition to her alluring personality – a euphemism, he now has to admit, for her somewhat meagre snatch, which was the part that fascinated him, and he apologizes for that, but such is the case with hormone-sodden adolescent males, and it's nature's plan, and he thought he was in love, so fuckit – she offered the advantage of a tiny room.

Most of the SecretBurgers meatgirls couldn't even manage that: they shared overcrowded walkups, or squatted in repossessed and decaying houses, or hooked on the side to support some child or addicted relative or tinselly pimp. But Wynette was cautious and frugal, and hadn't squandered, and could afford some privacy. Her place was located above a corner store that sold alcohol tasting of troll piss and paint remover, but Zeb wasn't too choosy at that time, so he used to grab a bottle of it to ply Wynette with before sex because she said it helped her relax.

"Was it as good?" asks Toby.

"Was what as good? As good as what?"

"Sex with Wynette. As good as the decapitated Lady Jane Greys."

"Apples and oranges," says Zeb. "No point comparing them."

"Oh, give it a try," says Toby.

"Okay. The Lady Jane Greys were repeatable. Reality's not. And since you're wondering, they're both good sometimes. But it can be disappointing either way."

Snowman's
Progress

Floral Bedsheet

Sunlight wakes her, coming in through her cubicle window. Birdsong, the voices of Craker children, the bleating of Mo'Hairs. Nothing unhappy.

She pushes herself upright, tries to remember what day it is. The Feast of Cyanophyta? *Thank you, Oh Lord, for creating the Cyanophyta, those lowly blue-green Algae so overlooked by many, for it is through them, so many millions of years ago – which timespan however is merely an eyeblink in Thy sight – that our oxygen-rich atmosphere came to be, without which we could not breathe, nor indeed could the other land-dwelling Zooforms, so various, so beautiful, so new each time we are able to see them, and intuit Your Grace through them...*

But on the other hand it may be Saint Jane Goodall's Day. *Thank you, Oh Lord, for blessing the life of Saint Jane Goodall, fearless Friend of God's Junglefolk, who braved many a risky situation and also biting Insect to reach out across the Species gap, and through her love for and labour with our close cousins the Chimpanzees, led us to understand the value of opposable thumbs and big toes, and also our own deep...*

Our own deep what? Toby rummages for the next phrase. She's slipping: she ought to write such things down. Keep a daily journal, as she did when she was alone at the AnooYoo Spa. She could go further, and record the ways and sayings of the now-vanished God's Gardeners for the future; for generations yet unborn, as politicians used to say when they were fishing for extra votes. If there is anyone in the future, that is; and if they'll be able to read; which, come to think of it, are two big *if*s. And even if reading persists, will anyone in the future be interested in the doings of an obscure and then outlawed and then disbanded green religious cult?

Maybe acting as if she believes in such a future will help to create it, which is the kind of thing the Gardeners used to say. She doesn't have any paper, but she could ask Zeb to bring some back on his next gleaning expedition; if he can find any that isn't damp, or nibbled for mouse nests, or eaten by ants. Oh, and pencils too, she'll add. Or pens. Or crayons. Then she could make a start.

Though it's hard to concentrate on the idea of a future. She's too immersed in the present: the present contains Zeb, and the future may not.

She longs for tonight, she longs to skip the day that's just begun and plunge headlong into the night as if into a pool; a pool with the moon reflected in it. She longs to swim in liquid moonlight.

But it's dangerous to live for the night. Daytime becomes irrelevant. You can get careless, you can overlook details, you can lose track. These days she'll find herself upright, in the middle of the room, one sandal in her hand, wondering how she got there; or outside under a tree, watching the leaves riffle, then prodding herself: *Move. Move now. Get moving. You need to...* But what exactly is it that she needs to do?

It isn't only her, and it isn't only her nightlife that's causing it. She's noticed others slacking off as well. Standing still for no reason, listening though no one's talking. Then jerking themselves back to the tangible, visibly making an effort. Busying themselves with the garden, the fence, the solar, the extension to the cobb house . . . It's tempting to drift, as the Crakers seem to. They have no festivals, no calendars, no deadlines. No long-term goals.

She remembers this floating mood so well from the months that she spent holed up in the AnooYoo Spa, waiting out the plague virus that was killing everyone else. Then – after there was no more crying, no more pleading and pounding at the door, no more bodies collapsing on the lawn – just waiting. Waiting for a sign that there was someone else left alive. Waiting for meaningful time to resume.

She'd stuck to her daily routine: keeping herself fed and watered, filling up the hours with small activities, writing in her daily journal.

Pushing back the voices that tried to get into her head, as such voices do when you're solitary. Fending off the temptation to wander away, wander off into the woods, open the door to whatever was going to happen to her or, more honestly, to put an end to her. An ending.

It was like a trance, or sleepwalking. *Give yourself up. Give up. Blend with the universe. You might as well.* It was as if something or someone was whispering, enticing her into the darkness: *Come in, come over here. Finish. It will be a relief. It will be completeness. It won't hurt much.*

She wonders if that sort of whispering is beginning in the ears of some of the others. Hermits in the desert heard those voices, and prisoners in dungeons. But maybe no one's hearing them now: it's not like the AnooYoo Spa here, it's not an isolation cell; everyone has other people. Still, she's conscious of counting heads each morning, making sure all the MaddAddamites and former Gardeners are still in place: that none among them has strayed away during the night, into the labyrinth of leaves and branches, of birdsong and windsong and silence.

There's a tapping on the wall beside her door. "Are you inside, Oh Toby?" It's little Blackbeard, come to check up on her. Perhaps on some level he shares her fears and doesn't want her to vanish.

"Yes," she says. "I'm here. You wait out there." She hurries to put on her bedsheet of the day. Something less austere and geometrical than usual: more floral, more sensuous. Roses, full-blown. Vines, entwining. Is she being vain? No, it's a celebration of renewed life, hers: that's her excuse. Does she look ridiculous, mutton dressed as lamb? Hard to tell without a mirror. The main thing is to keep the shoulders back, stride forth with confidence. She pushes her hair behind her ears, twists it into a knot. There, no waving tendrils. Best to show some restraint.

"I will take you to Snowman-the-Jimmy," Blackbeard says importantly, once she's ready. "So you can help him. With the maggots." He's proud of having learned this word, so he says it again: "The maggots!" He smiles radiantly. "The maggots are good. Oryx made them. They will not hurt us." A glance up at her, scanning her face to make sure he's got it right, then another smile. "And soon Snowman-the-Jimmy will not be sick." He takes her by the hand, tugs her forward. He knows the drill, he's her little shadow, he's absorbing everything.

If I'd had a child, thinks Toby, would he have been like this? No. He would not have been like this. Don't repine.

Jimmy's still asleep, but his colour is better and his high temperature is gone. She spoons some honey-and-water into him, along with the mushroom elixir. His foot is healing rapidly; soon he won't need the maggots any more.

"Snowman-the-Jimmy is walking," the Crakers tell her. Four of them are on duty this morning, three men and a woman. "He is walking very quickly, inside his head. Soon he will be here."

"Today?" she asks them.

"Today, tomorrow," they say. "Soon." They smile at her. "Do not be worried, Oh Toby," the woman says. "Snowman-the-Jimmy is safe now. Crake is sending him back to us."

"And Oryx too," says the tallest man: Abraham Lincoln, possibly. She really must try to sort out their names. "She, too, is sending him."

"She told her Children not to harm him," says the woman. Empress Josephine?

"Even though his piss is weak, and they did not understand at first that they could not eat him."

"Our piss is strong. The piss of our men. The Children of Oryx understand such piss."

"The Children with sharp teeth eat those with weak piss."

"The Children with tusks eat them, sometimes."

"The Children who are like a bear, big, with claws. We have not seen a bear. Zeb ate one, he knows what is a bear."

"But Oryx told them not to."

"Not to eat Snowman-the-Jimmy."

"Crake sent Snowman-the-Jimmy to take care of us. And Oryx sent him too."

"Yes, Oryx too," the others agree. One of them begins to sing.

Girl Stuff

The breakfast table is lively this morning.

Ivory Bill, Manatee, Tamaraw, and Zunzuncito have cleared their plates and are deep into a discussion of epigenetics. How much of Craker behaviour is inherited, how much is cultural? Do they even have what you could call a culture, separate from the expression of their genes? Or are they more like ants? What about the singing? Granted, it must be some form of communication, but is it territorial, like the singing of birds, or might it be termed art? Surely not the latter, says Ivory Bill. Crake couldn't account for it and didn't like it, says Tamaraw, but the team hadn't been able to eliminate it without producing affectless individuals who never went into heat and didn't last long.

The mating cycle is genetic, obviously, says Zunzuncito, as are the changes in female abdominal and genital pigmentation that accompany estrus, and the male equivalent, leading to the polysexual acts. Which in a deer or a sheep you'd have to call rutting, says Ivory Bill, but in the Crakers, would these phenomena vary with circumstances? There'd been no chance to test it, back there in the Paradice dome, which was a pity, they all agree. They could have made some variations, run studies on them, says Manatee. But Crake ruled with an iron hand, says Tamaraw, and he was so dogmatic: he didn't want to hear about any possible improvements apart from those he thought up himself. And he sure as hell didn't want his prize experiment ruined via the introduction of possibly inferior segments, says Zunzuncito, because the Crakers were going to be a mega-money-spinner. Or that was his story, says Tamaraw.

"Of course he was bullshitting us all along," said Zunzuncito.

"True, but he got results," says Ivory Bill.

"For what they're worth," says Manatee. "The fucker."

"The question is more *why* than how," says Ivory Bill, gazing up at the sky as if Crake really is up there and could send down a thunderous answer. "Why did he do it? The lethal wipeout virus in the Blyss-Pluss pills? Why did he want the human race to go extinct?"

"Maybe he was just very, very messed up," says Manatee.

"For the sake of argument, and to do him justice, he might have thought that everything else was," says Tamaraw. "What with the biosphere being depleted and the temperature skyrocketing."

"And if the Crakers were his solution, he'd have known he'd need to protect them from the likes of us, with our aggressive if not murderous ways," says Ivory Bill.

"That's what megalomaniac fuckers like him always think," says Manatee.

"He'd have seen the Crakers as indigenous people, no doubt," says Ivory Bill. "And *Homo sapiens sapiens* as the greedy, rapacious Conquistadors. And, in some respects . . ."

"Well, we came up with Beethoven," says Manatee. "And, you know, the major world religions, and whatnot. Fat chance of anything like that with this bunch."

White Sedge is beside them, gazing at them attentively but possibly not listening. If anyone's hearing voices, thinks Toby, it might be her. She's a pretty girl, perhaps the prettiest of the MaddAddamites. Yesterday she proposed that they start a morning yoga and meditation group, but there weren't any takers. She's wearing a grey bedsheet with white lilies on it; her black hair's knotted into a chignon.

Amanda's at the end of the table. She's still pallid and listless; Lotis Blue and Ren are fussing over her, urging her to eat.

Rebecca's having a cup of what they've all agreed to call coffee. She turns as Toby sits down.

"It's ham again," she says to Toby. "And kudzu pancakes. Oh, and if you want, there's some Choco-Nutrino."

"Choco-Nutrino?" says Toby. "Where'd you get that?" Choco-Nutrino had been a desperate stab at a palatable breakfast cereal for children after the world chocolate crop had failed. It was said to contain burnt soy.

"Zeb and Rhino and them gleaned it somewhere," says Rebecca. "And Shackie. It's not what you'd call fresh, don't even ask about the sell-by date, so I figure we better eat it now."

"You think so?" says Toby. The Choco-Nutrinos are in a bowl. They're like tiny pebbles, brown and alien-looking, granules from Mars. People used to eat this kind of stuff all the time, she thinks. They took it for granted.

"Last-chance café," says Rebecca. "Kind of a nostalgia trip. Yeah, I used to think it was disgusting too, but it's not bad with Mo'Hair milk. Anyway it's fortified with vitamins and minerals. Says so on the box. So we won't have to eat mud for a while."

"Mud?" says Toby.

"You know, for the trace elements," says Rebecca. Sometimes Toby can't tell if she's joking.

Toby sticks with the ham and the kudzu pancakes. "Where are the others?" she asks, keeping her voice neutral. Rebecca counts them off: Crozier has already eaten and is taking the Mo'Hairs out to pasture. Beluga and Shackleton are with him, one spraygun between them, covering his back. Black Rhino and Katuro did sentry last night, so they are sleeping in.

"Swift Fox?" says Toby.

"Taking her time," says Rebecca. "Having a doze. I heard her thrashing around in the bushes last night. With a gentleman caller or two." Her smile says, *Like you.*

No Zeb yet. Toby tries not to peer around too obviously. Is he, too, having a doze?

As she's finishing her bitter coffee, Swift Fox joins them. Today she's wearing a pale gauzy shift, shorts, and a floppy hat, pastel green and pink. She's done her hair in pigtails, with plastic Hello Kitty clips. It's the schoolgirl look, and if it were former times she'd never get away with it, thinks Toby. She'd been a highly qualified gene artist, so she'd have feared ridicule and loss of status, and dressed like a grown-up to advertise her rank. But that kind of rank and status have peeled away, so what exactly is she advertising now?

Don't be so hard on her, Toby tells herself. After all, she took a big risk: she was an undercover MaddAddamite informant before Crake hijacked her and made her a whitecoat brainiac serf inside the Paradice dome, along with the rest of the kidnapped MaddAddamites. He'd scooped most of them.

But not Zeb: Crake never managed to corner him. He'd covered his tracks too well.

"Hi, everyone," Swift Fox says, stretching her arms up, lifting her breasts, aiming them at Ivory Bill. "Ooh, I could go right back to bed! Hope you slept well. I fucking didn't! We need to do something about the bugs."

"There's spray," says Rebecca. "We've still got some of that citrus stuff."

"It wears off," says Swift Fox. "Then they bite and you wake up, and then you can hear people talking and etcetera, like in one of those not-your-real-name motels with cardboard walls." She smiles at Ivory Bill again, ignoring Manatee, who's staring at her, his mouth tight. Is it disapproval or extreme lust? Toby wonders. With some men it's hard to tell the difference.

"I think we should have a curfew on vocal cords," Swift Fox continues, with a sideways glance at Toby. *I heard you*, that look says. *If you must indulge in dusty, ridiculous middle-aged sex, at least put a sock in it.* Toby feels herself blushing.

"Dear lady," says Ivory Bill. "I trust our sometimes heated nocturnal discussions did not awaken you. Manatee and Tamaraw and I – "

"Oh, it wasn't you, and it wasn't a discussion," says Swift Fox. "Are those Choco-Nutrinos? I threw up a whole bowlful of those once, back when I still got hangovers."

Amanda stands up from the table, clamps her hand over her mouth, hurries away. Ren follows her.

"There's something wrong with that girl," says Swift Fox. "It's like she's pithed or something. Was she always such a dimwit?"

"You know what she went through," says Rebecca, frowning a little.

"Yeah, sure, but it's time for her to snap out of it. Do some work like the rest of us."

Toby feels a rush of anger. Swift Fox is never the first to volunteer for chores, nor has she been within spitting distance of a Painballer: used like a prostibot, leashed like a dog, practically disembowelled. Amanda's worth ten of her. But apart from that, Toby knows she's resenting the snide innuendoes Swift Fox aimed at her earlier, not to mention the gauzy shift and the cute shorts. And the breast weaponry, and the girly-girl pigtails. They don't go with your budding wrinkles, she feels like saying. Tanning takes a toll.

Swift Fox smiles again, but not at Toby: right past Toby. It's a full-disclosure teeth display and dimple trigger. "Hey," she says in a softer voice. Toby swivels: it's Rhino and Katuro.

And Zeb. Of course, of course.

"Morning, everyone," Zeb says evenly: nothing special for Swift Fox. Nor for Toby either: the night is the night, the day is the day. "Anybody want anything?" he says. "We're doing a quick scan around the area, couple of hours, just checking. We'll pass a few stores." He doesn't spell out his real object because he doesn't have to: they all know he'll be looking for signs of the Painballers. It's a patrol.

"Baking soda," says Rebecca. "Or baking powder, whichever. I don't know what I'll do when it runs out. If you're going to a mini-super . . ."

"Did you know that baking soda comes from the trona deposits in Wyoming?" says Ivory Bill. "Or it used to come from there."

"Oh, Ivory Bill," says Swift Fox, favouring him with a smile. "With you around, who needs Wikipedia?" Ivory Bill gives a semi-grin: he thinks it's a compliment.

"Yeast," says Zunzuncito. "Wild yeast, if you still have the flour. You can make sourdough that way."

"I guess," says Rebecca.

"I'll come too," says Swift Fox to Zeb. "I need a drugstore."

There's a pause. Everyone looks at her.

"Just tell us your list," says Black Rhino. He's scowling at her bare legs. "We'll get it for you."

"Girl stuff," she says. "You wouldn't know where to look." She glances in the direction of Ren and Lotis Blue, who are over by the pump, sponging off Amanda. "I'm gleaning for all of us."

Another pause. Menstrual wadding, thinks Toby. She has a point:

the stash in the storeroom is dwindling. No one wants to fall back on torn-up bedsheets. Or moss. Though we'll come to that sooner or later.

"Bad plan," says Zeb. "Those two guys are still out there. They've got a spraygun. They're third-time Painballers, there's nothing left of their empathy circuits. You wouldn't want them to grab you, they won't bother with the formalities. You saw what happened with Amanda. She was lucky to escape with her kidneys."

"I totally agree. It is in fact a very bad plan for you to leave the confines of our cozy little enclave here. I will go," says Ivory Bill gallantly, "if you will trust me with your shopping list, and – "

"But you'll be there with me," says Swift Fox to Zeb. "As protection." She lowers her eyelashes. "I'll be so safe!"

Zeb says to Rebecca: "Got any coffee? Or whatever you call that crap?"

"It's okay, I'll change my outfit," Swift Fox says, switching her tone to brisk. "I can keep up, I won't be a drag. I know how to handle, you know, a spraygun," she adds with a little drawl, letting her eyes drift downward. Then she resumes pertness. "Hey, we can pack a lunch! Have a picnic somewhere!"

"Get it together then," says Zeb, "because we're leaving right after we eat."

Rhino starts to say something, stops. Katuro is gazing upwards. "I think it will not rain," he says.

Rebecca looks over at Toby, lifts her eyebrows. Toby keeps her own face as flat as possible. Swift Fox is eyeing her sideways.

Fox by name, fox by nature, she thinks. Handle a spraygun, indeed.

Snowman's Progress

"Oh Toby, come and see! Come now!" It's little Blackbeard, tugging at her bedsheet.

"What is it?" says Toby, trying not to sound irritated. She wants to stay here, say goodbye to Zeb, even though he's not going very far, or for long. Just a few hours. She wants to put some sort of mark on him, is that it? In front of Swift Fox. A kiss, a squeeze. *Mine. Stay away.*

Not that it would be any use. She would make a fool of herself.

"Oh Toby, Snowman-the-Jimmy is waking up! He is waking up now," says Blackbeard. He sounds both anxious and supercharged, the way kids used to sound if it was a parade or a fireworks display – something brief and miraculous. She doesn't want to disappoint him, so she allows herself to be piloted. She looks behind once: Zeb and Rhino and Katuro are sitting at the table, forking up their breakfasts. Swift Fox is hurrying away, to shed that stupid hat and the lookit-my-legs shorts and don some bottom-hugging camouflage.

Toby. Take charge of yourself. This is not high school, she tells herself. But in some ways, it more or less is.

Over at Jimmy's hammock there's a crowd. Most of the Crakers are gathered around, adults and children both, looking happy and as excited as they ever look. Some of them are already beginning to sing.

"He is with us! Snowman-the-Jimmy is with us once more!"

"He has come back!"

"He will bring the words of Crake!"

Toby makes her way to the hammock. Two of the Craker women are propping Jimmy up. His eyes are open; he looks dazed.

"Greet him, Oh Toby," says the tall man called Abraham Lincoln. They're all watching, they're listening intently. "He has been with Crake. He will bring us words. He will bring a story."

"Jimmy," she says. "Snowman." She puts her hand on his arm. "It's me. Toby. I was there at the campfire, down near the beach. Remember? With Amanda, and the two men."

Jimmy looks up at her. His eyes are surprisingly clear, the whites white, the pupils a little dilated. He blinks. There's no recognition. "Crap," he says.

"What is this word, Oh Toby?" says Abraham Lincoln. "Is it a word of Crake?"

"He's tired," says Toby. "No. Not this word."

"Shit," says Jimmy. "Where's Oryx? She was here. She was in the fire."

"You've been sick," says Toby.

"Did I kill anyone? One of those . . . I think I had a nightmare."

"No," she says. "You didn't kill anyone."

"I think I killed Crake," he says. "He had hold of Oryx, he had a knife, he cut . . . Oh God. There was blood all over the pink butterflies. And then I, then . . . I shot him."

Toby's alarmed. What does he mean? More importantly, what will the Crakers make of such a tale? Nothing, she hopes. It will make no sense to them, it will sound like gibberish, because Crake lives in the sky and cannot possibly be dead. "You've had a nightmare," she says gently.

"No. I didn't. Not about that. Oh fuck." Jimmy lies back, closes his eyes. "Oh fuck."

"Who is this *Fuck*?" says Abraham Lincoln. "Why is he talking to this Fuck? That is not the name of anyone here."

It takes Toby a moment to figure it out. Because Jimmy said "Oh fuck" rather than plain "fuck," they think it's a term of address, like "Oh Toby." How to explain to them what "Oh fuck" means? They would never believe that the word for copulation could mean something bad: an expression of disgust, an insult, a failure. To them, as far as she can tell, the act is pure joy.

"You can't see him," says Toby a little desperately. "Only Jimmy, only Snowman-the-Jimmy can see him. He's — "

"Fuck is a friend of Crake's?" asks Abraham Lincoln.

"Yes," says Toby. "And a friend of Snowman-the-Jimmy."

"This Fuck is helping him?" says one of the women.

"Yes," says Toby. "When something goes wrong, Snowman-the-Jimmy calls on him for help." Which is true, in a way.

"Fuck is in the sky!" says Blackbeard triumphantly. "With Crake!"

"We would like to hear the story of Fuck," says Abraham Lincoln politely. "And of how he has helped Snowman-the-Jimmy."

Jimmy opens his eyes again, squints. Now he's looking at the quilt covering him, with its Hey-Diddle-Diddle motifs. He strokes the cat and the fiddle, the smiling moon. "What's this? Fucking cow. Brain spaghetti." He raises his hand to blot out the light.

"He would like you to move back a little," says Toby. She leans in close, hoping she'll block out whatever Jimmy says next.

"I fucked it up, didn't I," he says. Luckily he's almost whispering. "Where's Oryx? She was right here."

"You need to sleep," says Toby.

"Fucking pigoons almost ate me."

"You're safe now," says Toby. It's not uncommon for someone waking from a coma to hallucinate. But how to describe "hallucinate" to the Crakers? *It's when you see something that isn't there. But if it isn't there, Oh Toby, how can you see it?*

"What almost ate you?" she says patiently.

"Pigoons," says Jimmy. "The giant pigs. I think they did; sorry. It's all spaghetti. Inside of my head. Who were those guys? The ones I didn't shoot."

"You don't need to worry about anything right now," says Toby. "Are you hungry?" They'll have to start with small quantities, it's best after a fast. If only there were some bananas.

"Fucking Crake. I let him fuck me over. I fucking fucked up. Shit."

"It's okay," says Toby. "You did fine."

"Fucking not," says Jimmy. "Can I have a drink?"

The Crakers have been standing respectfully at a distance, but now they move forward. "We must purr, Oh Toby," says Abraham Lincoln. "To make him strong. In his head there is something tangled."

"You are right," says Toby. "There is something tangled."

"It is because of the dreaming. And the walking here," says Abraham Lincoln. "We will purr now."

"After that he will tell us the words of Crake," says the ebony woman.

"And the words of Fuck," says the ivory woman.

"We will sing to this Fuck."

"And to Oryx."

"And to Crake. Good, kind . . ."

"I'll get him some fresh water," says Toby. "And some honey."

"Got any booze?" says Jimmy. "Crap. I feel like shit."

Ren and Lotis Blue and Amanda are sitting on the low stone wall near the outdoor pump.

"How's Jimmy?" says Ren.

"He's awake," says Toby. "But he's not very lucid. That's normal when you've been out so long."

"What did he say?" says Ren. "Is he asking for me?"

"Do you think we could see him?" says Lotis Blue.

"He said the inside of his head feels like spaghetti," says Toby.

"It was always like spaghetti anyway," says Lotis Blue. She laughs.

"You knew him?" says Toby. She's aware that there was a connection between Jimmy and Ren in the early days, and then between Jimmy and Amanda. But Lotis Blue?

"Yeah," says Ren, "we figured it out. She did."

"I was his lab partner at HelthWyzer High," says Lotis Blue. "In Bio. Intro to Gene Splicing. Before I took the bullet train out west with my family, that time."

"Wakulla Price. He told me," says Ren, "that he had such a crush on you! He says you broke his heart. But you never came across for him, did you?"

"He was so full of bullshit," says Lotis Blue. Her tone is fond, as if Jimmy is a naughty but adorable child.

"And then he broke my heart," says Ren. "And God knows what he told Amanda, after he dumped me. Most likely he said that I broke *his* heart."

"I'd say he had a commitment problem," says Lotis Blue. "I knew guys like that."

"He used to like spaghetti," says Amanda: more words than Toby's heard her speak since the night of the Painballers.

"At high school it was fish fingers," says Ren.

"Twenty per cent real fish, remember?" says Lotis Blue. "Who knows what was really in them." They both laugh.

"They weren't all that bad, though," says Ren.

"Labmeat goo," says Lotis Blue. "But what did we know? Hey. We ate them."

"I wouldn't mind one of those right now," says Ren. "And a Twinkie." She sighs. "They were so retro-nouveau revival!"

"You felt like you were eating upholstery," says Lotis Blue.

"I'm going over there," says Amanda. She stands up, straightens her bedsheet, pushes back her hair. "We should say hello, see if he needs anything. He's been through a lot."

Finally, thinks Toby, a sign of the former Amanda, the girl she'd known at the Gardeners. Some of that energy, that resourcefulness: backbone, it used to be called. It was Amanda who'd been the initiator, the transgressor of boundaries. Even the larger boys had given her space, back then.

"We'll come too," says Lotis Blue.

"We'll say, *Surprise!*" says Ren. The two of them giggle.

So much for broken hearts, thinks Toby: Ren's doesn't appear to have anything fractured about it any more, or not in connection with Jimmy. "Maybe you should wait a little," she says. What will it do to Jimmy's state of mind if he opens his eyes and sees three of his former beloveds bending over him like the three Fates? Demanding his everlasting love, his apologies, his blood in a cat food saucer? Or worse: the chance to baby him, play nursie, smother him with kindness? Though maybe he'd like that.

But she needn't have worried, because when they get there Jimmy's eyes are closed. Lulled by the purring, he's gone back to sleep.

The gleaner team has moved off along the street, or what used to be a street. Zeb first, then Black Rhino, then Swift Fox, with Katuro bringing up the rear. They're moving slowly, carefully, in and around the rubble. They'll be scoping out possible ambushes, taking no chances.

Toby wants to run after them, like a left-behind kid – *Wait! Wait! Let me come with you! I have a rifle!* – but no point in that.

Zeb hadn't asked if there was anything he could bring for her. If he had, what would she have said? A mirror? A floral bouquet? She should have requested at least the paper and the pencils. But somehow she couldn't.

Now they're out of sight.

The day moves on. The sun travels up and across the sky, the shadows flatten, food appears and is eaten, words are spoken; dining table objects are gathered together and washed. Sentries take turns. The cobb-house wall rises a little higher, the fence around it gains a coil of wire, weeds are removed from the garden, laundry is deployed. The shadows begin to stretch again, the afternoon clouds gather. Jimmy is carried inside, and the rain rains, with impressive thunder. Then the skies clear, the birds resume their contests, the clouds begin to redden in the west.

No Zeb.

The Mo'Hairs and their shepherds return, Crozier and Beluga and Shackleton, adding three hormonally charged males to the in-camp population mix. Crozier is dangling around Ren, Shackleton edging up to Amanda, Zunzuncito and Beluga are both eyeing Lotis Blue: the intrigues of love are unfolding as they do among the young, and as they do as well among the snails on the lettuce and the shiny green beetles that plague the kale. Murmurings, the shrug of a shoulder, the step forward, the step back.

Toby proceeds through her tasks as if in a monastery, steadily, dutifully, counting the hours.

Still no Zeb.

What could have happened to him? She blots out the pictures. Or she tries to blot them out. Animal, with teeth and claws involved. Vegetable, a falling tree. Mineral, cement, steel, broken glass. Or human.

Suppose he were suddenly not there. A vortex opens: she closes it. Never mind her own loss. What about the others? The other humans. Zeb has valuable skills, he has knowledge that can't be replaced.

They're so few in number, so necessary to one another. Sometimes this encampment feels like a vacation of sorts, but it isn't. They aren't escaping from daily life. This is where they live now.

She tells the Crakers there will be no story tonight, because Zeb has left the story of Zeb inside her head, but some of that story is hard to understand and she needs to put it in order before she can tell it to them. They ask her if a fish would help, but she says not now. Then she goes to sit by herself in the garden.

You've lost, she tells herself. You've lost Zeb. By now Swift Fox must already have him, firmly clamped in her arms and legs and whatever orifices appeal. He's tossed Toby herself aside like an empty paper bag. Why not? No promises were given.

The breeze dies, damp heat rises from the earth, the shadows blend together. Mosquitoes whine. Here's the moon, not so full any more. The hour of the moth comes round again.

No moving lights approach, no voices. Nothing and no one.

She spends the midnight watch with Jimmy in his cubicle, listening to him breathe. There's a single candle. In its light the nursery-rhyme pictures on his quilt waver and swell. The cow grins, the dog laughs. The dish runs away with the spoon.

Drugstore Romance

In the morning Toby avoids the group at the breakfast table. She's in no mood for lectures on epigenetics, or for curious glances, or for speculation about how she's taking the defection of Zeb. He could have said a firm no to Swift Fox, but he didn't. The message was clear.

She goes around to the cooking shed, helps herself to some cold pork and burdock root from yesterday that's withering under an upside-down bowl: Rebecca doesn't like to throw out food.

She sits down at the table, checks the neighbourhood. In the background the Mo'Hairs mill around, waiting for Crozier to let them out and lead them off to eat the weeds along the pathways. Here he comes now, in his biblical bedsheet getup, holding a long stick.

Over by the swing set Ren and Lotis Blue are walking Jimmy to and fro in an awkward six-legged assemblage. His muscle tone isn't great, but he'll build up his strength quickly enough: underneath the wear and tear he's still young. Amanda's there too, sitting on one of the swings; and several of the Crakers, nibbling on the ubiquitous kudzu vines and watching, puzzled but not frightened.

From a distance the scene is bucolic, though there are off-notes: the missing or escaped Mo'Hair is still escaped or missing, Amanda is apathetic and gazing down at the ground, and from the set of Crozier's tight shoulders and the way he turns his back on Ren, he's jealous of her Jimmy-pampering. Toby herself is an off-note, though she must appear calm to anyone watching. It's best to look that way, and through long Gardener training she knows how to keep her face flat, her smile gentle.

But where is Zeb? Why isn't he back yet? Has he found Adam One?

If Adam's injured, he'll need to be carried. That would slow them down. What's happening out there in the ruined city, where she can't see? If only the cellphones still worked. But the towers are down; even if there were still a power source, no one here would know how to repair the tech. There's a hand-cranked radio, but it ceased to function.

We'll have to learn smoke signals all over again, she thinks. One for he loves me, two for he loves me not. Three for smouldering anger.

She spends the day working in the garden, on the theory that it will be soothing. If only she had some beehives to care for. She could share the daily news with the bees, as she and old Pilar used to do, back on the God's Gardeners' rooftop garden before Pilar died. Ask them for advice. Request that they fly out and explore and then report back to her, as if they were cyberbees.

Today we honour Saint Jan Swammerdam, first to discover that the Queen Bee is not a King, and that all worker Bees in a hive are sisters; and Saint Zosima, eastern patron of Bees, who lived the selfless monastic life in the desert, as we, too, are doing in our own way; and Saint C. R. Ribbands, for his meticulous observations on Bee communication stratagems. And let us thank the Creator for the Bees themselves, for their gifts of Honey and Pollen, for their priceless work of fertilization among our Fruits and Nuts and our flowering Vegetables, yes, and for the comfort they bring to us in times of stress, with, as Tennyson once wrote, the murmuring of innumerable Bees...

Pilar had taught her to rub a little royal jelly into her skin before working with the bees: that way, they wouldn't see her as a threat. They'd walk on her arms and face, their tiny feet touching as gently as eyelashes, as lightly as a cloud passing over. The bees are messengers, Pilar used to say. They carry the news back and forth between the seen world and the unseen one. If a loved one of yours has crossed the shadow threshold, they will tell you.

Suddenly, today, there are dozens of honeybees in the garden, busying themselves among the bean flowers. There must be a new wild swarm nearby. One bee alights on her hand, tastes the salt on it. Is Zeb dead? she asks it silently. Tell me now. But it lifts off again without signalling.

Had she believed all that? Old Pilar's folklore? No, not really; or not exactly. Most likely Pilar hadn't quite believed it either, but it was a reassuring story: that the dead were not entirely dead but were alive in a different way; a paler way admittedly, and somewhere darker. But still able to send messages, if only such messages could be recognized and deciphered. People need such stories, Pilar said once, because however dark, a darkness with voices in it is better than a silent void.

In the late afternoon, once the thunder is over, the gleaner team returns. Toby sees them walking down the street, weaving in and out among the abandoned trucks and solarcars, backlit in the declining sun, and counts their silhouettes even before she can identify them. Yes, there are four. Nobody's missing. But also, no one's been added.

As they approach the fence around the cobb house Ren and Lotis Blue run to meet them, with a posse of Craker children following. Amanda runs too, though not as fast as the others. Toby walks.

"It was intense!" Swift Fox is saying as she comes up. "But at least we made it to the drugstore." She's flushed, a little sweaty; smudged, jubilant. She sets down her pack, opening it. "Wait'll you see what I got!"

Zeb and Black Rhino look wiped; Katuro less so.

"What happened?" Toby says to Zeb. She doesn't say, "I was worried sick." Surely he knows that.

"Long story," Zeb says. "Tell you later. I need a shower. Any trouble?"

"Jimmy woke up," she says. "He's kind of weak. And thin."

"Good," says Zeb. "Let's fatten him up and get him walking. We could use some more help around here." Then he's moving away from her, over towards the back of the cobb house.

Toby feels a blip of rage travelling through her body. Gone for almost two days and that's all he has to say about it? She's not a wife, she has no nagging rights, but she can't stop the images: Zeb rolling around in the aisles of the deserted drugstore with Swift Fox, tearing off her camouflage outfit among the bottles of conditioner and shampoo-in colour, more than thirty exciting tints; or were they a couple of aisles over, near the condoms and sensation-enhancing gels? Maybe they'd squashed themselves in beside the cash register, or over by the baby products – finished off with a whole box of wet wipes. Something of the sort happened. It must have happened, to bring out that smug look on the face of Swift Fox.

"Nail polish, painkillers, toothbrushes! Look, tweezers!" she's saying now.

"Looks like you cleaned the place out," says Lotis Blue.

"There wasn't that much left," says Swift Fox. "Looters were through, looks like they were interested in the pharmaceuticals. The Oxy, the BlyssPluss pills, anything with codeine."

"Not much use for the hair products?" says Lotis Blue.

"No. And the girl stuff – they didn't take that," says Swift Fox. She starts unloading the packages of Heavy Days and tampons and Slimlines. "I made the guys carry some in their own packs. They scored some beer too. Now that was a minor miracle."

"Why did it take so long?" Toby asks. Swift Fox smiles at her, not snidely. Instead she's too friendly, too guileless, like a teenager who's broken curfew.

"We got kind of trapped," she says. "We poked around and gathered stuff, but then in the afternoon, right before we were going to head back, there was a herd of those huge pigs – the ones that used to try raiding the garden before we shot some of them.

"At first they were just lurking along behind us, but when we'd finished in the drugstore and were coming out, we saw they were heading us off. So we ran back into the drugstore, but the front windows were smashed, so there was nothing to keep them out. We managed to get up onto the roof through a little trapdoor in the storeroom ceiling – they can't climb."

"Did they look hungry?" says Ren.

"How can you tell with a pig?" says Swift Fox.

They're omnivorous, thinks Toby. They'll eat anything. But hungry or not, they'd kill in spite. Or for revenge. We've been eating them.

"So then?" says Ren.

"We stayed up on the roof for a while," says Swift Fox, "and then the pigs came out of the drugstore and saw we were up on the roof. They'd found a carton of potato chips, they dragged it outside and had a party, keeping an eye on us the whole time. They were flaunting those chips: they must've known we were hungry. Zeb said to count them in case they split up into groups, with some of them creating a distraction and the others waiting to ambush us. Then they went off to the west, not walking but trotting, as if they'd decided on a goal. And we looked, and there was something over there. There was smoke."

Every once in a while something in the city catches fire. An electrical connection, still attached to a solar unit; a pile of damp organics, going up in a fit of spontaneous combustion; a cache of carbon garboil, heated by the sun. So smoke is not unheard of, and Toby says so.

"This was different," says Swift Fox. "It was thinner, like a camping fire."

"Why didn't you shoot the pigs?" says Lotis Blue.

"Zeb said it would be a waste of time because there were too many of them. Also we didn't want to run out of energy packs for the sprayguns. Zeb thought we should go over there and take a look, but it was getting dark. So we stayed at the drugstore for the night."

"On the roof?" says Toby.

"In the storeroom," says Swift Fox. "We barricaded the door with some of the boxes in there. But nothing happened, except rats; there were a lot of those. Then in the morning we went over to where we saw the fire. Zeb and Black Rhino figured it was the Painball guys."

"Did you see them?" asks Amanda.

"We saw the remains of their fire," says Swift Fox. "Burnt out. Pig tracks all over it. Also what was left of our Mo'Hair. The one with the red braids? They'd been eating it."

"Oh no," says Lotis Blue.

"The Painballers or the pigs?" says Amanda.

"Both," says Swift Fox. "But we didn't see any two guys. Zeb says the pigs must've chased them away. We did find a dead piglet, a little farther along: spraygun kill, Zeb said. A hind leg cut off. He says we should go back for it later because those pigs aren't likely to throw themselves in our way again, not after one of their young has been killed, so we should make the most of any stray pork. But we heard some of those crazy vicious dog splices, so maybe we'll have to fight them for it. It's a zoo out there."

"If it really was a zoo there'd be fences," says Lotis Blue. "That Mo'Hair was stolen, right? It didn't just wander off. Those two guys must've been quite close to us and nobody saw them."

"That's creepy," says Ren.

Swift Fox isn't listening. "Look what else I got," she says. "Pregnancy tests, the kind where you pee on sticks. I figure we'll all be needing them. Or some of us will." She smiles, but she doesn't look at Toby.

"Count me out," says Ren. "Who'd bring a baby into this?" She sweeps her arm: the cobb house, the trees, the minimalism. "Without running water? I mean . . ."

"Not sure you'll have that option," says Swift Fox. "In the long run. Anyway, we owe it to the human race. Don't you think?"

"Who'd be the dads?" says Lotis Blue with some interest.

"I'd say take your pick," says Swift Fox. "The line forms to the left. Just choose the one with the longest tongue hanging out."

"Guess you'll be stuck with Ivory Bill then," says Lotis Blue.

"Did I say longest tongue?" says Swift Fox. She and Lotis Blue giggle, Ren and Amanda do not.

"Let's see those pee sticks," says Ren.

Toby stares into the darkness. Should she follow Zeb? He must have finished his shower by now: the cobb-house showers are never long, unless it's Swift Fox, using up all the sun-warmed water. But Zeb is not in evidence.

She stays awake in her cubicle, just in case. Moonlight silvering her eyes. Owls calling, in love with each other's feathers. Nothing she wants.

Weeding

No Zeb all morning. No one mentions him. She doesn't ask.

Lunch is soup, with meat of some kind – smoked dog? – and kudzu with garlic. Polyberries that could be riper. A salad of mixed greens. "We need to figure out how to get some vinegar," says Rebecca. "Then I can do a proper dressing."

"First we'd need to make the wine," says Zunzuncito.

"I'm all for that," says Rebecca. She's put some arugula seeds into the salad, for a peppery effect. She has a plan for making a saltworks – an evaporating pan, down by the shore. Once the coast is clear, she says. Once the Painballers are accounted for.

After lunch there's indoor time, undercover time. The sun's high and burning, the storm clouds not yet building. The air is sticky with moisture.

Toby stays in her cubicle, trying to nap but sulking instead. No sulking allowed, she tells herself. No wound-licking. She can't even be certain that there's a wound to lick. Though she does feel wounded.

Late afternoon, after the rain. Nobody's around, with the exception of Crozier and Manatee, standing sentinel. Toby's kneeling in the garden, killing slugs. It's an act that would once have made her feel guilty – *For are not Slugs God's creatures too*, Adam One would say, *with as much claim to breathe the air, as long as they do it somewhere else in a place that is more congenial for them than our Edencliff Rooftop Garden?* But right now killing them serves as an outlet for her. An outlet for what? She doesn't wish to ponder that.

Worse, she finds herself editorializing. *Die, evil slug!* She drops each plucked slug into a tin can with wood ash and water in the bottom. They'd used salt earlier, but there's little of that to spare. Perhaps a swift blow with a flat rock would be kinder to the slugs – the wood ash must be painful – but she's not in the mood to weigh the relative kindness of slug execution methods.

She yanks out a weed. *How thoughtlessly we label and dismiss God's Holy Weeds! But* Weed *is simply our name for a plant that annoys us by getting in the way of our Human plans. Consider how useful and indeed edible and delicious so many of them are!*

Right. Not this one. Ragweed, from the look of it. She tosses it onto the pile of discards.

"Hey there, Death Squad," says a voice. It's Zeb, grinning down at her.

Toby scrambles to her feet. Her hands are dirty; she doesn't know what to do with them. Has he been sleeping in until now, or what? She can't ask what happened with Swift Fox, or if anything did: she refuses to sound like a shrew.

"I'm glad you came back safe," she says. And she is glad, more glad than she can say, but even to herself her voice sounds fake.

"Me too," he says. "Trip was more than I bargained for. Wiped me out, slept like a log, must be getting old."

Is this a coverup? How suspicious can she get? "I missed you," she says. There. Was that so hard?

He grins more. "Counted on that," he says. "Brought you something." It's a compact, with a small round mirror.

"Thank you," she says. She manages a smile. Is it a guilt gift, an apology? The roses for the wife after the husband's furtive tumble with the office co-worker? But she's not a wife.

"Got you some paper too. Couple of school notebooks, drugstore still carried them, I guess for pleeb kids who couldn't afford the Wi-Fi tabs. Couple of rollerball pens, pencils. Felt markers."

"How did you know I wanted those?" she says.

"I worked with a mind reader, once upon a time," he says. "Cursive's a Gardener skill, right? Figured you'd want to be keeping track of the days. Hey, what about a hug?"

"I'd get you all muddy," she says, relenting, smiling.

"I've been dirtier."

How could she not put her arms around him, despite her slug-slippery fingers?

And the sun is shining, and there are bees, among the yellow squash flowers. "You know what I really need?" she says to Zeb's smoky beard. "Some reading glasses. And a hive."

"Consider them yours." There's a pause. "I wanted you to look at this."

From inside his sleeve he pulls out a shoe: a sandal. It's handmade, with recycled materials: tire-tread sole, bicycle inner tube straps, silver duct tape accents. Although earth-stained, it's not very worn. "Gardener," Toby says. She remembers the fashion well, or rather the lack of it. Then she qualifies: "Or maybe it is. Not that other people didn't make those, I guess."

Already she has a picture in her head: Adam One and the surviving Gardeners, hunkered down in one of their Ararat hidey holes — the old mushroom-growing cellars, for instance — cobbling away by candlelight at their handcrafted sandals like a burrowful of elves, nibbling on their stores of honey and soybits while above their heads the cities flamed and collapsed and the human race melted away to nothingness. She wants so much to believe it that it can't possibly be true.

"Where did you find it?" she asks.

"Near the piglet kill," Zeb says. "I didn't show the others."

"You think it's Adam. You think he's still alive. You think he left this for you — or for someone — on purpose." These aren't questions.

"So do you," says Zeb. "You think it too."

"Don't hope too much," she says. "Hope can ruin you."

"Okay. You're right. But still."

"If you're right," she says, "wouldn't Adam be looking for you?"

Blacklight
Headlamp

The Story of Zeb and Fuck

You don't need to tell them a story every time. Come with me, instead. You can skip a night.

I already skipped one night. I can't disappoint them too much. They might leave here and go back to the beach, and then they'd be easy to attack. Those Painballers would . . . I'd never forgive myself if . . .

Okay. But make it short?

I'm not sure that's possible. They ask a lot of questions.

Tell them to piss off.

They wouldn't understand that. They think piss is a good thing. Like *fuck* – they think there's an invisible entity called Fuck. A helper of Crake's in time of need. And of Jimmy's, because they heard him saying *Oh fuck*.

I'm with them. Fuck! An invisible entity! A helper in time of need! Dead right!

They want to hear a story about him. About him and you, actually. The two of you, having boyish adventures. You're both stars at the moment. They've been pestering me about it, that story.

Can I listen in?

No. You'd laugh.

See this mouth? Virtual duct tape! If I had some Krazy Glue, I could . . . Hey, I could glue my mouth to your . . .

Don't be so warped.

Life is warped. I'm just in synch.

Thank you for the fish.

See, I am wearing the red hat, and I have listened to the round shiny thing I wear on my arm.

Tonight I will tell you the story of Zeb and Fuck. As you have asked me to do.

Once Zeb had left his home, where his father and his mother were not kind to him, he wandered around in the chaos. He did not know where to go next, and he did not know where his brother, Adam, was, who was his only friend and helper.

Yes, Fuck was his friend and helper too, but he could not be seen.

No, that is not an animal over there in the dark behind the shrub. That is Zeb. He is not laughing, he is coughing.

So, Zeb's brother, Adam, was his only friend and helper that he could see and touch. Was Adam lost? Had he been stolen away? Zeb did not know, and that made him feel sad.

But Fuck kept him company and gave him advice. Fuck lived in the air and flew around like a bird, which was how he could be with Zeb one minute, and then with Crake, and then also with Snowman-the-Jimmy. He could be in many places at once. If you were in trouble and you called to him – *Oh Fuck!* – he would always be there, just when you needed him. And as soon as you said his name, you would feel better.

Yes, Zeb does have a bad cough. But you do not need to purr on him right now.

Yes, it would be good to have a friend and helper like Fuck. I wish I had one too.

No, Fuck is not my helper. I have a different helper, whose name is Pilar. She died, and took the form of a plant, and now she lives with the bees.

Yes, I talk to her even if I can't see her. But she is not quite so . . . she is not so abrupt as Fuck. She is less like thunder, and more like a breeze.

I will tell you the story of Pilar some other time.

So Zeb wandered deeper and deeper into dangerous places, where there were a great many bad men doing cruel and hurtful things. And then he came to a place where they cooked and ate the Children of Oryx, which he knew was wrong. And when he called on Fuck for advice, Fuck told him he had to leave that place. And then he lived in some houses with water all around, and he came to know a snake. But it was dangerous there; and he said, Oh Fuck! And Fuck flew through the air, and spoke to Zeb, and said he would help Zeb get away safely.

That's enough of the story for tonight. You already know that Zeb got away safely because he's sitting right over there, isn't he? And he's very happy to be hearing this story. That is why he is laughing now, and not coughing any more.

Thank you for saying good night. I am happy to know that you want me to sleep soundly, without bad dreams.

Good night to you, as well.

Yes, good night.

Good night!

That's enough. You can stop saying good night now.

Thank you.

Floating World

One day Zeb woke up next to Wynette, the SecretBurgers meatslinger, and realized that she smelled like grilled patties and stale cooking oil. As he did himself, granted, but that was different, because it always is, says Zeb, when it's your own smell. But it's not what you want the object of your lust to smell like. This is a primate thing, it's basic, they've done the tests. Ask any of the MaddAddamite biogeeks here.

And the onions, don't forget them, and the gruesome red sauce in squeeze bottles the customers craved so much it most likely had crack in it. When things got energetic and there was a brawl, someone would always go for that red sauce and start squirting it around. Then it would get mixed in with the scalp-wound splatter blood and you couldn't tell whether someone was bleeding to death or had only been doused with red sauce.

The way that combo of smells would seep into their clothing and hair and even the skin pores was unavoidable, working where the two of them did. You couldn't wash off that stink even when there was shower water available, and it didn't blend too well with the cheap glop Wynette would rub on herself to neutralize it: Delilah, it was called, in lotion and cologne forms both, and it was heavy going, like wading through a sea of dying lilies, or a clutch of elderly church-women of the kind that populated the Church of PetrOleum. Those two smells – the SecretBurgers, the Delilah – were okay if you were really hungry or really horny, or both. But not so sweet otherwise.

Fuck, Zeb thought, lying there newly awakened that morning and inhaling the dire potpourri. There's no future in this.

Or if there was a future, it was a negative one, because in addition to smelling funny Wynette was getting nosy. In the name of love and getting to know and understand the real, total him, she wanted to explore his deeper depths, figuratively speaking. She wanted his lid off. If she pried too hard – if she unwrapped one after another of his flimsy cover stories, which he hadn't constructed with enough care, he realized, and he vowed to do better next time he conned someone – if she did the unwrapping, there was nothing very convincing immediately underneath. And then if she kept going, she might make some guesses about where he'd come from and who he'd been originally, and then it would only be a matter of time before she weaselled on him so she could collect whatever greyland reward must be on offer, out there in the word-of-mouth rat networks of the pleeblands.

Zeb had no doubt that there was such a reward. There might even be some of his biometrics circulating, such as photos of his ears, and animated silhouettes of his walk, and his schooltime thumbprints. Wynette wasn't connected gangwise so far as he knew, and luckily she was too poor to own a PC or a tab. But there was cheap netstuff available on time-rental in cafés, and she might do some identity surfing if he pissed her off enough.

Already she was beginning to emerge from the initial sex-induced coma created by him through the magic of his first-contact-with-aliens puppy-on-speed gonadal enthusiasm. Young guys have no taste as such in sexual matters – no discrimination. They're like those penguins that shocked the Victorians, they'll bonk anything with a cavity, and Wynette had been the beneficiary in Zeb's case. Not to brag, but during their nightly tangles her eyes had rolled so far up into her head that she looked like the undead half the time, and the amplified rock-band noises she made had caused thumping and banging both from the alcohol store on the ground floor and from whatever nestful of mournful wage slaves lived above them.

But now she was mistaking Zeb's animal energies for something more profound. She wanted post-hump chat. She wanted them to share their essences, on a spiritual level. She was starting to ask things like, were her breasts big enough, and did this colour of lime green look good on her, and why weren't they doing it twice a night the way they did at first? Questions that mantrapped you any way you answered. These nightly interrogation sessions were becoming wearisome. Maybe, Zeb concluded, his feelings for Wynette hadn't been true love after all.

"Don't look at me like that. I was really young. And don't forget, I'd been improperly socialized," says Zeb.

"Look at you like what?" says Toby. "It's darker than the inside of a goat. You can't see me."

"I can feel the glacial chill of your stone-cold gaze."

"I just feel sorry for her, that's all," says Toby.

"No, you don't. If I'd stayed with her, I wouldn't be here with you, right?"

"Okay. True enough. I withdraw the sorrow. But still."

He wasn't a complete shit about it. He left Wynette some cash and a note of undying adoration, with a P.S. saying that his life had been threatened because of a dirty deal — he didn't say what kind — and he couldn't bear the thought of putting her in peril because of him.

"You used that word?" says Toby. "Peril?"

"She liked romance," says Zeb. "Knights and stuff. She had some old paperbacks; they'd been in the room when she rented it. Falling apart."

"And you didn't want to play the knight?"

"Not for her," says Zeb. "For you" — he kisses the tips of her fingers — "swords at dawn, any time."

"I can't believe that," says Toby. "You've just told me what a liar you are!"

"At least I take the trouble to lie, for you," says Zeb. "Lying's more work than the bare-naked truth. Think of it as a courtship display. I'm aging badly, I've got wear and tear, I don't have a giant blue dong like our Craker friends out there, so I need to use my wits. What's left of them."

Zeb travelled hastily south on the Truck-A-Pillar route, coming to rest in the remnants of Santa Monica. The rising sea had swept away the beaches, and the once-upmarket hotels and condos were semi-flooded. Some of the streets had become canals, and nearby Venice was living up to its name. The district as a whole was known as the Floating World, and it really was floating most of the time, especially when the full moon brought a spring tide.

None of the original owners lived there any more. Unable to collect insurance – for what was the encroaching sea but an Act of God? – they'd fled uphill. Squatters and transients of many kinds had moved in, though there were no municipal services left: the sewage system and the water mains were kaput, and the electricity had been cut off some time ago.

But the district had acquired a raunchy cachet, and middle-aged punters from posher locations on higher ground were willing to venture down to the Floating World for the odd dose of bohemian thrill, navigating the drowned streets in tiny runabout water taxis with solar putt-putt engines on them. They came for the gambling and the illegal-substance dealing and the girls, but also for the real-time carny acts that operated from building to crumbling building, moving shop when the premises got too waterlogged or when a violent storm had swept away yet more of the shoreline and the real estate.

Much was on offer in the Floating World; profitably so, since none of the operators paid rent or taxes. There was a crap game in progress morning and night, with a revolving set of bleary-eyed players left unsatisfied by online gaming and craving the addictive nerve-jangle of potential danger. In addition, they wanted freedom from oversight: they believed that the internet was as full of peepholes as a Truck-A-Pillar motel, and they didn't want to leave any of their virtual DNA on it.

There was a moppet shop, with a mix of real girls and prostibots, depending on how much pre-programmed interaction you wanted, not that you could always tell the difference. There was a group of street acrobats who did torch-lit high-wire acts on ropes strung across the flooded streets, and sometimes fell and broke parts of themselves, such as their necks. The possibility of injury or death was a strong attraction: as the online world became more and more pre-edited and slicked up, and as even its so-called reality sites raised questions about authenticity in the minds of the viewers, the rough, unpolished physical world was taking on a mystic allure.

Among the carny acts there was a magician, a sad-eyed guy of maybe fifty, with a baggy-kneed suit he must have purloined from a thrift store: there wasn't a lot of margin in what he did. He'd set up a makeshift stage on the rapidly mildewing mezzanine floor of a former platinum-grade hotel, where he manipulated cards and coins and handkerchiefs, and sawed women in half and made them disappear from cabinets, and read minds. Those delights had vanished from television and online, since such displays of skill lacked tangibility in the digital realm and were therefore distrusted: how could you tell it wasn't just special effects? But when the Floating World magician put a handful of needles into his mouth you could see they were real needles, and when they emerged threaded you could touch the thread; and when he threw a pack of cards up into the air and the ace of spades stayed there on the ceiling, you'd seen that happen in real time, right in front of your eyes.

The mezzanine was always crowded on Friday and Saturday nights when the Floating World magician put on his shows. He called himself Slaight of Hand, after Allan Slaight, a twentieth-century historian of the hermetic arts. Though few in the audience would know that.

Zeb learned it, however, because it was with Slaight of Hand that he found work. He played Lothar, the muscular assistant, clad in a cornball outfit made of faux-fur leopard skin. He'd heave the cabinet around, turning it upside down to show there was nothing in it, or he'd place the beautiful girl assistant into the box in which she would be sawn in two. Though sometimes he posed as an audience member, gathering information for the mind-reading act, or expressing amazement and thus distracting attention. In the daytimes he was sent on shopping errands outside the Floating World, to where there were mini-supermarkets and people who were awake during the day.

"I learned a lot from old Slaight of Hand," Zeb says.

"How to saw a woman in half?"

"That too, though anyone can saw a woman in half. The trick is to have them smile while you're doing it."

"I guess that takes mirrors," Toby says. "And smoke."

"I'm sworn to secrecy. Best thing old Slaight taught me was mis-direction. Make them look at something else, away from what you're really doing, and you can get away with a lot. Slaight called each one of his beautiful assistants Miss Direction. It was his generic name for them."

"Maybe he couldn't tell one from another?"

"Maybe not. They didn't interest him in that way. But they had to look good in sequins, not very many sequins. The Miss Direction of the moment was Katrina Wu, a lynx-eyed Asian-Fusion hybrid from Palo Alto. I thought of her as Katrina WooWoo, and tried to get friendly with her – Wynette the SecretBurgers meatslinger had opened up a whole world of possibility, and I was feeling reckless – but Miss Direction WooWoo was having none of it. I held her in my arms every weekend while stuffing her into boxes and cabinets to be sawed and disappeared and laying her out on a table so she could be levitated, and I'd give her the odd squeeze and what I must've thought was a marrow-melting leer, but she'd hiss at me through her smile: *Stop that right now.*"

"You do a good hiss. Maybe getting sawed in half was using up all her vital fluids."

"Nope. One of the high-wire acrobats was taking care of those. During the week, when she wasn't working for Slaight of Hand, this guy was teaching her trapeze dancing; the two of them were working on a high-wire strip act. She had a couple of outfits for that: a bird one, a snakeskin one. For the snake act she also had a real snake: some sort of lobotomized python. Its name was March because, according to Miss WooWoo, March was a month of hope, and her python was always hopeful.

"She appeared to like the thing; she'd drape it around her neck during some of her acts, let it do some writhing on her. I got friendly with March, I used to catch mice for it. I figured those terrorized mice could be a way to the WooWoo heart, but no dice."

"What is it about women and snakes?" says Toby. "Or women and birds, for that matter."

"We like to think you're wild animals," says Zeb. "Underneath the decorations."

"You mean stupid? Or subhuman?"

"Cut me some slack here. I mean, ferociously out of control, in a good way. A scaly, feathery woman is a powerful attraction. She's got an edge to her, like a goddess. Risky. Extreme."

"Okay, we'll split the difference. So then what?"

"*Then what* was that Katrina WooWoo and the high-wire guy took off one day. And March the python – March went with them. That bothered me at the time, not the snake so much, but Miss WooWoo. Infected as I was by Cupid's festering dart. I confess I moped."

"I can't imagine you moping," says Toby.

"I did, though. Pain in the butt, I was. Not that anyone noticed, so I was mostly a pain in the butt to myself. Word on the street was that Katrina and the trapeze guy had headed east to make their fortune. Couple of years later I found out that they'd used the snake-and-bird motif and launched an upmarket gents' joint called Scales and Tails. Started small, became a franchise. That was before the sex trades got taken over by the Corps."

"Like the Scales in the Sinkhole, near the Edencliff Rooftop Garden? Adult entertainment?"

"You got it. Where the Gardener kids used to glean leftover wine, for making the vinegar. Same franchise. Anyway, saved my ass at a crucial moment, but I'll tell you about that later."

"Is this going to be about you and that snake woman? You finally scored? I can hardly wait to hear. Was the python in on it too?"

"Ease up. I'm trying to stick with the chronological order here. And hey, not everything's about my sex life."

Toby wants to say that a lot of it has been so far, but she refrains: it's not fair to demand the whole story and then object to it, she does realize that. "Okay, fire away," she says.

"After Katrina WooWoo disappeared from the Floating World, old Slaight of Hand wandered away in search of another Miss Direction, and maybe a more aesthetically attractive performance space that wasn't falling into the water. I was at loose ends, which was most likely good, since – being on the lookout for the next best thing, with eyes open and ears pricked – I noticed a couple of guys hanging around who were making too much of an effort to fit in, riffraff-wise. You can tell when a man is new to his greasy ponytail, his raggedy 'stache, and his garish nose jewellery: too much face fiddling. And their pants were wrong. They hadn't made the mistake of new ones, like Chuck, but their rips and tears and smears were too artful. Or that was my judgment. So I was on the next Truck-A-Pillar I could hitch a ride with.

"This time I went all the way down to Mexico. I figured that whatever tentacles the Rev could stretch out weren't likely to reach that far."

The Hackery

There was a surplus of paranoid drug peddlers in Mexico who assumed that Zeb was a paranoid drug peddler too, and that their interests clashed with his. After a few too many episodes in which men with arcane tattoos and designs of tulips razored onto their scalps gave him the full frontal scowl, plus a couple of near-misses with knives to make things clear, he moved down the map, shedding spare change all the way. For incidentals he paid cash only: he didn't want to leave a cyber-trail, even the cybertrail of someone named John and then Roberto and then Diaz.

From Cozumel he hopped through the Caribbean Islands, then over to Colombia. But although he further honed the skill of drinking with strangers in bars, and survived those lessons and a few others, nothing in Bogotá held any possibilities for him; in addition to which, he stood out too much.

Rio was another story. Its nickname then was The Hackery; that was before the mini-drone raids and the electrical-grid sabotage events that sent the truly serious operators — those who'd survived — into the Cambodian jungles to set up shop anew. But Rio then was at its zenith. It was said to be the Wild West of the web, filled with youthful bristle-faced blackhat cyberhustlers of every possible nationality. There were hordes of potential customers: businesses were spying on businesses, politicians were setting nets for other politicians, and then there were the military interests: these paid the most of all, though they also did a moderately full security check on prospective employees, and Zeb didn't want that. But all in all, Rio was a seller's market: quick hands for hire, no questions asked, and no matter what you looked like you'd blend in down there as long as you looked odd enough.

He was out of practise keyboard-wise, considering the time he'd spent slinging meat, aiding Slaight of Hand, ogling Miss Direction, and python-wrestling, but it didn't take him long to get his flexibility back. Then he went looking for work. He found an opening suitable to his talents within a week.

His first employer was Ristbones, an outfit that specialized in the hacking of electronic voting machines. That had been easy in the first decade of the century, and also profitable – if you controlled the machines, you could slip in whichever candidate you wanted, as long as the real vote was close to being split – but outrage had been expressed and fusses had been made, and the appearance of democracy was still considered worth preserving back then; so firewalls had been installed and the pickwork was now more complex.

It was also boring – sort of like crocheting, working through the fairly elementary lacework that was more for show than for actual prevention. You could zizz off on the job trying to interest yourself. So when he had an offer from Hacksaw Inc. he took it, a little too rapidly as it turned out. He wasn't drunk at the time, but vodka was involved. That, and a lot of backslapping and loud comradely laughs and compliments. The pickup was made by three suave guys, one with large hands and another with large money. The third was probably the eliminator: he didn't say much.

Hacksaw was located on a joyboat moored off Rio and posing as an anything-goes sex bazaar. Not just a pose, either, because you could get everything there from chicken soup to nuts, on or off the bone, screams-for-sale extra. He spent a nervous four weeks on that deathstar working for a pod of seedy Russian pussy-smugglers who were tiring of the whininess and bleediness and need-to-feed of their human merchandise and were aiming to supplement their income in ways that required less soft tissue. They put Zeb to work hacking into online PachinkoPoker for skimming purposes, and it was a mite stressful because – said the other code slaves – the Hacksaw folk were known to heave you into the luminous krill if they thought you were taking too long unravelling the digital embroidery.

Or else if you were befriending the software. Misusing it was fine, so long as not much in the way of merchandise was damaged, since damage was a privilege reserved for paying customers. A few weekly free-time coupons for hackstaff were included in the paypacket, along with some complimentary gambling chips and the meals and drinks. But sentimental attachments were strictly off-limits.

The sex bazaar side of the Hacksaw business was beyond tawdry; especially the kids, they were lifting them from the favelas on a limited-time-use basis, turning them over, and fishfooding them at a fast clip. That part was too close to the Rev and his child-rearing practises for Zeb's tastes, and he must've let that show because the cordiality of the jovial comrades was waning rapidly. After working only a month of his contract he'd managed to sneak a go-fast boat by sharing a few vodkas with the Russian guard and then whacking him and pocketing his identity and overboarding him. That was the first time he'd killed anyone, and it was too bad for the guard, a non-too-bright bullet-head who should've known better than to trust a callow though not small and – by definition, considering he was working for Hacksaw – devious youth like Zeb.

He took a few lines of Hacksaw code with him, and a few passwords. Those could come in handy. He also took one of the girls. He'd sweet-talked her into acting as his very own Miss Direction: he used his coupons to book an hour of her time, then got her to walk past the booze-addled guard in what passed for her nightie – some shred of cheeseclothy fabric – looking just seductive enough and just furtive enough – *Where you going?* – to get the coconut-brain to turn his head.

Zeb could have left the girl on the joyboat, but he felt sorry for her. The comrades would figure out that she'd acted the decoy, wittingly or unwittingly they wouldn't care, and they'd mash her like a potato. She was only on the boat because she'd been lured away from her home town in rustbucket Michigan by spurious enticements and a few chunks of third-rate flattery. She'd been told she had talent; she'd been told the job was dancing.

He hadn't been so thick as to take the go-fast boat to a regular marina. The comrades might already have noticed the two absences – three, including the guard – and be on the prowl. He docked at one of the shore hotels and hid the girl behind an ornamental fountain until he could gain entrance to the corridors by booking a room with the guard's identity. Then he worked out the master code, snuck into a well-stocked bedroom, and lifted some clothes for her, and a shirt for himself as well: too small, but he rolled up the sleeves. He left a threatening Miss Direction note scrawled on the bathroom mirror in soap: *I Come Back Later. Revenge.* Chances were that nine-tenths of the guys staying in places like that would have at least one violent and resentful thug in their past, and would thus leave the hotel rapidly without complaining about their missing wardrobe items.

Or their car keys. Or their car.

Once they were far enough away, he found a net café where he could lilypad to one of his .09 per cent secret stashes, then transfer a lump of that to a different account and pay it out to himself; after which, he erased all traces. Then he borrowed another car that just happened to be available. People were careless.

So far, so good; but then there was the girl. Her name was Minta, which made him think of organic chewing gum. Fresh, green. She'd held firm during their escape, she hadn't lost her nerve, she'd been silent. Most likely she'd also been in shock, because she hadn't lasted. There was decay from the inside, whether mental or physical he couldn't tell.

She was all right when they were in view, on the street or in a store – she could act normal for short periods – but when they were inside, in this room or that room or even in a car, zigzagging their way north and west, she would spend the time at her two specialties, crying hopelessly and staring vacantly. Television was no distraction for her, nor was sex. Understandably enough she didn't want Zeb to touch her, though out of gratitude and as a form of payment she offered anything he might want in the way of his being touched himself.

"So you took her up on it?" Toby says, keeping her voice light. How can she be jealous of such a wreck, such a wraith?

"No, as a matter of fact," Zeb says. "No joy in that. Might as well hire a prostibot wank robot in a mall. It was more fun for me to tell her she didn't have to. After that she did let me hug her a little. I thought it might calm her down, but it only made her shiver."

Minta started hearing things – stealthy footsteps, heavy breathing, a metallic clanking sound − and she was frightened every time she went out of whatever squalid hotel room they were staying in. Zeb could have afforded classier lodgings, but it was better to keep to the deep pleeblands, in the shadows.

Sad to say, Minta ended by jumping off a balcony in San Diego. He wasn't in the room at the time, he'd been out getting her a coffee, but he saw the crowd gathering and heard the siren. Which meant he had to leave town in a hurry to avoid the investigation, if any; which in turn meant that his description might be top of the list as a murder suspect, supposing the authorities decided to follow up, which increasingly they didn't. Anyway, where would they start? Minta had no identity. He'd abandoned nothing of his − he made a point of taking everything with him whenever he left a room − but who knows if there were security cameras anywhere near? Not likely in the pleeb shadowlands, but you never knew.

He made it up to Seattle, where he took a quick peek into the *Birth of Venus* zephyr dropbox he shared with Adam. There was a message for him: "Confirm you're still in the body." Adam sometimes echoed the Rev's speech patterns in a creepy way.

"In whose body?" Zeb posted in reply.

It was an old joke of his: he always used to make fun of that pious no-longer-in-the-body funeral talk of the Rev's. He made that joke so Adam would know it was really him, not some decoy impersonator. In fact, Adam had most likely planted that in-body query on purpose because he'd know Zeb couldn't resist it; whereas a fake Zeb would just give a straight answer. Adam was usually a few twists ahead of the curve.

His next move was up to Whitehorse. He'd heard about Bearlift in a Rio bar and figured it would be a good place to hide out, since nobody would be expecting him to go there. Not Hacksaw, who had a score to settle: they'd look for him in some other hackers' hotspot, such as Goa. And not the Rev either: Zeb had never shown the least interest in wildlife.

"So that," says Zeb, "is how I wound up on the Mackenzie Mountain Barrens wearing a bear skin, and jumping onto a trail biker, and getting mistaken for Bigfoot the Sasquatch."

"Understandable," says Toby. "They might have thought that even without the bear skin."

"You being snarky?"

"It's a compliment."

"I'll mull that over. Anyway, I wasn't sad about the way it turned out."

Fast-forward to Whitehorse again: there he was, washed, dressed, and in his right mind, supposing there was such a thing. He was avoiding the Bearlift headquarters and the usual drinking holes because those people thought he was dead, and why would he want to sacrifice the advantages that non-existence can bring? So he was spending a fair amount of time in the motel room eating faux-peanut objects and sending out for pizza and watching pay-per-view, never mind what, and trying to figure out his next move. Where to go from Whitehorse? How to get out? What was his next incarnation of choice?

Also he was wondering, Who set Chuck up to stick that needle into him? Which of the several parties with an interest in his ill-being would use an inept, A-sombrero dink like Chuck as their choice of poison-dart launcher?

Cold Dish

He existed in two states: his actual camouflaged mode, an anyface with a bogus name; and, in his previous guise, fried to a crisp in a 'thopter crash. Pity about that, some might say, but very convenient for others. And convenient for himself as well.

But he didn't want Adam to think he was dead – there'd been a long communications hiatus during the Bearlift caper – so he needed to make contact before news of that kind leaked out.

He put on all his clothes, including the aviator helmet, the fake goosedown puffy jacket, and the sunglasses, and made a foray to one of the two local net cafés, a tidy operation called Cubs' Corner that served turgid organic soy beverages and undercooked giant muffins. He ordered both: eating the local foods was a principle of his. Then he paid cash for a half-hour of net time and sent a message to Adam via the zephyr dropbox. "Some shithead tried to mort me. Everyone thinks I'm f-ing dead."

He picked up the answer in ten minutes: "Renouncing profanity will improve your digestion. Stay dead. May have job opportunity. Get to New New York area ASAP, connect with me then."

"OK, get me jobcheck ID?" he sent back.

"Y. Will be waiting," Adam replied. Where was he? No clue about that. But he must have landed in a place where he felt safe, or safe enough. That was a relief to Zeb. Losing Adam would be like losing an arm and a leg. And the top part of his head.

He went back to his motel room and thought through the logistics of getting himself to New New York. As a dead person, and with the aid of the temporary patchwork ID he'd put together, he might chance the bullet train once he'd Truck-A-Pillared as far as, say, Calgary.

But the main puzzle was still bothering him. Who'd wanted to nab him via Chuck? He tried to narrow it down. First of all, who could've figured out where he was? Fingered him at Bearlift? By that time his name was Devlon, and before that it was Larry, and before that, Kyle. He didn't look much like a Kyle, but sometimes it was better to go counter-type. And he'd been through at least six earlier names.

He'd bought the better part of the identities on the greyer than grey market, and there was no upside for those guys to sell him out: they had their businesses to run, they had to maintain customer confidence, and anyway they wouldn't have been able to pinpoint a buyer for him. To them he was just one more shirker on the run from bad debts, or rapacious wives, or embezzlement from a Corp, or IP theft, or robbing a convenience store, or a string of psycho murders involving crossdressing and crowbars; they didn't care what. They'd do a preliminary ask, they pretended to have standards and ethics – no baby-fuckers – and he'd serve them up some platters of refried bullshit they both knew was crap. But it was polite to exchange this kind of pewl, just like they'd say, "Happy to help" and so forth, which meant "Let's see the cash."

So for any cybersleuth to pry him out of his layers of fake shell would've meant the expenditure of considerable resources. He'd covered his trail well enough unless they'd known exactly where to look. Whoever it was would need to be very motivated.

He more or less ruled out Ristbones because what did he have on them that could mess them up if leaked? Voting machine hacking was an open secret, but though there was grumbling in the so-called press, nobody really wanted to go back to the old paper system, and the Corp that owned the machines, picked the winners, and took the kickbacks had done a lunar PR job, so anyone who objected too much was smeared as a twisted Commie bent on spoiling everyone's fun, even the fun of those who weren't having any fun. But spoiling the fun they might have later. Their fun-in-the-sky.

So he was no threat to Ristbones because even if he did try to rouse some sort of mouldy civil-society rabble, anyone who'd listen to him would be credited with a terminal case of brain herpes. If he'd been crazy, he might've tried to double-hack the machines – code in his own virtual senator or something – just as a demo project about how easy it was.

"But you weren't crazy," says Toby.

"I might have done it for the lulz, if I'd had the time. It would have been one of those ephemeral pranks by which sulky keyboard geniuses like me used to signal their ineffectual objections to the system."

"So, not Ristbones, then," says Toby. "Must have been Hacksaw?"

"They had a case for payback," says Zeb. "I'd fishfooded their guard, pilfered their boat, robinhooded one of their maidens in distress; but worse, I'd made them look sloppy. I could see them wanting to stage-manage a public example of me − string me up in chains from a bridge or similar, minus a leg and all my blood; turn me into a gristle display. But in order to capitalize on the publicity they'd have to reveal what I'd done to them, so they'd still lose face.

"Anyway I couldn't see them tracking me as far as Bearlift, way up there in Whitehorse. It was very far from Rio, and most likely they thought it was covered with snow and igloos, if they ever thought about it at all. But more than that, I couldn't see a tightass like Chuck working for those guys. I couldn't even picture them in the same bar together. The Hacksaw types needed to be in a bar with you before they'd take you on, and Chuck didn't compute. He had the wrong wardrobe. None of the Hacksaw guys would be caught dead hiring a guy with such dorky pants."

The more he thought about Chuck − about the yucky-clean Chuckiness of Chuck − the more he figured that was the key. The smarmy friendliness, the fake white-toothed geniality . . . He had to be Church of PetrOleum. But no way the Rev and his buds, even hired professional buds, could've tracked Zeb through all his twists and turns. Just no fucking way.

Then he figured he was looking at the whole thing backwards. The Rev, and the whole Church, and their religious joined-at-the-hippers like the Known Fruits, and their political pals − they were all death on ecofreaks. Their ads featured stuff like a cute little blond girl next to some particularly repellent threatened species, such as the Surinam toad or the great white shark, with a slogan saying: *This?* or *This?* Implying that all cute little blond girls were in danger of having their throats slit so the Surinam toads might prosper.

By extension, anyone who liked smelling the daisies, and having daisies to smell, and eating mercury-free fish, and who objected to giving birth to three-eyed infants via the toxic sludge in their drinking water was a demon-possessed Satanic minion of darkness, hell-bent on sabotaging the American Way and God's Holy Oil, which were one and the same. And Bearlift, despite its fuzzy reasoning and its clumsy delivery system, was in a geographical area where more oil might well be discovered, or through which it might well be piped, with the usual malfunctions, spills, and coverups.

So naturally the Rev and his circle would've tried to infiltrate Bearlift. Which was none too choosy about who it let in. Chuck must've been a true PetrOleum believer, sent there to keep an eye on the furfuckers and report on the evils they were concocting. He wouldn't have been looking for Zeb in particular, though when he stumbled across him he would've recognized him. He'd been close to the Rev, then: family picture sharing. *The ungrateful son. But you... The son I wish I'd had.* Sigh. Wistful smile. Hand on shoulder. Gruff, manly pat-pat. Like that.

The rest would have followed: the snitch report by Chuck, the instructions from the Rev, the obtaining of the knockout needle, the failed attempt in the 'thopter. The flaming wreckage.

Which made Zeb feel angry all over again.

He put on all his clothes once more and sallied forth to send another batch of messages. This time he used the other net café in town, PrestoThumbs, a seedier place in a mini-mall. It was right next to a haptic-feedback remote-sex emporium called The Real Feel: "The Real Feel, The Real Deal! Keep It Safe! Thrills, Spills, No Microbes!" But he resisted nostalgia and walked past The Real Feel and logged on at Thumbs.

First he sent a message to the ranking Elder at the Church of PetrOleum, attaching the Rev's embezzlement data and informing him that the actual cash would be found not in the Canary Islands Grand Cayman bank account, where it actually was, but in the form of stocks, in a metal box buried under Trudy's rock garden. He advised the Elder to take not only six men with shovels but also a team of security minions armed with tasers, as the Rev was armed and could be dangerous. He signed the message "Argus." The hundred-eyed giant from Greek mythology, that was him: there were pictures of the guy on the same site that hosted *The Birth of Venus*. Not that having a hundred eyes made you attractive from an aesthetic point of view. There was a goddess on there with a hundred tits, yet another illustration of the fact that more is not always better.

Having ruined — he hoped — the Rev's upcoming evening, he cleaned out the Rev's secret Cayman account. He'd peeked at it from time to time during his travels to make sure the Rev had followed instructions and was leaving it alone. Yup, it was all still there. He transferred the whole works to an account he'd set up for Adam under the name of Rick Bartleby, for whom he'd also created a convincing identity: Rick was an undertaker in Christchurch, New Zealand. He left Adam a message saying he'd find an account number and a password and a big surprise via the right nipple of Venus. It did him good to picture Adam clicking — finally — on a nipple.

He felt it was only right to send a message to Bearlift as well: let them know they'd been infiltrated by Chuck, say maybe they should do more of a background check on smarmy rear-lickers who turned up out of the blue, especially in new clothes with too many pockets, and maybe alert them to the fact that not everyone found them and their furfucking ways as charming as they found themselves. He signed that message "Bigfoot," which he regretted as soon as he'd hit Send: it was a little too close to a hint.

Then he went back to his crappy motel and sat in the bar where they had a flat-screen, and waited for results from the Rev-O-Rama Show. Sure enough, the discovery of the bones and shreds of Fenella made the evening TV news all over the country. There was the Rev, covering his face while being led away; there was Trudy, sweet as a milkshake, dabbing at her eyes, saying she'd had no idea, and how frightening to have been living all these years with a ruthless killer.

Smart play, points to Trudy: there was no way they could pin anything on her. By that time she must've known about the Rev's secret stash of cash — the Elders would have questioned her about the embezzled funds — and guessed he'd been planning to ditch her. To head out to an offshore safe house, where he could do some basking, and some fondling of underage children, or some flaying of them, whichever appealed to him at the moment. Because of course she'd known, she'd known about his twistiness all along. But she'd chosen not to know.

He got into his winter layers again and hiked to Cubs' Corner, where he sent another message to Adam — a short one, just the URL for where the news item on the arrest was to be found. Adam would surely be pleased: with the Rev out of commission or at least seriously curtailed, both of them could breathe a little easier.

But he needed to leave Whitehorse immediately. The criminal justice folks or equivalent could be trying to trace the message he'd sent to the PetrOleum Elder, and, if they succeeded, they'd start sifting through Whitehorse, which wasn't huge. They wouldn't be looking for Zeb as such — he was dead — but any looking would be bad looking, and it wouldn't take them long to crosshair his position. Maybe they already had: he was getting a bad feeling about that.

So he didn't go back to the motel. Instead he loped out to the nearest highway Truck-A-Pillar stop and hopped a convoy. Once in Calgary, he was able to slide himself onto the sealed bullet train, and after a couple of changes, and before you could say Maybe I Just Did a Really Stupid Thing, he was in New New York.

"A really stupid thing?" says Toby.

"Turning the Rev in and grabbing all his money maybe wasn't so bright," says Zeb. "He must've guessed then that I wasn't really dead. You know what they say about revenge — it's a dish that should be eaten cold, meaning you shouldn't do it out of anger because you'll fuck it up."

"But you didn't," says Toby. "Fuck it up."

"It was almost a fuckup. But I was lucky," says Zeb. "Look, here comes the moon. Some people would call that romantic."

Sure enough, there it is, rising above the trees to the east, almost full, almost red.

Why is it always such a surprise? thinks Toby. The moon. Even though we know it's coming. Every time we see it, it makes us pause, and hush.

Blacklight Headlamp

New New York was on the Jersey shore, or what was now the shore. Not many people lived in Old New York any more, though it was officially a no-go zone and thus a no-rent zone so a few denizens were still willing to take their chances in the disintegrating, waterlogged, derelict buildings. Not Zeb, though; he didn't have webbed feet and a death wish, and New New York – though no paradise – had more people in it, and therefore more background and cover. More of a crowd to blend into.

Once arrived, he ducked into a shoddy soft-pretzel-infested net café and sent a checking-in message to Adam – *Plan A Yay, What's Plan B?* – then cooled his heels while Adam took his time, wherever the fuck he was, whatever the fuck he was up to. His latest terse communication had read merely *CU soon*.

Zeb had gone to ground in an erstwhile high-life pool-enabled party-roomed condo complex called Starburst – after a firework, perhaps, but at present suggestive of charred interstellar debris. Starburst had reached its half-life some time ago: the once-expensive iron scrollwork gate served mainly as a dogwiddle station, and the mouldy, leaking buildings had been turned into divided-space unit rentals. These hosted a coral-reef ecosystem of dealers and addicts and pilotfish and drunks and hookers and pyramid scheme fly-by-nighters and jackals and shell-gamers and rent-gougers, all parasitizing one another.

Meanwhile the Starburst owners dodged the needed repairs and waited for the next spin cycle. First the low-rent artists would move in, full of piss and vinegar and resentment and the delusion that they could change the world. Then the startup designers and graphics companies, hoping a sheen of grubby cool would rub off on them. After that would come the questionable gene-peddler storefronts and the fashion pimps and pseudo galleries and latest-thing restaurant openings, with molecular-mix fusion involving dry ice and labmeat and quorn, and daring little garnishes of dwindling species: starling's tongue pâté had been a fad of late, in such places. The Starburst owners were most likely a bunch of guys who'd cashed in via some superCorp and wanted to fool around in real estate. Once the starling's tongue pâté phase had kicked in, they'd knock down the decaying unit rentals and erect a whole batch of new limited-shelf-life upmarket condos.

But Starburst was nowhere near that sweet spot yet, so Zeb was safe there as long as he minded his own business and shambled enough so anyone looking would think he was just another brain-damaged stoner. He stayed away from everyone and anything because he didn't want to attract any Chuck-like infiltrators.

He knew from his dips into the news that although the Rev was awaiting trial, he was out on bail and issuing statements about his innocence: he was the victim of an anti-religion and anti-Oleum leftwing cabal that had kidnapped and murdered his saintly first wife, Fenella, and then had maliciously spread the rumour that she'd run away to partake of an immoral life; which, since the Rev had believed it, had been an ongoing torture to him. This dastardly cabal had then planted Fenella in the Rev's yard for the sole purpose of casting dirt upon his name and of sullying the reputation of the Holy Oleum itself.

The Rev on bail would therefore be living in his house, and would thus have access to his Church of PetrOleum network – if not the *true* true believers, who were no doubt shunning him because of the embezzlement charges, then at least the more cynical wing, the ones who were in it for the money. And he'd be filled to the brim with cold, rancorous vengefulness because he would deeply suspect who was to blame for the tipoff about Fenella's pitiful bones turning to plant nutrients in his rock garden.

Meanwhile, main-chance Trudy had sold an autobiographical plaint and was doing numerous online interviews. How deceived she'd been by the Rev, having been convinced when she married him that he was a grieving widower dedicated to the greater good, and she so much wanted to be a partner in his pious works, and a mother to Fenella's son, little Adam. No wonder that young man could not be found, as he was very sensitive, and would hate the glare of publicity as much as she did. How shattering it had been to awaken to the truth of the Rev's murderous nature! Since learning of it, she'd prayed for Fenella's soul and begged her forgiveness, even though she'd had no idea at the time about what had really happened. Because, like everyone else, she, Trudy, had believed the story about Fenella running off with some trashy Tex-Mex or other. She is ashamed of herself for having been so falsely judgmental.

And now some of her very own church members — people she'd thought of as brothers and sisters — were refusing to speak to her, and had even accused her of having been in on the Rev's gory and larcenous activities all along. Only her faith had seen her through this testing and trying ordeal; and she longed for just one glimpse of her beloved lost son, Zebulon, who had strayed from the path, and no wonder, considering what sort of a father he had. But she prayed for him, wherever he was.

That beloved lost son fully intended to stay lost; though the temptation to hack into one of Trudy's online weepies and impersonate a ghostly spirit voice and denounce her was very great. A fine line of DNA he'd inherited: a psychopath of a con artist for a dad, a selfish liar of a mother with an obsessive love of pelf. He could only hope that in addition to her narcissism and greed, Trudy was secretly a skanky cheat who'd pulled a fast one on the Rev and had it off with a dark stranger in the garden tool shed. If so, it was possibly from his real, nameless father — an itinerant spade and sod artist prone to bonking the be-ringed and be-bangled wives of his upper-echelon clients — that Zeb had inherited his more dubious talents: babe-charming, the knack for sneaking in and out of windows both real and virtual, discretion as the better part of valour, and a not always reliable cloak of invisibility.

Maybe that's why the Rev hated Zeb so much: he knew Trudy had saddled him with a cuckoo in the nest, but he couldn't get back at her directly because of their shared digging activities. He had to either kill her or put up with her, her and her sluttish ways. If only Zeb had thought to purloin some of the Rev's DNA — a few hairs or toenail clippings — then he could get the tests done and set his mind at rest. Or not. But at least he'd be sure of his parentage, one way or the other.

No doubt about Adam, though: a definite Rev resemblance there. Though refined by the contribution of Fenella, of course. The poor girl was most likely a pious type — scrubbed hands, no nail polish, pulled-back hairdo, white panties devoid of trim — longing to do good and help people. A sitting duckie. His Warpiness had no doubt sold her on the idea that she would be a precious helpmeet to him and that this was a higher calling, though he'd have told her that one must forgo joy and pleasure as such in the service of him and his mission. Zeb guessed he'd have had no patience with the female orgasm. Crappy sex the two of them must have had, in any normal terms.

This was what Zeb thought about while watching daytime TV in his dank Starburst lair, or tossing on his lumpy, stained mattress while listening to the shouting and screaming going on outside his flimsily locked door. Animal spirits, drug-induced hilarity, hatred, fear, craziness. There were gradations to screams. It was the ones that stopped in the middle that you had to worry about.

Finally Adam came through. A meetup address, a time, and some instructions about what to wear. No red, no orange, a plain brown T-shirt if possible. No green: it was a politically charged colour, what with the vendetta against ecofreaks.

The address was a nondescript Happicuppa in New Astoria, not too near the semi-submerged and dangerously unstable buildings of the waterfront. Zeb sat crammed in behind one of the chi-chi little Happicuppa tables, on one of the teensy chairs that reminded him of kindergarten — he hadn't fitted into those chairs either — nursing his Happicappuccino and fortifying himself with half a Joltbar, and wondering what sort of spitball Adam was about to toss his way. He'd have a job lined up for Zeb — otherwise he wouldn't be calling for a meet — but what sort of job? Worm picker? Nightwatchman at a puppy mill? What order of contacts might Adam have been cultivating, wherever he had been?

Adam had hinted that he'd use an intermediary as the meetup courier, and Zeb worried about safety: the two of them had always been wary about trusting anyone except each other. True, Adam would be cautious. But he was methodical, and methodology could give you away. The only sure camouflage was unpredictability.

From his cramped chair Zeb eyed the entering customers, hoping to spot the courier. Was it this blond hermaphrodite in the halter top and sequined three-horned headdress? He hoped not. This plump, gum-chewing woman with the cream-coloured shorts and the wedgie and the retro cinch belt? She looked too vacuous, though vacuousness was a nearly foolproof disguise, at least for girls. Was it this mild, geeky-looking boy of the type that would some day machine-gun an auditorium full of his pimply fellow classmates? Nope, not him either.

But suddenly, surprise: there was Adam himself. It startled Zeb to see him materialize in the chair opposite, which had been empty just the moment before. Ectoplasmic, you could say.

Adam looked like a passport photo of himself, one that was already fading to light and shadow. It was as if he'd returned from the dead: he had that glowing-eyeball thing about him. His T-shirt was beige, his baseball cap sloganless. He'd bought himself a Happimocha to make it seem as if this was just two oddfellow buddies taking a break from their nerdwork, or else doing a meeting about some startup doomed to implode like a drowning blimp. Happimocha and Adam didn't go together: Zeb was curious to see if he'd actually drink any of the stuff – something so impure.

"Don't raise your voice," were the first words Adam spoke. Not two seconds back in Zeb's life and already he was giving orders.

"I was thinking of fucking yelling," said Zeb. He waited to be told not to use profanity, but Adam didn't take the bait. Zeb stared at him: there was something different. His eyes were just as round and blue, but his hair was paler. Could it be turning white? There was a new beard too, also pale. "Nice to see you too," he added.

Adam smiled: a flicker of a smile. "You'll be going into Helth-Wyzer West near San Francisco," he said. "As a data inputter. I've fixed it up. When you leave here, pick up the shopping bag beside your left knee. Everything you'll need is in there. You'll have to get the scans and prints inserted in the ID – I've put the address for that.

And you'll need to scrap the old ID: delete anything online. But I don't have to tell you that."

"Where've you been, anyway?" said Zeb.

Adam smiled in that maddening, saintly way he had. Butter wouldn't melt; it never had melted. "Classified," he said. "Other lives involved." That was the kind of thing that made Zeb long to put a toad in his bed.

"Right, slap my wrist. Okay, what's this HelthWyzer West, and what'm I supposed to be doing in there?"

"It's a Compound," said Adam. "Research and innovation. Drugs, the medical kind; enriched vitamin supplements; materials for transgenic splices and gene enhancement, specifically the hormone blends and simulators. It's a powerful Corp. There are a lot of top brains there."

"How'd you get me in?" said Zeb.

"I have some new acquaintances," said Adam, continuing his nonstop I-know-more-than-you smile. "They'll watch out for you. You'll be safe." He looked past Zeb's shoulder, then at his watch. Or he appeared to look at his watch. Zeb knew a good piece of misdirection when he saw it: Adam was scanning the room, checking for shadows.

"Cut the bullshit," said Zeb. "You want me to do something for you."

Adam held his smile. "You'll be a blacklight headlamp," he said. "Be extra careful checking in online, once you're there. Oh, and there's a new dropbox, and a new gateway into it. Don't return to that zephyr site, it may have been compromised."

"What's a blacklight headlamp?" said Zeb. But Adam had already stood up and straightened his beige tee and was halfway to the door. He hadn't drunk any of his Happimocha, so Zeb obligingly drank it for him. An unconsumed Happimocha might raise eyebrows in a pleeb like this, where only pimps had money to burn.

Zeb took his time getting back to Starburst. The back of his neck prickled all the way there, he was so sure he was being watched. But nobody tried to mug him. Once inside his door he looked up "blacklight headlamp" on his most recent cheap toss-at-will cellphone. "Blacklight" was a novelty item from the first decades of the century, he was told: it let you see in the dark, or it let you see some things in the dark. Eyeballs. Teeth. White bedsheets. Glo in the Dark Hair Gel. Fog. As for "headlamp," it was what it said. Bicycle shops sold them, and camping suppliers. Not that anyone really went camping any more except inside derelict buildings.

Thanks a pile, Adam, thought Zeb. That is so fucking instructive.

Then he opened Adam's shopping bag. There was his new skin, all neatly laid out for him. What he had to do now was Truck-A-Pillar over to San Francisco, and then crawl into it.

Intestinal Parasites, the Game

Adam's preparations had been thorough. There was a burn-this to-do list, and a big envelope stuffed with cash because Zeb would need some to pay off the grey marketeer designated to fake his passes. There was plastic as well, so Zeb could get himself the kind of wardrobe Adam thought he should have. He'd supplied descriptions: casual geekwear, with brown cord pants and neutral Ts and plaid shirts — brown and grey — and a pair of round-eyed glasses that didn't magnify anything. As for the footgear, the recommendation was trainers with so much rubber cross-strapping Zeb would look like a gay Morris dancer or some fugitive from a session of Robin Hood cosplay. Hat, a steampunk bowler from the 2010s: those were back in style. Though how would Adam know that? He'd never appeared to take any interest in vestments, but no interest was of course an interest. He must've been noting what other people wore so he could not wear it himself.

Zeb's assigned name was Seth. A little biblical joke of Adam's: Seth meant "appointed," as they were both aware, since they'd had the main biblical names and stories drilled into their skulls with a figurative screwdriver. Seth was the third son of Adam and Eve, deputized to take the place of the murdered Abel, who wasn't entirely dead, however, because he still had talking blood that cried out from the ground. So "Seth" was replacing the departed and presumed dead Zeb. By appointment, courtesy of Adam. Very funny.

Adam requested that Zeb/Seth test the new chatroom before entering HelthWyzer, and then check in once a week to signal he was still walking the planet. So the next day, while making his circuitous way to the grey marketeer to get his prints and iris scans inserted into his fake docs, he chose a net café at random and followed the lilypad trail laid out for him by Adam. (*Memorize, then destroy*, said the note, as if Zeb was a fucking idiot.)

The main gateway was a biogeek challenge game called Extinctathon. Monitored by MaddAddam, it said: *Adam named the living animals, MaddAddam names the dead ones. Do you want to play?* Zeb entered the codename supplied to him by Adam – Spirit Bear – and the password, which was *shoelaces*, and found himself inside the game.

It seemed to be a variant of Animal, Vegetable, Mineral. Using obscure clues provided by your opponent, you had to guess the identities of various extirpated beetles, fish, plants, skinks, and so forth. A roll call of the already erased. It was a certified yawner: even the CorpSeCorps would be put to sleep by this one, plus they'd have no clue as to most of the answers. As – to be fair – Zeb himself did not, despite his time spent with the Bearlifters and their obscure forms of one-upmanship. *You haven't heard of Steller's sea cow? Really?* Tiny, self-satisfied smirk.

Five minutes inside Extinctathon and any self-respecting Corps-Man would run screaming in search of alcoholic beverages. A terminally boring game was almost as effective as a vacuous stare, disguise-wise; plus they'd never think there was anything hidden inside a location that was right out in the open and so obviously eco-freakish. Instead, they'd be combing through bimplant ads and sites where you could shoot exotic animals online without leaving your office chair. Full Points to Adam, thought Zeb.

Could it be that Adam had designed this game himself? A game with his own name embedded as the Monitor? But he'd never shown much interest in animals, as such. Though, come to think of it, he'd been known to view with mild contempt the Rev's interpretation of Genesis, which was that God had made the animals for the sole pleasure and use of man, and you could therefore exterminate them at whim. Was Extinctathon a piece of anti-Rev counterinsurgency on the part of Adam? Had he somehow got mixed up with the ecofreaks? Maybe he'd had a conversion moment while smoking too much of some brain-damaging hallucinogenic and bonded with a plant fairy. Though that was unlikely: it was Zeb who'd been the chemicals risk-taker, not Adam. But Adam was mixed up with someone, for sure, because he'd never be able to pull off something like this on his own.

Zeb continued along the pathway. He chose *Yes* to show readiness and was redirected. *Welcome, Spirit Bear. Do you want to play a general game, or do you want to play a Grandmaster?* The second was the choice to make, said Adam's instructions, so Zeb clicked on it.

Good. Find your playroom. MaddAddam will meet you there.

The path to the playroom was complicated, zigzagging from one coordinate to another through pixels located here and there on innocuous sites: ads, for the most part, though some were lists: TOP TEN SCARY EASTER BUNNY PICS, TEN SCARIEST MOVIES OF ALL TIME, TEN SCARIEST SEA MONSTERS. Zeb found a portal through the buck teeth of a deranged purple plush rabbit with a terrorized infant perched on its knee, from there to a tombstone in a still from *Night of the Living Dead*, the original, and finally to the eye of a coelacanth. Then he was in the chatroom.

Welcome to MaddAddam's playroom, Spirit Bear. You have a message.

Zeb clicked on *Deliver message.*

Hello, said the message. *You see, it works. Here are the coordinates for next week's chatroom. A.*

Minimalist bugger, thought Zeb. He's not going to tell me a thing.

He bought the suggested outfit, or most of it: the round glasses were too much to take, as were the shoes. He broke in the pants and the shirts — spilled food on them, frayed them a little, ran them through the wash a few times. Then he tossed his previous clothes into various dumpsters and wiped his biotraces off his cheesy Starburst room as much as he could.

After paying up at Starburst — no sense in having the skip-tracers on your tail, if avoidable — he made the cross-continent trek to San Francisco. Then he reported at HelthWyzer West as instructed, presented his fraudulent docs, and underwent the welcoming *Hi, Buddy, Happy You're Here, We'll Help You Feel at Home* minuet of the podge-faced greeter.

Nobody said boo. He was expected, he was accepted. Smooth as grease.

Inside HelthWyzer West he was assigned a bachelor condo unit in the residential tower. Nothing rundown about these facilities: nice landscaping around the entranceway, swimming pool on the roof, and the plumbing and electricals all worked, though the interior design was a little Spartan. There was a queen-sized bed, an optimistic signal. Bachelor did not mean celibate in the world of HelthWyzer West, it appeared.

The workspace high-rise had a cafeteria where he was issued a swipe card that would record his consumption: everyone had a points allowance, which they could use on anything on the menu. The food was real food, not spurious glop like the stuff he'd eaten at Bearlift. The drinks had alcohol in them, which was the least you could expect in a drink.

The HelthWyzer women were brisk, and had jobs to do and not much time for small talk, and – he guessed – no tolerance at all for cheap pickup lines, so he didn't even bother; but though he'd vowed to be careful about personal involvements because of the kinds of questions they could generate, he wasn't made of stone. Already a couple of the younger females had looked at his *Seth* name tag – name tags were a fashion statement at HelthWyzer – and one of them had asked him if he was new because she couldn't recall seeing him before, but of course she was kind of new herself.

Was there a little twist of the shoulders, a giveaway flutter of the eyelids? *Marjorie*, he read, not lingering too long on her name tag, which was perched on a breast of no more than ordinary prominence: obvious bimplants were not common inside the HelthWyzer walls. Marjorie had a blunt-nosed, brown-eyed, acquiescent face, like a spaniel, and in ordinary circumstances he would have proceeded, but as it was he said he hoped he'd see her around. Such a hope was not the top hope on his list of hopes – that spot was reserved for not getting caught – but it was not the bottom hope either.

The job description for Seth was that of a routine low-level IT guy, dime a dozen. Data inputting, using a packet of snoreworthy but serviceable software designed to record and compare the various factoids and buckets o'data the HelthWyzer brainiacs were coming up with. Glorified digital secretary, that's all he was supposed to be.

The duties weren't challenging: he could do the job with two fingers of one hand in much less time than was allotted for it. The Helth-Wyzer project managers didn't supervise much, they just wanted him to keep current with the inputting. Meanwhile he could ferret around in the HelthWyzer databank unimpeded. He ran a few IT security tests of his own to see whether any outside pirates were trying to hack in: if they were, it would be useful to know about it.

At first he didn't uncover any telltale signs; but during one of his deep dives he pinpointed something that looked as if it might be a cryptic tunnel. He wiggled through it, found himself outside the HelthWyzer burning ring of firewalls, then lilypadded his way into the Extinctathon chatroom. A message was waiting for him: *Use only when needed. Don't spend long. Wipe all prints. A.* He logged out quickly, then erased his trail. He'd need to build another portal, because whoever was using this tunnel might work out that someone else had been through it.

He decided Seth needed to be known as a guy who did a lot of gaming so that checking into Extinctathon wouldn't stand out should anyone be snooping. That was the operational reason; but also he just wanted to test out the games, and to see how easy it was to fool around during work hours without being reprimanded — staff weren't supposed to waste time in this way, or not too much time — and also how easy it was to cheat. He thought of it as keeping his hand in.

Some of the games on recreational offer were standard — weapons, explosions, and so on — but others were posted by the staff at Helth-Wyzer West: biogeeks were just as geeky as other geeks, so naturally they designed games of their own. Spandrel was one of the better ones: it let you devise extra, functionally useless features for a bioform, then link them to sexual selection and fast-forward to see what the evolution machine would churn out. Cats with rooster-like wattles on their foreheads, lizards with big red lipstick-kiss lips, men with enormous left eyes — whatever the females chose was favoured, and you could manipulate their bad taste in male attributes, just like real life. Then you played predators against prey. Would the supersexy span-

drels impede hunting skills or slow down escape? If your guy wasn't
sexy enough, he wouldn't get laid and you'd go extinct; if he was too
sexy, he'd get eaten and you'd go extinct. Sex versus dinner: it was a
fine balance. Packets of random mutations could be purchased for a
small sum.

Weather Monsters wasn't bad either: the game threw extreme
weather events at your player – a puny human avatar of either gender – and you tried to see how long your player could survive them.
With points won, you could purchase tools for your avatar: boots that
allowed it to run faster and jump higher, lightning-proof clothing,
floating planks for floods and tsunamis, wet handkerchiefs for covering its nose during brush fires, Joltbars for when it was trapped under
a thick wad of snow due to an avalanche. A shovel, some matches, an
axe. If your avatar survived the giant mudslide – a killer event – you'd
get a whole toolbox and a thousand extra points for your next game.

The one Zeb played the most was called Intestinal Parasites – a
nasty gucklunch the biogeeks thought was hilarious. The parasites
were truly ugly, with rebarbed hooks all around their mouths and no
eyes, and you had to nuke them with toxic pills or deploy an arsenal of
nanobots or moteins before they could lay thousands of eggs in you or
creep through your brain and out your tear ducts, or split themselves
into regenerating segments and turn the inside of your body into a
festering patty-melt. Were they real, or had the biogeeks made them
up? Worse, were they gene-splicing them right now as part of a bio-
weaponry project? Impossible to know.

Play Intestinal Parasites too much and you'd get nightmares, guaranteed, said the game's running slogan. So, never one to do as he was
told, Zeb did play it too much, and he did get nightmares.

Which didn't stop him from creating an alias of the game, then
reworking one of the hideous mouths so that it functioned as a gateway. He stashed his code in a triple-locked thumbdrive for safekeeping, then parked it at the back of his supervisor's desk drawer in a nest
of rubber bands, used nosewipes, and orphaned cough drops. No one
would ever look there.

Bone Cave

Cursive

Toby is at work on her journal. She doesn't really have the energy for it, but Zeb went to all that trouble to bring her the materials and he's bound to notice if she doesn't use them. She's writing in one of the cheap schooltime drugstore notebooks. The cover has a bright yellow sun, several pink daisies, and a boy and a girl, rudimentary figures of the kind children used to draw. Back when there were human children — how long ago? It seems like centuries since the plague swept through. Though it's less than half a year.

The boy has blue shorts, a blue cap, and a red shirt; the girl has pigtails, a triangular skirt, red, and a blue top. They both have smudgy black blob eyes and thick red upcurved mouths; they're laughing fit to kill.

Fit to die. They are only paper children, but they seem dead now anyway, like all the real children. She can't look at this notebook cover too much because it hurts.

Better to concentrate on the task at hand. Don't brood or mope. Take one day at a time.

Saint Bob Hunter and the Feast of Rainbow Warriors, Toby writes. This may not be accurate, time-wise — she's probably out by a day or two — but it will have to do because how can she check? There's no central authority any more for days of the month. But Rebecca might know. There were special recipes for the Festivals and Feasts. Maybe she's memorized them; maybe she's kept track.

Moon: Waxing gibbous. Weather: Nothing unusual. Noteworthy occurrences: Group pig aggression displayed. Painballer evidence sighted by Zeb's expedition: piglet shot and partly butchered. Discovery of a tire tread sandal, possible clue to Adam. No definite sign of Adam One and the Gardeners.

She thinks a minute, then adds: *Jimmy is conscious and improving. Crakers continue friendly.*

"What are you making, Oh Toby?" It's little Blackbeard: she didn't hear him come in. "What are those lines?"

"Come over here," she says. "I won't bite you. Look. I'm doing *writing*: that is what these lines are. I'll show you."

She runs through the basics. *This is paper, it is made from trees.*

Does it hurt the tree? No, because the tree is dead by the time the paper is made – a tiny lie, but no matter. *And this is a pen. It has a black liquid in it, it is called ink, but you do not need to have a pen to do writing.* Just as well, she thinks: those rollerballs will run out soon.

You can use many things to make writing. You can use the juice of elderberries for the ink, you can use the feather of a bird for the pen, you can use a stick and some wet sand to write on. All of these things can be used to make writing.

"Now," she says, "you have to draw the letters. Each letter means a sound. And when you put the letters together they make words. And the words stay where you've put them on the paper, and then other people can see them on the paper and hear the words."

Blackbeard looks at her, squinting with puzzlement and unbelief. "Oh Toby, but it can't talk," he says. "I see the marks you have put there. But it is not saying anything."

"You need to be the voice of the writing," she says. "When you *read* it. *Reading* is when you turn these marks back into sounds. Look, I will write your name."

She tears a page carefully from the back of the notebook, prints on it: BLACKBEARD. Then she sounds out each letter for him. "See?" she says. "It means you. Your name." She puts the pen in his hand, curls his fingers around it, guides the hand and the pen: the letter *B*.

"This is how your name begins," she says. "B. Like bees. It's the same sound." Why is she telling him this? What use will he ever have for it?

"That is not me," says Blackbeard, frowning. "It is not bees either. It is only some marks."

"Take this paper to Ren," says Toby, smiling. "Ask her to read it, then come back and tell me if she says your name."

Blackbeard stares at her. He doesn't trust what she's told him, but he takes the piece of paper anyway, holding it gingerly as if it's coated with invisible poison. "Will you stay here?" he says. "Until I come back?"

"Yes," she says. "I'll be right here." He backs out the doorway as he always does, keeping his eyes on her until he turns the corner.

She turns back to her journal. What else to write, besides the bare-facts daily chronicle she's begun? What kind of story — what kind of history will be of any use at all, to people she can't know will exist, in the future she can't foresee?

Zeb and the Bear, she writes. *Zeb and MaddAddam. Zeb and Crake.* All of these stories could be set down. But why, but for whom? Only for herself because it gives her a chance to dwell upon Zeb?

Zeb and Toby, she writes. But surely that will be only a footnote.

Don't jump to conclusions, she tells herself. He came to the garden, bringing gifts. You could be misinterpreting, about Swift Fox. And even if not, so what? Take what the moment offers. Don't close doors. Be thankful.

Blackbeard slips into the room again. He's carrying the sheet of paper, holding it in front of him like a hot shield. His face is radiant.

"It did, Oh Toby," he says. "It said my name! It told my name to Ren!"

"There," she says. "That is *writing*."

Blackbeard nods: now he's grasping the possibilities. "I can keep this?" he says.

"Of course," says Toby.

"Show me again. With the black thing."

Later — after it's rained, after the rain has stopped — she finds him at the sandbox. He has a stick, and the paper. There's his name in the sand. The other children are watching him. All of them are singing.

Now what have I done? she thinks. What can of worms have I opened? They're so quick, these children: they'll pick this up and transmit it to all the others.

What comes next? Rules, dogmas, laws? The Testament of Crake? How soon before there are ancient texts they feel they have to obey but have forgotten how to interpret? Have I ruined them?

Swarm

Breakfast is kudzu and other assorted forage greens, bacon, a strange flatbread with unidentified seeds in it, steamed burdock. Coffee from a blend of toasted roots: dandelion, chickory, something else. It has an undertaste of ashes.

They're running out of sugar, and there's no honey. But there is Mo'Hair milk. Another of the ewes – a blue-haired one – has given birth to twins, a blonde and a brunette. There have been some jokes about lamb stew, but no one wants to go there: somehow it would be hard to slaughter and eat an animal with human hair; especially human hair that so closely resembles, in its sheen and stylability, the shampoo ads of yore. Every time one of those Mo'Hairs shakes itself it's like watching the back view of a TV hair beauty: the shining mane, the flirtatious ripple and swirl. At any minute, thinks Toby, you expect them to come out with a product spiel. *Every day a bad-hair day? My hair was driving me crazy, but then ... I died.*

Don't be so dark, Toby, it's only hair. It's not the end of the world.

Over the coffee they discuss other food options. Protein variety is lacking, they're all agreed on that. Rebecca says she'd kill for some live chickens because then they could keep them in a henhouse and have eggs; but where are such chickens to be found? There are seabird eggs on top of the derelict towers offshore, down by the beach – there must be, the birds are nesting there – but who is willing to make the perilous trip down to the seashore through the increasingly overgrown Heritage Park that may harbour the Painballers, not to mention a squadron or two of large, malevolent pigs? And they shouldn't even think about climbing up the inner stairs of those towers, which must be very unstable by now.

A debate follows. One side points to the fact that the Crakers wander back and forth at will, singing their polyphonic music. They visit their home base by the shore, a hollow jumble of cement blocks. They keep it protected from animals by peeing in a circle around it, a circle they believe the pigoons and wolvogs and bobkittens won't cross. They spear the ritual fish to present to Toby so she will fulfill the functions of Snowman-the-Jimmy and tell them stories. No animal has molested the Crakers on their woodland walks, or not so far. As for the Painballers, they must be quite far away by now, judging from the location of the last known sign of them, which was the carcass of that recently killed piglet.

The other side argues that the Crakers appear to have ways of keeping the wildlife at bay while in transit, apart from the pissing defence. Maybe it's the singing? If so, and needless to point out, that won't work for normal human beings, whose vocal cords aren't made of organic glass or whatever it is that accounts for those digital-keyboard theremin sounds. As for the Painballers, they could easily have circled back by now, and might be lurking in ambush around the very next kudzu-smothered corner. You can never be too careful, and better safe than sorry, and they cannot afford to sacrifice one or two of their number for the sake of a few gull eggs, which are likely green and taste like fish guts anyway.

An egg is an egg, say the pro-eggers. Why not send a couple of human beings with the Crakers? That way the humans will be protected from wild animals via the Crakers, and the Crakers will be protected from the Painballers via the sprayguns toted by the Madd-Addamites. No point in giving sprayguns to the Crakers, since you could never teach them about shooting and killing people. They just aren't capable, not being human as such.

Not so fast: that case has not yet been proven, says Ivory Bill. "If they can crossbreed with us, then case made. Same species. If not, then not." He leans forward, peers into his coffee cup. "Any more?" he asks Rebecca.

"Only half true," says Manatee. "A horse plus a donkey gives you a mule, but it's sterile. We wouldn't know for sure until the next genera-tion."

"I've only got enough for tomorrow," says Rebecca. "We need to dig some dandelions. We've used up the ones around here."

"It would be an interesting experiment," says Ivory Bill. "But of course we would need the co-operation of the ladies." He inclines his head courteously towards Swift Fox, who's wearing a winsome floral print sheet, with bouquets of pink and blue flowers tied with pink and blue bows.

"You've seen those dicks of theirs?" says Swift Fox. "Too much of a good thing. If I find a dick in my mouth, I want to know it came in at the head end." Ivory Bill turns away, visibly shocked, silently angry. Laughter from some, frowns from others. Swift Fox likes to potty-mouth the crowd, especially the men; to demonstrate that she isn't just a pretty body, is Toby's guess. She wants to have it both ways.

Zeb is down at the other end of the table. He came late; he hasn't been joining in the debate. He appears to be engrossed in the flatbread. Swift Fox tosses him a glance: is he her intended audience? He pays no attention; but then he wouldn't, would he? That's what those lovelife advisers blogging about office romances used to say: you can tell the guilty parties by the way in which they studiously avoid each other.

"Those guys don't need any co-operation," says Crozier. "They jump anything with a c – Sorry, Toby. Anything with a skirt."

"A skirt!" says Swift Fox, laughing again, showing her white teeth. "Where've you been? You've seen any of us wearing skirts? Bedsheet wraps don't count." She twists her shoulders back and forth, as if on a fashion runway. "You like my skirt? It goes all the way up to my armpits!"

"Leave him alone, he's underage," says Manatee. Crozier is mak-ing a strange face: anger? Embarrassment? Ren's sitting beside him. He gives her a sheepish grin, puts his hand on her arm. She frowns at him like a spouse.

"They're the most fun, the underage ones," says Swift Fox. "Frisky. They're packed with endorphins, and their nucleotide sequences are to die for – miles of telomeres left." Ren stares at her, stone-faced.

"He's not underage," she says. Swift Fox smiles.

Do the men at the table see it? Toby wonders. The silent mud-wrestle in the air? No, probably not. They're not on the progesterone wavelength.

"They only do that under the right conditions," says Manatee. "The group copulation. The woman has to be in heat."

"That's fine for their own women," says Beluga. "They've got clear hormonal signals there, both visual and olfactory. But our women register to them as in heat all the time."

"Maybe they are," says Manatee, grinning. "They just won't admit it."

"Point being: two different species," says Beluga.

"Women aren't dogs," says White Sedge. "I am finding this exchange offensive. I don't think you should refer to us like that." Her voice is calm but her spine's like a ramrod.

"This is merely an objective scientific discussion," says Zunzuncito.

"Hey," says Rebecca. "All I said is, it would be neat to have some eggs."

Morning worktime, the sun not yet too hot. Bright pink kudzu moths hang in the shade, flocks of butterflies in blue and magenta kite-fight in the air, golden honeybees flock on the polyberry flowers.

Toby's on garden duty again, weeding and deslugging. Her rifle leans against the inside of the fence: she prefers it within reach, wherever she is, because you never know. All around her the plants are growing, weeds and cultivars both. She can almost hear them pushing up through the soil, their rootlets sniffing for nutrients and crowding the rootlets of their neighbours, their leaves releasing clouds of airborne chemicals.

Saint Vandana Shiva of Seeds, she wrote in her notebook this morning. *Saint Nikolai Vavilov, Martyr.* She added the traditional God's Gardener invocation: *May we be mindful of Saint Vandana and Saint Vavilov, fierce preservers of ancient seeds. Saint Vavilov, who collected the seeds and preserved them throughout the siege of Leningrad, only to fall victim to the tyrant Stalin; and Saint Vandana, tireless warrior against biopiracy, who gave of herself for the good of the Living Vegetable World in all its diversity and beauty. Lend us the purity of your Spirits and the strength of your resolve.*

Toby has a flash of memory: herself, back when she was Eve Six among the Gardeners, reciting this prayer along with old Pilar just before they set to work on the bean rows, doing their required stint of slug and snail relocation. Sometimes the homesickness for those days is so strong and also so unexpected that it knocks her down like a rogue wave. If she'd had a camera then, if she'd had a photo album, she'd be poring over the pictures. But the Gardeners didn't believe in cameras, or in paper records; so all she has is the words.

There would be no point in being a Gardener now: the enemies of God's Natural Creation no longer exist, and the animals and birds – those that did not become extinct under the human domination of the planet – are thriving unchecked. Not to mention the plant life.

Though maybe we could do with fewer of some plants, she thinks as she snips off the aggressive kudzu vines already climbing the garden fence. The stuff gets in everywhere. It's tireless, it can grow a foot in twelve hours, it surges up and over anything in its way like a green tsunami. The grazing Mo'Hairs do a little to keep it down, and the Crakers munch away at it, and Rebecca serves it up like spinach, but that hardly makes a dent in it.

She's heard some of the men discussing a plan to make it into wine, but she has mixed feelings about that. She can't imagine the taste – Pinot Grigio crossed with mashed lawn rakings? Pinot Vert with a whiff of compost pile? But apart from that, can their tiny group really afford to indulge in alcohol in any form? It dulls awareness, and they're too vulnerable for that. Their little enclave is poorly defended. One drunken sentry, then infiltration, then carnage.

"Found a swarm for you," says Zeb's voice. He's come up behind her unseen: so much for her own alertness.

She turns, smiling. Is it a real smile? Not entirely, because she still doesn't know the truth about Swift Fox. Swift Fox and Zeb. Did they or didn't they? And if he simply took the open door, so to speak – if he didn't think twice about it – why should she? "A swarm?" she says. "Really? Where?"

"Come into the forest with me," he says, grinning like a fairy-tale wolf, holding out his paw of a hand. So of course she takes it, and forgives him everything. For the moment. Even though there may not be anything to forgive.

They walk towards the tree edge, away from the cobb-house clearing. It does feel like a clearing now, though the MaddAddamites didn't clear anything. But now that the vegetation is moving in they're working to keep it clear, so maybe that counts.

It's cooler under the trees. Also more ominous: the green crosshatching of leaves and branches blocks the sight lines. There's a trail, indicated by bent twigs, showing the way Zeb must have come earlier.

"Are you sure this is safe?" Toby says. She's lowered her voice without even thinking about it. In the open you look, because a predator will be seen before it's heard. But among the trees you have to listen, because it will be heard before it's seen.

"I was just back here, I checked it out," says Zeb, too confidently for Toby.

There's the swarm, a large bee ball the size of a watermelon, hanging in the lower branches of a young sycamore. It's buzzing softly; the surface of the ball is rippling, like golden fur in a breeze.

"Thank you," says Toby. She ought to go back to the cobb-house enclave, find a container, and scoop the centre of the swarm into it to capture the queen. Then the rest of the swarm will follow. She won't even need to smoke the bees: they won't sting because they aren't defending a nest. She'll explain to them first that she means them well, and that she hopes they will be her messengers to the land of the dead. Pilar, her bee teacher at the Gardeners, told her this speech was necessary when persuading a swarm of wild bees to come with you.

"Maybe I should get a bag or something," she says. "They're already scouting for a good nest site. They'll be flying soon."

"You want me to babysit them?" asks Zeb.

"It's okay," she says. She'd like him to come back to the cobb house with her: she doesn't want to walk through the forest alone. "But could you just not listen to me for a minute? And look the other way?"

"You need to take a leak?" says Zeb. "Don't mind me."

"You know how this goes. You were a Gardener yourself," she says. "I need to talk to the bees." It's one of the Gardener practises that, viewed by an outsider, must seem weird; and it still does seem weird to her because part of her remains an outsider.

"Sure," says Zeb. "Hey. Do your stuff." He turns sideways, gazes into the forest.

Toby feels herself blushing. But she pulls the end of her bedsheet up to cover her head – essential, old Pilar said, or the bees would feel disrespected – and speaks in a whisper to the buzzing furball. "Oh Bees," she says. "I send greetings to your Queen. I wish to be her friend, and to prepare a safe home for her, and for you who are her daughters, and to tell you the news every day. May you carry messages from the land of the living to all souls who dwell in the land of shadows. Please tell me now whether you accept my offer."

She waits. The buzzing increases. Then several of the scout bees fly down and land on her face. They explore her skin, her nostrils, the corners of her eyes; it's as if a dozen tiny fingers are stroking her. If they sting, the answer is no. If they don't sting, the answer is yes. She breathes in, willing herself to be calm. They don't like fear.

The scout bees lift away from her, spiral back towards the swarm, blend into the moving golden pelt. Toby breathes out.

"You can look now," she says to Zeb.

There's a crackling, a thrashing: something's coming towards them through the undergrowth. Toby feels the blood leave her hands. Oh shit, she thinks. Pig, wolvog? We don't have a spraygun. And my rifle's back there in the garden. She scans around for a stone to throw. Zeb has picked up a stick.

Saint Dian, Saint Francis, Saint Fateh Singh Rathore: lend me your strength and wisdom. Speak to the animals now. May they turn away from us, and seek their meat from God.

But no, it's not an animal. There's a voice: it's people. There's no Gardener prayer against people. Painballers – they don't know we're here. What should we do? Run? No, they're too close now. Get out of the line of fire. If possible.

Zeb has stepped in front of her, pushed her back with one hand. He freezes. Then he laughs.

Bone Cave

Out of the bushes comes Swift Fox, straightening her pink and blue floral bedsheet. Right behind her is Crozier, similarly straightening, though his bedsheet is an understated black-and-grey stripe.

"Hi, Toby. Hi, Zeb," he says, overly casual.

"Taking a stroll?" says Swift Fox.

"Bee hunting," says Zeb. He doesn't seem upset. So maybe I've been wrong, thinks Toby: he's not feeling territorial about her, he doesn't care that she's been flailing among the weeds with Crozier.

As for Crozier, isn't he supposed to be pursuing Ren? Or has Toby been wrong about that as well?

"Bee hunting? Really? Hey, whatever works," says Swift Fox, laughing. "Us, we were foraging. For mushrooms. We foraged and foraged. We got down on our hands and knees, we looked everywhere. But we didn't find a single mushroom, did we, Croze?"

Crozier shakes his head, looking down at the ground. It's as if he's been caught with his pants down, but he's not wearing pants, only the striped bedsheet.

"See you," says Swift Fox. "Happy bee hunting." She heads back towards the cobb house, with Crozier following as if pulled on a string.

"C'mon, Bee Queen," Zeb says to Toby. "Let's get your supplies. I'll walk you home."

In a perfect world Toby would already have a Langstroth hive box, complete with supers and moveable frames. She should have prepared one ahead of time, on the off chance of finding a swarm; but, lacking foresight, she did not do this. Barring a proper hive box, what can she use that will appeal to the bees? Any cavity that's protected, with an entrance where they can go in and out; dry enough, cool enough, warm enough.

Rebecca offers a scavenged Styrofoam cooler; Zeb makes an entrance hole in the side, near the top, and several other ventilation holes. Toby and Zeb set it up in a corner of the garden, surround it with rocks for stability and extra shelter, then add a couple of vertical slabs of plywood, raising them above the bottom of the cooler with small stones. It's only a rough approximation of a hive, but it will have to do for now, and perhaps for a long time. The danger is that if the bees get established here they'll be very annoyed if she moves them later.

Toby improvises a catching bag out of a pillowcase, and they trek back into the woods to collect the bees. She uses a long stick, scrapes quickly. The core of the swarm tumbles gently into the bag. The densest part holds the magnet of the queen: like the heart in the body, she's invisible.

They carry the pillowcase to the garden, buzzing loudly; a cloud of loose bees trails behind them. Toby eases the bee ball into the cooler, waits until all strays have found their way out of the pillowcase, then waits some more while the bees explore their new home.

There's always an adrenalin rush for Toby when she's handling bees. It could go badly: she might smell wrong one day and find herself the centre of an angry, stinging horde. Sometimes she feels she could wash herself all over in bees, like a bubble bath; but that's the euphoria of bee handling, like an altitude high or the rapture of the deep. It would be stupid to actually try it.

When the swarm has settled down she closes the lid of the cooler and places a couple of stones on top. Soon the bees are winging in and out of the entrance hole and rummaging for pollen among the garden flowers.

"Thank you," she says to Zeb; and he says, "Any time," as if he's a crossing guard rather than a lover. But it's daytime, she reminds herself: he's always a little brisk in daytime. He lopes off, around the corner of the cobb house, out of sight; mission accomplished.

She covers her head. "May you be happy here, Oh Bees," she says to the Styrofoam cooler. "As your new Eve Six, I promise to visit you every day, if I can, and to tell you the news."

"Oh Toby, can we do the writing again? With the marks, on the paper?" It's her shadow, little Blackbeard. He's climbed up the garden fence on the outside and is hanging over it, resting his chin on his arms. How long has he been watching her?

"Yes," she says. "Maybe tomorrow, if you come early."

"What is that box? What are the stones? What are you doing, Oh Toby?"

"I'm helping the bees find a home," says Toby.

"Will they live in the box? Why do you want them to live there?"

Because I want to steal their honey, thinks Toby. "Because they will be safe there," she says.

"Were you talking to the bees, Oh Toby? I heard you talking. Or were you talking to Crake, as Snowman-the-Jimmy does?"

"I was talking to the bees," says Toby. Blackbeard's face lights up with a smile.

"I did not know you could do that," he says. "You talk with the Children of Oryx? As we do? But you can't sing!"

"You sing to the animals?" says Toby. "They like music?"

This question seems merely to puzzle him. "Music?" he says. "What is *music*?" The next minute he's dropped down behind the fence and has run off to join the other children.

Smelling of bees when you're not actually with them can attract unwanted insect company: already there are some green flies trying to settle on her, and some interested wasps. Toby goes over to wash her hands at the pump. As she's scrubbing, Ren and Lotis Blue come in search of her.

"We need to talk to you," says Ren. "It's about Amanda. We're really worried."

"Try to keep her busy," says Toby. "I'm sure she'll be back to normal in a while. She's had a shock, these things take time. Remember how you were at first, when you were recovering from your own Painballers attack? I'll give her some mushroom elixir, to build up her strength."

"No, you don't understand," says Ren. "She's pregnant."

Toby dries her hands on the towel hanging beside the pump. She does it slowly, giving herself time to think. "Are you sure?" she says.

"She peed on the stick," says Lotis Blue. "It was positive. The fucking thing showed a happy face."

"A pink happy face! That stick is so mean! It's horrible!" says Ren. She starts to cry. "She can't have that baby, not after what they did to her! Not a baby with a Painballer dad!"

"She's walking around like a zombie," says Lotis Blue. "She's so depressed. She's just really, really down."

"I'll talk to her," says Toby.

Poor Amanda. Who could expect her to give birth to a murderer's child? To the child of her rapists, her torturers? Though there's another possibility, as far as the father goes. Toby recalls the flowers, the singing, the enthusiastic tangle of Craker limbs in the light from the campfire on that chaotic Saint Julian's evening. What if Amanda is harbouring a baby Craker? Is that even possible? Yes, unless they're a different species altogether. But if so, won't it be dangerous? The Craker children are on a different developmental clock, they grow much faster. What if the baby gets too big, too fast, and can't make its way out?

It's not as if there are any hospitals. Or even any doctors. As far as facilities go it will be like giving birth in a cave.

"She's over at the swing set," says Lotis Blue.

Amanda is sitting on one of the children's swings, moving gently back and forth. She doesn't quite fit the swing; it's close to the ground, and her knees are sticking up awkwardly. Slow tears are rolling down her cheeks.

Standing around her are three of the Craker women, touching her forehead, her hair, her shoulders. They're all purring. Ivory, ebony, gold.

"Amanda," says Toby. "It's all right. Everyone will help you."

"I wish I was dead," says Amanda. Ren bursts into tears and kneels down, throwing her arms around Amanda's waist.

"Don't say that!" she says. "We got this far! You can't give up now!"

"I want this thing out of me," says Amanda. "Can't I drink some kind of poison? Some of your mushroom stuff?" At least she's showing some energy, thinks Toby. And it's true, there are plants that were once used. She remembers Pilar mentioning various seeds and roots: Queen Anne's lace, evening primrose. But she's not sure of the quantities: it would be too risky to try such a thing. And if it's a Craker baby, none of that may work on it anyway. They have a different biochemistry, according to the MaddAddamites.

The ivory Craker woman stops purring. "This woman is not blue any more," she says. "Her bone cave is no longer empty. That is good."

"Why is she sad, Oh Toby?" says the gold woman. "We are always happy when our bone cave is full."

Bone cave. That's what they call it; beautiful in a way, and accurate, but right now all Toby herself can visualize is a cave full of gnawed bones. Which is how it must feel to Amanda: death in life. What can Toby do to make this story better? Not much. Remove all knives and ropes, arrange constant companions.

"Toby," says Ren. "Can't you . . ."

"Please try," says Amanda.

"No," says Toby. "I don't have that knowledge." It was Marushka Midwife who did the ob/gyn, at the Gardeners. Toby herself stuck to illnesses and wounds, but maggots and poultices and leeches are no use for this. "It might not be as bad as you think," she continues. "The father might not be a Painballer. Remember that night, around the campfire, on Saint Julian's, when they jumped on . . . where there was a cultural misunderstanding? It might be a Craker baby."

"Terrific," says Ren. "Great choices! An ultracriminal or some kind of gene-spliced weirdo monster. She wasn't the only one, anyway, with the cultural misunderstanding or whatever you want to call it. For all I know, I've got one of those Frankenbabies inside me too. I'm just scared of peeing on the stick."

Toby tries to think of something to say – something upbeat and soothing. Genes aren't a total destiny? Nature versus nurture, good can come of evil? There are the epigenetic switches to be considered, and maybe the Painballers just had very, very bad nurturing? Or how about: the Crakers may be more human than we think? But none of it sounds very convincing, even to her.

"Oh Toby, do not be sad," says a child's voice: Blackbeard, nudging up beside her. He takes her hand, pats it. "Oryx will help, and the baby will come out of the bone cave, and then Amanda will be happy. Everyone is very happy when there is a baby that has just come out."

"Lift up, you're lying on my arm," says Zeb. "What's wrong?"

"I'm worried about Amanda," says Toby, which is accurate, though not the whole story. "It seems that she's pregnant. She's not overjoyed."

"Three cheers," says Zeb. "First little pioneer born into our brave new world."

"Anyone ever mention you can be callous at times?"

"Never," says Zeb. "I'm all quivering heart. The dad's most likely a Painballer though, judging from what went on, which would triple suck. Then we'd have to drown it like a kitten."

"Fat chance," says Toby. "Those Craker women just love babies. They'd go berserk if you did cruel and hurtful things to it."

"Women are strange," says Zeb. "Not that I couldn't have used a mom like that: protective, cuddly, and so forth."

"It could be a hybrid. Half a Craker," says Toby. "In view of the mob action during the Saint Julian's festivities. But if it is, the baby might kill her. Their fetal growth rates are different, their heads are bigger when they're born, judging from the kids some of those women are toting around, so it could get stuck. I wouldn't even begin to know how to do a C-section. And even before that, what if there's a blood incompatibility?"

"Ivory Bill and those others know anything about that? The genetic blood stuff?"

"I haven't asked them," says Toby.

"Okay, let's put it on the crisis list. One pregnancy. Call a group meeting. But if the MaddAddams don't know what's likely to happen, I guess it's wait and see?"

"It's wait and see anyway," says Toby. "It can't be aborted; no one here has that skill, and it would be way too risky to try it. There's some herbs, but if you don't know what you're doing they can be toxic. Nothing else to be done, unless someone at the group meeting has a brilliant suggestion. But before that, I need to do some consulting."

"With who? None of our brainiacs are doctors."

"Don't laugh at me for what I'm about to say."

"Tongue bitten, mouth stapled. Fire away."

"Okay, this is going to sound demented: with Pilar. Who, as you know, is dead."

A pause. "How you planning to do that?"

"I thought I could pay a visit to her, you know, where we . . ."

"To her shrine? Like a saint?"

"Something like that. Do an Enhanced Meditation. Remember where we buried her, in the park? On the day of her composting? We dressed up as park keepers, we dug a hole in the . . ."

"Yeah, I know the place. You wore those green parkie overalls I stole for you. We planted an elderberry bush on top of her."

"Yes. That's where I'd like to go. I know it's a bit crazy, as the Exfernal World would have said."

"First you talk to bees, now you want to talk to dead people? Even the Gardeners never went that far."

"Some of them did. Think of it as a metaphor. I'll be accessing my inner Pilar, as Adam One would have put it. He'd be right onside with this."

Another pause. "Well, you can't do it alone."

"I know." Now it's her turn to pause.

A sigh. "Okay, babe, whatever you want. I volunteer. I'll get Rhino and Shackie to come. We'll keep you covered. One spraygun, plus your rifle. How long you figure it'll take?"

"I'll do the short-form Enhanced Meditation. I don't want to hog too much time."

"You expect to hear voices? Just so I know."

"I've got no idea what I'll hear," says Toby truthfully. "Most likely nothing. But I need to do it anyway."

"That's what I like about you. You're game for anything." Some rustling, some shifting. Another pause. "Something else eating you?"

"No," Toby lies. "I'm good."

"You're into prevarication?" says Zeb. "Fine with me."

"Prevarication. That's a lot of syllables," says Toby.

"Let me guess. You think I should tell you what happened out in the wilds of the shopping strip with what's-her-name. Little Miss Fox. Whether I groped her or vice versa. Whether sexual congress took place."

Toby thinks about it. Does she want bad news about what she fears or good news she won't believe? Is she turning into a clinging invertebrate with tentacles and suction cups? "Tell me something more interesting," she says.

Zeb laughs. "Good one," he says.

So. Stalemate. It's for him to know and for her to try to refrain from finding out. He loves encryption. Even though she can't see him in the dark, she can feel him smiling.

They set out the next morning just at sunrise. The vultures that top the taller, deader trees are spreading their black wings so the dew on them will evaporate; they're waiting for the thermals to help them lift and spiral. Crows are passing the rumours, one rough syllable at a time. The smaller birds are stirring, beginning to cheep and trill; pink cloud filaments float above the eastern horizon, brightening to gold at the lower edges. Some days the sky looks like old paintings of heaven: there should be a few angels floating around, their white robes deployed like the skirts of archaic debutantes, their pink toes daintily pointed, their wings aerodynamically impossible. Instead, there are gulls.

They're walking along what is still a trail, through what is still recognizable as the Heritage Park. The little gravelled paths leading off to the side have vines creeping across them, but the picnic tables and cement barbecues have not yet been obscured. If there are ghosts here, they're the ghosts of children, laughing.

Every one of the drum-shaped trash containers has been tipped over, the lids pried off. That wouldn't have been people. Something has been busy. Not rakunks, though: the trash containers were made to be rakunk-proof. The earth around the picnic tables is rutted and muddy: something's been trampling, and wallowing.

The asphalted main pathway is wide enough for a Heritage Park vehicle, like the one Zeb and Toby used to transport Pilar to the site of her composting. Already there are weed shoots nosing up through. The force they can exert is staggering: they'll have a building cracked like a nut in a few years, they'll reduce it to rubble in a decade. Then the earth swallows the pieces. Everything digests, and is digested. The Gardeners found that a cause for celebration, but Toby has never been reassured by it.

Rhino walks ahead with a spraygun. Shackleton is at the rear. Zeb's in the middle, beside Toby, keeping a close eye on her. He's carrying the rifle for safekeeping, since she's already drunk the short-form Enhanced Meditation mixture. Luckily there were some *Psilocybe* species from the old Gardener mushroom beds among the assortment of dried mushrooms she'd saved over the years and brought with her from the AnooYoo Spa. To the soaked dried mushrooms and the mixed ground-up seeds she'd added a pinch of *muscaria*. Just a pinch: she doesn't want all-out brain fractals, just a low-level shakeup – a crinkling of the window glass that separates the visible world from whatever lies behind it. The effects are beginning: already there's a wavering, a shift.

"Hey, what're you doing here?" says a voice. Shackleton's voice, coming to her along a dark tunnel. She turns: it's Blackbeard.

"I wish to be with Toby," he says.

"Oh fuck," says Shackleton. Blackbeard smiles happily. "And with Fuck too," he says.

"It's all right," says Toby. "Let him come."

"You can't stop him, anyway," says Zeb. "Short of braining him. Though I could tell him to fuck the fuck off."

"Please," says Toby. "Don't confuse him."

"Where are you going, Oh Toby?" says Blackbeard.

Toby takes the hand he holds up to her. "To visit a friend," she says. "But it's a friend you can't see." Blackbeard asks no questions; he simply nods.

Zeb looks ahead, looks left, looks right. He's singing to himself, a habit he's had ever since Toby's known him. It usually means he's feeling stressed.

Now we're in the muck,
And that can really suck,
And this is why we're out of luck,
Because we don't know fuck…

"But Snowman-the-Jimmy knows him," says Blackbeard. "And Crake. He knows him too." He beams up at Toby and Zeb for verification, pleased with himself.

"You're right there, pal," says Zeb. "That's what they know. Both of them."

Toby can feel the full strength of the Enhanced Meditation formula kicking in. Zeb's head against the sun is circled with a halo of what she realizes must be split ends – he could really use a trim, she must get hold of some scissors – but which nevertheless appears to her as a radiant burst of electric energy shooting out of his hair. A morpho-splice butterfly floats down the path, luminescent. Of course, she remembers, it's luminescent anyway, but now it's blue-hot, like a gasfire. Black Rhino looms up out of his own footsteps, an earth giant. Nettles arc from the sides of the walkway, the stinging hairs on their leaves gauzy with light. All around there are sounds, noises, almost-voices: hums and clicks, tappings, whispered syllables.

And there is the elderberry bush, where they planted it on Pilar's grave so long ago. It's much larger now. White bloom cascades from it, sweetness fills the air. A vibration surrounds it: honeybees, bumblebees, butterflies large and small.

"You stay here, with Zeb," Toby says to Blackbeard. She lets go of his hand, steps forward, kneels in front of the elderberry.

She gazes at the clustered flowers, thinks, *Pilar.* The wizened old face, the brown hands, the gentle smile. All so real, once. Gone to ground. *I know you're here, in your new body. I need your help.*

There's no voice, but there's a space. A waiting.

Amanda. Will she die, will this baby kill her? What should I do?

Nothing. Toby feels abandoned. But really, what did she expect? There is no magic, there are no angels. It was always child's play.

But she can't help asking anyway. *Send me a message. A signal. What would you do in my place?*

"Watch it," says the voice of Zeb. "Stay still. Look slowly. To the left."

Toby turns her head. Crossing the path, within stone-throw, there's one of the giant pigs. A sow, with farrow: five little piglets, all in a row. Soft gruntings from the mother, high screechy pipings from the young. How pink and brightly shining are their ears, how crystalline their hooves, how . . .

"I've got you covered," Zeb says. He's slowly lifting the rifle.

"Don't shoot," says Toby. Her own voice in her ears is distant, her mouth feels huge and numbed. Her heart's becalmed.

The sow, turns sideways: a perfect target. She looks at Toby out of her eye. The five little ones gather in her shadow, under the nipples, which are all in a row too, like vest buttons. Her mouth upturns in a smile, but that's only the way it's made. Glint of light on a tooth.

Little Blackbeard moves forward. He's golden in the sun, his green eyes lambent, his hands outstretched.

"Get back here," says Zeb.

"Wait," Toby says. Such enormous power. A bullet would never stop the sow, a spraygun burst would hardly make a dent. She could run them down like a tank. Life, life, life, life, life. Full to bursting, this minute. Second. Millisecond. Millennium. Eon.

The sow does not move. Her head remains up, her ears pricked forward. Huge ears, calla lilies. She gives no sign of charging. The piglets freeze in place, their eyes red-purple berries. Elderberry eyes.

Now there's a sound. Where is it coming from? It's like the wind in branches, like the sound hawks make when flying, no, like a songbird made of ice, no, like a . . . Shit, thinks Toby. I am so stoned.

It's Blackbeard, singing. His thin boy's voice. His Craker voice, not human.

The next moment, the sow and her young have vanished. Blackbeard turns to smile at Toby. "She was here," he says. What does he mean?

"Crap," says Shackleton. "There go the spareribs."

So, thinks Toby. Go home, take a shower, sober up. You've had your vision.

Vector

The Story of how Crake got born

"Still a little buzzed, are you?" says Zeb as they walk towards the trees where Jimmy's hammock was once strung up and where the Crakers are waiting. It's the gloaming: deeper, thicker, more layered than usual, the moths more luminous, the scents of the evening flowers more intoxicating: the short-term Enhanced Meditation formula has that effect. Zeb's hand in hers is rough velvet: like a cat's tongue, warm and soft, delicate and raspy. It sometimes takes half a day for this stuff to wear off.

"I'm not sure *buzzed* is the appropriate word to use of a mystical quasi-religious experience," says Toby.

"That's what it was?"

"Possibly. Blackbeard's telling people that Pilar appeared in the skin of a pig."

"No shit! And her a vegetarian. How'd she get in there?"

"He says she put on the skin of the pig just the way you put on the skin of the bear. Except she didn't kill and eat the pig."

"What a waste."

"Also she spoke to me, Blackbeard says. He says he heard her do it."

"That what you think too?"

"Not exactly," says Toby. "You know the Gardener way. I was communicating with my inner Pilar, which was externalized in visible form, connected with the help of a brain chemistry facilitator to the wavelengths of the Universe; a universe in which — rightly understood — there are no coincidences. And just because a sensory impression may be said to be 'caused' by an ingested mix of psychoactive substances does not mean it is an illusion. Doors are opened with keys, but does that mean that the things revealed when the doors are opened aren't there?"

"Adam One really did a job on you, didn't he? He could spout that crap for hours."

"I can follow his line of reasoning, so I guess in that sense he did a job, yes. But when it comes to 'belief,' I'm not so sure. Though as he'd say, what is 'belief' but a willingness to suspend the negatives?"

"Yeah, right. I never knew myself how much of it he really believed himself, or believed so much that he'd stick his arm in the fire for it. He was such a slippery bugger."

"He said that if you acted according to a belief, that was the same thing. As having the belief."

"Wish I could find him," says Zeb. "Even if he's dead. I'd like to know what happened, either way."

"They used to call that 'closure,'" says Toby. "In some cultures, the spirit couldn't be freed unless the person got a decent burial."

"Funny old thing, the human race," says Zeb. "Wasn't it? So, here we are. Do your stuff, Story Lady."

"I'm not sure I can. Not tonight. I'm still a little foggy."

"Give it a try. At least turn up. You don't want to start a riot."

Thank you for the fish.

I will not eat it right now, because first I have something important to tell you.

Yesterday I listened to Crake on the shiny thing.

Please don't sing.

And Crake said, It is best to cook the fish a little longer. Until it is hot all the way through. Never leave it out in the sun before you cook it. Or keep it overnight. Crake says that is the best way, with a fish, and it is the way Snowman-the-Jimmy always wanted it to be cooked. And Oryx says that if it is the turn of her Fish Children to be eaten, she wants them to be eaten in the best way. Which means cooked all the way through.

Yes, Snowman-the-Jimmy is feeling better, though right now he is sleeping inside, in his own room. His foot does not hurt much any more. It is very good you did so much purring on it. He can't run fast yet, but he is practising his walking every day. And Ren and Lotis Blue are helping him.

Amanda can't help him because she is too sad.

We don't need to talk about why she is sad right now.

Tonight I will not tell a story, because of the fish. And the way it needs to be cooked. Also I am feeling a little . . . I am feeling tired. And that makes it harder for me to hear the story, when I put on the red hat of Snowman-the-Jimmy.

I know you are disappointed. But I will tell you a story tomorrow. What story would you like to hear?

About Zeb? And Crake too?

A story with both of them in it. Yes, I think there is a story like that. Maybe.

Was Crake ever born? Yes, I think he was. What do you think?

Well, I'm not sure. But he must have been born, because he looked like a — he looked like a person, once upon a time. Zeb knew him then. That's how there can be a story with both of them in it. And Pilar is in that story too.

Blackbeard? You have something to say about Crake?

He wasn't really born out of a bone cave, he only got inside the skin of a person? He put it on like clothes? But he was different inside? He was round and hard, like the shiny thing? I see.

Thank you, Blackbeard. Could you put on the red hat of Jimmy-the-Snowman, I mean Snowman-the-Jimmy, and tell us all of that story?

No, the hat won't hurt you. It won't turn you into someone else. No, you won't grow an extra skin; you won't grow clothes like mine. You can keep your very own skin.

It's all right. You don't have to put on the red hat. Please don't cry.

"Well, that was a bit of a fiasco," says Toby. "I didn't know they were afraid of it — that old red baseball cap."

"I was afraid of the Red Sox myself," says Zeb. "When I was a kid. I was a gambler at heart even then."

"It seems to be a sacred object to them. The hat. Sort of taboo. They can carry it around but they can't put it on."

"Cripes, can you blame them? That thing is filthy! Bet it has lice."

"I'm trying to have an anthropological discussion here."

"Have I told you recently you've got a fine ass?"

"Don't be complex," says Toby.

"*Complex* is another word for pathetic jerkoff?"

"No," says Toby. "It's just that . . ." Just that what? Just that she can't believe he means it.

"Okay, it's a compliment. Remember those? Guys give them to women. It's a courtship move – now that's anthropology. So just think of it as a bouquet. Deal?"

"Okay, deal," says Toby.

"Let's start again. I spotted that fine ass of yours way back when, on that day we composted Pilar. When you took off those baggy Gardener-lady clothes and put on the parkie overalls. Filled me with longing, it did. But you were inaccessible then."

"I wasn't really. I was . . ."

"Yeah, you kinda were. You were Miss Total God's Gardener Purity, as far as I could tell. Adam One's devoted altar girl. Wondered if he was having it off with you, to tell the truth. I was jealous of that."

"Absolutely not," says Toby. "He never, ever . . ."

"I believe you. Thousands wouldn't. Anyway, I was hooked up with Lucerne at the time."

"That stopped you? Mister Babe Magnet?"

A sigh. "I was magnetized to babes, naturally. Back when I was young. It's a hormone thing, it comes with the hairy balls. Wonders of nature. But babes weren't always magnetized to me." A pause. "Anyway, I'm loyal. To whoever I'm with, if I'm really with them. A serial monogamist, you could say."

Does Toby believe this? She isn't sure.

"But then Lucerne left the Gardeners," she says.

"And you were Eve Six. Talking to the bees, measuring out the head trips. You were like a Mother Superior. Figured you'd slap me down. Inaccessible Rail," he says, using her old MaddAddam chat-room codename. "That was you."

"And you were Spirit Bear," says Toby. "Hard to find, but good luck if you happen to see one. That's what the stories said, before those bears went extinct." She starts to sniffle. The Meditation formula does that too: it melts the fortress walls.

"Hey. What? Did I say something bad?"

"No," says Toby. "I'm just sentimental."

All those years you were my lifeline, she wants to say. But doesn't.

Young Crake

"Now I have to come up with something," says Toby. "A story with Crake in it, and you as well. Crake did know Pilar when he was younger, I figured that out. But what am I going to say about you?"

"As it happens, that part's actually true," says Zeb. "I knew him before the Gardeners even got started. But he wasn't Crake then, not even close. He was just a fucked-up kid named Glenn."

Once Zeb was inside HelthWyzer West, he learned its memes and set about mimicking them as fast as he could. Displaying the right memes was the yellow brick road to blending in and thus surviving, so that when the giant Rev monster eye came looking for him via the giant Corps network, as it might at any moment, it would pass right over his head. Protective colouration, that's what he needed.

The officially promoted view of HelthWyzer West was that it was one big happy family, dedicated to the pursuit of truth and the betterment of humankind. To dwell too much on the improvement in value for the shareholders was considered bad taste, but on the other hand there was an employee options package. All staff were expected to be unremittingly cheerful, to meet their assigned goals diligently, and – as in real families – not to ask too much about what was really going on.

Again like real families, there were no-go zones. Some were conceptual, but some were purely physical. The pleebland outside the HelthWyzer Compound was one of these, unless you had a pass and designated protection. The firewalls around IP had become thick and in some cases impenetrable, unless you had an inside track; so if you couldn't hack the system, you grabbed the primary source material. Brainiacs from Corps of all kinds were being kidnapped and smuggled abroad, or – some said – into rival Corps Compounds – and then strip-mined for the gold and jewels their heads were assumed to contain.

This was a cause for serious concern at HelthWyzer West – which meant there was some fairly important stuff going on behind locked doors – and barriers had been put in place. The top biogeeks carried alarm beepers that registered their whereabouts, though these had sometimes been adroitly hacked and then used as a means of targeting their bearers and tracking them down. Here and there on the walls of hallways and meeting rooms, posters reminded the unwary of ever-present perils. FOLLOW THE SAFETY RULES AND KEEP YOUR HEAD! AND ITS CONTENTS! Or: YOUR MEMORY IS OUR IP, SO WE'LL PROTECT IT FOR YOU!

Or: BRAINS ARE LIKE MEADOWS: A CULTIVATED ONE IS WORTH MORE. On this last poster, someone had written with a Sharpie: *Get more cultivated! Eat more shit!* So, thought Zeb, there was at least some hidden dissent among the smiley faces.

As part of the happy family ethos, HelthWyzer West threw a barbe-cue every Thursday in the central parkette of the Compound. Adam had told Zeb that these affairs should not be missed, as they were prime territory for eavesdropping and figuring out the invisible power filaments. Those wearing the most casual clothing would most likely be the alphas. Adam also said that Zeb would find some of the rec-reational pursuits of interest, especially the board games; though he hadn't said why.

So Zeb turned up at the HelthWyzer West barbecue on the first Thursday after his arrival. He sampled the eats: SoYummie ice cream for the kids, pork ribs for the carnivores, SoyOBoy products and quorn-burgers for the vegans. NevRBled Shish-K-Buddies for those who wanted to eat meat without killing animals – the cubes were lab-cultured from cells ("No Animal Suffered"), and he figured that with enough beer they wouldn't taste too bad. But he intended to limit his drinking because he needed to stay alert, so he stuck with the ribs. You didn't have to be half-cut to appreciate those.

Around the edges of the crowd, various geeky sports were in progress. Croquet and bocci in the sun, ping-pong and foosball under the awnings. Circle games for the under-sixes, variations of tag for the older ones. And for the serious and superintelligent and potentially Aspergerian child brainiacs, a row of umbrella-shaded computers where they could do obsessive-compulsive things online – within HelthWyzer firewalls, of course – and challenge each other to combat without making eye contact.

Zeb scoped out the games: Three-Dimensional Waco, Intestinal Parasites, Weather Challenge, Blood and Roses. Also Barbarian Stomp, a new one on him.

Here came Marjorie with the spaniel's eyes, making a beeline towards him, her beseeching smile at the ready, enhanced by a smear of ketchup on the chin. Time to duck and cover: she had the look of a woman who'd already staked out a claim, and would go through a guy's pants pockets while he was asleep in search of rivals, and would most likely read his email. Though maybe he was being paranoid. But best not to take chances.

"Want to go a round with me?" he said to the nearest youthful brainiac, a thin boy in a dark T-shirt with a stack of gnawed pork ribs on the paper plate beside him. Was that a cup of coffee? Since when was coffee allowable for a kid that age? Where were the parents?

The boy looked up at him with large, green, opaque but possibly mocking eyes. Even the children wore name tags to these barbecues, it seemed: *Glenn*, Zeb read.

"Sure," said young Glenn. "Conventional chess?"

"As opposed to?" said Zeb.

"Three-dimensional," said Glenn indifferently. If Zeb didn't know that, then he couldn't be a very good player. Blatantly obvious.

So that was how Zeb first met Crake.

"But like I said, he wasn't Crake yet," says Zeb. "He was just a kid then. Not too much bad stuff had happened to him, though 'not too much' is always a matter of taste."

"Really?" says Toby. "That long ago?"

"Would I lie to you?" says Zeb.

Toby thinks about it. "Not about this," she says.

Zeb generously and also patronizingly let Glenn play White, and Glenn walloped him, though Zeb put up an honourable fight. After that they did a round of Three-Dimensional Waco, and Zeb beat Glenn, who immediately wanted another game. This one ended in a tie. Glenn looked at Zeb with a small increase of respect and asked him where he'd come from.

Zeb then told a couple of lies, but they were entertaining lies: he put in Miss Direction and the Floating World, and some of the bears from Bearlift, though he changed the name and the location and left out anything about dead Chuck. Glenn had never been outside a Compound, or not that he could remember, so these tales must have had mythic dimensions for him. Though he made a point of not looking impressed.

In any case, Glenn started turning up in Zeb's vicinity at the Thursday barbecue events and hanging around at lunchtimes. It wasn't hero-worship, not exactly; nor did Glenn want Zeb to be his dad. More like an older brother, Zeb decided. There weren't that many kids his age at HelthWyzer West for Glenn to play games with. Or not ones as smart as him. Not that Glenn thought Zeb was up to scratch, smarts-wise, but he was within range. Though there was a slight air of command performance about these proceedings: Glenn as the crown prince and Zeb as the somewhat dim courtier.

How old exactly was Glenn? Eight, nine, ten? It was hard for Zeb to tell because he didn't like to remember what his own life had been like when he'd been eight or nine or ten. He'd spent too much time in the dark back then, one way or another. All of that needed to be forgotten, and he'd worked at forgetting it. Still, when he saw a boy of that age the first thing he wanted to say was, *Run away! Run away very fast!* And the second thing was, *Grow bigger! Grow very big!* If you could grow very big, then whoever they were would cease to have power over you. Or so much power. Though it hadn't worked for whales, he reflected. Or tigers. Or elephants.

There must have been a *they* in the life of young Glenn, or maybe an *it*: something that was haunting him. He had that look about him, a look Zeb used to catch glimpses of when he saw himself unawares in the mirror: a wary, distrustful look, as if he didn't know what bush or parking lot or piece of furniture was going to chasm suddenly to reveal the lurking enemy or the bottomless pit. Though Glenn had no scars, no bruises, and no difficulty eating his meals, or not that Zeb could see; so what was that haunting entity? Nothing definite, perhaps. More like a lack, a vacuum.

After several Thursdays and some close observation, Zeb concluded that neither of Glenn's parents had a lot of time for him. Nor for each other: from the body language, they were well past the stage of irritation or even occasional dislike and were deep into active hatred. When they met in public they resorted to iceman stares and monosyllables, and to walking quickly away. There was a pot of boiling rage on a private stove behind their closed curtains: that bubbling cauldron was taking all their attention, with Glenn relegated to a footnote or else a trading card. Maybe the kid gravitated to Zeb for the same reason children like dinosaurs: when feeling abandoned in a world of forces beyond your control, it's comforting to have a huge, scaly beast who is your friend.

Glenn's mother was on the food admin staff, tracking supplies and devising meal plans. Glenn's dad was a semi-top researcher – an expert in unusual microbes, wonky viruses, odd antigens, and offbeat variants of anaphylaxis biovectors. Ebola and Marburg were among his specialties, but right now he was working on a rare allergic reaction to red meat that was linked to tick bites. An agent in the salivary proteins of ticks caused it, said Glenn.

"So," said Zeb, "a tick drools into you and then you can't have steak any more without bursting out in hives and suffocating to death?"

"Bright side," said Glenn. He was going through a phase: he'd say "bright side," then add some gruesome sidebar. "Bright side, if they could spread it through the population – those tick saliva proteins embedded in, say, the common aspirin – then everyone would be allergic to red meat, which has a huge carbon footprint and causes the depletion of forests, because they're cleared for cattle grazing; and then ..."

"Not my idea of a bright side," said Zeb. "For argument: we're hunter-gatherers, we evolved to eat meat."

"And to develop lethal allergies to tick saliva," said Glenn.

"Only in those slated to be eliminated from the gene pool," said Zeb. "Which is why it's rare."

Glenn grinned, not something he did often. "Point," he said.

While Zeb and Glenn were playing onscreen games at the Thursday events, Glenn's mother, Rhoda, would sometimes drift over to watch, leaning a little too close to Zeb's shoulder, sometimes even touching it with — what? The business end of her tit? Felt like it: that nubbin shape. Certainly not a finger. Her breath, scented with beer, would riffle the fine hairs near his ear. She never touched Glenn, however. In fact, nobody ever touched Glenn. He somehow arranged it that way: he'd erected an invisible no-fly zone around himself.

"You guys," Rhoda would say. "You should get out there and run around. Play some croquet." Glenn didn't acknowledge these motherly interventions, nor did Zeb: Glenn's mother, although not wizened, was past the optimum freshness date as far as he was concerned, though if he'd been marooned on a liferaft with her. . . . But he wasn't, so he ignored the nipple nudges and the breath-to-ear signals and concentrated on the Blood part of Blood and Roses: eradicating the population of ancient Carthage and sowing the land with salt, enslaving the Belgian Congo, and murdering firstborn Egyptian babies.

Though why stop at firstborns? Some atrocities turned up by the virtual Blood and Roses dictated that the babies be tossed into the air and skewered on swords; others, that they be thrown into furnaces; yet others, that their brains be dashed out against stone walls. "Trade you a thousand babies for the Palace of Versailles and the Lincoln Memorial," he said to Glenn.

"No deal," said Glenn. "Unless you throw in Hiroshima."

"That's outrageous! You want these babies to die in agony?"

"They aren't real babies. It's a game. So they die, and the Inca Empire gets preserved. With all that cool gold art."

"Then kiss the babies goodbye," said Zeb. "Heartless little bugger, aren't you? Splat. There. Gone. And by the way, I'm cashing in my Wildcard Joker points to blow up the Lincoln Memorial."

"Who cares?" said Glenn. "I've still got the Palace of Versailles, plus the Incas. Anyway, there's too many babies. They make a huge carbon footprint."

"You guys are awful," said Rhoda, scratching herself. Zeb could hear the fingernails going behind his back, a sound like cat claws on felt. He wondered which part of herself she was scratching, then made an effort to stop wondering. Glenn had enough troubles without his one reliable friend making the double-backed beast with his unreliable mother.

Before he knew it, Zeb was giving young Glenn some extracurricular lessons in coding, which meant – practically speaking – in hacking as well. The kid was a natural, and he was finally impressed by some of the things Zeb knew and he didn't, and he caught on like magic. How tempting was it to take that talent and hone it and polish it and pass on the keys to the kingdom – the Open Sesames, the back doors, the shortcuts? Very tempting. So that is what Zeb did. It was a lot of fun watching the kid soak it all up, and who was to foresee the consequences? Which is usually the way with fun.

In return for Zeb's coding and hacking secrets, Glenn shared a few secrets of his own. For instance, he'd bugged his mother's room with an audio earlet concealed in her bedside lamp, by which means it became known to Zeb that Rhoda was having it off with an upper-middle-management type called Pete, usually right before lunchtime.

"My dad doesn't know," said Glenn. He considered for a moment, fixing Zeb with his uncanny green eyes. "Think I should tell him?"

"Maybe you shouldn't listen in on that shit," said Zeb.

Glenn gave him a cool stare. "Why not?"

"Because those things are for grown-ups," Zeb said, sounding prissy even to himself.

"You would, when you were my age," Glenn said, and Zeb couldn't deny that it was a thing he'd have done in a millisecond, given the opportunity and the tech. Avidly, gloatingly, without thinking twice.

On the other hand, maybe he wouldn't have done it if it involved his own parents. Even now he can't think about the Rev making umphing sounds while bobbing up and down on top of Trudy – who'd be slippery with perfumed lotion and lubricant, and would resemble an overstuffed pink satin pillow – without feeling queasy.

Grob's Attack

"Here comes the part where I meet Pilar," says Zeb.

"What on earth was Pilar doing at HelthWyzer West?" says Toby. "Working for a Corp, inside a Compound?"

But she knew the answer. A lot of the Gardeners had started out inside a Corp Compound, and a lot of the MaddAddamites had as well. Where else was a bioscience-trained person to work? If you wanted a job in research, you had to work for a Corp because that was where the money was. But you'd naturally be focused on projects that interested them, not on ones that interested you. And the ones that interested them had to have a profitable commercial application.

Zeb first met Pilar at one of the Thursday barbecues. He hadn't seen her there before. Some of the more senior people didn't attend the weekly ribfests: they were for younger people who might or might not be angling for a casual pickup or looking to exchange gossip and glean info, and Pilar was beyond that stage. As Zeb learned later, she was well up the seniority ladder.

But she was there that Thursday. All Zeb saw at first was a small, black-and-grey-haired older woman playing chess with Glenn, over on the sidelines. It was an odd combo — almost-old lady, uppity young kid — and odd combos intrigued him.

He sauntered up casually and loomed over Glenn's shoulder. He watched the game for a while, trying not to kibbitz. Neither side had an obvious advantage. The old dame played relatively quickly, though without fluster, while Glenn pondered. She was making him work.

"Queen to h5," Zeb said at last. Glenn was playing Black this time. Zeb wondered if he'd chosen it out of bravado or whether they'd flipped for White.

"Don't think so," said Glenn without looking up while moving his knight to block — Zeb now saw — a possible check. The older woman smiled at Zeb, one of those wrinkly-eyed brown-skinned gnome-in-the-woods smiles that could mean anything from *I like you* to *Watch out.*

"Who is your friend?" she said to Glenn.

Glenn frowned at Zeb, which meant he felt insecure about the game. "This is Seth," he said. "This is Pilar. Your move."

"Hey," said Zeb, nodding.

"A pleasure," said Pilar. "Good save," she said to Glenn.

"Catch you later," Zeb said to Glenn. He wandered off to eat some NevRBled Shish-K-Buddies — he was getting fond of them, despite their ersatz texture — topped off with a SoYummie cone, quasi-raspberry flavour.

He sucked on the cone while looking over the field and ranking all the women he could see. It was a harmless pastime. The scale was one to ten. There were no tens (In a Minute!), a couple of eights (With Mild Reservations), a clutch of fives (If Nothing Else Available), some definite threes (You'd Have to Pay Me), and an unfortunate two (Pay Me a Lot!) — when he felt a touch on his arm.

"Don't act surprised, Seth," said a low voice. He looked down: it was tiny, walnut-faced Pilar. Was she making a move on him? Surely not, but if so it could be a delicate moment, politeness-wise: how to say no in an acceptable manner?

"Your shoelaces are untied," she said.

Zeb stared at her. His shoes didn't have laces. They were slip-ons.

"Welcome to MaddAddam, Zeb," she said, smiling.

Zeb coughed out a chunk of SoYummie cone. "Fuck!" he said, but he had the presence of mind to say it softly. Adam and his idiot *shoe-laces* password. Who could have remembered?

"It's all right," said Pilar. "I know your brother. I helped bring you here. Look bored, as if we're making small talk." She smiled at him again. "I'll see you at the next Thursday barbecue. We should arrange to play a game of chess." Then she wafted serenely away towards the croquet game. She had excellent posture: Zeb sensed a yoga aficionado. Posture like that made him feel personally sloppy.

He longed to go online, zigzag into the Extinctathon MaddAddam chatroom, and ask Adam about this woman, but he knew that wouldn't be prudent. The least said the better online, even if you thought your space was secure. The net had always been just that — a net, full of holes, all the better to trap you with; and it still was, despite the fixes they claimed to be adding constantly, with the impenetrable algorithms and the passwords and thumb scans.

But what else did they expect? With code serfs like him in charge of the security keys, of course the thing was going to leak. The pay was too low, so the temptation to pilfer, snoop, snitch, and sell for high rewards was great. But the penalties were getting more extreme, which was a counterbalance of sorts. Online thieves were increasingly professional, like the outfits he'd worked with in Rio. Few were hacking for the pure lulz of it any more, or even to register protests, as they had in the golden years of legend that middle-aged guys wearing retro Anonymous masks got all nostalgic about in the dim, cobwebby, irrelevant corners of the web.

What good would registering a protest do you any more? The Corps were moving to set up their own private secret-service outfits and seize control of the artillery; not a month passed without the arrival of some new weapons law pretending to safeguard the public. Old-style demonstration politics were dead. You could get back at individual targets such as the Rev using underhanded means, but any kind of public action involving crowds and sign-waving and then storefront smashing would be shot off at the knees. Increasingly, everyone knew that.

He finished his SoYummie cone, fended off snub-nosed Marjorie, who wanted him to join a game of croquet and acted hurt when he said he was awkward with wooden balls, then meandered over to where Glenn was still sitting, staring at the chessboard. He'd set it up again and was playing against himself. "Who won?" Zeb asked.

"I almost did," said Glenn. "She pulled a Grob's Attack on me. It caught me off-guard."

"What exactly does she do here?" Zeb asked. "Is she in charge of something?"

Glenn smiled. He liked knowing things Zeb didn't know. "Mushrooms. Funguses. Mould. Want to play me?"

"Tomorrow," said Zeb. "Ate too much, it's dulling my brain."

Glenn grinned up at him. "Chickenshit," he said.

"Maybe just lazy. How come you know her?" said Zeb.

Glenn looked at him a little too long, a little too hard: green cat eyes. "I already said. She works with my dad. He's on her team. Anyway, she's in the chess club. Been playing her since I was five. She's not too stupid."

Which, in the high-praise area, was about as far as he went.

Vector

At the next Thursday barbecue, Glenn wasn't there. Nor had he been in evidence for a couple of days. He hadn't been mooching around the cafeteria, or asking Zeb to show him a few more hack moves on the computer. He'd become invisible.

Was he sick? Had he run away? Those were the only two possibilities that Zeb could think of, and he ruled out running away: the kid was surely too young for that, and it was too difficult to get out of HelthWyzer West without a pass. Though with Glenn's newfound robinhooding cryptic skills he could probably fake one.

There was another possibility: the little smartass had been colouring outside the digital lines. He'd broken into some sacrosanct Corps database or other and helped himself, just for the heck of it, because he couldn't possibly be into shady trading with the Chinese grey market, or worse – the Albanians, they were incandescent at the moment – and he'd got himself caught. In which case he'd be in a debriefing room somewhere having his brain pumped out. A person could come out of such affairs with nothing but a year-old dishrag north of the eyes. Would they do such a thing to a mere child? Yes. They would.

He really hoped it wasn't that: if it was, he himself would feel very guilty, because it would mean he'd been a bad teacher. "Rule Number One," he'd emphasized. "Don't get caught." But that was sometimes easier said than done. Had he been sloppy about the coding fretwork? Had he shown the kid a past-sell-by-date shortcut? Had he missed a few Detour signs, a few spoor marks that meant that he and Glenn were not the only ones on what he'd thought was his very own self-created poacher's jungle trail?

Though he was more than concerned, Zeb didn't want to start asking the teachers or even Glenn's lax and neglectful parents about him. He needed to keep his profile low, not draw attention.

Zeb scanned the barbecue crowd again. Still no Glenn. But Pilar was there, over to the side, under a tree. She was sitting in front of a chessboard, which she appeared to be studying. He assumed his casual saunter and made his way over there, hoping he looked random.

"Up for a game?" he said.

Pilar glanced up. "Certainly," she said with a smile. Zeb sat down.

"We'll toss for White," said Pilar.

"I like to play Black," said Zeb.

"So I've been told," said Pilar. "Very well."

She opened with a standard queen's pawn, and Zeb decided to opt for a queen's Indian defence. "Where's Glenn?" he asked.

"Things are not good," she answered. "Concentrate on the game. Glenn's father is dead. Glenn is naturally upset. The CorpSeCorps officers told him it was a suicide."

"No shit," said Zeb. "When did that happen?"

"Two days ago," said Pilar, moving her queen's knight. Zeb moved his bishop, pinning it down. Now she'd have a job developing her centre. "It's not when, however, it's how. He was pushed off an overpass."

"By his wife?" Zeb asked, remembering Rhoda's tit pressing against his back, and also the earlet concealed in her bedside lamp. It was a jokey kind of question — he should have been ashamed of himself. Sometimes that kind of thing shot out of his mouth like popcorn. But it was a serious question, as well: Glenn's dad could have found out about Rhoda's lunchtime interludes, they could have gone for a walk to discuss it, outside the walls of HelthWyzer for more privacy, and decided to stroll along the overpass, for the view of the oncoming traffic, and then they could have had a fight, and Glenn's mother could have upended his dad over the railing, a move he'd been unable to defend himself against . . .

Pilar was looking at him. Waiting for him to come to his senses, most likely.

"Okay, I take it back," he said. "It wasn't her."

"He found out something they're doing, inside HelthWyzer," said

Pilar. "He felt this practice was not only unethical but dangerous to public health, and therefore immoral. He threatened to make this knowledge public; or, well, not public as such, since the press probably wouldn't have touched it. But if he'd gone to a rival Corp, especially one outside the country, they'd have made damaging use of the information."

"He was on your research team, wasn't he?" said Zeb. He was trying to follow what she was saying, thus losing control of his game.

"Affiliated," said Pilar, dispatching one of his pawns. "He confided in me. And now I'm confiding in you."

"Why?" said Zeb.

"I'm being reassigned," said Pilar. "To the HelthWyzer headquarters, out east. Or that's where I hope I'm going, though it may be worse. They may think I'm lacking in enthusiasm, or suspect my loyalty. You'll have to leave here. I can't keep you safe once I've been transferred. Take my bishop with your knight."

"That's a bad move," said Zeb. "It opens the way to . . ."

"Just take it," she said calmly. "Then keep it in your hand. I have another one, I'll replace it in the box. No one will know there's a bishop missing."

Zeb palmed the bishop. He'd learned how to do that from Slaight of Hand, back in his Floating World days. Deftly he slid it up his sleeve.

"What am I supposed to do with it?" he said. With Pilar gone, he'd be isolated.

"Just deliver it," she said. "I'll fake you a day pass, with a cover story attached; they'll want to know your business in the pleeblands. Once you're outside the HelthWyzer West Compound, there'll be a new identity waiting. Take the bishop with you. There's a sex club franchise called Scales and Tails, you can look it up on the net. Go to the nearest branch. The password is *oleaginous*. They'll let you in. You'll be leaving the bishop there. It's a container, they'll know how to open it."

"Deliver it to who?" said Zeb. "What's in it, anyway? Who's *they*?"

"Vectors," said Pilar.

"In what sense?" said Zeb. "Like, math vectors?"

"Let's say biological. Vectors for bioforms. And these vectors are inside some other vectors that look like vitamin pills: three kinds, white, red, and black. And the pills are inside another vector, the bishop. Which will be carried by another vector, you."

"What's the thing inside the pills?" Zeb asked. "Brain candy? Code chips?"

"Definitely not. Best not to ask," said Pilar. "But whatever you do, don't eat any of them. If you think anyone's following you, shove the bishop down a drain."

"What about Glenn?" said Zeb.

"Check and mate," said Pilar, toppling his king. She stood up, smiling. "Glenn will make his way," she said. "He doesn't know they killed his father. He doesn't know yet. Or not directly. But he's very bright."

"You mean he'll figure it out," said Zeb.

"Not too soon, I hope," said Pilar. "He's too young for that kind of bad news. He might not be able to pretend ignorance, unlike you."

"Some of mine's real," said Zeb. "Like, right now, where do I switch identities? And how do I get the pass?"

"Go into the MaddAddam chatroom, there's a full package waiting for you. Then scramble your present gateway. You can't afford to leave your footprints on these computers."

"Does any of this involve different facial hair?" Zeb asked, to lighten things up. "For my new identity? And dorky pants?"

Pilar smiled. "I've had my beeper switched off all this time," she said. "We're allowed to do that on barbecue days, as long as we're in full view. I'm turning it back on now. Don't say anything you don't want overheard. Journey well."

Scales and Tails

Zeb retrieved his thumbdrive from the desk drawer where he'd hidden it, removed the cough drops that were stuck to it like barnacles, activated Intestinal Parasites on his computer, then slipped through the voracious maw of the blind nightmare worm and thence by lily-pad into the chatroom of MaddAddam. Sure enough, there was a how-to pack waiting for him, though no clue as to who had left it. He opened it, assimilated the contents, and scuttled backwards, whisking away his trail as he went. Then he ground the thumbdrive underfoot – or, more accurately, he placed it under one of his bed legs and then jumped on the bed, several times – and flushed the bits down several toilets. They wouldn't have gone down easily by themselves, being metal and plastic, but if you embed . . .

"It's okay," says Toby. "I get the picture."

Zeb's new name was Hector. Hector the Vector, was what he figured. Someone had a reasonably foul sense of humour, but he didn't think it was Pilar: she was not so much the humorous type.

But of course he'd only activate his new Hector identity once he was outside the walls and away from the security cameras of Helth-Wyzer West. Until then he was still Seth, a minor code-slave chained in the galleyship of data entry, in his geekwear with the brown corduroy pants. If anything, he was betting his change of identity would score him better pants. There was said to be an outfit waiting for him in the pleeblands, stashed in a dumpster he hoped no tramps or crazy people or sacked middle managers would be picking through before he could get to it.

The cover story for his Seth persona was that he was making a service call at a local branch of a beauty-and-mood-enhancing Corp called AnooYoo, which was a dubious affiliate of HelthWyzer. Health and Beauty, the two seductive twins joined at the navel, singing their eternal siren songs. A lot of people would pay through their nose jobs for either one.

HelthWyzer's products – the vitamin supplements, the over-the-counter painkillers, the higher-end disease-specific pharmaceuticals, the erectile dysfunction treatments, and so on – went in for scientific descriptions and Latin names on the labels. AnooYoo, on the other hand, was mining arcane secrets from Wiccan moon-worshippers and from shamans deep in the assassin-bug-rich rainforests of Dontgo-there. But Zeb could understand that there was an overlap of interests. If it hurts and you feel sick and it's making you ugly, take this, from HelthWyzer; if you're ugly and it hurts and you feel sick about it, take that, from AnooYoo.

Zeb readied himself for his mission by putting on a newly laundered pair of brown cords. He rearranged his face into his marginally shambolic Seth persona and winked at it in the bathroom mirror. "You're doomed," he said to it. He wouldn't be sorry to part company with Seth, who'd been foisted on him by Adam in an act of older-brother I-know-better bossiness. He longed to see Adam in person, if only to berate him for that. "You got any fucking idea of what those pants put me through?" he might say.

Time for Seth to go. He ambled in the direction of the front gate, exit pass in hand, humming to himself:

Hi ho, hi ho,
To jerkoff work I go,
With a hick hack here and a hick hack there,
Hi ho, hi ho, hi ho, hi ho!

Now to remember the cover story of Seth, junior code plumber. He was being sent to investigate the AnooYoo website, and to discover how it had been tampered with. Someone – maybe a jumped-up teen-aged hacker like his own younger self – had altered the online images so that when you clicked on any of the mood-enhancing, complexion-improving products, a squad of puce and orange insect animations would nibble into them at hyperspeed and then explode, legs twitching, yellow fumes coming out. It was silly but graphic.

HelthWyzer West didn't want anyone working on the problem from inside their own systems, naturally: the thing, simpleminded though it looked, could be a trap, with its planners hoping for just such an intervention so they could ram in through HelthWyzer's firewalls and filch its valuable IP. Therefore someone had to go to AnooYoo in person: someone minor and — since the gang-riddled pleebs were hazardous — someone expendable. That would be Seth, though at least they were providing a HelthWyzer car, with a driver. Nobody would likely go to the trouble of grabbing Seth for brain excavation: he wasn't inner circle. But still.

AnooYoo didn't want to find out who'd done the hack job, or why: that would be too expensive. They just wanted their firewall repaired. Their own guys hadn't been able to do it, ran the cover story, which wasn't — to Zeb — ultra plausible. But then, AnooYoo was a cheap operation — this was before its plusher days, when it set up the Spa-in-the-Park — so its IT bunch wasn't the A team, and maybe not even the B or C team: ultrabrights got snapped up by richer Corps. They were more like the F team. Obviously, since they'd failed.

But they were going to have a long wait, thought Zeb, because within the hour he would morph into Hector, and Seth would be no more. He had the chess bishop; it was in his baggy corduroy pants pocket, where he was also keeping his left hand just in case, and if anyone was looking they might conclude he was engaged in an act of self-abuse. Which he simulated in a restrained way, in case the car was equipped with spyware, as was likely. Better a wanker than a defector, and a contraband smuggler to boot.

AnooYoo was located in a seedy piece of real estate on the edge of a grey-market pleeb. So it wasn't alien to the streetscape to find an overturned SecretBurgers stand blocking the way, with a full-scale red-sauce fracas going on and a corona of yelling and honking surrounding it, plus flying squadrons of airborne meat patties. Zeb's own driver leaned on the horn, though he knew better than to roll down the window to yell.

But before you could say prestidigitation, the car was mobbed by a dozen Asian Fusions. One of them must've had a digilock popper keyed with the HelthWyzer car's passcode because up shot the lock buttons. In about one second the Fusion thugs had winkled out the thrashing, yelping driver and were going for his shoes and shucking him out of his clothing as if he was a cob of corn. Those pleeb gangs were fast and professional, you had to hand it to them. They'd get hold of the car keys, reverse, and be off like a shot, to sell the vehicle whole or strip it for parts, whichever paid more.

This was Zeb's moment. It had been paid for in advance: the Asian Fusions were dirty but they were also cheap, and happy to take small jobs. Checking first to make sure the driver's sightlines were blocked – they had to be, his entire head was now covered in red sauce – Zeb dove out the back door and frog-marched himself down the adjacent alleyway and around the corner, then around another corner, and then a third, where he kept his rendezvous with the designated dumpster.

The brown corduroy pants went into it, good riddance, and some well-aged jeans came out, with accessories to match. Black pleather jacket, black T that read ORGAN DONOR, TRY MINE FREE, reflector shades, baseball cap with a modestly sized red skull on the front. Gold clip-on tooth cap, fake 'stache, newly minted smirk, and Hector the Vector was ready to saunter. He'd taken care to keep the chess bishop safely to hand, and now he zipped it into the inside pocket of the pleather.

Off he went, in a hurry but not in any way looking it: best to seem unemployed. Also best to seem up to no good, in non-specific ways.

The Scales and Tails where he was heading was deeper into the pleeb. If he'd gone there in his geekwear he'd probably have had to defend his personal territory beginning with scalp, nose, and balls, but as it was he attracted not much more than a few narrow-eyed assessments. Worth taking on? Not, was the verdict. So his sauntering went unimpeded.

. . .

There it was, up ahead: ADULT ENTERTAINMENT in neon, *For Discerning Gentlemen* in subscript. Pics of reptilian lovelies in skintight green scales, most of them with impressive bimplants, some in contorted poses that suggested they had no backbones. A woman who could hook her legs around her own neck had something to offer in the way of novelty, though exactly what was unclear. And there was March the python, looped around the shoulders of a red-hot cobra lady who was swinging from a trapeze, and who greatly resembled Katrina WooWoo, the lovely snake trainer from the Floating World he'd so often helped to saw in half.

Not even very much older. So she was still keeping her hand in. As it were.

It was daytime: no customer traffic inbound. He reminded himself of the ludicrous password he'd been saddled with. *Oleaginous.* How to use it in a plausible sentence? "You're looking very oleaginous today?" That might get him a slap or a punch, depending on who he said it to. "Oleaginous weather we're having." "Turn off that oleaginous music." "Stop being so fucking oleaginous!" None of them sounded right.

He rang the doorbell. The door looked thick as a bank vault, with a lot of metal on it. An eye peered at him through the peephole. Locks clicked, the portal opened, and there was a bouncer as big as himself, only black. Shorn head, dark suit, shades. "What?" he said.

"Hear you've got some oleaginous girls," said Zeb. "Ones that butter you up."

The guy stared at him from inside his shades. "Say that again?" he said, so Zeb did. "Oleaginous girls," said the guy, rolling the phrase around in his mouth as if it was a doughnut hole. "Butter you up." His mouth upended at the corners. "Good one. Right. Inside." He checked the street before shutting the door. More locks clicking. "You want to see *her*," he said.

Down the hallway, purple-carpeted. Up the stairs: smell of a pleasure factory in the off hours, so sad. That moppet-shop smell that meant false raunchiness, that meant loneliness, that meant you got loved only if you paid.

The guy said something into his earpiece, which must have been very small because Zeb couldn't see it. Maybe it was inside a tooth: some were using those now, though if the tooth got knocked out and you swallowed the thing you might end up talking out your ass. An inner door marked HEAD OFFICE, BODY OFFICE TOO, with a shiny green winking-snake logo and the motto "We're Flexible."

"In," said the big guy once more – not a large vocabulary, him – and in Zeb went.

The room was an office of sorts, equipped with a lot of video screens and some expensive overstuffed furniture that was making a muffled statement, and a mini-bar. Zeb eyed the bar longingly – maybe there was a beer, all this running around and pretense had made him thirsty – but this was not the time.

There were two people in the room, each deep in a chair. One was Katrina WooWoo. She wasn't in her snake outfit: only an oversized sweatshirt that said BITCH #3, tight black jeans, and a pair of silver stilettos that would cripple a stilt dancer. She smiled at Zeb, one of those stage smiles she could always maintain while hissing. "Long time," she said.

"Not that long," said Zeb. "You still look easy to pick up and hard to put down."

She smiled. Zeb had to admit he longed to wend his way into her scaly underthings – that boyish yen hadn't faded – but he couldn't concentrate on such goals right then because the other person in the room was Adam. He was wearing a dorky caftan affair that looked as if it was put together by spastic ragpickers for a stage play about leprosy.

"Fuck," said Zeb. "Where'd you get that pixie nightshirt?" It was best not to show surprise: it would give Adam an advantage he didn't, at the moment, deserve.

"I note your tasteful T-shirt," said Adam. "It suits you. Nice motto, baby brother."

"Is this place bugged?" said Zeb. One more baby brother quip and he'd deck Adam. No, he wouldn't. He never could bear to hit the guy, not full-out: Adam was too ethereal.

"Of course," said Katrina WooWoo. "But we've turned everything off, courtesy of the house."

"I'm supposed to believe that?"

"She actually has turned it off," said Adam. "Think about it. She doesn't want any of our footprints on her establishment. She's doing us a big favour. Thanks," he said to Katrina. "We won't be long." She stilt-walked out of the room, teetering a little, casting them a smile over her shoulder: not a hissy smile this time. She was evidently keen on Adam, despite the caftan. "There's some food later, if you want it," she said. "In the girls' caf. I need to get changed, showtime coming up."

Adam waited until she'd closed the door. "You made it," he said. "Good."

"No thanks to you," said Zeb. "I might've been lynched because of those nerdy brown pants." He was in fact very pleased to know that Adam was still alive, but he wasn't going to straight-out admit it. "I looked like a fucking fuckwit in those fucking things," he added, piling on the profanity.

Adam ignored that part. "Have you got it?" he said.

"I take it you mean this fucking chess piece," Zeb said. He handed it over. Adam twisted the head, and off it came. He turned the bishop upside down: out slid the six pills: red, white, black, two of each colour. Adam looked at them, then put them back into the bishop and reattached the head.

"Thank you," he said. "We have to think of somewhere very safe for this."

"What is it?" said Zeb.

"Pure evil," said Adam. "If Pilar's right. But valuable pure evil. And very secret. Which is why Glenn's father is dead."

"What do they do?" said Zeb. "Supersex pills or what?"

"Cleverer than that," said Adam. "They're using their vitamin supplement pills and over-the-counter painkillers as vectors for diseases – ones for which they control the drug treatments. Whatever's in the white ones is in actual deployment. Random distribution, so no one will suspect a specific location of being ground zero. They make money all ways: on the vitamins, then on the drugs, and finally on the hospitalization when the illness takes firm hold. As it does, because the treatment drugs are loaded too. A very good plan for siphoning the victims' money into Corps pockets."

"So those are the white ones. What about the reds and the blacks?"

"We don't know," said Adam. "They're experimental. Possibly other diseases, possibly a faster-acting formula. We aren't even sure how to find out in any safe way."

Zeb took this in. "This is large," he said. "I wonder how many brainiacs it took to think that up."

"It's a small, designated group within HelthWyzer," said Adam. "Directed from the top. Glenn's father was being used by them. He thought he was working on a targeted cancer-treatment vector. When he realized the nature of it, the full scope, he couldn't go along with it. He slipped these to Pilar, before . . ."

"Shit," said Zeb. "They killed her too?"

"No," said Adam. "They don't even know she knows, or so we hope. She's just been transferred to HelthWyzer Central, on the east coast."

"Mind if I have a beer?" said Zeb. He didn't wait for an answer. "So now that you have this stuff," he said after the first refreshing swallow, "what next? You going to sell these things on the grey market? Foreign Corps would pay a lot."

"No," said Adam. "We couldn't do that. It would be firmly against our principles. All we can do in this world, now, is to learn what to avoid. We'll warn others about the vitamin supplements if we can, but if we were to try going public with this information we wouldn't be believed. We'd only sound paranoid, and after that we would have unfortunate accidents. The press is Corps-controlled, as you know, and any independent regulation is independent in name only. So we will keep the pills hidden until they can be analyzed without danger."

"Who's this *we*?" said Zeb.

"If you don't know, you can't tell," said Adam. "Safer for everyone, including you."

The Story of Zeb and the Snake Women

"How do I explain all of that to them?" says Toby. "The Scales and Tails girls, dressed up like snakes?"

"You could just leave it out."

"I don't think so. It needs to be in. It seems appropriate, a woman who is also a snake. It goes along with the Meditation, and whatever happened with that animal. With that sow. It . . . She really seemed to be communicating with me. And with Blackbeard."

"You think that thing is part human? A Pig Woman? You really drank the Kool-Aid." A chuckle.

"No, not exactly, but . . ."

"Too many peyote buttons in that mix of yours. Or whatever you put in."

"Maybe. No doubt you're right."

The story tells itself inside Toby's head. She doesn't seem to be thinking about the story, or directing it. She has no control over it; she just listens. Amazing what a few plant molecules will do to your brain, and how long that lasts.

This is the story of Zeb and the Snake Women. The Snake Women do not come into the story at first, they come in later. Important things often come into stories later, but also at the beginning. And in the middle as well.

But I have already told the beginning, so right now it's the middle. And Zeb is in the middle of the story about Zeb. He is in the middle of his own story.

I am not in this part of the story; it hasn't come to the part with me. But I'm waiting, far off in the future. I'm waiting for the story of Zeb to join up with mine. The story of Toby. The story I am in right now, with you.

Pilar, who lives in the elderberry bush and talks to us through the bees, was once in the form of an old woman. She gave Zeb a special important thing and told him he had to take care of it — a little thing, like a seed. And the seed would make you sick if you ate it. But some bad people from the chaos were telling all the other people that this seed would make them happy. And only Pilar and Zeb and a small number of other people knew the truth.

Why were the bad people doing that? Because of Money. Money was invisible, like Fuck. They thought that Money was their helper; they thought he was a better helper than Fuck. But they were wrong about that. Money was not their helper. Money goes away just when you need it. But Fuck is very loyal.

So Zeb took the seed, and he went out through the door, because if the bad men knew he had it they would chase him and take it away from him, and then do something very hurtful to him. And he was hurrying without seeming to hurry, and he said, Oh Fuck, and Fuck came flying through the air, very fast, as he always does when you call him; and he showed Zeb how to get to the house of the Snake Women. And the Snake Women opened their door, and took him in.

The Snake Women are . . . You have seen a snake, and you have seen women. The Snake Women were both. And they lived with several Bird Women and Flower Women. And they hid Zeb inside a giant . . . Inside a great big . . . A clam shell. No, a sofa. Or maybe they hid him inside a great big, an enormous . . . A flower. A very bright flower with lights on it.

Yes, a light-up flower. No one would look for Zeb inside a flower.

And Zeb's brother, Adam, was inside the flower too. That was nice. They were very happy to see each other, because Adam was the helper of Zeb and Zeb was the helper of Adam.

▪ ▪ ▪

The Snake Women sometimes bit people, but they didn't bite Zeb. They liked him. They made him a special drink, called a Champagne Cocktail, and then they did a special dance for him. It was a twisty dance, because after all they were snakes.

They were very kind. Because that is how Oryx made them. And they were her Children, because they were part snake. So they had nothing to do with Crake. Or not much.

And the Snake Women let Zeb sleep in a great big bed, a bed that was shiny and green. They said Fuck could sleep in there as well, because there was lots of room.

And Zeb said, Thank you, because the Snake Women were being so kind to him, and also to his invisible helper. And they made him feel much better.

No, they did not purr over him. Snakes can't purr. But they . . . they twined. Yes, that is what they did: some twining. And some constriction, they did that too. Snakes have very good muscles for constriction.

And Zeb was really, really tired, so he went to sleep at once. And the Snake Women and the Bird Women and the Flower Women took care of him, and made sure nothing bad would happen to him while he slept. They said they would protect him and hide him even if the bad men came there.

And the bad men did come. But that is in the next part of the story. And now I am really, really tired too. And I am going to sleep.

Good night.

That is what she'll say when it's time for the next story.

Piglet

Guru

The morning after her visit to Pilar's elderberry bush, Toby is still feeling the effects of the Enhanced Meditation mixture. The world's a little brighter than it should be, the scrim of its colours and shapes a little more transparent. She puts on a bedsheet in a calming neutral tone — light blue, no pattern — gives her face a quick wash at the pump, and makes it over to the breakfast table.

Everyone else seems to have eaten and gone. White Sedge and Lotis Blue are clearing off the dishes.

"I think there's some left," says Lotis Blue.

"What was it?" Toby asks.

"Ham and kudzu fritters," says White Sedge.

Toby has dreamt all night: piglet dreams. Innocent piglets, adorable piglets, plumper and cleaner and less feral than the ones she'd actually seen. Piglets flying, pink ones, with white gauzy dragonfly wings; piglets talking in foreign languages; even piglets singing, prancing in rows like some old animated film or out-of-control musical. Wallpaper piglets, repeated over and over, intertwined with vines. All of them happy, none of them dead.

They did love to depict animals endowed with human features, back in that erased civilization of which she had once been a part. Huggable, fluffy, pastel bears, clutching Valentine hearts. Cute cuddly lions. Adorable dancing penguins. Older than that: pink, shiny, comical pigs, with slots in their backs for money: you saw those in antique stores.

She can't manage the ham, not after a night full of waltzing piglets. And not after yesterday: what the sow communicated to her is still with her, though she couldn't put it into words. It was more like a current. A current of water, a current of electricity. A long, subsonic wavelength. A brain chemistry mashup. Or, as Philo of the Gardeners once said, Who needs TV? He'd done perhaps too many Vigils and Enhanced Meditations.

"Think I'll skip that," says Toby. "It's not so great warmed over. I'll go get some coffee."

"Are you all right?" says White Sedge.

"I'm fine," says Toby. She walks carefully along the path to the kitchen area, avoiding the places where the pebbles are rippling and dissolving, and finds Rebecca drinking a cup of coffee substitute. Little Blackbeard is there with her, sprawled on the floor, printing. He's got one of Toby's pencils, and he's swiped her notebook too. But useless to call it "swiping" – the Crakers appear to have no concept of personal property.

"You didn't wake up," he says, not reproachfully. "You were walking very far, in the night."

"Have you seen this?" Rebecca says. "The kid's amazing."

"What are you writing?" Toby says.

"I am writing the names, Oh Toby," says Blackbeard. And, sure enough, that's what he's been doing. TOBY. ZEB. CRAK. REBECA. ORIX. SNOWMANTHEJIMY.

"He's collecting them," says Rebecca. "Names. Who's next?" she says to Blackbeard.

"Next I will write Amanda," says Blackbeard solemnly. "And Ren. So they can talk to me." He scrambles up from the floor and runs off, clutching Toby's notebook and pencil. How am I going to get those back from him? she wonders.

"Honey, you look wiped," Rebecca says to her. "Rough night?"

"I overdid something," says Toby. "In the Enhanced Meditation mix. A few too many mushrooms."

"It's a hazard," says Rebecca. "Drink a lot of water. I'll make you some clover and pine tea."

"I saw a giant pig yesterday," says Toby. "A sow, with piglets."

"The more the merrier," says Rebecca. "So long as we've got sprayguns. I'm running out of bacon."

"No, wait," says Toby. "It – she gave me a very strange look. I got the feeling that she knew I'd shot her husband. Back at the AnooYoo Spa."

"Wow, you really went to town on the mushrooms," Rebecca says. "I once had a conversation with my bra. So, was she mad about the . . . I'm sorry, I just can't call it a husband! It was a pig, for chrissakes!"

"She wasn't pleased," says Toby. "But more sad than mad, I'd say."

"They're smarter than ordinary pigs, even without the Meditation booster," says Rebecca. "That's for sure. By the way, Jimmy came to breakfast today. No more invalid trays for him. He's doing well, but he'd like you to double-check his foot."

Jimmy has his own cubicle now. It's a new one, in the cobb-house addition they've finished at last. The cobb walls still smell a little damp, a little muddy; but there's a larger window than in the older part of the building, with a screen set into it and a curtain in a vibrant print of cartoon fish, with big curvy mouths and long-lashed eyes on the female ones. The males are playing guitars, with an octopus on the bongos. This is not the best thing for Toby to be looking at in her present state.

"Where did those come from?" she asks Jimmy, who's sitting up on his bed ledge with his feet on the floor. His legs are still thin, wasted; he'll need to build up the muscles again. "The curtains?"

"Who knows?" says Jimmy. "Ren, Wakulla – I mean, Lotis Blue. They felt I needed some cheerful interior decoration. It's like pre-school in here." He still has his Hey-Diddle-Diddle coverlet.

"You wanted me to look at your foot?" she says.

"Yeah. It's itchy. Driving me crazy. I just hope none of those maggot things got left inside."

"If they did, they'd have burrowed out by now," says Toby.

"Thanks a million," says Jimmy. The scar on his foot is red but sealed over. Toby examines it: no heat, no inflammation.

"That's normal," she says. "The itchiness. I'll get you something for it." A poultice: jewelweed, horsetail, red clover, she thinks. Horsetail might be the easiest to find.

"I heard you saw a pigoon," says Jimmy. "And it spoke to you."

"Who told you that?" says Toby.

"The Crakers, who else?" says Jimmy. "They're my radio. That kid Blackbeard gave them the whole story, it seems. They think you shouldn't have killed that boar, but they're forgiving you because maybe Oryx said you could. You know those pigs have human pre-frontal cortex tissue in their brains? Fact. I should know, I grew up with them."

"How did the Crakers learn about that?" Toby asks carefully. "Me shooting the boar?"

"The pigoon gal told Blackbeard. Don't give me that look, I'm just the messenger here. And according to Ren I've been hallucinating for a while, so hey. Maybe I'm not the best judge of reality." He gives her a lopsided grin.

"Mind if I sit down?" she says.

"Help yourself, thousands do," says Jimmy. "Fucking Crakers wander in here whenever the whim takes them. They want to know more shit about Crake. They think I'm his fucking guru. That he talks to me through my wristwatch. 'Course it's my own fucking fault because I made that up myself."

"And what do you tell them?" Toby asks. "About Crake?"

"I tell them to go ask you," says Jimmy.

"Me?" says Toby.

"You're the expert now. I need to take a nap."

"No, really, they always say you . . . they say you knew Crake, in person. When he was walking the earth."

"Like that's supposed to be first prize?" Jimmy gives a sour little laugh.

"It gives you a certain authority," says Toby. "In their eyes."

"That's like having a certain authority with a bunch of . . . Crap, I'm so wrecked I can't even think of a smartass comparison. Clams. Oysters. Dodos. What I'm saying is. Because, I'm tired. My guru juice is all used up. They wore me out a while ago, to tell you the truth. I never want to think about Crake again, ever, or listen to any more crapulous poop about how good and kind and all-powerful he is, or how he made them in the Egg and then sweetly wiped everybody else off the face of the planet, just for them. And how Oryx is in charge of the animals, and flies around in the shape of an owl, and even though you can't see her she's there anyway and will always hear them."

"As I understand it," says Toby, "that's consistent with what you've been telling them. It's Gospel as far as they're concerned."

"I know that's what I fucking told them!" says Jimmy. "They wanted to know the basic stuff, like where they came from and what all those decaying dead people were. I had to tell them something."

"So you made up a nice story," says Toby.

"Well, crap, I could hardly tell them the truth. So yes. And yes, I could've done a smarter job of it, and yes, I'm not a brainiac, and yes, Crake must've thought I had the IQ of an aubergine because he played me like a kazoo. So it makes me puke to hear them grovelling about fucking Crake and singing his fucking praises every time his stupid name comes up."

"But that's the story we've got," says Toby. "So we have to work with it. Not that I've grasped all the finer points."

"Whatever," says Jimmy. "It's over to you. Just keep doing what you're doing. You can add stuff in, go to town, they'll eat it up. I hear they're fanboys for Zeb these days. Stick with that plotline, it's got legs. Just keep them from finding out what a bogus fraud everything is."

"That's very manipulative," says Toby. "Shoving it all onto me."

"Yeah, I'm not denying it," says Jimmy. "I apologize. Though you're good at it, according to them. Your choice; you can always tell them to piss off."

"You realize we're under attack, in a manner of speaking," says Toby.

"The Painballers. Yeah. Ren told me," he says more soberly.

"So we can't let these people go wandering off on their own too much. They'd most likely be killed."

Jimmy thinks about that. "So, then?"

"You need to help me," says Toby. "We should get our stories straight. I've been flying in the dark."

"Nowhere else to fly on the subject of Crake," says Jimmy gloomily. "Welcome to my whirlwind. He cut her throat, did you know that? Good, kind Crake. She was so pretty, she was . . . Just thought I'd share that. But I shot the fucker."

"Whose throat?" Toby asks. "Who did you shoot?" But Jimmy's face is in his hands now, and his shoulders are shaking.

Piglet

Toby doesn't know what to do. Is a comforting maternal hug in order, supposing she's capable of giving one, or would Jimmy find that intrusive? How about a brisk, nurse-like *Chin up* or a feeble withdrawal, on tiptoe?

Before she can make up her mind, Blackbeard runs into the room. He's unusually excited. "They're coming! They're coming!" he says. It's almost a shout, which is rare for a Craker: even the kids aren't shouters.

"Who is?" she asks. "Is it the bad men?" Now where did she leave her rifle? That's the down side of Meditations: you forget how to be properly aggressive.

"They! Come! Come," he says, tugging at her hand, then at her bedsheet. "The Pig Ones. Very many!"

Jimmy lifts his head. "Pigoons. Oh fuck," he says.

Blackbeard is delighted. "Yes! Thank you for calling him, Snowman-the-Jimmy! We will need him, to help us," he says. "The Pig Ones have a dead."

"A dead what?" Toby asks him, but he's out the door.

The MaddAddamites have dropped their various tasks and are moving in behind the cobb-house fence. Some have armed themselves with axes, and rakes, and shovels.

Crozier, who must have set out to pasture with his flock of Mo'Hairs, is hurrying back along the pathway. Manatee's with him, carrying their spraygun.

"They're coming from the west," says Crozier. The Mo'Hairs surround him.

"They're . . . It's weird. They're marching. It's like a pig parade."

The Crakers are gathering by the swing set. They don't seem in any way frightened. They talk together in low voices, then the men begin to move west, as if to meet whatever's coming down the path. Several women go with them: Marie Antoinette, Sojourner Truth, two others. The rest stay behind with the children, who clump together and stand silently, though no one has ordered them to do that.

"Make them come back!" says Jimmy, who has joined the Madd-Addamite group. "Those things will rip them open!"

"You can't *make* them do anything," says Swift Fox, who is holding – somewhat awkwardly – a pitchfork from the garden.

"Rhino," says Zeb, handing over another spraygun. "Don't get trigger-happy," he says to Manatee. "You could hit a Craker. As long as the pigs don't charge us, don't fire."

"This is creepy," says Ren timorously. She's standing beside Jimmy now, holding on to his arm. "Where's Amanda?"

"Sleeping," says Lotis Blue, who's on the other side of Jimmy now.

"More than creepy," says Jimmy. "They're sly, the pigoons. They've got tactics. They almost cornered me one time."

"Toby. We'll need your rifle," says Zeb. "If they split into two groups, go around to the back. They can root under the fence fast if they've got us distracted out front. Then they'll attack from both sides."

Toby hurries to her cubicle. When she comes out carrying her old Ruger Deerfield, the herd of giant pigoons is already advancing into the clearing in front of the cobb-house fence.

There are fifty or so in all. Fifty adults, that is: several of the sows have litters of piglets, trotting along beside their mothers. In the centre of the group, two of the boars are moving side by side; there's something lying crossways on their backs. It looks like a mound of flowers – flowers and foliage.

What? thinks Toby. Is it a peace offering? A pig wedding? An altarpiece?

The largest pigs are acting as outriders; they seem nervous, pointing the moist discs of their snouts this way and that, snuffing the air.

They're glossy and greyish pink, rounded and plump and streamlined, like enormous nightmare slugs; but slugs with tusks, at least on the males. A sudden charge, an upward slash with those lethal scimitars, and you'd be gutted like a fish. And soon they'll be so close to the Crakers that even a direct hit with a spraygun wouldn't stop their momentum.

A low level of grunting is going on, from pig to pig. If they were people, Toby thinks, you'd say it was the murmuring of a crowd. It must be information exchange; but God knows what sort of information. Are they saying, "We're scared?" Or "We hate them?" Or possibly just a simple "Yum, yum?"

Rhino and Manatee are stationed just inside the fence. They've lowered their sprayguns. Toby has thought it best to conceal her rifle; she's carrying it at her side, a fold of her bedsheet tucked around it. No need to remind them of her boar-murdering exploits, though they probably need no reminders.

"Cripes," says Jimmy, who's standing behind Toby. "Would you look at that. They've got to be planning something."

Blackbeard has left the other Craker children and has clutched himself on to Toby. "Do not be afraid, Oh Toby," he says. "Are you afraid?"

"Yes, I am afraid," she says. Though not as afraid as Jimmy, she adds to herself, because I have a gun and he doesn't. "They have attacked our garden more than once," she says. "And we have killed some of them, to defend ourselves." She thinks uneasily of the pork roasts, the bacon, and the chops that have resulted. "And we have put them into soup," she says. "They have turned into a smelly bone. A lot of smelly bones."

"Yes, a smelly bone," says Blackbeard thoughtfully. "A lot of smelly bones. I have seen them near the kitchen."

"So they are not our friends," Toby says. "You are not the friend of those who turn you into a smelly bone."

Blackbeard thinks about this. Then he looks up at her, smiling gently. "Do not be afraid, Oh Toby," he says. "They are Children of Oryx and Children of Crake, both. They have said they will not harm you today. You will see." Toby's far from sure about that, but she smiles down at him anyway.

The advance deputation of Crakers has joined the herd of pigoons and is walking back with them. The rest of the Crakers wait silently by the swing set as the pigoons advance.

Now Napoleon Bonaparte and six other men step forward: piss parade, it looks like. Yes, they're peeing in a line. Aiming carefully, peeing respectfully, but peeing. Having finished, they each take a step back. Three curious little piglets scamper forward, snuffle at the ground, then run squealing back to their mothers.

"There," says Blackbeard. "See? It is safe."

The Crakers move into a semicircle behind their demarcation line of urine. They begin to sing. The herd of pigoons divides in two, and the pair of boars moves slowly forward. Then they roll to either side, and the flower-covered burden they've been carrying slips onto the ground. They heave to their feet again and move some of the flowers away, using their trotters and snouts.

It's a dead piglet. A tiny one, with its throat cut. Its front trotters are tied together with rope. The blood is still red, it's oozing from the gaping neck wound. There are no other marks.

Now the whole herd is deploying itself in a semicircle around the — what? The bier? The catafalque? The flowers, the leaves — it's a funeral. Toby remembers the boar she shot at the AnooYoo Spa — how, when she went to collect maggots from the carcass, there were fern fronds and leaves scattered over it. Elephants, she'd thought then. They do that. When someone they love has died.

"Crap," says Jimmy. "I hope it wasn't us who nuked that little porker."

"I don't think so," says Toby. She would have heard about it, surely. There would have been some culinary chitchat.

The two piglet-bearers have gone forward to the line of piss. Abraham Lincoln and Sojourner Truth are on the other side of it. They kneel so they're at the level of the pigoons: head facing head. The Crakers stop singing. There's silence. Then the Crakers start singing again.

"What's happening?" says Toby.

"They are talking, Oh Toby," says Blackbeard. "They are asking for help. They want to stop those ones. Those ones who are killing their pig babies." He takes a deep breath. "Two pig babies — one with a stick you point, one with a knife. The Pig Ones want those killing ones to be dead."

"They want help from . . ." She can't say *the Crakers*, it isn't what they call themselves. "They want help from your people?"

If killing is the request, how can the Crakers help? she wonders. According to the MaddAddamites, Crakers are nonviolent by nature. They don't fight, they can't fight. They're incapable of it. That's how they're made.

"No, Oh Toby," says Blackbeard. "They want help from you."

"Me?" says Toby.

"All of you. All those standing behind the fence, those with two skins. They want you to help them with the sticks you have. They know how you kill, by making holes. And then blood comes out. They want you to make such holes in the three bad men. With blood." He looks a little ill: he isn't finding this easy. Toby wants to hug him, but that would be condescending: he has chosen this duty.

"Did you say three men?" Toby asks. "Aren't there only two?"

"The Pig Ones say there are three," says Blackbeard. "They have smelled three."

"That's not so good," says Zeb. "They've found a recruit." He and Black Rhino exchange sombre glances.

"Changes the odds," says Rhino.

"They want you to make blood come out," says Blackbeard. "Three with holes in them, and blood."

"Us," says Toby. "They want us to do it."

"Yes," says Blackbeard. "Those with two skins."

"Then why aren't they talking to us?" says Toby. "Why are they talking to you?"

Oh, she thinks. Of course. We're too stupid, we don't understand their languages. So there has to be a translator.

"It is easier for them to talk to us," says Blackbeard simply. "And in return, if you help them to kill the three bad men, they will never again try to eat your garden. Or any of you," he adds seriously. "Even if you are dead, they will not eat you. And they ask that you must no longer make holes in them, with blood, and cook them in a smelly bone soup, or hang them in the smoke, or fry them and then eat them. Not any more."

"Tell them it's a deal," says Zeb.

"Throw in the bees and the honey," says Toby. "Make those off-limits too."

"Please, Oh Toby, what is a *deal*?" says Blackbeard.

"A deal means, we accept their offer and will help them," says Toby. "We share their wishes."

"Then they will be happy," says Blackbeard. "They want to go hunting for the bad men tomorrow, or else the next day. You must bring your sticks, to make the holes."

Something appears to have been concluded. The pigoons, who have been standing with ears cocked forward and snouts raised as if sniffing the words, turn away and head west, back from where they came. They've left the dead flower-strewn piglet on the ground.

"Wait," says Toby to Blackbeard. "They've forgotten their . . ." She almost said *their child*. "They've forgotten the little one."

"The small Pig One is for you, Oh Toby," says Blackbeard. "It is a gift. It is dead already. They have already done their sadness."

"But we have promised not to eat them any more," says Toby.

"Not kill and then eat, no. But they say you would not be killing it yourselves. Therefore it is permitted. They say you may eat it or not eat it, as you choose. They would eat it themselves, otherwise."

Curious funeral rites, thinks Toby. You strew the beloved with flowers, you mourn, and then you eat the corpse. No-holds-barred recycling. Even Adam and the Gardeners never went that far.

Palaver

The Crakers have moved apart, over to the swing set, where they are chewing away at the kudzu vines and talking together in low voices. The dead piglet lies on the ground, flies settling on it, encircled by a ring of MaddAddamites, pondering over it as if holding an inquest.

"So, you think those pricks were butchering it?" says Shackleton.

"Maybe," says Manatee. "But it wasn't hanging from a tree. That's what you'd do normally, to drain the blood."

"The pigs told my blue buddies it was just lying on the path," says Crozier. "In plain view."

"You think it's a message to us?" says Zunzuncito.

"Sort of like a challenge," says Shackleton. "Like they're calling us out."

"Maybe that's how come the rope. It was the rope on *them* last time," says Ren.

"Nah," says Crozier. "Why would they use a piglet for that?"

"Maybe like *This will be you next time.* Or *Look how close we can get.* They're triple-time Painball vets, remember. That's Painball style: freak you out," says Shackleton.

"Right," says Rhino. "They really want our stuff now. Must be running out of cellpack power, getting desperate."

"They'll try to sneak in at night," says Shackleton. "We'll have to double up on sentries."

"Better check the fences," says Rhino. "They're still pretty make-shift."

"They may have tools," says Zeb. "From some hardware store. Knives, wire cutters, stuff like that." He moves off, around the corner of the cobb house, with Rhino following.

"Maybe it's not the Painballers who killed it. Maybe it's persons unknown," says Ivory Bill.

"Maybe it's the Crakers," says Jimmy. "Hey, just joking, I know they'd never do that."

"Never say never," says Ivory Bill. "Their brains are more malleable than Crake intended. They've been doing several things we didn't anticipate during the construction phase."

"Maybe it's someone in our own group," says Swift Fox. "Someone who wanted sausages."

There's an uneasy, guilty laugh round the circle. Then a silence. "So. What next?" says Ivory Bill.

"What next is, do we cook it or not?" says Rebecca. "Suckling pig?"

"Oh, I couldn't," says Ren. "It would be like eating a baby." Amanda starts to cry.

"My dear lady, what's all this about?" says Ivory Bill.

"I'm sorry," says Ren. "I shouldn't have said *baby*."

"Okay, cards on the table," says Rebecca. "Hands up, anyone here who didn't know that Amanda's pregnant?"

"I appear to be the only one left in gynecological ignorance," says Ivory Bill. "Perhaps such intimate feminine material was considered unfit for my elderly ears."

"Or maybe you weren't listening," says Swift Fox.

"Okay, so that's clear," says Rebecca. "Now I would like to open up the circle, as we used to say at the Gardeners . . . Ren, you want to do this?"

Ren takes a breath. "I'm pregnant too," she says. She begins to sniffle. "I peed on the stick. It turned pink, it made a smiley face . . . Oh God." Lotis Blue pats her. Crozier makes a move towards her, then stops.

"Three's company," says Swift Fox. "Count me in. Bun in the oven, up the spout. Farrow in the barrow." At least she's cheerful about it, thinks Toby. But whose bun?

There's another silence. "I don't suppose there is any point," says Ivory Bill with heavy disapproval, "in speculating as to the paternity of these . . . these various imminent progenies."

"None whatsoever," says Swift Fox. "Or not in my case. I've been doing an experiment in genetic evolution. Reproduction of the fittest. Think of me as a petri dish."

"I find that irresponsible," says Ivory Bill.

"I'm not sure it's any of your business," says Swift Fox.

"Hey!" says Rebecca. "It is what it is!"

"With Amanda, it may be a Craker," says Toby. "From something that happened the night she was . . . the night we got her back, from . . . That's the best possibility. And that may be what happened with Ren too."

"It wasn't the Painballers, anyway," says Ren. "With me. I know it wasn't."

"You know that how?" says Crozier.

"I don't want to go into the gory details," says Ren, "because you'd think it was oversharing. It's girl stuff. We count the days. That's how."

"I can definitely rule out the Painballers," says Swift Fox. "In my case. And I can rule out a few other guys too." None of the men look at each other. Crozier suppresses a grin.

"And the Crakers as well?" says Toby, keeping her voice neutral. Who's on her checklist? Crozier, definitely, but who else? Have there been multitudes? Maybe Zeb was one of them, after all; if so, soon there may be an infant Zeb. Then what will she herself do? Pretend she doesn't notice? Knit babywear? Brood and sulk? The first two options would be preferable, but she's not sure she'll be up to them.

"I did have an interlude or two with the big blues," says Swift Fox. "When no one was looking, which didn't give me a huge window of opportunity, since everyone here is so snoopy. It was energetic, and I'm not sure I'd want to make a habit of it. Not much foreplay. But the pink smiley face doesn't lie, and I will soon be heavy with young. The question is, young what?"

"Guess we'll find out," says Shackleton.

Zeb and Black Rhino return from their inspection of the fences. "This place is hardly a fortress," Zeb says. "Thing is — if we take the weapons with us on the hunt, we leave everyone in the cobb house undefended."

"Which may be what they want," says Rhino. "Lure us out the front, sneak in the back. Make off with the women."

"We're not just packages," says Swift Fox. "We can fight back! You can leave us a couple of sprayguns."

"Good luck with that plan," says Rhino.

"We need to move our whole group out of here when we go hunting for those guys," says Crozier. "We can't leave anyone behind. Take the Mo'Hairs too. If we're all together, it's harder for them to ambush us."

"But easier to stampede us," says Zeb. "How fast can we all run?"

"I'm not running," says Rebecca. "And I need to point out here that there are three pregnant women in this crowd."

"Three?" says Zeb.

"Ren and Swift Fox," says Rebecca.

"When did that happen?"

"They told everyone else when you were checking the fences," says Rebecca.

"They got knocked up by elves overnight," says Jimmy.

"Not funny, Jimmy," says Lotis Blue.

"Point is, bad for them to run," says Rebecca.

"So, we can't keep our end of the deal? We can't go into battle with the pig militia?" says Shackleton. "They'll have to do it alone?"

"They can't," says Jimmy. "They're fucking lethal but they can't climb stairs. If the pigs chase those Painball guys into the city, they'll just move up a floor and shoot down. The pigoons will be decimated."

"Crozier's right, we should all relocate," says Toby. "To a more secure place, with doors that lock."

"Like where?" says Rebecca.

"We can go back to the AnooYoo Spa," says Toby. "I holed up in there for months. There's still some basic food left." And maybe some seeds, she thinks: I can collect seeds, for the garden. And more bullets, she'd left some there.

"They've got real beds," says Ren. "And towels."

"And solid doors," says Toby.

"Could be a plan," says Zeb. "Vote?"

Nobody votes no.

"Now we must prepare," says Katuro.

"First we should bury the piglet," Toby says. "It would be right. Under the circumstances."

So they do.

Fallback

It takes them a day to get organized. There are many things they need to take with them: the basic supplies for cooking, a change of daywear bedsheets, duct tape, rope. Flashlights, headlamps: most of the batteries are still good. The sprayguns, of course. Toby's rifle. And any sharp-edged tools, because you wouldn't want such things as knives and picks to fall into the hands of enemies.

"Keep it light," Zeb tells them. "If all goes well, we'll be back here in a few days."

"Or else this place may be burned to the ground," says Rhino.

"So if you really need it, take it with you," says Katuro.

Toby worries about her hive of bees. Will they be all right? What could attack them? She hasn't seen any bears, and the Pigoons have made a no-bees deal, or so she must believe. Do wolvogs like honey? No, they're carnivores. Rakunks, perhaps, but they'd be no match for an angry hive.

She covers her head and speaks to the hive, as she's been doing faithfully each morning. "Greetings, Bees. I bring news to you and your Queen. Tomorrow I must go away for a short time, so I will not be talking with you for several days. Our own hive is threatened. We are in danger, and we must attack those that threaten us, as you would in our place. Be steadfast, gather much pollen, defend your hive if need be. Tell this message to Pilar, and ask for the help of her strong Spirit, on our behalf."

The bees fly in and out of the hole in the Styrofoam cooler. They seem to like it here in the garden. Several of them come over to investigate her. They test her floral bedsheet, find it wanting, move to her face. Yes, they know her. They touch her lips, gather her words, fly away with the message, disappear into the dark. Pass through the membrane that separates this world from the unseen world that lies just underneath it. There is Pilar, with her calm smile, walking forward along a corridor that glows with hidden light.

Now, Toby, she tells herself. Talking pigs, communicative dead people, and the Underworld in a Styrofoam beer cooler. You're not on drugs, you're not even sick. You really have no excuse.

The Crakers watch the departure preparations with interest. The children hang around the kitchen, staring at Rebecca with their huge green eyes, keeping a distance between themselves and her flitch of bacon and her dried wolvog jerky.

The Crakers don't seem to fully understand why the MaddAddams are moving house, but they've made it clear that they themselves are coming too.

"We will help Snowman-the-Jimmy," they say. "We will help Zeb." "We will help Crozier, he is our friend, we must help him to piss better." "We will help Toby, she will tell us a story." "Crake wants us to go there," and so forth. They themselves have no possessions, so there's nothing they need to carry; but they want to carry other things. "I will bring this, it is a pot." "I will bring this, it is a wind-up radio, what is it for?" "I will bring this sharp one, it is a knife." "This one is a toilet paper, I will carry it."

"We will carry Snowman-the-Jimmy," one trio announces, but Jimmy says he can walk.

Blackbeard marches into Toby's cubicle. "I will bring the writing," he says importantly. "And the pen. I will bring those, for us to have there."

He views Toby's journal as a joint possession of theirs, which is fine, thinks Toby, as it lets her follow his writing progress. Though sometimes it's hard to get the journal away from him so she can write in it herself, and he has to be reminded not to leave it out in the rain.

So far he's concentrated mostly on names, though he's also fond of writing THANK YOU and GOOD NIGHT. CRAK GOODNIT GOOD BAD

FLOWR ZEB TOBY ORIX THAK YOU is a typical entry. Maybe one of these days she'll gain some new insights into how his mind works, though she can't say she's had any blinding illuminations as yet.

At sunrise the next day they set out from the cobb-house compound in the Tree of Life parkette. It's an exodus, a move away from civilization, such as it is.

Two Pigoons have arrived as escorts; the rest will meet them at the AnooYoo Spa, says Blackbeard. He's got Toby's binoculars, which he's figured out how to use. Every once in a while he steps off to the side, lifts the binocs, focuses. "Crows," he announces. "Vultures." The Craker women laugh gently. "Oh Blackbeard, but you knew that without the eye tube things," they say. Then he laughs too.

Rhino and Katuro walk ahead with the Pigoons, followed by Crozier and the flock of Mo'Hairs. Some of them have bundles tied onto their backs, which is new for them, though they don't seem to mind. With their human hair, curly and straight, and the lumpy packages on top of it, they look like avant-garde hats with legs.

Shackleton stays in the middle of the procession, with Ren, Amanda, and Swift Fox, who are surrounded in their turn by most of the Craker women, attracted by their pregnant state. The Crakers make cooing noises, they smile and laugh and pat and stroke. Swift Fox appears to find this annoying, but Amanda smiles.

The rest of the MaddAddamite group is behind them, and then the Craker men. Zeb brings up the rear.

Toby walks near the Craker women, rifle at the ready. It seems a long time since she came this way with Ren, searching for Amanda. Ren must be remembering those days as well: she drops behind to join Toby, slipping her arm through Toby's free left arm. "Thank you for letting me in," she says. "At the AnooYoo Spa. And for the maggots. I would have died if you hadn't taken care of me. You saved my life."

And you saved mine, thinks Toby. If Ren hadn't stumbled along, what would she have done? Waited and waited, shut up inside the AnooYoo by herself, until she went bonkers or dried up of old age.

. . .

They stick to the road that leads through the Heritage Park, heading northwest. There's Pilar's elderberry bush, covered with butterflies and bees. One of the Mo'Hairs grabs a mouthful of it on the way past.

Now they've reached the eastern gatehouse – pink, Tex-Mex retro – and the high fence that encloses the AnooYoo grounds. "We came here," Ren says. "That man was inside it. The Painballer, the worst one."

"Yes," says Toby. It was Blanco, her old enemy. He'd had gangrene, but he was bent on murder despite that.

"You killed him, didn't you?" says Ren. She must have known at the time.

"Let's say I helped him enter a different plane of being," says Toby. That was the Gardener way of putting it. "He would have died soon, but more painfully. Anyway, it was Urban Bloodshed Limitation." First rule: limit bloodshed by making sure that none of your own gets spilled.

She'd dosed Blanco with Amanita and Poppy: a painless exit, and better than he deserved. Then she'd dragged him onto the ornamental planting ringed with whitewashed stones, as a gift for the wildlife. Was the dose of Amanita strong enough to poison anything that ate him? She hopes not: she wishes the vultures well.

The heavy wrought-iron gate is wide open. Toby had tied it shut when they'd left, but the rope has been chewed apart. The two Pigoons trot through first, snuffle around the walkway to the gatehouse, nose their way in. They come back out, then trot over to Blackbeard. Subdued grunting, eye-to-eye staring.

"They say the three men have been there. But they are not there now," he says.

"Are they sure?" Toby asks. "There was a man in there earlier. A bad man. They don't mean that one?"

"Oh no," says Blackbeard. "They know about that one. He was dead, on the flowers. At first they wanted to eat him, but he had bad mushrooms in him. So they did not."

Toby checks out the ornamental flowerbed. It used to say WELCOME TO ANOOYOO in petunias; now it's a lush thicket of meadow weeds. Down among them, is that a boot? She has no desire to probe further.

She'd left Blanco's knife there, with the body. It was a good one:

sharp. But the MaddAddamites have other knives. She only hopes the Painballers haven't retrieved it; but they, too, must have other knives.

Now they're in the AnooYoo grounds proper. They keep to the main roadway, although there's a forest path: Toby and Ren had taken it earlier, to stay in the shade. That was where they'd come upon Oates, slaughtered by the Painballers and minus his kidneys, strung up in a tree.

He must still be there, thinks Toby. They should find him, cut him down, give him a proper burial. His brothers, Shackleton and Crozier, will welcome that. A true composting, with his own tree planted on top of him. Restore him to the cool peace of rootlets, the calm dissolve of earth. But now is not the time.

Dogs barking, off in the woods. They stop to listen. "If those things come over wagging their tails, you need to shoot them," says Jimmy. "Wolvogs; they're vicious."

"Ammunition's rationed," says Rhino. "Until we find more."

"They won't attack us now," says Katuro. "Too many people. Plus two Pigoons."

"We must've killed most of them by now," says Shackleton.

They pass a burnt-out jeep, then an incinerated solarcar. Then a crashed pink mini-van with the AnooYoo logo on it: kissy lips, winky eye.

"Don't look inside," says Zeb, who has already looked. "Not pretty."

And now there's the Spa building up ahead, solid pink, still standing: no one has burned it down.

The main force of the Pigoons is milling around outside, probably finishing off the organic kitchen garden, one-time source of garnishes for the clients' diet salads. Toby remembers the hours she'd spent alone in that garden after the Flood, hoping to raise enough edible plant life so she could keep going. It's all churned earth by now.

At least she left the door unlocked.

Shadow, mildew. Her old self, bodiless, wandering the mirrorless halls. She'd put towels over the glass to blot out her own reflection.

"Come in," she says to everyone. "Make yourselves at home."

Fortress AnooYoo

The Crakers are entranced by the AnooYoo Spa. They walk carefully along the hallways, bending to touch the smooth, polished floor. They lift the pink towels that Toby had hung over the mirrors, glimpse the people in there, look behind the mirrors; then, when they realize the people are themselves, they touch their hair and smile to make their reflections smile too. They sit on the beds in the bedrooms, gingerly, then stand up again. In the gymnasium the children bounce on the trampolines, giggling. They sniff at the pink soap in the washrooms. There is still a lot of pink soap.

"Is this the Egg?" they ask. Or the younger ones do. They have a faint memory of a similar place, with high walls and smooth floors. "Is this the Egg where we were made?" "No, the Egg is not the same." "The Egg is far. It is more far than this." "The Egg has Crake in it, the Egg has Oryx. They are not here." "Can we go to the Egg?" "We do not want to go to the Egg now, it is dark." "Does the Egg have the pink things in it, like this? The flower-smelling things we can eat?" "That is not a plant, that is a soap. We do not eat a soap," and so on.

At least they aren't singing, thinks Toby. They haven't sung much on the way here either. They've been looking and listening. They seem to know there is danger.

Fortunately there haven't been any leaks in the roof. Toby is happy about that: it means the beds, despite being slightly musty, are still sleepable. As de facto hostess, she assigns rooms. For herself she picks a Couples room. The Spa contained three of those, in the unlikely event that a husband and wife or equivalent would check in together, to undergo joint facials and cleansings and tweaks and polishes. But this offering was not popular, or not among heterosexual couples — usually women liked to have such adjustments done in private so they could emerge like butterflies from a perfumed cocoon and astound the multitudes with their ravishing beauty. Toby used to run this place, so she knows. She knows, also, about the disappointment felt by these women, when, despite the large amounts of money they'd spent, they did not look very much better.

In the closet she stashes her belongings, such as they are. Her well-worn binoculars: she hasn't had much use for them at the cobb house because there were few vistas there, but they'll be essential now. Her rifle, and the ammunition. She left a cache of bullets here at the Spa, so she can top up her supply now. Once that's gone the rifle will be of no use, unless she can learn to make gunpowder.

She places her toothbrush in the ensuite bathroom. She needn't have bothered bringing the one from the cobb house: there are a lot of toothbrushes at the Spa, all pink; and, in the supply room, a whole shelf of AnooYoo's guest mini-toothpastes, two kinds: Cherry Blossom Organic, biodegradable with anti-plaque micro-organisms; and Kiss-in-the-Dark Chromatic Sparkle Enhancer.

The second one claims to make your entire mouth glow in the dark. Toby never tried it out, but some women swore by it. She wonders how Zeb would react if he were to be confronted with a disembodied glowing mouth. Tonight will not be the night to find out, however: she'll be on sentry duty, up on the rooftop, and a light-up mouth would make an excellent target for a sniper.

Her old journals; she's gathered them up from where she'd slept on one of the massage tables, out of some nun-like sense of penitence. Here they are, written in AnooYoo appointment books, with the kissy-mouth logo and the winking eye. She'd recorded the Gardener days, the Feasts and Festivals, and the phases of the moon; and the daily happenings, if any. It had helped to keep her sane, that writing. Then, when time had begun again and real people had entered it, she'd abandoned it here. Now it's a whisper from the past.

Is that what writing amounts to? The voice your ghost would have, if it had a voice? If so, why is she teaching this practice to little Blackbeard? Surely the Crakers would be happier without it.

She slides the journals into a dresser drawer. She'd like to read them over sometime, but there's no space for that right now.

The toilets still have water in them, plus a lot of dead flies. She flushes: the collector barrels on the roof must be functional, which is a blessing. And there's a vast supply of pink toilet paper, with flower petals pressed into it. Some of the earlier AnooYoo botanical-items toilet paper experiments had not gone well, as there had been some unexpected allergies.

She needs to post a Boil Water advisory, however. Seeing water actually coming out of a tap, some people might get carried away.

After washing her face and putting on a clean pink top-to-toe from the Housekeeping closet, she rejoins the others. There's a heated discussion going on in the main foyer: what to do with the Mo'Hairs overnight? The broad AnooYoo lawn is now thigh-high in meadow growth, so grazing them in the daytime won't pose a problem, but they'll need to be sheltered or guarded once darkness falls: there may be liobams. Crozier is all for herding them into the gym: he's become quite attached to them, and is worried. Manatee points out that the floor is slippery and they may skid and break their legs, not to mention the sheep-shit factor. Toby suggests the kitchen garden: it has a fence, which is still largely intact – the Pigoons have entered by means of the holes they dug, but these can be quickly filled. Then a sentry on the rooftop can keep an eye on the flock and report any unusual bleating.

But where will the Crakers sleep? They don't like sleeping inside buildings. They want to sleep in the meadow, where there are a lot of leaves for them to eat as well. But with the Painballers on the loose and possibly in a hunting mood, that's out of the question.

"On the roof," says Toby. "There are some planters up there in case they want a snack." So that's decided.

. . .

The afternoon thunderstorm comes and goes. Once it's over the Pigoons go for a dip in the swimming pool; the fact that it's growing algae and waterweeds and has a lively population of frogs does not deter them. They've solved the problem of how to get in and out of it by shoving a collection of poolside furniture into the shallow end: the deck chairs make a sort of ramp, which provides a foothold. The younger ones enjoy splashing and squealing; the older sows and boars take brief dips, then watch over their piglets and shoats indulgently, lounging at poolside. Toby wonders if pigs get sunburn.

Dinner is somewhat haphazard, though served in grand style on the round tables and pink tablecloths of the main dining room. A foraging posse has scoured the meadow, so there's a hefty salad of wild greens. Rebecca has found a small unopened bottle of olive oil and made a classic French dressing. Steamed purslane, parboiled burdock root, wolvog jerky, Mo'Hair milk. There was a residual jar of sugar in the kitchen, so each of them has a teaspoonful of it for dessert. Toby isn't used to sugar any more: the potent sweetness goes through her head like a blade.

"I've got some news for you," says Rebecca when they're cleaning up. "Your pals caught a frog for you. They asked me to cook it."

"A frog?" says Toby.

"Yeah. They couldn't get a fish."

"Oh crap," says Toby. The Crakers will be asking for their night-time story. With any luck, they've forgotten to bring the red Snowman hat.

It's mellow evening now, the sun subsiding. Crickets trill, birds flock to roost, amphibians ribbet from the swimming pool or twang like rubber bands. Toby looks for something to wrap herself in while standing sentry: the rooftop can be cool.

As she's swaddling up in a pink bedspread, little Blackbeard sidles into her room. He spots himself in the mirror, smiles, waves at himself, does a tiny dance. Once that's over, he delivers his message: "The Pig Ones are saying that the three bad men are over there."

"Over where?" says Toby, her heart quickening.

"Across the flowers. Behind the trees. They can smell them."

"They shouldn't go too close," says Toby. "The bad men might have sprayguns. The sticks that make holes. With blood coming out."

"The Pig Ones know that," says Blackbeard.

Toby climbs the stairs to the rooftop, binoculars around her neck, rifle slung and ready. A number of the Crakers are already up there, waiting expectantly. Zeb is there too, leaning against the railing.

"You're very pink," he says. "The colour suits you. The silhouette too. Michelin Tire Man?"

"Are you being an asshole?"

"Not on purpose," he says. "Crows making a racket." And they are making one. *Caw caw caw* over at the edge of the forest. Toby lifts the binoculars: nothing to be seen.

"It could be an owl," she says.

"Could be," says Zeb.

"The Pigoons keep saying there are three men. Not two."

"I'd be surprised if they're wrong," says Zeb.

"Do you think it might be Adam?" says Toby.

"Remember what you said about hope?" says Zeb. "You said it can be bad for you. So I'm trying not to."

There's a flicker of something light, over among the branches. Is it a face? Gone again.

"The worst thing," says Toby, "is the waiting."

Blackbeard tugs at her bedspread. "Oh Toby," he says. "Come! It is time for us to hear the story that you will tell to us. We have brought the red hat."

The
Train
to
CryoJeenyus

The Story of the Two Eggs and Thinking

Thank you. I am happy that you remembered to bring the red hat.

And the fish. It is not a fish exactly, it is more like a frog. But you caught it in the water, and we are far from the ocean, so I am sure that Crake will understand, and will know that it was too far for you to go all the way to the ocean in order to catch a fish there.

Thank you for cooking it. For asking Rebecca to cook it. Crake has told me that I do not have to eat all of it. A nibble will be enough.

There.

Yes, the frog ... the fish has a bone in it. A smelly bone. That is why I spat it out. But we do not need to talk about the smelly bone right now.

Tomorrow is a very important day. Tomorrow, all of us with two skins must finish the work that Crake began — the work of clearing away the chaos. That work was the Great Rearrangement, and it made the Great Emptiness.

But that was only part of the work of Crake. The other part was when he made you. He made your bones out of the coral on the beach, which is white like bones but not smelly. And he made your flesh out of a mango, which is sweet and soft. He did all this inside the giant Egg, and he had some helpers there. And Snowman-the-Jimmy was his friend — he was inside the Egg as well.

And Oryx was there too. Sometimes she was in the form of a woman with green eyes like yours, and sometimes she was in the form of an owl. And she laid two smaller owl eggs, inside the giant Egg. One smaller owl egg was full of animals and birds and fish — all her Children. Yes, and bees. And butterflies too. And ants, yes. And beetles – very many beetles. And snakes. And frogs. And maggots. And rakunks, and bobkittens, and Mo'Hairs, and Pigoons.

Thank you, but I don't think we need to list every one of them.

Because we would be here all night.

Let us just say that Oryx made very many Children. And each one was beautiful in its own special way.

Yes, it was kind of her to make each and every one of them, inside the smaller owl egg that she laid. Except maybe the mosquitoes.

The other egg she laid was full of words. But that egg hatched first, before the one with the animals in it, and you ate up many of the words, because you were hungry; which is why you have words inside you. And Crake thought that you had eaten all the words, so there were none left over for the animals, and that was why they could not speak. But he was wrong about that. Crake was not always right about everything.

Because when he was not looking, some of the words fell out of the egg onto the ground, and some fell into the water, and some blew away in the air. And none of the people saw them. But the animals and the birds and the fish did see them, and ate them up. They were a different kind of word, so it was sometimes hard for people to understand the animals. They had chewed the words up too small.

And the Pigoons – the Pig Ones – ate up more of the words than any of the other animals did. You know how they love to eat. So the Pig Ones can think very well.

Then Oryx made a new kind of thing, called singing. And she gave it to you because she loved birds and she wanted you to be able to sing that way as well. But Crake did not want you to do the singing. It worried him. He thought that if you could sing like birds you would forget to talk like people, and then you would not remember him or understand his work – all the work that he had done to make you.

And Oryx said, You will just have to suck it up. Because if these people cannot sing, they will be like . . . they will be like nothing. They will be like stones.

Suck it up means . . . we will talk about that some other time.

Now I will tell a different part of the story, which is about why Crake decided to make the Great Emptiness.

. . .

For a long time, Crake thought. He thought and thought. He told no one about all his thoughts, though he told some of them to Snowman-the-Jimmy and some of them to Zeb and some of them to Pilar and some of them to Oryx.

This is what he thought:

The people in the chaos cannot learn. They cannot understand what they are doing to the sea and the sky and the plants and the animals. They cannot understand that they are killing them, and that they will end by killing themselves. And there are so many of them, and each one of them is doing part of the killing, whether they know it or not. And when you tell them to stop, they don't hear you.

So there is only one thing left to do. Either most of them must be cleared away while there is still an earth, with trees and flowers and birds and fish and so on, or all must die when there are none of those things left. Because if there are none of those things left, then there will be nothing at all. Not even any people.

But shouldn't you give those ones a second chance? he asked himself. No, he answered, because they have had a second chance. They have had many second chances. Now is the time.

So Crake made some little seeds that tasted very good; and they made people very happy at first, when they ate them. But then those who ate the seeds would become very sick, and would come to pieces, and would die. And he sprinkled the seeds over all the earth.

And Oryx helped to sprinkle the seeds, because she could fly like an owl. And the Bird Women and the Snake Women and the Flower Women helped too. Though they did not understand about the dying part, only the happy part, because Crake had not told them all of his thoughts.

And then the Great Rearrangement began to happen. And Oryx and Crake left the Egg and flew up into the sky. But Snowman-the-Jimmy stayed behind, to watch over you and to keep bad things away from you, and to help you, and to tell you the stories of Crake. And the stories of Oryx as well.

You can do the singing later.

That is the story of the two eggs.

Now we must all go to sleep, because we must get up very early tomorrow. Some of us will go looking for the three bad men. Zeb will go, and Rhino, and Manatee, and Crozier, and Shackleton. And Snowman-the-Jimmy. Yes, the Pig Ones will go too, many of them. Not the little ones, or their mothers.

But you will stay here, with Rebecca, and Amanda, and Ren. And Swift Fox. And Lotis Blue. And you must keep the door shut, and not let anyone in, no matter what they say. Unless it is ones you already know.

Don't be frightened.

Yes, I will go out looking for the bad men too. And Blackbeard will go, to help us talk with the Pig Ones.

Yes, we will come back. I hope we will come back.

Hope is when you want something very much but you do not know if that thing you want will really happen.

Now I will say good night.

Good night.

Shades

"This is where I waited for you," says Toby. "During the Waterless Flood. Up here on the rooftop. I kept expecting you'd stroll out of those woods at any moment."

The Crakers are all around them, sleeping peacefully. How trusting they are, thinks Toby. They've never learned real fear. Maybe they can't learn it.

"So you didn't think I was dead?" says Zeb.

"I was counting on you," says Toby. "I thought, if anyone knew how to stay alive through all of that, it would be you. Some days I did tell myself you were dead, though. I called that 'realism.' But the rest of the time I was waiting."

"Worth it?" says Zeb. Invisible grin in the darkness.

"You're having a failure of confidence? You need to ask?"

"Yeah, I kind of do," says Zeb. "Used to think I was God's gift, but that gets rubbed off a guy. From the first time I knew you, back at the Gardeners, I could see you were smarter than me, what with the mushrooms and the potions and all of that."

"But you were craftier," says Toby.

"Granted. Though I outcraftied myself sometimes. Now where was I?"

"You were living with the Snake Women," says Toby. "At Scales and Tails. Keeping yourself to yourself, your eyes open, your hands in your pockets, and your lip zipped."

"Right."

They made Zeb a bouncer. It was a fine disguise. He got the shaved head, the black suit, the shades, and the gold tooth that broadcast right into his mouth. Also the tasteful enamelled lapel pin in the shape of a snake eating its own tail: an ancient motif that meant regeneration, said Adam, though you could have fooled Zeb.

He rearranged his face parsley in the deep-pleeb bouncer fuzzdo of the day, which involved a very narrow shaver used to carve a crisscross design into a light layer of stubble, with an effect like a hairy waffle. It was at that time, too, that he got his ears recontoured, at the suggestion of Adam. They were using ears more in identities, said Adam, and it would be as well if Zeb were to rearrange his own so they couldn't be matched with some ear photo of yore, supposing anyone was looking. The actual plasti-cosmi job was courtesy of Katrina WooWoo, who had access to some Grade A flesh-and-fat sculptors. Zeb opted for a more pointy look at the top of the ear and a droopier blob of lobe.

"Don't look now," he says. "I got them done a couple of times after that. But for a while there I was sort of a pixie Buddha."

"It's how I think of you," says Toby.

Zeb's job was to stand around the bar area, not smiling broadly but not actively threatening: just more or less looming. His partner was a large black guy called — at that moment — Jebediah, though when he joined MaddAddam he became Black Rhino. Zeb and Jeb was how Zeb linked the two of them in his head.

Though he was not Zeb to those at Scales, nor was he Hector the Vector. He had yet another name, which was Smokey. Smokey the Bear, like the old mascot for the so-called Forest Service. It was a fitting name. "Only YOU can prevent wildfires," had been the slogan, and that was what he was supposed to do: prevent wildfires.

When there were signs of petulance among the clientele — glowering and scowling, verbal unpleasantness, unseemly grabbing and ripping of the feathery or scaly or petal-shaped fabrics decorating the floorshow, or the chimp-display shaking of beer cans that signalled an exchange of foam-streams followed by can-tossing, bottle-smashing, and punches — Zeb and Jeb would step in. They'd switch their passive looming to active surgical intervention, the goal being to take the aggressors out smoothly and cleanly without triggering an all-in brawl. So prompt action was a must, though of course you didn't want to piss off the clients unnecessarily: a clobbered client was not often a repeat client.

Also – increasingly – a lot of the customers were from the top layers of the Corps layer cake, and those guys liked to go slumming in the pleebs, though not in any life-endangering ways. Just enough so you could feel a little rebellious, a little cool, a little sexually functional. Scales and Tails was gaining a reputation as a sanitary and discreet place in which to get shitfaced and indiscreet, and you could take a prospective business partner there as a complicated form of bribery without fear of exposure.

Thus the light touch was essential when it came to conflict resolution. The best way was to drape a companionable arm around the shoulders of the dickhead in question and to growl warmly into the ear: "House Special, just for you, sir. Compliments of the management." Overjoyed to be getting something for free and doubtless already suffering from nano-brain-death due to what he'd already guzzled, the guy would be shepherded down a few hallways and around a few corners with his tongue hanging out a yard. He'd be ushered into a large room with feather decorations and a green satin bedspread, and invisible video surveillance. There he would be lovingly undressed by a couple of the Snake Women, those with the knack of making an actuarial report sound like hot porn, while Zeb or Jeb loomed in the middle distance just out of sight, to keep the guy civil.

Then in would come a lurid mixture in a cocktail glass that might be orange or purple or blue depending on what had been ordered, topped with a green cherry that had a green plastic snake stuck into it. This would be hand-delivered by an orchid or a gardenia or a flamingo or a fluorescent blue skink on stilts, shimmering all over with sequins and tiny LED lights and scales or petals or feathers, with huge tits and a lip-licking smile. *Itchy-kitchy-coo*, this hallucination would say, or words to that effect. *Drinkie-poo!* What red-blooded hominid could say no? Down the hatch would go the mystery liquid, followed quickly by sweet dreams for Mr. Self-Styled Alpha Male, with minimal wear and tear on the hired help.

The chosen one would awaken ten hours later, convinced that he'd just had the time of his life. Which he would have done, said Zeb, because all experience registered by the brain is real, no? Even if it didn't happen in 3-D so-called real time.

This act usually worked fine with Corp exec types, a naive and trusting bunch when it came to the duplicitous mores of the pleeblands. Zeb knew their kind from the Floating World: out for thrills during their night on the town, eager for something they mistook for experience. They led sheltered lives inside their Corp Compounds and the other guarded spaces where they hung out, such as courthouses, statehouses, and religious institutions, and they were gullible about anything outside their walls. It was touching how easily they drank the Kool-Aid on offer, how rapidly they hit the hay or, in fact, the green satin bedspread, how softly they slept, and how cheerily they awoke.

But a different sort of client was establishing a presence at Scales: a less agreeable type, not easily deflected from his own angers. Hate-fuelled, hardened in the fire, bent on carnage and broken glassware. These were rockier cases, and called for an all-points alert.

"I speak of the Painballers, as you must've guessed," says Zeb. "Painball had just begun back then."

Painball Arenas were at that time highly illegal, like cockfighting and the slaughter and eating of endangered species. But, like them, Painball existed and was expanding, hidden from public view. Spectator positions were reserved for the upper echelons, who liked to watch duels to the death involving skill, cunning, ruthlessness, and cannibalism: it was Corp life in graphic terms. A lot of money was already changing hands at Painball in the form of highroller betting. So the Corps paid indirectly for the infrastructure and the upkeep of the Painball players, and those providing the locations and the services paid directly if caught, and sometimes with their lives when there were turf wars.

This arrangement suited the CorpSeCorps – in its adolescence then – as it provided ample blackmail material through which the CorpSeCorps men could tighten their hold on those considered to be the pillars of what still passed for society.

If you were already locked up in an ordinary prison, you could elect the Painball option: fight your fellow prisoners, eliminate them, and win big prizes, such as getting out of jail free and landing a stint as a pleebland grey-market enforcer. Perks all round. Of course, once you'd elected to enter Painball, the alternative to winning was death. That was why it was so much fun to watch. Those who survived it did so through guile, the ability to wrongfoot their opponents, and superior murderousness: the eating of gouged-out eyes was a favourite party trick. In a word, you had to be prepared to knife and fillet your best friend.

Once they'd graduated from a stint in Painball, the Painball vets had very high status in the deeper pleebs and also on the higher heights, as Roman gladiators must once have had. Corps wives would pay to have sex with them, Corps husbands would invite them to dinner for the thrill of astounding their friends and watching them smash up the champagne flutes, though security enforcers would always be present in case things looked like they were getting seriously out of hand. A little rampaging was acceptable on these occasions, but uncontrolled mayhem was not.

Fuelled by their greyworld celebrity position, the Painball vets were pumped full of I-won hormones and thought they could tackle anyone, and they welcomed the chance to take a poke at a large, solid-looking bouncer such as Zeb the Smokey Bear. He was warned by Jeb never to turn his back on a Painballer: they'd whack you in the kidneys, blam you on the skull with anything handy, squeeze your neck till your eyes popped out of your ears.

How to recognize them? The facial scars. The blank expressions: some of their human mirror neurons had gone missing, along with big chunks of the empathy module: show a normal person a child in pain and they'd wince, whereas these guys would smirk. According to Jeb you had to get quick at reading the signs because if you were dealing with a psycho you needed to know it. Otherwise they could mangle the female talent before you could say *snapped neck*, and this could be costly: trapeze dancers who could do an artistic strip while hanging from one foot high above the crowd didn't come cheap. Or, for that matter, an orgasm-enhancing near-strangulation with a python. A Painball vet might well feel that biting off a python's head would be an unbeatable slice of alpha-chimp display, and even if the bite were to be intercepted, a damaged python would be hard to replace.

Scales kept a regularly updated register of Painballer identities, complete with face pics and ear profiles, which Katrina WooWoo obtained through some obscure back door using God-knows-what as trading cards. She must've been acquainted with someone on the running end of Painball – someone who wanted something she could supply, or else could withhold. Favours and anti-favours were the most respected currency of the deeper pleeblands.

"Hit first and hit dirty, was our rule for those Painball assholes," says Zeb. "As soon as they started to get twitchy. Sometimes we'd spike their drinks, but sometimes we took them out permanently, because if we didn't they'd be back for revenge. We had to be careful what we did with the bodies, though. They might have affiliates."

"What *did* you do with the bodies?" says Toby.

"Let's just say there was always a demand in the deeper pleebs for condensed protein packages, to be utilized for fun, profit, or pet food. But back then, in the early days, before the CorpSeCorps decided to make Painball legal and run it on TV, there weren't very many out-of-control Painballers, so body disposal wasn't a regular thing. More like an improvisation."

"You make it sound like a leisure-time amusement," says Toby. "These were human lives, whatever they'd done."

"Yeah, yeah, I know, slap my wrist, we were bad. Though you didn't get into Painball unless you were already a multiple killer.

"Point of this whole recital being that it wasn't unknown for us bar guards – me and Jeb – to take a personal interest in what went into the mixed drinks. Sometimes we even mixed them."

Kicktail

All this time the white chess bishop with the six mystery pills in it had been kept safely hidden pending further instructions. The only people who knew where it was were Zeb himself, Katrina WooWoo, and Adam.

The hiding place was cunning, and right in plain view, a ploy Zeb had learned from old Slaight of Hand: the obvious is invisible. On a glass shelf behind the bar there was an array of novelty corkscrews, nutcrackers, and salt-and-peppers in the shapes of naked women. The arrangement of their parts was ingenious: the legs would open, the corkscrew would be revealed; the legs would open, the nut would be inserted, the legs would close, the nut would be cracked; the legs would open, the head would be screwed around, the salt or pepper would descend. Laughter all round.

The white bishop had been inserted into the salt cavity of one of these iron maidens, a green lady with enamelled scales. Her head still turned, salt still came out from between her thighs, but the bartenders had been told that this one was fragile – no man was too keen to have his salty sex toy's head come off in mid-screw – so they should use the others instead, on the occasions when salt was required. Which were not frequent, though some liked to sprinkle salt in their beer and on their bar snacks.

Zeb kept an eye on the scaly green girl with the inner bishop. He felt he owed it to Pilar. Still, he was jumpy about the chosen location. What if someone got hold of the thing when he wasn't there, fooled around with it, and found the pills? What if they thought the colourful little oblongs were brain candy, and took one or two just to try them?

Since Zeb had no idea what the pills might actually do to a person, that possibility made him nervous.

Adam, on the other hand, was remarkably cool about it, taking the view that no one would think to look inside a salt shaker unless it ran out of salt. "Though I don't know why I'm saying 'remarkably,'" says Zeb. "He was always a cool little bugger."

"He was living there too?" asks Toby. "At Scales and Tails?" She can't picture it. What would Adam One have done there all day, among the exotic dancers and their unusual fashion items? When she'd known him – once he'd been Adam One – he'd been quietly disapproving of female vanity, and of colour and ostentation and cleavage and leg in a woman's outfit. But there was no way he could have implemented the Gardener religion at Scales or convinced its workers to follow the simple life. Those women must have had expensive manicures. They wouldn't have put up with being required to dig and delve and relocate slugs and snails, even if there had been any vegetable-plot space available at Scales: ladies of the night do not weed by day.

"Nope, he wasn't living at Scales," says Zeb. "Or not living as such. He came and went. It was like a safe house for him."

"You have any idea what he was doing when he wasn't there?" asks Toby.

"Learning things," said Zeb. "Tracking ongoing stories. Watching for storm clouds. Gathering the disaffected under his wing. Making converts. He'd already had his big insight, or whatever you want to call it – the part where God lightning-bolted a message into the top of his skull. *Save my beloved Species in whom I am well pleased*, and all of that: you know the palaver. I never got one of those messages, personally, but it seems Adam did.

"By that time he was well on the way to assembling the God's Gardeners. He'd even bought the flat-roofed pleeb-slum building for the Edencliff Garden using some of the ill-gotten gains we'd hacked out of the Rev's account. Pilar was sending him secret recruits from inside HelthWyzer; she was already planning to join him at Edencliff. However, I didn't know any of that yet."

"Pilar?" asks Toby. "But she can't have been Eve One! She was way too old!" Toby has always wondered about Eve One: Adam had been Adam One, but there had never been any mention of an Eve.

"Nope, it wasn't her," Zeb says.

One of the ongoing stories Adam was tracking was that of their mutual father, the Rev. After a pleasing flurry of activity surrounding his embezzlements from the Church of PetrOleum and the tragic discovery that the Rev's first wife, Fenella, was buried in the rock garden, and then the scandalous publication of the tell-all memoir by his second wife, Trudy, the whole affair had fizzled out.

There was a trial, yes, but the evidence had been inconclusive, or so the jury had decided. Trudy had taken the proceeds from her memoir and gone on vacation to a Caribbean island with – some said – a Tex-Mex lawn-maintenance expert, and had been found washing about in the surf after an impetuous naked moonlight swim. Such dangerous things, undertows, said the local police. She must have been dragged down, and hit her head on a rock. Her companion, whoever he was, had vanished. Understandable, since he might have been blamed; though a whisper was going around that he might also have been paid.

So Trudy was not able to give evidence at the trial, and, without that, what could be proven about anything? The skeleton of Fenella had lain so long in the ground: anyone at all might have put it there. Anonymous men, immigrants as a rule, were always walking around with shovels in the more affluent areas of cities, ready to bang trusting, innocent, horticulturally minded ladies on the head, stuff gardening gloves into their mouths, ravish them in the potting shed despite their muffled screams, and plant hens and chicks on top of them, not to mention lamb's ears and snow-in-summer and other drought-resistant succulents. It was a well-known hazard for female homeowners who took an interest in landscaping.

As for his sizable embezzlements, which were beyond a doubt, the Rev had gone the tried and true route: a public confession of temptation, followed by an account of his sinfulness in failing to resist it, then by a further account of the discovery of that sinfulness, which had been a bitter herb, but through his humiliation had saved him from himself. This was topped up with a grovelling, tearful request for forgiveness from both God and man, in particular from the members of the Church of PetrOleum. Bingo, he was absolved, washed clean of stains, and ready for a new start. For who could find it in his heart to withhold forgiveness from a fellow human being who was so obviously contrite?

"He's on the loose," said Adam. "Exonerated, reinstated. His Oil-Corps associates got him off."

"Fucker," said Zeb. "Make that plural."

"He'll be wanting to hunt us down, and now he'll be able to access the cash to do it," said Adam. "His OilCorps friends will supply it. So be alert."

"Right," said Zeb. "The world needs more lerts." It was an old joke of his. It used to make Adam laugh, or rather smile, but he didn't smile that time.

One evening, when Zeb was loitering around the Scales bar in his Smokey the Bear shades and black suit and snake lapel pin, wearing his non-smile, non-frown, and listening to the chatter from the faux-gold tooth in his mouth, he heard something from one of the guys at the front door that made him stand up a little straighter.

It wasn't a Painballer warning this time. On the contrary.

"Top of the pyramid, four of them, coming in," said the voice. "Three OilCorps, one Church of PetrOleum. That preacher who was on the news."

Zeb felt the adrenalin shooting through his veins. It had to be the Rev. Would the twisted, kiddie-bashing, wife-murdering sadist recognize him or not? He checked the location of every potential missile within reach, in case there might be a need for one. If there was a cry of "Seize that man" or any similar melodrama, he'd hurl a few cut-glass decanters and run like shit. His muscles were so taut they were twanging.

Here they came now, in a festive mood, judging from the japes and laughter and the modified backslaps — more like tentative pats — that were the main phrases of the quasi-brotherly body language permitted at the top levels of the Corps. They were on their way to champagne and tidbits, and everything that went with them. Tips would be lavish, supposing they could all get it up. Why be rich if you can't flaunt it by bestowing patronizing sums of dosh on those who aid you in your quest for self-aggrandizement?

The cool thing for high-status Corps dudes was to pass by the paid security drudges at Scales as if they didn't exist – why make eye contact with a hedge? – which, says Zeb, has probably been the style ever since you could say *Roman emperor*. And that was lucky for Zeb, because the Rev didn't even toss him a glance. Not that he would have spotted Zeb beneath his hairy face waffle and dark shades, with the shaved head, the pointy ears, and all, had he bothered to look. But he didn't bother. Zeb looked at him, though, and the more he looked, the less he liked the view.

The mirror balls were going round and round, sprinkling the clientele and the talent with a dandruff of light. The music was playing, a canned retro tango. Five Scalies in sequins were contorting themselves on the trapezes, tits pointing floorward, bodies curved into a C-shape, one leg on either side of their heads. Their smiles glowed in the blacklight. Zeb backed up to the glass bar shelving, palmed the green lady with the bishop up her snatch, and slid her into his sleeve. "Taking a leak," he said to his partner, Jeb. "Cover for me."

Once in the can, he unscrewed the bishop and abstracted three of the magic beans: a white, a red, and a black. He licked the salt from his fingers and tucked the pills into a front jacket pocket, then returned to his post and eased the scaly lady back into position on the shelf with not even a clink. No one would notice she'd been gone.

The Rev's foursome was having a high old time. It was a celebration, Zeb figured: most likely in aid of the Rev's return to what they all considered to be his normal life. Slithery lovelies were plying them with drinks, while above them the trapeze dancers did boneless twists and spineless twines. They showed bits of this and that, but never the royal flush: Scales was tonier than that, you had to pay extra if you wanted the full peepshow. Manners demanded a display of appreciative lust: the acrobatic sin charade wasn't really the Rev's thing because nobody was suffering, but he was doing a convincing job of pretending. His smile had that Botox look, as if it was a product of nerve damage.

Katrina WooWoo came over to the bar. Tonight she was dressed as an orchid, in a luscious peach colour with lavender accents. March, her python, was draped around her neck, and also over one bare shoulder.

"They've ordered the House Special for their pal," she said to the bartender. "With the Taste of Eden."

"Heavy on the tequila?" said the barkeep.

"Everything in," said Katrina. "I'll tell the girls."

The House Special involved a private feather room with a green satin bedspread and three reptilian Scalies billed as catering to your every whim, and the Taste of Eden was a headbender kicktail guaranteed to deliver maximum bliss. Once that thing had been swallowed the client would be off in a world of wonders all his own. Zeb had tried some of the stuff on offer at Scales, but he'd never drunk the Taste of Eden kicktail. He was afraid of the visions he might have.

There it was now, standing on the counter. It was dark orange and fizzing slightly, and had a swizzle stick with a plastic snake curled around it, skewering a maraschino cherry. The snake was green and sparkly, with big eyes and a smiling lipstick mouth.

Zeb should have resisted his evil impulses. What he did was reckless, he admits that freely. But you only live once, he told himself, and maybe the Rev had used up his once. Zeb wondered which of the three pills to slip into the drink — the white, the red, or the black. But why be stingy? he admonished himself. Why not all?

"Down the hatch, good buddy." "Have a wild trip!" "Up and at 'em!" "Knock 'em dead!" Were such archaic chunks of joshery still uttered on occasions like this? It appeared so. The Rev was patted and treated to a bouquet of softly knowing haw-haws, then led away for his treat by three lithe snakelets. All four of them were *giggling*: eerie to remember that, in retrospect.

Zeb longed to excuse himself from bar duty and slide into the video viewing cubicle where a couple of Scales security personnel monitored the private feather rooms for trouble. He didn't know how those pills would act. Did they make you very sick, and if so, how? Maybe the effect was long-term: maybe those babies didn't kick in for a day, a week, a month. But if it was anything more rapid, he sure as hell wanted to watch.

Doing so, however, would finger him as the perpetrator. So he waited stoically though tensely, ears pricked, humming silently to himself to the tune of "Yankee Doodle":

> *My dad loved walloping little kids,*
> *He loved it more than nooky,*
> *I hope he bleeds from every pore,*
> *And chucks up all his cookies.*

After a few too many repetitions of that, there was some tooth static: someone else was talking to the gatekeeper guys at the front. After what seemed like a long time but wasn't, Katrina WooWoo came through the doorway that led to the private rooms. She was trying to appear casual, but the clicking of her high heels was urgent.

"I need you to come backstage," she whispered to him.

"I'm on bar duty," he said, feigning reluctance.

"I'll call in Mordis from the front. He'll take over. Come right now!"

"Girls okay?" He was stalling: if something bad was happening to the Rev, he wanted it to keep on happening.

"Yes. But they're frightened. It's an emergency!"

"Guy go berserk?" he said. They sometimes did: the effects of the Taste of Eden weren't always predictable.

"Worse than that," she said. "Bring Jeb too."

Raspberry Mousse

The feather room was a cyclone site: a sock here, a shoe there, smears of unidentified substances, bedraggled feathers everywhere. That lump in the corner must've been the Rev, covered by the green satin bedspread. Oozing out from under it was a hand-span of red foam that looked like a badly diseased tongue.

"What happened?" Zeb asked innocently. It was hard to look really innocent with shades on – he'd tried in the mirror – so he took them off.

"I've sent the girls to take showers," said Katrina WooWoo. "They were so upset! One minute they were ..."

"Peeling the shrimp," said Zeb. It was the staff slang for getting a dink out of his clothes, the underpants in particular. There was an art to it, as to everything, said the Scalies. Or a craft. A slow unbuttoning, a long, sensuous unzipping. Hold the moment. Pretend he's a box of candies, lick-a-licious. "Lick-a-licious," Zeb said out loud. He's shaken: the effect on the Rev had been far worse than he'd imagined. He hadn't intended actual death.

"Yes, well, good thing they didn't get that far, because he, well, he simply dissolved, according to the monitors in the video room. They've never seen anything like it. Raspberry mousse, is what they said."

"Crap," said Jeb, who'd lifted a corner of the bedspread. "We need a water-vac, it's like a very sick swimming pool under there. What hit him?"

"The girls say he just started to froth," said Katrina. "And scream, of course. At first. And tear out feathers – those are ruined, they'll have to be destroyed, what a waste. Then it was no longer screaming, it was gurgling. I'm so worried!" She was understating: scared was more like it.

"He had a meltdown. Must be something he ate," said Zeb. He meant it for a joke; or he meant it to be mistaken for a joke.

Katrina didn't laugh. "Oh, I don't think so," she said. "Though you're right, it might have been in food. Nothing he ate here though, no way! It has to be a new microbe. Looks like a flesh-eater, only so speeded up! What if it's really contagious?"

"Where could he have caught it?" said Jeb. "Our girls are clean."

"Off a doorknob?" said Zeb. Another lame joke. Shut up, pinhead, he told himself.

"Lucky our girls had their Biofilm Bodygloves on," said Katrina. "Those will have to be burned. But none of the – none of what came out of – none of whatever it is touched them."

Zeb was getting an incoming call on his tooth: it was Adam. Since when does he have tooth broadcasting privileges? thought Zeb.

"I understand there's been an incident," said Adam. He was tinny and far away.

"It's fucking creepy having your voice in my head," said Zeb. "You sound like a Martian."

"No doubt," said Adam. "But that is not your number-one problem right now. The man who died was our mutual parent, I'm told."

"You were told right," said Zeb, "but who told you?"

He'd gone into a corner of the room so the conversation would be semi-private, out of consideration for others: it was annoying to have to listen to a person talking to their own tooth. Katrina was in another corner with her intramural cell, calling in the Scales cleanup squad, who were bound to be taken aback. Similar things had been known to occur with older guys during the course of House Specials – the kick-tails could be overly powerful for those of diminished bodily abilities and functions – but nothing very similar. Usually it was a stroke or a heart attack. This kind of frothing was unprecedented.

"Katrina called me. Naturally," said Adam. "She keeps me informed."

"She knows he's our . . . ?"

"Not exactly. She knows I have an interest in anything concerning the Corps bookings – especially the OilCorps – so she notified me of the four-party reservation, and of the special surprise arrangements made by three of the clients as a gift to the fourth. Then she sent me the headshots generated automatically by the doorware at the front, and of course I recognized him at once. I was already on the premises, so I came to the front of the house in case I might be needed. I'm out in the bar area now; I'm right beside the glass shelves, where the novelty corkscrews and the salt shakers are displayed."

"Oh," said Zeb. "Good," he added lamely.

"Which one did you use?"

"Which one of what?" said Zeb.

"Don't play innocent," said Adam. "I can count. Six minus three is three. The white, the red, or the black?"

"All of them," said Zeb. There was a pause.

"Too bad," said Adam. "That will make it more difficult for us to determine what exactly was in each one. A more controlled approach would have been preferable."

"Aren't you going to tell me I'm a fucking stupid fuckwit," said Zeb, "for doing such a stupid fucking dickwit thing? Though not in so many words, I guess."

"It was a little spontaneous of you," said Adam, "but worse things could have happened. In the event, it was fortuitous that he didn't recognize you."

"Wait a minute," said Zeb. "You knew he was walking in the door? You didn't warn me?"

"I counted on you to act as the situation would dictate," said Adam. "Nor was my confidence misplaced."

Zeb was outraged: his cunning bastard of a big brother had set him up, the shit! But he'd also trusted Zeb to be competent enough to deal with whatever mayhem might result, so in addition to the outrage he felt all warm and vindicated. *Thank you* didn't really fit the case, so instead he said, "You fucking smartass!"

"Regrettable," said Adam. "And I do regret it. But may I point out that, as a result, that man is permanently off our case. Now, and this is important: get them to collect as much of him – of it – as they can. Put it in a CryoJeenyus Frasket – Katrina always keeps a few on hand for clients with CryoJeenyus contracts. The full-body model would be preferable to the head-only. Many Scales customers who are no longer young have made such arrangements. The protocol is that if they have a — what CryoJeenyus calls 'a life-suspending event' — and when speaking of those who have had their lives suspended, please do avoid the word *death*, as CryoJeenyus employees do, since you will shortly be impersonating one of them. If such a life-suspending event occurs, the client is flash-frozen immediately in the Frasket and shipped to CryoJeenyus for re-animation later, once CryoJeenyus has developed the biotech to do that."

"Which is when pigs can fly," says Zeb. "I hope Katrina's got a giant ice-cube tray."

"Use buckets if necessary," said Adam. "We need to get him — we need to get the effluent to Pilar's cryptic team, out on the east coast."

"Pilar's what?"

"Cryptic team. Our friends," says Adam. "They have day jobs in the biotech Corps: OrganInc, HelthWyzer Central, RejoovenEsense, even CryoJeenyus. But they're helping us at night, *cryptic* being a bio-term for camouflage in, say, caterpillars."

"Since when are you so palsy with caterpillars?" said Zeb. "Are you warping your brain lurking in that dumb MaddAddam Extinctathon name-the-dead-beetle game site?" Adam overrode him.

"The cryptic team will find out what it was, inside the pills. Or is. Let's hope it can't go airborne; we don't think it can yet, or anyone who was in that room will have been contaminated. It appears to be very rapid-acting, so they'd be showing symptoms. As things stand, we believe it's contact-only. Don't let any of the — of the residue touch you."

And don't stick my finger in the goo and then shove it up my ass, Zeb thought. "I'm not a fucking idiot," he said out loud.

"Live up to that pledge. I know you can," said Adam. "I'll see you on the sealed bullet train, with the Frasket."

"We're going where?" said Zeb. "You're coming too?" But Adam had rung off, or hung up, or logged out; whatever you did on the other end of a tooth.

While the plastic-film-dressed and face-masked cleanup team was water-vaccing the Rev into enamelled pails and then funnelling him into sealable freezer-friendly metal flasks, Zeb headed off to become a tidier and sweeter version of Smokey the Bear. He disposed of his black outfit, doomed to incineration, and took a quick antimicrobial-enhanced shower – same product the Scalies used – lathering his face, sanctifying his pits, and Q-tipping his pointy ears.

> *I'm gonna wash that Rev right offa my head,*
> *'Cause he's not only dead, he's red,*
> *He's a red red goo, and a good thing too,*
> *'Cause Daddy I'm through and so are you,*
> *A boobity-doop-de-doop-de-doop-de-doo!*

He did a little two-step, a little hip-wiggle. He liked to sing in the shower, especially when danger threatened.

One more river, he sang while putting on a fresh black suit. *And that's the river of boredom! One more molar, There's one more molar to floss.*

Then he resumed his duties, standing sentinel behind Katrina WooWoo – now dressed as a fruit cluster with a fetching set of tooth marks embroidered on one apple-shaped boob – while she and March the python broke the lamentable news to the three OilCorps execs, having first ordered frozen daiquiris on the house, all around, and a platter of mini-fish-fingers, PeaPod Good-as-Real Scallops – No Bottoms Dragged for These, said the label, as Zeb knew from mooching them in the kitchen – some Gourmet's Holiday Poutine, and a plate of deep-fried NeverNetted Shrimps, a new lab-grown splice.

"Your friend has unfortunately had a life-suspending event," she told the OilCorps execs. "Total bliss can be taxing on the system. But as you know, he had – excuse me, he *has* a contract with CryoJeenyus – full-body, not head-only – so all is well. I'm so sorry for your temporary loss."

"I didn't know that," said one of the execs. "About the contract. I thought you wore a CryoJeenyus bracelet or something; I never saw his."

"Some gentlemen prefer not to advertise the possibility of life suspension," said Katrina smoothly. "They choose the tattoo option, which is applied in a concealed and very private location. Of course, at this enterprise we become aware of all such tattoos, as a casual business acquaintance might not." One more thing to admire about her, thought Zeb, trying not to peer down the front of her apples: she was a tip-top liar. He couldn't have done better himself.

"Makes sense," said the dominant exec.

"In any case, we did discover this fact in time," said Katrina, "and, as you know, the procedure has to be carried out immediately in order to be effective. Luckily we have a fast-track Premium Platinum-level agreement with CryoJeenyus, and their trained operatives are always on call. Your friend is already in a Frasket, and will be on his way to the central CryoJeenyus facility on the east coast almost at once."

"We can't see him?" said the second exec.

"Once the Frasket is sealed and vacuumized — as it now is — it would defeat the purpose to open it," Katrina said, smiling. "I can provide a certificate of authentication from CryoJeenyus. Would you like another frozen daiquiri?"

"Shit," said the third exec. "What do we tell that nutbar church of his? *Fell over getting fracked in a moppet shop* won't go down too well."

"I agree," said Katrina, a little more coldly. She felt Scales was much more than a moppet shop: it was a *total aesthetic experience*, ran the blurb on the website. "But Scales and Tails is well known for its discretion in such matters. That is why it is the number-one choice among discerning gentlemen such as yourselves. With us, you do get what you pay for, and more; and that includes a good cover story."

"Any bright ideas?" said the second exec. He had eaten all the NeverNetted Shrimps and was starting on the scallops. Death made some people hungry.

"Contracted viral pneumonia while working with disadvantaged children in the deeper pleeblands, would be my first suggestion," said Katrina. "That would be a popular choice. But we have our own trained PR personnel to assist you."

"Thank you, ma'am," said the third exec, watching her through narrowed and slightly reddened eyes. "You've been very helpful."

"My pleasure," said Katrina, smiling graciously and leaning forward to let her hand be shaken and then her fingertips kissed while disclosing enough but not too much of her upper torso real-estate. "Anytime. We're here for you."

. . .

"What a gal," says Zeb. "She could have run any of the top Corps with one thumb, no problem."

Toby feels the familiar snarly tendrils of jealousy knotting round her heart. "So did you ever?" she asks.

"Ever what, babe?"

"Ever get into her scaly underthings."

"It's one of my life-span regrets," says Zeb, "but no. I didn't even give it a try. Hands stayed in the pockets, firmly clenched. Jaw clenched likewise. It was an effort to restrain myself, but that's the bare-naked truth: I didn't give it a single grope. Not even a wink."

"Because?"

"One, she was my boss when I was working at Scales. It's not a smart move to roll around on the floor with a woman boss. It confuses them."

"Oh please," says Toby. "That's so twentieth century!"

"Yeah, yeah, I'm a sexist-wexist pig and so forth, but that happens to be accurate. Hormone overdrive craps up efficiency. I've watched it in action – women bosses getting all coy and weird about issuing orders to some bullet-headed stud who's just erased their rational faculties and blown off the top of their heads and made them growl like a rakunk in heat and scream like a dying rabbit. It alters the power hierarchy. 'Take me, take me, write my speech, get me a coffee, you're fired.' So there's that." He pauses. "Plus."

"Plus what?" She's hoping for some revolting feature on the part of Katrina WooWoo, whom, granted, she has never seen, and who is 99.999 per cent likely to be dead; but envy crosses all borders. Maybe she was knock-kneed, or had halitosis or hopeless taste in music. Even a pimple would have been some comfort.

"Plus," says Zeb, "Adam loved her. No doubt of it. I'd never poach in his goldfish pond. He was – he's my brother. He's my family. There's limits."

"You're kidding!" says Toby. "Adam One? In love? With Katrina WooWoo?"

"She was Eve One," says Zeb.

The Train to CryoJeenyus

"That's hard to believe," says Toby. "How do you know?"

Zeb is silent. Will this be a painful story? It's likely: most stories about the past have an element of pain in them, now that the past has been ruptured so violently, so irreparably.

But not, surely, for the first time in human history. How many others have stood in this place? Left behind, with all gone, all swept away. The dead bodies evaporating like slow smoke; their loved and carefully tended homes crumbling away like deserted anthills. Their bones reverting to calcium; night predators hunting their dispersed flesh, transformed now into grasshoppers and mice.

There's a moon now, almost full. Good luck for owls; bad luck for rabbits, who often choose to cavort riskily but sexily in the moonlight, their brains buzzing with pheromones. There's a couple of them down there now, jumping about in the meadow, glowing with a faint greenish light. Some used to think there was a giant rabbit up there on the moon: they could clearly make out its ears. Others thought there was a smiling face, yet others an old woman with a basket. What will the Crakers decide about that when they get around to astrology, in a hundred years, or ten, or one? As they will, or will not.

But is the moon waxing or waning? Her moontime sense isn't as sharp as it used to be in the days of the Gardeners. How many times had she watched over Vigils when the moon was full? Wondering, from time to time, why there was an Adam One but no Eve One, nor ever any mention of such. Now she'll find out.

"Picture it," says Zeb. "Adam and me were on the sealed bullet train together for three days. I'd only seen him twice since we cleared out the Rev's bank account and went our separate ways: in the Happicuppa joint, in the back room at Scales. No time to dig down. So naturally I asked him stuff."

Zeb had to sacrifice his face waffle, of which he'd become moderately fond despite the meticulous upkeep, what with those stubbly mini-squares to sculpt. He clear-cut the thing with a shaver: all that remained of it was a goatee. He had some new head growth – an unconvincing Mo'Hair glue-on from the early days of that Corp – in a shade of glossy pimp-oil brown.

Luckily he could cover up some of the more fraudulent effects with the dorky hat that was part of the CryoJeenyus outfit for the position that would have once been called "undertaker's assistant," though CryoJeenyus used the label Temporary Inertness Caretaker instead. The hat was a modified turban, referencing both magicians and genies. It was reddish in colour and had a flame design on the front.

"Ever-burning flame of life, right?" says Zeb. "When they showed that third-rate magic-show headrag to me, I said, 'You can't be fucking serious! I'm not wearing a boiled tomato on my head!' But then I saw the beauty of it. With it, and with the rest of the ensemble – a purple thing like pyjamas, or maybe a karate concept, with the CryoJeenyus logo plastered across the front – no one could mistake me for anything but an overgrown dim bulb who couldn't get any other job. Frasket-sitting on a train – how pathetic was that? 'If you're where no one expects you to be,' old Slaight of Hand used to say, 'you're invisible.' "

Adam had the same uniform, and he looked even stupider in it than Zeb did. So that was some comfort. Anyway, who was going to see them? They were locked into the special CryoJeenyus car with the Frasket plugged into its own separate generator to keep it sub-zero inside. CryoJeenyus prided itself on being extra secure: DNA theft, not to mention the pilfering of other, larger body parts, was a worry among those who were in love with their own carbon structures: in those circles, the theft of Einstein's brain had not been forgotten.

Thus an armed guard travelled with all Frasket-sitters, riding shotgun near the door. On bona fide CryoJeenyus missions, this individual would have been a member of the consolidated and ever-expanding CorpSeCorps and would have been armed with a spraygun. But since everything about this particular caper was bogus, the role was played by a Scales manager named Mordis. He looked the part: tough, bright eyes like a shiny black beetle, smile impartial as a falling rock.

His weaponry wasn't real, however: the cryptic team could imitate clothing, but they couldn't reproduce that kind of triple-security moving-part tech. So the spraygun was a cunning plastic and painted-foam imitation, which wouldn't matter at all unless someone got close enough to be hit with a fist.

But why would they? As far as anyone else was concerned, this was just a routine dead-run. Or rather, *a ferrying of the subject of a life-suspending event from the shore of life on a round trip back to the shore of life*. It was a mouthful, but CryoJeenyus went in for that kind of evasive crapspeak. They had to, considering the business they were in: their two best sales aids being gullibility and unfounded hope.

"It was the most bizarre trip I ever took," says Zeb. "Dressed up like Aladdin, sitting in a locked train compartment with my brother, who was wearing half a squashed pumpkin on his head, and between us a Frasket containing our dad in the form of soup stock. Though we did put the bones and teeth in there, as well. Those didn't dissolve. There was some discussion at Scales about the osseous materials — you could get a good price for human bones in the deeper pleeblands, where carved artisanal human-products jewellery was a fashion: Bone Bling, it was called. But the cooler heads of Adam and Katrina and, I have to say, your humble self overruled the enthusiasts, because even if you boiled those things there was no telling what microbes might remain. As yet, we knew nothing about them."

A tisket, a tasket, a green and yellow Frasket, Zeb sang.

Adam took out a little notebook and a pencil and wrote: *Watch what you say. We're most likely bugged.*

After showing it to Zeb under cover of his hand, he erased it, and wrote: *And please do not sing. It is very irritating.*

Zeb motioned for the little notebook. After a slight hesitation,

Adam handed it over. Zeb wrote: *FU+PO.* Then he wrote, underneath them: *Fuck You and Piss Off.* Then: *You manage to get yourself laid yet?*

Adam read this and blushed. Watching him blush was a novelty: Zeb had never witnessed such a thing before. Adam was so pale you could almost see his capillaries. He wrote: *None of your business.*

Zeb wrote: *Haha, was it K and did you pay?* Since he had long suspected which way the wind of Adam was blowing.

Adam wrote: *I refuse to have that lady spoken about in such a manner. She has been a devoted furtherer of our efforts.*

Zeb should have written: *What efforts?* Then he would have known more. Instead he wrote, *Haha, hole in one for my score, so to speak :D!! At least you're not gay! :D :D*

Adam wrote: *You are beneath vulgar.*

Zeb wrote: *That would be me! Never mind, I respect true love.* He drew a heart, then a flower. He almost added, *Even if she is running a fancypants blowjob emporium,* but he thought better of it: Adam was getting very huffy, and he might forget himself and take a swipe at Zeb for just about the first time in his life. Then there would be an unseemly scuffle over the remains of their liquefied parent that would not end well for Zeb because he could never bear to deck Adam, not really; so he'd just have to let the pallid little weenie beat him up.

Adam looked mollified – maybe it was the heart and the flower – but still ruffled. He crumpled up all the notebook pages they'd been writing on, then tore them into pieces and went to the can, where – Zeb assumed – he flushed them onto the tracks. Even if some nosy spyster managed to gather them up and stick them together they'd hardly learn anything of interest. Just a bunch of low-calorie dirty talk, of the kind a Frasket-sitter might be expected to employ while killing time out of the hearing of the paying customers.

The rest of the trip passed in silence, Adam with arms folded and a frowny but sanctimonious expression on his face, Zeb humming under his breath while the continent zipped past outside the window.

At the east coast end, the CryoJeenyus dedicated carriage was met by Pilar, posing as a concerned relative of the stiff – or, rather, of the temporarily life-suspended client – and three members from, Zeb assumed, the cryptic team.

"You know two of them," says Zeb. "Katuro and Manatee. The third was a gal we lost during Crake's scoop of the MaddAddamites, when he was designing the Crakers and gathering up the brainslaves for his Paradice Project. She tried to run, and I can only assume she went over an overpass and got turned into car tire mush. But none of that had happened yet."

Pilar shed a few croc tears into a hanky just in case there were any mini-drones or spyware installations around. Then she supervised discreetly as the Frasket was loaded into a long vehicle. CryoJeenyus did not call those vehicles "hearses": they were "Life2Life Shuttles." They were boiled tomato colour and had the perky ever-burning flame of life on the doors: nothing dark to spoil the festive mood.

So into the L2LS went the Rev in his Frasket, headed for an extreme security biosampling unit – not at CryoJeenyus, they weren't equipped for that, but at HelthWyzer Central. Pilar got in as well, and also Zeb. Mordis would change his outfit and head to the local Scales and Tails, where they needed a tougher manager.

Adam would change into his increasingly bizarre streetwear and shuffle off to do whatever it was that Adam did, out there in the deep pleebs. He gave the white bishop to Pilar, having extracted it from the salty cavity of the girl salt shaker: the cryptic team wanted to take a close look at the contents of those pills, and they thought they finally had the equipment to do so without exposing themselves to contagion.

Zeb was slated for yet another identity, which Pilar had already prepared for him: he was to be embedded right inside HelthWyzer Central.

"Do me a favour," said Zeb to Pilar, once she had assured them that the L2LS had been thoroughly swept for spyware. "Run a DNA comparison for me. On the Rev. The guy in the Frasket." He'd never shaken his childhood notion that the Rev was not his real father, and this was surely his last chance to find out.

Pilar said it would be no problem. He handed over a cheek swab sample of himself, improvised on a piece of tissue, and she tucked it carefully inside a small plastic envelope that contained what looked like a dried-up elf ear, wrinkly in appearance, yellow in colour.

"What's that?" he asked her. He wanted to say, "What the fuck's that," but proximity to Pilar did not encourage swearing. "Gremlin from outer space?"

"It's a chanterelle," she said. "A mushroom. An edible variety, not to be confused with the false chanterelle."

"So, will I come out with the DNA of a fungus?"

Pilar laughed. "There's not much chance of that," she said.

"Good," said Zeb. "Tell Adam."

Only problem was, he thought later that night, when drifting off to sleep in his Spartan but acceptable HelthWyzer accommodations – only problem was that if Pilar ran the DNA comparison and the Rev wasn't his dad, then Adam wouldn't be his brother. Adam would be no relation to him at all. No blood relation.

Thus:

Fenella + the Rev = Adam.
Trudy + Unknown Semen Donor = Zeb.
= No shared DNA.

If that was the truth, did he really want to know it?

Lumiroses

Zeb's new title at HelthWyzer Central was that of Disinfector, First Rank. He got a pair of lurid green overalls with the HelthWyzer logo and a big luminous orange *D* on the front; he got a hairnet to keep his own shed follicle-ware from littering the desk spaces of his betters; he got a nose filter cone that made him look like a cartoon pig; he got an endless supply of protective liquid-repelling nanobioform-impermeable gloves and shoes; and, most importantly, he got a passkey.

Only for the bureaucratic offices, however: not for the labs. Those were in another building. But you never could tell what sort of intel a nimble-fingered robinhooder with a few lines of entry code slipped to him by underground cryptics might be able to scoop off an untended computer, late at night, when all good citizens were sound asleep in other people's beds. HelthWyzer was somewhat porous in the spouse department.

Once upon a time Zeb's Disinfector position would have been called "cleaner," and before that "janitor," and before that "charwoman"; but this was the twenty-first century and they'd added some nanobioform consciousness to the title. To deserve that title Zeb was supposed to have passed a rigid security check, for what hostile Corp — possibly from a foreign clime — wouldn't think of disguising one of their keyboard pirates as a minor functionary and ordering him to grab whatever he could find?

To qualify as a Disinfector, Zeb was also supposed to have taken a training course replete with updated modern babble about where germs might lurk and how to render them unconscious. Needless to say, he hadn't taken it; but Pilar had given him the condensed version before he started.

Germs were said to hang out on the usual toilet seats, floors, sinks, and doorknobs, of course. But also on elevator buttons, on telephone receivers, and on computer keyboards. So he had to wipe down all of these with antimicrobial cloths and zap them with death rays, in addition to the floor-washing in hallways and such, and the dust-sucking on the carpets in the plushier offices to pick up anything the daily robots might have missed. Those things were always rolling to and fro, backing up to wall outlets to plug themselves in and replenish their battery power, then scuttling away again, emitting beeping sounds so you wouldn't trip over them. It was like navigating a beach littered with giant crabs. When he was alone on a floor he used to kick them into corners or turn them over on their backs, just to see how fast they could recover.

In addition to the outfit he got a new name, which was Horatio.

"Horatio?" says Toby.

"Laughter is uncalled for," says Zeb. "It was someone's idea of what a semi-legal Tex-Mex family who snuck under the Wall might have called a son they hoped would make good in the world. They thought I looked kind of Tex-Mex, or maybe like a hybrid that contained some of that DNA. Which I do, as was discovered not long after that."

"Oh," says Toby. "Pilar ran the DNA comparison."

"You got it," says Zeb. "Though it took a while for me to access the news. She couldn't really be seen with me, because why would she know me? Anyway we'd have to go out of our way to meet, we were on different shifts. So we'd fixed up a fallback code when I gave her my cell sample.

"Before then, when I was on my way in the CryoJeenyus train car and she was putting my Disinfector identity together and getting it slotted into the system, she'd already learned I'd be cleaning the women's washroom down the hall from the lab where she was working. I was night shift — it was all male Disinfectors for that shift, they didn't want any groping or screaming, which might have taken place with a gender mix. So I had the run of the floor after dark. Second cubicle from the left: that was the one I needed to watch."

"She left a note inside the toilet tank?"

"Nothing so obvious. Those toilet tanks were routinely checked; only an amateur would stash anything important in there. The drop-box was that square container thing they have in those washrooms, for what-have-you. Those items you aren't supposed to flush. But it wouldn't be a note, way too telltale."

"So, a signal?" Toby wonders what kind. One for joy, two for sorrow? But one and two of what?

"Yeah. Something that wouldn't be out of place, but wouldn't be the usual. Pits, was what she decided."

"Pits? What do you mean, pits?" Toby tries to visualize pits. Armpits, holes in the ground? "Like peach pits?" she guesses.

"Correct. Might be from a lunch that got eaten in the washroom. Some of the secretary-type women did that – they sat in the can for some peace and quiet. I did find sandwich remains in those boxes: the odd bacon rind, the odd cheesefood fragment. There was a lot of time pressure in HelthWyzer, and more of it the farther down the status ladder you were, so they liked to sneak breathers."

"What was the pit selection?" Toby asks. "For the yes and the no?" The way Pilar thought has always intrigued her: she wouldn't have made the fruit selections haphazardly.

"Peach pit for no: no relationship to the Rev. Date pit for yes: worse luck, the Rev is your dad, hear it and weep because you're at least half psychopath."

The peach choice makes sense to Toby: peaches were valued among the Gardeners as having been one of the possible candidates for the Fruit of Life in Eden. Not that the Gardeners disparaged dates, or any other fruit that had not been chemically sprayed.

"HelthWyzer must have had access to some pretty expensive fruit. I thought the peach and apple yields plummeted around then, when the big bee die-off was going on. And the plums," she adds. "And the citrus varieties."

"HelthWyzer was making a lot of money," says Zeb. "Raking it in, from their vitamin pill business and the medical drugs end. So they could afford the cyber-pollinated imports. It was one of the perks of working at HelthWyzer, the fresh fruit. Only for the higher-ups, naturally."

"Which did you find?" says Toby. "Pit-wise."

"Peach. Two pits. She'd underlined it."

"How did you feel about that?" Toby asks.

"About the overkill on the expensive fruit?" says Zeb. He's dodging emotion.

"About finding out that your father wasn't your father," says Toby patiently. "You must have felt something."

"Okay. I felt, *I knew it*," says Zeb. "I always like to be right, who doesn't? Also less guilty about, you know. Frothing him to death."

"You felt guilty about that?" says Toby. "Even if he had been your father, he was such a . . ."

"Yeah, I know. But still. Blood is thicker than blood. It would've bothered me some. The downside was the Adam end of it. I didn't feel so good about that: all of a sudden he was no relation to me. No genetic relation, that is."

"Did you tell him?" Toby asks.

"Nope. As far as I was concerned, I figured he was my brother. Joined at the head. We shared a lot of stuff."

"Now I'm coming to a part you won't like much, babe," says Zeb.

"Because it's about Lucerne?" says Toby. Zeb's not stupid. He must have suspected for a long time how she'd felt about Lucerne, his live-in at the Gardeners. Lucerne the Irritating, dodger of communal weeding duties, shirker of women's sewing groups, sufferer from frequent excuse-making headaches, whiny possessor of Zeb, neglectful mother of Ren. Lucerne the Luscious, one-time denizen of the HelthWyzer Corp, married to a top geek. Lucerne, the romantic fantasist who'd run away with the raggle-taggle Zeb because she'd seen too many movies in which beautiful women did that.

Zeb, in Lucerne's version, had been crazed with irresistible and relentless desire for her. He'd been cross-eyed with lust when he'd spotted her in her pink negligee at the AnooYoo Spa while he was planting lumiroses in his capacity as gardener, and he'd made mad passionate love to her right there and then, on the dew-damp morning grass. Toby had heard that story many times from Lucerne herself, back at the Gardeners, and she'd liked it less every time. If she leaned over the railing and spat, she might be able to hit the very spot where Zeb and Lucerne had first rolled around on the lawn. Or near enough.

"Right," says Zeb. "Lucerne. That's what came next in my life. I can skip over it if you like."

"No," says Toby. "I've never heard your side of it. But Lucerne told me about the lumirose petals. How you strewed them over her pulsating body and so forth." She tries not to sound envious, but it's difficult. Has anyone ever strewn lumirose petals over her own pulsating body, or even thought about it? No. She lacks the temperament for petal-strewing. She would spoil the moment – "What are you doing with those silly petals?" Or she would laugh, which would be fatal. Right now she needs to shut up and hold back on the commentary or she won't get the story.

"Yeah, well, petal-strewing comes naturally to me, I used to be in the magic biz," says Zeb. "It distracts the attention. But some of what she told you was most likely true."

The first time Zeb and Lucerne set eyes on each other was not at the AnooYoo Spa, however. It was in the women's washroom that Zeb was supposed to be cleaning – was cleaning, in fact – while pawing through the detritus in the metal box for pits, whether peach or date. He hadn't found any yet – it was before Pilar had the results of the Rev mix 'n' match DNA test, or possibly before she could amass the necessary pits – so he was emerging from the second cubicle from the left empty-handed, pit-wise. When who should come into the Women's Room but Lucerne.

"This was the middle of the night?" says Toby.

"Affirmative. What was she doing there? I asked myself. Either she was a robinhooder like me, in which case she was really inept because she'd got caught out of place. Or else she was having it off with some HelthWyzer exec who'd given her an access key to the building so they could flail on his fancy carpet while he was supposed to be working late at the office and she was supposed to be at the gym. Though it was late even for that."

"Or both," says Toby. "The having it off and the robinhooding, both."

"Yeah. They combine well: each can provide an excuse for the other. *Oh no, I wasn't pilfering, I was only cheating on my husband. Oh no, I wasn't cheating, I was only pilfering.* But it was the first one of those, for sure. No mistaking the symptoms."

Lucerne gave a little scream when she saw Zeb emerging from the cubicle in his impermeable gloves and his alien-from-outer-space nose cone. It wasn't the first time that night she'd given a little scream, in his opinion: she was flushed and breathless, and what you might call dishevelled. Or maybe unbuttoned. Or, if you were being fancy, in disarray. Needless to say, she was very attractive at that moment.

Oh, needless to say, thinks Toby.

"What are you doing in the Ladies?" Lucerne said accusingly. The first rule: when caught wet-handed, accuse first. She did say Ladies, not Women's. That was a clue in itself.

"To what?" says Toby.

"Her character. She had a pedestal complex. She wanted to be on one. Ladies was a step higher than Women."

Zeb shoved his nose cone up onto his forehead: now he looked like a blunted rhinoceros. "I'm a Disinfector, First Rank," he added impressively but pompously. There's something about a gorgeous woman who's obviously been shagging another man that brings out the pompous in a guy: it's a wound to his ego. "What are *you* doing in this *building*?" he counter-accused. He noted the wedding ring. Aha, he thought. Caged lioness. Needs a holiday from the tedium.

"I had some work to finish up," Lucerne lied, as convincingly as she could. "My presence here is entirely legitimate. I have a pass." Zeb could have called her on it, but he admired a woman who could use the word *legitimate* in such a fraudulent context. So he did not march her off to Security, which would have triggered a check via the spouse, and set off unpleasant repercussions for the lover, and would almost certainly have resulted – come to think of it – in Zeb himself being fired. So he let her get away with it.

"Right, okay, sorry," he said with acceptable hangdog servility.

"Now, if you don't mind, this is the *Ladies*, and I'd like some privacy, Horatio," she said, caressing the name on his tag. She gazed deep into his eyes. It was a plea — *Don't rat me out* — and also a promise: *One day I'll be yours.* Not that she intended to honour that promise.

Well played, thought Zeb as he made his exit.

Thus, when he and Lucerne encountered each other for the second time, in the first flush of dawn, she barefoot and inadequately concealed in a diaphanous pink negligee, he with a phallic spade and an ardent lumirose bush in hand, right down there on the freshly sodded lawn of the just-completed AnooYoo Spa in the middle of Heritage Park, she recognized him. And she remembered that he'd once been Horatio, but was now, mysteriously — as his AnooYoo Spa grounds-keeper's name tag had it — Atash.

"You were at HelthWyzer," she'd said. "But you weren't . . ." So, naturally, he'd kissed her, fervently and with unrestrainable passion. Because she couldn't talk and kiss at the same time.

"Naturally," says Toby. "You were supposed to be who? What's *Atash?*"

"Iranian," says Zeb. "Immigrant grandparents. Why not? There were a lot of them came over in the late twentieth. It was safe enough as long as I never bumped into any other Iranians and they started asking genealogy stuff, and where was your family from. Though I'd memorized the whole identity, just in case. I had a good backstory — just enough disappearances and atrocities in it to account for any time/place discrepancies."

"So Lucerne meets Atash, and suspects he's really Horatio," says Toby. "Or vice versa." She wants to get over the hurtful parts as quickly as possible: with luck, the hot, irresistible sex and the petal-strewing that Lucerne had never tired of describing to Toby won't be mentioned again.

"Right. And that wasn't good, because I'd had to go missing from HelthWyzer very fast. One of the computers had an alarm on it I didn't spot until too late, and it showed that somebody'd been in there. I could tell I'd triggered it right after I did it, and they were going to start tracking who'd been in the building at the time, and that would pinpoint me. I used the MaddAddam chatroom and called for emergency help, and the cryptics got hold of Adam. He had a contact who could stick me into the AnooYoo Spa gardening job, though we both realized it was a stopgap and I'd have to move on soon."

"So, she knows, and you know she knows, and she knows you know she knows," says Toby. "At the lawn encounter."

"Correct. I had two choices: murder or seduction. I chose the most attractive."

"Understood," says Toby. "I'd have done the same." He's made it sound like a seduction of convenience, but they both know there was more to it than that. Diaphanous pink negligees are their own excuse for being.

Lucerne was bad luck in some ways, said Zeb. Though she was good luck in others, because you couldn't deny that she —

"You can skip that part," says Toby.

"Okay, short version: she had me by the nuts, more ways than one. But I hadn't ratted on her that time in the washroom, and she was inclined to return the favour as long as I was attentive enough to her. Then she got hooked on me, and you know the rest: nothing would do but an elopement with a mystery man first spotted when wearing a nose of a pig.

"I moved us around inside the deeper pleeblands, which she found romantic at first. Luckily no one — no one in the CorpSeCorps — was much interested in her disappearance, because she hadn't stolen any IP. Wives did skedaddle from the Compounds out of sheer boredom, it wasn't unheard of. The CorpSeCorps regarded such defections as private, insofar as they regarded anything as private. They didn't bother with them much, especially if the husband wasn't agitating. Which it appears that Lucerne's husband did not.

"Trouble is, Lucerne took Ren with her. Cute little girl, I liked her. But it was way too dangerous for her in the deeper pleeblands. Kids like that could get snatched for the chicken-sex trade just walking along the street, even if they were with adults. There'd be a pleebrat mob scuffle, some SecretBurgers red sauce tossing, an overturned stand or solarcar — in other words, a honking big misdirection — and when you looked again, your child would be gone. I couldn't risk that."

· · ·

Zeb got a few more alterations done to his ears and fingerprints and irises – they'd know by now he'd been up to no good on the Helth-Wyzer computers, they'd be looking for him – and then . . .

"And then the three of you turned up at the God's Gardeners," says Toby. "I remember that; I wondered from the first what you were doing there. You didn't fit in with the rest of them."

"You mean I hadn't taken the vow of whatnot and drunk the Elixir of Life? God loves you, and he also loves aphids?"

"More or less."

"No. I hadn't. But Adam had to put up with me anyway, didn't he? I was his brother."

Edencliff

"Adam already had his ecofreakshow up and running by that time," says Zeb. "At the Edencliff Rooftop Garden. You were there. So were Katuro and Rebecca. Nuala — wonder what happened to her? Marushka Midwife, and the others. And Philo. Too bad about him."

"Freakshow?" says Toby. "That's not very kind. Surely the God's Gardeners was more than that."

"Yeah, it was," says Zeb. "Granted. But the pleebland slumfolk tagged it as a freakshow. Just as well: best to be thought of as harmless and addled and poor, in those parts. Adam did nothing to discourage that view; in fact, he encouraged it. Roaming around in the pleebs wearing the simple but eye-catching garb of a lunatic recycler with his choir in tow singing nutbar hymns, then preaching the love of hoofed animals in front of SecretBurger stands — you'd have to be lobotomized to do that, was the street verdict."

"If he hadn't done those things I wouldn't be here," says Toby. "Him and the Gardener kids grabbed me during a street brawl. I was working — I was trapped at SecretBurgers at the time, and the manager had a thing for me."

"Your pal Blanco," says Zeb. "Third-time Painball vet, as I recall."

"Yes. Girls he had a thing for ended up dead, and I was next on the list. He was already at the violent stage, he was working up to the kill; you could feel it. So I owe a lot to Adam — to Adam One, as I always knew him. Freakshow or not," she says defensively.

"Don't get it wrong," says Zeb. "He's my brother. We had our disagreements, and he had his way of doing things and I had mine, but that's different."

"You didn't mention Pilar," says Toby to deflect the conversation from Adam One. It's uncomfortable for her to listen to criticism of him. "She was there too. At Edencliff."

"Yeah, HelthWyzer finally got too much for her. She'd been feeding inside stuff to Adam, which was useful to him — he liked to know who might jump ship from a Corp, come over to the side of virtue, which was his side, naturally. But she said she couldn't stay there any longer. With the CorpSeCorps takeover of so-called law-and-order functions, the Corps had the power to bulldoze and squash and erase anything they liked. Their addiction to making a buck was becoming toxic for her: it was poisoning, I quote, her soul.

"The cryptics helped her put together a cover story that allowed her to vanish without inspiring any trackers: she'd had an unfortunate stroke, with instant shipment to CryoJeenyus in a Frasket, and presto, there she was on top of a pleebland tenement building, dressed in a cloth bag and mixing potions."

"And growing mushrooms, and teaching me about maggots, and keeping bees. She was very good at it," says Toby a little ruefully. "Convincing. She had me talking to the bees. I was the one who told them when she died."

"Yeah. I remember all of that. But she wasn't bullshitting," said Zeb. "She believed the whole sackful, in a way. That's why she was willing to run the risks she did at HelthWyzer. Remember what happened to Glenn's dad? She could have gone off an overpass, like him. If they'd caught her; especially if they'd caught her with that white bishop and the three pills."

"She held on to those?" says Toby. "I thought she was going to have them analyzed. After Adam gave them to her."

"She decided it was too dangerous," says Zeb. "For anyone to open them up and maybe let out whatever was inside them. They didn't know how to get rid of them. So that bishop stayed right inside HelthWyzer Central as long as she was there. She brought it out with her when she left, and slipped those pills into her own white bishop, in the set she hand-carved. We played with that set of hers, you and me, that time I was recovering. From getting sliced up on one of those pleeb missions I was running for Adam."

Toby has an image of it: Zeb in the shade, on a hazy afternoon. His arm. Her own hand, moving the white bishop, the death-carrier. Unknown to her then, like so much.

"You always played Black," she says. "What happened to that bishop when Pilar died?"

"She willed her set to Glenn, along with a sealed letter. She'd taught him to play chess, back at HelthWyzer West, when he was little. But by the time she died, his mother had married the guy she'd been fooling around with — so-called Uncle Pete — and they'd been upgraded to HelthWyzer Central. Pilar kept in touch with Glenn through the cryptics, and Glenn was the one who arranged the cancer tests for her, found out she was terminal."

"What was in the letter?"

"It was sealed. How to open the bishop, is my guess. I would have filched it, but Adam had firm control of it."

"So Adam just handed that stuff over, the chess set with the pills inside? To Glenn — to Crake? He was only a teenager."

"Pilar said he was mature for his age, and Adam felt Pilar's death-bed wishes should be respected."

"What about you? It was before I became an Eve, but you were on the council then. They discussed important decisions like that. You must have had an opinion. You were an Adam — Adam Seven."

"The others agreed with Adam One. I thought it was a bad idea. What if the kid tried those things out on someone without knowing exactly what they'd do, the way I had?"

"He must have, later," says Toby. "With some additions of his own. That must've been the core of the BlyssPluss pills: what you got after you'd experienced the bliss."

"Yeah," says Zeb. "I think you're right."

"Do you think Pilar knew what use he'd make of those microbes or viruses or whatever they were?" she asks. "Eventually?" She remembers Pilar's wrinkled little face, her kindness, her serenity, her strength. But underneath, there had always been a hard resolve. You wouldn't call it meanness or evil. Fatalism, perhaps.

"Let's put it this way," says Zeb. "All the real Gardeners believed the human race was overdue for a population crash. It would happen anyway, and maybe sooner was better."

"But you weren't a real Gardener."

"Pilar thought I was, because of my Vigil. Part of the deal with Adam One was that I had to take on a title, that Adam Seven thing: he said it would confer the needed authority, as he put it. Status enhancer. To become one of those, you had to undergo a Vigil. See what was going on with your spirit animal."

"I did that," said Toby. "Talking tomato plants, in-depth stars."

"Yeah, all of that. I don't know what old Pilar mixed into the enhancer, but it was potent."

"What did you see?"

A pause. "The bear. The one I killed and ate, when I was walking out of the Barrens."

"Did it have a message for you?" says Toby. Her own spirit animal had been enigmatic.

"Not exactly. But it gave me to understand that it was living on in me. It wasn't even pissed with me. It seemed quite friendly. Amazing what happens when you fuck with your own neurons."

Once he was Adam Seven, Zeb could install himself and Lucerne and little Ren as bona fide members of the God's Gardeners. They didn't meld very well. Ren was homesick for the Compound and her father, and Lucerne had too great an interest in nail polish to make it as a female Gardener. Her investment in vegetable preparation was nil, and she hated the required outfits – the dark, baggy dresses, the bib aprons. Zeb ought to have known she wasn't going to stick with this arrangement, over time.

Zeb himself had no affinity for slug and snail relocation or soap-making or kitchen cleanup, so he and Adam came to an understanding about what his duties would be. He taught the kids survival skills, and Urban Bloodshed Limitation, which was street fighting viewed from a loftier perspective. As the Gardeners gathered members and expanded, and set up branch locations in different cities, he ran courier among the different groups. The Gardeners refused to use cellphones or technology of any kind; apart, that is, from the one secret souped-up computer that Zeb kept at his own disposal, and fitted out with spyware so he could snoop on the CorpSeCorps, and firewalled up the yin-yang.

* * *

Running courier for Adam had its advantages — he was away from home, so he didn't have to listen to Lucerne's complaints. But it also had its disadvantages — he was away from home, which gave Lucerne more to complain about. She liked to nag on about his commitment issues: why, for instance, had he never asked her to go through the God's Gardeners Partnership ceremony with him?

"Where you jumped over a bonfire together and then traded green branches while everyone stood in a circle, and then they had some kind of pious banquet," says Zeb. "She really wanted me to do that with her. I said as far as I was concerned it was a meaningless empty symbol. Then she'd accuse me of humiliating her."

"If it was meaningless, why didn't you do it?" says Toby. "It might have satisfied her. Made her happier."

"Fat chance," says Zeb. "I just didn't want to. I hated being pushed."

"She was right, you had commitment issues," says Toby.

"Guess so. Anyway, she dumped me. Went back to the Compounds, took Ren with her. And then I wanted the Gardeners to get more activist, and everything unravelled."

"I wasn't there any more, by that time," says Toby. "Blanco got out of Painball and went after me. I was a liability to the Gardeners. You helped me change my identity."

"Years of practice." He sighs. "After you left, things got severe. The God's Gardeners was getting too big and successful for the CorpSe-Corps. To them, it looked like a resistance movement in the making.

"Adam was using the Garden as a safe house for escapees from the BioCorps, and they were beginning to figure that out; so the CorpSemen were paying the pleebmobs to attack us. Being a pacifist, Adam One couldn't bring himself to weaponize the Garden. I could've helped him turn a toy potato gun into an effective short-range shrapnel thrower, but he wouldn't hear of it. It was too unsaintly for him."

"You're making fun," says Toby.

"Just describing. No matter what was at stake, he couldn't go on the offensive, not directly. Remember, he was the firstborn; the Rev got hold of him early, before either of us figured out what a fraud the murderous old bugger actually was. What stuck with Adam was that he had to be good. Gooder than good, so God would love him. Guess he was going to do the Rev thing himself, but do it right – everything the Rev had pretended to be, he would be in reality. It was a tall order."

"But none of that stuck with you."

"Not so I noticed. I was the devil-kid, remember? That let me off the goodness hook. Adam depended on that: he never would have turned the Rev into a raspberry soda with his own two hands. He just put me in the way of it. Even so, he had some guilt issues: the Rev was his father, like it or not, and honour your parents, etcetera, even if one of them had buried the other one in the rock garden. He felt he should be forgiving. He beat himself up a lot, Adam did. It was worse after he lost Katrina WooWoo."

"She went off with someone else?"

"Nothing so pleasant. The Corps decided to take over the sex trade: it was so lucrative. They bought a few politicians, got it legalized, set up SeksMart, forced everyone in the trade to roll in. Katrina played at first, but then they wanted to institute policies she found unaccept-able. 'Institute policies,' that's how they put it. She had scruples, so she became inconvenient. They got rid of the python too."

"Oh," says Toby. "I'm sorry."

"So was I," says Zeb. "Adam was more than sorry. He pined, he dwindled. Something went missing in him. I think he'd had a dream of installing Katrina in the Garden. Not that it would have worked out. Wrong wardrobe preferences."

"That's very sad," says Toby.

"Yeah. It was. I should've been more understanding. Instead, I picked a fight."

"Oh," says Toby. "Only you?"

"Maybe both of us. But it was no holds barred. I said he was just like the Rev, really, only inside out, like a sock: neither one of them gave a shit about anyone else. It was always their way or zero. He said I'd always had criminal tendencies, and that was why I couldn't understand pacifism and inner peace. I said that by doing nothing he was colluding with the powers that were fucking the planet, especially the OilCorps and the Church of PetrOleum. He said I had no faith, and that the Creator would sort the earth out in good time, most likely very soon, and that those who were attuned and had a true love for the Creation would not perish. I said that was a selfish view. He said I listened to the whisperings of earthly power and I only wanted attention, the way I always had as a child when I pushed the boundaries." He sighs again.

"Then what?" says Toby.

"Then I got mad. So I said something I wish I'd never said." A pause. Toby waits. "I said he wasn't really my brother, not genetically. He was no relation to me." Another pause. "He didn't believe me at first. I backed it up, I told him about the test Pilar had done. He just crumpled."

"Oh," says Toby. "I'm sorry."

"I felt terrible right away, but I couldn't unsay it. After that we tried to patch it up and paper it over. But things festered. We had to go our own ways."

"Katuro went with you," says Toby. She knows this for a fact. "Rebecca. Black Rhino. Shackleton, Crozier, and Oates."

"Amanda, at first," says Zeb. "She got out, though. Then new ones joined. Ivory Bill, Lotis Blue, White Sedge. All of them."

"And Swift Fox," says Toby.

"Yeah. And her. We thought Glenn — we thought Crake was our inside guy, feeding us stuff from the Corps through the MaddAddam chatroom. But all along, he was setting us up so he could drag us into the Paradice dome to do his people-splicing for him."

"And his plague-virus-mixing?" says Toby.

"Not from what I hear," says Zeb. "He did that on his own."

"To make his perfect world," says Toby.

"Not perfect," says Zeb. "He wouldn't claim that. More like a reboot. And he succeeded in his own way. Up to now."

"He didn't anticipate the Painballers," says Toby.

"He should have. Or something like them," says Zeb.

It's very quiet, down there in the forest. A Craker child is singing a little in its sleep. Around the swimming pool the Pigoons are dreaming, emitting small grunts like puffs of smoke. Far away something cries: a bobkitten?

There's a faint cool breeze; the leaves go about their business, which is rustling; the moon travels through the sky, moving towards its next phase, marking time.

"You should get some sleep," says Zeb.

"Both of us should," says Toby. "We'll need our energy."

"I'll spell you – two on, two off. Wish I was twenty years younger," says Zeb. "Not that those Painball guys are in great shape, you'd think. God knows what they've been eating."

"The Pigoons are fit enough," says Toby.

"They can't pull triggers," says Zeb. He pauses. "If we both come out of this tomorrow, maybe we should do the bonfire thing. With the green branches."

Toby laughs. "I thought you said it was a meaningless empty symbol."

"Even a meaningless empty symbol can mean something some-times," says Zeb. "You rejecting me?"

"No," says Toby. "How could you even think it?"

"I fear the worst," says Zeb.

"Would that be the worst? Me rejecting you?"

"Don't push a guy when he's feeling skinless."

"I just have trouble believing you're serious," says Toby.

Zeb sighs. "Get some sleep, babe. We'll work it out later. Tomor-row's on the way."

Eggshell

Muster

Peach-coloured haze in the east. Day is breaking, so cool and delicate at first, the sun not yet a hot spotlight. The crows are abroad, signalling to one another. *Caw! Cawcaw! Caw!* What are they saying? *Look out! Look out!* Or maybe: *Party time soon!* Where there are wars, there will be crows, the carrion-fanciers. And ravens too, the warbirds, the eyeball gourmands. And vultures, the holy birds of yore, old connoisseurs of rot.

Dump the morbid soliloquies, Toby tells herself. What's needed is a positive outlook. That was what trumpet fanfares were for, and drums, and march music. We are invincible, that music told the soldiers. They had to believe in them, those lying melodies, because who can walk intrepidly towards death without? The bear-shirted berserkers were said to have doped themselves up before battle with northern hallucinogenic fungus: *Amanita muscaria*, perhaps, or so said Pilar, at the Gardeners. *Historical Mushroom Practices, for senior students only.*

Maybe I should spike the water bottles, she thinks. Poison your brain, then stride forth and kill people. Or be killed.

She stands, unwinds herself from the pink bedspread, shivers. There's been a dew: dampness beads her hair, her eyebrows. Her foot's asleep. Her rifle is where she left it, within reach; and the binoculars as well.

Zeb's already up, leaning on the railing. "I dozed off last night," she says to him. "Not much of a watchperson. Sorry."

"So did I," he says. "It's okay, the Pigoons would've sounded the alarm."

"Sounded?" she says, laughing a little.

"You're such a stickler. Okay, grunted the alarm. Our porky pals have been busy."

Toby looks where he's looking: over and down. The Pigoons have levelled the meadow, all the way around the spa building, wherever there were tall weeds or shrubs. Five of the larger ones are still at work, trampling and rolling on anything higher than an ankle.

"Nobody's going to be sneaking up on them, that's for sure," says Zeb. "Clever buggers, they know about cover." They've left one tuft of foliage in the middle distance, Toby notes. She peers at it with the binoculars. It must mark the remains of that boar she'd killed, back when there was a turf war between her and the Pigoons over the subject of the AnooYoo garden. Oddly enough they hadn't devoured the carcass, though they'd seemed willing enough to eat their dead piglet. Was there a hierarchy in such matters, among them? Sows eat their farrow, but nobody eats the boars? What next, commemorative statues?

"Too bad about the lumiroses," she says.

"Yeah, planted them myself. But they'll grow back. Darn things are as hard to kill as kudzu, once they get going."

"What will the Crakers have for breakfast, though?" says Toby. "Now that the foliage is gone. We can't have them wandering over there, close to the forest."

"The Pigoons thought of that too," says Zeb. "Look beside the swimming pool."

Sure enough, there's a heap of fresh fodder. The Pigoons must have gathered it, since there's no one else around.

"That's considerate," says Toby.

"Crap, they're smart," says Zeb. "Speaking of which." He points.

Toby lifts the binoculars. Three medium-sized Pigoons, two spotted ones and a third that's mostly black, are approaching from the north at a brisk trot. The squad of huge bulldozing Pigoons assiduously levelling the meadow roll themselves upright and lollop out to meet them. There's some grunting, some nuzzling. All ears are forward, all tails are curled and twirling: they're not frightened or angry, anyway.

"I wonder what they're saying?" Toby asks.

"We'll find out," says Zeb, "when they're damn ready to tell us. We're just the infantry as far as they're concerned. Dumb as a stump, they must think, though we can work the sprayguns. But they're the generals. I'd bet they've got their strategy all worked out."

Rebecca must have been ferreting around, discovering odds and ends. For breakfast they have soybits that have been soaked in Mo'Hair milk and sweetened with sugar. On the side, for a treat, a teaspoonful of Avocado Body Butter. The AnooYoo Spa had gone in for cosmetic products that sounded a lot like food: Chocolate Mousse Facial, Lemon Meringue Exfoliating Masque. And the various body butters, so rich in essential lipids.

"There was some of that stuff left?" says Toby. "I was sure I ate it all."

"It was in the kitchen, hidden in one of the big soup tureens," says Rebecca. "Maybe you put it there yourself, and forgot. You must've been building up an Ararat cache somewhere in this building, all the time you worked here."

"Yes, but it was in the supply room," says Toby. "Here and there. I disguised it inside the colon cleanser bulk packaging. I wouldn't have left any of my own supplies in the kitchen; someone might have found them. It was most likely one of the staff who hid it. They used to try that – make off with a little of the high-end AnooYoo line, sell it on the pleebland grey market. But I did an inventory every two weeks, so usually I caught them."

Not that she always reported them: the help was not overpaid. Why wreck a life?

Breakfast concluded, they assemble in the main foyer, where once a welcoming pink fruit-based drink, with or without alcohol, was served to the arriving clients. The MaddAddamites are all present, and the former God's Gardeners. One of the boars is also in attendance, and, staying close to it, little Blackbeard. The rest of the Crakers are still out by the swimming pool munching on their pile of breakfast fodder. So are the rest of the Pigoons, similarly munching.

"So," says Zeb. "Here's where we stand. We know the direction the enemy is taking. There are three of them, not two. The pigs – the Pigoons – are sure of that. They haven't seen these guys clearly – the pig scouts kept well out of sight to avoid being shot – but they've tracked them."

"How far away?" says Rhino.

"Far enough. They've got a head start on us. But, in our favour, the Pigoons say they can't go really fast because one of the three is limping. Dragging a foot. That right?" he says to Blackbeard, who nods.

"A smelly foot," he says.

"That's the good news. The bad news is that they're heading towards the RejoovenEsense Compound. Which most likely means the Paradice dome."

"Oh fuck," says Jimmy. "The spraygun cellpacks! They'll find them!"

"Think they're going for those?" says Zeb. "Sorry. Stupid question. We have no way of knowing what they intend."

"If they aren't just wandering around, we can assume they have a goal," says Katuro. "The third one – he might be directing them."

"We need to head them off," says Rhino. "Keep them out of there. Otherwise they'll be well armed, and for a long time."

"And after a short time we won't be," says Shackleton. "We're already running low on the cellpacks."

"So, only question," says Zeb. "Who comes with us, who stays here. Some of that's self-evident. Rhino, Katuro, Shackleton, Crozier, Manatee, Zunzuncito, coming. And Toby, of course. All the pregnant women, staying. Ren, Amanda, Swift Fox. Anyone else with a bun . . . anyone else declaring?"

"Gender roles suck," says Swift Fox.

Then you should stop playing them, thinks Toby.

"Granted," says Zeb, "but that's reality now. We can't have anyone doing an unscheduled bleedout in the middle of. . . . In the middle. Any more than necessary. White Sedge?"

"She's a pacifist," says Amanda unexpectedly. "And Lotis Blue has, you know. Cramps."

"Staying, then. Anyone else have disabilities, or else qualms?"

"I want to come," says Rebecca. "And I am definitely not pregnant."

"Can you keep up?" says Zeb. "That's the next question. Be honest. You may pose a danger to self and others. Veteran Painballers don't fool around. There's only three of them, but they'll be lethal. This picnic is not for the squeamish."

"Okay, scratch that," says Rebecca. "Know yourself, out of shape, hand up. Not to mention squeamish. I'll stay here."

"Me too," says Beluga.

"And I," says Tamaraw.

"And I," says Ivory Bill. "There comes a time in a man's life when, no matter how agile the spirit, the earthly carapace develops its limitations. Not to mention the knees. And on the subject of the . . ."

"Right. And Blackbeard comes with us. We'll need him: he seems to have a fix on whatever it is the Pigoons want to convey."

"No," says Toby. "He should stay here. He's only a child." She doesn't think she could live with herself if little Blackbeard got killed, especially in the ways the Painballers would kill him if they got hold of him. "And he has no fear — or none that's realistic — when it comes to people. He might go running right out into the open, into crossfire. Or get snatched as a hostage. What would happen then?"

"Yeah, but I don't see how we can manage without him," says Zeb. "He's our only liaison with the pigs, and they're essential. We'll have to take the risk."

Blackbeard himself has been following this exchange. "Do not worry, Oh Toby," he says. "I need to come, the Pig Ones have said so. Oryx will be helping me, and Fuck. I have already called Fuck, he is flying to here, right now. You will see." There's no way Toby can contradict any of this: she herself can't see Oryx or the helpful Fuck, nor can she understand the Pigoons. In the world of Blackbeard she's deaf and blind.

"If they point a stick at you," she says to him, "those men, you must fall flat on the ground. Or get behind a tree. If there is a tree. Or else a wall."

"Yes, thank you, Oh Toby," he says politely. This is evidently old news to him.

"Right then," says Zeb. "Are we clear?"

"I'm coming too," says Jimmy. Everyone looks at him: they've assumed he'd stay behind. He's still skinny as a twig and pale as a puffball.

"Are you sure?" says Toby. "What about your foot?"

"It's fine. I can walk. I have to come."

"Not sure that's wise," says Zeb.

"Wise," says Jimmy. He grins a little. "Never been accused of that. But if we're heading to the Paradice dome, I really have to go."

"Because?" says Zeb.

"Because Oryx is there." An embarrassed silence: this is demented. Jimmy looks around the circle, grinning nervously. "Okay, I'm not crazy, I know she's dead. But you need me," he says.

"Why?" says Katuro. "Not meaning to be rude, but . . ."

"Because I've been back there already. Since the Flood," says Jimmy.

"So?" says Zeb, voice level. "Nostalgia?" Toby guesses the meaning of that levelness: rid me of this brain-damaged dweeb.

Jimmy stands his ground. "So, I know where everything is. Such as the cellpacks. And the sprayguns: there's a stash of them too."

Zeb sighs. "Okay," he says. "But if you lag behind, we'll have to send you back. Under non-hominid escort."

"You mean those werewolf pigs," says Jimmy. "Been there, done that: they think I'm tripe. Forget the escort. I can keep up."

Sortie

Toby changes into a Spa track suit, with a pillowcase torn open for a sun cover on her head. Too bad about the kissy lips and winky eye on the sweatshirt — not very military — and too bad also about the colour pink, which could make her a target. But there are no khaki textiles at AnooYoo.

She checks her rifle, tucks some of her extra bullets into a pink Spa carrybag. There's some Spa cotton half-socks with fluffy pom-poms at the backs: she puts on a pair of those, takes an extra pair. If Zeb says anything about her getup she'll be tempted to smack him.

In the main foyer she distributes the water bottles, filled with water that's been properly boiled by Rebecca earlier with the aid of Ren and Amanda. The AnooYoo Spa emphasized the need for proper hydration during gym workouts, so there are enough plastic bottles. The MaddAddamites have brought some Joltbars with them from the cobb house, and some cold kudzu fritters. "Enough energy to run on, not too much or it weighs you down," says Zeb. "Keep some for later." He looks at Toby, her kissy-lipped pink outfit.

"You auditioning for something?" he says.

"It's vivid," says Jimmy.

"Like a rock star," says Rhino. "Kinda."

"Good camouflage," says Shackleton.

"They'll think you're a hibiscus," says Crozier.

"This is a rifle," says Toby. "I'm the only one here who knows how to use it. So button up." They all grin.

. . .

Then they set forth.

The three Pigoon scouts are out in front, snuffling along the ground. To either side of them, two more act as outriders, testing the air with the wet disks of their snouts. Odour radar, thinks Toby. What vibrations well beyond our blunted senses are they picking up? As falcons are to sight, these are to scent.

Six younger Pigoons – barely more than shoats – are running messages between the scouts and outriders and the main van of older and heavier Pigoons: the tank battalion, had they been armoured vehicles. Despite their bulk, they can move surprisingly fast. At the moment they're keeping a steady pace, conserving their energy: a marathon gait, not a sprint. There's not much grunting going on, and no squealing: like soldiers on a long march, they're saving their breath. Their tails are curled but inactive, their pink ears are aimed forward. Lit by the morning sun, they look almost like a cartoon version of cute, huggable, smiling pigs, Valentine pigs clutching red heart-shaped candy boxes, the kind with Cupid wings: If This Little Piggie Could Fly He'd Bring You My Love!

But only almost. These pigs aren't smiling.

If we were carrying a flag, thinks Toby, what would be on it?

At first the going is easy. They cross the flattened part of the meadow, which still has a few handbags and boots and bones poking out of the ground from where the plague victims had fallen. If they'd been covered by weeds these objects might have tripped up the marchers, but because they're visible they're easy to avoid.

The Mo'Hairs have been turned loose and are grazing on the far edge of the meadowland that's been left for pasture. Five young Pigoons have been deputized to watch over them. They don't seem to be taking their duties very seriously, which means they smell no danger. Three are rooting around in the plant life, one is rolling in a damp patch of mud, and the fifth is dozing. Would the five of them be a match for a liobam, should one attack? No doubt of it. A pair of liobams? Possibly even that. But before they'd even get close, the youngsters would have the entire Mo'Hair flock rounded up and trotting back to the Spa.

After leaving the meadow the procession takes the roadway to the north, cutting through the forest that borders the AnooYoo grounds and conceals its perimeter fence. The northern gatehouse is deserted: no sign of life in or around it, apart from a rakunk that's sunning itself on the walkway. It stands up as they approach but doesn't bother to run away. Overly friendly, those animals: in a harsher world they'd all be hats by now.

The city streets that come next are harder to navigate. Crashed and deserted vehicles clog the pavement, which is littered with shattered glass and twists of metal. Already the kudzu vines are thrusting in, covering the broken shapes with a soft fledging of green. The Pigoons pick their way daintily, avoiding injury to their trotters; the humans have thick footgear. Still, they need to proceed carefully and glance down often.

Toby has anticipated the problems Blackbeard might have on these streets, with their shards and cutting edges. True, his feet have an extra-thick layer of skin on them, and that's fine for earth and sand and even pebbles; but, as a precaution, Toby has rummaged through the MaddAddamites' stockpile of gleaned footgear and fitted Blackbeard with a pair of Hermes Trismegistus cross-trainers. At first he was very worried about putting such things on his feet – would they hurt, would they stick to him, would he ever be able to get them off? But Toby showed him how to put them on and then take them off again, and said that if his feet got cut by sharp things he wouldn't be able to come any farther, and then who would be able to tell them what the Pigoons were thinking? So after several practice sessions he has agreed to wear them. The shoes have appliquéd green wings on them and lights that flash with every step he takes – the batteries haven't run down yet – and he is now perhaps a little too delighted with them.

He's up at the front of the main body, listening to the intelligence reports of the Pigoon scouts, if you could call it listening: receiving them, in any case, however he does that. Evidently he hasn't learned anything yet that's important enough to pass along. He glances back now and then, keeping track of Zeb, and also of Toby. There's that jaunty little wave of his hand again, which must mean *All is well*. Or maybe just *I see you*, or *Here I am*, or even, just possibly, *Look at my cool shoes!* His high, clear singing comes to her on the air in short bursts: the Morse code of Crakerdom.

The Pigoons alongside tilt their heads to look up at their human allies from time to time, but their thoughts can only be guessed. Compared with them, humans on foot must seem like slowpokes. Are they irritated? Solicitous? Impatient? Glad of the artillery support? All of those, no doubt, since they have human brain tissue and can therefore juggle several contradictions at once.

They appear to have assigned three guards to each of the gunbearers. The guards don't crowd, they don't herd or dictate, but they keep within a two-yard radius of their charges, their ears swivelling watchfully. The MaddAddamites without sprayguns have one Pigoon each. Jimmy, on the other hand, has five. Are they conscious of his fragility? So far he's been keeping up, but he's beginning to sweat.

Toby drops back to check on him. She hands him her water bottle: he seems already to have emptied his own. All eight Pigoons – her three, his five – shift their positions to surround both of them.

"The Great Wall of Pork," says Jimmy. "The Bacon Brigade. The Hoplites of Ham."

"Hoplites?" says Toby.

"It was a Greek thing," says Jimmy. "Citizens' army type of arrangement. A wall of interlocked shields. I read it in a book." He's a little short of breath.

"Maybe it's an honour guard," says Toby. "Are you okay?"

"These things make me nervous," says Jimmy. "How do we know they aren't leading us astray so they can ambush us and gobble our giblets?"

"We don't know that," says Toby. "But I'd say the odds are against it. They've already had the opportunity."

"Occam's razor," says Jimmy. He coughs.

"Pardon?" says Toby.

"It was a Crake thing," says Jimmy sadly. "Given two possibilities, you take the simplest. Crake would have said 'the most elegant.' The prick."

"Who was Occam?" says Toby. Is that a slight limp?

"Some kind of a monk," says Jimmy. "Or bishop. Or maybe a smart pig. Occ Ham." He laughs. "Sorry. Bad joke."

They walk on for a block or two in silence. Then Jimmy says, "Sliding down the razor blade of life."

"Excuse me?" Toby says. She'd like to feel his forehead. Is he running a temperature?

"It's an old saying," says Jimmy. "It means you're on the edge. Plus, you may get your nuts sliced off." He's limping more visibly now.

"Is your foot all right?" Toby asks. No answer: he stumps doggedly onward. "Maybe you should go back," she says.

"No fucking way," says Jimmy.

The street ahead is blocked by the rubble from a partially fallen condo. There's been a fire in it — most likely caused by an electrical short, says Zeb, who has halted the march while the scouts reconnoitre a detour. The smell of burning is still in the air. The Pigoons don't like it: several of them snort.

Jimmy sits down on the ground.

"What?" says Zeb to Toby.

"His foot again," says Toby. "Or something."

"So, we need to send him back to the Spa."

"He won't go," says Toby.

Jimmy's five Pigoons are snuffling at him, but from a respectful distance. One of them moves forward to sniff his foot. Now two of them nudge him, one on either arm.

"Get away!" says Jimmy. "What do they want?"

"Blackbeard, please," says Toby, beckoning him over. He huddles with the Pigoons. There's a silent interchange, followed by a few notes of music.

"Snowman-the-Jimmy must ride," says Blackbeard. "They say his . . ." There's a word Toby can't decipher, that sounds like a grunt and a rumble. "They say that part of him is strong. In the middle he is strong, but his feet are weak. They will carry him."

One of the Pigoons steps forward, not the fattest. She lowers herself beside Jimmy.

"They want me to do what?" says Jimmy.

"Please, Oh Snowman-the-Jimmy," says Blackbeard. "They say you must lie down on the back and hold on to the ears. Two others will go beside you to keep you from falling off."

"This is dumb," says Jimmy. "I'll slide off!"

"That's your only option," says Zeb. "Catch a ride, or else you stay here."

Once Jimmy is in position, Zeb says, "Got any of that rope? It might help a bit."

Jimmy is tied onto the Pigoon like a parcel, and they all set off once more. "So, its name is Dancer, or Prancer, or what?" says Jimmy. "Think I should pat it?"

"Please, Oh Snowman-the-Jimmy, thank you," says Blackbeard. "The Pig Ones are telling me that a scratching behind the ears is a good thing."

When reciting the story in later years, Toby liked to say that the Pigoon carrying Snowman-the-Jimmy flew like the wind. It was the sort of thing that should be said of a fallen comrade-in-arms, and especially one that performed such an important service – a service that resulted, not incidentally, in the saving of Toby's own life. For if Snowman-the-Jimmy had not been transported by the Pigoon, would Toby be sitting here among them tonight, wearing the red hat and telling them this story? No, she would not. She would be composting under an elderberry bush, and assuming a different form. A very different form indeed, she would think to herself privately.

So, in her story, the Pigoon in question flew like the wind.

The telling was complicated by the fact that Toby could not pronounce the flying Pigoon's name in any way that resembled the grunt-heavy original. But nobody in the Craker audience seemed to mind, though they laughed at her a little. The children made up a game in which one of them played the heroic Pigoon flying like the wind, wearing a determined expression, and a smaller one played Snowman-the-Jimmy, also with a determined expression, clinging to its back.

Her back. The Pigoons were not objects. She had to get that right. It was only respectful.

At the time, things are somewhat different. The progress of the Jimmy-porting Pigoon is lumpy, and its back is rounded and slippery. Jimmy bumps up and down, and is in danger of sliding off, first on one side, then on the other. When this happens the flanking Pigoons give him a sharp upward nudge with their snouts, under the armpits, which causes him to yell maniacally because it tickles.

"For fuck's sake, can't you get him to shut up?" says Zeb. "We might as well be playing the bagpipes."

"He can't help it," says Toby. "It's a reflex."

"If I bonk him on the head, that'll be a reflex too," says Zeb.

"They probably know we're coming," says Toby. "They may have seen the scouts."

They're following the lead of the Pigoons, but it's Jimmy who provides the verbal guidelines. "We're still in the pleebs," he says. "I remember this part." Then: "We're coming up to No Man's Land, cleared buffer zone before the Compounds."

Then: "Main security perimeter coming up." After a while: "Over there, CryoJeenyus. Next up, Genie-Gnomes. Look at that fucking light-up genie sign! The solar must still be working."

Then: "Here comes the biggie. The RejoovenEsense Compound." Crows on the wall: four, no, five. One crow, sorrow, Pilar used to say; more, and they were protectors, or else tricksters, take your choice. Two of the crows lift off, circle overhead, sizing them up.

The Rejoov gates stand open. Inside, dead houses, dead malls, dead labs, dead everything. Tatters of cloth, derelict solarcars.

"Thank God for the pigs," says Jimmy. "Without them, needle in a haystack. The place is a labyrinth."

But the Pigoons are sure of the trail. They trot steadily forward, not hesitating. A corner turned, another corner.

"There it is," says Jimmy. "Up ahead. The gates of Paradice."

Eggshell

Crake had planned the Paradice Project himself. There was a tight security perimeter around it, in addition to the Rejoov barrier wall. Inside that was a park, a microclimate-modifying planting of mixed tropical splices, tolerant alike to drought and downpour. At the centre of it all was the Paradice dome, climate-controlled, airlocked, an impenetrable eggshell harbouring Crake's treasure trove, his brave new humans. And at the very centre of the dome he'd placed the artificial ecosystem where the Crakers themselves in all their strange perfection had been brought into being and set to live and breathe.

They reach the perimeter gate, stop to reconnoitre. No one in the gatehouses to either side, according to the Pigoons: their inactive tails and ears are semaphoring as much.

Zeb signals a rest stop: they need to gather their energy. The humans resort to their water bottles and eat half a Joltbar each. The Pigoons have found an avomango tree and are gobbling down the windfalls, the orange ovals pulped by their jaws, the fatty seeds crushed. Fermented sweetness fills the air.

I hope they aren't getting drunk, thinks Toby. That wouldn't be good, drunk Pigoons. "How are you doing?" she asks Jimmy.

"I remember this place," says Jimmy. "In every detail. Shit. I wish I didn't."

Ahead of them is the roadway leading through the forest. Untrimmed branches reach into the corridor of light above it, opportunist weeds push into it from the margins, renegade vines overhang it. Out of the swelling foam of vegetation the curved dome rises like the white half-eye of a sedated patient. It must once have seemed so bright and shining, that dome; so much like a harvest moon, or like a hopeful sunrise, but without the burning rays. Now it looks barren. More than that, it looks like a trap: for who can tell what's hidden in it, and what's hiding?

But that's only because of what we know, thinks Toby. There's nothing in the image itself that would signal death to an innocent observer.

"Oh Toby!" says Blackbeard. "Look! It is the Egg! The Egg where Crake made us!"

"Do you remember it?" says Toby.

"I don't know," says Blackbeard. "Not very much. Trees were growing in it. It rained, but it did not thunder. Oryx came to visit us every day. She taught us many things. We were happy."

"It might not be the same any more," says Toby.

"Oryx is not there," says Blackbeard. "She flew out because she wanted to help Snowman-the-Jimmy when he was sick, didn't she?"

"Yes, I'm sure she did," says Toby.

The young Pigoon scouts have been sent ahead to sniff out possible roadside ambushes. They're racing back now, along the leaf-strewn asphalt. Their ears are back, their tails out straight behind them: cause for alarm.

The elders leave their rooting party among the fallen avomangoes; Blackbeard runs over to them; there's a quick huddle. The Madd-Addamites gather around. "What's up?" Zeb asks.

"They say the bad ones are near the Egg," says Blackbeard. "Three. One with ropes tied on. He has white feathers on his face."

"What's he wearing?" Toby asks. Is it for instance a caftan, like those Adam One always wore? But how to ask that? She revises: "Does he have a second skin?"

"Shit," says Jimmy. "Keep them out of the emergency storeroom! They'll get all the sprayguns, and then we're toast!"

"Yes, he has a second skin, like you," says Blackbeard. "Only not pink. It is different colours. It is dirty. He has only one of these, on his foot. A shoe."

"How'll we do that?" says Rhino. "We can't move fast enough."

"We send some of the pigs," says Zeb. "The faster ones. They can cut through the woods."

"Then what?" says Rhino. "They can't hold the main door. Those guys have a spraygun. We don't know how much of their cellpack is left."

"We can't just let the Pigoons be shot down like rats in a barrel," says Toby. "Jimmy. When you go through the Paradice entranceway, where's the storeroom?"

"There's the two doors, the airlock door, the inner one. They're both open, I left them open. You go down the hall to the left, take a right, another left. The fucking pigs need to get into that room and hold the door shut from the inside."

"Okay, how do we tell them this?" says Zeb. "Toby?"

"Right and left could be a problem," says Toby. "I don't think the Crakers know about those."

"Think hard," says Zeb. "Clock's ticking."

"Blackbeard?" says Toby. "This is a picture of the Egg, if you were up at the top looking down at it." She draws a round circle in the dirt, with a stick. "Do you see?"

Blackbeard looks at it and nods, though not with much assurance. We hang by a thread, thinks Toby. "Good," she says with false heartiness. "Can you say this to the Pig Ones? Tell them they need to run very fast. Five of them, through the trees. They need to go past the bad men, right into the Egg. Then they need to go here" – she traces with the stick – "and in here. That right?" she asks Jimmy.

"Right enough," says Jimmy.

"They need to shut the door. They need to lean against it, to keep the bad ones from going into that room," says Toby. "Can you tell them all of that?"

Blackbeard looks puzzled. "Why do the men want to go into the Egg?" he asks. "The Egg is for making. They are already made."

"They want to find some killing things," says Toby. "The sticks that make holes."

"But the Egg is good. It does not have killing things."

"It does now," says Toby. "We have to hurry. Can you tell them?"

"I will try," says Blackbeard. He kneels on the ground. Two of the largest Pigoons lower their huge heads, one to either side of his face. There's a white tusk right beside his neck. Toby shivers. He begins to sing while tracing over Toby's marks in the sand with her stick. The Pigoons sniff at the diagram. Oh no, thinks Toby. This isn't going to work. They think it's something to eat.

But then the Pigoons lift their snouts and move to join the others. Low grunting, restless tail movements. Indecision?

Five of the medium-sized ones detach from the group and head off at a canter, two to the left of the road, three to the right. The undergrowth swallows them up.

"Looks like they got it," says Rhino. Zeb grins.

"Good," he says to Toby. "Always knew you had potential."

"They are going to the Egg," says Blackbeard. "They say they will not move too close to those men. They will be careful about the stick things, with blood coming out."

"Hope they make it," says Zeb. "Let's hike."

"It's not far," says Jimmy. "Anyway, they can't shoot us from the windows because there aren't any windows." He laughs feebly.

"Zeb?" says Toby as they move off down the road. "The third guy? I'm not sure. But I think it's Adam One."

"Yeah, I know," says Zeb. "I figured that for a while."

"What can we do to get him back?"

"They'll want to trade him," says Zeb.

"For what?"

"Sprayguns, supposing the pigs block them out. Other stuff."

"Like, for instance?"

"Like, for instance, you," says Zeb. "In their place, it's what I'd do."

Right, thinks Toby. They'll want revenge.

The Paradice dome lies in front of them. All is silent. The airlock door is open. Three shoats go through it, then come out again. "They are inside, the men," says Blackbeard. "But far inside. Not near the door."

"I need to go in first," says Jimmy. "Just for a minute." Toby stays close behind him.

There are two destroyed skeletons on the floor of the airlock. The bones have been gnawed and jumbled, no doubt by animals. Rags of mouldering cloth, a small pink and red sandal.

Jimmy falls to his knees; his hands are over his face. Toby touches his shoulder. "We need to go now," she says, but he says, "Leave me alone!"

There's a dirty pink ribbon tied in the long black hair of one of the skulls: hair decays very slowly, the Gardeners always said. Jimmy unties the bow, twists the ribbon in his fingers. "Oryx. Oh God," he says. "You fucker, Crake! You didn't have to kill her!"

Zeb is standing beside Toby now. "Maybe she was already sick," he says to Jimmy. "Maybe he couldn't live without her. Come on, we need to get in there."

"Oh fuck, spare me the fucking clichés!" says Jimmy.

"We can just leave him here for now, he'll be safe; let's go in," says Toby. "We need to be sure they didn't get into the storage room."

The others are right outside the doorway – the MaddAddamites, the main body of the Pigoons. "What's up?" says Rhino.

Little Blackbeard is tugging at her hand. "Please, Oh Toby, what is *clichés*?" he says.

Toby hardly knows what she answers, because now the truth is hitting him: Oryx and Crake are these skeletons. He heard Jimmy say that; it registered. He turns his frightened face up to her: she can see the sudden fall, the crash, the damage.

"Oh Toby, is this Oryx, and is this Crake?" he says. "Snowman-the-Jimmy said! But they are a smelly bone, they are many smelly bones! Oryx and Crake must be beautiful! Like the stories! They cannot be a smelly bone!" He begins to cry as if his heart will break.

Toby kneels, folds her arms around him, hugs him tight. What to say? How to comfort him? In the face of this terminal sorrow.

The Story of the Battle

Toby cannot tell the story tonight. She is too sad, because of the dead ones. The ones who became dead, in the battle. So now I will try to tell this story to you. I will tell it in the right way, if I can.

First I am putting the red hat on my head, the hat of Snowman-the-Jimmy. These markings on it — look, it is a voice, and it is saying: RED. And it is saying: SOX.

SOX is a special word of Crake. We do not know what it means. Toby does not know either. Maybe we will know later.

But see — the red hat is on my head, and it does not hurt me. I am not growing an extra skin, I have my own skin, the same. I can take the hat off, I can put it back on again. It does not stick to my head.

Now I will eat the fish. We do not eat a fish, or a smelly bone; that is not what we eat. It is a hard thing to do, eating a fish. But I must do it. Crake did many hard things for us, when he was on the earth in the form of a person. He cleared away the chaos for us, and . . .

You do not have to sing.

. . . and he did many other hard things, so I will try to do this hard thing of eating the smelly bone fish. It is cooked. It is very small. Perhaps it will be enough for Crake if I put it into my mouth and take it out again.

There.

I am sorry for making the noises of a sick person.

Please take the fish away and throw it into the forest. The ants will be happy. The maggots will be happy. The vultures will be happy.

Yes, it does taste very bad. It tastes like the smell of a smelly bone, or the smell of a dead one. I will chew many leaves to get rid of that taste. But if I did not do the hard thing with the bad taste, I would not be able to hear the story Crake is telling me, and then tell it to you. That is the way it was with Snowman-the-Jimmy, and that is the way it is with Toby. The hard thing of eating the fish, the smelly bone taste — that is what needs to be done. First the bad things, then the story.

Thank you for the purring. I am not feeling so sick now.

This is the Story of the Battle. It tells how Zeb and Toby and Snowman-the-Jimmy and the other two-skinned ones and the Pig Ones cleared away the bad men, just as Crake cleared away the people in the chaos to make a good and safe place for us to live.

And Toby and Zeb and Snowman-the-Jimmy and the two-skinned ones and the Pig Ones needed to clear away the bad men, because if they did not do it, our place would never be safe. The bad men would kill us as they killed the Pig One baby, with a knife. Or with a stick that makes holes with blood coming out. So that is why.

Toby told this reason to me. It is a good reason.

And the Pig Ones helped them, because they did not want any more of their Pig One babies to be killed with a knife. Or a stick thing. Or in any other way, such as a rope.

The Pig Ones can smell better than any. We can smell better than the ones with two skins, but the Pig Ones can smell better than us. So they helped, by smelling the footprints of the bad men, and showing where they had gone. And by helping to chase after them.

And I was there too, so that I could tell the others what the Pig Ones were saying. I had shoes on my feet. You see those shoes, they are here, see? They have lights on them, and wings. They are a special thing from Crake, and I am grateful for having them, and I say, Thank you. But I do not need to put them on unless there is danger, and other bad men that must be cleared away. So I do not have them on my feet right now. But I have them here beside me, because they are part of the story.

But that time I put those shoes on my feet, and we walked a long way, into the place where the buildings are, where we do not go because they can fall down. But I went there that time, and I saw many things.

I saw things left over from the chaos, many. I saw empty buildings, many. I saw empty skins, many. I saw metal and glass things, many. And the Pig Ones carried Snowman-the-Jimmy.

Then the Pig Ones were following the bad men with their noses, and they found where they had gone. And the bad men went into the Egg, even though the Egg should only be for making, not for killing. And some of the Pig Ones went into the Egg also, to the room where the killing things were, so the bad men could not get those things. So the bad men were running, and they were hiding inside the Egg, in the hallways of the Egg. And at first we could not see them.

The Egg was dark, not light, as it used to be. We could see when we were inside the Egg, I do not mean that kind of dark. The Egg had a dark feeling. It had a dark smell.

And Snowman-the-Jimmy went into the first doorway of the Egg, and he found a pile of smelly bones and another pile of smelly bones, all mixed together, and he was very sad, and he fell down onto his knees, and he cried. And Toby wanted to purr on him, but he said, "Leave me alone!"

And then he took a pink twisty thing from the hair of one of the smelly bone piles, and he held it in his hands, and he said, "Oryx. Oh God." And then he said, "You fucker, Crake! You didn't have to kill her!"

And Toby and Zeb were there. And Zeb said, "Maybe she was already sick. Maybe he couldn't live without her." And Snowman-the-Jimmy said, "Oh Fuck, spare me the fucking clichés!"

And I said to Toby, "What is *clichés*?" And Toby said that it was a word to help people get through a trouble when they couldn't think of anything else. And I hoped that Fuck was flying very quickly to help Snowman-the-Jimmy, because he was in very much trouble.

And I was in very much trouble too, because Snowman-the-Jimmy said these bone piles were Oryx and Crake. And I felt a very bad feeling, and I was frightened. And I said, "Oh Toby, is this Oryx, and is this Crake? But they are a smelly bone, they are many smelly bones! Oryx and Crake must be beautiful! Like the stories! They cannot be a smelly bone!" And I cried, because they were dead ones, very dead ones, and all fallen apart.

But Toby said the bone piles were not the real Oryx and Crake any more, they were only husks, like an eggshell.

And the Egg wasn't the real Egg, the way it is in the stories. It was only an eggshell, like the shells that are broken and left behind when the birds hatch out of them. And we ourselves were like the birds, so we did not need the broken eggshell any more, did we?

And Oryx and Crake had different forms now, not dead ones, and they are good and kind. And beautiful. The way we know, from the stories.

So I felt better then.

Please do not sing yet.

And then after that we went all the way into the Egg. It was not bright there but it was not dark either, because the sun shone through the eggshell. But the feeling of darkness was all the way through the air. And then they were having a battle. A *battle* is when some wish to clear others away, and the others want to clear them away as well.

We do not have battles. We do not eat a fish. We do not eat a smelly bone. Crake made us that way. Yes, good, kind Crake.

But Crake made the two-skinned ones so they could have a battle. He made the Pig Ones that way too. They do a battle with their tusks, and the others do a battle with the sticks that punch holes and blood comes out. That is how they are made.

I don't know why Crake made them that way.

The Pig Ones chased the bad men. They chased them through the hallways, and they chased them into the centre of the Egg, where there were many dead trees. Not as when we were made there: then, there were trees with many leaves, and beautiful water, and it rained, and the stars were shining in the sky. But now there were no stars, only a ceiling.

The Pig Ones told me later of all the places where they chased the bad men. Toby would not let me go with them because she said I might get holes with blood, or else the bad ones might grab hold of me, and that would be worse. So I could not see everything that happened, but there was shouting, and the Pig Ones were screaming, and it hurt my ears. Pig One voices when screaming are very, very loud.

And there was the sound of galloping, and footsteps with shoes on. And then it would be silent, and that was when thinking was happening: the thinking of the bad ones, and the thinking of the Pig Ones, and the thinking of Zeb, and Toby, and Rhino. They wanted the Pig Ones to chase the bad men past where they were so they could make holes in them with the sticks, but it did not happen. There were many, many hallways inside the Egg.

And one of the Pig Ones came and told me that there were only two bad men being chased through the hallways. But three had gone into the Egg. And the third one was above us: they could smell him. He was above us, but they did not know where.

And I told that to Zeb and Toby, and Zeb said, "They've stashed Adam on the second floor somewhere. Where's the stairs?" And Snowman-the-Jimmy said there were fire stairs in four places. And Toby said, "Can you take us there?" And Snowman-the-Jimmy said, "So you go up one stairway and they come down another stairway and run away, and then what?" And Zeb said, "Shit."

Three of the Pig Ones became hurt when they were chasing the bad men in the hallways, and one of them fell down and did not get up again. It was the one who carried Snowman-the-Jimmy. And I saw that part of the battle, and I made the noises of a sick person. And I cried.

Then the two bad men ran up some of the stairs. *Stairs* are – I will tell you what stairs are later. But the Pig Ones cannot climb stairs. And when the bad ones reached the top, we could not see them.

And Zeb and Toby and the other two-skinned people told me to tell the Pig Ones to find the other stair places, and to scream if the bad ones tried to come down. Then they brought wood in from outside, and they made a fire, with smoke. And the smoke went up the stairs. And they put cloths over their faces and waited near the bottom of the stairs where the men had run up, and when there was much smoke – very much smoke, I saw it, I coughed! – two of the bad men came to the top of the stairs, and they were pushing the third man in front of them, and holding him by the arms, one on each side. And he had ropes on his hands. And he had only one shoe. On his foot. But that shoe did not have wings, and lights. Not like the shoes here, that were on my feet.

And Toby said, "Adam!"

And that one began to say something, and a bad one hit him, the one with short feathers on his face. Then the bad one with the long feathers said, "Let us past or he gets it." And I did not know what he would get.

And Zeb said, "Okay, free pass, hand him over." And the other bad man said, "Throw in the bitch, and we'll take the sprayguns too. And call off the fucking pigs!"

But the man Adam with the ropes on his hands shook his head, which meant no. And then he pulled away from them where they were holding him by the tops of the arms, and he jumped forward, and he fell, and he rolled down the stairs. And one of the bad men made a hole in him with his stick.

And Zeb ran forward to Adam, and Toby raised her gun thing and pointed it, and it made a sound, and the bad man that made the hole in Adam dropped the stick; and he fell down, holding on to his leg and screaming.

And Toby wanted to run to help Zeb with the man Adam, at the bottom of the stairs, and Snowman-the-Jimmy was trying to hold her back with one hand on her pink second skin. And Snowman-the-Jimmy pushed me behind him, but I could still see.

The other bad man was partway behind a wall, but his head and arm came out, and he had the stick now, and he was pointing it at Toby. But Snowman-the-Jimmy saw it, and he went very fast in front of her, and he had the holes punched in him instead. And he fell down too, with blood coming out, and he did not get up.

And then Zeb used his stick thing, and the second bad man dropped his own stick thing and took hold of his own arm. And he screamed as well. And I put my hands over my ears because there was so much pain. It hurt me very much.

And Rhino and Shackleton and the other ones with two skins went up the stairs, and caught the two men, and tied them with ropes, and pulled them down the stairs. But Zeb and Toby were with Adam, and also with Snowman-the-Jimmy. And they were sad.

And we all went outside the Egg, which had smoke coming out, and then flames. And we walked very fast away from it. And there were some loud noises from inside.

And Zeb was carrying Adam, who was very thin and white-looking; and Adam was still breathing. And Zeb said, "I've got you, best buddy. You're gonna be okay." But his face was all wet.

And Adam said, "I'll be fine. Pray for me." And he smiled at Zeb and said, "Don't worry. I wouldn't have lasted long. Plant a good tree."

And I said to Toby, "Oh Toby, who is *Bestbuddy*? This one is Adam, that is his name, you said so."

And Toby said that Bestbuddy was another name for *brother*, because Adam was the brother of Zeb.

But after that, the man Adam stopped breathing.

And it was evening, and we walked slowly back, with the bad men being carried by the Pig Ones because of the holes in them, and the ropes. The Pig Ones were angry because of the deads, and they wanted to stick their tusks into those men, and roll on them, and trample on them, but Zeb said it was not the time.

And Snowman-the-Jimmy and Adam were carried too, and the dead Pig One. And in the night we reached the building where the children were, and the mothers, and the Mo'Hairs, and the Pig One mothers and babies, and the other two-skinned ones – Ren and Amanda and Swift Fox and Ivory Bill and Rebecca, and the others. And they came to meet us, and all of the people said very many things, such as "I was so worried" and "What happened?" and "Oh God!"

And we, the Children of Crake, we sang together.

We slept there that night, and ate. And all who had been in the battle were very tired. They talked in low voices, and looked very carefully at the dead one Adam, and said he was not dead because of the chaos-clearing seed that Crake made but because of the holes with blood coming out. And they said anyway that it was a mercy that he was not dead of the Crake seed thing.

I will ask Toby later what a *mercy* is. She is tired now, she is sleeping.

. . .

And they wrapped the man Adam in a pink bedsheet, with a pink pillow under his head, and they were very quiet and sad. And some of the Pig Ones went swimming in the pool, which they liked very much.

And the next day we walked here, to the cobb house. And the Pig Ones carried Adam, on branches, with flowers, and the dead Pig One too, which was harder for them because she was big and heavy.

And they carried Snowman-the-Jimmy in the same way, though he was not dead, not when we began to walk. And Ren walked beside him, holding his hand and crying, because she was his friend; and Crozier walked on the other side of her, and he helped her.

But Snowman-the-Jimmy was travelling in his head, far, far away, as he had travelled before, when he was in the hammock and we purred. But this time he went so far away that he could not come back.

And Oryx was there with him, and she was helping him. I heard him talking to her, just before he went too far, out of sight, and stopped breathing. And now he is with Oryx. And with Crake too.

That is the Story of the Battle.

Now we can sing.

Moontime

Trial

The next morning they hold a trial.

They sit around the dining table – or the MaddAddamites and the God's Gardeners sit. The Pigoons sprawl on the grass and pebbles; the Crakers graze nearby, chewing their eternal mouthfuls of leaf, taking it all in.

The prisoners themselves are not present. They don't need to be there: what they've done isn't in question. The trial is about the verdict only.

"So, we're here to decide their fates," says Zeb. "Worse luck we didn't blow them away in the heat of the proceedings, but since we didn't, we have to make some decisions in cold blood. Vote now, or is there any discussion?"

Toby says, "Are they common prisoners? Or prisoners of war? Because it's different, no?" She feels impelled to advocate for them in some way, but why? Is it simply because they don't have a lawyer?

"How about soul-dead neurotrash?" says Rebecca.

"Fellow human beings," says White Sedge. "Though I realize that this in itself is not a defence."

"They killed our brother," says Shackleton.

"Scumsucking fuckbuckets," says Crozier.

"Rapists and murderers," says Amanda.

"They shot Jimmy," says Ren, starting to cry. Amanda puts an arm around her, gives her a hug. She herself is not crying: she looks flinty-eyed, like a wood carving of herself. She'd make a good executioner, thinks Toby.

"Who cares what we call them," says Rhino. "So long as it's not *people*."

Hard to choose a label, thinks Toby: three sessions in the once notorious Painball Arena have scraped all modifying labels away from them, bleached them of language. Triple Painball survivors have long been known to be not quite human.

"I vote for all of the above," says Zeb. "Now let's get on with it."

White Sedge enters a halfhearted clemency plea. "We shouldn't judge," she says. "Surely their viciousness is a result of what was done to them earlier in their lives, by others. And considering the plasticity of the brain and how their behaviour was shaped by harsh experience, how are we to know that they had any control over what they did?"

"Are you fucking serious?" says Shackleton. "They ate my little brother's fucking kidneys! They butchered him like a Mo'Hair! I want to rip out all their teeth! Through their assholes," he adds, perhaps unnecessarily.

"Let's not get too fired up," says Zeb. "Hold the outrage. We all have cause. Though some more than others." He looks older, thinks Toby. Older and grimmer. Finding Adam and then losing him again has dragged him down. We're all in mourning: even the Pigoons. Their tails are drooping, their ears are limp; they nuzzle one another in a consoling way.

"We shouldn't fight over what should be a purely philosophical and practical decision," says Ivory Bill. "The question is, do we have the facilities for correctional guardianship, or, on the other hand, the theoretical justification for . . ."

"It's not a time for hair-splitting," says Zeb.

"Taking life under any circumstances is reprehensible," says White Sedge. "We shouldn't let our own moral standards slip, just because —"

"Just because most of the human race has been wiped out and the surviving remnant can hardly get enough solar going to run a light bulb?" says Shackleton. "So you want to let these two cesspools bash your brains out?"

"I don't know why you're being so hostile," says White Sedge. "Adam One would have advocated clemency."

"Maybe he'd have been wrong," says Amanda. "You weren't there, you don't know what they did to us. Me and Ren. You don't know what they're like."

"Though, with so few true humans left," says Ivory Bill, "perhaps we shouldn't waste any increasingly rare human DNA. Even if the individuals in question must be eliminated, possibly their . . . their generative fluids should be, as it were, siphoned off, to provide genetic variety. An ingrown gene pool must be avoided."

"Avoid it yourself," says Swift Fox. "Personally, the mere idea of having sex with those two festering bedsores just to capture their rancid DNA makes me nauseous."

"You wouldn't need to have sex with them, as such," says Ivory Bill. "We could use a turkey baster."

"Use it on your own self," says Swift Fox rudely. "Men are always telling women what to do with their uteruses. Excuse me, their uteri."

"I'd rather slit my wrists than let any of their fucking generative fluids near me ever again," says Amanda. "It's bad enough as it is. How do I know my own kid won't be one of theirs?"

"Anyway, a child with such warped genes would be a monster," says Ren. "The mother couldn't love it. Oh, sorry," she says to Amanda.

"It's okay," says Amanda. "If it's theirs, I'll hand it over to White Sedge and she can love it. Or the Pigoons can eat the thing; they'd appreciate it."

"We could try rehabilitation," says White Sedge serenely. "Incorporate them into the community, keep them in a safe place at night, let them help out. Sometimes, when people feel they can contribute, it makes for a genuine change in . . ."

"Look around," Zeb says. "See any social workers? See any jails?"

"Contribute to what?" says Amanda. "You want to let them be in charge of the day care?"

"They'd put everyone else at risk," says Katuro.

"There's no safe place to store them except a hole in the ground," says Shackleton.

"The vote," says Zeb.

They use pebbles: black for death, white for mercy. It has an archeological feel. The old symbol systems follow us around, thinks Toby, as she collects the pebbles in Jimmy's red hat. There's only one white pebble.

The Pigoons vote collectively, through their leader, with Blackbeard as their interpreter. "They all say *dead*," he tells Toby. "But they will not eat those ones. They do not want those ones to be part of them."

The rest of the Crakers are puzzled. They clearly do not understand what *vote* means, or *trial*, or why pebbles should be put into the hat of Snowman-the-Jimmy. Toby tells them it is a thing of Crake.

The Story of the Trial

The two bad men were put in a room at night, with ropes tying them. We could feel that the rope was hurting them, and making them sad and also angry. But we did not untie the rope the way we did before. Toby told us not to, because it would only cause more killing. And we told the children not to go too close, because the bad ones might bite them.

And then they were given soup, with a smelly bone.

In the morning there was a Trial. You all saw it. It was at the table. Many words were said. The Pig Ones were also at the Trial.

Perhaps we will understand it later, this Trial.

And after the Trial, all the Pig Ones went down to the seashore. And Toby went with them, and she had her gun thing that we should not touch. And Zeb went. And Amanda went, and Ren. And Crozier and Shackleton. But we did not go, we Children of Crake, because Toby said it would be hurtful to us.

And after a while they all came back, without the two bad ones. They looked tired. But they were more peaceful.

Toby said that now we would be safe from the bad ones. And the Pig Ones said their babies were now safe too. And they said also that even though the Battle was over now, they would keep the pact they made with Toby, and with Zeb, and they would not hunt and eat any of the two-skinned ones, and they would also not dig up their garden any more. Or eat the honey of the bees.

And Toby told me the words to say to them, which were: We agree to keep the pact. None of you, or your children, or your children's children, will ever be a smelly bone in a soup. Or a ham, she added. Or a bacon.

And Rebecca said, Worse luck.

And Crozier said, What're they saying, what the fuck is going on? And Toby said, Watch your language, it's confusing for him.

And I said that Crozier did not need to call Fuck right now because we were not in trouble and did not need his help. And Toby said, That's right, he doesn't like to be summoned on trivial matters. And Zeb coughed.

After the Pig Ones had gone away, Toby told us that the two bad men had been washed away in the sea. They had been poured away, as Crake poured away the chaos. So everything was much cleaner now.

Yes, good, kind Crake.

Please don't sing.

Because when you sing I can't hear the words that Crake is telling me to say, and also when we sing about him he can't tell me any words of the story, because he has to listen to the singing.

So that is the Story of the Trial. It is a thing from Crake. We do not have to have a Trial, among us. Only the two-skinned ones and the Pig Ones have to have a Trial.

And that is a good thing, because I did not like the Trial.

Thank you. Good night.

Rites

The Feast of Cnidaria, Toby writes. *Waxing gibbous moon.*

The Cnidaria phylum contains the jellyfish, the corals, the sea anemones, and the hydra. The Gardeners had been thorough – no phylum or genus was left out of their list of feasts and festivals, if they could help it – though some celebrations had been odder than others. The Festival of Intestinal Parasites, for instance, had been memorable, though not what you would call delightful.

The Feast of Cnidaria, however, had been an especially beautiful one. There had been paper lanterns in the shapes of jellyfish, and many decorations fashioned from objects found in dumpsters. A creative use was made of spent balloons and inflated rubber gloves with trailing filaments of string, sea anemones were created from modified round dish-scrubbing brushes, and hydras crafted from transparent plastic sandwich bags.

The children would do a little jellyfish dance, festooned with streamers and waving their arms slowly, and one year they'd composed and performed an interminable play on the subject of the life cycle of the jellyfish, which was uneventful. *First I was an egg, Then I grew and grew, Now I am a jellyfish, Green and pink and blue.* Though when the Portuguese Man O' War had made its entrance, drama had been possible: *I drifted here, I drifted there, My tentacles so fine to view, But don't get tangled up with me, Or I will put an end to you.*

Had Ren helped with that play? Toby wonders. Had Amanda? The song, the grabbing of a smaller child playing a fish, the stinging to death – they had the earmarks of Amanda; or of the streetwise pleebrat Amanda of those days, who, since the disposal of the two malignant Painballers, appears to have been reborn.

"After the disposal of the two malignant Painballers," she writes. *Disposal* makes them sound like garbage, as in garbage disposal. She wonders if this kind of name-calling is worthy of her one-time position as Eve Six, decides it's not, leaves it anyway.

"After the disposal of the two malignant Painballers, Ren and Shackleton and Amanda and Crozier and I walked back along the AnooYoo forest path. We came to the tree where the Painballers had left poor Oates hanging with his throat slit. There wasn't much left of him — the crows had been assimilating him, and God knows what else — but Shackleton shinnied up the tree and cut the rope, and he and Crozier gathered together the bones of their younger brother and tied them up in a bedsheet.

"Then it was time for the composting. The Pigoons wished to carry Adam and Jimmy to the site for us, as a sign of friendship and inter-species co-operation. They collected more flowers and ferns, which they piled on top of the bodies. Then we walked to the site in procession. The Crakers sang all the way."

She adds, ". . . which was somewhat hard on the nerves." But then, reflecting that Blackbeard is making so much progress in his writing that he might someday be able to read her entries, she scratches it out.

"Following a short discussion, the Pigoons understood that we did not wish to eat Adam and Jimmy, nor would we wish the Pigoons to do that. And they concurred. Their rules in such matters appear complex: dead farrow are eaten by pregnant mothers to provide more protein for growing infants, but adults, and especially adults of note, are contributed to the general ecosystem. All other species are, however, up for grabs.

Amanda added that she did not see a transition through pigshit as an acceptable phase in Jimmy's life cycle, but this remark was not translated by Blackbeard. There was not enough left of Oates for it to be an issue in his case.

"We buried all three of them near Pilar, and planted a tree on top of each. For Jimmy, Ren, Amanda, and Lotis Blue had made a trip to the Botanical Gardens, to the section called Fruits of the World — under the guidance of the Pigoons, who of course knew where it was, being fond of fruit — and had chosen a Kentucky coffeetree, which has heart-shaped leaves and produces berries that can be used as a coffee substitute. Many in our group will be pleased by that, as the roasted-root coffee is beginning to pall.

"For Oates, Crozier and Shackleton chose an oak tree, because it echoed his name. The Pigoons were delighted by that, as later on there would be acorns.

"For Adam One, Zeb as next of kin had the choice of tree. He selected a native crabapple, somewhat biblical — he said — and also fitting. Its apples would have the added virtue of making a good jelly, which would have pleased Adam: the Gardeners, though conscious of symbolism, were practical in such matters.

"The Pigoons had their own funeral rites. They did not bury the dead Pigoon, but set her down in a clearing near one of the park picnic tables. They heaped her with flowers and branches, and stood silently, tails drooping. Then the Crakers sang."

"Oh Toby, what have you been writing?" says Blackbeard, who's come into her cobb-house cubicle — unannounced, as usual — and is now standing at her elbow. He's peering into her face with his large, green, luminous, uncanny eyes.

How had Crake devised those eyes? How do they light up from within like that? Or give the appearance of lighting up. It must be a luminosity feature, perhaps from a deep-sea bioform. She's often wondered.

"I am writing the story," she says. "The story of you, and me, and the Pigoons, and everyone. I am writing about how we put Snowman-the-Jimmy and Adam One into the ground, and Oates too, so that Oryx can change them into the form of a tree. And that is a happy thing, isn't it?"

"Yes. It is a happy thing. What is wrong with your eyes, Oh Toby? Are you crying?" says Blackbeard. He touches her eyebrow.

"I'm just a little tired," says Toby. "And my eyes are tired as well. Writing makes them tired."

"I will purr on you," says Blackbeard.

Among the Crakers, the small children do not purr. Blackbeard is growing quickly – they do grow faster, these children – but is he big enough to purr? Apparently so: already his hands are on her forehead, and the mini-motor sound of Craker purring is filling the air. She's never been purred on before: it's very soothing, she has to admit.

"There," says Blackbeard. "Telling the story is hard, and writing the story must be more hard. Oh Toby, when you are too tired to do it, next time I will write the story. I will be your helper."

"Thank you," says Toby. "That is kind."

Blackbeard smiles like daybreak.

Moontime

The Festival of Bryophyta-the-Moss. Waning crescent moon.

I am Blackbeard, and this is my voice that I am writing down to help Toby. If you look at this writing I have made, you can hear me (I am Blackbord) talking to you, inside your head. That is what writing is. But the Pig Ones can do that without writing. And sometimes we can do it, the Children of Crake. The two-skinned ones cannot do it.

Today Toby said Bryophyta is moss. I said if it is moss, then I must write *moss*. Toby says it has two names, like Snowman-the-Jimmy. So I am writing Bryophyta-the-Moss. Like this.

Today we made the pictures of Snowman-the-Jimmy, and of Adam as well. We did not know Adam, but we made the picture for Zeb and Toby, and for the other ones who did know him. For Snowman-the-Jimmy we used a mop, from the beach, and we used a jar lid and some pebbles, and more things. But not the red hat, because we need to keep it for the stories.

For Adam we used a cloth skin that we found, with two arms, and a white bag of plastic for the head, with feathers we took from a gull that did not need them any longer, and some blue glass from the beach, because his eyes were blue.

We made a picture of Snowman-the-Jimmy once before, to call him back, and it did call him back. These pictures will not call Snowman-the-Jimmy and Adam back this time, but it will make Zeb and Toby and Ren and Amanda feel better. That is why we made the pictures. They like pictures.

Thank you. Good night.

The Feast of Saint Maude Barlow, of Fresh Water. New moon.

Zeb has been recovering from the death of Adam. He and the others are working on an extension to the cobb house because they will soon need a nursery. The pregnancies are advancing much faster than is usual, and most of the women believe that all three of the babies will be Craker hybrids.

The garden is progressing well. The Mo'Hair flock is increasing — there have been three new additions to it, one blue-haired, one a red-head, and one blond — though one of the lambs was lost to a liobam. The liobams, too, appear to be on the increase.

"One of the Crakers reports seeing something that sounds like a bear," Toby writes. "It wouldn't be surprising. Perhaps we should set a guard for the beehives? There are two hives now, as another swarm was captured.

"Deer are proliferating: they are an acceptable source of animal protein. They are much leaner than pork, though not as tasty. Venison does not make top-quality bacon. But Rebecca says it is healthier."

The Festival of Gymnosperms. Full moon.

Toby made the mistake of announcing to the others that this was the God's Gardener Festival of Gymnosperms. Several bad jokes about gymnasts and sperms and even male Crakers were made, one of them by Zeb, which is a good sign. Perhaps his time of mourning is coming to an end.

Three more functioning solar units have been installed. An existing one has gone out of commission. One of the violet biolets is malfunctioning. Shackleton and Crozier have experimented with making charcoal: the results have been mixed. Rhino, Katuro, and Manatee have gone fishing down by the shore. Ivory Bill is designing a coracle.

Two young Pigoons — barely more than piglets — dug under the garden fence and were discovered eating the root vegetables, the carrots and beets in particular. The MaddAddamites had slacked off their vigilance as regards the Pigoons, thinking that their agreement would hold. And it is holding, with the adults; but juveniles of all kinds push the rules.

A conference was called. The Pigoons sent a delegation of three adults, who seemed both embarrassed and cross, as adults put to shame by their young usually are. Blackbeard stood as interpreter.

It would not happen again, said the Pigoons. The young offenders had been threatened with a sudden transition to a state of bacon and soup bones, which seems to have made the desired impression.

The Festival of Saint Geyikli Baba of Deer. New moon.

The bees are productive: the first honey harvest has taken place. White Sedge has begun a Meditation to Music group, which many of the Crakers enjoy. Beluga is helping her. Tamaraw has been experimenting with sheep cheese, both hard and soft; also yogurt. The nursery has been finished, just in time. Very soon now, the three babies will be born, though Swift Fox claims she is having twins. Cradles are being discussed.

"Blackbeard has his own journal now," Toby writes. "I have given him his own pen, and a pencil. I would like to know what he is writing but I don't wish to pry. He's as tall as Crozier now. Already he is showing signs of blueness; very soon he will be grown up. Why does this make me sad?"

The Feast of Saint Fiacre of Gardens.

This is my voice, the voice of Blackbeard that you are hearing in your head. That is called *reading*. And this is my own book, a new one for my writing and not the writing of Toby.

Today Toby and Zeb did a strange thing. They jumped over a small fire and then Toby gave Zeb a green branch and Zeb gave Toby a green branch. And then they kissed each other. And all those with two skins watched, and then they cheered.

And I (Blackbeard) said, "Oh Toby, why are you doing this?"

And Toby said, "It is a custom we have. It shows that we love each other."

And I (Blackberd) said, "But you love each other anyway."

And Toby said, "It is hard to explain." And Amanda said, "Because it makes them happy." Blackbeard (I am ~~Blackbard~~ Blackbeard) does not see why. But what makes them happy or not happy is strange.

Soon Blacbeard will be ready for his first mating. When the next woman turns blue, he will turn very blue also, and gather flowers; and maybe he will be chosen. He (I, Blackbeard) asked Toby if the green branches were like that, like the flowers that we give, to be chosen, and then we sing; and she said yes, it was something like that. So now I understand it better.

Thank you. Good night.

The Festival of Quercus. The Feast of Pigoons. Full moon.

"I have taken the liberty of adding the Pigoons to the regular calendar of Gardener feasts," Toby writes. "They deserve to have a day named in their honour. I've attached them to the Festival of Quercus, the oak tree day. I thought it was fitting, because of the acorns."

The Feast of Artemis, Mistress of the Animals. Full moon.

Over the past two weeks, all three births have taken place. Or all four, because Swift Fox gave birth to twins, a boy and a girl. Each of the twins has the green eyes of the Crakers, which is a great relief to Toby; she'll have no tiny Zebs to contend with. She has made four small sunbonnets for them, out of a flowered bedsheet. The Craker women find these hilarious: what are such hats for? Their own babies do not sunburn.

Amanda's baby is fortunately of Craker descent, not Painballer: the large green eyes are unmistakable. The birth was difficult, and Toby and Rebecca had to perform an episiotomy. Toby did not want to give too much Poppy, for fear of damaging the newborn; so there was pain. Toby worried that Amanda might reject the baby, but she didn't. She appears to be quite fond of it.

Ren's baby is also a green-eyed Craker hybrid. What other features might these children have inherited? Will they have built-in insect repellent, or the unique vocal structures that enable purring and Craker singing? Will they share the Craker sexual cycles? Such questions are much discussed around the MaddAddamite dinner table.

The three mothers and the four children are all doing well, and the Craker women are ever-present, purring, tending, and bringing gifts. The gifts are kudzu leaves and shiny pieces of glass from the beach, but they are well meant.

Lotis Blue is now pregnant herself, though she claims the father is not a Craker: Manatee was her choice. He is attentive to her, when not down at the beach fishing, or out deer hunting.

Crozier and Ren appear united in their desire to raise Ren's child together. Shackleton is supporting Amanda, and Ivory Bill has offered his services as soi-disant father to the Swift Fox twins. "We all have to pitch in," he said, "because this is the future of the human race."

"Good luck to it," said Swift Fox, but she tolerates his help.

"Zeb and Rhino and I risked a trip to the drugstore," Toby writes, "and managed to scrounge several sackfuls of disposable diapers. But are they even necessary? The Craker babies are not cumbered with them."

The Feast of Kannon-the-Oryx, and of Rhizomes-the-Roots. Full moon.

Toby says that Kannon is like Oryx. She says that Rhizomes is like roots. So I (Blackbeard) have written those things down.

Here are the names of the babies who have been born:

The baby of Ren is called Jimadam. Like Snowman-the-Jimmy, and like Adam too. Ren says she wanted the name of Jimmy to still be spoken in the world, and alive; and she wanted the same for the name of Adam.

The baby of Amanda is called Pilaren. That is like Pilar, who lives in the elderberry bush, with the bees; and also like Ren, who is Amanda's very good friend and helper, through thick and thin, she said. I (Blackbeard) will ask Toby what *thick and thin* means.

The babies of Swift Fox are called Medulla and Oblongata. Medulla is a girl and Oblongata is a boy. Swift Fox says these names are for a reason that is hard to understand. It is about something inside a head.

All of the babies make us very happy.

I (Blackbeard) had his first mating, with SarahLacy, who chose his flower, so he is more happy than everyone. Soon there will be another baby, SarahLacy has told us, because he (Blackbeard) and the other three fourfathers did their dance of mating very well.

And their singing.

Thank you. Good night.

Book

Book

Now this is the Book that Toby made when she lived among us. See, I am showing you. She made these words on a *page,* and a page is made of *paper.* She made the words with *writing,* that she marked down with a stick called a *pen,* with black fluid called *ink,* and she made the *pages* join together at one side, and that is called a *book.* See, I am showing you. This is the Book, these are the Pages, here is the Writing.

And she showed me, Blackbeard, how to make such words, on a page, with a pen, when I was little. And she showed me how to turn the marks back into a voice, so that when I look at the page and read the words, it is Toby's voice that I hear. And when I speak these words out loud, you too are hearing Toby's voice.

Please don't sing.

And in the book she put the Words of Crake, and the Words of Oryx as well, and of how together they made us, and made also this safe and beautiful World for us to live in.

And in the Book too are the Words of Zeb, and of his brother, Adam; and the Words of Zeb Ate A Bear; and how he became our Defender against the bad men who did cruel and hurtful things; and the Words of Zeb's Helpers, Pilar and Rhino and Katrina WooWoo and March the Snake, and of all the MaddAddamites; and the Words of Snowman-the-Jimmy, who was there in the beginning, when Crake made us, and who led our people out of the Egg to this better place.

And the Words of Fuck, though these Words are not very long. See, there is only one page about Fuck.

Yes, I know he helps us when we are in trouble, and comes flying. He was sent by Crake, and we speak his name in Crake's honour. But there is not very much about him in this writing.

Please don't sing yet.

And Toby set down also the Words about Amanda and Ren and Swift Fox, our Beloved Three Oryx Mothers, who showed us that we and the two-skinned ones are all people and helpers, though we have different gifts, and some of us turn blue and some do not.

So Toby said we must be respectful, and always ask first, to see if a woman is really blue or is just smelling blue, when there is a question about blue things.

And Toby showed me what to do when there should be no more pens of plastic, and no more pencils either; for she could look into the future, and see that a time would come when no pens or pencils or paper could be found any more, among the buildings of the city of chaos, where they used to grow.

And she showed me how to use the quill feathers of birds to make the pens, though we also made some pens from the ribs of a broken umbrella.

An *umbrella* is a thing from the chaos. They used it for keeping the rain off their bodies.

I don't know why they did that.

And Toby showed me how to make the black marks with ink that is made of walnut shells, mixed with vinegar and salt; and this ink is brown. And ink of different colours can be made from berries, and we made some purple ink from the elderberries with Pilar's Spirit in them, and we wrote the Words of Pilar in that ink. And Toby showed me how to make more paper out of plants.

And Toby gave warnings about this Book that we wrote. She said that the paper must not get wet, or the Words would melt away and would be heard no longer, and mildew would grow on it, and it would turn black and crumble to nothing. And that another Book should be made, with the same writing as the first one. And each time a person came into the knowledge of the writing, and the paper, and the pen, and the ink, and the reading, that one also was to make the same Book, with the same writing in it. So it would always be there for us to read.

And that at the end of the Book we should put some other pages, and attach them to the Book, and write down the things that might happen after Toby was gone, so that we might know all of the Words about Crake, and Oryx, and our Defender, Zeb, and his brother, Adam, and Toby, and Pilar, and the three Beloved Oryx Mothers. And about ourselves also, and about the Egg, where we came from in the beginning.

And I have taught all of these things about the Book and the paper and the writing to Jimadam, and to Pilaren, and to Medulla and Oblongata, who were born to Ren and Amanda and Swift Fox, our Beloved Three Oryx Mothers.

And they wanted to learn, although it is hard. But they learned these things, to help all of us together. And when I am no longer here among us but have gone where Toby and Zeb have gone, as Toby said I will go one day, then Jimadam and Pilaren and Medulla and Oblongata will teach these things to the younger ones.

Now I have added to the Words, and have set down those things that happened after Toby stopped making any of the Writing and putting it into the Book. And I have done this so we will all know of her, and of how we came to be.

And these new Words I have made are called the Story of Toby.

The Story of Toby

I am putting on the red hat of Snowman-the-Jimmy. See? It is on my head. And I have put the fish into my mouth, and taken it out again. Now it is time to listen, while I read to you from the Story of Toby that I have written down at the end of this Book.

One day Zeb went on a journey to the south. He went there because when he was out hunting for deer, he saw a tall smoke. And it was not smoke made by a forest on fire, but it was a thin smoke. And he watched it for some days, and it did not become any bigger or smaller, but stayed the same. But then one day it moved closer. And the day after that it moved closer still.

So Zeb told us that there might be others — more people from before the chaos, from before Crake cleared the chaos away. But would they be good people, or would they be bad and cruel men that would hurt us? There was no way to tell. But he did not want those people to get very close to us unless he could find out the answer to that question. If the answer was that they were good, then we would be their helpers, and they would be our helpers as well. But if they were not good, then he would not let them come near us, and hurt us, but would clear them away.

And Abraham Lincoln and Albert Einstein and Sojourner Truth and Napoleon wanted to go with him, to help; and I, Blackbeard, wanted to go as well, as I was not a child any more but had become a man, with blueness and strength. But Zeb said it might be too harsh, what would happen. And we were not sure what *harsh* meant. And

Zeb said he hoped we would never have to find out. And Toby said we needed to stay behind, because it might be a Battle; and if we went, the others would be very sad if we did not come back. And Toby said she had asked Oryx and also the Spirit of Pilar, and they both said we should stay, and not go with Zeb. And so we did not go.

And Zeb took with him Black Rhino and Katuro. And Manatee and Zunzuncito and Shackleton and Crozier wanted to go too, but Zeb said they needed to stay, because there were young children to be protected. And Toby had to stay as well, with the gun thing we should not touch. So they did not go. And Zeb said that it was just a scouting trip, to see; and if it was bad news he would set a fire, another fire, and we would see the smoke, and then more could be sent to help him, and the Pig Ones could be told, though first we would have to find them, because they move from one place to another.

And we waited a long time, but Zeb did not return. And Shackleton took three of our blue men to see if the tall and thin smoke was still there. And they came back and told us it was not there any more. Which meant those making it had not been good, and Zeb our Defender must have done a sudden Battle, to make sure that those ones did not get any closer to us. But because he did not come back, he too must have died in the Battle, and Rhino, and Katuro as well.

And when she heard that, Toby cried.

Then we were all sad. But Toby was more sad than anyone, because Zeb was gone. And although we purred over her, she did not ever become happy again.

Then she became thinner and thinner, and shrunken; and after several months, she told us that she had a wasting sickness that was eating parts of her away, inside her body. And it could not be healed with purring, or with maggots, or with anything that she knew of; and the wasting sickness was increasing, and soon she would not be able to walk. And we said we could carry her wherever she wanted to go, and she smiled and said, Thank you.

Then she called each one of us to her, and said good night, a thing she herself taught us long ago. And it is a way of hoping that the other person will sleep well, and will not be troubled by bad dreams. And we said good night to her as well. And we sang for her.

Then Toby took her very old packsack, which was pink; and into it she put her jar of Poppy, and also a jar with mushrooms in it that we were told never to touch. And she walked away slowly into the forest, with a stick to help her, and asked us not to follow her.

Where she went I cannot write in this Book, because I do not know. Some say that she died by herself, and was eaten by vultures. The Pig Ones say that. Others say she was taken away by Oryx, and is now flying in the forest, at night, in the form of an Owl. Others said that she went to join Pilar, and that her Spirit is in the elderberry bush.

Yet others say that she went to find Zeb, and that he is in the form of a Bear, and that she too is in the form of a Bear, and is with him today. That is the best answer, because it is the happiest; and I have written it down. I have written down the other answers too. But I made them in smaller writing.

The three Beloved Oryx Mothers cried very much when Toby went away. We cried as well, and purred over them, and after a while they felt better. And Ren said, Tomorrow is another day, and we said we did not understand what that meant, and Amanda said, Never mind because it was not important. And Lotis Blue said it was a thing of hope.

Then Swift Fox told us that she was pregnant again and soon there would be another baby. And the fourfathers were Abraham Lincoln and Napoleon and Picasso and me, Blackbeard; and I am very happy to have been chosen for that mating. And Swift Fox said that if it was a girl baby it would be named Toby. And that is a thing of hope.

This is the end of the Story of Toby. I have written it in this Book. And I have put my name here – Blackbeard – the way Toby first showed me when I was a child. It says that I was the one who set down these words.

Thank you.

Now we will sing.

Acknowledgements

Although *MaddAddam* is a work of fiction, it does not include any technologies or biobeings that do not already exist, are not under construction, or are not possible in theory.

Most of the central characters in *MaddAddam* appear in the first two books in this series, *Oryx and Crake* and *The Year of the Flood*. Several of their names originated through donations in aid of various causes, including the Medical Foundation for the Care of Victims of Torture ("Amanda Payne") and *The Walrus* magazine ("Rebecca Eckler"). Joining them in *MaddAddam* are "Allan Slaight," courtesy of his daughter, Maria (his biography is called *Sleight of Hand*); "Katrina Wu," courtesy of Yung Wu; and "March," courtesy of a blind draw on Wattpad.com that was won by Lucas Fernandes. Saint Nikolai Vavilov came from Sona Grovenstein, and beekeeping tips from Carmen Brown of Honey Delight in Canberra, Australia.

My gratitude, as always, to my editors, Ellen Seligman of McClelland & Stewart (Canada), Nan Talese of Doubleday (U.S.A.), and Alexandra Pringle of Bloomsbury (U.K.).

Thanks also to my first readers: Jess Atwood Gibson; my U.K. agents, Vivienne Schuster, Karolina Sutton, and Betsy Robbins of Curtis Brown; and Phoebe Larmore, my North American agent; and to Timothy O'Connell. Thanks also to Ron Bernstein. And special thanks to Heather Sangster of Strongfinish.ca for the marathon copyediting session, after which she was faced with a blizzard and a car that wouldn't start.

And thanks to my office staff, Sarah Webster and Laura Stenberg; and to Penny Kavanaugh; and to VJ Bauer, vjbauer.com, VFX artist; and to Joel Rubinovich and Sheldon Shoib. And to Michael Bradley and Sarah Cooper, and to Coleen Quinn and Xiaolan Zhao. Also, to Louise Dennys, LuAnn Walther, and Lennie Goodings, and to my many agents and publishers around the world. I'd also like to thank Dr. Dave Mossop and Grace Mossop, and Barbara and Norman Barricello, all of Whitehorse, Yukon; and the many readers who have encouraged the writing of this book, including those on Twitter and Facebook.

Finally, my special thanks to Graeme Gibson, with whom I wander through the afternoon woods of life, foraging for nutritious bioforms, battling hostile ones wherever they appear, and eating them when possible.

"Atwood is a wry wizard at world-building. . . . Fans . . . should grab a biohazard suit, crawl into a hermetically sealed fallout shelter, and dive right in."   —*The Christian Science Monitor*

"Atwood scores a ten."   —*The Philadelphia Inquirer*

"Atwood's latest is a fiercely imagined tale of suffering that rivals Job's. . . . As dark as Atwood's vision may be, the bonds among her women give her work a bittersweet power."   —*People*

"Richly imagined. . . . Thought-provoking, unexpectedly funny and utterly original."   —*The Denver Post*

"Engrossing and suspenseful."   —*The New York Review of Books*

"Vintage Atwood: It's artfully edgy, casting a pitiless eye on her fellow creatures. . . . A powerful indictment of the way human beings have long treated the planet and themselves."   —*Chicago Tribune*

"Mesmerizing. . . . *Flood*'s relentlessly fabulous inventions and despondent predictions become almost unbearable, especially told in such gorgeously trenchant prose." —*Time Out New York* (five out of five stars)

"With Atwood's characteristic brainy humor. . . it entertains, spins out suspense and rewards a reader's basic impulse, all the while subtly and expertly maintaining its literary respectability."
                                  —*Minneapolis Star Tribune*

"[Atwood] is emerging as literature's queen of the apocalypse. . . . Gripping and scary, provocative and quite humorous."
                                  —Associated Press

"A marvelously absorbing novel. . . . Vivid and remarkably drawn."
                                  —*The Onion*

MARGARET ATWOOD
THE YEAR OF THE FLOOD

Margaret Atwood, whose work has been published in over thirty-five countries, is the author of more than forty books of fiction, poetry, and critical essays. In addition to *The Handmaid's Tale*, her novels include *Cat's Eye*, shortlisted for the Booker Prize; *Alias Grace*, which won the Giller Prize in Canada and the Premio Mondello in Italy; *The Blind Assassin*, winner of the Booker Prize; and her most recent, *Oryx and Crake*, shortlisted for the Booker Prize. She lives in Toronto with writer Graeme Gibson.

www.yearoftheflood.com

The Journals of Susanna Moodie
Procedures for Underground
Power Politics
You Are Happy
Selected Poems
Two-Headed Poems
True Stories
Interlunar
Selected Poems II: Poems Selected and New 1976–1986
Morning in the Burned House

NONFICTION

Survival: A Thematic Guide to Canadian Literature
Days of the Rebels 1815–1840
Second Words
Strange Things: The Malevolent North in Canadian Literature
Two Solicitudes: Conversations (with Victor-Lévy Beaulieu)
Negotiating with the Dead: A Writer on Writing
Writing with Intent: Essays, Reviews, Personal Prose 1983–2005

FOR CHILDREN

Up in the Tree
Anna's Pet (with Joyce Barkhouse)
For the Birds
Princess Prunella and the Purple Peanut
Rude Ramsay and the Roaring Radishes
Bashful Bob and Doleful Dorinda

Anchor Books
A Division of Random House, Inc.
New York

A NOVEL

THE
YEAR
OF THE
FLOOD

MARGARET
ATWOOD

FIRST ANCHOR BOOKS EDITION, JULY 2010

Copyright © 2009 by O. W. Toad Ltd.

The Library of Congress has cataloged the
Nan A. Talese/Doubleday edition as follows:
Atwood, Margaret, 1939–
The year of the flood : a novel / Margaret Atwood. —1st ed.
p. cm.
1. Environmental disasters—Fiction. 2. Regression (Civilization)—Fiction.
I. Title.
PR9199.3.A8Y43 2009
813'.54—dc22
2009005901

Anchor ISBN: 978-0-307-45547-5

www.anchorbooks.com

Printed in the United States of America
20 19 18 17 16 15

For Graeme and Jess

CONTENTS

THE GARDEN

Who is it tends the Garden,
The Garden oh so green?

'Twas once the finest Garden
That ever has been seen.

And in it God's dear Creatures
Did swim and fly and play;

But then came greedy Spoilers,
And killed them all away.

And all the Trees that flourished
And gave us wholesome fruit,

By waves of sand are buried,
Both leaf and branch and root.

And all the shining Water
Is turned to slime and mire,

And all the feathered Birds so bright
Have ceased their joyful choir.

Oh Garden, oh my Garden,
I'll mourn forevermore

Until the Gardeners arise,
And you to Life restore.

From *The God's Gardeners Oral Hymnbook*

THE YEAR
OF THE FLOOD

1

TOBY

YEAR TWENTY-FIVE, THE YEAR OF THE FLOOD

In the early morning Toby climbs up to the rooftop to watch the sunrise. She uses a mop handle for balance: the elevator stopped working some time ago and the back stairs are slick with damp, and if she slips and topples there won't be anyone to pick her up.

As the first heat hits, mist rises from among the swath of trees between her and the derelict city. The air smells faintly of burning, a smell of caramel and tar and rancid barbecues, and the ashy but greasy smell of a garbage-dump fire after it's been raining. The abandoned towers in the distance are like the coral of an ancient reef – bleached and colourless, devoid of life.

There still is life, however. Birds chirp; sparrows, they must be. Their small voices are clear and sharp, nails on glass: there's no longer any sound of traffic to drown them out. Do they notice that quietness, the absence of motors? If so, are they happier? Toby has no idea. Unlike some of the other Gardeners – the more wild-eyed or possibly overdosed ones – she has never been under the illusion that she can converse with birds.

The sun brightens in the east, reddening the blue-grey haze that marks the distant ocean. The vultures roosting on hydro poles fan out their wings to dry them, opening themselves like black umbrellas. One and then another lifts off on the thermals and spirals upwards. If they plummet suddenly, it means they've spotted carrion.

Vultures are our friends, the Gardeners used to teach. *They purify the earth. They are God's necessary dark Angels of bodily dissolution. Imagine how terrible it would be if there were no death!*

Do I still believe this? Toby wonders.

Everything is different up close.

The rooftop has some planters, their ornamentals running wild; it has a few fake-wood benches. There was once a sun canopy for cocktail hour, but that's been blown away. Toby sits on one of the benches to survey the grounds. She lifts her binoculars, scanning from left to right. The driveway, with its lumirose borders, untidy now as frayed hairbrushes, their purple glow fading in the strengthening light. The western entrance, done in pink adobe-style solarskin, the snarl of tangled cars outside the gate.

The flower beds, choked with sow thistle and burdock, enormous aqua kudzu moths fluttering above them. The fountains, their scallop-shell basins filled with stagnant rainwater. The parking lot with a pink golf cart and two pink AnooYoo Spa minivans, each with its winking-eye logo. There's a fourth minivan farther along the drive, crashed into a tree: there used to be an arm hanging out of the window, but it's gone now.

The wide lawns have grown up, tall weeds. There are low irregular mounds beneath the milkweed and fleabane and sorrel, with here and there a swatch of fabric, a glint of bone. That's where the people fell, the ones who'd been running or staggering across the lawn. Toby had watched from the roof, crouched behind one of the planters, but she hadn't watched for long. Some of those people had called for help, as if they'd known she was there. But how could she have helped?

The swimming pool has a mottled blanket of algae. Already there are frogs. The herons and the egrets and the peagrets hunt them, at the shallow end. For a while Toby tried to scoop out the small animals that had blundered in and drowned. The luminous green rabbits, the rats, the rakunks, with their striped tails and racoon bandit masks. But now she leaves them alone. Maybe they'll generate fish, somehow. When the pool is more like a swamp.

Is she thinking of eating these theoretical future fish? Surely not. Surely not yet.

She turns to the dark encircling wall of trees and vines and fronds and shrubby undergrowth, probing it with her binoculars. It's from there that any danger might come. But what kind of danger? She can't imagine.

In the night there are the usual noises: the faraway barking of dogs, the tittering of mice, the water-pipe notes of the crickets, the occasional grumph of a frog. The blood rushing in her ears: *katoush, katoush, katoush*. A heavy broom sweeping dry leaves.

"Go to sleep," she says out loud. But she never sleeps well, not since she's been alone in this building. Sometimes she hears voices – human voices, calling to her in pain. Or the voices of women, the women who used to work here, the anxious women who used to come, for rest and rejuvenation. Splashing in the pool, strolling on the lawns. All the pink voices, soothed and soothing.

Or the voices of the Gardeners, murmuring or singing; or the children laughing together, up on the Edencliff Garden. Adam One, and Nuala, and Burt. Old Pilar, surrounded by her bees. And Zeb. If any one of them is still alive, it must be Zeb: any day now he'll come walking along the roadway or appear from among the trees.

But he must be dead by now. It's better to think so. Not to waste hope.

There must be someone else left, though; she can't be the only one on the planet. There must be others. But friends or foes? If she sees one, how to tell?

She's prepared. The doors are locked, the windows barred. But even such barriers are no guarantee: every hollow space invites invasion.

Even when she sleeps, she's listening, as animals do – for a break in the pattern, for an unknown sound, for a silence opening like a crack in rock.

When the small creatures hush their singing, said Adam One, it's because they're afraid. You must listen for the sound of their fear.

2

YEAR TWENTY-FIVE, THE YEAR OF THE FLOOD

Beware of words. Be careful what you write. Leave no trails.

This is what the Gardeners taught us, when I was a child among them. They told us to depend on memory, because nothing written down could be relied on. The Spirit travels from mouth to mouth, not from thing to thing: books could be burnt, paper crumble away, computers could be destroyed. Only the Spirit lives forever, and the Spirit isn't a thing.

As for writing, it was dangerous, said the Adams and the Eves, because your enemies could trace you through it, and hunt you down, and use your words to condemn you.

But now that the Waterless Flood has swept over us, any writing I might do is safe enough, because those who would have used it against me are most likely dead. So I can write down anything I want.

What I write is my name, *Ren*, with an eyebrow pencil, on the wall beside the mirror. I've written it a lot of times. *Renrenren*, like a song. You can forget who you are if you're alone too much. Amanda told me that.

I can't see out the window, it's glass brick. I can't get out the door, it's locked on the outside. I still have air though, and water, as long as the solar doesn't quit. I still have food.

I'm lucky. I'm really very lucky. Count your luck, Amanda used to say. So I do. First, I was lucky to be working here at Scales when the Flood hit. Second, it was even luckier that I was shut up this way in the Sticky Zone, because it kept me safe. I got a rip in my Biofilm Bodyglove – a client got carried away and bit me, right through the green sequins – and I was waiting for my test results. It wasn't a wet rip with secretions and membranes involved, it was a dry rip near the elbow, so I wasn't that worried. Still, they checked everything, here at Scales. They had a reputation to keep up: we were known as the cleanest dirty girls in town.

Scales and Tails took care of you, they really did. If you were talent, that is. Good food, a doctor if you needed one, and the tips were great, because the men from the top Corps came here. It was well run, though it was in a seedy area – all the clubs were. That was a matter of image, Mordis would say: seedy was good for business, because unless there's an edge – something lurid or tawdry, a whiff of sleaze – what separated our brand from the run-of-the-mill product the guy could get at home, with the face cream and the white cotton panties?

Mordis believed in plain speaking. He'd been in the business ever since he was a kid, and when they outlawed the pimps and the street trade – for public health and the safety of women, they said – and rolled everything into SeksMart under CorpSeCorps control, Mordis made the jump, because of his experience. "It's who you know," he used to say. "And what you know about them." Then he'd grin and pat you on the bum – just a friendly pat though, he never took freebies from us. He had ethics.

He was a wiry guy with a shaved head and black, shiny, alert eyes like the heads of ants, and he was easy as long as everything was cool. But he'd stand up for us if the clients got violent. "Nobody hurts my best girls," he'd say. It was a point of honour with him.

Also he didn't like waste: we were a valuable asset, he'd say. The cream of the crop. After the SeksMart roll-in, anyone left outside the system was not only illegal but pathetic. A few wrecked, diseased old women wandering the alleyways, practically begging. No man with even a fraction of his brain left would go anywhere near them. "Hazardous waste," we Scales girls used to call them. We shouldn't have been so scornful; we should have had compassion. But compassion takes work, and we were young.

That night when the Waterless Flood began, I was waiting for my test results: they kept you locked in the Sticky Zone for weeks, in case you had something contagious. The food came in through the safety-sealed hatchway, plus there was the minifridge with snacks, and the water was filtered, coming in and out both. You had everything you needed, but it got boring in there. You could exercise on the machines, and I did a lot of that, because a trapeze dancer needs to keep in practice.

You could watch TV or old movies, play your music, talk on the phone. Or you could visit the other rooms in Scales on the intercom videoscreens. Sometimes when we were doing plank work we'd wink at the cameras in mid-moan for the benefit of whoever was stuck in the Sticky Zone. We knew where the cameras were hidden, in the snake-skin or featherwork on the ceilings. It was one big family, at Scales, so even when you were in the Sticky Zone, Mordis liked you to pretend you were still participating.

Mordis made me feel so secure. I knew if I was in big trouble I could go to him. There were only a few people in my life like that. Amanda, most of the time. Zeb, sometimes. And Toby. You wouldn't think it would be Toby – she was so tough and hard – but if you're drowning, a soft squashy thing is no good to hold on to. You need something more solid.

CREATION
DAY

CREATION DAY

YEAR FIVE.

OF THE CREATION, AND OF THE NAMING OF THE ANIMALS.
SPOKEN BY ADAM ONE.

Dear Friends, dear Fellow Creatures, dear Fellow Mammals:

On Creation Day five years ago, this Edencliff Rooftop Garden of ours was a sizzling wasteland, hemmed in by festering city slums and dens of wickedness; but now it has blossomed as the rose.

By covering such barren rooftops with greenery we are doing our small part in the redemption of God's Creation from the decay and sterility that lies all around us, and feeding ourselves with unpolluted food into the bargain. Some would term our efforts futile, but if all were to follow our example, what a change would be wrought on our beloved Planet! Much hard work still lies before us, but fear not, my Friends: for we shall move forward undaunted.

I am glad we have all remembered our sunhats.

Now let us turn our minds to our annual Creation Day Devotion.

The Human Words of God speak of the Creation in terms that could be understood by the men of old. There is no talk of galaxies or genes, for such terms would have confused them greatly! But must we therefore take as scientific fact the story that the world was created in six days, thus making a nonsense of observable data? God cannot be held to the narrowness of literal and materialistic interpretations, nor measured by Human measurements, for His days are eons, and a thousand ages of our time are like an evening to Him. Unlike some other religions, we have never felt it served a higher purpose to lie to children about geology.

Remember the first sentences of those Human Words of God: the Earth is without form, and void, and then God speaks Light into being.

This is the moment that Science terms "The Big Bang," as if it were a sex orgy. Yet both accounts concur in their essence: Darkness; then, in an instant, Light. But surely the Creation is ongoing, for are not new stars being formed at every moment? God's Days are not consecutive, my Friends; they run concurrently, the first with the third, the fourth with the sixth. As we are told, "Thou sendeth forth thy Spirit, they are created: and Thou renewest the face of the Earth."

We are told that, on the fifth day of God's Creating activities, the waters brought forth Creatures, and on the sixth day the dry land was populated with Animals, and with Plants and Trees; and all were blessed, and told to multiply; and finally Adam – that is to say, Mankind – was created. According to Science, this is the same order in which the species did in fact appear on the Planet, Man last of all. Or more or less the same order. Or close enough.

What happens next? God brings the Animals before Man, "to see what he would call them." But why didn't God already know what names Adam would choose? The answer can only be that God has given Adam free will, and therefore Adam may do things that God Himself cannot anticipate in advance. Think of that the next time you are tempted by meat-eating or material wealth! Even God may not always know what you are going to do next!

God must have caused the Animals to assemble by speaking to them directly, but what language did He use? It was not Hebrew, my Friends. It was not Latin or Greek, or English, or French, or Spanish, or Arabic, or Chinese. No: He called the Animals in their own languages. To the Reindeer He spoke Reindeer, to the Spider, Spider; to the Elephant He spoke Elephant, to the Flea He spoke Flea, to the Centipede He spoke Centipede, and to the Ant, Ant. So must it have been.

And for Adam himself, the Names of the Animals were the first words he spoke – the first moment of Human language. In this cosmic instant, Adam claims his Human soul. To Name is – we hope – to greet; to draw another towards one's self. Let us imagine Adam calling out the Names of the Animals in fondness and joy, as if to say, *There you are, my dearest! Welcome!* Adam's first act towards the Animals was thus one of loving-kindness and kinship, for Man in his unfallen state was not yet a carnivore. The Animals knew this, and did not run away. So it must have been on that unrepeatable Day – a peaceful gathering at which every living entity on the Earth was embraced by Man.

How much have we lost, dear Fellow Mammals and Fellow Mortals! How much have we wilfully destroyed! How much do we need to restore, within ourselves!

The time of the Naming is not over, my Friends. In His sight, we may still be living in the sixth day. As your Meditation, imagine yourself rocked in that sheltering moment. Stretch out your hand towards those gentle eyes that regard you with such trust – a trust that has not yet been violated by bloodshed and gluttony and pride and disdain.

Say their Names.

Let us sing.

WHEN ADAM FIRST

When Adam first had breath of life
All in that golden place,
He dwelt in peace with Bird and Beast,
And knew God face to face.

Man's Spirit first went forth in speech
To Name each Creature dear;
God called to all in Fellowship,
They came without a fear.

They romped in play, and sang, and flew –
Each motion was a praise
For God's great Creativity
That filled those early days.

How shrunk, how dwindled, in our times
Creation's mighty seed –
For Man has broke the Fellowship
With murder, lust, and greed.

Oh Creatures dear, that suffer here,
How may we Love restore?
We'll Name you in our inner Hearts,
And call you Friend once more.

From *The God's Gardeners Oral Hymnbook*

3

TOBY. PODOCARP DAY

YEAR TWENTY-FIVE

It's daybreak. The break of day. Toby turns this word over: break, broke, broken. What breaks in daybreak? Is it the night? Is it the sun, cracked in two by the horizon like an egg, spilling out light?

She lifts her binoculars. The trees look as innocent as ever; yet she has the feeling that someone's watching her – as if even the most inert stone or stump can sense her, and doesn't wish her well.

Isolation produces such effects. She'd trained for them during the God's Gardeners Vigils and Retreats. The floating orange triangle, the talking crickets, the writhing columns of vegetation, the eyes in the leaves. Still, how to distinguish between such illusions and the real thing?

The sun's fully up now – smaller, hotter. Toby makes her way down from the rooftop, covers herself in her pink top-to-toe, sprays with SuperD for the bugs, and adjusts her broad pink sunhat. Then she unlocks the front door and goes out to tend the garden. This is where they used to grow the ladies' organic salads for the Spa Café – their garnishes, their exotic spliced vegetables, their herbal teas. There's overhead netting to thwart the birds, and a chain-link fence because of the green rabbits and the bobkittens and the rakunks that might wander in from the Park. These weren't numerous before the Flood, but it's astonishing how quickly they've been multiplying.

She's counting on this garden: her supplies in the storeroom are getting low. Over the years she'd stashed what she thought would be enough for an emergency like this, but she'd underestimated, and now she's running out of soybits and soydines. Luckily, everything in the garden is doing well: the chickenpeas have begun to pod, the beananas are in flower, the polyberry bushes are covered with small brown nubbins of different shapes and sizes. She picks some spinach, flicks off the iridescent green beetles on it, steps on them. Then, feeling remorseful, she makes a thumbprint grave for them and says the words for the freeing of the soul and the asking of pardon. Even though no one's watching her, it's hard to break such ingrained habits.

She relocates several slugs and snails and pulls out some weeds, leaving the purslane: she can steam that later. On the delicate carrot fronds she finds two bright-blue kudzu-moth caterpillars. Though developed as a biological control for invasive kudzu, they seem to prefer garden vegetables. In one of those jokey moves so common in the first years of gene-splicing, their designer gave them a baby face at the front end, with big eyes and a happy smile, which makes them remarkably difficult to kill. She pulls them off the carrots, their mandibles chewing ravenously beneath their cutie-pie masks, lifts the edge of the netting, and tosses them outside the fence. No doubt they'll be back.

On the way back to the building, she finds the tail of a dog beside the path – an Irish setter, it looks like – its long fur matted with burrs and twigs. A vulture's dropped it there, most likely: they're always dropping things. She tries not to think of the other things they dropped in the first weeks after the Flood. Fingers were the worst.

Her own hands are getting thicker – stiff and brown, like roots. She's been digging in the earth too much.

4

TOBY. SAINT BASHIR ALOUSE DAY

YEAR TWENTY-FIVE

She takes her baths in the early mornings, before the sun's too hot. She keeps a number of pails and bowls up on the rooftop, for collecting the afternoon-storm rainwater: the Spa has its own well, but the solar system's broken so the pumps are useless. She does her laundry on the rooftop too, spreading it out on the benches to dry. She uses the grey-water to flush her toilet.

She rubs herself with soap – there's still a lot of soap, all of it pink – and sponges off. My body is shrinking, she thinks. I'm puckering, I'm dwindling. Soon I'll be nothing but a hangnail. Though she's always been on the skinny side – *Oh Tobiatha*, the ladies used to say, *if only I had your figure!*

She dries herself off, slips on a pink smock. This one says, *Melody*. There's no need to label herself now that nobody's left to read the labels, so she's begun wearing the smocks of the others: *Anita, Quintana, Ren, Carmel, Symphony*. Those girls had been so cheerful, so hopeful. Not Ren, though: Ren had been sad. But Ren had left earlier.

Then all of them had left, once the trouble hit. They'd gone home to be with their families, believing love could save them. "You go ahead, I'll lock up," Toby had told them. And she had locked up, but with herself inside.

She scrubs her long dark hair, twists it into a wet bun. She really must cut it. It's thick and too hot. Also it smells of mutton.

As she's drying her hair she hears an odd sound. She goes cautiously to the rooftop railing. Three huge pigs are nosing around the swimming pool – two sows and a boar. The morning light shines on their plump pinky-grey forms; they glisten like wrestlers. They seem too large and bulbous to be normal. She's spotted pigs like this before, in the meadow, but they've never come this close. Escapees, they must be, from some experimental farm or other.

They're grouped by the shallow end of the pool, gazing at it as if in thought, their snouts twitching. Maybe they're sniffing the dead rakunk floating on the surface of the scummy water. Will they try to retrieve it? They grunt softly to one another, then back away: the thing must be too putrid even for them. They pause for a final sniff, then trot around the corner of the building.

Toby follows the railing, tracking them. They've found the garden fence, they're looking in. Then one of them begins to dig. They'll tunnel under.

"Get away from there!" Toby shouts at them. They peer up at her, dismiss her.

She scrambles down the stairs as fast as she can without slipping. Idiot! She should keep the rifle with her at all times. She grabs it from her bedside, hurries back up to the roof. She holds one of the pigs in the scope – the boar, an easy shot, he's sideways – but then she hesitates. They're God's Creatures. Never kill without just cause, said Adam One.

"I'm warning you!" she yells. Amazingly they seem to understand her. They must've seen a weapon before – a spraygun, a stun gun. They squeal in alarm, then turn and run.

They're a quarter of the way across the meadow when it occurs to her they'll be back. They'll dig under at night and root up her garden in no time flat, and that will be the end of her long-term food supply. She'll have to shoot them, it's self-defence. She squeezes off a round, misses, tries again. The boar falls down. The two sows keep running. Only when they've reached the forest rim do they turn and look back. Then they meld with the foliage and are gone.

Toby's hands are shaking. You've snuffed a life, she tells herself.

You've acted rashly and from anger. You ought to feel guilty. Still, she thinks of going out with one of the kitchen knives and sawing off a ham. She'd taken the Vegivows when she joined the Gardeners, but the prospect of a bacon sandwich is a great temptation right now. She resists it, however: animal protein should be the last resort.

She murmurs the standard Gardener words of apology, though she doesn't feel apologetic. Or not apologetic enough.

She needs to do some target practice. Shooting the boar, missing at first, letting the sows get away – that was clumsy.

In recent weeks she's grown lax about the rifle. Now she vows to cart it around with her wherever she goes – even up to the rooftop for a bath, even to the toilet. Even to the garden – especially to the garden. Pigs are smart, they'll keep her in mind, they won't forgive her. Should she lock the door when she goes out? What if she has to run back into the Spa building in a hurry? But if she leaves the door unlocked, someone or something could slip in when she's working in the garden and be waiting for her inside.

She'll need to think of every angle. *An Ararat without a wall isn't an Ararat at all*, as the Gardener children used to chant. *A wall that cannot be defended is no sooner built than ended.* The Gardeners loved their instructive rhymes.

5

Toby went in search of the rifle a few days after the first outbreaks. It was the night after the girls had fled from AnooYoo, leaving their pink smocks behind them.

This was not an ordinary pandemic: it wouldn't be contained after a few hundred thousand deaths, then obliterated with biotools and bleach. This was the Waterless Flood the Gardeners so often had warned about. It had all the signs: it travelled through the air as if on wings, it burned through cities like fire, spreading germ-ridden mobs, terror, and butchery. The lights were going out everywhere, the news was sporadic: systems were failing as their keepers died. It looked like total breakdown, which was why she'd needed the rifle. Rifles were illegal and getting caught with one would have been fatal a week earlier, but now such laws were no longer a factor.

The trip would be dangerous. She'd have to walk to her old pleeb – no transport would be functioning – and locate the tacky little split-level that had so briefly belonged to her parents. Then she'd have to dig the rifle up from where it had been buried, hoping no one would see her doing it.

Walking that far would be no problem: she'd kept herself in shape. The hazard would be other people. The rioting was everywhere, according to what fitful news she could still pick up from her phone.

She left the Spa at dusk, locking the door behind her. She crossed the wide lawns and made her way to the northern entrance along the woodland walk where the customers used to take their shady strolls: she'd be less visible there. There were still some glowlights marking the pathway. She met no one, though a green rabbit hopped into the bushes and a bobkitten crossed in front of her, turning to stare with its lambent eyes.

The entrance gate was ajar. She slid through cautiously, half expecting a challenge. Then she set out across Heritage Park. People were hurrying past, singly and in groups, trying to get out of the city, hoping to make their way through the pleebland sprawl and seek out refuge in the countryside. There was coughing, a child's wail. She almost stumbled over someone on the ground.

By the time she reached the Park's outer edge, it was pitch-dark. She moved from tree to tree along the verge, hugging the shadows. The boulevard was jammed with cars, trucks, solarbikes, and buses, their drivers honking and shouting. Some of the vehicles had been overturned and were burning. In the shops, the looting was in full swing. There were no CorpSeCorpsMen in sight. They must have been the first to desert, heading for their gated Corporation strongholds to save their skins, and carrying – Toby certainly hoped – the lethal virus with them.

From somewhere there were gunshots. So backyards were already being dug up, thought Toby: hers was not the only rifle.

Up the street there was a barricade, cars wedged together. It had its defenders, armed with what? As far as Toby could see they were using metal pipes. The crowd was screaming at them in fury, throwing bricks and stones: they wanted past, they wanted to flee the city. What did the barricade-holders want? Plunder, no doubt. Rape and money, and other useless things.

When the Waterless Waters rise, Adam One used to say, the people will try to save themselves from drowning. They will clutch at any straw. Be sure you are not that straw, my Friends, for if you are clutched or even touched, you too will drown.

Toby turned away from the barricade – she'd have to circle around it. She held herself back in the darkness, crouching along behind the foliage and skirting the Park's rim. Now she'd reached the open space where the

Gardeners used to hold their markets, and the cobb house where the kids once played. She hid behind it, waiting for a distraction. Soon enough there was a crash and an explosion, and while all heads were turned she ambled across. It's best not to run, Zeb had taught: running away makes you a prey.

The side streets were awash with people; she dodged to avoid them. She'd worn surgical gloves, a bulletproof vest made of silk from a spider/goat splice lifted from the AnooYoo guardhouse a year ago, and a black nose-cone air filter. From the garden shed she'd brought a shovel and a crowbar, both of which could be lethal if used decisively. In her pocket was a bottle of AnooYoo Total Shine Hairspray, an effective weapon if aimed at the eyes. She'd learned a lot of things from Zeb in his Urban Bloodshed Limitation classes: in Zeb's view, the first bloodshed to be limited should be your own.

She headed northeast, through upmarket Fernside, then through Big Box with its tracts of smallish, badly built houses, slipping along the narrowest streets, which were dimly lit and not crowded. Several people passed her, intent on their own stories. Two teenagers paused as if to try a mugging, but she began coughing and croaked out, "Help me!" and they scurried away.

Around midnight, and after a few wrong turns – the streets in Big Box looked so much alike – she reached her parents' former house. No lights were on, the door to the garage was open, and the plate-glass window at the front was smashed, so she didn't think anyone was in there. The current occupants were either dead or elsewhere. It was the same with the identical house next door, the one where the rifle was buried.

She stood for a moment, calming herself down, listening to the blood in her head: *katoush, katoush, katoush.* Either the rifle was still there or it was gone. If it was there, she'd have a rifle. If it was gone, she wouldn't have one. Nothing to panic about.

She opened the neighbours' garden gate, stealthy as a thief. Darkness, no movement. The scent of night flowers: lilies, nicotiana. Mixed with that, a whiff of smoke from something burning, blocks away: she could see the flare. A kudzu moth flickered against her face.

She stuck the crowbar under a patio stone, lifted, grabbed the edge, heaved the stone over. Did it again, and again. Three patio stones. Then she dug with the shovel.

A heartbeat, then another.

It was there.

Don't cry, she told herself. Just cut open the plastic, grab the rifle and the ammunition, and get out of here.

It took her three days to get back to AnooYoo, skirting the worst rioting. There were muddy footprints on the outside steps, but no one had broken in.

6

The rifle is a primitive weapon – a Ruger 44/99 Deerfield. It had been her father's. He was the one who'd taught her to shoot, when she was twelve, back in those days that seem now like some mushroom-induced Technicolour brain vacation. Aim for the centre of the body, he'd said. Don't waste your time with heads. He said he just meant animals.

They'd been living in the semi-country, before the sprawl had rolled over that stretch of landscape. Their white frame house had ten acres of trees around it, and there were squirrels, and the first green rabbits. No rakunks, those hadn't been put together yet. There were a lot of deer; they'd get into her mother's vegetable garden. Toby had shot a couple, and helped to dress them; she can still remember the smell, and the slither of shining viscera. They'd eaten deer stew, and her mother had made soup with the bones. But mostly Toby and her father shot tin cans, and rats at the dump – there'd still been a dump. She'd practised a lot, which had pleased her dad. "Great shot, pal," he'd say.

Had he wanted a son? Perhaps. What he'd said was that everyone needed to know how to shoot. His generation believed that if there was trouble all you'd have to do was shoot someone and then it would be okay.

Then the CorpSeCorps had outlawed firearms in the interests of public security, reserving the newly invented sprayguns for themselves, and suddenly people were officially weaponless. Her father had buried his rifle and a supply of ammunition under a pile of discarded picket fencing and shown Toby where it was in case she ever needed it. The CorpSeCorps could have found it with their metal detectors – they were rumoured to be doing sweeps – but they couldn't look everywhere, and her father was innocuous from their point of view. He sold air conditioning. He was a small potato.

Then a developer wanted to buy his land. The offer was good, but Toby's father refused to sell. He liked it where he was, he said. So did Toby's mother, who ran the HelthWyzer supplements franchise in the nearest shopping area. They turned down another offer, then a third. "We'll build around you," said the developer. Toby's father said that was okay with him: by this time it had become a matter of principle.

He thought the world was still the way it had been fifty years before, thinks Toby. He shouldn't have been so stubborn. Already, back then, the CorpSeCorps were consolidating their power. They'd started as a private security firm for the Corporations, but then they'd taken over when the local police forces collapsed for lack of funding, and people liked that at first because the Corporations paid, but now CorpSeCorps were sending their tentacles everywhere. He should have caved.

First he'd lost his job with the air-conditioning corp. He got another one selling thermal windows, but it paid less. Then Toby's mother came down with a strange illness. She couldn't understand it, because she'd always been so careful about her health: she worked out, she ate a lot of vegetables, she took a dose of HelthWyzer Hi-Potency VitalVite supplements daily. Franchise operators like her got a deal on the supplements – their own customized package, just like the ones for the higher-ups at HelthWyzer.

She took more supplements, but despite that she became weak and confused and lost weight rapidly: it was as if her body had turned against itself. No doctor could give her a diagnosis, though many tests were done by the HelthWyzer Corp clinics; they took an interest because she'd been such a faithful user of their products. They arranged for special care, with their own doctors. They charged for it, though, and even with the discount for members of the HelthWyzer Franchise Family it was a lot of money; and because the condition had no name, her parents' modest health insurance plan refused to cover the costs. Nobody could get public wellness coverage unless they had no money of their own whatsoever.

Not that you'd want to go to one of those public dump bins anyway, thought Toby. All they did was poke at your tongue and give you a few germs and viruses you didn't already have, and send you home.

Toby's father took out a second mortgage and poured the money into the doctors and the drugs and the hired nurses and the hospitals. But Toby's mother continued to wither away.

Her father had to sell their white frame house then, for a much lower price than the one he'd first been offered. The day after the sale closed, the bulldozers flattened the place. Her father bought another house, a tiny split-level in a new subdivision – the one nicknamed Big Box because it was flanked by a whole flotilla of megastores. He'd dug up his rifle from under the picket fencing, smuggled it to the new house, and buried it again, this time under the patio stones in the barren little backyard.

Then he'd lost his thermal-window job because he'd taken too much time off due to his wife's illness. His solarcar had to be sold. Then the furniture disappeared, piece by piece; not that Toby's father could get much for it. People can smell desperation on you, he said to Toby. They take advantage.

This conversation took place over the phone because Toby had made it to college despite the lack of family cash. She'd got a meagre scholarship from the Martha Graham Academy, which she was fleshing out by waiting tables in the student cafeteria. She wanted to come home and help out with her mother, who'd been shipped back from the hospital and was sleeping on the main-floor sofa because she couldn't climb stairs, but her father said no, Toby should stay at college, because there was nothing she could do.

Finally even the tacky Big Box house had to be put up for sale. The sign was on the lawn when Toby came home for her mother's funeral. Her father by that time was a wreck; humiliation, pain, and failure had eaten away at him until there was almost nothing left.

Her mother's funeral was short and dreary. After it, Toby sat with her father in the stripped-down kitchen. They drank a six-pack between them, Toby two, her father four. Then, after Toby had gone to bed, her father went into the empty garage and stuck the Ruger into his mouth, and pulled the trigger.

Toby heard the shot. She knew at once what it was. She'd seen the rifle standing behind the door in the kitchen: he must have dug it up for a reason, but she hadn't allowed herself to imagine what that reason might be.

She couldn't face what was in the garage. She lay in bed, skipping ahead in time. What to do? If she called the authorities – even a doctor or an ambulance – they'd find the bullet wound, and then they'd demand the rifle, and Toby would be in trouble as the daughter of an admitted lawbreaker – one who'd owned a forbidden weapon. That would be the least of it. They might accuse her of murder.

After what seemed hours, she forced herself to move. In the garage, she tried not to look too closely. She wrapped what was left of her father in a blanket, then in plastic heavy-duty garbage bags, sealed him with duct tape, and buried him under the patio stones. She felt terrible about it, but it was a thing he'd have understood. He'd been a practical man, but sentimental under that – power tools in the shed, roses on birthdays. If he'd been nothing but practical he'd have marched into the hospital with the divorce papers, the way a lot of men did when something too debilitating and expensive struck their wives. Left her mother to be tossed out onto the street. Stayed solvent. Instead, he'd spent all their money.

Toby wasn't much for standard religion: none of her family had been. They'd gone to the local church because the neighbours did and it would have been bad for business not to, but she'd heard her father say – privately, and after a couple of drinks – that there were too many crooks in the pulpit and too many dupes in the pews. Nevertheless, Toby had whispered a short prayer over the patio stones: *Earth to earth.* Then she'd brushed sand into the cracks.

She'd wrapped up the rifle in its plastic again and buried it under the patio stones of the house next door, which seemed to be empty: windows dark, no car in evidence. Maybe they'd been foreclosed. She'd taken that chance, trespassing on the neighbours, because if her father's body settled and they dug up the yard, and she'd buried the rifle beside him, it would be found too, and she wanted it to stay where it was. "You never know," her father used to say, "when you might need it," and that was right: you never did know.

It's possible a neighbour or two saw her digging around in the dark, but she didn't think they'd tell. They wouldn't want to draw the lightning down anywhere near their own possibly weapon-filled backyards.

She hosed the blood off the garage floor, then took a shower. Then she went to bed. She lay in the darkness, wanting to cry, but all she felt was cold. Though it wasn't cold at all.

She couldn't sell the house without revealing that she was the owner now because her father was dead, thus unleashing a whole dumpster-load of garbage onto her own head. Where, for instance, was the corpse, and how had it become one? So in the morning, after a sparse breakfast, she put the dishes in the sink and walked out of the house. She didn't even take a suitcase. What was there to pack?

Most likely the CorpSeCorps wouldn't bother tracing her. There was nothing in it for them: one of the Corporation banks would get the house anyway. If her disappearance was of interest to anyone, such as maybe her college – where was she, was she ill, had she been in an accident – the CorpSeCorps would spread it about that she'd been last seen with a cruising pimp on the lookout for fresh recruits, which is what you'd expect in the case of a young woman like her – a young woman in desperate financial straits, with no visible relations and no nest egg or trust fund or fallback. People would shake their heads – a shame but what could you do, and at least she had something of marketable value, namely her young ass, and therefore she wouldn't starve to death, and nobody had to feel guilty. The CorpSeCorps always substituted rumour for action, if action would cost them anything. They believed in the bottom line.

As for her father, everyone would assume he'd changed his name and vanished into one of the seedier pleebs to avoid paying for her mother's funeral with money he didn't have. That sort of thing was happening all the time.

7

The period that followed was a bad time for Toby. Though she'd hidden the evidence and managed to disappear, there was still a chance the CorpSeCorps might come after her for her father's debts. She didn't have any money they could seize, but there were stories about female debtors being farmed out for sex. If she had to make her living on her back, she at least wanted to keep the proceeds.

She'd burned her identity and didn't have the cash to buy a new one – not even a cheap one, without the DNA infusion or the skin-colour change – so she couldn't get a legitimate job: those were mostly controlled by the Corporations. But if you sank deep down – down where names disappeared and no histories were true – the CorpSeCorps wouldn't bother with you.

She rented a tiny room – she had enough money left from her cafeteria savings for that. A room of her own, which might save her few possessions from theft by some dubious roommate. It was on the top floor of a fire-trap commercial building in one of the worst pleebs – Willow Acres was its name, though the locals called it the Sewage Lagoon because a lot of shit ended up in it. She shared the bathroom with six illegal Thai immigrants, who kept very quiet. It was said that the CorpSeCorps had decided that expelling illegals was too expensive, so they'd resorted to the method used by farmers who found a diseased cow in the herd: shoot, shovel, and shut up.

On the floor below her there was an endangered-species luxury couture operation called Slink. They sold Halloween costumes over the counter to fool the animal-righter extremists and cured the skins in the backrooms. The fumes came up through the ventilation system: though Toby tried stuffing pillows into the vent, her cubicle stank of chemicals and rancid fat. Sometimes there was roaring and bleating as well – they killed the animals on the premises because the customers didn't want goat dressed up as oryx or dyed wolf instead of wolverine. They wanted their bragging rights to be genuine.

The skinned carcasses were sold on to a chain of gourmet restaurants called Rarity. The public dining rooms served steak and lamb and venison and buffalo, certified disease-free so it could be cooked rare – that was what "Rarity" pretended to mean. But in the private banquet rooms – key-club entry, bouncer-enforced – you could eat endangered species. The profits were immense; one bottle of tiger-bone wine alone was worth a neckful of diamonds.

Technically, the endangered trade was illegal – there were high fines for it – but it was very lucrative. People in the neighbourhood knew about it, but they had their own worries, and who could you tell, without risk? There were pockets within pockets, with a CorpSeCorps hand in each one of them.

Toby got a job as a furzooter: cheap day labour, no identity required. The furzooters put on fake-fur animal suits with cartoon heads and hung advertising signs around their necks, and worked the higher-end malls and the boutique retail streets. But it was hot and humid inside the furzoots, and the range of vision was limited. In the first week she suffered three attacks by fetishists who knocked her over, twisted the big head around so she was blinded, and rubbed their pelvises against her fur, making strange noises, of which the meows were the most recognizable. It wasn't rape – no part of her actual body was touched – but it was creepy. Also it was distasteful dressing up as bears and tigers and lions and the other endangered species she could hear being slaughtered on the floor below her. So she stopped doing that.

Then she made a lump of quick cash by selling her hair. The hair market hadn't yet been decimated by the Mo'Hair sheep breeders – that happened a few years later – so there were still scalpers who'd buy from anyone, no questions asked. She'd had long hair then, and although it was medium brown – not the best colour, they preferred blond – it had fetched a decent sum.

After the money from the hair was used up, she'd sold her eggs on the black market. Young women could get top dollar for donating their eggs to couples who hadn't been able pay the required bribe or else were so truly unsuitable that no official would sell them a parenthood licence anyway. But she could only pull the egg stunt twice because the second time the extraction needle had been infected. At that time the egg traders were still paying for treatment if anything went wrong; still, it took her a month to recover. When she tried a third time, they told her there were complications, so she could never donate any more eggs, or – incidentally – have any children herself.

Toby hadn't known until then that she'd wanted any children. She'd had a boyfriend back at Martha Graham who used to talk about marriage and a family – Stan was his name – but Toby had said they were far too young and poor to consider it. She was studying Holistic Healing – Lotions and Potions, the students called it – and Stan was in Problematics and Quadruple-Entry Creative Asset Planning, at which he was doing well. His family wasn't rich or he wouldn't have been at a third-rate institution like Martha Graham, but he was ambitious, and fully intended to prosper. On their more tranquil evenings, Toby would rub her flower preparations and herbal extract projects on him, and after that there would be a round of crisp, botanical-remedy-flavoured sex, followed by a shower-off and some popcorn, without salt or fat.

But once her family hit the downdraft, Toby knew she couldn't afford Stan. She also knew her days at college were numbered. So she'd cut off contact. She didn't even answer his reproachful text messages, because there was no future in it: he wanted a two-professionals marriage, and she was no longer in the running. Better to do the weeping sooner rather than later, she told herself.

But it seems she'd wanted children after all, because when she was told she'd been accidentally sterilized she could feel all the light leaking out of her.

After getting that news, she'd blown her hoarded egg-donation money on a drug-fuelled holiday from reality. But waking up with various men she'd never seen before had lost its thrill very quickly, especially when she'd found they had a habit of pocketing her spare change. After the fourth or fifth time she knew she had to make a decision: did she want to live or did she want to die? If *die*, there were quicker ways. If *live*, she had to live differently.

Through one of her single-nighters – a man with the Sewage Lagoon equivalent of a kind soul – she found a job at a pleebmob business. Pleebmob businesses didn't ask for identity and didn't need references: if you dipped into the till they'd simply cut your fingers off.

Toby's new job was with a chain called SecretBurgers. The secret of SecretBurgers was that no one knew what sort of animal protein was actually in them: the counter girls wore T-shirts and baseball caps with the slogan *SecretBurgers! Because Everyone Loves a Secret!* The job paid rock-bottom wages, but you got two free SecretBurgers a day. Once she was with the Gardeners and had taken the Vegivows, Toby suppressed the memory of eating these burgers; but as Adam One used to say, hunger is a powerful reorganizer of the conscience. The meat grinders weren't 100 per cent efficient; you might find a swatch of cat fur in your burger or a fragment of mouse tail. Was there a human finger-nail, once?

It was possible. The local pleebmobs paid the CorpSeCorpsMen to turn a blind eye. In return, the CorpSeCorps let the pleebmobs run the low-level kidnappings and assassinations, the skunkweed gro-ops, the crack labs and street-drug retailing, and the plank shops that were their stock-in-trade. They also ran corpse disposals, harvesting organs for transplant, then running the gutted carcasses through the SecretBurgers grinders. So went the worst rumours. During the glory days of Secret-Burgers, there were very few bodies found in vacant lots.

If there was a so-called reality TV exposé, the CorpSeCorps would make a pretense at investigation. Then they'd list the case as Unsolved and discard it. They had an image to uphold among those citizens who still paid lip service to the old ideals: defenders of the peace, enforcers of public security, keeping the streets safe. It was a joke even then, but most people felt the CorpSeCorps were better than total anarchy. Even Toby felt that.

The year before, SecretBurgers had gone too far. The CorpSeCorps had closed them down after one of their high-placed officials went slumming in the Sewage Lagoon and his shoes were discovered on the feet of a SecretBurgers meat-grinder operator. So for a while stray cats breathed easier at night. But a few months later the familiar grilling booths were sizzling again, because who could say no to a business with so few supply-side costs?

8

Toby was pleased to learn she'd got the SecretBurgers job: she could pay the rent, she wouldn't starve. But then she discovered the catch.

The catch was the manager. His name was Blanco, though behind his back the SecretBurgers girls called him the Bloat. Rebecca Eckler, who worked Toby's shift, told her about him right away. "Stay off his radar," she said. "Maybe you'll be okay – he's doing that girl Dora, and he mostly does just the one at a time, and you're kind of scrawny and he likes the curvy butts. But if he tells you to come to the office, look out. He's real jealous. He'll take a girl apart."

"Has he asked you?" said Toby. "To the office?"

"Praise the Lord and spit," said Rebecca. "I'm too black and ugly for him, plus he just likes the kittens, not the old cats. Maybe you should wrinkle yourself up, sweetheart. Knock out a few of your teeth."

"You're not ugly," said Toby. Rebecca was in fact beautiful in a substantial way, with her brown skin and her red hair and her Egyptian nose.

"I don't mean ugly like that," said Rebecca. "Ugly to deal with. Us Jelacks, we're two kinds of folks you don't want to mess with. He knows I'd get the Blackened Redfish onto him, and they're one mean gang. Plus maybe the Wolf Isaiahists. Way too much grief!"

Toby had no such backups. She kept her head down when Blanco was around. She'd heard his story. According to Rebecca, he'd been a bouncer at Scales, the classiest club in the Lagoon. Bouncers had status; they strolled around in black suits and dark glasses, looking suave but tough, and they had women swarming all over them. But Blanco had blown it big time, said Rebecca. He'd ripped up a Scales girl – not a smuggled illegal-alien temporary, they got ripped up all the time, but one of the top talent, a star pole dancer. You couldn't have a guy like that around – someone who'd mess up the works because he couldn't keep his cool – so they'd fired him. Lucky for him he had friends in the CorpSeCorps or he'd have ended up minus some body parts in a carbon garboil dumpster. As it was, they'd stuck him in to run the Sewage Lagoon SecretBurgers outlet. It was a big comedown and he was bitter about it – why should he suffer because of some slut? – so he hated the job. But he figured the girls were his perks. He had two pals, ex-bouncers like himself, who acted as his bodyguards, and they got the leavings. Supposing there was anything left.

Blanco was still bouncer-shaped – oblong and hefty – though running to fat: too much beer, said Rebecca. He'd kept the signature bouncer ponytail at the back of his balding head, and he sported a full set of arm tattoos: snakes twining his arms, bracelets of skulls around his wrists, veins and arteries on the backs of his hands so they looked flayed. Around his neck was a tattooed chain, with a lock on it shaped like a red heart, nestled into the chest hair he displayed in the V of his open shirt. According to rumour, that chain went right down his back, twined around an upside-down naked woman whose head was stuck in his ass.

Toby kept her eye on Dora, who'd arrive at the grilling booth to take over when Toby's shift was done. She'd begun as a plump optimist, but over the weeks she'd been shrinking and sagging; on the white skin of her arms, the bruises bloomed and faded. "She wants to run away," Rebecca whispered, "but she's scared. Maybe you should get out of here yourself. He's been looking at you."

"I'll be okay," said Toby. She didn't feel okay, she felt scared. But where else could she go? She lived from pay to pay. She had no money.

The next morning, Rebecca signalled Toby over. "Dora's dead," she said. "Tried to run. I just heard it. Found her in a vacant lot, neck broke, cut to bits. Saying it was some crazy."

"But it was him?" said Toby.

"Course it was him," Rebecca sniffed. "He's bragging."

At noon that same day, Blanco ordered Toby to his office. He sent his two pals with the message. They walked on either side of her, just in case she might get flighty ideas. As they went along the street, the heads turned. Toby felt she was on the way to her own execution. Why hadn't she quit when she had the chance?

The office was through a grimy door tucked behind a carbon garboil dumpster. It was a small room with a desk, filing cabinet, and battered leather couch. Blanco heaved himself out of his swivel chair, grinning.

"Skinny bitch, I'm promoting you," he said. "Say thank you."

Toby could only whisper: she felt strangled.

"See this heart?" said Blanco. He pointed to his tattoo. "It means I love you. And now you love me too. Right?"

Toby managed to nod.

"Smart girl," said Blanco. "Come here. Take off my shirt."

The tattoo on his back was just as Rebecca had described it: a naked woman, wound in chains, her head invisible. Her long hair waving up like flames.

Blanco put his flayed hands around her neck. "Cross me up, I'll snap you like a twig," he said.

9

Ever since her family had died in such sad ways, ever since she herself had disappeared from official view, Toby had tried not to think about her earlier life. She'd covered it in ice, she'd frozen it. Now she longed desperately to be back there in the past – even the bad parts, even the grief – because her present life was torture. She tried to picture her two faraway, long-ago parents, watching over her like guardian spirits, but she saw only mist.

She'd been Blanco's one-and-only for less than two weeks, but it felt like years. His view was that a woman with an ass as skinny as Toby's should consider herself in luck if any man wanted to stick his hole-hammer into her. She'd be even luckier if he didn't sell her to Scales as a temporary, which meant temporarily alive. She should thank her lucky stars. Better, she should thank him: he demanded a thank you after every degrading act. He didn't want her to feel pleasure, though: only submission.

Nor did he give her any time off from her SecretBurgers duties. He demanded her services during her lunch break – the whole half-hour – which meant she got no lunch.

Day by day she was hungrier and more exhausted. She had her own bruises now, like poor Dora's. Despair was taking her over: she could see where this was going, and it looked like a dark tunnel. She'd be used up soon.

Worse, Rebecca had gone away, no one knew exactly where. Off with some religious group, said the street rumour. Blanco didn't care, because Rebecca hadn't been part of his harem. He filled her SecretBurgers place quickly enough.

Toby was working the morning shift when a strange procession approached along the street. From the signs they were carrying and the singing they were doing, she guessed it was a religious thing, though it wasn't a sect she'd ever seen before.

A lot of fringe cults worked the Sewage Lagoon, trolling for souls in torment. The Known Fruits and the Petrobaptists and the other rich-people religions kept away, but a few wattled old Salvation Army bands shuffled through, wheezing under the weight of their drums and French horns. Groups of turbaned Pure-Heart Brethren Sufis might twirl past, or black-clad Ancients of Days, or clumps of saffron-robed Hare Krishnas, tinkling and chanting, attracting jeers and rotting vegetation from the bystanders. The Lion Isaiahists and the Wolf Isaiahists both preached on street corners, battling when they met: they were at odds over whether it was the lion or the wolf that would lie down with the lamb once the Peaceable Kingdom had arrived. When there were scuffles, the pleebrat gangs – the brown Tex-Mexes, the pallid Lintheads, the yellow Asian Fusions, the Blackened Redfish – would swarm the fallen, rooting through their draperies for anything valuable, or even just portable.

As the procession drew nearer, Toby had a better view. The leader had a beard and was wearing a caftan that looked as if it had been sewn by elves on hash. Behind him came an assortment of children – various heights, all colours, but all in dark clothing – holding their slates with slogans printed on them: *God's Gardeners for God's Garden! Don't Eat Death! Animals R Us!* They looked like raggedy angels, or else like midget bag people. They'd been the ones doing the singing. *No meat! No meat! No meat!* they were chanting now. She'd heard of this cult: it was said to have a garden somewhere, on a rooftop. A wodge of drying mud, a few draggled marigolds, a mangy row of pathetic beans, broiling in the unforgiving sun.

The procession drew up in front of the SecretBurgers booth. A crowd was gathering, readying itself to jeer. "My Friends," said the leader, to the crowd at large. His preaching wouldn't go on for long, thought Toby, because the Sewage Lagooners wouldn't tolerate it. "My dear Friends. My name is Adam One. I, too, was once a materialistic, atheistic meat-eater. Like you, I thought Man was the measure of all things."

"Shut the fuck up, ecofreak," someone yelled. Adam One ignored this. "In fact, dear Friends, I thought measurement was the measure of all things! Yes – I was a scientist. I studied epidemics, I counted diseased and dying animals, and people too, as if they were so many pebbles. I thought that only numbers could give a true description of Reality. But then –"

"Piss off, dickhead!"

"But then, one day, when I was standing right where you are standing, devouring – yes! – devouring a SecretBurger, and revelling in the fat thereof, I saw a great Light. I heard a great Voice. And that Voice said –"

"It said, 'Get stuffed!'"

"It said, Spare your fellow Creatures! Do not eat anything with a face! Do not kill your own Soul! And then . . ."

Toby felt the crowd, the way they were poised to surge. They'd stomp this poor fool into the ground, and the little Gardener children with him. "Go away!" she said as loudly as she could.

Adam One gave her a courtly little bow, a kindly smile. "My child," he said, "do you have any idea what you're selling? Surely you wouldn't eat your own relatives."

"I would," Toby said, "if I was hungry enough. Please go!"

"I see you've had a difficult time, my child," said Adam One. "You have grown a callous and hard shell. But that hard shell is not your true self. Inside that shell you have a warm and tender heart, and a kind Soul . . ."

It was true about the shell; she knew she'd hardened. But her shell was her armour: without it she'd be mush.

"This asshole bothering you?" said Blanco. He'd loomed up behind her, as he was in the habit of doing. He put his hand on her waist, and she could see it even without looking at it: the veins, the arteries. Raw flesh.

"It's okay," said Toby. "He's harmless."

Adam One showed no sign of dislodging himself. He carried on as if no one else had spoken. "You long to do good in this world, my child –"

"I'm not your child," said Toby. She was more than aware that she wasn't anyone's child, not any more.

"We are all one another's children," said Adam One with a sad look.

"Scram," said Blanco. "Before I knot you!"

"Please leave or you'll get injured," said Toby as urgently as she could. This man had no fear. She lowered her voice, hissed at him: "Piss off! Now!"

"It is you who will be injured," said Adam One. "Every day you stand here selling the mutilated flesh of God's beloved Creatures, it's injuring you more. Join us, my dear – we are your friends, we have a place for you."

"Get your fuckin' paws off my worker, you fuckin' pervert!" Blanco shouted.

"Am I bothering you, my child?" said Adam One, ignoring him. "I certainly haven't touched . . ."

Blanco came out from behind the booth and lunged, but Adam One seemed used to being attacked: he stepped to the side, and Blanco rocketed forward into the group of singing children, knocking some of them down and falling down himself. A teenaged Linthead promptly hit him over the head with an empty bottle – Blanco wasn't a neighbourhood favourite – and he sank down, bleeding from a gash on his head.

Toby ran around to the front of the grilling booth. Her first impulse was to help him up because she'd be in big trouble later if she didn't. A pack of Redfish pleebrats was mauling him, and some Asian Fusions were working on his shoes. The crowd moved in around him, but now he was struggling to right himself. Where were his two bodyguards? Nowhere to be seen.

Toby felt curiously exhilarated. Then she kicked Blanco's head. She did it without even thinking. She felt herself grinning like a dog, she felt her foot connect with his skull: it was like a towel-covered stone. As soon as she'd done it she realized her mistake. How could she have been so dumb?

"Come away, my dear," said Adam One, taking her by the elbow. "It would be best. You've lost your job in any case."

Blanco's two thug pals were back now, and were beating off the pleebrats. Although he was groggy, his eyes were open and they were fixed on Toby. He'd felt that kick; worse, he'd been humiliated by her in public. He'd lost face. Any minute now he'd haul himself up and pulverize her. "Bitch!" he croaked. "I'll slice off your tits!"

Then Toby was surrounded by a crowd of children. Two of them took hold of her hands, and the others formed themselves into an honour guard, front and back. "Hurry, hurry," they were saying as they pulled and pushed her along the street.

There was a roar from behind: "Get back here, bitch!"

"Quick, this way," said the tallest boy. With Adam One covering the rear they jogged through the streets of the Sewage Lagoon. It was like a parade: people stared. In addition to her panic Toby felt unreal, and a little dizzy.

Now the crowds were becoming thinner and the smells less pungent; fewer shops were boarded up. "Faster," said Adam One. They ran up an alleyway and turned several corners in quick succession, and the shouting faded away.

They came to an early modern red-brick factory building. On the front was a sign saying, PACHINKO, over a smaller one that read, STARDUST PERSONAL MASSAGE, SECOND FLOOR, ALL TASTES INDULGED, NOSE JOBS EXTRA. The children ran around to the side of the building and began climbing up the fire escape, and Toby followed. She was out of breath, but they scampered up like monkeys. Once they'd reached the rooftop, each of them said, "Welcome to our Garden" and hugged her, and she was enveloped in the sweet, salty odour of unwashed children.

Toby couldn't remember being hugged by a child. For the children it must have been a formality, like hugging a distant aunt, but for her it was something she couldn't define: fuzzy, softly intimate. Like being nuzzled by rabbits. But rabbits from Mars. Nevertheless she found it touching: she'd been touched, in an impersonal but kindly way that was not sexual. Considering how she'd been living lately, with Blanco's the only hands touching her, the strangeness must have come in part from that.

There were adults too, holding out their hands in greeting – the women in dark baggy dresses, the men in coveralls – and here, suddenly, was Rebecca. "You made it, sweetheart," she said. "I told them! I just knew they'd get you out!"

The Garden wasn't at all what Toby had expected from hearsay. It wasn't a baked mudflat strewn with rotting vegetable waste – quite the reverse. She gazed around it in wonder: it was so beautiful, with plants and flowers of many kinds she'd never seen before. There were vivid butterflies; from nearby came the vibration of bees. Each petal and leaf was fully alive, shining with awareness of her. Even the air of the Garden was different.

She found herself crying with relief and gratitude. It was as if a large, benevolent hand had reached down and picked her up, and was holding her safe. Later, she frequently heard Adam One speak of "being flooded with the Light of God's Creation," and without knowing it yet that was how she felt.

"I'm so glad you have made this decision, my dear," said Adam One.

But Toby didn't think she'd made any decision at all. Something else had made it for her. Despite everything that happened afterwards, this was a moment she never forgot.

That first evening, there was a modest celebration in honour of Toby's advent. A great fuss was made over the opening of a jar of preserved purple items – those were her first elderberries – and a pot of honey was produced as if it was the Holy Grail.

Adam One made a little speech about providential rescues. The brand plucked from the burning was mentioned, and the one lost sheep – she'd heard of those before, at church – but other, unfamiliar examples of rescue were used as well: the relocated snail, the windfall pear. Then they'd eaten a sort of lentil pancake and a dish called Pilar's Pickled Mushroom Medley, followed by slices of soybread topped with the purple berries and the honey.

After her initial elation, Toby was feeling stunned and uneasy. How had she got up here, to this unlikely and somehow disturbing location? What was she doing among these friendly though bizarre people, with their wacky religion and – right now – their purple teeth?

10

Toby's first weeks with the Gardeners were not reassuring. Adam One gave her no instructions: he simply watched her, by which she understood that she was on probation. She tried to fit in, to help when needed, but at the routine tasks she was inept. She couldn't sew tiny stitches, the way Eve Nine – Nuala – wanted, and after she'd bled into a few salads, Rebecca told her to lay off the vegetable chopping. "If I want it to look like beets I'll put in beets," was what she said. Burt – Adam Thirteen, in charge of garden vegetables – discouraged her from weeding after she'd uprooted some of the artichokes by mistake. She could clean out the violet biolets, though. It was a simple chore that took no special training. So that is what she did.

Adam One was well aware of her efforts. "The biolets aren't so bad, are they?" he said to her one day. "After all, we're strict vegetarians here." Toby wondered what he meant, but then she realized: less smelly. Cow rather than dog.

Figuring out the Gardener hierarchy took her some time. Adam One insisted that all Gardeners were equal on the spiritual level, but the same did not hold true for the material one: the Adams and the Eves ranked higher, though their numbers indicated their areas of expertise rather than their order of importance. In many ways it was like a monastery, she thought. The inner chapter, then the lay brothers. And the lay sisters, of course. Except that chastity was not expected.

Since she was accepting Gardener hospitality, and under false pretenses at that – she wasn't really a convert – she felt she should pay by working very hard. To the violet biolet cleaning she added other tasks. She carted fresh soil up to the rooftop via the fire escape – the Gardeners had a supply of it, gathered from deserted building sites and vacant lots – to be mixed with compost, and with violet biolet by-products. She melted down soap ends and decanted and labelled vinegar. She packaged worms for the Tree of Life Natural Materials Exchange, she mopped the floor of the Run-For-Your-Light Treadmills gym, she swept out the dormitory cubicles on the level below the Rooftop where the single members of the group slept every night on futons stuffed with dried plant materials.

After several months of this, Adam One suggested that she put her other talents to work. "What other talents?" said Toby.

"Didn't you study Holistic Healing?" he asked. "At Martha Graham?"

"Yes," Toby said. There was no point in asking how Adam One knew that about her. He just knew things.

So she set to work making herbal lotions and creams. There wasn't much chopping involved, and she had a strong arm with the mortar and pestle. Soon after that, Adam One asked her to share her skills with the children, so she added several daily classes to her routine.

By now she was used to the dark, sack-like garments the women wore. "You'll want to grow your hair," said Nuala. "Get rid of that scalped look. We Gardener women all wear our hair long." When Toby asked why, she was given to understand that the aesthetic preference was God's. This kind of smiling, bossy sanctimoniousness was a little too pervasive for Toby, especially among the female members of the sect.

From time to time she thought of deserting. For one thing, she was swept with periodic but shameful cravings for animal protein. "You ever feel like eating a SecretBurger?" she asked Rebecca. Rebecca was from her former world: such things could be discussed with her.

"I must admit it," said Rebecca. "I do have those thoughts. They put something in them – it has to be. Some addictive thing."

The food was pleasant enough – Rebecca did her best with the limited materials available – but it was repetitious. In addition to that, the prayers were tedious, the theology scrambled – why be so picky about lifestyle details if you believed everyone would soon be wiped off the face of the planet? The Gardeners were convinced of impending disaster, through no solid evidence that Toby could see. Maybe they were reading bird entrails.

A massive die-off of the human race was impending, due to overpopulation and wickedness, but the Gardeners exempted themselves: they intended to float above the Waterless Flood, with the aid of the food they were stashing away in the hidden storeplaces they called Ararats. As for the flotation devices in which they would ride out this flood, they themselves would be their own Arks, stored with their own collections of inner animals, or at least the names of those animals. Thus they would survive to replenish the Earth. Or something like that.

Toby asked Rebecca whether she really believed the Gardener total-disaster talk, but Rebecca wouldn't be drawn. "They are good people," was all she'd say. "What comes just comes, so what I say is, *Relax*." Then she'd give Toby a honey/soy doughnut.

Good people or not, Toby couldn't see herself sticking it out among these fugitives from reality for long. But she couldn't just walk away openly. That would be too blatantly ungrateful: after all, these people had saved her skin. So she pictured herself slipping down the fire escape, past the sleeping level and the pachinko joint and the massage parlour on the floors below, and running off under cover of darkness, then hitching a solarcar ride to some other city farther north. Planes were out of the question, being far too expensive and intensely scrutinized by the CorpSeCorps. Even if she'd had the money for it, she couldn't take the bullet train – they checked identities there, and she didn't have one.

Not only that, but Blanco would still be on the lookout for her, down on the pleeb streets – him and his two thug pals. No woman ever got away from him, was his boast. Sooner or later he'd track her down and make her pay. That kick of hers would be very expensive. It would take a publicly advertised gang rape or her head on a pole to wipe the slate.

Was it possible that he didn't know where she was? No: the pleebrat gangs must have picked up such knowledge the way they picked up every rumour and sold it to him. She'd been avoiding the streets, but what was to stop Blanco from coming after her up the fire escape and onto the rooftop? Finally she shared her fears with Adam One. He knew about Blanco and what he was likely to do – he'd seen him in action.

"I don't want to put the Gardeners in danger," was how Toby put it.

"My dear," said Adam One, "you are safe with us. Or moderately safe." Blanco was Sewage Lagoon pleebmob, he explained, and the Gardeners were next door, in the Sinkhole. "Different pleebs, different mobs," he said. "They don't trespass unless they're having a mob war. In any case, the CorpSeCorps run the mobs, and according to our information they've declared us off-limits."

"Why would they bother to do that?" asked Toby.

"It would be bad for their image to eviscerate anything with God in its name," said Adam One. "The Corporations wouldn't approve of it, considering the influence of the Petrobaptists and the Known Fruits among them. They claim to respect the Spirit and to favour religious toleration, as long as the religions don't take to blowing things up: they have an aversion to the destruction of private property."

"They can't possibly *like* us," said Toby.

"Of course not," said Adam One. "They view us as twisted fanatics who combine food extremism with bad fashion sense and a puritanical attitude towards shopping. But we own nothing they want, so we don't qualify as terrorists. Sleep easier, dear Toby. You're guarded by angels."

Curious angels, thought Toby. Not all of them angels of light. But she did sleep easier, on her mattress of rustling husks.

THE FEAST OF ADAM
AND ALL PRIMATES

THE FEAST OF ADAM AND ALL PRIMATES

YEAR TEN.

OF GOD'S METHODOLOGY IN CREATING MAN.
SPOKEN BY ADAM ONE.

Dear Fellow Gardeners in the Earth that is God's Garden:

How wonderful to see you all assembled here in our beautiful Edencliff Rooftop Garden! I have enjoyed viewing the excellent Tree of Creatures created by our Children from the plastic objects they've gleaned – such a fine illustration of evil materials being put to good uses! – and I look forward to our coming meal of Fellowship, featuring the turnips we stored from last year's harvest in Rebecca's delicious turnip pie, not to mention the Pickled Mushroom Medley, courtesy of Pilar, our Eve Six. We also celebrate the promotion of Toby to full teaching status. By her hard work and dedication, Toby has shown us that a person can overcome so many painful experiences and inner obstacles once they have seen the light of Truth. We are very proud of you, Toby.

On the Feast of Adam and All Primates, we affirm our Primate ancestry – an affirmation that has brought down wrath upon us from those who arrogantly persist in evolutionary denial. But we affirm, also, the Divine agency that has caused us to be created in the way that we were, and this has enraged those scientific fools who say in their hearts, "There is no God." These claim to prove the non-existence of God because they cannot put Him in a test tube and weigh and measure Him. But God is pure Spirit; so how can anyone reason that the failure to measure the Immeasurable proves its non-existence? God is indeed the No Thing, the No-thingness, that through which and by which all material things exist; for if there were not such a No-thingness, existence would be so crammed full of materiality that no one thing could be distinguished from another. The mere existence of separate material things is a proof of the No-thingness of God.

Where were the scientific fools when God laid the foundations of the Earth by interposing his own Spirit between one blob of matter and another, thus giving rise to forms? Where were they when "the morning stars sang together"? But let us forgive them in our hearts, for it is not our task today to reprimand, but to contemplate our own earthly state in all humility.

God could have made Man out of pure Word, but He did not use this method. He could also have formed him from the dust of the Earth, which in a sense He did, for what else can be signified by "dust" but atoms and molecules, the building blocks of all material entities? In addition to this, He created us through the long and complex process of Natural and Sexual Selection, which is none other than His ingenious device for instilling humility in Man. He made us "a little lower than the Angels," but in other ways – and Science bears this out – we are closely related to our fellow Primates, a fact that the haughty ones of this world do not find pleasant to their self-esteem. Our appetites, our desires, our more uncontrollable emotions – all are Primate! Our Fall from the original Garden was a Fall from the innocent acting-out of such patterns and impulses to a conscious and shamed awareness of them; and from thence comes our sadness, our anxiety, our doubt, our rage against God.

True, we – like the other Animals – were blessed, and ordered to increase and multiply, and to replenish the Earth. But by what humiliating and aggressive and painful means this replenishing frequently takes place! No wonder we are born to a sense of guilt and disgrace! Why did He not make us pure Spirit, like Himself? Why did he embed us in perishable matter, and a matter so unfortunately Monkey-like? So goes the ancient cry.

What commandment did we disobey? The commandment to live the Animal life in all simplicity – without clothing, so to speak. But we craved the knowledge of good and evil, and we obtained that knowledge, and now we are reaping the whirlwind. In our efforts to rise above ourselves we have indeed fallen far, and are falling farther still; for, like the Creation, the Fall, too, is ongoing. Ours is a fall into greed: why do we think that everything on Earth belongs to us, while in reality we belong to Everything? We have betrayed the trust of the Animals, and defiled our sacred task of stewardship. God's commandment to "replenish the Earth" did not mean we should fill it to overflowing with ourselves, thus wiping out everything else. How many other Species have we already annihilated? Insofar as you do it unto the least of God's Creatures, you do it unto Him. Please consider that, my Friends, the next time you crush a Worm underfoot or disparage a Beetle!

We pray that we may not fall into the error of pride by considering ourselves as exceptional, alone in all Creation in having Souls; and that we will not vainly imagine that we are set above all other Life, and may destroy it at our pleasure, and with impunity.

We thank Thee, oh God, for having made us in such a way as to remind us, not only of our less than Angelic being, but also of the knots of DNA and RNA that tie us to our many fellow Creatures.

Let us sing.

OH LET ME NOT BE PROUD

Oh let me not be proud, dear Lord,
Nor rank myself above
The other Primates, through whose genes
We grew into your Love.

A million million years, Your Days,
Your methods past discerning,
Yet through Your blend of DNAs
Came passion, mind, and learning.

We cannot always trace Your path
Through Monkey and Gorilla,
Yet all are sheltered underneath
Your Heavenly Umbrella.

And if we vaunt and puff ourselves
With vanity and pride,
Recall Australopithecus,
Our Animal inside.

So keep us far from worser traits,
Aggression, anger, greed;
Let us not scorn our lowly birth,
Nor yet our Primate seed.

From *The God's Gardeners Oral Hymnbook*

11

When I'm thinking back over that night – the night the Waterless Flood first began – I can't recall anything out of the ordinary. Around seven o'clock I was feeling hungry, so I got a Joltbar from the minifridge and ate half of it. I only ever ate half of anything because a girl with my body type can't afford to blimp up. I once asked Mordis if I should get bimplants, but he said I could play underage in a dim light, and there was heavy demand for the schoolgirl act.

I ran through some chin-ups and did my Kegel floor exercises, and then Mordis called in on my videophone to see if I was okay: he missed me, because no one could work the crowd like me. "Ren, you make them shit thousand-dollar bills," he said, and I blew him a kiss.

"Keeping your butt in shape?" he said, so I held the videophone behind me.

"Chickin' lickin' good," he said. Even if you were feeling ugly, he made you feel pretty.

After that I hit the Snakepit video, to check the action and dance along to the music. It was strange to watch everything going on without me, as if I'd been erased. Crimson Petal was teasing the pole, Savona was subbing for me on the trapeze. She looked good – glittery and green and sinuous, with a new silver Mo'Hair. I was considering one of those myself – they were better than wigs, they never came off – but some girls said the smell was like lamb chops, especially in the rain.

Savona was a little clumsy. She wasn't a trapeze girl, she was a pole girl, and she was top-heavy – she'd blown herself up like a beach ball.

Stick her on stilettos, breathe on her from behind, and she'd do a vertical face-plant. "Whatever works," she'd say. "And, baby, this works."

Now she was doing the upside-down splits move with the one-handed midstroke. She didn't convince me, but the men down there were never much interested in art: they'd think Savona was great unless she laughed instead of moaning, or actually fell off the trapeze.

I left the Snakepit and flipped through the other rooms, but nothing much was going on. No fetishists, nobody who wanted to be covered in feathers or slathered in porridge or strung up with velvet ropes or writhed on by guppies. Just the daily grind.

Then I called Amanda. We're each other's family; I guess when we were kids we were both stray puppies. It's a bond.

Amanda was in the Wisconsin desert, putting together one of the Bioart installations she's been doing now that she's into what she calls the art caper. It was cow bones this time. Wisconsin's covered with cow bones, ever since the big drought ten years ago when they'd found it cheaper to butcher the cows there rather than shipping them out – the ones that hadn't died on their own. She had a couple of fuel-cell front-end loaders and two illegal Tex-Mexican refugees she'd hired, and she was dragging the cow bones into a pattern so big it could only be seen from above: huge capital letters, spelling out a word. Later she'd cover it in pancake syrup and wait until the insect life was all over it, and then take videos of it from the air, to put into galleries. She liked to watch things move and grow and then disappear.

Amanda always got the money to do her art capers. She was kind of famous in the circles that went in for culture. They weren't big circles, but they were rich circles. This time she had a deal with a top CorpSeCorps guy – he'd get her up in the helicopter, to take the videos. "I traded Mr. Big for a whirly," was how she told me – we never said CorpSeCorps or helicopter on the phone, because they had robots listening in for special words like those.

Her Wisconsin thing was part of a series called The Living Word – she said for a joke that it was inspired by the Gardeners because they'd repressed us so much about writing things down. She'd begun with one-letter words – *I* and *A* and *O* – and then done two-letter words like *It*, and then three letters, and four, and five. Now she was up to six. They'd been written in all different materials, including fish guts and toxic-spill-killed birds and toilets from building demolition sites filled with used cooking oil and set on fire.

Her new word was *kaputt*. When she'd told me that earlier, she'd said she was sending a message.

"Who to?" I'd said. "The people who go to the galleries? The Mr. Rich and Bigs?"

"That's who," she'd said. "And the Mrs. Rich and Bigs. Them too."

"You'll get in trouble, Amanda."

"It's okay," she said. "They won't understand it."

The project was going fine, she said: it had rained, the desert flowers were in bloom, there were a lot of insects, which was good for when she'd pour on the syrup. She already had the *K* done, and she was halfway through the *A*. But the Tex-Mexicans were getting bored.

"That makes two of us," I said. "I can hardly wait to get out of here."

"Three," said Amanda. "There's two of them – the Tex-Mexicans. Plus you. Three."

"Oh. Right. You're looking great – that khaki outfit suits you." She was tall, she had that rangy girl-explorer look. A pith-helmet look.

"You're not bad yourself," said Amanda. "Ren, you take care."

"You take care too. Don't let the Tex-Mex guys jump you."

"They won't. They think I'm crazy. Crazy women cut your dong off."

"I didn't know that!" I was laughing. Amanda liked to make me laugh.

"Why would you?" said Amanda. "You're not crazy, you've never seen one of those things wriggling on the floor. Sweet dreams."

"Sweet dreams too," I said. But she'd clicked off.

I've lost track of the Saints' Days – I can't remember which one it is today – but I can count the years. I've used my eyebrow pencil on the wall to add up how long I've known Amanda. I've done it like those old cartoons of prisoners – four strokes and then one through them to make five.

It's been a long time – over fifteen years, ever since she came into the Gardeners. So many people from my earlier life were from there – Amanda, and Bernice, and Zeb; and Adam One, and Shackie, and Croze; and old Pilar; and Toby, of course. I wonder what they'd think of me – of what I ended up doing for a living. Some of them would be disappointed, like Adam One. Bernice would say I was backslidden and it served me right. Lucerne would say I'm a slut, and I'd say takes one to know one. Pilar would look at me wisely. Shackie and Croze would laugh. Toby would be mad at Scales. What about Zeb? I think he'd try to rescue me because it would be a challenge.

Amanda knows already. She doesn't judge. She says you trade what you have to. You don't always have choices.

12

When Lucerne and Zeb first took me away from the Exfernal World to live among the Gardeners, I didn't like it at all. They smiled a lot, but they scared me: they were so interested in doom, and enemies, and God. And they talked so much about Death. The Gardeners were strict about not killing Life, but on the other hand they said Death was a natural process, which was sort of a contradiction, now that I think about it. They had the idea that turning into compost would be just fine. Not everyone might think that having your body become part of a vulture was a terrific future to look forward to, but the Gardeners did. And when they'd start talking about the Waterless Flood that was going to kill everybody on Earth, except maybe them – that gave me nightmares.

None of it scared the real Gardener kids. They were used to it. They'd even make fun of it, or the older boys would – Shackie and Croze and their pals. "We're all gonna diiiiie," they'd say, making dead-person faces. "Hey, Ren. Want to do your bit for the Cycle of Life? Lie down in that dumpster, you can be the compost." "Hey, Ren. Want to be a maggot? Lick my cut!"

"Shut up," Bernice would say. "Or you're going into that dumpster yourself because I'm shoving you in!" Bernice was mean, and she stood her ground, and most kids would back off. Even the boys would. But then I'd owe Bernice, and I'd have to do what she said.

Shackie and Croze would tease me, though, when Bernice wasn't around to push back at them. They were slug-squeezers, they were beetle-eaters. They tried to gross you out. They were trouble – that's what Toby called them. I'd hear her saying to Rebecca, "Here comes trouble."

Shackie was the oldest; he was tall and skinny, and he had a spider tattoo on the inside of his arm that he'd punched in himself with a needle and some candle soot. Croze was a stumpier shape, with a round head and a missing side tooth, which he claimed had been knocked out in a street battle. They had a little brother whose name was Oates. They didn't have any parents; they'd had some once, but their father had gone off with Zeb on some special Adam trip and had never come back, and then their mother had left, telling Adam One she'd send for them when she'd got herself established. But she never had.

The Gardener school was in a different building from the Rooftop. It was called the Wellness Clinic because that's what used to be in there. It still had some leftover boxes full of gauze bandages, which the Gardeners were gleaning for crafts projects. It smelled of vinegar: across the hallway from the schoolrooms was the room the Gardeners used for their vinegar making.

The benches at the Wellness Clinic were hard; we sat in rows. We wrote on slates, and they had to be wiped off at the end of each day because the Gardeners said you couldn't leave words lying around where our enemies might find them. Anyway, paper was sinful because it was made from the flesh of trees.

We spent a lot of time memorizing things and chanting them out loud. The Gardener history, for instance – it went like this:

> *Year One, Garden just begun; Year Two, still new; Year
> Three, Pilar started bees; Year Four, Burt came in the
> door; Year Five, Toby snatched alive; Year Six, Katuro
> in the mix; Year Seven, Zeb came to our heaven.*

Year Seven should have said that I came too, and my mother, Lucerne, and anyway it wasn't heaven, but the Gardeners liked their chants to rhyme.

Year Eight, Nuala found her fate; Year Nine, Philo
began to shine.

I wanted Year Ten to have Ren in it, but I didn't think it would.

The other things we had to memorize were harder. Mathematical and science things were the worst. We also had to memorize every saint's day, and every single day had at least one saint and sometimes more, or maybe a feast, which meant over four hundred of those. Plus what the saints had done to get to be saints. Some of them were easy. Saint Yossi Leshem of Barn Owls – well, it was obvious what the answer was. And Saint Dian Fossey, because the story was so sad, and Saint Shackleton, because it was heroic. But some of them were really hard. Who could remember Saint Bashir Alouse, or Saint Crick, or Podocarp Day? I always got Podocarp Day wrong because what was a Podocarp? It was an ancient kind of tree, but it sounded like a fish.

Our teachers were Nuala for the little kids and the Buds and Blooms Choir and Fabric Recycling, and Rebecca for Culinary Arts, which meant cooking, and Surya for Sewing, and Mugi for Mental Arithmetic, and Pilar for Bees and Mycology, and Toby for Holistic Healing with Plant Remedies, and Burt for Wild and Garden Botanicals, and Philo for Meditation, and Zeb for Predator-Prey Relationships and Animal Camouflage. There were some other teachers – when we were thirteen, we'd get Katuro for Emergency Medical and Marushka Midwife for the Human Reproductive System, whereas all we'd had so far was Frog Ovaries – but those were the main ones.

The Gardener kids had nicknames for all of the teachers. Pilar was the Fungus, Zeb was the Mad Adam, Stuart was the Screw because he built the furniture. Mugi was the Muscle, Marushka was the Mucous, Rebecca was the Salt and Peppler, Burt was the Knob because he was bald. Toby was the Dry Witch. Witch because she was always mixing things up and pouring them into bottles and Dry because she was so thin and hard, and to tell her apart from Nuala, who was the Wet Witch because of her damp mouth and her wobbly bum, and because you could make her cry so easily.

In addition to the learning chants, the Gardener kids had rude ones they made up themselves. They'd chant softly – Shackleton and Crozier and the older boys would start, but then we'd all join in:

> *Wet Witch, Wet Witch,*
> *Big fat slobbery bitch,*
> *Sell her to the butcher, make yourself rich,*
> *Eat her in a sausage, Wet Wet Witch!*

It was especially bad about the butcher and the sausage, because meat of any kind was obscene as far as the Gardeners were concerned. "Stop that," Nuala would say, but then she'd sniffle, and the older boys would give each other a thumbs-up.

We could never make Dry Witch Toby cry. The boys said she was a hardass – she and Rebecca were the two hardest asses. Rebecca was jolly on the outside, but you did not push her buttons. As for Toby, she was leathery inside and out. "Don't try it, Shackleton," she would say, even though her back was turned. Nuala was too kind to us, but Toby held us to account, and we trusted Toby more: you'd trust a rock more than a cake.

13

I lived with Lucerne and Zeb in a building about five blocks from the Garden. It was called the Cheese Factory because that's what it used to be, and it still had a faint cheesy smell to it. After the cheese it was used for artists' lofts, but there weren't any artists left, and nobody seemed to know who owned it. Meanwhile the Gardeners had taken it over. They liked living in places where they didn't have to pay rent.

Our space was a big room, with some cubicles curtained off – one for me, one for Lucerne and Zeb, one for the violet biolet, one for the shower. The cubicle curtains were woven of plastic-bag strips and duct tape, and they weren't in any way soundproof. This wasn't great, especially when it came to the violet biolet. The Gardeners said digestion was holy and there was nothing funny or terrible about the smells and noises that were part of the end product of the nutritional process, but at our place those end products were hard to ignore.

We ate our meals in the main room, on a table made out of a door. All of our dishes and pots and pans were salvaged – gleaned, as the Gardeners said – except for some of the thicker plates and mugs. Those had been made by the Gardeners back in their Ceramics period, before they'd decided that kilns used up too much energy.

I slept on a futon stuffed with husks and straw. It had a quilt sewed out of blue jeans and used bathmats, and every morning I had to make the bed first thing, because the Gardeners liked neatly made beds, though they weren't squeamish about what they were made of. Then I'd take my clothes down from the nail on the wall and put them on. I got clean ones every seventh day: the Gardeners didn't believe in wasting water and soap on too much washing. My clothes were always dank, because of the humidity and because the Gardeners didn't believe in dryers. "God made the sun for a reason," Nuala used to say, and according to her that reason was for drying our clothes.

Lucerne would still be in bed, it being her favourite place. Back when we'd lived at HelthWyzer with my real father she'd hardly ever stayed inside our house, but here she almost never went out of it, except to go over to the Rooftop or the Wellness Clinic and help the other Gardener women peel burdock roots or make those lumpy quilts or weave those plastic-bag curtains or something.

Zeb would be in the shower: *No daily showers* was one of the many Gardener rules Zeb ignored. Our shower water came down a garden hose out of a rain barrel and was gravity-fed, so no energy was used. That was Zeb's reason for making an exception for himself. He'd be singing:

> *Nobody gives a hoot,*
> *Nobody gives a hoot,*
> *And that is why we're down the chute,*
> *Cause nobody gives a hoot!*

All his shower songs were negative in this way, though he sang them cheerfully, in his big Russian-bear voice.

I had mixed feelings about Zeb. He could be frightening, but also it was reassuring to have someone so important in my family. Zeb was an Adam – a leading Adam. You could tell by the way the others looked up to him. He was large and solid, with a biker's beard and long hair – brown with a little grey in it – and a leathery face, and eyebrows like a barbed-wire fence. He looked as if he ought to have a silver tooth and a tattoo, but he didn't. He was strong as a bouncer, and he had the same menacing but genial expression, as if he'd break your neck if necessary, but not for fun.

Sometimes he'd play dominoes with me. The Gardeners were skimpy on toys – *Nature is our playground* – and the only toys they approved of were sewed out of leftover fabric or knitted with saved-up string, or they'd be wrinkly old-person figures with heads fashioned from dried crabapples. But they allowed dominoes, because they carved the sets themselves. When I won, Zeb would laugh and say, "Atta girl," and then I'd get a warm feeling, like nasturtiums.

Lucerne was always telling me to be nice to him, because although he wasn't my real father he was *like* my real father, and it hurt his feelings if I was rude to him. But then she didn't like it much when Zeb was nice to me. So it was hard to know how to act.

While Zeb was singing in the shower I'd get myself something to eat – dry soybits or maybe a vegetable patty left over from dinner. Lucerne was a fairly terrible cook. Then I'd go off to school. I was usually still hungry, but I could count on a school lunch. It wouldn't be great, but it would be food. As Adam One used to say, Hunger is the best sauce.

I couldn't remember ever being hungry at the HelthWyzer Compound. I really wanted to go back there. I wanted my real father, who must still love me: if he'd known where I was, he'd surely have come to take me back. I wanted my real house, with my own room and the bed with pink bed curtains and the closet full of different clothes in it. But most of all I wanted my mother to be the way she used to be, when she'd take me shopping, or go to the Club to play golf, or off to the AnooYoo Spa to get improvements done to herself, and then she'd come back smelling nice. But if I mentioned anything about our old life, she'd say all that was in the past.

She had a lot of reasons for running off with Zeb to join the Gardeners. She'd say their way was best for humankind, and for all the other creatures on Earth as well, and she'd acted out of love, not only for Zeb but for me, because she wanted the world to be healed so life wouldn't die out completely, and didn't it make me happy to know that?

She herself didn't seem all that happy. She'd sit at the table brushing her hair, staring at herself in our one small mirror with an expression that was glum, or critical, or maybe tragic. She had long hair like all the Gardener women, and the brushing and the braiding and the pinning up was a big job. On bad days she'd go through the whole thing four or five times.

On the days when Zeb was away, she'd barely talk to me. Or she'd act as if I'd hidden him. "When did you last see him?" she'd say. "Was he at school?" It was like she wanted me to spy on him. Then she'd be apologetic and say, "How are you feeling?" as if she'd done something wrong to me.

When I'd answer, she wouldn't be listening. Instead she'd be listening for Zeb. She'd get more and more anxious, even angry; she'd pace around and look out our window, talking to herself about how badly he treated her; but when he'd finally turn up, she'd fall all over him. Then she'd start nagging – where had he been, who had he been with, why hadn't he come back sooner? He'd just shrug and say, "It's okay, babe, I'm here now. You worry too much."

Then the two of them would disappear behind their plastic-strip and duct-tape curtain, and my mother would make pained and abject noises I found mortifying. I hated her then, because she had no pride and no restraint. It was like she was running down the middle of the mallway with no clothes on. Why did she worship Zeb so much?

Now I can see how that can happen. You can fall in love with anybody – a fool, a criminal, a nothing. There are no good rules.

The other thing I disliked so much at the Gardeners was the clothes. The Gardeners themselves were all colours, but their clothes weren't. If Nature was beautiful, as the Adams and the Eves claimed – if the lilies of the field were our models – why couldn't we look more like butterflies and less like parking lots? We were so flat, so plain, so scrubbed, so dark.

The street kids – the pleebrats – were hardly rich, but they were glittery. I envied the shiny things, the shimmering things, like the TV camera phones, pink and purple and silver, that flashed in and out of their hands like magician's cards, or the Sea/H/Ear Candies they stuck into their ears to hear music. I wanted their gaudy freedom.

We were forbidden to make friends with the pleebrats, and on their part they treated us like pariahs, holding their noses and yelling, or throwing things at us. The Adams and the Eves said we were being persecuted for our faith, but it was most likely for our wardrobes: the pleebrats were very fashion-conscious and wore the best clothes they could trade or steal. So we couldn't mingle with them, but we could eavesdrop. We got their knowledge that way – we caught it like germs. We gazed at that forbidden worldly life as if through a chain-link fence.

Once I found a beautiful camera phone, lying on the sidewalk. It was muddy and the signal was dead, but I took it home anyway, and the Eves caught me with it. "Don't you know any better?" they said. "Such a thing can hurt you! It can burn your brain! Don't even look at it: if you can see it, it can see you."

14

I first met Amanda in Year Ten, when I was ten: I was always the same age as the Year, so it's easy to remember when it was.

That day was Saint Farley of Wolves – a Young Bioneer scavenging day, when we had to tie sucky green bandanas around our necks and go out gleaning for the Gardeners' recycled-materials crafts. Sometimes we collected soap ends, carrying wicker baskets and making the rounds of the good hotels and restaurants because they threw out soap by the shovelful. The best hotels were in the rich pleebs – Fernside, Golfgreens, and the richest of all, SolarSpace – and we'd hitch rides to them, even though it was forbidden. The Gardeners were like that: they'd tell you to do something and then prohibit the easiest way to do it.

Rose-scented soap was the best. Bernice and me would take some home, and I'd keep mine in my pillowcase, to drown out the mildew smell of my damp quilt. We'd take the rest to the Gardeners, to be simmered into a jelly in the black-box solarcookers on the Rooftop, then cooled and cut up into slabs. The Gardeners used a lot of soap, because they were so worried about microbes, but some of the cut-up soaps would be set aside. They'd be rolled up in leaves and have strands of twisted grass tied around them, to be sold to tourists and gawkers at the Gardeners' Tree of Life Natural Materials Exchange, along with the bags of worms and the organic turnips and zucchinis and the other vegetables the Gardeners hadn't used up themselves.

That day wasn't a soap day, it was a vinegar day. We'd go to the back entrances of the bars and nightclubs and strip joints and pick through their dump boxes, and find any leftover wine, and pour it into our Young Bioneer enamel pails. Then we'd lug it off to the Wellness Clinic building, where it would be poured into the huge barrels in the Vinegar Room and fermented into vinegar, which the Gardeners used for household cleaning. The extra was decanted into the small bottles we'd gather up during our gleaning, which would have Gardeners labels glued onto them. Then they'd be offered for sale at the Tree of Life, along with the soap.

Our Young Bioneer work was supposed to teach us some useful lessons. For instance: Nothing should be carelessly thrown away, not even wine from sinful places. There was no such thing as garbage, trash, or dirt, only matter that hadn't been put to a proper use. And, most importantly, everyone, including children, had to contribute to the life of the community.

Shackie and Croze and the older boys sometimes drank their wine instead of saving it. If they drank too much, they'd fall down or throw up, or they'd get into fights with the pleebrats and throw stones at the winos. In revenge, the winos would pee into empty wine bottles to see if they could trick us. I never drank any piss myself: all you had to do was smell the opening of the bottle. But some kids had deadened their noses by smoking the butt ends of cigarettes or cigars, or even skunkweed if they could get it, and they'd upend the bottle, then spit and swear. Though maybe those kids drank from the peed-in bottles on purpose, to give themselves an excuse for the swearing, which was forbidden by the Gardeners.

As soon as they were out of sight of the Garden, Shackie and Croze and those boys would take off their Young Bioneer bandanas and tie them around their heads, like the Asian Fusions. They wanted to be a street gang too – they even had a password. "Gang!" they'd say, and the other person was supposed to say, "Grene." So, gangrene. The "gang" part was because they were a gang, and the "grene" stood for "green," like their head scarves. It was supposed to be a secret thing just for their gang members, but we all knew about it anyway. Bernice said it was a really good password for them, because gangrene was flesh rot and they were totally rotten.

"Big joke, Bernice," said Crozier. "P.S., you're ugly."

We were supposed to glean in groups, so we could defend ourselves against the pleebrat street gangs, or the winos who might grab our pails and drink the wine, or the child-snatchers who might sell us on the chicken-sex market. But instead we'd break up in twos or threes because that way we could cover the territory faster.

On this particular day I started out with Bernice, but then we had a fight. We squabbled constantly, which I took as a sign of our friendship because no matter how viciously we fought we'd always make up afterwards. Some bond held us together: not hard like bone, but slippery, like cartilage. Most likely we both felt insecure among the Gardener kids; we were each afraid to be left without an ally.

This time our fight was over a beaded change purse with a starfish on it that we'd picked out of a trash pile. We coveted finds like that and were always looking for them. The pleeblanders threw a lot of stuff away, because – said the Adams and Eves – they had short attention spans and no morals.

"I saw it first," I said.

"You saw it first last time," said Bernice.

"So what? I still saw it first!"

"Your mother's a skank," said Bernice. That was unfair because I thought so myself and Bernice knew it.

"Yours is a vegetable!" I said. "Vegetable" shouldn't have been an insult among the Gardeners, but it was. "Veena the Vegetable!" I added.

"Meat-breath!" said Bernice. She had the purse, and she was keeping it.

"Fine!" I said. I turned and walked away. I loitered, but I didn't look around, and Bernice didn't hurry after me.

This happened at the mallway, which was called Apple Corners. This was the official name of our pleeb, though everyone called it the Sinkhole because people vanished into it without a trace. We Gardener kids walked through the mallway whenever we could, just looking.

Like everything else in our pleeb, this mallway had once been classier. There was a broken fountain full of empty beer cans, there were built-in planters with a lot of Zizzy Froot cans and cigarette butts and used condoms covered (said Nuala) in festering germs. There was a holospinner booth that must once have spun out suns and moons, and rare animals, and your own image if you put money in, but it had been trashed some time ago and now stood empty-eyed. Sometimes we went inside it and pulled the tattered star-sprinkled curtain across, and read the messages left on the walls by the pleebrats. *Monica sucks. So does Darf only betr. UR $? 4 U free, baBc8s! Brad UR ded.* Those pleebrats were so daring, they'd write anywhere or anything. They didn't care who saw it.

The Sinkhole pleebrats went into the holospinner to smoke dope – the booth reeked of it – and they had sex in there: we could tell because of the condoms and sometimes the panties they'd leave behind. Gardener kids weren't supposed to do either one of those things – hallucinogenics were for religious purposes, and sex was for those who'd exchanged green leaves and jumped the bonfire – but the older Gardener kids said they'd done them anyway.

The shops that weren't boarded up were twenty-dollar stores called Tinsel's and Wild Side and Bong's – names like that. They sold feather hats, and crayons for drawing on your body, and T-shirts with dragons and skulls and mean slogans. Also Joltbars, and chewing gum that made your tongue glow in the dark, and red-lipped ashtrays that said, Let Me Blow It For You, and In-Your-Skin Etcha-Tattoos the Eves said would burn your skin down to the veins. You could find expensive stuff at bargain prices that Shackie said were boosted from the SolarSpace boutiques.

Tawdry rubbish, all of it, the Eves would say. If you're going to sell your soul, at least demand a higher price! Bernice and I paid no attention to that. Our souls didn't interest us. We'd peer in the windows, giddy with wanting. *What would you get?* we'd say. *The LED-light wand? That's baby! The Blood and Roses video? Gross, that's for boys! The Real Woman Stick-on Bimplants, with responsive nipples? Ren, you suck!*

After Bernice had left that day, I wasn't sure what to do. I thought maybe I should just go back, because I didn't feel too safe, alone. Then I saw Amanda, standing on the other side of the mallway with a group of Tex-Mexican pleeb girls. I knew that group by sight, and Amanda had never been with them before.

Those girls were wearing the sort of clothes they usually wore: miniskirts and spangled tops, candyfloss boas around their necks, silver gloves, plasticized butterflies clipped into their hair. They had their Sea/H/Ear Candies and their burning-bright phones and their jellyfish bracelets, and they were showing off. They were playing the same tune on their Sea/H/Ear Candies and they were dancing to it, swivelling their bums, sticking out their chests. They looked as if they already owned everything from every single store and were bored with it. I envied that look so much. I just stood there, envying.

Amanda was dancing too, except she was better. After a while she stopped and stood a little apart, texting on her purple phone. Then she stared straight at me and smiled, and waved her silver fingers. That meant *Come here.*

I checked that no one was looking. Then I crossed the mallway.

15

"You want to see my jellyfish bracelet?" Amanda said once I got there. I must have seemed pathetic to her, with my orphanish clothes and chalky fingers. She held up her wrist: there were the tiny jellyfish, opening and closing themselves like swimming flowers. They looked so perfect.

"Where did you get it?" I asked. I hardly knew what to say.

"Lifted," said Amanda. That was how the pleebrat girls mostly got things.

"How do they stay alive in there?"

She pointed to the silver knob where the bracelet fastened. "This is an aerator," she said. "It pumps in oxygen. You add the food twice a week."

"What happens if you forget?"

"They eat each other," said Amanda. She gave a little smile. "Some kids do that on purpose, they don't add the food. Then it's like a miniwar in there, and after a while there's just one jellyfish left, and then it dies."

"That's horrible," I said.

Amanda kept the same smile. "Yeah. That's why they do it."

"They're really pretty," I said in a neutral voice. I wanted to please her, and I couldn't tell whether she thought *horrible* was good or bad.

"Take it," said Amanda. She held out her wrist. "I can lift another one."

I wanted that bracelet so badly, but I wouldn't know how to buy the food and the jellyfish would die. Or else the bracelet would be discovered, no matter how well I hid it, and I'd be in trouble. "I can't," I said. I took a step back.

"You're one of *them*, aren't you?" said Amanda. She wasn't taunting, she seemed merely curious. "The Goddies. The Godawfuls. They say there's a bunch of them around here."

"No," I said, "I'm not." The lie must have stood out all over me. There were a lot of shabby people in the Sinkhole pleeb, but they weren't shabby on purpose the way the Gardeners were.

Amanda tilted her head a little to one side. "Funny," she said. "You look like them."

"I only live with them," I said. "I'm just more or less visiting them. I'm not really like them at all."

"Of course you aren't," said Amanda, smiling. She gave my arm a little pat. "Come over here. I want to show you something."

Where she took me was the alleyway that led to the back of Scales and Tails. We Gardener kids weren't supposed to go there, but we did anyway because when we were collecting you could get a lot of vinegar wine if you were early enough to beat out the winos.

That alleyway was dangerous. Scales and Tails was a dirt den, said the Eves. We should never, ever go into it, especially not girls. It said, ADULT ENTERTAINMENT in neon over the door, which was guarded at night by two enormous men in black suits who wore sunglasses even though it was dark. One of the older Gardener girls claimed these men had said to her, "Come back in a year and bring your sweet little ass." But Bernice said she was just bragging.

Scales had pictures on either side of the entrance – light-up holophotos. The pictures were of beautiful girls covered completely with shining green scales, like lizards, except for the hair. One of them was standing on a single leg with the other leg hooked around her neck. I thought that it must hurt to stand like that, but the girl in the picture was smiling.

Did the scales grow or were they were pasted on? Bernice and I disagreed about that. I said they were pasted, Bernice said they grew because the girls had been operated on, like getting bimplants. I told Bernice that was nuts because nobody would have such an operation. But secretly I sort of believed her.

One day we'd seen a scaly girl running down the street in daytime, with a black-suited man chasing her. She sparkled a lot because of her shiny green scales; she'd kicked off her high heels and she was running in her bare feet, dodging in and out among the people, but then she hit a patch of broken glass and fell. The man caught up with her and scooped her up, and carried her back to Scales with her green snakeskin arms dangling down. Her feet were bleeding. Whenever I thought of that, a chill went all through me, like watching someone else cut their finger.

At the back of the alleyway beside Scales there was a small square yard where the trash bins were kept – the ones for the carbon garboil trash and the other kind. Then there was a board fence, and on the other side of it there was a vacant lot where a building had burned down. Now it was just hard earth with pieces of cement and charred wood and broken glass, and weeds growing on it.

Sometimes the pleebrats hung out around there, and they'd jump us when we were emptying the wine bottles. They'd yell, "Goddie, goddie, stinky body" and snatch the pails and run off with them or empty them onto us. That happened to Bernice once and she reeked of wine for days.

Sometimes we went into that vacant lot with Zeb on our Outdoor Classroom days: he said it was the closest thing to a meadow we'd ever find in our pleeb. When he was with us, the pleebland kids didn't bother us. Zeb was like having your own private tiger: tame to you, savage to everyone else.

Once, we found a dead girl there. She didn't have any hair or clothes: she only had a few green scales left clinging to her. *Pasted on*, I thought. *Or something. Anyway, not growing. So I was right.*

"Maybe she's sunbathing," said one of the older boys, and the rest of them snickered.

"Don't touch her," said Zeb. "Have some respect! We'll have our lesson on the Rooftop Garden today." When we came back for our next Outdoor Classroom, she was gone.

"I bet she's carbon garboil," Bernice whispered to me. Carbon garboil was made from any sort of carbon garbage – slaughterhouse refuse, old vegetables, restaurant tossout, even plastic bottles. The carbs went into a boiler, and oil and water came out, plus anything metal. Officially you couldn't put in human corpses, but the kids made jokes about that. Oil, water, and shirt buttons. Oil, water, and gold pen nibs.

"Oil, water, and green scales," I whispered to Bernice.

At first glance the vacant lot was empty. No winos, no pleebrats, no dead naked women. Amanda led me over to the far corner, where there was a flat slab of concrete. A syrup bottle was leaning against it, the squeeze kind.

"Look at this," she said. She'd written her name in syrup on the slab, and a stream of ants was feeding on the letters, so that each letter had an edging of black ants. That was how I first learned Amanda's name – I saw it written in ants. Amanda Payne.

"Cool, huh?" she said. "Want to write your own name?"

"Why are you doing that?" I said.

"It's neat," said Amanda. "You write things, then they eat your writing. So you appear, then you disappear. That way no one can find you."

Why did this make sense to me? I don't know, but it did. "Where do you live?" I asked.

"Oh, around," said Amanda carelessly. That meant she didn't really live anywhere: she was sleeping in a squat somewhere, or worse. "I used to live in Texas," she added.

So she was a refugee. A lot of Texas refugees had turned up after the hurricanes and then the droughts. They were mostly illegal. Now I could see why Amanda would be so interested in disappearing.

"You can come and live with me," I said. I hadn't planned that, it just came out of my mouth.

At that moment Bernice squeezed through the gap in the fence. She'd relented, she'd returned to collect me, except now I didn't want her.

"Ren! What're you *doing*!" she yelled. She came clomping across the vacant lot in that purposeful way she had. I found myself thinking she had big feet, and her body was too square and her nose too small, and her neck ought to be longer and thinner. More like Amanda's.

"Here comes a friend of yours, I guess," said Amanda, smiling. I felt like saying, *She's not my friend*, but I wasn't brave enough to be that treacherous.

Bernice came up to us, red-faced. She always got red when she was mad. "Come on, Ren," she said. "You're not supposed to talk to her." She spotted Amanda's jellyfish bracelet, and I could tell she wanted it as much as I did. "You're evil," she said to Amanda. "Pleebrat!" She stuck her arm through mine.

"This is Amanda," I said. "She's coming to live with me."

I thought Bernice would fly into one of her rages. But I was giving her my stony-eyed stare, the one that said I wasn't going to give in. She'd risk losing face in front of a stranger if she pushed too hard, so instead she gave me a silent, calculating look. "Okay then," she said. "She can help carry the vinegar wine."

"Amanda knows how to steal things," I said to Bernice as we trudged back to the Wellness Clinic. I meant this as a peace offering, but Bernice only grunted.

16

I knew I couldn't really take Amanda home with me like a stray kitten: Lucerne would've told me to put her back where I found her, because Amanda was a pleebrat and Lucerne hated pleebrats. According to her they were ruined children, thieves and liars all, and once a child had been ruined it was like a wild dog, it could never be trained or trusted. She was afraid to walk along the street from one Gardener place to another because of the pleebrat gangs that could swarm you and run off with anything they could grab. She never learned about picking up stones and hitting back and yelling. It was because of her earlier life. She was a hothouse flower: that's what Zeb called her. I used to think this was a compliment, because of the word *flower*.

So Amanda would be sent packing, unless I got Adam One's permission first. He loved people joining the Gardeners, especially kids – he was always going on about how the Gardeners should mould young minds. If he said Amanda should live with us, Lucerne wouldn't be able to say no.

The three of us found Adam One at the Wellness Clinic, helping to bottle the vinegar. I explained that I'd picked up Amanda – "gleaned" her, I said – and that she wished to join us, having seen the Light, and could she live at my house?

"Is that true, my child?" Adam One asked Amanda. The other Gardeners had stopped work and were eyeing Amanda's miniskirt and silver fingers.

"Yes, sir," said Amanda in a respectful voice.

"She'll be a bad influence on Ren," said Nuala, who had come over. "Ren is too easily led. We should place her with Bernice."

Bernice gave me a triumphant look: *See what you've done!* "That would be fine," she said neutrally.

"No!" I said. "I found her!" Bernice glared at me. Amanda said nothing.

Adam One considered the three of us. He knew a lot of things. "Perhaps Amanda herself should decide," he said. "She should meet the families in question. That will help to settle the matter. That would be fairest, no?"

"My place first," said Bernice.

Bernice lived in the Buenavista Condos. The Gardeners didn't exactly own the building, because ownership was wrong, but somehow they controlled it. It had "Luxury Lofts for Today's Singles" on it in faded gold lettering, but I knew it wasn't Luxury: the shower in Bernice's apartment was clogged, the tiles in the kitchen were cracked and gap-toothed, the ceilings oozed when it rained, the bathroom was slick with mildew.

The three of us went into the lobby, past the middle-aged Gardener lady on security duty there – she was busy with some snarled-up macramé craft object and hardly noticed us. We had to climb six flights of stairs to get to Bernice's floor because the Gardeners didn't believe in elevators except for old people and paraplegics. There were forbidden objects in the stairwell – needles, used condoms, spoons, candle ends. The Gardeners said pleeb crooks and thugs and pimps got in at night and used the stairwell for nasty parties; we'd never seen any of these, though we'd once caught Shackie and Croze and their pals drinking wine dregs in there.

Bernice had her own plastikey; she unlocked the door and let us in. The apartment smelled like unwashed clothes left under a dripping sink, or like other kids' plugged sinuses, or like diapers. Through these odours drifted another one – a rich, fertile, spicy, earthy aroma. Maybe it was wafting up through the hot-air vents from the Gardener mushroom beds in the basement.

But this smell – all the smells – seemed to be coming from Bernice's mother, Veena, who was sitting on the worn plush-covered sofa as if rooted there, staring at the wall. She had on her usual shapeless dress; her knees were covered with an old yellow baby blanket; her pale hair hung limply on either side of her round, soft, whitish face; her hands lay curled slackly, as if her fingers were broken. On the floor in front of her was a scattering of dirty plates. Veena didn't cook: she ate what Bernice's father gave her; or else she didn't eat it. But she never tidied up. She hardly ever spoke, and she didn't speak now. Her eyes flickered as we went past her though, so maybe she saw us.

"What's the matter with her?" Amanda whispered to me.

"She's Fallow," I whispered back.

"Yeah?" Amanda whispered. "She just looks really stoned."

My own mother said Bernice's mother was "depressed." But my mother wasn't a real Gardener, as Bernice was always telling me, because a real Gardener would never say *depressed*. The Gardeners believed that people who acted like Veena were in a Fallow state – resting, retreating into themselves to gain Spiritual insight, gathering their energy for the moment when they would burst out again like buds in spring. They only appeared to be doing nothing. Some Gardeners could remain in a Fallow state for a very long time.

"This is my place," said Bernice.

"Where would I sleep?" said Amanda.

We were looking at Bernice's room when Burt the Knob came in. "Where's my little girl?" he called.

"Don't answer," said Bernice. "Close the door!" We could hear him moving around in the main room; then he came into Bernice's room and scooped her up. He stood there holding her under the armpits. "Where's my little girl?" he said again, which made me cringe. I'd seen him do this before, not only to Bernice. He just loved girls' armpits. He'd corner you in behind the bean rows when you were doing slug and snail relocation and pretend to be helping you. Then along would come the hands. He was such a knob.

Bernice was scowling and wriggling. "I'm not your little girl," she said, which could mean: *I'm not little*, or *I'm not yours*, or even *I'm not a girl*. Burt took this as a joke.

"Then where's my little girl gone?" he repeated in a woebegone voice.

"Put me down," Bernice shouted. I felt sorry for her, and also I felt lucky – because whatever I felt about Zeb, it wasn't embarrassment.

"I'd like to look at your place now," said Amanda. So the two of us went back down the stairs, leaving Bernice behind us, redder and angrier than ever. I did feel bad about that, but not bad enough to give up Amanda.

Lucerne wasn't pleased to find that Amanda had been added to our family, but I told her that Adam One had ordered it; so what could she do? "She'll have to sleep in your room," she said crossly.

"She won't mind," I said. "Will you, Amanda?"

"No, indeed," said Amanda. She had a very polite manner she could put on, as if she was the one doing you the favour. It grated on Lucerne.

"And she'll have to get rid of those flashy clothes," said Lucerne.

"But they aren't worn out yet," I said innocently. "We can't just throw them away! That would be wasteful!"

"We'll sell them," said Lucerne tightly. "We can certainly use the money."

"Amanda should get the money," I said. "They're her clothes."

"It's okay," said Amanda, softly but regally. "They didn't cost me anything." Then we went into my cubicle and sat on the bed, and laughed behind our hands.

When Zeb got back that evening, he had no comment at first. We all ate dinner together, and Zeb chewed away at the soybit and green bean casserole and watched Amanda with her graceful neck and silver fingers picking daintily away at what was on her plate. She hadn't yet taken off her gloves. Finally he said to her, "You're a sly little operator, aren't you?" It was his friendly voice, the one he used for saying, "Atta girl" at dominoes.

Lucerne, who was dishing him out a second helping, stiffened in mid-motion, the big spoon straight up in the air like some kind of metal detector. Amanda gazed at him straight-faced, with her eyes wide open. "Excuse me, sir?"

Zeb laughed. "You're very good," he said.

17

Having Amanda living with me was like having a sister, only better. She had Gardeners' clothing now, so she looked like the rest of us; and pretty soon she smelled like the rest of us too.

In the first week I showed her all around. I took her to the Vinegar Room, the Sewing Room, and up to the Run-For-Your-Light Treadmills gym. Mugi was in charge of that; we called him Mugi the Muscle because he only had one muscle left. Amanda made friends with him, though. She made friends with everyone by asking them the right way to do things.

Burt the Knob explained how to relocate the slugs and snails in the Garden by heaving them over the railing into the traffic, where they were supposed to crawl off and find new homes, though I knew they really got squashed. Katuro the Wrench, who fixed the leaks and took care of the water systems, showed her how the plumbing worked.

Philo the Fog didn't say much to her; he just smiled at her a lot. The older Gardeners said he'd transcended language and was travelling with the Spirit, though Amanda said he was just wasted. Stuart the Screw, who made our furniture out of recycled junk, didn't like people much, but he liked Amanda. "That girl's got a good eye for wood," he'd say.

Amanda didn't like sewing, but she pretended to, so Surya praised her. Rebecca called her *sweetheart* and said she had good food taste, and Nuala cooed over her singing in the Buds and Blooms Choir. Even Dry Witch Toby would brighten up when she saw Amanda coming. She was the hardest nut to crack, but Amanda took a sudden interest in mushrooms, and helped old Pilar stamp bees on the honey labels, and that pleased Toby, though she tried not to show it.

"Why are you sucking up so much?" I asked Amanda.

"It's how you find stuff out," she said.

We told each other a lot of things. I told her about my father and my house in the HelthWyzer Compound, and how my mother ran off with Zeb.

"I bet she had hot panties for him," said Amanda. We were whispering all of this in our cubicle, at night, with Zeb and Lucerne right nearby, so it was hard not to hear the sex noises they'd make. Before Amanda came I'd found all of that shameful, but now found it funny because Amanda did.

Amanda told me about the droughts in Texas – how her parents had lost their Happicuppa coffee franchise and couldn't sell their house because no one would buy it, and how there were no jobs and they'd ended up in a refugee camp with old trailers and a lot of Tex-Mexicans. Then their trailer was demolished in one of the hurricanes and her father was killed by a piece of flying metal. A lot of people drowned, but she and her mother held on to a tree and got rescued by some men in a rowboat. They were thieves, said Amanda, looking for stuff they could lift, but they said they'd take Amanda and her mother to dry land and a shelter if they'd do a trade.

"What kind of trade?" I said.

"Just a trade," said Amanda.

The shelter was a football stadium with tents in it. There was a lot of trading going on: people would do anything for twenty dollars, Amanda said. Then her mother got sick from the drinking water, but Amanda didn't because she traded for sodas. And there was no medicine, so her mother died. "A lot of people shat to death," said Amanda. "You should have smelled that place."

Amanda snuck away after that because more people were getting sick and no one was taking away the crap and garbage or bringing food. She changed her name, because she didn't want to be put back in the football stadium: the refugees were supposed to be farmed out to work in whatever job they were told to. "No free lunch," people were saying: you had to pay for everything, one way or another.

"What did you change it from?" I asked her. "Your name."

"It was a white-trash name. Barb Jones," said Amanda. "That was my identity. But I don't have an identity now. So I'm invisible." It was one more thing I could admire about her – her invisibility.

Amanda walked north, along with thousands of other people. "I tried to hitch, but I only got one lift, with a guy who said he was a chicken farmer," she said. "He pushed his hand between my legs; you can tell that's coming when they breathe funny. I stuck my thumbs in his eyes and got out of there fast." She made it sound like thumbs in the eyes was normal in the Exfernal World. I wanted to learn how to do it, but I didn't think I could work up the nerve.

"Then I had to get past the Wall," she said.

"What wall?"

"Don't you watch the news? The Wall they're building to keep the Tex refugees out, because just the fence wasn't enough. There's men with sprayguns – it's a CorpSeCorps wall. But they can't patrol every inch – the Tex-Mex kids know all the tunnels, they helped me get through."

"You could've been shot," I said. "Then what?"

"Then I worked my way up here. For food and stuff. It took a while."

In her place I would have just laid down in a ditch and cried myself to death. But Amanda says if there's something you really want, you can figure out a way to get it. She says being discouraged is a waste of time.

I worried that there might be trouble with the other Gardener kids: after all, Amanda was a pleebrat – one of our enemies. Bernice hated her, of course, but she didn't dare say so because like everyone else she was in awe of her. First of all, no Gardener kid could dance, and Amanda had excellent moves – it was like her hips were dislocated. She'd teach me when Lucerne and Zeb weren't there. We'd get the music off her purple phone, which she kept hidden in our mattress, and when the card was used up she'd lift another one. She had some flashy pleeblander clothes hidden away as well, so when she needed to lift something she'd put those clothes on and go off to the Sinkhole mallway.

I could see that Shackleton and Crozier and the older boys were in love with her. She was very pretty, with her tawny skin and her long neck and her big eyes, but you could be pretty and still get called a carrot-sucker or a meat-hole on legs by those boys; they had a bunch of sick names for girls.

Not for Amanda, though: she had their respect. She had a piece of glass with duct tape along one edge to hold it with, and she said this glass had saved her life more than once. She showed us how to ram a guy in the crotch or trip him up and then kick him under the chin and break his neck. There were lots of tricks like that, she said – ones you could use if you had to.

But on Festival days or at Buds and Blooms Choir practice, no one was as pious as her. You'd think she'd been washed in milk.

THE FESTIVAL OF ARKS

THE FESTIVAL OF ARKS

YEAR TEN.

OF THE TWO FLOODS AND THE TWO COVENANTS.
SPOKEN BY ADAM ONE.

Dear Friends and Fellow Mortals:

Today the Children have built their little Arks and launched them on the Arboretum Creek to carry their messages of respect for God's Creatures to other children who may happen to find them on the seashore. In an increasingly endangered world, what a caring act that is! Let us remember: It is better to hope than to mope!

This evening we will share a special Festival meal – Rebecca's delicious lentil soup, representing the First Flood, with Noah's Ark dumplings stuffed with vegetable Animal forms. One of those dumplings contains a turnip Noah, and whoever finds that Noah will get a special prize – thus teaching us not to gobble our food in a heedless manner.

That prize is a picture painted by Nuala, our talented Eve Nine: Saint Brendan the Voyager, shown with the essential items we must include in our Ararat storerooms in preparation for the Waterless Flood. In this artwork, Nuala has given the tinned soydines and the soybits their due prominence. But let us remind ourselves to refresh our Ararats regularly. You wouldn't want to open that tin of soydines on the day of need and find that the contents have gone bad.

Burt's worthy wife, Veena, is in a Fallow state and cannot be with us for this Festival, but we look forward to welcoming her among us very soon.

Now let us turn to our Devotion for the Festival of Arks.

On this day we mourn, but we also rejoice. We mourn the deaths of all those Creatures of the land that were destroyed in the First Flood of extinctions – whenever those occurred – but we rejoice that the Fishes and Whales, and the Corals, and the Sea Turtles and the Dolphins, and the Sea Urchins, yea, also the Sharks – we rejoice that they were spared, unless a change in ocean temperature and salinity caused by the great downpour of fresh waters did harm to some Species unknown to us.

We mourn the carnage that took place among the Animals. God was evidently willing to do away with numerous Species, as the fossil records attest, but many were saved until our times, and these are the ones He bequeathed anew to our care. If you had composed a splendid symphony, would you want it to be obliterated? The Earth and the music thereof, the Universe and the harmony therein – these are God's works of Creativity, of which Man's creativity is but a poor shadow.

According to the Human Words of God, the task of saving the chosen Species was given to Noah, symbolizing the aware ones among Mankind. He alone was forewarned; he alone took upon himself Adam's original stewardship, keeping God's beloved Species safe until the waters of the Flood had receded and his Ark was beached upon Ararat. Then the rescued Creatures were set loose upon the Earth, as if at a second Creation.

At the first Creation all was rejoicing, but the second event was qualified: God was no longer so well pleased. He knew something had gone very wrong with his last experiment, Man, but that it was too late for him to fix it. "I will not again curse the ground any more for man's sake; for the imagination of man's heart is evil from his youth; neither will I again smite every thing living, as I have done," say the Human Words of God in Genesis 8:21.

Yes, my Friends – any further cursing of the ground would be done not by God but by Man himself. Consider the southern shores of the Mediterranean – once fruitful farmland, now a desert. Consider the ruinations wrought in the Amazon River basin; consider the wholesale slaughter of ecosystems, each one a living reflection of God's infinite care for detail . . . but these are subjects for another day.

Then God says a noteworthy thing. He says, "And the fear of you" – that is, Man – "and the dread of you shall be upon every beast of the earth, and upon every fowl of the air . . . into your hand are they delivered." Genesis 9:2. This is not God telling Man that he has a right to destroy all the Animals, as some claim. Instead it is a warning to God's beloved Creatures: *Beware of Man, and of his evil heart.*

Then God establishes his Covenant with Noah, and with his sons, "and with every living creature." Many recall the Covenant with Noah, but forget the Covenant with all other living Beings. However, God does not forget it. He repeats the terms "all flesh" and "every living creature" a number of times, to make sure we get the point.

No one can make a Covenant with a stone: for a Covenant to exist, there must be a minimum of two live and responsible parties to it. Therefore the Animals are not senseless matter, not mere chunks of meat. No; they have living Souls, or God could not have made a Covenant with them. The Human Words of God affirm this: "But ask now the beasts," says Job 12, "and they shall teach thee; and the fowls of the air, and they shall tell thee . . . and the fishes of the sea shall declare unto thee."

Let us today remember Noah, the chosen caregiver of the Species. We God's Gardeners are a plural Noah: we too have been called, we too forewarned. We can feel the symptoms of coming disaster as a doctor feels a sick man's pulse. We must be ready for the time when those who have broken trust with the Animals – yes, wiped them from the face of the Earth where God placed them – will be swept away by the Waterless Flood, which will be carried on the wings of God's dark Angels that fly by night, and in airplanes and helicopters and bullet trains, and on transport trucks and other such conveyances.

But we Gardeners will cherish within us the knowledge of the Species, and of their preciousness to God. We must ferry this priceless knowledge over the face of the Waterless Waters, as if within an Ark.

Let us construct our Ararats carefully, my Friends. Let us provision them with foresight, and with canned and dried goods. Let us camouflage them well.

May God deliver us from the snare of the fowler, and cover us with his feathers, and under his wings may we trust, as it says in Psalm 91; and thou shalt not be afraid of the pestilence that walketh in darkness, nor for the destruction that wasteth at noonday.

May I remind you all about the importance of hand-washing, seven times a day at least, and after every encounter with a stranger. It is never too early to practise this essential precaution.

Avoid anyone who is sneezing.

Let us sing.

MY BODY IS MY EARTHLY ARK

My body is my earthly Ark,
It's proof against the Flood;
It holds all Creatures in its heart,
And knows that they are good.

It's builded firm of genes and cells,
And neurons without number;
My Ark enfolds the million years
That Adam spent in slumber.

And when Destruction swirls around,
To Ararat I'll glide;
My Ark will then come safe to land
By light of Spirit's guide.

With Creatures all, in harmony
I'll pass my mortal days,
While each in its appointed voice
Sings the Creator's praise.

From *The God's Gardeners Oral Hymnbook*

18

YEAR TWENTY-FIVE

In the northern meadow the dead boar is still lying. The vultures have been at it, though they can't get through the tough hide: they're limited to eyes and tongue. They'll have to wait until it rots and bursts before they can really dig in.

Toby turns her binoculars skyward, at the crows racketing around. When she looks back, two liobams are crossing the meadow. A male, a female, strolling along as if they own the place. They stop at the boar, sniff briefly. Then they continue their walk.

Toby stares at them, fascinated: she's never seen a liobam in the flesh, only pictures. Am I imagining things? she wonders. No, the liobams are actual. They must be zoo animals freed by one of the more fanatical sects in those last desperate days.

They don't look dangerous, although they are. The lion-sheep splice was commissioned by the Lion Isaiahists in order to force the advent of the Peaceable Kingdom. They'd reasoned that the only way to fulfil the lion/lamb friendship prophecy without the first eating the second would be to meld the two of them together. But the result hadn't been strictly vegetarian.

Still, the liobams seem gentle enough, with their curly golden hair and twirling tails. They're nibbling flower heads, they don't look up; yet she has the sense that they're perfectly aware of her. Then the male opens its mouth, displaying its long, sharp canines, and calls. It's an odd combination of baa and roar: a bloar, thinks Toby.

Her skin prickles. She doesn't relish the thought of one of those creatures leaping on her from behind a shrub. If it's her fate to be mangled and devoured, she'd prefer a more conventional beast of prey. Still, they are astounding. She watches them while they gambol together, then sniff the air and saunter away to the edge of the forest, vanishing into dappled shade.

How Pilar would have enjoyed seeing those, she thinks. Pilar, and Rebecca, and little Ren. And Adam One. And Zeb. All dead now.

Stop it, she tells herself. Just stop that right now.

She sidesteps carefully down the stairs, using her mop handle for balance. She keeps expecting – still – that the elevator doors will open, the lights blink on, the air conditioning begins to breathe, and someone – who? – will step out.

She goes down the long hall, walking softly on the increasingly spongy carpet, past the line of mirrors. There's no shortage of mirrors in the Spa: the ladies needed to be reminded by harsh light of how bad they looked, and then by soft light of how good they might yet appear with a little costly help. But after her first few weeks alone she'd covered the mirrors with pink towels to avoid being startled by her own shape as it flitted from one frame to the next.

"Who lives here?" she says out loud. Not me, she thinks. This thing I'm doing can hardly be called living. Instead I'm lying dormant, like a bacterium in a glacier. Getting time over with. That's all.

She spends the rest of the morning sitting in a kind of stupor. Once, this would have been meditation, but she can hardly call it that now. Paralyzing rage can still take hold of her, it seems: impossible to know when it will strike. It begins as disbelief and ends in sorrow, but in between those two phases her whole body shakes with anger. Anger at whom, at what? Why has she been saved alive? Out of the countless millions. Why not someone younger, someone with more optimism and fresher cells? She ought to trust that she's here for a reason – to bear witness, to transmit a message, to salvage at least something from the general wreck. She ought to trust, but she can't.

It's wrong to give so much time over to mourning, she tells herself. Mourning and brooding. There's nothing to be accomplished by it.

During the heat of the day, she naps. Trying to stay awake through the noontime steambath is a waste of energy.

She sleeps on a massage table in one of the cubicles where the Spa clients took their organic-botanic treatments. There are pink sheets and pink pillows, and pink blankets too – soft cuddly colours, pampering infant colours – though she doesn't need the blankets, not in this weather.

She's been having some difficulty waking up. She must fight against lethargy. It's a strong desire – to sleep. To sleep and sleep. To sleep forever. She can't live only in the present, like a shrub. But the past is a closed door, and she can't see any future. Maybe she'll go on from day to day and year to year until she simply withers, folds in on herself, shrivels up like an old spider.

Or she could take a shortcut. There's always the Poppy in its red bottle, there are always the lethal amanita mushrooms, the little Death Angels. How soon before she sets them loose inside herself and lets them fly away with her on their white, white wings?

To cheer herself up, she opens her jar of honey. It's the last one remaining from the honey she extracted so long ago – she and Pilar – up on the Edencliff Rooftop. She's been saving it all these years as if it's a protective charm. Honey doesn't decay, said Pilar, as long as you keep water out of it: that's why the ancients called it the food of immortality.

She swallows one fragrant spoonful, then another. It was hard work collecting that honey: the smoking of the hives, the painstaking removal of the combs, the extracting. It took delicacy and tact. The bees had to be spoken to and persuaded, not to mention temporarily gassed, and sometimes they'd sting, but in her memory the whole experience is one of unblemished happiness. She knows she's deceiving herself about that, but she prefers to deceive herself. She desperately needs to believe such pure joy is still possible.

19

Gradually, Toby stopped thinking she should leave the Gardeners. She didn't really believe in their creed, but she no longer disbelieved. One season blended into the next – rainy, stormy, hot and dry, cooler and dry, rainy and warm – and then one year into another. She wasn't quite a Gardener, yet she wasn't a pleeblander any more. She was neither the one nor the other.

She'd venture out onto the street now, though she didn't go far from the Garden, and she'd cover herself well and wear a nose cone and a wide sunhat. She still had nightmares about Blanco – the snakes on his arms, the headless women chained to his back, his skinless-looking blue-veined hands coming for her neck. *Say you love me! Say it, bitch!* During the worst times with him, during the most terror, the most pain, she'd focus on those hands coming off at the wrists. The hands, other parts of him. Grey blood gushing out. She'd picture him stuffed into a garboil boiler, alive. Those had been violent thoughts, and since joining the Gardeners she'd sincerely tried to erase them from her brain. But they kept coming back. She was told by those in nearby sleeping cubicles that she some-times made what they called "signals of distress" in her sleep.

Adam One was aware of these signals. She had come, over time, to realize it would be a mistake to underestimate him. Though his beard had now turned an innocent feathery white and his blue eyes were round and guileless as a baby's, though he seemed so trusting and vulnerable, Toby felt she would never encounter anyone as strong in purpose. He didn't wield this purpose like a weapon, he simply floated along inside it and let it carry him. That would be hard to attack: like attacking the tide.

"He's in Painball now, my dear," he told her one fine Saint Mendel's Day. "He may not ever be released. Perhaps he will return to the elements there."

Toby's heart fluttered. "What did he do?"

"Killed a woman," said Adam One. "The wrong kind of woman. A woman from one of the Corps who was seeking excitement in the pleeblands. I wish they wouldn't do that. The CorpSeCorps were forced to act, this time."

Toby had heard about Painball. It was a facility for condemned criminals, both political ones and the other kind: they had a choice of being spraygunned to death or doing time in the Painball Arena, which wasn't an arena at all, but more like an enclosed forest. You got enough food for two weeks, plus the Painball gun – it shot paint, like a regular paintball gun, but a hit in the eyes would blind you, and if you got the paint on your skin you'd start to corrode, and then you'd be an easy target for the throat-slitters on the other team. For everyone who went in was assigned to one of two teams: the Red, the Gold.

Woman criminals didn't choose Painball much, they chose the sprayguns. So did most of the politicals. They knew they wouldn't stand a chance in there, they preferred to just get it over with. Toby could understand that.

For a long time they'd kept the Painball Arena secret, like cock-fighting and Internal Rendition, but now, it was said, you could watch it onscreen. There were cameras in the Painball forest, hidden in trees and built into rocks, but often there wasn't much to see except a leg or an arm or a blurry shadow, because the Painballers were understandably stealthy. But once in a while there'd be a hit, right on screen. If you survived for a month, you were good; longer than that, very good. Some got hooked on the adrenalin and didn't want to come out when their time was up. Even the CorpSeCorps professionals were scared of the long-term Painballers.

Some teams would hang their kill on a tree, some would mutilate the body. Cut off the head, tear out the heart and kidneys. That was to intimidate the other team. Eat part of it, if food was running low or just to show how mean you were. After a while, thought Toby, you wouldn't just cross the line, you'd forget there ever were any lines. You'd do whatever it takes.

She had a quick vision of Blanco, headless, hanging upside down. What did she feel about that? Pleasure? Pity? She couldn't tell.

She asked to do a Vigil, and spent it on her knees, attempting to mind-meld with a plantful of green peas. The vines, the flowers, the leaves, the pods. So green and soothing. It almost worked.

One day, old walnut-faced Pilar – Eve Six – asked Toby if she wanted to learn about bees. Bees and mushrooms – these were Pilar's specialties. Toby liked Pilar, who seemed kind, and who had a serenity she envied; so she said yes.

"Good," said Pilar. "You can always tell the bees your troubles." So Adam One wasn't the only person to have registered Toby's worry.

Pilar took her to visit the beehives, and introduced her to the bees by name. "They need to know you're a friend," she said. "They can smell you. Just move slowly," she cautioned as the bees coated Toby's bare arm like golden fur. "They'll know you next time. Oh – if they do sting, don't slap them. Just brush the sting off. But they won't sting unless they're frightened, because stinging kills them."

Pilar had a fund of bee lore. A bee in the house means a visit from a stranger, and if you kill the bee, the visit will not be a good one. If the beekeeper dies, the bees must be told, or they will swarm and fly away. Honey helps an open wound. A swarm of bees in May, worth a cool day. A swarm of bees in June, worth a new moon. A swarm of bees in July, not worth a squashed fly. All the bees of a hive are one bee: that's why they'll die for the hive. "Like the Gardeners," Pilar said. Toby couldn't tell whether or not she was joking.

The bees were agitated by her at first, but after a while they accepted her. They allowed her to extract the honey by herself, and she got stung only twice. "The bees made a mistake," Pilar told her. "You must ask permission of their Queen, and explain to them that you mean them no harm." She said you had to speak out loud because the bees couldn't read your mind precisely, any more than a person could. So Toby did speak, though she felt like a fool. What would anyone down there on the sidewalk think if they saw her talking to a swarm of bees?

According to Pilar, the bees all over the world had been in trouble for decades. It was the pesticides, or the hot weather, or a disease, or maybe all of these – nobody knew exactly. But the bees on the Rooftop Garden were all right. In fact, they were thriving. "They know they're loved," said Pilar.

Toby doubted this. She doubted a lot of things. But she kept her doubts to herself, because *doubt* wasn't a word the Gardeners used much.

After a while, Pilar took Toby down to the dank cellars below the Buenavista Condos and showed her where the mushrooms were grown. Bees and mushrooms went together, said Pilar: the bees were on good terms with the unseen world, being the messengers to the dead. She tossed that crazed little factoid off as if it was something everyone knew, and Toby pretended to ignore it. Mushrooms were the roses in the garden of that unseen world, because the real mushroom plant was underground. The part you could see – what most people called a mushroom – was just a brief apparition. A cloud flower.

There were mushrooms for eating, mushrooms for medicinal uses, and mushrooms for visions. These last were used only for the Retreats and the Isolation Weeks, though sometimes they might be good for certain medical conditions, and even to ease people through their Fallow states, when the Soul was refertilizing itself. Pilar said that everyone had a Fallow state sometime. But it was dangerous to stay Fallow too long, "It's like going down the stairs," she said, "and never coming back up. But the mushrooms can help with that."

There were three kinds of mushrooms, said Pilar – Never Poisonous, Employ with Caution and Advice, and Beware. They all had to be memorized. Puffballs, any species: Never Poisonous. The psilocybins: Employ with Caution and Advice. All amanitas, and especially amanita phalloides, the Death Angel: Beware.

"Aren't those very dangerous?" said Toby.

Pilar nodded. "Oh yes. Very dangerous."

"Then why do you grow them?"

"God wouldn't have made poisonous mushrooms unless He intended us to use them sometimes," said Pilar.

Pilar was so mild-mannered and gentle that Toby couldn't believe she'd just heard this. "You wouldn't poison anyone!" she said.

Pilar gave her a straight look. "You never know, dear," she said. "When you might have to."

Now Toby spent all her spare hours with Pilar – tending the Edencliff beehives and the crops of buckwheat and lavender grown for the bees on adjacent rooftops, extracting the honey and storing it in jars. They stamped the labels with the little bee stamp that Pilar used instead of lettering, and set some jars aside to add to the preserved foods in the Ararat that Pilar had built behind a moveable cinder block in the Buenavista cellar wall. Or they cared for the Poppy plants and collected the thick juice from their seed pods, or pottered among the mushroom beds in the Buenavista cellar, or simmered elixirs and remedies and the honey-and-rose liquid skin emulsion they'd sell at the Tree of Life Natural Materials Exchange.

Thus the time passed. Toby stopped counting it. In any case, time is not a thing that passes, said Pilar: it's a sea on which you float.

At night, Toby breathed herself in. Her new self. Her skin smelled like honey and salt. And earth.

20

New people kept arriving among the Gardeners. Some were genuine converts, but others didn't stay long. They'd be there for a while, wearing the same baggy, concealing clothes as everyone else, working at the most menial tasks, and, if they were women, weeping from time to time. Then they'd be gone. They were shadow people, and Adam One was moving them around in the shadows. As he'd moved Toby herself.

This was guesswork: it hadn't taken Toby long to realize that the Gardeners did not welcome personal questions. Where you'd come from, what you'd done before – all of that was irrelevant, their manner implied. Only the Now counted. Say about others as you would have them say about you. In other words, nothing.

There were a lot of things Toby remained curious about. For instance, had Nuala ever got laid, and if not, was that why she flirted so much? Where had Marushka Midwife learned her skills? What exactly had Adam One done before the Gardeners? Had there ever been an Eve One, or even a Mrs. Adam One, or any child Adam Ones? If she came too close to such territory Toby would be granted a smile and a change of subject, and a hint that she might try avoiding the original sin of desiring too much knowledge, or possibly too much power. Because the two were connected – didn't dear Toby agree?

Then there was Zeb. Adam Seven. Toby didn't believe Zeb was a true Gardener, any more than she was. She'd seen a lot of men of that general shape and hairiness during her SecretBurger days, and she'd bet that he had some game going; he had that kind of alertness. Now what was a man like that doing at the Edencliff Rooftop?

Zeb came and went; sometimes he'd vanish for days, and when he turned up again he might be wearing pleeblander clothes: solarbiker fleather gear, groundsman's coveralls, bouncer black. At first she'd worried that he was a Blanco affiliate, come to spy her out, but no, it wasn't that. Mad Adam, the kids nicknamed him, but he appeared sane enough. A little too sane to be hanging out with this clutch of sweet but delusional eccentrics. And what was the bond between him and Lucerne? Lucerne had pampered Compound wife written all over her: every time she broke a nail she went into a pout. She was an unlikely choice of partner for a man like Zeb – a bullet-spitter, he'd have been called in Toby's childhood, back when bullets were common.

Though maybe it was the sex, Toby thought. A mirage of the flesh, a hormone-fuelled obsession. It happened to a lot of people. She could remember a time when she herself might have been part of such a story, given the right man, but the longer she stayed with the Gardeners, the more that time receded.

She'd had no sex recently, nor did she miss it: during her immersion in the Sewage Lagoon she'd had far too much sex, though not the kind anyone would want. Freedom from Blanco was worth a lot: she was lucky she hadn't ended up fucked into a purée and battered to a pulp and poured out onto a vacant lot.

There had been one sex-linked incident at the Gardeners: old Mugi the Muscle had leapt on her when she was putting in an hour on one of the Run-For-Your-Light Treadmills in the former party room at the top of the Boulevard Condos. He'd pulled her off the treadmill and tussled her to the floor, then fallen heavily on top of her and groped under her denim skirt, wheezing like a faulty pump. But she was strong from all the soil-hauling and stair-climbing, and Mugi wasn't as fit as he must have been once, and she'd dug her elbow into him and levered him off, and left him sprawled and gasping on the floor.

She'd told Pilar about it, as she now told her everything that puzzled her. "What should I do?" she said.

"We never make a fuss about such things," said Pilar. "There's no harm in Mugi really. He's tried that on more than one of us – even me, some years ago." She gave a dry little chuckle. "The ancient Australopithecus can come out in all of us. You must forgive him in your heart. He won't do it again, you'll see."

So that was that, as far as sex went. Maybe it's temporary, thought Toby. Maybe it's like having your arm go to sleep. My neural connections for sex are blocked. But why don't I care?

It was the afternoon of Saint Maria Sibylla Merian of Insect Metamorphosis Day, said to be a propitious time for working with bees. Toby and Pilar were extracting the honey. They had on their wide veiled hats; for the smoke they used a bellows, and a smudge of decaying wood.

"Your parents – are they living?" said Pilar, from behind her white veil.

Toby was surprised by such a question, uncharacteristically direct for a Gardener. But Pilar wouldn't have asked such a thing without good reason. Toby couldn't bring herself to discuss her father, so instead she told Pilar about her mother's mysterious illness. What was so odd, she said, was that her mother had always been so keen on health: by weight she would have been half vitamin supplement.

"Tell me," said Pilar. "What supplements was she taking?"

"She ran a HelthWyzer franchise, so she took those."

"HelthWyzer," said Pilar. "Yes. We've heard of this before."

"Heard of what?" said Toby.

"This kind of illness, coupled with those supplements. No wonder the HelthWyzer people wanted to treat your mother themselves."

"What do you mean?" said Toby. She felt chilly, even though the morning sun was hot.

"Did it ever occur to you, my dear," said Pilar, "that your mother may have been a guinea pig?"

It hadn't occurred to Toby, but it occurred to her now. "I kind of wondered," she said. "Not about the pills, but . . . I thought it was the developer who wanted Dad's land. I figured maybe they'd put something in the well."

"In that case you'd all have been ill," said Pilar. "Now, promise me that you will never take any pill made by a Corporation. Never buy such a pill, and never accept any such pill if offered, no matter what they say. They'll produce data and scientists; they'll produce doctors – worthless, they've all been bought."

"Surely not all of them!" said Toby, shocked by Pilar's vehemence: she was usually so calm.

"No," said Pilar. "Not all. But all who are still working with any of the Corporations. The others – some have died unexpectedly. But those still alive – those with any shred of the old medical ethic left in them . . ." She paused. "There are doctors like that, still. But not at the Corps."

"Where are they?" Toby asked.

"Some of them are here, with us," said Pilar. She smiled. "Katuro the Wrench used to be an internist. He does our plumbing now. Surya was an eye surgeon. Stuart was an oncologist. Marushka was a gynecologist."

"And the other doctors? If they aren't here?"

"Let's just say they're safe, elsewhere," said Pilar. "For the moment. But now you must promise me: those Corporation pills are the food of the dead, my dear. Not our kind of dead, the bad kind. The dead who are still alive. We must teach the children to avoid these pills – they're evil. It's not only a rule of faith among us, it's a matter of certainty."

"But how can you be so sure?" Toby asked. "The Corps – nobody knows what they're doing. They're locked into those Compounds of theirs, nothing gets out . . ."

"You'd be surprised," said Pilar. "No boat was ever built that didn't spring a leak eventually. Now, promise me."

Toby promised.

"One day," said Pilar, "when you're an Eve, you'll understand more."

"Oh, I don't think I'll ever be an Eve," said Toby lightly. Pilar smiled.

Later that same afternoon, when Pilar and Toby had finished the honey extraction and Pilar was thanking the hive and the queen for their co-operation, Zeb came up the fire-escape stairs. He was wearing a black fleather jacket of the kind favoured by solarbikers. They slashed those jackets to let the hot air circulate while they were riding, but there were extra slashes in this one.

"What happened?" said Toby. "What can I do?" Zeb's tree-stump hands were clutched to his stomach; blood was coming out from between his fingers. She felt a little sick. At the same time she felt an urge to say, "Don't drip on the bees."

"Fell down and cut myself," said Zeb. "Broken glass." He was breathing heavily.

"I don't believe that," said Toby.

"Didn't think you would," said Zeb, grinning at her. "Here," he said to Pilar. "Brought you a present. SecretBurger special." He reached a hand into the pocket of his fleather jacket and brought out a fistful of ground meat. For a moment, Toby had the horrible impression that this was part of Zeb himself, but Pilar smiled.

"Thank you, dear Zeb," she said. "I can always rely on you! Come with me, now, we'll fix it up. Toby, could you find Rebecca and ask her to bring some clean kitchen towels? And Katuro. Him too." She didn't seem at all flustered by the sight of blood.

How old will I be, thought Toby, before I can be that calm? She felt cut open.

21

Pilar and Toby carried Zeb over to the Fallows Recovery Hut on the northwest corner of the Rooftop, which was used by Gardeners on Vigils, or those emerging from a Fallow state, or those who were moderately ill. As they were helping him to lie down, Rebecca came out from the enclosed shed at the back of the Rooftop, carrying a stack of dishtowels. "Now who did that?" she said. "That's a glass job! Bottle fight?"

Katuro arrived, peeled the jacket off Zeb's stomach, took a professional look. "Stopped by ribs," he said. "Slash, not stab. No deep punctures – lucky."

Pilar handed the ground meat to Toby. "It's for the maggots," she said. "Could you take care of it this time, dear?" The meat was already going off, from the smell of it.

Toby wrapped it in gauze from the Wellness Clinic as she'd seen Pilar do, and lowered the bundle over the edge of the rooftop on a string. In a couple of days, after the flies had laid their eggs and the eggs had had time to hatch, they'd haul it up again and harvest the maggots, because where there was rotting flesh, maggots were sure to follow. Pilar kept a supply of maggots always on hand for therapeutic use in case of need, but Toby had never seen them in action.

According to Pilar, maggot therapy was very ancient. It had been discarded as out of date along with leeches and bleeding, but during the First World War the doctors had noticed that soldiers' wounds healed much faster if maggots were present. Not only did the helpful creatures eat the decaying flesh, they killed necrotic bacteria, and were thus a great help in preventing gangrene.

The maggots created a pleasant sensation, said Pilar – a gentle nibbling, as of minnows – but they needed to be watched carefully, because if they ran out of decay and began to invade the living flesh there would be pain and bleeding. Otherwise, the wound would heal cleanly.

Pilar and Katuro sponged Zeb's cuts with vinegar, then rubbed on honey. Zeb was no longer bleeding, though he was pale. Toby got him a drink of Sumac.

Katuro said that pleebland street-fight glass was notoriously septic, so they should apply the maggots right away to avoid blood poisoning. Pilar used tweezers to place her stored maggots inside a fold of gauze, taping the gauze to Zeb. By the time the maggots had chewed through the gauze, Zeb would surely be festering enough to be attractive to them.

"Someone has to stay on maggot watch," said Pilar. "Twenty-four hours a day. In case the maggots start to eat our dear Zeb."

"Or in case I start to eat them," said Zeb. "Land shrimp. Same body plan. Very nice fried. Great source of lipids." He was keeping up a good front, but his voice was weak.

Toby took the first five hours. Adam One had heard about Zeb's accident and came to visit. "Discretion is the better part of valour," he said mildly.

"Yeah, well, there were too many of them," said Zeb. "Anyway I put three of them in the hospital."

"Not a thing to be proud of," said Adam One. Zeb frowned.

"Foot soldiers use their feet," he said. "That's why I wear boots."

"We'll discuss this later, when you're feeling better," said Adam One.

"I'm feeling fine," Zeb growled.

Nuala bustled in to take over from Toby. "Have you made him some Willow?" she said. "Oh dear, I hate those maggots! Here, let me prop you up! Can't we raise the screening? We need a breeze through!

Zeb, is this what you mean by Urban Bloodshed Limitation? You are so naughty!" She was twittering, and Toby felt like kicking her.

Lucerne arrived next, blotting tears. "This is terrible! What's happened, who did . . ."

"Oh, he's been so bad!" said Nuala conspiratorially. "Haven't you, Zeb? Fighting with the pleeblanders," she whispered delightedly.

"Toby," said Lucerne, ignoring Nuala, "how serious is it? Will he . . . is he . . ." She sounded like some old-time TV actress playing a death-bed scene.

"I'm fine," said Zeb. "Now buzz off and leave me alone!"

He didn't want anyone fiddling with him, he said. Except Pilar. And Katuro, if absolutely necessary. And Toby, because at least she was silent. Lucerne went away, weeping angrily, but there was nothing Toby could do about that.

Rumour was the daily news among the Gardeners. The older boys heard quickly about Zeb's battle – it had now become a battle – and the next afternoon Shackleton and Crozier came to see him. He was asleep – Toby had slipped some Poppy into his Willow tea – so they tiptoed around him, speaking in low voices and trying for a peek at his wound.

"He ate a bear once," said Shackleton. "When he was flying for Bearlift, that time they were trying to save the polar bears. His plane crashed and he walked out – it took months!" The older boys had many such heroic tales about Zeb. "He said bears look just like a man when they're skinned."

"He ate the co-pilot. After he was dead, though," Crozier said.

"Can we see the maggots?"

"Has he got gangrene?"

"Gang! Grene!" shouted little Oates, who'd tagged along after his brothers.

"Shut up, Oatie!"

"Ow! You meat-breath!"

"Off you go now," said Toby. "Zeb – Adam Seven needs his rest."

Adam One persisted in thinking that Shackleton and Crozier and young Oates would turn out just fine, but Toby had her doubts. Philo the Fog was supposed to be their stand-in father, but he wasn't always mentally available.

Pilar took the night watches: she didn't sleep much at night anyway, she said. Nuala volunteered for the mornings. Toby took over during the afternoons. She checked the maggots every hour. Zeb had no temperature, and there was no fresh blood.

Once he began healing he was restless, so Toby played dominoes with him, then cribbage, and finally chess. The chess set was Pilar's: black was ants, white was bees; she'd carved it herself. "They used to think the queen of the bees was a king," Pilar said. "Since if you killed that bee, the rest lost their purpose. That's why the chess king doesn't move around much on the board – it's because the queen bee always stays inside the hive." Toby wasn't sure this was true: did the queen bee always stay inside the hive? Except for swarming, of course, and for nuptial flights . . . She stared at the board, trying to see the pattern. From outside the Fallows Recovery Hut came the sound of Nuala's voice mingling with the chirping of the smaller children. "The five senses, through which the world comes to us . . . seeing, hearing, feeling, smelling, tasting . . . what do we use for tasting? That's right . . . Oates, there is no need for you to lick Melissa. Now pop your tongues back into your tongue containers and close the lids." Toby had an image – no, a taste. She could taste the skin of Zeb's arm, the salt on it . . .

"Checkmate," said Zeb. "Ants win again." Zeb always played Ants, to give Toby an opening advantage.

"Oh," said Toby. "I didn't see that." Now she was wondering – unworthy thought – whether there was something going on between Nuala and Zeb. Though overblown, Nuala was lush, and oddly babyish. Some men found that quality alluring.

Zeb swept the pieces from the board and began to set them up again. "Do me a favour?" he said. He didn't wait for a yes.

Lucerne was having a lot of headaches, he said. His voice was neutral, but there was an edge to it, by which Toby understood that the headaches might not be real; or else that they were real enough, but Zeb found them boring anyway.

Could Toby stop by with some of her bottles the next time Lucerne had a migraine, he said, and see what she could manage? Because he himself sure as hell couldn't do anything for Lucerne's hormones, if that's what it was. "She's been giving me a lot of grief," he said. "For being away too much. Makes her jealous." He grinned like a shark. "Maybe she'll hear sense, from you."

So. The bloom is off the rose, thought Toby. And the rose doesn't like it.

22

Saint Allan Sparrow of Clean Air: not a Day that had so far lived up to its name. Toby picked her way through the crowded pleebland streets, carrying her bag of dried herbals and bottled medicinals hidden under her loose coverall. The afternoon thunderstorm had cleared the fumes and particulate somewhat, but she was wearing a black nose cone any-way, in honour of Saint Sparrow. As was the custom.

She felt safer on the street since Blanco had been put into Painball; still, she never strolled or loitered, but – remembering Zeb's instructions – also she didn't run. It was best to look purposeful, as if you were on a mission. She ignored the passing stares, the anti-Gardener slurs, but she was alert to sudden movement or to anyone coming too close. A pleebrat gang had once grabbed her mushrooms; luckily for them, she hadn't been carrying anything lethal that time.

She was heading towards the Cheese Factory building to fulfil Zeb's request. This was the third time she'd gone. If Lucerne's headaches were real and not just a bid for attention, an over-the-counter double-strength painkiller/soporific from HelthWyzer could have handled the problem, either by curing her or killing her. But Corps pills were taboo among the Gardeners, so she'd been using extract of Willow, followed by Valerian, with some Poppy mixed in; though not too much Poppy, as it could be addictive.

"What's in this?" Lucerne would say each time Toby had treated her. "It tastes better when Pilar makes it."

Toby would refrain from saying that Pilar had in fact made it, and would urge Lucerne to swallow the dose. Then she'd put a cold compress on her forehead and sit by her bedside, trying to tune out Lucerne's whining.

The Gardeners were expected to avoid any broadcasting of their personal problems: foisting your mental junk on others was frowned on. For drinking Life there are two cups, Nuala taught the small children. What's in each of them might be exactly the same, but my, oh my, the taste is so different!

> *The No Cup is bitter, the Yes Cup is yummy –*
> *Now, which one would you rather have in your tummy?*

This was a basic Gardener credo. But though Lucerne could mouth the slogans, she hadn't internalized the teachings: Toby could tell a sham when she saw one, being a sham herself. As soon as Toby was locked into the ministering position, everything that was festering inside Lucerne would come roiling out. Toby would nod and say nothing, hoping to convey the impression of sympathy, though in reality she'd be considering how many drops of Poppy it would take to knock Lucerne unconscious before she, Toby, gave in to her worst impulses and throttled her.

As she quick-stepped through the streets, Toby anticipated Lucerne's complaints. If true to pattern, they'd be about Zeb: why was he never there when Lucerne needed him? How had she ended up in this unsanitary septic tank with this clutch of dreamers – *I don't mean you, Toby, you've got some sense* – who didn't understand the first thing about how the world really worked? She was buried alive here with a monster of egotism, with a man who cared only about his own needs. Talking to him was like talking to a potato – no, to a stone. He didn't hear you, he never told you what he was thinking, he was hard as flint.

Not that Lucerne hadn't tried. She wanted to be a responsible person, she really did believe that Adam One was right about so many things, and nobody loved animals more than she did, but really there was a limit and she did not believe for one instant that slugs had any central nervous system, and to say they had souls was to make a mockery of the whole idea of souls, and she resented that, because nobody had more respect for souls than she did, she'd always been a very spiritual person. As for saving the world, nobody wanted to save the world as much as she did, but no matter how much the Gardeners deprived themselves of proper food and clothing and even proper showers, for heaven's sake, and felt more high and mighty and virtuous than everyone else, it wouldn't really change anything. They were just like those people who used to whip themselves during the Middle Ages – those flagrants.

"Flagellants," Toby had said, the first time this came up.

Then Lucerne had said she didn't mean it about the Gardeners, she was just feeling gloomy because of the headache. Also because they looked down on her for coming from a Corps, and for ditching her husband and running away with Zeb. They didn't trust her. They thought she was a slut. They made dirty jokes about her behind her back. Or the children did – didn't they?

"The children make dirty jokes about everyone," Toby had said. "Including me."

"You?" Lucerne had said, opening her large eyes with their dark lashes. "Why would they make dirty jokes about you?" Nothing sexual about *you*, was what she meant. Flat as a board, back and front. Worker bee.

There was a plus to that: at least Lucerne wasn't jealous of her. In that respect, Toby stood alone among the Gardener women.

"They don't look down on you," Toby had said. "They don't think you're a slut. Now just relax and close your eyes and picture the Willow moving through your body, up to your head, where the pain is."

It was true that the Gardeners didn't look down on Lucerne, or not for the reasons she thought they did. They might resent the way she slacked off on chores and could never learn how to chop a carrot, they might be scornful of the messiness of her living space and her pathetic attempt at windowsill tomato-growing and the amount of time she spent in bed, but they didn't care about her infidelity, or her adultery, or whatever it had once been called.

That was because the Gardeners didn't bother with marriage certificates. They endorsed fidelity as long as a pair-bonding was current but there was no record of the first Adam and the first Eve going through a wedding, so in their eyes neither the clergymen of other religions nor any secular official had the power to marry people. As for the CorpSeCorps, they favoured official marriages only as a means for capturing your iris image, your fingerscans, and your DNA, all the better to track you with. Or so the Gardeners claimed, and this was one claim of theirs that Toby could believe without reservation.

Among the Gardeners, weddings were simple affairs. Both parties had to proclaim in front of witnesses that they loved each other. They exchanged green leaves to symbolize growth and fertility and jumped over a bonfire to symbolize the energy of the universe, then declared themselves married and went to bed. For divorces they did the whole thing in reverse: a public statement of non-love and separation, the exchange of dead twigs, and a swift hop over a heap of cold ashes.

A standing complaint of Lucerne's – which was sure to come up if Toby wasn't quick enough with the Poppy – was that Zeb had never invited her to do the green-leaf and bonfire-leaping ceremony with him. "Not that I think it means anything," she'd say. "But he must think it does, because he's one of them, right? So by not doing it, he's refusing commitment. Don't you agree?"

"I never know what anyone thinks," Toby would say.

"But if it was you, wouldn't you feel he was shirking his responsibility?"

"Why don't you ask him?" Toby would say. "Ask why he hasn't . . ." Was *proposed* the right word?

"He'd just get angry." Lucerne would sigh. "He was so different when I first knew him!"

Then Toby would be treated to the story of Lucerne and Zeb – a story Lucerne never tired of telling.

23

The story went like this. Lucerne met Zeb at the AnooYoo Spa-in-the-Park – did Toby know the AnooYoo? Oh. Well, it was a fantastic place to unwind and get yourself resurfaced. This was right after it was built and they were still putting in the landscaping. The fountains, the lawns, the gardens, the bushes. The lumiroses. Didn't Toby just love lumiroses? She'd never seen them? Oh. Well, maybe sometime . . .

Lucerne loved to get up at dawn, she was an early riser then, she liked to watch the sunrise; it was because she'd always been so sensitive to colour and light, she'd paid so much attention to the aesthetic values in her homes – the homes she'd decorated. She loved to include at least one room in sunrise colours – the sunrise room, she would think of that room.

Also she was restless in those days. She was really very restless, because her husband was cold as a crypt, and they never made love any more because he was too busy with his career. And she was a sensual person, she always had been, and her sensual nature was being starved to death. Which was bad for the health, and especially for the immune system. She'd read the studies on that!

So there she was, prowling around at dawn in her pink kimono and crying a little, and contemplating a divorce from her HelthWyzer Corp husband, or a separation at least, though she realized it would not be the best thing for Ren, so young then and fond of her father, not that he paid enough attention to Ren either. And suddenly there was Zeb, in the rising light, like a – well, like a vision, all by himself, planting a lumirose bush. One of those roses that glow in the dark, the scent was so divine – had

Toby ever smelled them? – she didn't suppose so because the Gardeners were death on anything new, but those roses were really pretty.

So there was a man, in the dawn, kneeling on the ground and looking as if he was holding a bouquet of live coals.

What restless woman can resist a man with a shovel in one hand and a glowing rose bush in the other, and a moderately crazed glitter in his eyes that might be mistaken for love? thought Toby. On Zeb's part there must have been something to be said for an attractive woman in a pink kimono, a loosely tied pink kimono, on a lawn in a pearly sunrise, especially when tearful. Because Lucerne was attractive. Simply from a visual point of view, she was very attractive. Even if whining, which was the way Toby saw her mostly.

Lucerne had wafted across the lawn, aware of her bare feet on the damp cool grass, aware of the brush of fabric across her thighs, aware of the tightness around her waist and the looseness below her collarbone. Billowing, like waves. She'd stopped in front of Zeb, who'd been watching her come towards him as if he'd been a sailor dumped into the ocean by mistake and she'd been either a mermaid or a shark. (Toby supplied these images: Lucerne said *Fate.*) They were both just so *aware*, she told Toby; she'd always been aware of other peoples' awareness, she was like a cat, or, or . . . she had that talent, or was it a curse – that was how she knew. So she could feel from the inside what Zeb was feeling as he watched her. That was overwhelming!

It was impossible to explain this in words, she'd say, as if nothing of the sort could ever have happened to Toby herself.

Anyway, there they stood, though they'd already foreseen what was about to happen – what had to happen. Fear and lust pushed them together and held them apart, equally.

Lucerne did not call it lust. She called it longing.

At this point, Toby would have an image of the set of salt and pepper shakers that used to be on the kitchen table in her long-ago childhood home: a little china hen, a little china rooster. The hen had been the salt, the rooster had been the pepper. Salty Lucerne had stood there in front of peppery Zeb, smiling and looking up, and she'd asked him a simple question – how many rose bushes would there be or something, she couldn't remember, so mesmerized was she by Zeb's . . . (Here Toby would turn off her attention because she didn't want to hear about the biceps, triceps, and other muscular attractions of Zeb. Was she herself immune to them? No. Was she therefore jealous of this part of the story? Yes. We must be mindful of our own animal-nature tendencies and biases at all times, said Adam One.)

And then, Lucerne would say, hooking Toby back into her story – and then a strange thing had happened: she'd recognized Zeb.

"I've seen you before," she'd said. "Didn't you used to be at HelthWyzer? But you weren't working on the grounds then! You were –"

"Mistaken identity," said Zeb. And then he'd kissed her. That kiss had gone right into her like a knife, and she'd crumpled into his arms like – like a dead fish – no – like a petticoat – no – like damp tissue paper! And then he'd picked her up and laid her down on the lawn, right where anyone could have seen, which was an unbelievable turn-on, and then he'd undone her kimono and pulled the petals off the roses he was holding and scattered them all over her body, and then the two of them . . . It was like a high-speed collision, said Lucerne, and she'd thought, How can I survive this, I'm going to die right here and now! And she could tell he felt the same.

Later – quite a lot later, after they were living together – he'd told her she'd been right. Yes, he'd been at HelthWyzer, but for reasons he wouldn't go into he'd had to leave in a hurry, and he trusted her not to mention that earlier time and place he'd once inhabited, not to anybody. Which she hadn't mentioned. Or not very much. Except right now, to Toby.

Back then, though, during her Spa sojourn – thank god she hadn't been having any skin procedure that would have made her scabby, she'd just been there for a tuneup – back then, they'd had several more appetizer-sized helpings of each other, locked into one of the showers in the Spa pool's changeroom, and after that she was stuck to Zeb like a wet leaf. As he was to her, she added. They couldn't get enough of each other.

And then, after her Spa sessions were over and she was back at her so-called home, she'd slip out of the Compound on one pretext or another – shopping errands, mostly, the things you could buy in the Compound were so predictable – and they'd met secretly in the pleeb-lands – it was so exciting at first! – such funny places, junky little love hotels and rent-a-rooms, you took them by the hour, so far away from the buttoned-down ambiance of the HelthWyzer Compound; and then, when he'd had to travel in a hurry – there was some trouble, she'd never understood why, but he needed to get away very fast – and, well, she couldn't bear to be apart from him.

So she'd left her so-called husband, not that it didn't serve him right for being so inert. And they'd moved around from one city to another, from one trailer park to another, and Zeb had bought a few black-market procedures, for his fingers and his DNA and so on; and then, when it was safe, they'd come back, right here, to the Gardeners. Because Zeb had told her he'd been a Gardener all along. Or so he'd said. Anyway, he seemed to know Adam One quite well. They'd been to school together. Or something like that.

So Zeb was forced into it, Toby thought. He was ex-Corps, on the run; maybe he'd been black-marketing some proprietary item, such as a nanotechnology or a gene splice. That could be fatal if you were caught. And Lucerne had put face and ex-name together, and he'd had to dis-tract her with sex, then take her with him to ensure her loyalty. It was either that or kill her. He couldn't leave her behind: she would have felt scorned, she'd have set the CorpSeCorps dogs on him. Still, what a risk he'd taken. The woman was like an amateur car bomb: you never knew when she'd blow up or who she'd take down with her when she did. Toby wondered whether Zeb had ever thought of stuffing a cork down her epiglottis and slotting her into a carbon garboil dumpster.

But maybe he loved her. In his way. Hard though that was for Toby to picture. However, perhaps the love had run out, because he wasn't doing enough maintenance work on her at the moment.

"Hasn't your husband looked for you?" Toby had asked the first time she'd heard this tale. "The one at HelthWyzer?"

"I don't consider that man to be my husband any more," Lucerne said in an offended tone.

"Excuse me. Your former husband. Haven't the CorpSeCorps . . . did you leave him a message?" The trail of Lucerne, if followed, would lead right to the Gardeners – not only to Zeb, but to Toby herself, and to her own former identity. Which could be uncomfortable for her: the CorpSeCorps never wrote off skipped debts, and what if anyone had dug up her father?

"Why would they spend the money?" said Lucerne. "I'm not important to them. As for my former husband" – she gave a little grimace – "he ought to have married an equation. Maybe he doesn't even notice I've gone."

"What about Ren?" said Toby. "She's a lovely little girl. Surely he misses her."

"Oh," said Lucerne. "Yes. He probably does notice that."

Toby wanted to ask why Lucerne hadn't simply left Ren behind with her father. Stealing her away, leaving no information – it seemed like a petty act of spite. But asking such a question would simply make Lucerne angry – it would sound too much like criticism.

Two blocks away from the Cheese Factory, Toby ran into a pleebrat street fight – Asian Fusions versus Blackened Redfish, with a few Lintheads shouting around the edges. These kids were only seven or eight, but there were a lot of them, and when they spotted her they stopped yelling at one another and started yelling at her. *Goddie goddie, whitey bitch! Get her shoes!*

She swivelled so her back was against a wall and prepared to fend them off. It was difficult to kick them really hard when they were that young – as Zeb had pointed out in his Urban Bloodshed Limitation class, there was a species inhibition against hurting children – but she knew she'd have to, because they could be deadly. They'd aim for her stomach, ram her with their hard little heads, try to pull her down. The smaller ones had a nasty habit of hoisting the Gardener women's baggy skirts and diving in under them, then biting whatever they could find once they were in there. But she was ready for them: when they got close enough, she'd twist their ears or chop their necks with the side of her hand, or bang two of their little skulls together.

Suddenly, however, they swerved like a school of fish, rushed past her, and disappeared into an alleyway.

She turned her head, saw why. It was Blanco. He wasn't in Painball at all. He must have been let out. Or got out, somehow.

Panic gripped her heart. She saw his red-and-blue flayed hands, she felt her bones crumbling. This was her worst fear.

Take hold, she told herself. He was across the street, and she was inside her baggy coverall and had her nose cone on, so maybe he couldn't recognize her. And he'd given no sign yet that he'd noticed her. But she was alone, and he wasn't above a random stomp-and-rape. He'd drag her up that very same alleyway, the one where the pleebrats had gone. Then he'd rip off the cone and see who she was. And that would be the end, but it wouldn't be a quick end. It would be as slow as he could make it. He'd turn her into a flesh billboard – a not-quite-living demonstration of his rank finesse.

She turned quickly and marched away as fast as she could, before he'd had a chance to focus his malevolence on her. Breathless, she turned the corner, went half a block, glanced back. He wasn't there.

For once she was more than happy to reach the door of Lucerne's apartment. She raised her nose cone, twitched the muscles of her professional smile, and knocked.

"Zeb?" Lucerne called. "Is that you?"

SAINT EUELL OF WILD FOODS

SAINT EUELL OF WILD FOODS

YEAR TWELVE.

OF THE GIFTS OF SAINT EUELL.
SPOKEN BY ADAM ONE.

My Friends, my Fellow Creatures, my dear Children:

This day marks the beginning of Saint Euell's Week, during which we will be foraging for the Wild Harvest gifts that God, through Nature, has put at our disposal. Pilar, our Eve Six, will lead us in a ramble through the Heritage Park, hunting for Fungi, and Burt, our Adam Thirteen, will aid us with the Edible Weeds. Remember – if in doubt, spit it out! But if a mouse has eaten it, you can probably eat it too. Though not invariably.

The older children will have a demonstration by Zeb, our respected Adam Seven, concerning the trapping of small Animals for survival food in times of pressing need. Remember, nothing is unclean to us if gratitude is felt and pardon asked, and if we ourselves are willing to offer ourselves to the great chain of nourishment in our turn. For where else lies the deep meaning of sacrifice?

Burt's esteemed wife, Veena, is still in her Fallow state, though we hope to welcome her back among us very soon. Let us wish Light around her.

Today we meditate upon Saint Euell Gibbons, who flourished upon this Earth from 1911 to 1975, so long ago but so close to us in our hearts. As a boy, when his father left home to seek work, Saint Euell provided for his family through his Natural knowledge. He went to no high school but Yours, oh Lord. In Your Species he found his teachers, often strict but always true. And then he shared those teachings with us.

He taught the uses of Your many Puffballs, and the other wholesome Fungi; he taught the dangers of the poisonous species, which however can also be of Spiritual value, if taken in judicious quantities.

He sang the virtues of the wild Onion, of the wild Asparagus, of the wild Garlic, that toil not, neither do they spin, nor do they have pesticides sprayed upon them, if they happily grow far enough away from agribusiness crops. He knew the roadside medicines: the bark of the Willow in respect of pains and fevers, the root of the Dandelion as a diuretic in the shedding of excess fluid. He taught us not to waste; for even the lowly Nettle, so often wrenched up and thrown away, is a source of many vitamins. He taught us to improvise; for if there is no Sorrel, there may be Cattails; and if there are no Blueberries, the wild Cranberry may perhaps abound.

Saint Euell, may we sit with you in Spirit at your table, that lowly tarpaulin spread upon the ground; and dine with you upon wild Strawberries, and upon spring Fiddleheads, and upon young Milkweed pods, lightly simmered, with a little butter substitute if it can be obtained.

And in the time of our greatest need, help us to accept whatever Fate may bring us; and whisper into our inner and Spiritual ears the names of the Plants, and their seasons, and the locations in which they may be found.

For the Waterless Flood is coming, in which all buying and selling will cease, and we will find ourselves thrown back upon our own resources, in the midst of God's bounteous Garden. Which was your Garden also.

Let us sing.

Oh sing we now the Holy Weeds
That flourish in the ditch,
For they are for the meek in needs,
They are not for the rich.

You cannot buy them at the mall,
Nor at the superstore,
They are despised because they all
Grow freely for the poor.

The Dandelion shoots, for spring,
Before their flowers burst;
The Burdock root is best in June
When it is fat with juice;

When autumn comes, the Acorn's ripe,
The Walnut black is too;
Young Milkweed pods are sweet when boiled,
And Milkweed shoots when new.

The inner bark of Spruce and Birch
For extra Vitamin C –
But do not take too much of each,
Or you will kill the tree.

The Purslane, Sorrel, Lamb's Quarters,
And Nettles, too, are good;
The Hawthorn, Elder, Sumac, Rose –
Their berries wholesome food.

The Holy Weeds are plentiful
And beautiful to see –

For who can doubt God put them there,
So starved we'll never be?

From *The God's Gardeners Oral Hymnbook*

24

I remember what the dinner was, that night in the Sticky Zone: it was ChickieNobs. I couldn't deal with meat very well ever since the Gardeners, but Mordis said that ChickieNobs were really vegetables because they grew on stems and didn't have faces. So I ate half of them.

Then I did some dancing to keep in practice. I had my own Sea/H/Ear Candy, and I sang along. Adam One said music was built into us by God: we could sing like the birds but also like the angels, because singing was a form of praise that came from deeper than just talking, and God could hear us better when we were singing. I try to remember that.

Then I looked in on the Snakepit again. There were three guys from Painball in the Snakepit – ones who'd just got out. You could always tell because they were freshly shaved, with new haircuts, and new clothes too, and they had a stunned look, like they'd been kept in a dark closet for a long time. Also they had a little tattoo at the base of their left thumb – a round circle, red or bright yellow, depending on whether they were Red Team or Gold Team. The other customers were sort of moving back from them, giving them room, but respectfully – as if they were webstars or sports heroes instead of Painball criminals. Rich guys loved to imagine themselves as Painball players. They gambled on the teams as well: Red against Gold. A lot of money changed hands over Painball.

There were always two or three CorpSeCorps guys minding the Painball vets – they could go berserk and do a lot of damage. We Scalies were never allowed to be alone with them: they didn't understand make-believe, they never knew when to stop, and they could break a lot more than the furniture. It was best to get them wasted, but it had to be fast or they'd go into full rage mode.

"I'd bar those assholes myself," said Mordis. "Nothing much human left inside that scar tissue of theirs. But SeksMart pays us a big-time extra bonus when it's them."

We'd feed them drinks and pills, with a shovel if we could. There was something new they'd started using just after I went into the Sticky Zone – BlyssPluss, it was called. Hassle-free sex, total satisfaction, blow you right out of your skin, plus 100 percent protection – that was the word on it. Scales girls weren't allowed to do drugs on the job – we weren't paid to enjoy ourselves, said Mordis – but this was different, because if you took it you didn't need a Biofilm Bodyglove, and a lot of customers would pay extra that way. Scales was testing the BlyssPluss for the ReJoov Corp, so they weren't handing it out like candy – it was mostly for the top customers – but I could hardly wait to try it.

We always got huge tips on Painball nights, though none of us regular Scales girls had to do plank duty with the new vets because we were skilled artists and any damage to us would be pricey. For the basic bristle work they brought in the temporaries – smuggled Eurotrash or Tex-Mexicans or Asian Fusion and Redfish minors scooped off the streets because the Painball guys wanted membrane, and after they were finished you'd be judged contaminated until proved otherwise, and Scales didn't want to spend Sticky Zone money either testing these girls or fixing them up. I never saw them twice. They walked in the door, but I don't think they walked out. In a shoddier club they'd have been used for the guys acting out their vampire fantasies, but that involved mouth-to-blood contact, and as I said, Mordis liked to keep it clean.

That night one of the Painball guys had Starlite on his lap, giving him the signature twist. She was in her peagret-feather outfit with the headdress, and maybe she was terrific from the front, but from my angle of vision it looked like the guy had a big blue-green duster working him over – like a dry carwash.

The second guy was gazing up at Savona with his mouth open and his head so far back it was almost at right angles to his spine. If her grip slips, she'll snap his neck. If that happens, I thought, he won't be the first guy to be carted out the back door of Scales and dumped in a vacant lot with no clothes on. He was an older guy, bald on top, with a ponytail at the back, and a lot of arm tattoos. There was something familiar about him – maybe he was a repeat – but I didn't get a very good look.

The third one was drinking himself into mud. Maybe he was trying to forget what he'd done inside the Painball Arena. I never watched the Painball Arena website myself. It was too disgusting. I only knew about it because men talk. It's amazing what they'll tell you, especially if you're covered with shiny green scales and they can't see your real face. It must be like talking to a fish.

Nothing else was happening, so I called Amanda on her cell. But she wasn't answering. Maybe she was asleep, rolled up in her sleeping bag out there in Wisconsin. Maybe she was sitting around a campfire and the two Tex-Mexicans were playing their guitars and singing, and Amanda was singing too because she knew the Tex-Mex language. Maybe there was a moon up above and some coyotes howling in the distance, just like an old movie. I hoped so.

25

Things changed in my life when Amanda came to live with me, and they changed again in the Saint Euell's Week when I was almost thirteen. Amanda was older: she'd already grown real tits. It's strange how you measure time that way.

That year, Amanda and I – and Bernice as well – would be joining the older kids for Zeb's Predator-Prey Relationship demonstration, when we'd have to eat real prey. I had a faint memory of meat-eating, back at the HelthWyzer Compound. But the Gardeners were very much against it except in times of crisis, so the idea of putting a chunk of bloody muscle and gristle into my mouth and pushing it down inside my throat was nauseating. I vowed not to throw up, though, because that would embarrass me a lot and make Zeb look bad.

I wasn't worried about Amanda. She was used to eating meat, she'd done it lots of times before. She used to lift SecretBurgers whenever she could. So she'd be able to chew and swallow as if there was nothing to it.

On the Monday of Saint Euell's Week, we put our clean clothes on – clean yesterday – and I braided Amanda's hair, and then she braided mine. "Primate grooming," Zeb called it.

We could hear Zeb singing in the shower:

Nobody gives a poop.
Nobody gives a poop;

And that is why we're in the soup,
Cause nobody gives a poop!

I'd come to find this morning singing of his a comforting sound. It meant things were ordinary, at least for that day.

Usually Lucerne stayed in bed until we were gone, partly to avoid Amanda, but today she was in the kitchen area, wearing her dark-coloured Gardener dress, and she was actually cooking. She'd been making that effort more often lately. Also she was keeping our living space tidier. She was even growing a raggedy tomato plant in a pot on the sill. I think she was trying to make things nice for Zeb, though they were having more fights. They made us go outside when they were fighting, but that didn't mean we couldn't listen in.

The fights were about where Zeb was when he wasn't with Lucerne. "Working," was all he'd say. Or "Don't push me, babe." Or "You don't need to know. It's for your own good."

"You've got someone else!" Lucerne would say. "I can smell bitch all over you!"

"Wow," Amanda would whisper. "Your mom's got a foul mouth!" and I didn't know whether to be proud or ashamed.

"No, no," Zeb would say in a tired voice. "Why would I want anyone but you, babe?"

"You're lying!"

"Oh, Christ in a helicopter! Get off my fucking case!"

Zeb came out of the shower cubicle, dripping on the floor. I could see the scar where he'd got slashed that time, back when I was ten: it gave me a shivery feeling. "How're my little pleebrats today?" he said, grinning like a troll.

Amanda smiled sweetly. "Big pleebrats," she said.

For breakfast we had mashed-up fried black beans and soft-boiled pigeon's eggs. "Nice breakfast, babe," Zeb said to Lucerne. I had to admit that it was actually quite nice, even though Lucerne had cooked it.

Lucerne gave him that syrupy smile of hers. "I wanted to be sure you all get a good meal," she said. "Considering what you'll be eating the rest of the week. Old roots and mice, I suppose."

"Barbecued rabbit," said Zeb. "I could eat ten of those suckers, with a side of mice and some deep-fried slugs for dessert." He leered over at Amanda and me: he was trying to gross us out.

"Sounds real good," said Amanda.

"You're such a monster," said Lucerne, giving him her cookie eyes.

"Too bad I can't get a beer with it," said Zeb. "Join us, babe, we need some decoration."

"Oh, I think I'll sit this one out," said Lucerne.

"You're not coming with us?" I said. Usually during Saint Euell's Week, Lucerne would trail along on the woodland walks, picking the odd weed and complaining about the bugs and keeping an eye on Zeb. I didn't really want her to come this time, but also I wanted things to stay normal, because I had a feeling that everything was about to be rearranged again, as it was when I'd been yanked out of the HelthWyzer Compound. It was just a feeling, but I didn't like it. I was used to the Gardeners, it was where I belonged now.

"I don't think I can," she said. "I've got a migraine headache." She'd had a migraine headache yesterday too. "I'll just go back to bed."

"I'll ask Toby to drop around," said Zeb. "Or Pilar. Make that mean ol' pain go away."

"Would you?" A suffering smile.

"No problem," said Zeb. Lucerne hadn't eaten her pigeon's egg, so he ate it for her. It was only about the size of a plum anyway.

The beans were from the Garden, but the pigeon's eggs were from our own rooftop. We didn't have any plants up there, because Adam One said it was not a suitable surface, but we had pigeons. Zeb lured them with crumbs, moving softly so they felt safe. Then they'd lay eggs, and then he'd rob their nests. Pigeons weren't an endangered species, he said, so it was okay.

Adam One said that eggs were potential Creatures, but they weren't Creatures yet: a nut was not a Tree. Did eggs have souls? No, but they had potential souls. So not a lot of Gardeners did egg-eating, but they didn't condemn it either. You didn't apologize to an egg before joining its protein to yours, though you had to apologize to the mother pigeon, and thank her for her gift. I doubt Zeb bothered with any apologizing. Most likely he ate some of the mother pigeons too, on the sly.

Amanda had one pigeon's egg. So did I. Zeb had three, plus Lucerne's. He needed more than us because he was bigger, Lucerne said: if we ate like him we'd get fat.

"See you later, warrior maidens. Don't kill anyone," said Zeb as we went out the door. He'd heard about Amanda's knee-in-the-groin and eye-gouging moves, and her piece of glass with the duct tape; he made jokes about them.

26

We had to pick up Bernice at the Buenavista before school. Amanda and I had wanted to quit, but we knew we'd get in trouble from Adam One if we did, for being un-Gardener. Bernice still didn't like Amanda, but she didn't exactly hate her either. She was wary of her the way you might be of some animals, like a bird with a very sharp beak. Bernice was mean, but Amanda was tough, which is different.

Nothing could change the way things were, which was that Bernice and I had once been best friends and we weren't any longer. That made me uneasy when I was around her: I felt guilty in some way. Bernice was aware of this, and she'd try to find ways to twist my guilt around and turn it against Amanda.

Still, things were friendly on the outside. The three of us walked to and from school together, or did chores or Young Bioneer collecting. That sort of thing. Bernice never came over to the Cheese Factory, though, and we never hung out with her after school.

On the way to Bernice's that morning, Amanda said, "I've found out something."

"What?" I said.

"I know where Burt goes between five and six, two nights a week."

"Burt the Knob? Who cares!" I said. We both felt contempt for him because he was such a pathetic armpit-groper.

"No. Listen. He goes to the same place Nuala goes," said Amanda.

"You're joking! Where?" Nuala flirted, but she flirted with all men. It was only her way, like giving you the stone-eye was Toby's way.

"They go into the Vinegar Room when no one's supposed to be there."

"Oh no!" I said. "Really?" I knew this was about sex – most of our jokey conversations were. The Gardeners called sex "the generative act" and said it was not a fit subject for ridicule, but Amanda ridiculed it anyway. You could snigger at it or trade it or both, but you couldn't respect it.

"No wonder her bum's so wobbly," said Amanda. "It's getting worn out. It's like Veena's old sofa – all saggy."

"I don't believe you!" I said. "She couldn't be doing it! Not with Burt!"

"Cross my heart and spit," said Amanda. She spat: she was a good spitter. "Why else would she go there with him?"

We Gardeners kids often made up rude stories about the sex lives of the Adams and Eves. It took away some of their power to imagine them naked, either with each other or with stray dogs, or even with the green-skinned girls in the pictures outside Scales and Tails. Still, Nuala moaning and flailing around with Burt the Knob was hard to picture. "Well, anyway," I said, "we can't tell Bernice!" Then we laughed some more.

At the Buenavista we nodded at the dowdy Gardener lady behind the lobby desk, who was doing string knotwork and didn't look up. Then we climbed the stairs, avoiding the used needles and condoms. The Buenavista Condom was Amanda's name for this building, so I called it that now too. The mushroomy, spicy Buenavista smell was stronger today.

"Someone's got a gro-op," said Amanda. "It reeks of skunkweed." She was an authority: she'd lived out there in the Exfernal World, she'd even done some drugs. Not much though, she said, because you lost your edge with drugs, you should only buy them from people you trusted because anything could have anything in it, and she didn't trust anybody much. I'd nag her to let me try some, but she wouldn't. "You're a baby," she'd say. Or else she'd say she had no good contacts since she'd been with the Gardeners.

"There can't be a gro-op in here," I said. "This building's Gardener. It's only the pleebmobs who have gro-ops. It's just – kids smoke it in here, at night. Pleeb kids."

"Yeah, I know," said Amanda, "but this isn't smoke. It's more of a gro-op smell."

As we reached the fourth-floor level, we heard voices – men's voices, two of them, on the other side of the landing door. They didn't sound friendly.

"That's all I got," said one voice. "I'll have the rest tomorrow."

"Asshole!" said the other. "Don't jerk me around!" There was a thud, as if something had hit the wall; then another thud, and a wordless yell, of pain or anger.

Amanda poked me. "Climb," she said. "Fast!"

We ran up the rest of the stairs as quietly as we could. "That was serious," said Amanda when we'd reached the sixth floor.

"How do you mean?"

"Some trade going bad," said Amanda. "We never heard this. Now, act normal." She looked scared, which scared me too because Amanda didn't scare easily.

We knocked at Bernice's door. "Knock, knock," said Amanda.

"Who's there?" said Bernice's voice. She must've been waiting for us right inside the door, as if she was afraid we might not come. I found this sad.

"Gang," said Amanda.

"Gang who?"

"Gangrene," said Amanda. She'd adopted Shackie's password, and the three of us used it now.

When Bernice opened the door I had a glimpse of Veena the Vegetable. She was sitting on her brown plush sofa as usual, but she was looking at us as if she actually saw us. "Don't be late," she said to Bernice.

"She spoke to you!" I said to Bernice once she was out in the hall with the door closed behind her. I was trying to be friendly, but Bernice froze me out. "Yeah, so?" she said. "She's not a moron."

"Didn't say she was," I said coldly.

Bernice gave me a short glare. Even her glaring power wasn't what it used to be, ever since Amanda had come.

27

When we got to the vacant lot behind Scales for our Outdoor Classroom Predator-Prey demonstration, Zeb was sitting on a folding canvas camp-stool. There was a cloth bag at his feet with something in it. I tried not to look at the bag. "We're all here? Good," said Zeb. "Now. Predator-Prey Relations. Hunting and stalking. What are the rules?"

"Seeing without being seen," we chanted. "Hearing without being heard. Smelling without being smelled. Eating without being eaten!"

"You forgot one," said Zeb.

"Injuring without being injured," said one of the oldest boys.

"Correct! A predator can't afford a serious injury. If it can't hunt, it'll starve. It must attack suddenly and kill quickly. It must choose the prey that's at a disadvantage – too young, too old, too crippled to run away or fight back. How do we avoid being prey?"

"By not looking like prey," we chanted.

"By not looking like the prey *of that predator*," said Zeb. "A surf-boarder looks like a seal, to a shark, from underneath. Try to imagine what you look like from the predator's point of view."

"Don't show fear," said Amanda.

"Right. Don't show fear. Don't act sick. Make yourself look as big as possible. That will deter the larger hunting animals. But we ourselves are among the larger hunting animals, aren't we? Why would we hunt?" said Zeb.

"To eat," said Amanda. "There's no other good reason."

Zeb grinned at her as if this was a secret only the two of them knew. "Exactly," he said.

Zeb lifted up the cloth bag, untied it, and reached his hand in. He left his hand inside for what seemed a very long time. Then he took out a dead green rabbit. "Got it in Heritage Park. Rabbit trap," he said. "Noose. You can use them for the rakunks too. Now we're going to skin and gut the prey."

It still makes me feel sick to think about that part. The older boys helped him – they didn't flinch, though even Shackie and Croze seemed a bit strained. They always did whatever Zeb said. They looked up to him. It wasn't only because of his size. It was because he had lore, and it was lore they respected.

"What if the rabbit isn't, like, dead?" Croze asked. "In the snare."

"Then you kill it," said Zeb. "Smash it on the head with a rock. Or take it by the hind legs and bash it on the ground." You wouldn't kill a sheep like that, he added, because sheep had hard skulls: you'd slit its throat. Everything had its own most efficient way of being killed.

Zeb went on with the skinning. Amanda helped with the part where the furry green skin turned inside out like a glove. I tried not to look at the veins. They were too blue. And the glistening sinews.

Zeb made the chunks of meat really small so everyone could try, and also because he didn't want to push us too far by making us eat big pieces. Then we grilled the chunks over a fire made with some old boards.

"This is what you'll have to do if worst comes to worst," said Zeb. He handed me a chunk. I put it into my mouth. I found I could chew and swallow if I kept repeating in my head, "It's really bean paste, it's really bean paste . . ." I counted to a hundred, and then it was down.

But I had the taste of rabbit in my mouth. It felt like I'd eaten a nosebleed.

That afternoon we had the Tree of Life Natural Materials Exchange. It was held in a parkette on the northern edge of Heritage Park, across from the SolarSpace boutiques. It had a sand pit and a swing-and-slide set for small kids. There was a cobb house too, made of clay and sand and straw. It had six rooms and curved doorways and windows, but no doors or glass. Adam One said it was ancient greenies who'd built it, at least thirty years ago. The pleebrats had sprayed their tags and messages all over the walls: *I LV pssys (BBQd). Sk my dk, it's organic! UR ded FKn GreeNeez!*

The Tree of Life wasn't just for Gardeners. Everyone in the Natmart Net sold there – the Fernside Collective, the Big Box Backyarders, the Golfgreens Greenies. We looked down on these others because their clothes were nicer than ours. Adam One said their trading products were morally contaminated, though they didn't radiate synthetic slave-labour evil the way the flashy items in the mallway did. The Fernsiders sold their overglazed ceramics, plus jewellery they'd made from paper clips; the Big Box Backyarders did knitted animals; the Golfgreeners made artsy handbags out of rolled paper from vintage magazines, and grew cabbages around the edges of their golf course. Big deal, said Bernice, they still spray the grass there so a few cabbages won't save their souls. Bernice was getting more and more pious. Maybe it was her substitute for not having any real friends.

A lot of upmarket trendies came to the Tree of Life. Affluents from the SolarSpace gated communities, Fernside showoffs, even people from the Compounds, coming out for a safe pleebland adventure. They claimed to prefer our Gardener vegetables to the supermarkette kinds and even to the so-called farmers' markets, where – said Amanda – guys in farmer drag bought stuff from warehouses and tossed it into ethnic baskets and marked up the prices, so even if it said Organic you couldn't trust it. But the Gardener produce was the real thing. It stank of authenticity: the Gardeners might be fanatical and amusingly bizarre, but at least they were ethical. That's how they talked while I was wrapping up their purchases in recycled plastic.

The worst thing about helping at the Tree of Life was that we had to wear our Young Bioneer neck scarves. This was humiliating, as the trendies would often bring their kids. These kids wore baseball caps with words on them and stared at us and our neck scarves and drab clothing

as if we were freaks, whispering among themselves and laughing. I'd try
to ignore them. Bernice would stomp up to them and say, "What're you
staring at?" Amanda's mode was smoother. She'd smile at them, then
take out her piece of glass with the duct tape and cut a line on her arm
and lick the blood. Then she'd run her bloody tongue around her lips, and
hold out her arm, and they'd back off fast. Amanda said if you want
people to leave you alone you should act crazy.

The three of us were told to help at the mushroom booth. Usually
it was Pilar and Toby there, but Pilar wasn't well so it was only Toby.
She was strict: you had to stand up straight and be extra polite.

I checked out the affluents as they walked past. Some had pastel
jeans and sandals, but others were overloaded with expensive skin –
alligator slingbacks, leopard minis, oryx-hide handbags. They'd give
you this defensive look: *I didn't kill it, why let it go to waste?* I wondered
what it would be like to wear those things – to feel another creature's
skin right next to your own.

Some of them had the new Mo'Hairs – silver, pink, blue. Amanda
said there were Mo'Hair shops in the Sewage Lagoon that lured girls
in, and once you were in the scalp-transplant room they'd knock you
out, and when you woke up you'd not only have different hair but different fingerprints, and then you'd be locked in a membrane house and
forced into bristle work, and even if you escaped you'd never be able to
prove who you were because they'd stolen your identity. This sounded
really extreme. And Amanda did tell lies. But we'd made a pact never to
lie to each other. So I thought maybe it was true.

After an hour selling mushrooms with Toby we were told to go over to
Nuala's booth to help with the vinegar. By this time we were feeling
bored and silly, and every time Nuala bent over to get more vinegar from
the box under the counter, Amanda and I made wiggly motions with our
bums and sniggered under our breaths. Bernice was getting redder and
redder because we weren't letting her in. I knew this was mean, but I
couldn't somehow stop myself.

Then Amanda had to go to the violet porta-biolet, and Nuala said she needed a word with Burt, who was selling leaf-wrapped soap at the next booth. As soon as Nuala's back was turned, Bernice grabbed my arm and twisted it two ways at once. "Tell me!" she hissed.

"Let go!" I said. "Tell you what?"

"You know what! What's so funny with you and Amanda?"

"Nothing!" I said.

She twisted harder. "Okay," I said, "but you won't like it." Then I told her about Nuala and Burt and what they'd been doing in the Vinegar Room. I must have been longing to tell her anyway, because it all came out in a rush.

"That is a stinking lie!" she said.

"What's a stinking lie?" said Amanda, back from the porta-biolet.

"My father is not humping the Wet Witch!" hissed Bernice.

"I couldn't help it," I said. "She twisted my arm." Bernice's eyes were all red and watery, and if Amanda hadn't been there she would've hit me.

"Ren gets carried away," Amanda said. "The fact is, we don't know for sure. We just *suspect* that your father is humping the Wet Witch. Maybe he isn't. But you could understand him doing it, with your mother in a Fallow state so much. He must get very horny – that's why he's always groping little girls' armpits." She said all of this in a virtuous, Eve sort of voice. It was cruel.

"He's not," said Bernice. "He doesn't!" She was close to tears.

"If he is," said Amanda in her calm voice, "it's something you should be aware of. I mean, if I had a father, I wouldn't want him humping someone's generative organ, other than my mother's. It's a filthy habit – so unsanitary. You'd have to worry about his germy hands touching *you*. Though I'm sure he doesn't –"

"I really, really hate you!" said Bernice. "I hope you burn and die!"

"That's not very *forgiving*, Bernice," said Amanda in a reproachful voice.

"So, girls," said Nuala as she bustled towards us. "Any customers? Bernice, why are your eyes so red?"

"I'm allergic to something," said Bernice.

"Yes, she is," said Amanda solemnly. "She's not feeling well. Maybe she should go home. Or maybe it's the bad air. Maybe she should get a nose cone. Don't you think, Bernice?"

"Amanda, you are a very thoughtful girl," said Nuala. "Yes, Bernice dear, I do think you should leave right away. And we'll see about a nose cone for you, tomorrow, for the allergies. I'll walk you partway, dear." And she put her arm around Bernice's shoulders and led her away.

I couldn't believe what we'd just done. I had that sinking feeling in my stomach, like when you drop a heavy thing and you know it's going to land on your foot. We'd gone way too far, but I didn't know how to say that without Amanda thinking I was sermonizing. Anyway, there was no way of taking it back.

28

Right then a boy I'd never seen before came to our booth – a teenage boy, older than us. He was thin and dark-haired and tall, and he wasn't wearing the sort of clothes the affluents wore. Just plain black.

"How may I help you, sir?" said Amanda. We sometimes imitated SecretBurger wage-slaves when we were working the booths.

"I need to see Pilar," he said. No smile, nothing. "There's something wrong with this." He took a jar of Gardener honey out of his backpack. That was strange, because what could be wrong with honey? Pilar said it never went bad unless you got water in it.

"Pilar's not feeling well," I said. "You should talk to Toby about it – she's right over there, with the mushrooms."

He looked all around, as if he was nervous. He didn't seem to be with anyone else – no friends, no parents. "No," he said. "It has to be Pilar."

Zeb came over from the vegetable stand, where he was selling burdock roots and lamb's quarters. "Something wrong?" he said.

"He wants Pilar," said Amanda. "About some honey." Zeb and the boy looked at each other, and I thought I saw the boy give a small shake of his head.

"Would I do?" Zeb said to him.

"I think it should be her," said the boy.

"Amanda and Ren will take you over," said Zeb.

"What about selling the vinegar?" I said. "Nuala had to leave."

"I'll keep an eye on it," said Zeb. "This is Glenn. Take good care of him. Don't let them eat you alive," he said to Glenn.

We walked through the pleeb streets, heading to the Edencliff Rooftop Garden. "How come you know Zeb?" said Amanda.

"Oh, I used to know him," said the boy. He wasn't talkative. He didn't even want to walk beside us: after a block, he dropped a little behind.

We reached the Gardener building and climbed up the fire escape. Philo the Fog and Katuro the Wrench were up there – we never left the place empty, in case pleebrats tried to sneak in. Katuro was fixing one of the watering hoses; Philo was just smiling.

"Who is this?" sad Katuro when he saw the boy.

"Zeb told us to bring him here," said Amanda. "He's looking for Pilar."

Katuro nodded over his shoulder. "Fallows Hut."

Pilar was lying in a deck chair. Her chess game was set up beside her, the pieces all in place: she hadn't been playing. She didn't look well at all – she was kind of sunken in. Her eyes were closed, but she opened them when she heard us coming in. "Welcome, dear Glenn," she said, as if she was expecting him. "I hope you didn't have any trouble."

"No trouble," said the boy. He took out the jar. "Not good," he said.

"Everything's good," said Pilar. "In the big picture. Amanda, Ren, would you get me a glass of water?"

"I'll go," I said.

"Both of you," said Pilar. "Please."

She wanted us out of there. We left the Fallows Hut as slowly as we could. I wished I could hear what they were saying – it wouldn't be about honey. The way Pilar looked was frightening me.

"He's not pleeb," Amanda whispered. "He's Compound."

I thought that myself, but I said, "How can you tell?" The Compounds were where the Corps people lived – all those scientists and business people Adam One said were destroying old Species and making new ones and ruining the world, though I couldn't quite believe my real father in HelthWyzer was doing that; but in any case, why would Pilar even say hello to someone from there?

"I just have a feeling," said Amanda.

When we came back with the glass of water, Pilar had her eyes closed again. The boy was sitting beside her; he'd moved a few of her chess pieces. The white queen was boxed in: one more move and she'd be gone.

"Thank you," said Pilar, taking the glass of water from Amanda. "And thank you for coming, dear Glenn," she said to the boy.

He stood up. "Well, goodbye," he said awkwardly, and Pilar smiled at him. Her smile was bright but weak. I wanted to hug her, she looked so tiny and frail.

Going back to the Tree of Life, Glenn walked along beside us. "There's something really wrong with her," said Amanda. "Right?"

"Illness is a design fault," said the boy. "It could be corrected." Yes – he was definitely Compound. Only brainiacs from there talked like that: not answering your question up front, then saying some general kind of thing as if they knew it for a fact. Was that the way my real father had talked? Maybe.

"So, if you were making the world, you'd make it better?" I said. Better than God, was what I meant. All of a sudden I was feeling pious, like Bernice. Like a Gardener.

"Yes," he said. "As a matter of fact, I would."

29

The next day we went to pick up Bernice from the Buenavista Condos as usual. I think we were both feeling ashamed of ourselves because of what we'd done the day before – at least I was. But when we knocked on the door and said, "Knock, knock," Bernice didn't say, "Who's there?" She said nothing.

"It's Gang," Amanda called. "Gang grene!" Still nothing. I could almost feel her silence.

"Come on, Bernice," I said. "Open the door. It's us."

The door opened, but it wasn't Bernice. It was Veena. She was looking right at us, and she didn't seem in any way Fallow. "Go away," she said. Then she shut the door.

We looked at each other. I had a very bad feeling. What if we'd done some kind of permanent damage to Bernice, with our story about Burt and Nuala? What if it wasn't even true? It had just been a joke, at first. But it didn't seem like a joke any more.

Any other Saint Euell's Week we'd have gone to the Heritage Park to look for mushrooms with Pilar and Toby. It was exciting to go there because you never knew what you'd see. There'd be pleebland families having cookouts and family fights, and we'd hold our noses to avoid the stink of frizzling meat; there'd be couples thrashing around in the bushes, or homeless people drinking from bottles or snoring under the trees, or tangle-haired crazies talking to themselves or shouting, or druggies shooting up. If we got down as far as the beach, there might be girls in bikinis lying in the sun, and Shackie and Croze might say, *Skin cancer* to them, to get their attention.

Or there could be some CorpSeCorps guys on public-service patrol telling people to put their trash in the containers provided, though really – said Amanda – they were looking for small dealers doing business without cutting their mob friends in. Then you might hear the hot *zipzipzip* of a spraygun and some screams. Offering violence, they'd say to the bystanders as they dragged the guy away.

But our Heritage Park trip was cancelled that day because of Pilar being ill. So instead we had Wild Botanicals with Burt the Knob, in the vacant lot behind Scales and Tails.

We had our slates and chalk because we always drew the Wild Botanicals to help us memorize them. Then we'd wipe off our drawings, and the plant would be in our heads. There's nothing like drawing a thing to make you really see it, Burt would say.

Burt hunted around the vacant lot, picked something, held it up for us to see. "*Portulaca oleracea,*" he said. "Common name, Purslane. Found cultivated and in the wild. Prefers disturbed earth. Notice the red stem, the alternate leaves. A good source of omega 3s." He paused, frowned at us. "Half of you aren't looking and the other half aren't drawing," he said. "This could save your lives! We're talking about sustenance here. *Sustenance.* What is sustenance?"

Blank stares, silence. "Sustenance," said the Knob, "is what sustains a person's body. It's food. Food! Where does food come from? Class?"

We recited together: "All food comes from the Earth."

"Right!" said Burt. "The Earth! And then most people buy it from the supermarkette. What would happen if suddenly there were no more supermarkettes? Shackleton?"

"Grow it on the roof," said Shackie.

"Suppose there weren't any roofs," said the Knob, beginning to go pink in the face. "Where would you get it then?" Blank stares again. "You'd *forage*," said the Knob. "Crozier, what do we mean by *foraging*?"

"Finding stuff," said Croze. "Stuff you don't pay for. Like, stealing." We laughed.

The Knob ignored this. "And where would you look for this *stuff*? Quill?"

"At the mallway?" said Quill. "In behind, like. Where they throw stuff out, like, old bottles, and . . ." He was kind of dim, Quill, but also he was acting dim. The boys did that to make the Knob lose it.

"No, no!" the Knob shouted. "There won't *be* anyone to throw stuff out! You've never been outside this pleeb, have you? You've never seen a *desert*, you've never been in a *famine*! When the Waterless Flood hits, even if you personally last it out you'll starve. Why? Because you haven't been paying any attention! Why do I waste my time on you?" Every time the Knob took a class, he'd tip over some invisible edge and start yelling.

"Well then," he said, winding down. "What is this plant? Purslane. What can you do with it? Eat it. Now then, keep on drawing. Purslane! Notice the oval shape of those leaves! Notice their shininess! Look at the stem! Memorize it!"

I was thinking, It can't be true. I didn't see how anyone – even Wet Witch Nuala – could do sex with Burt the Knob. He was so bald and sweaty. "Cretins," he was muttering to himself. "Why do I bother?"

Then he went very still. He was looking at something behind us. We turned around: Veena was standing there, beside the gap in the fence. She must have squeezed through. She was still in her slippers; her yellow baby blanket was draped over her head like a shawl. Beside her was Bernice.

They just stood there. They didn't move. Then two CorpSeMen came through the fence as well. They were Combat, in their shimmering grey suits that made them look like a mirage. They had their sprayguns out. I felt all the blood drain out of my face; I thought I was going to throw up.

"What's wrong?" shouted Burt.

"Freeze!" said one of the CorpSeMen. His voice was very loud because of the mike in his helmet. They moved forward.

"Stay back," Burt said to us. He looked as if he'd been tasered.

"Come with us, sir," said the first CorpSeMan when they'd reached us.

"What?" said Burt. "I haven't done anything!"

"Illegal growing of marijuana for black-market profit, sir," said the second one. "It would be safer not to resist arrest."

They walked Burt towards the gap in the fence. We all trailed silently along behind – we couldn't understand what was happening.

As they came up to Veena and Bernice, Burt held out his arms. "Veena! How did this happen?"

"You fucking degenerate!" she said to him. "Hypocrite! Fornicator! How dumb do you think I am?"

"What are you talking about?" said Burt in a pleading voice.

"I guess you thought I was so high on that poisonous weed of yours that I couldn't see straight," said Veena. "But I found out. What you're doing with that cow Nuala! Not that she's the worst of it. You twisted asshole!"

"No," said Burt. "I swear! I never really . . . I was just . . ."

I was looking at Bernice: I couldn't tell what she was feeling. Her face wasn't even red. It was blank, like a chalkboard. Dusty white.

Adam One stepped in through the gap in the fence. He always seemed to know if there was something unusual going on. Amanda said it was just like he had a phone. He laid his hand on Veena's yellow baby blanket. "Veena, dear, you've come out of your Fallow state," he said. "How wonderful. We've been praying for that. Now, what seems to be the matter?"

"Move out of the way, please, sir," said the first CorpSeMan.

"Why did you do this to me?" Burt howled at Veena as they pushed him forward.

Adam One took a deep breath. "This is regrettable," he said. "Perhaps it would be wise to reflect on our shared Human frailties . . ."

"You're an idiot," Veena said to him. "Burt's been running a major gro-op in the Buenavista, right under your sacred Gardener noses. He's been dealing right under your noses too, at that stupid market of yours.

Those cute bars of soap wrapped up in leaves – not all of it was soap! He's been making a killing!"

Adam One looked mournful. "Money is a terrible temptation," he said. "It is a sickness."

"You fool," Veena said to him. "Organic botanics, what a joke!"

"Told you there was a gro-op in the Buenavista," Amanda whispered to me. "The Knob's in very deep shit."

Adam One said we should all go home, so that's what we did. I felt really bad about Burt. All I could imagine was that Bernice had gone back that day after we'd been so mean to her at the Tree of Life, and told Veena about Burt and Nuala having sex, and also about the armpit-groping, and that had made Veena so jealous or angry that she'd got in contact with the CorpSeCorps and made an accusation. The CorpSeCorps encouraged you to do that – to turn in your neighbours and family members. You could even get money for it, said Amanda.

I hadn't meant any harm, or not that kind of harm. But now look what had happened.

I thought we should go to Adam One and tell him what we'd done, but Amanda said what good would that do, it wouldn't fix things, it would just land us in more trouble. She was right. But that didn't make me feel any better.

"Lighten up," said Amanda. "I'll steal something for you. What d'you want?"

"A phone," I said. "Purple. Like yours."

"Okay," said Amanda. "I'll take care of it."

"That's nice of you," I said. I tried to put a lot of energy into my voice so she'd know I appreciated it, but she could tell I was faking.

30

The next day, Amanda said she had a surprise that would cheer me up without fail. It was at the Sinkhole mallway, she said. And it really was a surprise, because when we got there Shackie and Croze were hanging around near the wrecked holospinner booth. I knew they both had a crush on Amanda – all the boys did – though she never spent time with them except in a group.

"Have you got it?" she said to them. They grinned at her shyly. Shackie had grown a lot lately: he was tall and rangy, with dark eyebrows. Croze had grown too, but sideways as well as up; he had the beginnings of a straw-coloured beard. Before this I hadn't thought too much about what they looked like – not in detail – but now I found myself seeing them in a different way.

"In here," they said. They seemed not scared exactly, but alert. They checked that no one was watching, and then we all crammed into the booth where people used to get their image spun out into the mallway. It was designed for just two, so we had to stand close together.

It was hot in there. I could feel the heat from our bodies, as if we were infected and burning with fever, and I could smell the dried-sweat and old cotton and grime and oily scalp smell from Shackie and Croze – which was what we all smelled like – mixed with their older-boy smell, a mushroom and wine-dregs blend; and the flowery smell of Amanda, with a musky undertone and a hint of blood.

I couldn't tell what I smelled like to them. They say you can never really smell your own smell because you're so used to yourself. I wished

I'd known about this surprise in advance, because then I could have used one of my saved-up rose soap ends. I hoped I didn't smell like dirty underwear or cooped-up feet.

Why do we want other people to like us, even if we don't really care about them all that much? I don't know why, but it's true. I found myself standing there and smelling all those smells, and hoping a lot that Shackie and Croze thought I was pretty.

"Here it is," Shackie said. He brought out a piece of cloth with something wrapped up in it.

"What is it?" I said. I could hear my own voice: girly and squeaky.

"It's the surprise," said Amanda. "They got some of that superweed for us. The stuff Burt the Knob was growing."

"No way!" I said. "You bought it? From the CorpSeCorps?"

"Lifted it," said Shackie. "We snuck in the back of the Buenavista – we've done that lots. The CorpSe guys were going in and out the front door, they didn't pay any attention to us."

"There's a loose set of bars on one of the cellar windows – we used to get in there and party in the stairwell," said Croze.

"They've put bags of it in the cellar," said Shackie. "They must've harvested all the gro-op rooms. You could get blasted just breathing."

"Show," said Amanda. Shackie unrolled the cloth: dried shredded leaves.

I knew how Amanda felt about doing drugs: you lost control of your mind, and that was risky because it gave other people the edge. Also you could do too much, like Philo the Fog, and then you wouldn't have any mind left to speak of so no one would care whether you lost control of it or not. And you should only smoke with people you trusted. Did she trust Shackie and Croze?

"Have you tried this stuff?" I whispered to Amanda.

"Not yet," Amanda whispered back. Why were we whispering? The four of us were so close together that Shackie and Croze could hear everything.

"Then I don't want to," I said.

"But I traded!" said Amanda. She sounded fierce. "I traded a lot!"

"I've done this shit," said Shackie. He used his toughest voice for *shit.* "It's awesome!"

"Me too, you feel like you're airborne," said Croze. "Like a fucking bird!" Shackie was already rolling the shredded leaves, already lighting up, already sucking in.

There was someone's hand on my bum, I didn't know whose. It was creeping up, trying to find a way in under my Gardener one-piece dress. I wanted to say, Stop that, but I didn't.

"Just give it a try," said Shackie. He took hold of my chin and stuck his mouth down on mine and blew me full of smoke. I coughed, and he did it again, and I felt very dizzy. Then I had a clear blinding-bright fluorescent image of the rabbit we'd eaten that week. It was glaring at me with its dead eyes, only the eyes were orange.

"That was too much," said Amanda. "She's not used to it!"

Then I felt sick to my stomach, and then I threw up. I think I must have hit all of them. Oh no, I thought, what an idiot. I don't know how long all of that lasted because time was like rubber, it stretched out like a long, long elastic rope or a huge piece of chewing gum. Then it snapped shut into a tiny black square and I passed out.

When I woke up I was sitting against the broken fountain in the mallway. I was still dizzy, though not so sick: it was more like floating. Everything seemed far away and translucent. Maybe I can stick my hand through the cement, I thought. Maybe everything's lacework – made of specks, with God in between, just like Adam One says. Maybe I'm smoke.

The mallway store window across from us was like a boxful of fireflies, like living sequins. There was a party going on in there, I could hear the music. Tinkly and strange. A butterfly party: they must be dancing on their spindly butterfly legs. If I could only stand up, I thought, I could dance too.

Amanda had her arm around me. "It's okay," she said. "You're fine." Shackie and Croze were still there, and they were sounding pissed off. Or Croze was, more than Shackie, because Shackie was almost as whacked as I was.

"So, when'll you pay up?" said Croze.

"It didn't work," said Amanda. "So, never."

"That wasn't the trade," said Croze. "The trade was, we bring the stuff. We brought it. So, you owe us."

"The trade was, Ren gets happy," said Amanda. "She didn't. End of story."

"No way," said Croze. "You owe us. Pay up."

"Make me," said Amanda. Her voice had that dangerous edge, the one she'd use on pleebrats when they got too close.

"Whatever," said Shackie. "Whenever." He didn't seem too bothered.

"You owe us two fucks," said Croze. "One each. We ran a big risk, we could've got killed!"

"Don't bug her," said Shackie. "I just want to touch your hair," he said to Amanda. "You smell like toffee." He was still flying.

"Piss off," said Amanda. And I guess they did, because the next time I looked for them they weren't there.

I was feeling more normal by then. "Amanda," I said. "I can't believe you traded with them." I wanted to say, For me, but I was afraid I'd cry.

"Sorry it didn't work," she said. "I only wanted you to feel better."

"I do feel better," I said. "Lighter." That was true, partly because I'd puked up a lot of water weight, but partly because of Amanda. I knew she used to do that kind of trade, for food, when she was so hungry after the Texas hurricane, but she'd told me she'd never liked it and it was strictly business, so she never did it any more because she didn't have to. And she didn't have to this time, but she'd done it anyway. I didn't know she liked me so much.

"Now they're mad at you," I said. "They'll get even." It didn't seem really important, though, because I was still high as a bee.

"I'm not worried," said Amanda. "I can take care of them."

MOLE DAY

䷜

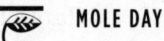

YEAR TWELVE.

OF THE LIFE UNDERGROUND.
SPOKEN BY ADAM ONE.

Dear Friends, dear Fellow Mammals, dear Fellow Creatures:

I point no fingers, for I know not where to point; but as we have just seen, malicious rumours can spread confusion. A careless remark can be as the cigarette butt casually tossed into the dumpster, smouldering until it bursts into flame and engulfs a neighbourhood. Do guard your words in future.

It is inevitable that certain friendships may lend themselves to undue comment. But we are not Chimpanzees: our females do not bite rival females, our males do not jump up and down on our females and hit them with branches. Or not as a rule. All pair-bondings are subject to stress and temptation – but let us not add to that stress nor misinterpret that temptation.

We miss the presence of our erstwhile Adam Thirteen, Burt, and his wife, Veena, and little Bernice. Let us forgive what needs to be forgiven, and put Light around them in our hearts.

Moving forward, we have identified an abandoned automobile repair establishment that can be turned into cozy homes, once our proposed Rat relocation has been carried out. I am sure the Rats of the FenderBender Body Shop will be very happy in the Buenavista once they have understood the food opportunities it has to offer.

You'll be pleased to know that though our Buenavista mushroom beds are lost to us, Pilar has kept some spawn on hand for each of our treasured species, and we will set up our mushroom beds in a cellar room at the Wellness Clinic until a damper location can be found.

Today we celebrate Mole Day, our Festival of Underground Life. Mole Day is a Children's festival, and our Children have been busily at work, decorating our Edencliff Rooftop Garden. The Moles with their little claws fashioned from hair combs, the Nematodes wrought from transparent plastic bags, the Earthworms of stuffed pantyhose and string, the Dung Beetles – what a testimony to our God-given powers of creativity, through which even the useless and discarded may be redeemed from meaninglessness.

We are inclined to overlook the very small that dwell among us; yet, without them, we ourselves could not exist; for every one of us is a Garden of sub-visual life forms. Where would we be without the Flora that populate the intestinal tract, or the Bacteria that defend against hostile invaders? We teem with multitudes, my Friends – with the myriad forms of Life that creep about beneath our feet, and – I may add – under our toenails.

True, we are sometimes infested with nanobioforms we would prefer to be without, such as the Eyebrow Mite, the Hookworm, the Pubic Louse, the Pinworm, and the Tick, not to mention the hostile bacteria and viruses. But think of them as God's tiniest Angels, doing His unfathomable work in their own way, for these Creatures, too, reside in the Eternal Mind, and shine in the Eternal Light, and form a part of the polyphonic symphony of Creation.

Consider also His workers in the Earth! The Earthworms and Nematodes and Ants, and their endless tilling of the soil, without which it would harden into a cement-like mass, extinguishing all Life. Think of the antibiotic properties of the Maggots and of the various Moulds, and of the honey that our Bees make, and also of the Spider's web, so useful in the stopping of bloodflow from a wound. For every ill, God has provided a remedy in His great Medicine Cabinet of Nature!

Through the work of the Carrion Beetles and the putrefying Bacteria, our fleshly habitations are broken down, and returned to their elements to enrich the lives of other Creatures. How misguided were our ancestors in their preserving of corpses – their embalmings, their adornings, their encasings in mausoleums. What a horror – to turn the Soul's husk into an unholy fetish! And, in the end, how selfish! Shall we not repay the gift of Life by regifting ourselves to Life when the time comes?

When next you hold a handful of moist compost, say a silent prayer of thanks to all of Earth's previous Creatures. Picture your fingers giving each and every one of them a loving squeeze. For they are surely here with us, ever present in that nourishing matrix.

Now let us join our Buds and Blooms Choir in singing our traditional Mole Day Children's Hymn.

WE PRAISE THE TINY PERFECT MOLES

We praise the tiny perfect Moles
That garden underground;
The Ant, the Worm, the Nematode,
Wherever they are found.

They live their whole lives in the dark,
Unseen by Human sight;
The earth is like the air to them,
Their day is like our night.

They turn the soil and till it,
They make the plants to thrive;
The Earth would be a desert,
If they were not alive.

The little Carrion Beetles
That seek unlikely places
Return our Husks to Elements,
And tidy up our spaces.

And so for God's small Creatures
Beneath the field and wood,
Let us today give joyful thanks,
For God has found them good.

From *The God's Gardeners Oral Hymnbook*

31

While the Flood rages, you must count the days, said Adam One. You must observe the risings of the Sun and the changings of the Moon, because to everything there is a season. On your Meditations, do not travel so far on your inner journeys that you enter the Timeless before it is time. In your Fallow states, do not descend to a level that is too deep for any resurgence, or the Night will come in which all hours are the same to you, and then there will be no Hope.

Toby's been keeping track of the days on some old AnooYoo Spa-in-the-Park notepaper. Each pink page is topped with two long-lashed eyes, one of them winking, and with a lipstick kiss. She likes these eyes and smiling mouths: they're companions of a sort. At the top of each fresh page she prints the Gardener Feast Day or Saint's Day. She can still recite the entire list off by heart: Saint E.F. Schumacher, Saint Jane Jacobs, Saint Sigrithur of Gullfoss, Saint Wayne Grady of Vultures; Saint James Lovelock, The Blessed Gautama Buddha, Saint Bridget Stutchbury of Shade Coffee, Saint Linnaeus of Botanical Nomenclature, The Feast of Crocodylidae, Saint Stephen Jay Gould of the Jurassic Shales, Saint Gilberto Silva of Bats. And the rest.

Under each Saint's Day name she writes her gardening notes: what was planted, what was harvested, what phase of the moon, what insect guests.

Mole Day, she writes now. *Year Twenty-five. Do the laundry. Gibbous Moon.* Mole Day was part of Saint Euell's Week. It wasn't such a good anniversary.

On the bright side, there should be some polyberries by now, ripe ones. The strength of the polyberry gene splice is that it produces at all seasons. Perhaps in the late afternoon she'll go down and pick them.

Two days back – on Saint Orlando Garrido of Lizards – she made an entry that wasn't about gardening. *Hallucination?* she'd written. She ponders this entry now. It did seem like a hallucination at the time.

It was after the daily thunderstorm. She was up on the roof, check-ing the rain barrel connections: the flow from the single tap she's kept open downstairs was blocked. She found the problem – drowned mouse clogging the intake – and was turning to go back down the stairs when she heard an odd sound. It was like singing, but not any singing she'd ever heard before.

She scanned with the binoculars. At first there was nothing, but then at the far end of the field a strange procession appeared. It seemed to consist entirely of naked people, though one man walking at the front had clothes on, and some sort of red hat, and – could it be? – sunglasses. Behind him there were men and women and children, every known skin colour; as she focused, she could see that several of the naked people had blue abdomens.

That was why she's decided it must have been a hallucination: the blueness. And the crystalline, otherworldly singing. She'd seen the figures for only a moment. They were there, then they'd vanished, like smoke. They must have gone in among the trees, to follow the walkway there.

Her heart had leapt with joy – she couldn't help it. She'd felt like running down the stairs, running outside, running after them. But it was far too much to hope for, other people – so many other people. Other people who looked so healthy. They couldn't possibly be real. If she allowed herself to be lured outside by such a siren mirage – lured into the pig-ridden forest – she wouldn't be the first person in history to have been destroyed by the overly optimistic projections of her own mind.

Confronted by too much emptiness, said Adam One, the brain invents. Loneliness creates company as thirst creates water. How many sailors have been wrecked in pursuit of islands that were merely a shimmering?

She takes her pencil and scratches out the question mark. *Hallucination*, it says now. Pure. Simple. No doubt about it.

She sets down her pencil, gathers her mop handle and her binoculars and the rifle, and trudges up the stairs to the rooftop to survey her domain. All is quiet this morning. No movement out there in the field – no large animals, no naked blue-tinged singers.

32

How long ago was that Mole Day, the last one Pilar was alive? Year Twelve, it must have been.

Right before it had come the disaster of Burt's arrest. After he'd been taken away by the CorpSeMen and Veena and Bernice had left the vacant lot, Adam One had called all the Gardeners together for an emergency meeting up on the Edencliff Rooftop. He'd told them the news, and when they'd grasped it, the Gardeners had gone into shock. The revelation was so painful, and so shameful! How had Burt managed to run a gro-op in the Buenavista without anyone suspecting?

Through trust, of course, thinks Toby. The Gardeners mistrusted everyone in the Exfernal World, but they trusted their own. Now they'd joined the long list of the religious faithful who'd woken one morning to find that the vicar had made off with the church building fund, leaving a trail of molested choirboys behind him. At least Burt hadn't done any choirboy molesting, or not as far as was known. There'd been gossip among the children – crude remarks of the kind children made – but they hadn't been about boys. Just girls, and just groping.

The only one of the Gardeners who hadn't been surprised and horrified by the gro-op was Philo the Fog, but he was never surprised or horrified by anything. "I'd like to try that shit, see if it's any good," was all he had to say.

Adam One had asked for volunteers to take in the families that had been so suddenly displaced – they couldn't go back to the Buenavista, he'd said, because it would be overrun with CorpSeMen, so they should consider their material possessions as lost to them. "If the building was on fire, you wouldn't run back into it to save a few baubles and trinkets," he said. "It is God's way of testing your attachment to the realm of useless illusion." The Gardeners weren't supposed to be bothered by that part: they'd gleaned their material possessions in junkyards and dumpsters so they could always glean others, went the theory. Nevertheless there was some weeping over a lost crystal glass, and a puzzling fuss about a broken waffle iron with sentimental value.

Adam One then asked all present not to talk about Burt and the Buenavista, and especially the CorpSeCorps. "Our enemies may be listening," he'd said. He'd been saying that more and more frequently: Toby sometimes wondered whether he was paranoid.

"Nuala, Toby," he'd said as the others were leaving. "A moment. Can you go by there and check?" he said to Zeb. "Though I don't suppose there's anything to be done."

"Nope," said Zeb cheerfully. "Not a fuckworth. But I'll take a look."

"Wear your pleebland clothes," said Adam One.

Zeb nodded. "The solarbiker outfit." He strolled away towards the fire-escape stairs.

"Nuala, my dear," said Adam One. "Can you cast any light? On what Veena said, about you and Burt?"

Nuala began sniffling. "I have no idea," she said. "It's such a lie! It's so disrespectful! It's so hurtful! How could she think such a thing, about me and . . . and Adam Thirteen?"

Not too hard, thought Toby, considering the way you rub up against pant legs. Nuala flirted with anything male. But Veena had been in a Fallow state while the flirting had been going on, so what had aroused her suspicion?

"None of us believes it, my dear," said Adam One. "Veena must have listened to some rumour-monger – perhaps an *agent provocateur* sent by our enemies to sow dissention among us. I will ask the Buenavista gatekeepers if Veena had any unusual visitors in recent days. Now, dear

Nuala, you should dry your tears and go to the Sewing Room. Our displaced congregation members will need many cloth items, such as quilts, and I know you're happy to be of use."

"Thank you," said Nuala gratefully. She gave him her only-you-understand-me look and hurried away towards the fire escape.

"Toby, my dear. Do you think you could see it in your heart to take over Burt's duties?" Adam One asked, once Nuala had gone. "The Garden Botanics, the Edible Weeds. We'd make you an Eve, of course. I've meant to do that for some time, but Pilar has so appreciated your help as her assistant, and I believe you've been happy in that role. I didn't want to steal you away from her."

Toby thought. "I'd be honoured," she said at last. "But I can't accept. To be a full-fledged Eve . . . it would be hypocritical." She'd never managed to repeat the moment of illumination she'd felt on her first day with the Gardeners, though she'd tried often enough. She'd gone on the Retreats, she'd done an Isolation Week, she'd performed the Vigils, she'd taken the required mushrooms and elixirs, but no special revelations had come to her. Visions, yes, but none with meaning. Or none with any meaning she could decipher.

"Hypocritical?" said Adam One, wrinkling his forehead. "In what way?"

Toby chose her words carefully: she didn't wish to hurt his feelings. "I'm not sure I believe in all of it." An understatement: she believed in very little.

"In some religions, faith precedes action," said Adam One. "In ours, action precedes faith. You've been acting as if you believe, dear Toby. *As if* – those two words are very important to us. Continue to live according to them, and belief will follow in time."

"That's not much to go on," said Toby. "Surely an Eve ought to be . . ."

Adam One sighed. "We should not expect too much from faith," he said. "Human understanding is fallible, and we see through a glass, darkly. Any religion is a shadow of God. But the shadows of God are not God."

"I wouldn't want to be a poor example," said Toby. "Children can spot faking – they'll see I'm just going through the motions. That might be harmful to what you're trying to accomplish."

"Your doubts reassure me," said Adam One. "They show how trustworthy you are. For every No there is also a Yes! Will you do one thing for me?"

"What thing?" said Toby cautiously. She didn't want the responsibilities of Evehood – she didn't want to close down her choices. She wanted to feel free to quit if she needed to. I've just been timeserving, she thought. Taking advantage of their goodwill. Such a fraud.

"Just ask for guidance," said Adam One. "Do an overnight Vigil. Pray for the strength to face your doubts and fears. I feel confident that a positive answer will be provided to you. You have gifts that should not be wasted. We would all welcome you as an Eve among us, I can assure you."

"All right," said Toby. "I can do that." For every Yes, she thought, there is also a No.

Pilar was the keeper of the Vigil materials and the other Gardener out-of-body voyaging substances. Toby hadn't spoken with her for several days because of her illness – a stomach virus, it was said. But in their conversation Adam One hadn't mentioned anything about this illness, so maybe Pilar was well again. Those bugs never lasted more than a week.

Toby sought out Pilar's tiny cubicle at the back of the building. Pilar was lying propped up on her futon; a beeswax candle flickered in a tin can on the floor beside her. The air was close, and smelled of vomit. But the bowl beside Pilar was empty, and clean.

"Dear Toby," said Pilar. "Come and sit beside me." Her little face was more like a walnut than ever, though her skin was pale, or as pale as brown skin could get. Greyish. Muddy.

"Are you feeling better?" said Toby, taking Pilar's sinewy claw in both of her own hands.

"Oh yes. Much better," said Pilar, smiling sweetly. Her voice was not strong.

"What was it?"

"I ate something that disagreed with me," said Pilar. "Now, what can I do for you?"

"I wanted to make sure you were all right," said Toby, who'd just discovered that this was true. Pilar looked so wan, so depleted. She recognized fear in herself: what if Pilar – who'd seemed eternal, who'd surely always been there, or if not always, at least for a very long time, like a boulder or an ancient stump – what if she were suddenly to vanish?

"That's very kind of you," said Pilar. She squeezed Toby's hand.

"And Adam One asked me to become an Eve."

"I suppose you said no?" said Pilar, smiling.

"That's right," said Toby. Pilar could usually guess what she was thinking. "But he wants me to do an overnight Vigil. To pray for guidance."

"That would be best," said Pilar. "You know where I keep the Vigil things. It's the brown bottle," she said as Toby lifted the rubber-band-and-string curtain in front of the storage shelves. "The brown one, to the right. Five drops only, and two from the purple one."

"Have I done this mix before?" asked Toby.

"Not this exact one. You'll get an answer of some kind, on this. It never fails. Nature never does betray us. You do know that?"

Toby knew no such thing. She measured the drops into one of Pilar's chipped teacups, then replaced the bottles. "Are you sure you're better?" she asked.

"I'm fine," said Pilar, "for the moment. And the moment is the only time we can be fine in. Now, you go along, Toby dear, and have a lovely Vigil. It's a gibbous moon tonight. Enjoy it!" Sometimes, when doling out the head trips, Pilar sounded like the supervisor of a kiddie carnival ride.

For the site of her Vigil, Toby chose the tomato section of the Edencliff Rooftop Garden. She posted the site on the Vigil sign-in slate, as required: those on Vigils sometimes went wandering away, and in tracing them it was helpful to know where they were supposed to have been.

Adam One had recently taken to placing gatekeepers on every floor, beside the landings. So I can't get down the Garden stairs without someone seeing me, thought Toby. Unless I fall off the roof.

She waited till dusk, then took the drops with a mix of Elderflower and Raspberry to disguise the taste: Pilar's Vigil potions always tasted like mulch. Then she sat down in meditation position, near a large tomato plant, which in the moonlight looked like a contorted leafy dancer or a grotesque insect.

Soon the plant began to glow and twirl its vines, and the tomatoes on it started to beat like hearts. There were crickets nearby, speaking in tongues: quarkit quarkit, ibbit ibbit, arkit arkit . . .

Neural gymnastics, thought Toby. She closed her eyes.

Why can't I believe? she asked the darkness.

Behind her eyelids she saw an animal. It was a golden colour, with gentle green eyes and canine teeth, and curly wool instead of fur. It opened its mouth, but it did not speak. Instead, it yawned.

It gazed at her. She gazed at it. "You are the effect of a carefully calibrated blend of plant toxins," she told it. Then she fell asleep.

33

The next morning Adam One came to see how Toby's Vigil had gone. "Did you get an answer?" he asked her.

"I saw an animal," said Toby.

Adam One was delighted. "What a successful outcome! Which animal? What did it say to you?" But before Toby could answer, he looked over her shoulder. "We have a messenger," he said.

In her hazy post-Vigil state, Toby thought he meant some kind of mushroom angel or plant spirit, but it was only Zeb, breathing hard from his climb up the fire escape. He was still wearing his pleeblander disguise: black fleather vest, grimy jeans, battered solarbike boots. He looked hungover.

"Were you up all night?" said Toby.

"You too, looks like," said Zeb. "I'll get shit for it back at the nest – Lucerne hates it when I work at night." He didn't seem too concerned about that. "You want to call a general meeting," he said to Adam One, "or hear the bad news first yourself?"

"Bad news first," said Adam One. "We may have to edit it for wider consumption." He nodded towards Toby. "She doesn't panic."

"Right," said Zeb. "Here's the story."

His sources of information were unofficial, he said: in pursuit of the truth, he'd been forced to sacrifice himself by spending an evening watching the girls gyrate at Scales and Tails, where the CorpSeCorps guys hung out when off-duty. He didn't like to get too close to the CorpSeMen, he said – he had a history of sorts, he might be recognized despite the alterations he'd had done to himself. But he knew a few of the girls, so he'd mined them for rumours.

"You paid them?" said Adam One.

"Nothing's free," said Zeb. "But I didn't pay too much."

Burt had indeed been running a gro-op in the Buenavista, he said. It was the usual method – unoccupied apartments, windows blacked out, electricity hijacked. Full-spectrum gro-lights, automatic sprinkler systems, all top of the line. But it wasn't just ordinary skunkweed, not even West Coast superweed: it was a stratospheric splice, with some peyote genes and psilocybins, and even a little ayahuasca – the good part, though they hadn't completely eliminated the part that made you puke your guts out. A lot of people who'd tried this would kill to do it again, and there wasn't much being made yet, so it was going for a very high price on the market.

It was a CorpSeCorps operation, naturally. The HelthWyzer labs had developed the splice, the CorpSeCorpsMen were the wholesalers. They ran it the way they ran everything illegal, through the pleebmobs. They'd thought it was a joke to get one of the Adams to front it, and to plant the gro-op in a building the Gardeners controlled. They'd been paying Burt well enough, but then he'd tried to cheat by selling on his own. He'd been getting away with it too, said Zeb, until the CorpSeCorps got an anonymous tip. Traced to a cellphone tossed into a dumpster. No DNA on it. Woman's voice, though. Very pissed-off woman.

That would be Veena, thought Toby. I wonder where she got the phone? Word had it that she'd taken Bernice to the West Coast, with the money the CorpSeCorps had paid her.

"Where is he now?" said Adam One. "Adam Thirteen? Former Adam Thirteen. Is he still alive?"

"Can't tell you," said Zeb. "No word on it."

"Let us pray," said Adam One. "He'll talk about us."

"If he was in that deep with them, he already has," said Zeb.

"Did he know about Pilar's tissue samples?" said Adam One. "And our contact in HelthWyzer? Our young courier with the honey jar?"

"No," said Zeb. "That was just you and me and Pilar. We never discussed it in Council."

"Fortunate," said Adam One.

"Let's hope he'll have an accident with a gutting knife," said Zeb. "You didn't hear any of this," he said to Toby.

"Fear not!" said Adam One. "Toby's truly one of us now. She's going to be an Eve."

"I didn't get an answer!" Toby protested. An animal yawn was not very definitive, as visions went.

Adam One smiled benignly. "You'll make the right decision," he said.

Toby spent the rest of the afternoon mixing up a scent combo that would be irresistible to rats, and could be laid down as a trail from the Fender-Bender Body Shop to the Buenavista Condos. The goal was to remove the rats from the former and rehouse them in the latter, without loss of life: the Gardeners didn't want to displace a fellow Species without offering them accommodation of equal value.

She used meat scraps from the stash Pilar kept for maggots, some honey, some peanut butter – she'd sent Amanda to buy that at a supermarkette. Some rancid cheese; beer dregs for the liquid element. When it was ready, she sent for Shackleton and Crozier and gave them their instructions.

"That is really putrid," said Shackleton, sniffing with admiration.

"Think you can stand it?" said Toby. "Because if you can't . . ."

"We'll do it," said Crozier, straightening his shoulders.

"Can I come too?" said little Oates, who'd followed them.

"No thumbsuckers," said Crozier.

"Be careful," said Toby. "We don't want to find you spraygunned in a vacant lot. Minus your kidneys."

"I know what I'm doing," said Shackleton proudly. "Zeb's gonna help us. We're wearing pleeb stuff – see?" He opened his Gardener shirt: underneath it was a black T-shirt that read, DEATH: A GREAT WAY TO LOSE WEIGHT! Underneath the slogan was a skull and crossbones, in silver.

"Those Corps guys are so dumb," said Crozier, grinning. He had a T-shirt too: STRIPPERS LOVE MY POLE. "We'll walk right past them!"

"Not a thumbsucker," said Oates, kicking Crozier in the shin. Crozier batted him on the side of the head.

"We're under their radar," said Shackleton. "They won't even see us."

"Pig-eater!" said Oates.

"Oates, that is enough language out of you," said Toby. "You can come and help me feed the worms. Off you go," she said to the other two. "Here's the bottle. Don't spill it inside FenderBender, and especially not on wood, or some unlucky people will have to live with it for a long time." She added, to Shackleton, "We're depending on you." It was good to let boys that age believe they were doing the jobs of men, so long as they didn't get carried away.

"Ciao, bedwetter," said Crozier.

"You totally stink," said Oates.

34

The next morning Toby was giving a class at the Wellness Clinic: Affective Herbs, for the twelve- to fifteen-year-olds. Manic Botanics, the kids called it, which was better than what they called some of the other subjects: Poop and Goop for violet biolet instruction, Guck and Muck for Compost-Pile Building.

"Willow," she said. "Analgesic. A-N-A-L-G-E-S-I-C, spell it on your slates." There was the squeaking of chalk – too much squeaking. "Stop that, Crozier," said Toby, without looking. Crozier was a chronic squeaker. Had she heard a whisper of *Dry Witch*? "I heard that, Shackleton," she said. The class was more restless than usual: after-shocks from the uproar caused by Veena. "Analgesic. What do we mean by that?"

"Painkiller," said Amanda.

"Correct, Amanda," said Toby. Amanda, always suspiciously well behaved in class, was even more so today. She was sly, Amanda. Too well versed in the ways of the Exfernal World. But Adam One believed the Gardeners had been of great benefit to her, and who was to say that Amanda was not undergoing a life change?

Still, it was unfortunate that Ren had been swept into Amanda's all-too-attractive orbit. Ren was overly pliable – she risked being always under somebody's thumb.

"What part of the Willow do we use to make the analgesic?" she went on. "The leaves?" said Ren. Too eager to please, the wrong answer anyway, and even more anxious than usual. Ren must be feeling the loss of Bernice, or maybe the guilt: how ruthlessly Bernice had been shouldered aside, once Amanda had appeared on the scene. They think we don't see them, thought Toby. They think we don't know what they're up to. Their snobberies, their cruelties, their schemes.

Nuala stuck her head in the door. "Toby, dear," she said, "could I have a word with you?" Her tone was lugubrious. Toby stepped out into the corridor.

"What's happened?" she said.

"You need to go and see Pilar," said Nuala. "Right now. She's chosen her time." Toby felt her heart contract. So Pilar had lied to her. No, not lied; just not told the whole truth. It had been something she'd eaten, but not by accident. Nuala squeezed Toby's arm to show deep sympathy. Get your moist palms off me, Toby thought, I'm not a man.

"Could you take my class?" she said. "Please. I'm teaching Willow."

"Of course, Toby dear," said Nuala. "I'll do 'The Weeping Willow' with them." This sugary song was a favourite of Nuala's; she'd composed it for small children. Toby could imagine the rolling eyes among these older kids. But since Nuala didn't really know much about botanicals, having them sing it would at least fill the time.

Toby hurried away to the sound of Nuala's voice: "Toby has been called away on an errand of mercy, so let us help her by singing the Weeping Willow song!" Her intense, slightly flat contralto rose above the lacklustre voices of the children:

> Weeping willow, weeping willow, branches waving like the sea,
> While I'm lying on my pillow, come and take my pain from me . . .

Hell would be an eternity of Nuala's lyrics, thought Toby. Anyway it wasn't the Weeping Willow, it was the White Willow, *salix alba*, with its available salicylic acid. That's what killed the pain.

Pilar was lying in her cubicle, on her bed, with her beeswax candle still burning in its tin container. She stretched out her thin brown fingers. "Dearest Toby," she said. "Thank you for coming. I wanted to see you."

"You did it yourself!" said Toby. "You didn't tell me!" She was so sad she was angry.

"I didn't want you to waste your time in worrying," said Pilar. Her voice had dwindled to a whisper. "I wanted you to have your nice Vigil. Now come and sit beside me, and tell me what you saw last night."

"An animal," said Toby. "Sort of like a lion, but not a lion."

"Good," whispered Pilar. "That's a good sign. You'll be helped with strength when you need it. I'm glad it wasn't a slug." She gave a tiny laugh; then her face contorted in pain.

"Why?" said Toby. "Why did you?"

"I got the diagnosis," said Pilar. "It's cancer. Very advanced. So, best to go now, while I still know what I'm doing. Why linger?"

"What diagnosis?" said Toby.

"I sent in some biopsy samples," said Pilar. "Katuro did it for me – took the tissue samples. We hid them in a jar of honey and smuggled them to the diagnostic labs at HelthWyzer West – under a different identity, of course."

"Who smuggled them?" said Toby. "Was it Zeb?"

Pilar smiled as if enjoying a private joke. "A friend," she said. "We have many friends."

"We could take you to a hospital," said Toby. "I'm sure Adam One would authorize –"

"Don't backslide, my Toby," said Pilar. "You know our views on hospitals. I might as well be thrown into a cesspool. Anyway, there's no cure for what I've taken. Now, please hand me that glass – the blue one."

"Not yet!" said Toby. How to postpone, delay? Keep Pilar with her.

"It's just water, and a little Willow and Poppy," Pilar whispered. "Deadens the pain without knocking you out. I want to stay awake as long as possible. I'm good for a while."

Toby watched while Pilar drank. "Another pillow," said Pilar.

Toby handed her one of the husk-filled sacks from the bottom of the bed. "You've been my family here," she said. "More than the others." She was finding it hard to talk, but she refused to cry.

"And you've been mine," said Pilar simply. "Remember to tend the Buenavista Ararat. Keep it renewed."

Toby didn't want to tell her that the Buenavista Ararat was lost to them because of Burt. Why upset her? She propped Pilar up with the pillow: she was strangely heavy. "What did you use?" she asked. Her throat was tightening.

"I've trained you well," said Pilar. Her eyes crinkled at the edges, as if the whole thing was a prank. "Let's see if you can guess. Symptoms: cramps and vomiting. Then a respite period during which the patient appears to improve. But meanwhile, the liver is slowly being destroyed. No antidote."

"One of the amanitas," said Toby.

"Clever girl," Pilar whispered. "The Death Angel, a friend in need."

"But it will be so painful," said Toby.

"Don't worry about that," said Pilar. "There's always the Poppy concentrate. It's the red bottle – that one. I'll let you know when. Now, listen to me carefully. This is my will. As we say, shrouds have no pockets – all earthly things must be passed from the dying to the living, and that includes our knowledge. I want you to have everything I've assembled here – all my materials. It's a good collection, and it confers great power. Guard it well and use it well. I trust you to do that. You're familiar with some of these bottles. I've made a paper list of the rest, which you must memorize and then destroy. The list is inside the green jar – that one. Do you promise?"

"Yes," said Toby. "I promise."

"Deathbed promises are sacred among us," said Pilar. "You know that. Don't cry. Look at me. I'm not sad."

Toby knew the theory: Pilar believed that she was donating herself to the matrix of Life through her own volition, and she also believed that this should be a matter for celebration.

But what about me? thought Toby. I'm being deserted. It was like the time her mother died, and then her father. How many times did she have to go through the process of being orphaned? Don't whine, she told herself sternly.

"I want you to be Eve Six," Pilar said. "In my place. No one else has the talent, and the knowledge. Can you do that for me? Promise?"

Toby promised. What else could she say?

"Good," Pilar whispered, breathing out. "Now, I think it's time for the Poppy. The red bottle, that's the one. Wish me well on my journey."

"Thank you for all you've taught me," said Toby. I can't stand this, she thought. I'm killing her. No: I'm helping her to die. I'm fulfilling her wishes.

She watched as Pilar drank.

"Thank you for learning," said Pilar. "I'm going to sleep now. Don't forget to tell the bees."

Toby sat beside Pilar until she stopped breathing. Then she pulled the coverlet up over her tranquil face and snuffed out the candle. Was it her imagination or had the candle flared up at the moment of Pilar's death as if a little surge of air had passed it? Spirit, Adam One would say. An energy that cannot be grasped or measured. Pilar's immeasurable Spirit. Gone.

But if Spirit wasn't material in any way, it couldn't influence a candle flame. Could it?

I'm getting as mushy as the rest of them, thought Toby. Addled as an egg. Next thing I'll be talking to flowers. Or snails, like Nuala.

But she went to tell the bees. She felt like an idiot doing it, but she'd promised. She remembered that it wasn't enough just to think at them: you had to say the words out loud. Bees were the messengers between this world and the other worlds, Pilar had said. Between the living and the dead. They carried the Word made air.

Toby covered her head – as was the custom, Pilar had claimed – and stood in front of the Rooftop's hives. The bees were flying around as usual, coming and going, bringing their leg-loads of pollen, waggling in their figure-eight semaphoric dances. From inside the hives came the humming of wings as they fanned the air, cooling it, ventilating the cells and passageways. One bee is all the bees, Pilar used to say, so what's good for the hive is good for the bee.

Several bees flew around her head, golden in their fur. Three lit on her face, tasting her.

"Bees," she said. "I bring news. You must tell your Queen."

Were they listening? Perhaps. They were nibbling gently at the edges of her dried tears. For the salt, a scientist would say.

"Pilar is dead," she said. "She sends you her greetings, and her thanks for your friendship over many years. When the time comes for you to follow her to where she has gone, she will meet you there." These were the words Pilar had taught her. She felt like such a dolt, saying them out loud. "Until then, I am your new Eve Six."

Nobody was listening, though if they had been they wouldn't have found anything odd, not up here on the Rooftop. Whereas down below at ground level they'd have labelled her as a crazy woman, wandering the streets, talking out loud to nothing.

Pilar used to bring the news to the bees every morning. Would Toby be expected to do the same? Yes, she would. It was one of the functions of the Eve Six. If you didn't tell the bees everything that was going on, Pilar said, their feelings would be hurt and they'd swarm and go elsewhere. Or they'd die.

The bees on her face hesitated: maybe they could feel her trembling. But they could tell grief from fear, because they didn't sting. After a moment they lifted up and flew away, blending with the circling multitudes above the hives.

35

Once she'd pulled herself together and arranged her face, Toby went to tell Adam One. "Pilar died," she said. "She took care of it herself."

"Yes, my dear. I know," said Adam One. "We discussed it. She used the Death Angel, and then the Poppy?" Toby nodded. "But – this is a delicate matter, and I am counting on your discretion – she didn't feel the Gardeners at large should be told the entire truth. Final self-journeying is a moral option only for the experienced and, I have to say, only for the terminally ill, as Pilar was; but it's not one we should make widely available – especially not to our young people, who are impressionable and prone to indulge in morbid sulking and false heroics. I trust you've taken charge of those medicine bottles of Pilar's? We wouldn't want any accidents."

"Yes," said Toby. I need to get a box made, she thought. A metal one. With a lock.

"And now you're Eve Six," said Adam One, beaming. "I'm so pleased, my dear!"

"You discussed that with Pilar too, I suppose," said Toby. The whole Vigil thing was just a stall, she thought. Keeping me on hold until Pilar could clinch the sale.

"It was her earnest desire," said Adam One. "She had such a deep love and respect for you."

"And I hope to be worthy of her," she said.

So the two of them had trapped her. What could she say? She found herself stepping into ritual as if into a pair of stone shoes.

▬▬
▬▬
▬▬

Adam One called a general Gardeners meeting, at which he made a lying speech. "Unfortunately," he began, "our dear Pilar – Eve Six – passed away tragically earlier today after making a species identification error. She had many years of impeccable practice to her credit – but perhaps this was God's way of harvesting our beloved Eve Six for His greater purposes. Let me remind you of the importance of learning our mushrooms thoroughly; and do confine your mushrooming activities to well-known species, such as the Morels, the Shaggy Manes, and the Puffballs – those about which there cannot be any confusion.

"While she was alive, Pilar expanded our mushroom and fungus collection enormously, adding a number of wild specimens. Some of these can be an aid to meditation during your Retreats, but please, do not try them without taking informed advice, and watch for those telltale cups and rings – we do not want any more unfortunate incidents of this nature."

Toby felt outrage: how could Adam One disparage Pilar's mycological expertise? Pilar would never have made such a mistake: the older Gardeners must know that. But maybe it was only a way of talking, just as suicide used to be called "death by misadventure."

"I am happy to announce," Adam One continued, "that our worthy Toby has agreed to fill the position of Eve Six. This was Pilar's wish, and I'm sure you'll all agree that there is no one more suited to the position than she. I myself rely upon her completely for . . . for many things. Her great gifts include not only her extensive knowledge, but also her good sense, her fortitude in adversity, and her kind heart. This is why she was Pilar's choice." There was some subdued nodding and smiling in Toby's direction.

"Our beloved Pilar wished to be composted in Heritage Park," Adam One continued. "She herself thoughtfully selected the shrub she wished planted on top of her – a fine specimen of Elderberry – so that in time we may expect some foraging dividends. As you know, an unofficial composting is a risk, as it incurs heavy penalties – the Exfernal World believes that even death itself should be regimented and, above all, paid for – but we will prepare for this event with caution and carry it out with discretion. Meanwhile, those of you who desire to see Pilar for the last time may do so at her cubicle. If you wish to present a floral tribute, may I suggest the nasturtiums, which are plentiful at this season. Please do not pick any of the garlic flowers, as we are saving them for propagation."

There were some tears, and some outright sobbing from the children – Pilar had been well loved. Then the Gardeners filed away. Some smiled again at Toby to show they were pleased by her promotion. Toby herself stayed where she was, because Adam One was holding on to her arm.

"Forgive me, dear Toby," he said when the rest had gone. "I apologize for my excursion into fiction. I must sometimes say things that are not transparently honest. But it is for the greater good."

Toby and Zeb were chosen to select the location for Pilar's composting, and to pre-dig the hole. Time was of the essence, said Adam One: the Gardeners did not go in for refrigeration and the weather was warm, so if they didn't compost Pilar soon she was likely to undertake the process a little too rapidly herself.

Zeb had a couple of Heritage Park groundsman suits – green overalls and shirts, with the Park logo in white. The two of them put these on and set off with a couple of shovels and rakes and a mattock and a pitchfork rattling around in the back of their truck. It was news to Toby that the Gardeners had a truck, but they did. It was a compressed-air pickup, which they kept in a pet store over in the Sewage Lagoon. An abandoned pet store – not much call for pet pampering in the Lagoon, said Zeb, because if you did have a cat there it was likely to end up in someone else's deep fryer.

The Gardeners painted different things on their truck, said Zeb, according to need. At the moment it had a Heritage Park logo on it, impeccably forged. "There's a number of ex-graphic artists in the Gardeners," said Zeb. "Of course, there's a number of ex-everything."

They drove along through the Sinkhole, honking to get the plee-brats out of their path and shooing away any who tried to force-clean their windows. "Have you done this before?" Toby asked.

"By 'this,' you mean burying old ladies illegally in public parkland? Nope," said Zeb. "No Eves died on my watch until this. But there's a first time for everything."

"How dangerous is it?" said Toby.

"Guess we'll find out," said Zeb. "Course, we could just leave her in a vacant lot for the scavengers, but she might end up in a SecretBurger. Animal protein's getting very pricey. Or she could get sold to the garboil folks, they'll take anything. We're saving her from that: old Pilar was death on oil, it was contra to her religion."

"Not to yours?" said Toby.

Zeb chuckled. "I leave the finer points of doctrine to Adam One. I just use what I have to, to get where I need to go. C'mon, let's grab a Happicuppa." He swerved into a mallway lot.

"We're drinking Happicuppa?" said Toby. "Gen-mod, sun-grown, sprayed with poisons? It kills birds, it ruins peasants – we all know that."

"We're in deep cover," said Zeb. "You have to act the part!" He winked at her, then reached across her and opened the truck door. "Cut yourself some slack. I bet you used to be a babe until the Gardeners got to you."

Used to be, thinks Toby. That about sums up everything. Never-theless she was pleased: she hadn't had a gender-weighted compliment for some time.

Happicuppa had once been a feature of such lunch breaks as she'd been able to snatch, back when she worked at SecretBurgers; it seemed a lifetime since she'd drunk any of the stuff. She ordered a Happicappuchino. She'd forgotten how delicious they could be. She drank it in sips: it could be years before she got another, if she ever did get one.

"We better go," said Zeb before she was quite finished. "We've got a hole to dig. Put your cap on, stick your hair up under it, that's how the girl parkies wear it."

"Hey, Park bitch," said a voice behind her. "Show us your shrub!" Toby was afraid to glance around. But Blanco was back in Painball again, Adam One had told her – that was the word on the street.

Zeb picked up on her fear. "If any guy bothers you, I'll hit him with the mattock," he said.

Back in the truck, they mowed their way through the pleebland streets until they reached the Heritage Parkland north gate. Zeb waved his forged pass at the gatekeepers and they drove through. The Park was officially pedestrian, so there were no vehicles other than theirs.

Zeb drove slowly, passing families of pleeblanders seated at the picnic tables with their barbecues going full blast. Rowdy groups of pleebrats were drinking and messing around. A rock bounced off the truck: the Heritage Parkies weren't armed, and the pleebrats knew that. There'd been swarmings and even fatalities, Zeb told her. Something about a bunch of trees made people think they could cut loose. "Wherever there's Nature, there's assholes," he said cheerfully.

They found a good location – a patch of open ground where the Elderberry shrub would get enough sunlight, and where they might not encounter too many tree roots while digging. Zeb set to work with the mattock, loosening the dirt; Toby shovelled. They'd put out a stand-alone sign: Planting Courtesy of HelthWyzer West. "If anyone asks, I've got the authorization," said Zeb. "Right here in my pocket. Didn't even cost that much."

When the hole was deep enough they packed up, leaving the sign in place.

Pilar's composting took place that afternoon. Pilar travelled to the site by truck, in a burlap sack labelled Mulch, with the Elderberry and a five-gallon water tank beside her. Nuala and Adam One marched the Buds and Blooms Choir through the Park, right past the burial spot, so anyone in the vicinity would be looking at them rather than at Zeb and Toby and their shrub planting. They were singing the "Mole Day Hymn" at the top of their lungs. When they came to the final verse, Shackleton and Crozier in their pleebrat T-shirt disguises jeered at them from the pathside. When Crozier tossed a bottle, the Buds and Blooms yelled and broke ranks and ran down the pathway. All the pleeblanders watched the chase with interest, hoping for violence. Zeb deftly slotted Pilar into the hole, still in her burlap sack, and positioned the Elderberry shrub on top of her. Toby shovelled and tamped; then they watered.

"Don't look mournful," Zeb told her. "Act like it's only a job."

There was another onlooker, a tall dark-haired boy. He wasn't distracted by the Buds and Blooms sideshow; he stood leaning against a tree, as if indifferent. He was wearing a black T-shirt with a slogan that said, THE LIVER IS EVIL AND MUST BE PUNISHED.

"You know that boy?" said Toby. The T-shirt looked wrong. If he was a real pleebrat it would have fit him better.

Zeb glanced over. "Him? Why?"

"He's taking an interest in us." CorpSeCorps, she thought? No. Surely too young.

"Don't stare," said Zeb. "He knew Pilar. I let him know we'd be here."

36

According to Adam One, the Fall of Man was multidimensional. The ancestral primates fell out of the trees; then they fell from vegetarianism into meat-eating. Then they fell from instinct into reason, and thus into technology; from simple signals into complex grammar, and thus into humanity; from firelessness into fire, and thence into weaponry; and from seasonal mating into an incessant sexual twitching. Then they fell from a joyous life in the moment into the anxious contemplation of the vanished past and the distant future.

The Fall was ongoing, but its trajectory led ever downward. Sucked into the well of knowledge, you could only plummet, learning more and more, but not getting any happier. And so it was with Toby, once she'd become an Eve. She could feel the Eve Six title seeping into her, eroding her, wearing away the edges of what she'd once been. It was more than a hair shirt, it was a shirt of nettles. How had she allowed herself to be sewn into it this way?

She knew more now, however. As with all knowledge, once you knew it, you couldn't imagine how it was that you hadn't known it before. Like stage magic, knowledge before you knew it took place before your very eyes, but you were looking elsewhere.

For instance: the Adams and Eves had a laptop. Toby had been shocked to discover this – wasn't such a device in direct contravention of Gardener principles? – but Adam One had reassured her: they never went online with it except with extreme precaution, they used it mostly for the storage of crucial data pertaining to the Exfernal World, and they took care to conceal such a dangerous object from the Gardener membership at large – especially the children. Nevertheless, they had one. "It's like the Vatican's porn collection," Zeb told her. "Safe in our hands."

They kept their laptop in a concealed wall compartment in the small room behind the vinegar barrels, which was also where they held the bi-weekly Adam and Eve meetings. There was a door to this room, but before Eveship had closed in around her Toby had been told there was only a closet behind it, used for bottle storage. There were indeed some shelves for empty bottles, but the whole shelf unit swung open to reveal the room's actual door. Both doors were kept locked: only the Adams and Eves had keys. Now Toby had a key too.

She ought to have realized the Adams and the Eves had some way of meeting together. They appeared to move and think as one, and they didn't use phones or computers, so how would they have made their group decisions except face to face? She must have supposed they exchanged information chemically, like trees. But no, nothing so vegetable: they sat around a table like any other conclave and hammered out their positions – theological as well as practical – as ruthlessly as medieval monks. And, as with the monks, there was increasingly much at stake. That was worrying to Toby, for the Corporations tolerated no opposition, and the Gardener stance against commercial activities in the larger sense might well come to be construed as that. So Toby was not wrapped in some otherworldly sheepfold-like cocoon, as she'd once supposed. Instead she was walking the edge of a real and potentially explosive power.

For the Gardeners, it seemed, were no longer a tiny localized cult. They were growing in influence: far from being confined to the Sinkhole Edencliff Rooftop Garden and its neighbouring rooftops and the other buildings they controlled, they had branches in different pleebs, and even in other cities. They also had cells of hidden Exfernal sympathizers embedded at every level, even within the Corporations themselves. The information provided by these sympathizers was indispensable, according to Adam One: by means of it, the intentions and movements of their enemies could be monitored, at least in part.

The cells were referred to as Truffles because they were underground, rare, and valuable, because you never could tell where they might appear next, and because pigs and dogs were employed to sniff them out. Not that the Gardeners had anything against actual Pigs and Dogs, Adam One made haste to explain – only against their enslavement by the forces of darkness.

Although they'd hidden their distress from the mass of the Gardeners, the Adams and Eves had been badly frightened by the arrest of Burt. Some claimed the CorpSeCorps would offer the age-old devil's bargain – information in exchange for your life. But the CorpSeCorps didn't need to make deals, Zeb said grimly, because once they got started on their Internal Rendition procedures a person would say anything. Who knew how many buckets of incriminating lies were being squeezed out of poor Burt, along with his blood, shit, and vomit?

So the Adams and Eves expected a CorpSeCorps raid on the Garden at any moment. They set their rapid-evacuation plans in place, and alerted the Truffle cells, who could be counted on to hide them. Then Burt had been discovered in the vacant lot behind Scales and Tails, with freezer burns on his skin and minus his vital organs.

"They want it to look like a mob hit," Zeb said at the Council meeting behind the Vinegar Room. "But it's not convincing. A mob would do more gratuitous mutilation. Fun stuff."

Nuala said it was disrespectful of Zeb to use the word *fun* in this context. Zeb said he was speaking ironically. Marushka Midwife, who rarely said anything, said that irony was overvalued. Zeb said he hadn't noticed such overvaluation much among the Gardeners. Rebecca – who was now a powerful new Eve – Eve Eleven of Nutriment Combining – said everyone should get a grip and bite their tongues. Adam One said that a house divided against itself could not stand.

A spirited debate then took place concerning the disposal of Burt's body. Burt had been an Adam, said Rebecca: he deserved to be illegally composted in the Heritage Park, like any other Adam or Eve. That would be fair. Philo the Fog – who was less foggy inside the Council Room than outside it – said this would be too dangerous: what if the CorpSeCorps had planted Burt's cadaver as bait and were watching to see who came to collect it? Stuart the Screw said the CorpSeCorps already knew Burt had been a Gardener, so what would they learn by that? Zeb said maybe dead Burt was a message from the CorpSeCorps to the pleebmobs, to tell them to tighten up their operations and root out maverick freeloaders.

Nuala said, well, if they couldn't compost poor Burt, maybe they could just go at night and sprinkle a spoonful of earth on him as a symbolic thing: she personally would feel a lot better in the Spirit if she could do that. Mugi said Burt was a meat-breath pig-eater who'd betrayed them, and he didn't know why they were even talking about this. Adam One said they should take a moment of silence and put Light around Burt in their hearts, and Zeb said they'd already put so much light around him the guy was probably burning like a suicide bomber in a fried-chicken franchise. Nuala said Zeb was being frivolous. Adam One said they should meditate overnight and perhaps the solution would arrive by visionary inspiration. Philo said in that case he'd toke up.

But the next day, Burt's corpse was no longer in the vacant lot: he'd been scooped by the early-bird garboil collectors, Zeb informed them, and was doubtless fuelling some Corps employee's cityvan. Toby asked how he was sure of that, and Zeb grinned and said he had connections among the pleebrat gangs who'd snitch on anyone if you paid them.

Adam One made a speech to the Gardener membership at large in which he outlined the fate of Burt, called him a victim seduced by the spirit of materialist greed whom they should pity rather than condemn, and asked them all to be extra vigilant and to report any overly curious tourists and especially any unusual activities.

But no unusual activities were reported. Months went by, then more months. The daily chores and teaching hours went on as usual, and the Saints' Days and Festivals kept their appointed rounds. Toby took up macramé, hoping it would cure her of idle daydreaming and fruitless desires, and increase her focus on the moment. The bees increased and multiplied, and Toby delivered the news to them every morning. The moon emerged from darkness, then plumped out, then dwindled. Several babies appeared, and an infestation of shiny green beetles, and a number of new Gardener converts. The sands of time are quicksands, said Adam One. So much can sink into them without a trace. And what a blessing when those things that sink away are needless worries.

APRIL FISH

YEAR FOURTEEN.

OF THE FOOLISHNESS WITHIN ALL RELIGIONS.
SPOKEN BY ADAM ONE.

Dear Friends, dear Fellow Creatures and Fellow Mortals:

What a fun-filled April Fish Day we have had, here on our Edencliff Rooftop Garden! This year's Fish lanterns, modelled on the phosphorescent Fish that adorn the depths of the Ocean, are the most effective yet, and the Fish cakes look delectable! We have Rebecca and her special helpers, Amanda and Ren, to thank for these toothsome confections.

Our Children always enjoy this day, as it allows them to make fun of their elders; and as long as that fun does not get out of hand, we elders welcome it, as it reminds us of our own childhoods. It never hurts us to remember how small we felt then, and how we depended on the strength, knowledge, and wisdom of our elders to keep us safe. Let us teach our Children tolerance, and loving-kindness, and correct boundaries, as well as joyful laughter. As God contains all things good, He must also contain a sense of playfulness – a gift he has shared with Creatures other than ourselves, as witness the tricks Crows play, and the sportiveness of Squirrels, and the frolicking of Kittens.

On April Fish Day, which originated in France, we make fun of one another by attaching a Fish of paper, or, in our case, a Fish of recycled cloth, to the back of another person and then crying out, "April Fish!" Or, in the original French, "Poisson d'Avril!" In anglophone countries, this day is known as April Fool's Day. But April Fish was surely first a Christian festival, as a Fish image was used by the early Christians as secret signals of their faith in times of oppression.

The Fish was an apt symbol, for Jesus first called as his Apostles two fishermen, surely chosen by him to help conserve the Fish population.

They were told to be fishers of men *instead of* being fishers of Fish, thus neutralizing two destroyers of Fish! That Jesus was mindful of the Birds, the Animals, and the Plants is clear from his remarks on Sparrows, Hens, Lambs, and Lilies; but he understood that most of God's Garden was under water and that it, too, needed tending. Saint Francis of Assisi preached a sermon to the Fish, not realizing that the Fish commune directly with God. Still, the Saint was affirming the respect due to them. How prophetic does this appear, now that the world's Oceans are being laid waste!

Others may take the Specist view that we Humans are smarter than Fish, and thus an April Fish is being marked as mute and foolish. But the life of the Spirit always seems foolish to those who do not share it: therefore we must accept and wear the label of God's Fools gladly, for in relation to God we are all fools, no matter how wise we may think we are. To be an April Fish is to humbly accept our own silliness, and to cheerfully admit the absurdity – from a materialist view – of every Spiritual truth we profess.

Please join me now in a Meditation on our Fish brethren.

Dear God, You who created the great and wide Sea, with its Creatures innumerable: we pray that You hold in your gaze those who dwell in Your underwater Garden, in which Life originated; and we pray that none may vanish from the Earth by Human agency. Let Love and aid be brought to the Sea Creatures in their present peril and great suffering; which has come to them through the warming of the Sea, and through the dragging of nets and hooks along the bottom of it, and through the slaughtering of all within it, from the Creatures of the shallows to the Creatures of the depths, the Giant Squid included; and remember your Whales, that You created on the fifth day, and set in the Sea to play therein; and bring help especially to the Sharks, that misunderstood and much-persecuted breed.

We hold in our minds the Great Dead Zone in the Gulf of Mexico; and the Great Dead Zone in Lake Erie; and the Great Dead Zone in the

Black Sea; and the desolate Grand Banks of Newfoundland, where the Cod once abounded; and the Great Barrier Reef, now dying and bleaching white and breaking apart.

Let them come to Life again; let Love shine upon them and restore them; and let us be forgiven for our oceanic murders; and for our foolishness, when it is the wrong kind of foolishness, being arrogant and destructive.

And help us to accept in all humility our kinship with the Fishes, who appear to us as mute and foolish; for in Your sight, we are all mute and foolish.

Let us sing.

OH LORD, YOU KNOW OUR FOOLISHNESS

Oh Lord, You know our foolishness,
And all our silly deeds;
You watch us scamper here and there,
Pursuing useless greeds.

We sometimes doubt that You are Love,
And we forget to thank;
We find the Sky an empty void,
The Universe a blank.

We fall into despondency,
And curse the hour that bore us;
We either claim You don't exist,
Or else that You ignore us.

So pardon us these vacant moods,
Our dour and gloomy sayings;
Today we own ourselves Your Fools,
And celebrate by playing.

We make a full acknowledgment
Of all in us that's vain –
Our petty strifes and tiny woes,
Our self-inflicted pain.

At April Fish we jest and sing
And laugh with childish glee;
We puncture pomp and puffed-up pride,
And smile at all we see.

Your starry World's beyond our thought,
And wondrous without measure;
We pray, among Your Treasures bright,
Your Fools You'll also treasure.

From *The God's Gardeners Oral Hymnbook*

37

I must have dozed off – being in the Sticky Zone makes you tired – because I was dreaming about Amanda. She was walking towards me in her khaki outfit through a wide field of dry grass with many white bones in it. There were vultures flying over her head. But she saw me dreaming her, and she smiled and waved at me, and I woke up.

It was too early to really go to sleep, so I did my toenails. Starlite liked the claw effect with spider-silk strengtheners, but I never used that because Mordis said it would be an image brainfry, like a bunny with spikes. So I stuck to the pastels. Shiny new toes make you feel all fresh and sparkling: if someone wants to suck your toes, those toes should be worth sucking. While the polish was drying I went to the intercom camera in the room I shared with Starlite. It cheered me up to connect with my own things – my dresser, my Robodog, my costumes on their hangers. I could hardly wait to be back in my normal life. Not that it was normal exactly. But I was used to it.

Then I surfed the Net, looking for the horoscope sites to see what sort of week was coming up, because I'd be out of the Sticky Zone very soon if my tests were clear. Wild Stars was my favourite: I liked it because it was so encouraging.

> The Moon in your sign, Scorpio, means your hormones are pumped this week! It's hot, hot, hot! Enjoy, but don't take this sexy flareup too seriously – it will pass.

You're working hard now at making your home a pleasure palace. Time to
buy those new satin sheets and slip between them! You'll be pampering
all your Taurean senses this week!

I was hoping that romance and adventure might be heading
my way, once I got out of the Sticky Zone. And maybe travel, or spiritual quests – sometimes they had those. But my own horoscope wasn't
so good:

Messenger Mercury in your sign, Pisces, means that things and people
from the past will surprise you in the coming weeks. Be prepared for
some quick transitions! Romance may take strange forms – illusion and
reality are dancing closely together right now, so tread carefully!

I didn't like the sound of romance taking strange forms. I got
enough of that at work.

When I checked in on the Snakepit again, it was really crowded. Savona
was still on the trapeze, and Crimson Petal was up there too, in a Biofilm
Bodysuit with extra genital ruffles so she looked like a giant orchid.
Down below, Starlite was still working away on her Painballer customer.
That girl could raise the dead, but he was so close to being unconscious
that I didn't think she'd be getting a big tip out of him.

The CorpSeCorps minders were hovering, but suddenly they all
looked in the direction of the entranceway, so I went to another camera
and had a look myself. Mordis was over there, talking to a couple more
CorpSeCorps guys. They had another Painballer in tow, who looked in
even worse shape than the first three. More explosive. Mordis wasn't
happy. Four of those Painballers – that was a lot to handle. And what if
they were from different teams and just yesterday they were trying to
disembowel each other?

Mordis was herding the new Painballer to the far corner. Now he
was barking into his cell; now three backup dancers were hurrying over:

Vilya, Crenola, Sunset. Block the view, he must've told them. Use your tits, why in hell did God make them? There was a shimmering, a flurry of feathers, six arms twining around him. I could almost hear what Vilya was saying into the guy's ear: *Take two, honey, they're cheap.*

A signal from Mordis and the music got louder: loud music distracts them, they're less likely to rampage with their ears full of sound. Now the dancers were all over this guy like anacondas. Two Scales bouncers on standby.

Mordis was grinning: situation solved. He'd steer this one into the feather-ceiling rooms, dump in some alcohol, stick some girls on top of him, and he'd be what Mordis called one blitzed-out brain-dead squeeze-dried happy zombie. And now that we had BlyssPluss, he'd get multiple orgasms and wuzzy comfy feelings, with no microbe-death downside. The furniture breakage at Scales had tanked since they'd been using that stuff. They were serving it in chocolate-dipped polyberries, and in Soylectable olives – though you had to make sure not to overdo it, said Starlite, or the guy's dick might split.

38

In Year Fourteen, we had April Fish Day as usual. On that day you were supposed to act silly and laugh a lot. I pinned a fish onto Shackie, and Croze pinned a fish onto me, and Shackie pinned a fish onto Amanda. A lot of kids pinned fish onto Nuala, but nobody pinned a fish onto Toby because you couldn't get behind her without her knowing. Adam One pinned a fish onto himself to make some point about God. That little brat Oates ran around shouting, "Fish fingers" and poking his fingers into people from behind until Rebecca made him stop. Then he was sad, so I took him into the corner and told him the story about the Littlest Vulture. He was a sweet boy when he wasn't being a pest.

Zeb was away on one of his trips – he'd been going away more lately. Lucerne stayed home: she said she had nothing to celebrate, and it was a stupid festival anyway.

It was my first April Fish without Bernice. We'd always decorated a Fish Cake together when we were little, before Amanda arrived. We'd fight all the time about what to put on it. Once we'd made our cake green, with spinach for the green colour, with eyes of carrot rounds. It looked really toxic. Thinking about that cake made me want to cry. Where was Bernice now? I felt ashamed of myself, for being so unkind to her. What if she was dead, like Burt? If she was, it was partly my fault. Mostly my fault. My fault.

Amanda and I walked back to the Cheese Factory, and Shackie and Croze walked with us – to protect us, they said. Amanda laughed at that but said they could come with us if they liked. The four of us were more or less friends again, though every once in a while Croze would say to Amanda, "You still owe us," and Amanda would tell him to get knotted.

By the time we got back to the Cheese Factory it was dark. We thought we'd be in trouble for being so late – Lucerne was always warning us about the dangers of the street – but it turned out that Zeb was back, and already they were having a fight. So we went into the hall to wait it out, because their fights took up all the room in our place.

This fight was louder than usual. A piece of furniture toppled over, or was thrown: Lucerne, it must have been, because Zeb wasn't a thrower.

"What's it about?" I said to Amanda. She had her ear against the door. She was shameless about eavesdropping.

"I dunno," she said. "She's yelling too loud. Oh wait – she says he's having sex with Nuala."

"Not Nuala," I said. "He wouldn't!" Now I knew how Bernice must have felt when we'd said all that about her father.

"Men'll have sex with anything, given the chance," said Amanda. "Now she's saying he's a pimp at heart. And he despises her and treats her like shit. I think she's crying."

"Maybe we should stop listening," I said.

"Okay," said Amanda. We stayed with our backs against the wall, waiting until Lucerne would start wailing. As she always did. Then Zeb would stomp out and slam the door, and we might not see him for days.

Zeb came out. "See you around, Queens of the Night," he said. "Watch your backs." He was joking with us the way he liked to do, but there wasn't any fun behind it. He looked grim.

Usually after their fights Lucerne would go to bed and cry, but this night she started packing a bag. The bag was a pink backpack Amanda and I had gleaned. There wasn't much for Lucerne put into it, so quite soon she finished her packing and came into our cubicle.

Amanda and I were pretending to be asleep, on our husk-filled futons, under our blue-jean quilts. "Get up, Ren," Lucerne said to me. "We're going."

"Where?" I said.

"Back," she said. "To the HelthWyzer Compound."

"Right now?"

"Yes. Why are you looking like that? It's what you've always wanted." It's true that I'd longed for the HelthWyzer Compound, once. I'd been homesick for it. But ever since Amanda'd moved in, I hadn't been thinking about it too much.

"Amanda's coming too?" I said.

"Amanda's staying here."

I felt very cold. "I want Amanda to come," I said.

"Out of the question," said Lucerne. Something else had now happened, it seemed: Lucerne had cast off her paralyzing spell, the spell of Zeb. She'd stepped out of sex as if out of a loose dress. Now she was brisk, decisive, no nonsense. Had she been like that before, long ago? I could scarcely remember.

"Why?" I said. "Why can't Amanda come?"

"Because they won't let her in at HelthWyzer. We can get our identities back there, but she doesn't have one, and I certainly don't have the money to buy her one. They'll take care of her here," she added, as if Amanda was a kitten I was being forced to abandon.

"No way," I said. "If she's not coming, I'm not!"

"And where would you live, here?" said Lucerne with contempt.

"We'll stay with Zeb," I said.

"He's never home," said Lucerne. "You don't think they'd let two young girls camp out by themselves!"

"Then we can live with Adam One," I said. "Or Nuala. Or maybe Katuro."

"Or Stuart the Screw," said Amanda hopefully. This was desperate – Stuart was dour and a loner – but I grabbed the idea.

"We can help him make furniture," I said. I imagined the whole scenario – Amanda and me collecting pieces of junk for Stuart, sawing and hammering and singing as we worked, making herbal tea . . .

"You won't be welcome," said Lucerne. "Stuart is a misanthrope. He only tolerates you kids because of Zeb, and it's the same with all the others."

"We'll stay with Toby," I said.

"Toby has other things to do. Now that's enough. If Amanda can't find someone who'll take her in, she can always go back to the pleebrats. She belongs with them, anyway. You don't. Now, hurry up."

"I need to put on my clothes," I said.

"Fine," said Lucerne. "Ten minutes." She left the cubicle.

"What'll we do?" I whispered to Amanda as I started to dress.

"I don't know," Amanda whispered back. "Once you're in there she'll never let you out. Those Compounds are like castles, they're like jails. She won't ever let you see me. She hates me."

"I don't care what she thinks," I whispered. "I'll get out somehow."

"My phone," Amanda whispered. "Take it with you. You can phone me."

"I'll get you in somehow," I said. By this time I was crying silently. I slipped her purple phone into my pocket.

"Hurry up, Ren," said Lucerne.

"I'll call you!" I whispered. "My dad will buy you an identity!"

"Sure he will," said Amanda softly. "Don't take shit, okay?"

In the main room, Lucerne was moving fast. She dumped out the sickly looking tomato plant she'd been growing on the windowsill. Underneath the soil there was a plastic bag full of money. She must've been ripping it off, from selling stuff at the Tree of Life – the soap, the vinegar, the macramé, the quilts. Money was old-fashioned, but people still used it for small things and the Gardeners wouldn't take virtual money because they didn't allow computers. So she'd been stashing away her escape money. She hadn't been such a doormat as I'd thought.

Then she took the kitchen shears and cut off her long hair, straight across at neck level. The cutting made a Velcro sound – scratchy and dry. She left the pile of hair in the middle of the dining-room table.

Then she took me by the arm and hauled me out of our place and down the stairs. She never went out at night because of the drunks and druggies on the street corners, and the pleebrat gangs and muggers. But right then she was white-hot with anger and filled with crackling energy: people on the street cleared out of our path as if we were contagious, and even the Asian Fusions and the Blackened Redfish left us alone.

It took us hours to get through the Sinkhole and the Sewage Lagoon, and then the richer pleebs. As we went along, the houses and buildings and hotels got newer looking, and the streets emptier of people. In Big Box we got a solarcab: we drove through Golfgreens and then past a big open space, and finally right up to the gates of the HelthWyzer Compound. It was so long since I'd seen that place it was like one of those dreams, where you don't recognize anything, yet also you do. I felt a little sick, but that might have been excitement.

Before we got into the cab, Lucerne had mussed up my hair and smeared dirt on her own face, and torn part of her dress. "Why'd you do that?" I said. But she didn't answer.

There were two guards at the HelthWyzer gateway, behind the little window. "Identities?" they said.

"We don't have any," said Lucerne. "They were stolen. We were forcibly abducted." She looked behind her, as if she was afraid someone was following us. "Please – you have to let us in, right away! My husband – he's in Nanobioforms. He'll tell you who I am." She started to cry.

One of them reached for the phone, pushed a button. "Frank," he said. "Main gate. Lady here says she's your wife."

"We'll need some cheek swabs, ma'am, for the communicables," said the second one. "Then you can wait in the holding room, pending bioform clearance and verification. Someone will be with you soon."

In the holding room we sat on a black vinyl sofa. It was five in the morning. Lucerne picked up a magazine – *NooSkins*, it said on the cover. *Why Live With Imperfection?* She riffled through it.

"Were we forcibly abducted?" I asked her.

"Oh, my darling," she said. "You don't remember! You were too young! I didn't want to tell you – I didn't want you to be frightened! They might have done something terrible to you!" Then she began to cry again, harder. By the time the CorpSeMan in the biosuit walked in, her face was all streaky.

39

Be careful what you wish for, old Pilar used to say. I was back at the HelthWyzer Compound and I was reunited with my father, just as I used to wish long ago. But nothing felt right. All that faux marble, and the reproduction antique furniture, and the carpets in our house – none of it seemed real. It smelled funny too – like disinfectant. I missed the leafy smells, of the Gardeners, the cooking smells, even the sharp vinegar tang; even the violet biolets.

My father – Frank – hadn't changed my room. But the four-poster bed and the pink curtains looked shrunken. It also looked too young for me. There were the plush animals I'd once loved so much, but their glass eyes looked dead. I stuffed them into the back of my closet so they wouldn't be able to look through me as if I was a shadow.

The first night, Lucerne ran a bath for me with fake-flower bath essence in it. The big white tub and the white fluffy towels made me feel dirty, and also stinky. I stank like earth – compost earth, before it's finished. That sour odour.

Also my skin was blue: it was the dye from the Gardener clothes. I'd never really noticed it because the showers at the Gardeners were so brief, and there weren't any mirrors. I hadn't noticed, either, how hairy I'd become, and that was more of a shock than my blue skin. I rubbed and rubbed at the blue: it wouldn't come off. I looked at my toes, where they stuck up out of the bath water. The toenails looked like claws.

"Let's put some polish on those," Lucerne said two days later, when she saw my feet in flip-flops. She was acting as if none of it had ever happened – not the Gardeners, not Amanda, and especially not Zeb. She was wearing crisp linen suits, she'd had her hair styled and streaked. She'd already had her own toes done – she'd wasted no time. "Look at all these colours I bought for you! Green, purple, frosted orange, and I got you some sparkly ones . . ." But I was angry with her, and I turned away. She was such a liar.

All those years I'd kept an outline of my father in my head, like a chalk line enclosing a father-shaped space. When I was little, I'd coloured it in often enough. But those colours had been too bright, and the outline had been too large: Frank was shorter, greyer, balder, and more confused-looking than what I'd had in mind.

Before he'd come to the HelthWyzer gatehouse to identify us, I'd thought he'd be overjoyed to find that we were safe and sound and not dead after all. But when he saw me, his face fell. Now I realize that he'd last known me when I was a small girl, so I was bigger than he expected, and probably bigger than he wanted. I was also shabbier – despite the drab Gardener clothes, I must have looked like one of the pleebrats he might have seen running around if he'd ever even been to the Sinkhole or the Sewage Lagoon. Maybe he was afraid I was going to pick his pockets or grab his shoes. He approached me as if I might bite, and put his arms awkwardly around me. He smelled of complex chemicals – the kind of chemicals used for cleaning off sticky things, like glue. A smell that could burn right down into your lungs.

On that first night I slept for twelve hours, and when I woke up I found that Lucerne had taken away my Gardener clothes and burnt them. Luckily I'd hidden Amanda's purple phone inside the plush tiger in my closet – I'd cut open the stomach. So the phone didn't get burnt.

I missed the smell of my own skin, which had lost its salty flavour and was now soapy and perfumy. I thought about what Zeb used to say about mice – if you take them out of the mouse nest for a while and then put them back, the other mice will tear them apart. If I went back to the Gardeners with my fake-flower smell, would they tear me apart?

‖
‖
‖

Lucerne took me to the HelthWyzer In-clinic so I could be checked for head lice and worms, and for being interfered with. That meant a couple of fingers up you, front and back. "Oh my goodness," the doctor said when he saw my blue skin. "Are these bruises, dear?"

"No," I said. "It's dye."

"Oh," he said. "They made you dye yourself?"

"It's in the clothes," I said.

"I see," he said. Then he made an appointment for me with the In-clinic psychiatrist, who had experience with people who'd been snatched by cults. My mother would have to be at those appointments as well.

Which was how I found out what Lucerne was telling them. We'd been grabbed off the street while in SolarSpace doing some boutique shopping, but she couldn't say exactly where we'd been taken because she'd never been allowed to know. She said it wasn't the fault of the cult itself – it was one of the male members who'd been obsessed with her and wanted her for his personal sex slave, and had taken away her shoes to keep her captive. This was supposed to be Zeb, though she said she didn't know his name. I'd been too young to realize what was going on, she said, but I'd been a hostage – she'd had to do the bidding of this madman, service his every twisted whim, it was revolting the things he'd made her do – or my life would have been in danger. But she'd finally been able to share her plight with one of the other cult members – a sort of nun. She must have meant Toby. It was this woman who'd helped her to escape – brought her shoes, given her money, lured the madman away so Lucerne could make a dash for freedom.

It was no use asking me anything, she said. The cult members had been nice to me, and anyway they'd been duped. She'd been the only one who'd known the truth: it was a burden she'd had to carry alone. What woman who loved her child as much as she loved me wouldn't have done the same?

Before our psychiatry sessions, she'd squeeze my shoulder and say, "Amanda's back there. Keep that in mind." Meaning that if I told anyone she'd been lying her hair off she'd suddenly remember where she'd been imprisoned, and the CorpSeCorps would go in there with their spray-guns, and who knew what might happen? Bystanders got killed a lot in spraygun attacks. It couldn't be helped, said the CorpSeCorps. It was in the interests of public order.

For weeks Lucerne hovered around to make sure I wouldn't try to run away or else rat on her. But at last I got a chance to take out Amanda's purple phone and call. Amanda had texted me with the number of the new phone she'd lifted, so I'd know where to reach her – she thought ahead about everything. I sat inside my closet to make the call. It had a light inside, like all the closets in the house. The closet itself was as big as my former sleeping cubicle.

Amanda answered right away. There she was on the screen, looking the same as ever. I longed to be back at the Gardeners.

"I really miss you," I said. "I'm running away as soon as I can." But I didn't know when that would be, I said, because Lucerne was keeping my identity locked in a drawer, and I wouldn't be allowed past the gate-house without it.

"Can't you trade?" said Amanda. "With the guards?"

"No," I said. "I don't think so. It's different here."

"Oh. What happened to your hair?"

"Lucerne made me cut it."

"It looks okay," said Amanda. Then she said, "They found Burt dumped in the vacant lot, out behind Scales. He had freezer burns."

"He'd been in a freezer?"

"What was left. There were parts missing – liver, kidneys, heart. Zeb says the mobs will sell the parts, then keep the rest in the freezer until they need to send a message."

"Ren! Where are you?" It was Lucerne, in my room.

"I have to go," I whispered. I tucked the phone back into the tiger. "In here," I said. My teeth were chattering. Freezers were so cold.

"What are you doing in the closet, darling?" said Lucerne. "Come and have some lunch! You'll feel better soon!" She sounded chirpy: the crazier and more disturbed I acted, the better it was for her, because the less anyone would believe me if I told on her.

Her story was that I'd been traumatized by being stuck in among the warped, brainwashing cult folk. I had no way of proving her wrong. Anyway maybe I had been traumatized: I had nothing to compare myself with.

40

Once I'd adjusted enough – *adjusted* was the word they used, as if I was a bra strap – Lucerne said I had to go to school because it was bad for me to be moping around the house: I needed to get out and make a whole new life for myself, as she was doing. It was a risk for her – I was a walking cluster bomb, the truth about her might come popping out of my mouth at any time. But she knew I was judging her silently, and that annoyed her, so she really wanted me elsewhere.

Frank seemed to have believed her story, though he didn't seem to care about it one way or the other. I could see now why Lucerne had run off with Zeb: at least Zeb had noticed her. And he'd noticed me, as well, whereas Frank treated me like a window: he never looked at me, only through me.

Sometimes I dreamed about Zeb. He'd be wearing a bear suit, and the fur would unzip down the middle like a pyjama bag, and Zeb would step out. He'd smell comforting, in the dream – like rained-on grass, and cinnamon, and the salty, vinegary, singed-leaf smell of the Gardeners.

The school was called HelthWyzer High. On the first day I put on one of the new outfits that Lucerne had picked out for me. It was pink and lemon yellow – colours the Gardeners never would have allowed because they'd show the dirt and waste the soap.

My new clothes felt like a disguise. I couldn't get used to how tight they were compared to my old loose dresses, and how my bare arms stuck out from the sleeves and my bare legs came out from the bottom of the knee-length, pleated skirt. But this was what the girls at HelthWyzer High all wore, according to Lucerne.

"Don't forget your sunblock, Brenda," she said as I headed towards the door. She was calling me Brenda now: she claimed it was my real name.

HelthWyzer sent a student to be my guide – walk me to the school, show me around. Her name was Wakulla Price; she was thin, with glossy skin like toffee. She was wearing a pastel yellow top like mine, but she had pants on the bottom. She gazed at my pleated skirt, her eyes wide. "I like your skirt," she said.

"My mother bought it," I said.

"Oh," she said in a *sorry* voice. "My mother bought me one like that two years ago." So I liked her.

On the way to school, Wakulla said, *What does your dad do, when did you get here*, and so on, but she didn't mention any cults; and I said, *How do you like the school, who are the teachers*, and that got us safely there. The houses we were passing were all different styles, but with solarskins. They had the latest tech in the Compounds, which Lucerne had pointed out a lot. *Really, Brenda, they're so much more truly green than those purist Gardeners so you don't have to worry about how much hot water you're using, and isn't it time you took another shower?*

The high-school building was sparkling clean – no graffiti, no pieces falling off, no smashed windows. It had a deep green lawn and some shrubs pruned into round balls, and a statue: "Florence Nightingale," it said on the plaque, "The Lady of the Lamp." But someone had changed the *a* to a *u*, so it said The Lady of the Lump.

"Jimmy did that," said Wakulla. "He's my lab partner in Nanoforms Biotech, he's always doing dumb things like that." She smiled: she had really white teeth. Lucerne had been saying how dingy my own teeth were and I needed a cosmetic dentist. She was already planning to redecorate our entire house, but she had some alterations planned for me as well.

At least I didn't have any cavities. The Gardeners were against refined sugar products and were strict about brushing, though you had to use a frayed twig because they hated the idea of putting either plastic or animal bristles inside their mouths.

The first morning at that school was very strange. I felt as if the classes were in a foreign language. All the subjects were different, the words were different, and then there were the computers and the paper notebooks. I had a built-in fear of those: it seemed so dangerous, all that permanent writing that your enemies could find – you couldn't just wipe it away, not like a slate. I wanted to run into the washroom and wash my hands after touching the keyboards and pages; the danger had surely rubbed off on me.

Lucerne said that our so-called personal history – the forcible abduction and so on – would be kept confidential by the officials at the HelthWyzer Compound. But someone had leaked because the kids at the school all knew. At least they hadn't heard about Lucerne's sex-slave lust-mad pervert story. But I knew I'd lie about that if I had to, in order to protect Amanda, and Zeb, and Adam One, and even the ordinary Gardeners. We are all in one another's hands, Adam One used to say. I was beginning to find out what that meant.

At lunch hour a group gathered around me. Not a mean group, just curious. *So, you lived with a cult? Weird! How crazy were they?* They had a lot of questions. Meanwhile they were eating their lunches, and there was meat smell everywhere. Bacon. Fish sticks, 20 per cent real fish. Burgers – they were called WyzeBurgers, and they were made of meat cultured on stretchy racks. So no animals had actually been killed. But it still smelled like meat. Amanda would've eaten the bacon to show she hadn't been brainwashed by the leaf-eaters, but I couldn't go that far. I peeled the bun off my WyzeBurger and tried to eat that, but it stank of dead animal.

"Like, how bad was it?" said Wakulla.

"It was just a greenie cult," I said.

"Like the Wolf Isaiahists," said one kid. "Were they terrorists?" They all leaned forward: they wanted horror stories.

"No. They were pacifists," I said. "We had to work on this rooftop garden." And I told them about the slug and snail relocation. It sounded so strange to me, when I told it.

"At least you didn't eat them," said one girl. "Some of those cults, they eat road kill."

"The Wolf Isaiahists do, for sure. It was on the Web."

"You lived in the pleebs, though. Cool." Then I realized I had an edge, because I'd lived in the pleeblands where none of them had ever been except maybe on a school trip, or dragged along with their slumming parents to the Tree of Life. So I could make up whatever I liked.

"You were child labour," one boy said. "A little enviroserf. Sexy!" They all laughed.

"Jimmy, don't be so dumb," said Wakulla. "It's okay," she said to me, "he always says stuff like that."

Jimmy grinned. "Did you worship cabbages?" he went on. "Oh Great Cabbage, I kiss your cabbagey cabbageness!" He went down on one knee and grabbed a handful of my pleated skirt. "Nice leaves, do they come off?"

"Don't be such a meat-breath," I said.

"A what?" he said, laughing. "A meat-breath?"

Then I had to explain how that was a harsh name to call someone, among the extreme greens. Like pig-eater. Like slug-face. This made Jimmy laugh more.

I saw the temptation. I saw it clearly. I would come up with more bizarre details about my cultish life, and then I would pretend that I thought all these things were as warped as the HelthWyzer kids did. That would be popular. But also I saw myself the way the Adams and the Eves would see me: with sadness, with disappointment. Adam One, and Toby, and Rebecca. And Pilar, even though she was dead. And even Zeb.

How easy it is, treachery. You just slide into it. But I knew that already, because of Bernice.

Wakulla walked home with me, and Jimmy came too. He fooled around a lot – made jokes, expected us to laugh – and Wakulla did laugh, in a polite way. I could see that Jimmy had a big crush on her, though Wakulla told me later that she couldn't see Jimmy in any way other than as a friend.

Wakulla turned off halfway to go to her house, and Jimmy said he'd continue along with me because it was on the way. He was irritating when there was more than one other person: maybe he felt it was better to make a fool of yourself than to have other people do it for you. But when he wasn't putting on an act he was much nicer. I could tell he was sad underneath, because I was that way myself. We were sort of like twins in that way, or so I felt at the time. He was the first boy I'd ever really had for a friend.

"So, it must be weird for you, being here in a Compound, after the pleeblands," he said one day.

"Yeah," I said.

"Was your mom really tied to the bed by a deranged maniac?" Jimmy would come right out with stuff other people might think but would never say.

"Where did you hear that?" I said.

"Locker room," said Jimmy. So Lucerne's fable had seeped out.

I took a deep breath. "This is between us, right?"

"Cross my heart," said Jimmy.

"No," I said. "She wasn't tied to the bed."

"Didn't think so," said Jimmy.

"But don't tell that to anyone. I really trust you not to."

"I won't," said Jimmy. He didn't say, *Why not*. He knew that if everyone heard Lucerne had been bullshitting, people would know she hadn't been kidnapped, she'd merely cheated big time. What she'd done had been for love, or just sex. And she was back at HelthWyzer with her loser of a husband because the other guy had tossed her over. But she'd rather die than admit it. Or else she'd rather kill someone.

All this time I was going into my closet and taking the purple cellphone out of my tiger and phoning Amanda. We'd text each other with the best times to call, and if the connection was good we could see each other onscreen. I asked a lot of questions about the Gardeners. Amanda told me she wasn't staying with Zeb any more – Adam One said she was almost grown up so she had to sleep in one of the singles cubicles, and that was pretty boring. "When can you get back here?" she said. But I didn't know how I could manage to run away from HelthWyzer.

"I'm working on it," I said.

The next time we were on the phone she said, "Look who's here," and it was Shackie, grinning at me sheepishly, and I wondered if they'd been having sex together. I felt as if Amanda had scooped some glittery piece of junk I wanted for myself, but that was stupid because I had no feelings for Shackie whatsoever. I did wonder whether it had been his hand on my bum, that night I passed out in the holospinner. But most likely it was Croze.

"How's Croze?" I said to Shackie. "And Oates?"

"They're fine," Shackie mumbled. "When're you coming back? Croze really misses you! Gang, right?"

"Grene," I said. "Gangrene." I was surprised he'd still use that old kidstuff password, but maybe Amanda had put him up to it so I'd feel included.

After Shackie went offscreen, Amanda said they were partners – the two of them were boosting things from malls. But it was a fair trade: she got someone watching her back and helping her lift stuff and sell it, and he got sex.

"Don't you love him?" I said.

Amanda said I was a romantic. She said love was useless, because it led you into dumb exchanges in which you gave too much away, and then you got bitter and mean.

41

Jimmy and I started doing our homework together. He was really nice about helping me with the parts I didn't know. Because of all that memorizing we'd had to do at the Gardeners, I could stare at a lesson and then see everything inside my head, like a picture. So although it was hard for me and I felt I was way behind, I started to catch up quite fast.

Because he was two years ahead of me, Jimmy wasn't in any of my classes except for Life Skills, which was supposed to help you structure your life, once you had one. They mixed up the age groups in Life Skills so we could benefit from sharing our different life experiences, and Jimmy traded desks so he was sitting right behind me. "I'm your body-guard," he whispered, which made me feel safe.

We went to my place to do our homework if Lucerne wasn't there; if she was, we went to Jimmy's. I liked Jimmy's place better because he had a pet rakunk – it was a new splice, half skunk but without the smell, half raccoon but without the aggression. Her name was Killer; she was one of the first ones they'd made. When I picked her up, she liked me right away.

Jimmy's mother seemed to like me as well, though the first time she saw me she looked at me very hard with her stern blue eyes and asked me how old I was. I liked her all right too, although she smoked too much, which made me cough. Nobody at the Gardeners smoked, or at least not cigarettes. She worked on a computer a lot, but I couldn't figure out what she did on it, because she didn't have a job. His father was hardly ever there – he was at the labs, figuring out how to transplant human stem cells and DNA into pigs, to grow new human pieces. I asked Jimmy what pieces, and he said kidneys, but maybe it was lungs too – in the future you'd be able to get your very own pig made, with second copies of everything. I knew what the Gardeners would think of that: they would think it was bad, because of having to kill the pigs.

Jimmy had seen these pigs: their nickname was pigoon, like pig balloon, because they were so big. The double-organ methods were proprietary secrets, he said: extra valuable. "Aren't you worried some foreign Corps will kidnap your dad and squeeze the secrets out of his brain?" I said. That was happening more often: they kept it out of the news, but there was gossip at HelthWyzer. Sometimes they got the kidnapped scientists back, sometimes they didn't. The security was getting tighter and tighter.

After doing our homework Jimmy and I would hang out at the HelthWyzer mall and play tame video games and drink Happicappuchinos. The first time, I told him Happicuppa was the brew of evil so I couldn't drink it, and he laughed at me. The second time I made an effort, and it tasted delicious, and soon I wasn't thinking too much about the evilness of it.

After a while Jimmy talked to me about Wakulla Price. He said she was the first girl he'd ever been in love with, but when he'd asked her to get serious with him she'd said they could only be friends. I knew that part already, but I said that was too bad, and Jimmy said he'd been a puddle of dog vomit for weeks and he still hadn't got over it.

Then he asked if I had a boyfriend back in the pleebs, and I said yes – which wasn't true – but since I had no way of getting back there I'd decided to forget about him because that was the best thing to do if you wanted someone you couldn't have. Jimmy was really sympathetic about my lost boyfriend, and he squeezed my hand. Then I felt guilty for telling such a lie; but I wasn't sorry about the squeezing.

By this time I had a diary – all the girls at school had them, it was a retro craze: people could hack your computer, but they couldn't hack a paper book. I wrote all of this down in my diary. It was like talking to someone. I didn't even think that writing things down was that dangerous any more: I guess that shows how far away from the Gardeners I'd grown already. I kept my diary in the closet, inside a stuffed bear, because I didn't want Lucerne snooping on me. The Gardeners were right about that part: reading someone else's secret words does give you power over them.

Then a new boy came to HelthWyzer High. His name was Glenn, and as soon as I saw him I knew he was the same Glenn who'd come to the Tree of Life on the Saint Euell's Week when Amanda and I had walked him over with that jar of honey to visit Pilar. I thought he gave me a little nod – did he recognize me? I hoped not, because I didn't want him to start talking about where he'd seen me last. What if the CorpSeCorps were still trying to track down Lucerne's pretend sex-slaver? What if they found Zeb through me and he ended up without his parts, in a freezer? That was a horrifying thought.

But surely even if he did remember me, Glenn wouldn't say anything because he wouldn't want them finding out about Pilar and the Gardeners and whatever he'd been doing with them. I was sure it was something illegal, or why would Pilar have sent Amanda and me away? It must have been to protect us.

Glenn acted like he didn't care about anybody, him and his black T-shirts. But after a while Jimmy started hanging out with him, and then I wasn't seeing so much of Jimmy.

"What do you do with that Glenn? He's creepy," I said one afternoon when we were doing our homework on the school library computers. Jimmy said they only played three-dimensional chess or online video games, at his place or else at Glenn's. I thought they were probably watching porn – most of the guys did, and a lot of girls too – so I asked what games. Barbarian Stomp, he said – that was a war game. Blood and Roses was like Monopoly, only you had to corner the genocide and atrocity market. Extinctathon was a trivia game you played with extinct animals.

"Maybe I could come over one day and play too," I said, but he didn't go for that. So I guessed that they really were watching porn.

≡

Then a really bad thing happened: Jimmy's mother disappeared. Not kidnapped, they said: she'd gone on her own. I heard Lucerne talking about it to Frank: it seemed that Jimmy's mother had made off with a lot of crucial data, so the CorpSeCorps were all over Jimmy's house like a rash. And since Jimmy was such a buddy of mine, said Lucerne, they might soon be swarming all over us as well. Not that we had anything to hide. But it would be a nuisance.

I texted Jimmy right away and said how sorry I was about his mother, and was there anything I could do. He wasn't at school, but he texted me later that week, then came over to my place. He was very depressed. It was bad enough that his mother was gone, he said, but also the CorpSeCorps had asked his dad to help them with their inquiries, which meant that his dad was carted off in a black solarvan; and now two female CorpSers were snooping around the house and asking him a lot of stupid questions. Worst of all, Jimmy's mother had stolen Killer to let her loose in the wild – she'd left him a note about it. But the wild was totally wrong for Killer, because she'd be eaten by bobkittens.

"Oh Jimmy," I said. "That's terrible." I put my arms around him and hugged him: he was sort of crying. I started crying too, and we stroked each other carefully, as if both of us had broken arms or diseases, and then we slid tenderly into my bed, still holding on to each other as if we were drowning, and we started kissing each other. I felt I was helping Jimmy and he was helping me at the same time. It was like a feast day back at the Gardeners, when we'd do everything in a special way because it was in honour of something. That's what this was like: it was *in honour*.

"I don't want to hurt you," Jimmy said.

Oh Jimmy, I thought. I'm putting Light around you.

42

After that first time I felt very happy, as if I was singing. Not a doleful song, more like a bird song. I loved being in bed with Jimmy, it made me feel so safe to have his arms around me, and it was amazing to me how slippery and silky one skin felt against another skin. The body has a wisdom of its own, Adam One used to say: he'd been talking about the immune system, but it was true in another way. That wisdom wasn't merely like singing, it was like dancing, only better. I was in love with Jimmy, and I had to believe that Jimmy was just as in love with me.

I wrote in my diary: JIMMY. Then I underlined it in red and drew a red heart. I still distrusted writing enough not to put in everything that was happening, but each time we had sex I drew another heart and coloured it in.

I wanted to phone Amanda and tell her about it, even though Amanda had said once that people telling you about their sex was as boring as people telling you about their dreams. But when I went into my closet and took out my plush tiger, the purple phone was no longer there.

I felt cold all over. My diary was still inside the bear, where I'd hidden it. But I had no phone.

Then Lucerne came into my room. She said, didn't I know that any phone inside the Compound had to be registered, so people couldn't phone out industrial secrets? It was a crime to have an unregistered phone, and the CorpSeCorps could track such phones. Didn't I know that?

I shook my head. "Can they tell who was called?" I said. She said they could trace the number, which could be really bad news for the callers at both ends. She didn't say, *really bad news*, she said, *unfortunate consequences*.

Then she said that despite my obvious belief that she was a bad mother, she did have my best interests at heart. For instance, if she happened to find a purple phone with a frequently called number, she might leave a text message at that called number, such as "Dump it!!" So if they did locate that second phone, it would be inside a dumpster. And she herself would dispose of the purple one. And now she was going to play golf, and she hoped I would think very carefully about what she'd just said.

I did think very carefully. I thought, *Lucerne went out of her way to save Amanda. She must've known that's who I was phoning. But she hates Amanda. So really, Lucerne went out of her way to save Zeb: despite everything, she still loves him.*

Now that I was in love with Jimmy I had more sympathy for Lucerne and the way she used to behave around Zeb. I could see how you could do extreme things for the person you loved. Adam One said that when you loved a person, that love might not always get returned the way you wanted, but it was a good thing anyway because love went out all around you like an energy wave, and a creature you didn't even know would be helped by it. The example he used was of someone being killed by a virus and then eaten by vultures. I hadn't liked that comparison, but the general idea was true; because here was Lucerne, sending that text message because she loved Zeb, but as a side effect saving Amanda, which hadn't been her original intention. So Adam One was right.

But meanwhile I'd lost touch with Amanda. I felt very sad about that.

Jimmy and I still did our homework together. Sometimes we really did do it, when there were other people around. The rest of the time we didn't. It would take us about a minute to get out of our clothes and into each other, and Jimmy would be running his hands all over me and saying I was so slender, like a sylph – he liked words like that, not that I always knew what they meant. He said sometimes he felt like a child molester.

Later I'd write down some of the things he'd said, as if they were prophecies. *Jimmy is so great he said Im a silf.* I didn't care that much about spelling, only about the feeling.

I loved him so much. But then I made a mistake. I asked him if he was still in love with Wakulla or did he love me instead? I shouldn't have asked that. He waited too long to answer and then he said, Did it matter? I wanted to say yes, but instead I said no. Then Wakulla Price moved to the West Coast, and Jimmy got moody and went back to spending more time with Glenn than he spent with me. So that was the answer, and it made me very unhappy.

Despite that we were still having sex, though not very often – the red hearts in my diary were getting farther and farther apart. Then I saw Jimmy by accident at the mall with this foul-mouthed older girl called LyndaLee, who was rumoured to be going through all the boys at school, one by one but fast, like eating soynuts. Jimmy had his hand right on her ass, and then she pulled down his head and kissed him. It was a long, wet kiss. I felt sick to my stomach at the thought of Jimmy with her, and I remembered something Amanda once said about diseases, and I thought, Whatever LyndaLee's got, I've got too. And I went home and threw up, and cried, and then I got into my big white bathtub and had a warm bath. But it wasn't much comfort.

Jimmy didn't know I knew about him and LyndaLee. A few days later he asked if he could come over as usual, and I said yes. I wrote in my diary, *Jimmy you nosy brat I know your reading this, I hate it just because I fucked you doesn't mean I like you so STAY OUT!* Two red lines under *hate*, three under *stay out*. Then I left the diary on the top of my dresser. Your enemies could use your writing against you, I thought, but also you could use it against them.

After the sex I took a shower by myself, and when I came out, Jimmy was reading my diary, and said why did I hate him all of a sudden? So I told him. I used words I'd never said out loud before, and Jimmy said he was wrong for me, he was incapable of commitment because of Wakulla Price, she'd turned him into an emotional dumpster, but maybe he was destructive by nature since he messed up every girl he touched.

And I asked exactly how many that would be? I couldn't stand it that he would just include me in a big basket of girls, as if we were peaches or turnips. Then he said he really liked me as a person, which was why he was being honest with me, and I told him to get stuffed. So we broke up on bad terms.

The stretch of time after that was very dark. I wondered what I was doing on the Earth: no one would care much if I wasn't on it any more. Maybe I should cast away what Adam One called my husk and transform into a vulture or a worm. But then I remembered how the Gardeners used to say, *Ren, your life is a precious gift, and where there is a gift there is a Giver, and when you've been given a gift you should always say thank you.* So that was some help.

Also I could hear Amanda's voice: Why are you being so weak? Love's never a fair trade. So Jimmy's tired of you, so what, there's guys all over the place like germs, and you can pick them like flowers and toss them away when they're wilted. But you have to act like you're having a spectacular time and every day's a party.

What I did next wasn't good, and I'm still ashamed of it. I walked up to Glenn in the cafeteria – it took a lot of courage because Glenn was so cool he was practically frozen. And I asked him if he'd like to hang out with me. What I had in mind was that I'd have sex with Glenn, and Jimmy would find out and be wrecked. Not that I wanted sex with Glenn, it would be like shagging a salad server. Kind of flat and wooden.

Glenn said, "Hang out?" in a puzzled way. "Aren't you with Jimmy?" I said it was over, and anyway it was never serious because Jimmy was such a clown. Then I blurted out the next thing that came into my head.

"I saw you with the Gardeners, at the Tree of Life," I said. "Remember? I was the one who walked you over to see Pilar. With that honey?" He looked alarmed, and said we should get a Happicappuchino and talk.

We did talk. We talked a lot. We hung out in the mall so much that kids started saying we were a thing, but we weren't – it was never a romance. What was it then? I guess Glenn was the only person at HelthWyzer I could talk to about the Gardeners, and it was the same for him – that was the bond. It was like being in a secret club. Maybe Jimmy was never my twin at all – maybe it was Glenn. Which is a strange thought, because he was a strange guy. More like a cyborg, which was what Wakulla Price used to call him. Were we friends? I wouldn't even call it that. Sometimes he looked at me as if I was an amoeba, or some problem he was solving in Nanobioforms.

Glenn already knew quite a lot about the Gardeners, but he wanted to know more. What it was like to live with them every day. What they did and said, what they really believed. He'd get me to sing the songs, he'd want me to repeat what Adam One said in his Saint and Feast Day speeches: Glenn never laughed at them the way Jimmy would have if I'd ever done that for him. Instead he'd ask things like, "So, they think we should use nothing except recycled. But what if the Corps stopped making anything new? We'll run out." Sometimes he'd ask me more personal things, like "Would you eat animals if you were starving?" and "Do you think the Waterless Flood is really going to happen?" But I didn't always know the answers.

He'd talk about other things too. One day, he said that what you had to do in any adversarial situation was to kill the king, as in chess. I said people didn't have kings any more. He said he meant the centre of power, but today it wouldn't be a single person, it would be the techno-logical connections. I said, you mean like coding and splicing, and he said, "Something like that."

Once he asked me if I thought God was a cluster of neurons, and if so, whether people having that cluster had been passed down by natural selection because it conferred a competitive edge, or whether maybe it was just a spandrel, such as having red hair, which didn't matter one way or another to your survival chances. A lot of the time I felt way out of my depth with him, so I'd say, "What do you think?" He always had an answer to that.

Jimmy did see us together at the mall, and he did seem taken aback; though not for long, because I caught him giving Glenn a thumbs-up, as if saying, *Go for it, buddy, be my guest!* As if I was his property and he was sharing.

Jimmy and Glenn graduated two years before I did and went off to college. Glenn went to Watson-Crick with all the brainiacs, and Jimmy went to the Martha Graham Academy, which was for kids with no math and science potential. So at least I didn't have to watch Jimmy at school any more, coming on to this or that new girl. But it was almost worse with Jimmy not there than with him there.

I put in the next two years somehow. My marks were poor, and I didn't think I'd get in anywhere for college – I'd end up as a minimum-wage meat slave, working at SecretBurgers or somewhere like that. But Lucerne pulled some strings. I heard her talking about it to one of her golf-club friends: "She's not stupid, but that cult experience ruined her motivation, so the Martha Graham Academy is the best we could do." So I'd be in the same space with Jimmy: that made me so nervous I felt sick.

The night before I left on the sealed bullet train, I reread my old diary, and then I knew what the Gardeners meant when they said, *Be careful what you write.* There were my own words from the time when I was so happy, except that now it was torture to read them. I took the diary down the street and around the corner and shoved it into a garboil dumpster. It would turn into oil and then all those red hearts I'd drawn would go up in smoke, but at least they would be useful along the way.

Part of me thought I would find Jimmy again at Martha Graham, and he would say it was me he'd loved all along, and could we get back together, and I'd forgive him and everything would be wonderful, the way it had been at first. But the other part of me realized that the chances of that were nothing. Adam One used to say that people can believe two opposite things at the same time, and now I knew it was true.

THE FEAST OF SERPENT WISDOM

THE FEAST OF SERPENT WISDOM

YEAR EIGHTEEN.

OF THE IMPORTANCE OF INSTINCTIVE KNOWING.
SPOKEN BY ADAM ONE.

Dear Friends, Fellow Mortals, Fellow Creatures:

Today is our Feast of Serpent Wisdom, and our Children have once again excelled in their decoration. We have Amanda and Shackleton to thank for the gripping mural of the Fox Snake ingesting a Frog – an apt reminder to us of the intertwined nature of the Dance of Life. For this Feast we traditionally feature the Zucchini, a Serpent-shaped vegetable. Thanks to Rebecca, our Eve Eleven, for her innovative Zucchini and Radish Dessert Slice. We are certainly looking forward to it.

But first I must alert you to the fact that certain individuals have been making unofficial inquiries about Zeb, our many-talented Adam Seven. In our Father's Garden there are many Species, and it takes all kinds to make an Ecosystem, and Zeb has chosen the non-violent option; so if questioned, do keep in mind that "I don't know" is always the best answer.

Our text for Serpent Wisdom is from Matthew 10:16: "Be ye therefore wise as Serpents, and harmless as Doves." To those former biologists among us who have made a study either of Serpents or of Doves, this sentence is puzzling. Serpents are expert hunters, paralyzing or strangling and crushing their prey, a gift that enables them to predate many Mice and Rats. Yet, despite their natural technology, one would not ordinarily call Serpents "wise." And Doves, though harmless to us, are extremely aggressive to other Doves: a male will harass and kill a less dominant male if occasion offers. The Spirit of God is sometimes pictured as a Dove, which simply informs us that this Spirit is not always peaceful: it has a ferocious side to it as well.

The Serpent is a highly charged symbol throughout the Human Words of God, though its guises are varied. Sometimes it is shown as an evil enemy of Humankind – perhaps because, when our Primate ancestors slept in trees, the Constrictors were among their few nocturnal predators. And for these ancestors – shoeless as they were – to step on a Viper meant certain death. Yet the Serpent is also equated with Leviathan, that great water-beast God made to humble Mankind, and also named to Job as an awe-inspiring example of His Inventiveness.

Among the Ancient Greeks, serpents were sacred to the god of healing. In other religions, the Serpent with its tail in its mouth refers to the cycle of Life, and to the beginning and end of Time. Because they shed their skins, Serpents have also symbolized Renewal – the Soul casting off its old self, from which it emerges resplendent. A complicated symbol, indeed. Therefore, how are we to be "wise as Serpents"? Are we to eat our own tails, or tempt people to wrongdoing, or coil around our enemies and squeeze them to death? Surely not – because in the same sentence, we are told to be as harmless as Doves.

Serpent Wisdom – I propose – is the wisdom of *feeling directly*, as the Serpent feels vibrations in the Earth. The Serpent is wise in that it lives in immediacy, without the need for the elaborate intellectual frameworks Humankind is endlessly constructing for itself. For what in us is belief and faith, in the other Creatures is inborn knowledge. No Human can truly know the full mind of God. The Human reason is a pin dancing on the head of an angel, so small is it in comparison to the Divine vastness that encircles us.

As the Human Words of God have put it, "Faith is the substance of things hoped for, the evidence of things not seen." That is the point: *not* seen. We cannot know God by reason and measurement; indeed, excess reason and measurement lead to doubt. Through them, we know that Comets and nuclear holocausts are among the possible tomorrows, not to mention the Waterless Flood, that we fear looms ever nearer. This fear dilutes our certainty, and through that channel comes loss of Faith; and then the temptation to enact malevolence enters our Souls; for if annihilation awaits us, why bother to strive for the Good?

We Humans must labour to believe, as the other Creatures do not. They *know* the dawn will come. They can sense it – that ruffling of the half-light, the horizon bestirring itself. Not only every Sparrow, not only every Rakunk, but every Nematode, and Mollusc, and Octopus, and Mo'Hair, and Liobam – all are held in the palm of His hand. Unlike us, they have no need for Faith.

As for the Serpent, who can tell where its head ends and its body begins? It experiences God in all parts of itself; it feels the vibrations of Divinity that run through the Earth, and responds to them quicker than thought.

This then is the Serpent Wisdom we long for – this wholeness of Being. May we greet with joy the few moments when, through Grace, and by the aid of our Retreats and Vigils and the assistance of God's Botanicals, we are granted an apprehension of it.

Let us sing.

GOD GAVE UNTO THE ANIMALS

God gave unto the Animals
A wisdom past our power to see:
Each knows innately how to live,
Which we must learn laboriously.

The Creatures need no lesson books,
For God instructs their Minds and Souls:
The sunlight hums to every Bee,
The moist clay whispers to the Mole.

And each one seeks its meat from God,
And each enjoys the Earth's sweet fare;
But none does sell and none does buy,
And none does foul its proper lair.

The Serpent is an arrow bright
That feels the Earth's vibrations fine
Run through its armoured shining flesh,
And all along its twining spine.

Oh, would I were, like Serpents, wise –
To sense the wholeness of the Whole,
Not only with a thinking Brain,
But with a swift and ardent Soul.

From *The God's Gardeners Oral Hymnbook*

43

The Feast of Serpent Wisdom. Old Moon. Toby enters the Feast Day and the moon phase on her pink notepaper with the winky eyes and kissy lips. Old moon is a pruning week, said the Gardeners. Plant by the new, slash by the old. A good time to apply sharp tools to yourself, hack off any extraneous parts that might need trimming. Your head, for instance.

"A joke," she says out loud. She should avoid such morbid thoughts.

Today she will pare her fingernails. Toenails, as well: they shouldn't be permitted to run rampant. She could give herself a manicure: there are lots of cosmetic supplies in this place, whole shelves of them. AnooYoo Luscious Polish. AnooYoo Plum Skin Plumper. AnooYoo Fountain of Yooth Total Immersion: *Shed That Scaly Epidermis!* But why bother to polish or plump or shed? But why not bother? Either choice is equally pointless.

Do it for Yoo, AnooYoo used to croon. *The Noo Yoo.* I could have a whole new me, thinks Toby. Yet another whole new me, fresh as a snake. How many would that add up to, by now?

She trudges up the stairs to the rooftop, hoists her binoculars, surveys her visible realm. There's motion in the weeds, over by the forest edge: could it be the pigs? If so, they're keeping a low profile. Vultures are still clustering around the dead boar. There'll be lots of nanobioforms at work on it: it must be getting ripe by now.

Here's something different. Closer to the building, a clump of sheep is grazing. Five of them: three Mo'Hairs – a green one, a pink one, and a bright purple one – and two other sheep that appear to be conventional. The long hair of the Mo'Hairs isn't in good shape – there are clot-like snarls in it, and twigs and dry leaves. Onscreen, in advertisements, their hair had been shiny – you'd see the sheep tossing its hair, then a beautiful girl tossing a mane of the same hair. *More hair with Mo'Hair!* But they're not faring so well without their salon treatments.

The sheep clump together, lift their heads. Toby sees why: crouching low in the weeds, two liobams are on the hunt. Maybe the sheep smell them, but the scent must be confusing – part lion, part lamb.

The purple Mo'Hair is the most jittery. Don't look like prey, Toby thinks at it. Sure enough, it's the purple one the liobams go after. They cut it out from the group and chase it for a short distance. The pathetic beast is impeded by its coiffure – it looks like a purple fright wig on legs – and the liobams quickly pull it down. Finding the throat under all that hair padding takes them a while, and the Mo'Hair scrambles to its feet several times before the liobams finish it off. Then they settle down to eat. The other sheep have run awkwardly away in a muddle of bleating, but now they're grazing again.

She'd intended to do some gardening today, pick some greens: her stock of preserved and dried foods is waning like the moon. But she decides against it because of the liobams. Cats of all kinds will set ambushes: one frisks around in the open to distract your attention while another one slips quietly up behind.

In the afternoon she takes a nap. An old moon draws the past, said Pilar: whatever arrives from the shadows you must greet as a blessing. And the past does come back to her: the white frame house of her childhood, the ordinary trees, the woodland in the background, tinged with blue as if there's haze. A deer is outlined against it, standing rigid as a lawn ornament, ears pricked. Her father's digging with a shovel, over by the pile of picket fencing; her mother's a momentary glimpse at the kitchen window. Perhaps she's making soup. Everything tranquil, as if it would never end. But where is Toby in this picture? For it is a picture. It's flat, like a picture on a wall. She's not there.

She opens her eyes: tears on her cheeks. I wasn't in the picture because I'm the frame, she thinks. It's not really the past. It's only me, holding it all together. It's only a handful of fading neural pathways. It's only a mirage.

Surely I was an optimistic person back then, she thinks. Back there. I woke up whistling. I knew there were things wrong in the world, they were referred to, I'd seen them in the onscreen news. But the wrong things were wrong somewhere else.

By the time she'd reached college, the wrongness had moved closer. She remembers the oppressive sensation, like waiting all the time for a heavy stone footfall, then the knock at the door. Everybody knew. Nobody admitted to knowing. If other people began to discuss it, you tuned them out, because what they were saying was both so obvious and so unthinkable.

We're using up the Earth. It's almost gone. You can't live with such fears and keep on whistling. The waiting builds up in you like a tide. You start wanting it to be done with. You find yourself saying to the sky, *Just do it. Do your worst. Get it over with.* She could feel the coming tremor of it running through her spine, asleep or awake. It never went away, even among the Gardeners. Especially – as time wore on – among the Gardeners.

44

The Sunday after Serpent Wisdom Day was Saint Jacques Cousteau's Day. It was Year Eighteen – the year of rupture, though Toby did not yet know that. She remembers negotiating the Sinkhole streets on her way to the Wellness Clinic for the regular Sunday-evening Adams and Eves Council. She wasn't looking forward to it: lately those meetings had been sliding into squabbles.

The week before, they'd spent all their time on theological problems. The matter of Adam's teeth, for starters.

"Adam's *teeth*?" Toby had blurted. She needed to work on controlling such expressions of surprise, which might be read as criticism.

Adam One had explained that some of the children were upset because Zeb had pointed out the differences between the biting, rending teeth of carnivores and the grinding, munching teeth of herbivores. The children wanted to know why – if Adam was created as a vegetarian, as he surely was – human teeth should show such mixed characteristics.

"Shouldn't have brought it up," Stuart had muttered.

"We changed at the Fall," Nuala had said brightly. "We evolved. Once Man started to eat meat, well, naturally . . ."

That would be putting the cart before the horse, said Adam One; they could not achieve their goal of reconciling the findings of Science with their sacramental view of Life simply by overriding the rules of the former. He asked them to ponder this conundrum, and propose solutions at a later date.

Then they turned to the problem of the animal-skin clothing provided by God for Adam and Eve at the end of Genesis 3. The troublesome "coats of skins."

"The children are very worried about them," Nuala had said. Toby could understand why they'd been so dismayed. Had God killed and peeled some of his beloved Creatures to make these skin coats? If so, He'd set a very bad example to Man. If not, where had these skin coats come from?

"Maybe those animals died a natural death." That was Rebecca. "And God didn't see them going to waste." She was adamant about using up leftovers.

"Maybe very small animals," Katuro had said. "Short life spans."

"That is one possibility," Adam One had said. "Let it stand for now, until a more plausible explanation presents itself."

Early in her Eveship, Toby had asked if it was really necessary to split such theological hairs, and Adam One had said that it was. "The truth is," he'd said, "most people don't care about other Species, not when times get hard. All they care about is their next meal, naturally enough: we have to eat or die. But what if it's God doing the caring? We've evolved to believe in gods, so this belief bias of ours must confer an evolutionary advantage. The strictly materialist view – that we're an experiment animal protein has been doing on itself – is far too harsh and lonely for most, and leads to nihilism. That being the case, we need to push popular sentiment in a biosphere-friendly direction by pointing out the hazards of annoying God by a violation of His trust in our stewardship."

"What you mean is, with God in the story there's a penalty," said Toby.

"Yes," said Adam One. "There's a penalty without God in the story too, needless to say. But people are less likely to credit that. If there's a penalty, they want a penalizer. They dislike senseless catastrophe."

What would the topic be today? Toby wondered. Which fruit Eve ate from the Tree of Knowledge? It couldn't have been an apple, considering the state of horticulture at that time. A date? A bergamot? The Council had long been deliberating over that one. Toby had thought of proposing a strawberry, but then, strawberries didn't grow on trees.

As she walked, Toby was conscious, as always, of the others on the street. She could see in front of her and to the sides, despite her sunhat. She made use of pauses in doorways, of reflections in windows to check behind. But she could never shake the feeling that someone was sneaking up on her – that a hand would descend on her neck, a hand with red and blue veining and a bracelet of baby skulls. Blanco hadn't been seen in the Sewage Lagoon for some time – still in Painball, said some; no, overseas fighting as a mercenary, said others – but he was like smog: there were always some of his molecules in the air.

There was someone behind her – she could feel it, like a tingling between her shoulders. She stepped into a doorway, turned to face the sidewalk, then sagged with relief: it was Zeb.

"Hi, babe," he said. "Hot enough?"

He strolled along beside her, singing to himself:

> *Nobody gives a snot,*
> *Nobody gives a snot,*
> *That is why we're on the fucking spot,*
> *Cause nobody gives a snot!*

"Maybe you shouldn't sing," said Toby neutrally. It wasn't good policy to call attention to yourself on a pleeb sidewalk, especially not for Gardeners.

"Can't help it," said Zeb cheerfully. "God's fault. Wove music into the fabric of our being. Hears you better when you sing, so He's listening to this right now. I hope He's enjoying it," he added in a pious, mocking Adam One voice – a voice he was using a lot, though not when Adam One was around.

Lurking insubordination, thought Toby: he's tired of being the Beta Chimp.

Since becoming an Eve she'd gained much insight into Zeb's status among the Gardeners. Each Gardener Rooftop site and Truffle cell ran its own affairs, but every half-year they'd send delegates to a central convention, which for security reasons was never held in the same abandoned warehouse twice. Zeb was always a delegate: he was well equipped to make it through the more jagged pleebland neighbourhoods and around the CorpSeCorps checkpoints without being mugged, swarmed, spraygunned, or arrested. Maybe that was why he was allowed to stretch the Gardeners' rules the way he did.

Adam One seldom attended the conventions. The journey was hazardous, and the implication was that although Zeb was expendable, Adam One was not. In theory the Gardener fellowship had no overall head, but in practice its leader was Adam One, revered founder and guru. The soft hammer of his word carried a lot of weight at the Gardener conventions, and since he was rarely there to use that hammer himself, Zeb wielded it for him. Which must be a temptation: what if Zeb were to jettison Adam One's decrees and substitute his own? By such methods had regimes been changed and emperors toppled.

"You've had some bad news?" Toby asked Zeb now. The singing was the clue: Zeb was annoyingly upbeat whenever the news was bad.

"In point of fact," said Zeb. "We've lost contact with one of our insiders in Compoundland – our boy courier. He's gone dark."

Toby had learned about the boy courier once she'd become an Eve. He'd run Pilar's biopsy samples and brought her the fatal diagnosis – both of them concealed in a jar of honey. But that was all she knew: information was shared among the Adams and Eves, but only as much as was necessary. Pilar's death was years ago: the boy courier couldn't be much of a boy any longer.

"Gone dark?" she said. "How?" Had he had a pigmentation makeover? Surely not that.

"He used to be at HelthWyzer, but now he's graduated from high school and moved over to the Watson-Crick Institute, and he's fallen off our screen. Not that we have that much of a screen, as such," he added.

Toby waited. With Zeb, there was no point in pushing or fishing.

"Between us, right?" he said after a while.

"Of course," said Toby. I'm just an ear, she thought. A doggie-type faithful companion. A well of silence. Nothing more to it. After Lucerne had flown the coop four years ago she'd wondered briefly if there might be more, sometime, between her and Zeb. But nothing had come of that hankering. I'm the wrong body type, she thought. Too muscular. No doubt he likes the jiggle.

"Council doesn't know about this, okay?" said Zeb. "Him going dark will just make them nervous."

"I'll forget I heard it," said Toby.

"His dad was a friend of Pilar's – she used to be Botanic Splices, at HelthWyzer. I knew them both, at that time. But he got unhappy when he found out they were seeding folks with illnesses via those souped-up supplement pills of theirs – using them as free lab animals, then collecting on the treatments for those very same illnesses. Nifty scam, charging top dollar for stuff they caused themselves. Troubled his conscience. So the dad fed us some interesting data. Then he had an accident."

"Accident?" said Toby.

"Went off an overpass at rush hour. Blood gumbo."

"That's a bit graphic," said Toby. "For a vegetarian."

"Sorry about that," said Zeb. "Suicide, was the rumour."

"It wasn't, I take it," said Toby.

"We call it Corpicide. If you're Corp and you do something they don't like, you're dead. It's like you shot yourself."

"I see," said Toby.

"Anyway, back to our young guy. The mother was Diagnostics at HelthWyzer, he'd hacked her lab sign-in code, he could run stuff through the system for us. Genius hacker. The mom's married a top corp guy at HelthWyzer Central and the kid went with her."

"Where Lucerne is," said Toby.

Zeb ignored this. "Burned through their firewalls, cooked up a few onscreen identities, got back in touch. We heard from him for a while, but then nothing."

"Maybe he's lost interest," said Toby. "Or else they caught him."

"Maybe," said Zeb. "But he's a three-dimensional chess player, he likes a challenge. He's nimble. Also he's got no fear."

"How many like that do we have?" Toby asked. "In the Compounds?"

"Nobody that good at hacking," said Zeb. "This guy's one of a kind."

45

They reached the Wellness Clinic and entered the Vinegar Room. Toby moved around behind the three huge barrels, unlocked the bottle shelf, and swung it out so she could open the inner door. She could hear Zeb sucking in his stomach to squeeze past the barrels: he wasn't softly fat, but he was large.

The inner room was almost filled by a table patched together from old floorboards, with a motley collection of chairs. On one wall there was a recent watercolour – Saint E.O. Wilson of Hymenoptera – done by Nuala in one of her too frequent moments of artistic inspiration. The Saint was shown with the sun behind him, giving him a halo effect. On his face was an ecstatic smile, in his hand was a collecting jar containing several black spots. These were the bees, Toby supposed, or possibly the ants. As was often the case with Nuala's paintings of Saints, one of the arms was longer than the other.

There was a gentle knock, and Adam One slipped through the door. The rest followed in their turn.

Adam One was a different person behind the scenes. Not entirely different – no less sincere – but more practical. Also more tactical. "Let us say a silent prayer for the success of our deliberations," he began. The meetings always opened this way. Toby had some difficulty praying in the close confines of the hidden room: she was too aware of stomach rumblings, of the waftings of clandestine odours, of the creaks and shiftings of bodies. But then, she had some difficulty praying anyway.

The silent prayer seemed to be on a timer. As heads lifted and eyes opened, Adam One glanced around the room. "Is that a new picture?" he said. "On the wall?"

Nuala beamed. "It's Saint E.O.," she said. "Wilson. Of Hymenoptera."

"So like him, my dear," said Adam One. "Especially the . . . You are blessed with such talent." He coughed slightly. "Now to a pressing practical matter. We have just received a very special guest, originally from HelthWyzer Central, though she has been, shall we say, travelling. Despite all obstacles, she's brought us a gift of genome codes, for which we owe her, not only temporary asylum, but secure Exfernal placement."

"They're looking for her," said Zeb. "She shouldn't have come back to this country. We'll have to move her out as fast as possible. Through the FenderBender and over to the Street of Dreams, as usual?"

"If it's a clear path," said Adam One. "We can't take unnecessary risks. We can always keep her hidden in this meeting room, if we have to."

The ratio of women to men fleeing the Corporations was roughly three to one. Nuala said it was because women were more ethical, Zeb said it was because they were more squeamish, and Philo said it amounted to the same thing. Such fugitives often brought contraband information with them. Formulae. Long lines of code. Test secrets, proprietary lies. What did the Gardeners do with it all? Toby wondered. Surely they didn't sell it as industrial corp espionage material, though it would fetch a bundle from foreign rivals. As far as she could tell, they just held on to it; though it was possible that Adam One harboured a dream of restoring all the lost Species via their preserved DNA codes, once a more ethical and technically proficient future had replaced the depressing present. They'd cloned the mammoth, so why not all? Was that his vision of the ultimate Ark?

"Our new guest wants to send a message to her son," said Adam One. "She's worried about having left him at what may have been a crucial time in his life. Jimmy is this lad's name. I believe he's now at the Martha Graham Academy."

"A postcard," said Zeb. "We'll say it's from Aunt Monica. Get me the address, I'll relay it through England – one of our Truffle cellfolk has a trip there next week. The CorpSeCorps will read it, of course. They read all the postcards."

"She wants us to say that his pet rakunk was released into the wilds of Heritage Park, where it is living a free and happy life. Its name is – ah – Killer."

"Oh, Christ in a Zeppelin!" said Zeb.

"That language is uncalled for," said Nuala.

"Sorry. But they make it so fucking complicated," said Zeb. "That's the third pet rakunk message this month. Next it'll be gerbils and mice."

"I think it's touching," said Nuala.

"Guess some people anyway practise what they preach," said Rebecca.

Toby was assigned as minder to the new refugee. Her code name was the Hammerhead, because upon leaving HelthWyzer she was said to have taken her husband's computer apart with a home handyman's toolkit to disguise the extent of her data thefts. She was thin and blue-eyed, and far from calm. Like all Corp defectors, she thought she was the only one ever to have taken the momentous and heretical step of defying a Corp; and like all of them, she desperately wanted to be told what a good person she was.

Toby obliged. She said how brave the Hammerhead had been, which was true, and how smart she'd been to take a winding and devious path, and how much they appreciated the information she'd brought them. In reality she hadn't told them anything they didn't already know – it was that old human-to-pig neocortex transplant material – but it would have been less than kind to say so. We must cast a wide net, said Adam One, although some of the fish may be small. Also we must be a beacon of hope, because if you tell people there's nothing they can do, they will do worse than nothing.

Toby shrouded the Hammerhead in a dark blue Gardener dress, adding a nose cone to conceal her face. But the woman was nervous and fidgety, and kept asking if she could have a cigarette. Toby said no

Gardener smoked – not tobacco – so to be caught doing so would blow her cover. Anyway there weren't any cigarettes up on the Rooftop.

The Hammerhead paced the floor and gnawed her fingernails until Toby felt like hitting her. We didn't ask you to come here and put all our necks in a noose over a teaspoonful of stale-dated crap, she wanted to say. In the end she gave the woman some chamomile tea with Poppy in it, just to take her off the airwaves.

46

The next day was Saint Aleksander Zawadzki of Galicia. A minor saint but one of Toby's favourites. He'd lived in turbulent times – what times in Poland had ever not been turbulent? – but had followed his own peaceful and slightly dotty pursuits nonetheless, cataloguing the flowers of Galicia, naming its beetles. Rebecca liked him too: she'd put on her apron with the butterfly appliqués and made beetle biscuits for the small children's snack time, ornamenting each one with an *A* and a *Z*. The children had made up their own little song about him: *Alexsander, Alexsander, beetle up your nose! Blow it on your handkerchief, stick it on a rose!*

It was midmorning. The Hammerhead was still sleeping off the effects of yesterday's Poppy: Toby had overdone it, but she didn't feel too guilty, and now she had some time for her regular chores. She'd garbed up in her bee veil and gloves and lit the smudge in her bellows: as she'd explained to the bees, she intended to spend the morning extracting the full honeycombs. Before she'd begun the smoking, however, Zeb appeared.

"Crappy news," he said. "Your Painball buddy's out again." Like everyone at the Gardeners, Zeb knew the story of Toby's rescue from Blanco by Adam One and the Buds and Blooms – it was part of oral history. But he also sensed her fear. Though they'd never discussed it.

Toby felt an ice needle shoot through her. She lifted up her veil. "Really?"

"Older and meaner," said Zeb. "Twisted fuck should have been vulture pellets long ago. He must have friends in high places, though, because he's back managing SecretBurgers, over in the Sewage Lagoon."

"As long as he stays there," said Toby. She tried to make her voice sound strong.

"The bees can wait," said Zeb. He took her arm. "You need to sit down. I'll do a snoop. Maybe he's forgotten all about you."

He took Toby to the kitchen. "Sweetheart, you look beat," said Rebecca. "What's wrong?" Toby told her.

"Oh shit," said Rebecca. "I'll make you some Rescue Tea, you look like you need it. Don't you worry – that man's karma will kill him one day." But, thought Toby, *one day* was far too distant.

It was afternoon. Many of the general-membership Gardeners were gathered on the roof. Some were retying the tomatoes and climbing zucchinis that had blown over in the storm, a more violent one than usual. Others sat in the shade, working at their knitting, their knotting, their mending. The Adams and Eves were restless, as they always were when they were harbouring a runaway – what if the Hammerhead had been followed? Adam One had posted sentinels; he himself was standing over by the roof's edge in one-legged meditation pose, keeping an eye on the street below.

The Hammerhead had woken up, and Toby had set her to work picking snails off the lettuces; she'd told the rank-and-file Gardeners this was a new convert, and shy. They'd seen so many new converts come and go.

"If we have a visit," Toby said to the Hammerhead, "anything like an inspection, pull your sunhat down and go on with the snails. Act like background." She herself was smoking the bees, on the theory that it was best to carry on as usual.

Then Shackleton and Crozier and young Oates came pounding up the fire-escape stairs, followed by Amanda, then Zeb. They headed straight over to Adam One. He motioned to Toby with his chin: *join us*.

"There's been a scuffle in the Sewage Lagoon," said Zeb after they'd grouped around Adam One.

"Scuffle?" said Adam One.

"We were just looking," said Shackleton. "But he saw us."

"He called us fucking meat-stealers," said Crozier. "He was drunk."

"Not drunk: wasted," said Amanda with authority. "He tried to hit me, but I did a *satsuma*." Toby smiled a little: it was a mistake to underestimate Amanda. She was a tall sinewy Amazon by now, and she'd been studying Urban Bloodshed Limitation with Zeb. As had her two devoted henchmen. There were three if you counted Oates, though he was merely at the hopeless crush level.

"Who is 'he'?" said Adam One. "Where was this?"

"SecretBurgers," said Zeb. "We were checking it out – we heard Blanco was back."

"Zeb pulled an *unagi* on him," said Shackleton. "It was neat!"

"Did you have to actually go there?" said Adam One, a little peevishly. "We have other ways of . . ."

"Then the Asian Fusions swarmed him," said Oates excitedly. "They had bottles!"

"He pulled a killer knife," said Croze. "He notched a couple."

"I hope there was no lasting damage," said Adam One. "Much as we deplore the very existence of SecretBurgers, and the depredations of this – this unlucky individual, we want no violence."

"Booth overturned, meat thrown around. All he suffered was cuts and bruises," said Zeb.

"That is unfortunate," said Adam One. "It's true that we sometimes have to defend ourselves, and we've had trouble with this – with him before. But on this occasion, do I have the impression that we attacked first?" He frowned at Zeb. "Or provoked an attack? Is this correct?"

"Asshole had it coming," said Zeb. "We should be getting medals."

"Our way is the way of peace," said Adam One, frowning even more.

"Peace goes only so far," said Zeb. "There's at least a hundred new extinct species since this time last month. They got fucking eaten! We can't just sit here and watch the lights blink out. Have to begin somewhere. Today SecretBurgers, tomorrow that fucking gourmet restaurant chain. Rarity. That needs to go."

"Our role in respect to the Creatures is to bear witness," said Adam One. "And to guard the memories and the genomes of the departed. You can't fight blood with blood. I thought we'd agreed on that."

There was a silence. Shackleton and Crozier and Oates and Amanda were staring at Zeb. Zeb and Adam One were staring at each other.

"Anyway, it's too late now," said Zeb. "Blanco's raging."

"Will he cross pleebmob boundaries?" said Toby. "Raid us here, in the Sinkhole?"

"Mood he's in, no question," said Zeb. "Ordinary mob guys don't scare him any more. He's multiple-session Painball."

Zeb warned the assembled Gardeners, posted a line of watchers around the roof, and stationed the strongest gatekeepers at the bottom of the fire-escape stairs. Adam One protested, saying that to act like one's enemies was to descend to their level. Zeb said that if Adam One wanted to handle defence matters in some other way he was free to do so, but if not he should keep his nose out of it.

"There's movement," said Rebecca, who was watching. "Three of them coming, it looks like."

"Whatever you do," Toby told the Hammerhead, "don't cut and run. Don't do anything that calls attention." She went over to the roof's edge to look.

Three heavyweights were muscling along the sidewalk. They had baseball bats. No sprayguns. Not CorpSeCorps then, just pleeb thugs: payback for the wreckage at SecretBurgers. One of the three was Blanco – she could spot him from any angle. What would he do? Bash her to death on the spot, or drag her away to do it more slowly elsewhere?

"What is it, my dear?" said Adam One.

"It's him," said Toby. "If he sees me, he'll kill me."

"Be of good cheer," he said. "Nothing bad will be done to you." But since Adam One thought that even the most terrible things happened for ultimately excellent though unfathomable reasons, Toby did not find this reassuring.

Zeb told her she'd better get their special guest out of sight, just in case, so she took the Hammerhead to her own cubicle and gave her a calming drink, heavy on the chamomile, with a little Poppy. The Hammerhead drifted off to sleep, and Toby sat watching her and hoping the two of them wouldn't end up cornered. She found herself looking around for weapons. I suppose I could hit them with the Poppy bottle, she thought. But it's not very big.

Then she walked back out to the Rooftop. She was still in her bee gear. She adjusted her heavy gloves, took up her bellows, and lowered her veil. "Stand by me," she said to the bees. "Be my messengers." As if they could hear.

The fight didn't last long. Later, Toby heard Shackleton and Crozier and Oates enacting the full battle story for the younger children, who'd been hurried out of the way by Nuala. According to them, it had been epic.

"Zeb was brilliant," said Shackleton. "He had it all planned out! They must've thought since we're so pacifist and all, they could just . . . Anyway, it was like an ambush – we backed up the stairs, with them following."

"And then, and then," said Oates.

"And then, at the top, Zeb let the first guy lunge at him, and then he got the end of the guy's baseball bat and kind of flung it, and the guy almost crashed into Rebecca, and she had this two-pronged fork, and then he went screaming right over the edge of the roof."

"Like this!" said Oates, arms flailing.

"Then Stuart sprayed the next one with the plant hydrator," said Crozier. "He says it works on cats."

"Amanda did something to him. Didn't you?" Shackleton said to her fondly. "Like, some Bloodshed Limitation move, like a *hamachi*, or – I don't know what she did, but he went over the railing too. Did you kick him in the nuts or what?"

"I relocated him," said Amanda demurely. "Like a snail."

"Then the third one ran away," said Oates. "The biggest guy. With bees all over him. Toby did that, it was wicked. Adam One wouldn't let us go after him."

"Zeb says this won't be the end of it," said Amanda.

Toby had her own version, in which everything had moved both very fast and very slowly. She'd placed herself behind the hives, and then the three of them had been right there, just emerging from the stair-top. A pale-faced man with a dark chin and a baseball bat, a scarred Redfish type, and Blanco. Blanco had spotted her immediately. "I see you, stringy-assed bitch!" he'd yelled. "You're meat!" Her bee veil was no disguise. He had his knife out; he was grinning.

The first man had tangled with Rebecca and gone over the railing somehow, screaming on the way down, but the second one was still coming. Then Amanda – who'd been standing off to the side, looking ethereal and harmless – had raised her arm. Toby had seen a flash of light: was that glass? But Blanco was almost upon her: there was nothing between them but the hives.

She pushed the hives over – three of them. She was veiled, Blanco was not. The bees poured out, whining with anger, and went for him like arrows. He fled howling down the fire-escape stairs, flailing and slapping, trailing a plume of bees.

It took some time for Toby to set the hives back up. The bees were furious, and several Gardeners got stung. Toby apologized to the victims, and she and Katuro treated them with calamine and chamomile; but she apologized much more profusely to the bees, once she'd smoked them enough to make them drowsy: they'd sacrificed many of their own in the battle.

47

The Adams and Eves had a tense meeting in the hidden room behind the vinegar barrels. "That shit wouldn't attack without authorization," said Zeb. "It's the CorpSeCorps behind it – they're aware of some of the folks we've been helping out, so they're working up to branding us as terrorist fanatics, like the Wolf Isaiahists."

"Nope, it's personal," said Rebecca. "That man is mean as a snake, no disrespect to Snakes, and he was after Toby, is all. Once he's stuck his pole in some hole, he thinks it's his." When Rebecca got worked up, she tended to revert to her earlier vocabulary and then regret it. "No offence, Toby," she said.

"Surely the proximate cause is among us," said Adam One. "The young people provoked him. And Zeb. We should have let sleeping dogs lie."

"Dogs is right," said Rebecca. "No disrespect to Dogs."

"Two dead bodies on the sidewalk will hardly do our peaceful reputation any good," said Nuala.

"Accidents. They fell off the roof," said Zeb.

"And one got his throat cut and the other had his eye put out on the way down," said Adam One. "As any forensic investigation will show."

"Dangerous, brick walls," said Katuro. "Things stick. Nails. Broken glass. Sharp things."

"Maybe you'd like a few dead Gardeners better?" said Zeb.

"If your premise is correct," said Adam One, "and this is a CorpSeCorps plot, has it occurred to you that those three may have been sent to provoke exactly such an incident? To cause us to break the law, thus providing an excuse for reprisals?"

"What was our choice?" said Zeb. "Let them squash us like bugs? Not that we squash Bugs," he added.

"He'll come back," said Toby. "Whatever the reason, CorpSeCorps or not. As long as I stay here, I'll be a target."

"I think," said Adam One, "that it would be best for your safety, dear Toby, and also for the safety of the Garden, if we were to place you in one of our Truffle niches in the Exfernal World. You can be of much use to us there. We'll ask our pleebrat connections to spread the news that you are no longer among us. Perhaps your foe may then lack motivation, and we will be protected from aggression from that quarter, at least for the moment. How soon can we move her?" he asked Zeb.

"Consider it done," said Zeb.

Toby went to her sleeping cubicle and packed her most necessary items – the bottled extracts, the dried herbs, the mushrooms. Pilar's honey, the last three jars. She left some of each thing behind for whoever might be filling her empty Eve Six shoes.

She remembered her early desire to leave the Garden, out of boredom and claustrophobia, and the desire for what she used to think of as a life of her own; but now that she was actually going, it felt like an expulsion. No: more like a wrenching, a severing, a skin peeling off. She resisted the urge to drink some Poppy, to dull the edge. She had to stay alert.

Another hurt: she was failing Pilar. Would she have time to say goodbye to the bees, and if she didn't, would the hives die? Who would take over as beekeeper? Who had the skills? She covered her head with a scarf and hurried out to the hives.

"Bees," she said out loud. "I have news." Did the bees pause in mid-air, were they listening? Several came to investigate her; they lit on her face, exploring her emotions through the chemicals on her skin. She hoped they'd forgiven her for tipping their hives. "You must tell your

Queen I've had to leave," she said. "Nothing to do with you, you've performed your duties well. My enemy is forcing me to go. I'm sorry. I hope that when we meet again it will be under happier circumstances." She always found herself using a formal style with the bees.

The bees buzzed and fizzed; they appeared to be discussing her. She wished she could take them with her like a large, golden, furry collective pet. "I'll miss you, bees," she said. As if in answer, one of them started crawling up her nostril. She breathed it sharply out. Maybe we wear hats for these interviews, she thought, so they won't go into our ears.

She went back to her cubicle, where an hour later Adam One and Zeb joined her. "You'd better wear this, dear Toby," said Adam One. He was carrying a furzoot – a fluffy pink duck with flapping red rubbery feet and a smiling yellow plastic bill. "The nose cone's built in. It's the latest fabric. Mo'Hair NeoBiofur – it exhales for you. Or so the label claims."

The two of them waited on the other side of the cubicle curtain while Toby took off her sombre Gardener dress and put on the furzoot. NeoBiofur or not, it was hot in there. And dark. She knew she was looking out through a pair of round white eyes with big black pupils, but it felt like peering through a keyhole.

"Flap your wings," said Zeb.

Toby moved her arms up and down inside the zoot arms and the duck suit quacked. It sounded like an old man blowing his nose.

"If you want to make the tail wiggle, stamp your left foot."

"How do I talk?" said Toby. She had to say it again, louder.

"Through the right earhole," said Adam One.

Oh great, thought Toby. You quack with your foot, you talk through your earhole. I won't ask how to do any of the other bodily functions.

She changed back into her dress, and Zeb stuffed the furzoot into a duffle bag. "I'll drive you in the truck," he said. "It's right out front."

"We'll be in touch very soon, my dear," said Adam One. "I regret . . . it's unfortunate that . . . Keep the Light around . . ."

"I'll try," said Toby.

The Gardeners' forced-air truck now had a logo on it that said, PARTY TIME. Toby sat in the front with Zeb. The Hammerhead was in the back, disguised as a box of balloons: Zeb said he was killing two birds with one stone.

"Sorry," he added.

"For what?" Toby asked. Sorry that she was going? She felt a small pulse-beat.

"Killing two birds. Not good to mention bird murder."

"Oh. Right," said Toby. "It's okay."

"We'll send the Hammerhead down the line," said Zeb. "We've got connections among the bag-heavers for the sealed bullet train; she can go as cargo, we'll mark her as Fragile. We've got a Truffle cell in Oregon – they'll keep her out of sight."

"How about me?" said Toby.

"Adam One wants you closer to the Garden," said Zeb, "in case Blanco gets Painballed again and you can come back. We've got an Exfernal spot for you, but it'll take a few days to set up. Meanwhile, just hang out in your zoot. Street of Dreams, where they peddle the custom genes – that place is crawling with furzooters, nobody will notice you. Now, better scrunch down – we're going through the Sewage Lagoon."

Zeb delivered Toby to the FenderBender Body Shop, where the resident Gardeners whisked her out of the truck and stashed her in the former hydraulic-lift pit, which they'd covered with trapdoor flooring. There she breathed ancient engine-oil fumes and ate a sparse meal of damp soybits and mashed turnips, washed down with Sumac. She slept on an old futon, using her furzoot as a pillow. There was no biolet in there, only a rusted Happicuppa coffee can. *Use what's to hand* was a cherished Gardener motto.

Not all the members of the FenderBender rat colony had been successfully relocated to the Buenavista Condos, she discovered. But those remaining were not overtly hostile.

The next morning she began her spurious job – waddling along the Street of Dreams inside a wodge of fake fur, quacking at intervals and wiggling her tail, wearing a sandwich board, and handing out brochures. On the front of the board it said, UGLY DUCKLINGS TO LOVELY SWANS AT THE ANOOYOO SPA-IN-THE-PARK! *Goose Your Self-Esteem!* On the back, ANOOYOO! DO IT FOR YOO! On the brochures it said, *Epidermal enhancement! Lower cost! Avoid gene errors! Fully reversible!* AnooYoo didn't sell gene therapy – nothing so radical or permanent. Instead it sold more superficial treatments. Herbal elixirs, system cleansers, dermal mood lifts; vegetable nanocell injections, mildew-formula micromesh resurfacing, heavy-duty face creams, rehydrating balms. Iguana-based hue changes, microbial spot removal, flat-wart leech peels.

She handed out many brochures, but she also got hassled by some of the gene-shop owners: on the Street of Dreams it was dream eat dream. There were a number of other furzooters working the Street – a lion, a Mo'Hair sheep, two bears, and three other ducks. Toby wondered how many of them were really who they claimed to be: if she was hiding out in plain view, others in need of invisibility must have discovered the same solution.

If she'd been working for a genuine furzoot outfit as she'd done once before, she'd have clocked her hours at day's end, climbed out of her zoot, and pocketed the receipt for her e-pay. As it was, Zeb collected her in the pickup. Its logo now said, BIGZOOT – SAY IT WITH FURORE! She rolled herself into the back, still inside her zoot, and Zeb ferried her to another Gardener enclave – an abandoned bank in the Sewage Lagoon. The various banking corps had once paid the local pleebmob for protection, but soon their Tex-Mex identity-theft specialists were skipping in and out as freely as mice. Finally the banks had given up and decamped, because no employee's idea of a business day well spent was lying on the floor with duct tape over your mouth while an identity filcher hacked the accounts, gaining access with your cut-off thumb.

The old-fashioned bank vault was a much better place to spend the night than the hydraulic-lift pit had been. Cool, rat-free, no gas fumes; a lingering odour of the gently oxidizing paper money of yesteryear. But then Toby started wondering what would happen if someone inadvertently closed and locked the vault door and then forgot about her, so she didn't sleep very well.

The next day it was the Street of Dreams again. The duck costume was intolerable in the heat, one of her rubber feet was coming loose, and the nose-cone filter was dysfunctional. What if the Gardeners abandoned her and she was left to eddy around in the Dreams-land, transformed into a non-existent bird-animal and dehydrating herself to death, to be found one day in a welter of damp pink faux feathers, clogging up the drains?

But finally Zeb picked her up. He drove her to a clinic at the back of a Mo'Hair franchise outlet. "We're doing the hair and skin," he said. "You're going dark. And the fingerprints, and the voiceprint. Plus a bit of recontouring." The biotech for changing iris pigment was risky – there'd been some unpleasant bulging effects, said Zeb – so she'd have to use contacts. Green ones – he'd picked out the colour himself.

"Higher voice, or lower?" he asked her.

"Lower," said Toby, hoping she wouldn't come out a baritone.

"Good choice," said Zeb.

The doctor was Chinese, and very smooth. There'd be an anaesthetic, and a recuperation time in the recovery unit upstairs – top of the line, said Zeb – and once Toby found herself inside it, the place did seem very clean. They didn't do much cutting and stitching. Her fingertips lost their sensitivity – it would come back, said Zeb – and her throat was sore from the voicework, and her head itched a lot while the Mo'Hair scalp was bonding. The skin pigmentation was uneven at first, but Zeb told her it would be fine in six weeks: until then, she'd have to keep strictly out of the sun.

She spent the six weeks of seclusion at a Truffle cell in SolarSpace. Her contact, whose name was Muffy, collected Toby from the clinic in a very expensive all-electric coupé. "If anyone asks," Muffy said, "just tell them you're the new maid. I do have to apologize," she continued, "but we have to eat meat at our place, it's part of our cover. We feel terrible about it, but just about everyone in SolarSpace is a carnivore, and they're very big on barbecues – organic, naturally, and some of it's stretchy-rack-grown, you know, they grow just the muscle tissue, no brain, no pain – and it would be suspicious if we ducked it. But I'll try to keep the cooking smells away from you."

Too late for such a warning: Toby had already smelled something that came close to the aroma of the bone-stock soup her mother used to make. Though she was ashamed of herself, it made her hungry. Hungry, and also sad. Maybe sadness was a kind of hunger, she thought. Maybe the two went together.

In her little maid's room Toby read e-magazines, and practised sticking her contact lenses onto her eyeballs, and listened to music on a Sea/H/Ear Candy. It was a surreal interlude. "Think of yourself as a chrysalis," Zeb had told her before the transformation process had begun. Sure enough, she'd gone in as Toby and had come out as Tobiatha. Less angla, more latina. More alto.

She looked at herself – her new skin, her new abundant hair, her more prominent cheekbones. Her new almond-shaped green eyes. She'd have to remember to put those lenses in every morning.

The alterations hadn't made her stunningly beautiful, but that wasn't the object. The object was to make her more invisible. Beauty is only skin deep, she thought. But why did they always say *only*?

Still, her new look wasn't bad. The hair was a nice change, though the family cats were taking an interest in it, probably because of the faint lamb-like smell. When she woke up in the morning she was likely to find one of them sitting on her pillow, licking her hair and purring.

48

Once her scalp was firmly rooted to her head and her skin tone was uniform, Toby was ready to move into her new identity. Muffy explained to her what this was to be.

"We thought, the AnooYoo Spa-in-the-Park," she said. "They're heavy on the botanics there, so you'd fit right in, because of the mushrooms and the potions and all, Zeb told me – so you can get up to speed on their products really fast. They have an organic garden for the café, they pride themselves on that, with a compost heap and all of that; and they're doing some plant splice tryouts you might find interesting. As for the rest, it's like organizing anything else – product in, value added, product out. Supervising the books and the supplies, managing the staff – Zeb says you're really good with people. The procedural templates are already in place – you'll just need to follow them."

"The product would be the customers?" said Toby.

"That's right," said Muffy.

"And the value added?"

"It's an intangible," said Muffy. "They feel they look better afterwards. People will pay a lot of money for that."

"Do you mind telling me how you got me this position?" Toby asked.

"My husband's on the AnooYoo board," said Muffy. "Don't worry, I didn't lie to him. He's one of us."

Once installed at the AnooYoo Spa, Toby settled into her role as Tobiatha, the vaguely Tex-Mex but discreet and efficient manager. The days were placid, the nights were calm. True, there was an electric fence around the whole place and four gatehouses with guards, but the identi-checks were lax and the guards never bothered Toby. It wasn't a high-security posting. The Spa had no big secrets to defend, so the guards did nothing but monitor the ladies who were going in, frightened by the first signs of droop and pucker, then going out again, buffed and tightened and resurfaced, irradiated and despotted.

But still frightened, because when might the whole problem – the whole *thing* – start happening to them again? The whole signs-of-mortality thing. The whole *thing* thing. Nobody likes it, thought Toby – being a body, a thing. Nobody wants to be limited in that way. We'd rather have wings. Even the word *flesh* has a mushy sound to it.

We're not selling only beauty, the AnooYoo Corp said in their staff instructionals. We're selling hope.

Some of the customers could be demanding. They couldn't under-stand why even the most advanced AnooYoo treatments wouldn't make them twenty-one again. "Our laboratories are well on the way to age reversal," Toby would tell them in soothing tones, "but they aren't quite there yet. In a few years . . ."

If you really want to stay the same age you are now forever and ever, she'd be thinking, try jumping off the roof: death's a sure-fire method for stopping time.

Toby took pains to be a convincing manager. She ran the Spa efficiently, she listened carefully to both staff and customers, she mediated disputes when necessary, she cultivated efficiency and tact. Having been an Eve Six helped: through that experience she'd discovered a talent within herself for gazing solemnly as if deeply interested, while saying nothing. "Remember," she'd tell her staff, "every customer wants to feel like a princess, and princesses are selfish and overbearing." Just don't spit in their soup, she wanted to counsel, but that would have been going too far out of her Tobiatha character.

On the most aggravating days she amused herself by viewing the Spa as if it were a tabloid 'zine: *Socialite corpse found on lawn, toxic facial suspected. Amanita implicated in exfoliation death. Tragedy stalks the pool.* But why take it out on the ladies? They only wanted to feel good and be happy, like everything else on the planet. Why should she begrudge them their obsessions with their puffy veins and tummy flubber? "Think pink," she told her girls as per the AnooYoo Corp instructional template, and then she'd tell herself the same thing. Why not? It was a nicer colour than bilious yellow.

After a cautious pause, she began stashing away a few supplies – building her own private Ararat. She wasn't sure she believed in the Waterless Flood – as time passed, the Gardeners and their theories seemed more and more remote, more fanciful, more creative – in a word, loonier – but she believed in it enough to take the rudimentary precautions. She was in charge of Spa inventory, so stockpiling was easy. She'd simply retrieve empty product containers from the recycling bins, a few at a time – those for AnooYoo Intestinal Whisk were especially useful, as they were large and had tops that snapped on – and fill them with soybits or dried seaweed or powdered milk substitute or tins of soydines. Then she'd replace the tops and store the containers at the very backs of the stockroom shelves. A couple of other staff members had the storeroom door code, but as Toby was known to be a strict inventory-taker and to be tough on pilferers, no one was likely to make off with any of her refilled containers.

She had an office of her own, and in that office there was a computer. She knew the hazards of out-of-bounds usage – some AnooYoo Corp functionary might be monitoring her searches and messages and checking to make sure staff wasn't watching porno flicks on company time – so most days she scanned only for general news, hoping that way to pick up any word of the Gardeners.

There wasn't much. From time to time there'd be a story on subversive acts by fanatical greenies, but there was a number of such groups by now. She glimpsed some Gardener faces in the crowd during the Boston Coffee Party, when they were dumping Happicuppa beans into the harbour, but she might have been wrong about that. Several people were wearing T-shirts with G IS G on them for "God Is Green," which proved nothing: the Gardeners themselves hadn't worn such T-shirts, not in the old days.

The CorpSeCorps could have shut down the Happicuppa riots. They could have spraygunned the lot, plus any TV camerafolk who happened to be nearby. Not that you could shut down coverage of such events completely: people used their cameraphones. Still, why didn't the CorpSeCorps move in openly, blitz their opponents right in plain view, and impose overt totalitarian rule, since they were the only ones with weapons? They were even running the army, now that it had been privatized.

She'd once put this question to Zeb. He'd said that officially they were a private Corporation Security Corps employed by the brand-name Corporations, and those Corporations still wanted to be perceived as honest and trustworthy, friendly as daisies, guileless as bunnies. They couldn't afford to be viewed by the average consumer as lying, heartless, tyrannical butchers.

"The Corps have to sell, but they can't force people to buy," he'd said. "Not yet. So the clean image is still seen as a must."

That was the short answer: people didn't want the taste of blood in their Happicuppas.

Muffy, her Truffle-cell minder, kept in touch with Toby by checking herself in for AnooYoo treatments. Occasionally she'd bring news: Adam One was well, Nuala sent regards, the Gardeners were still expanding their influence, but the situation was unstable. Once in a while she'd bring in a female fugitive in need of a temporary hide. She'd dress the woman in clothes like hers – rich SolarSpace matron colours, pastel blue, creamy beige – and book her in for treatments. "Just pile on the mud and smother her in towels, and no one will notice a thing," she'd say, which turned out to be true.

One of these emergency guests was the Hammerhead. Toby recognized her – the fidgety hands, the intense blue martyr's eyes – but she didn't recognize Toby. So the Hammerhead hadn't made it to a quiet life in Oregon after all, thought Toby: she's still in the area, taking the risks, on the run all the time. Most likely she'd been sucked into the urban green-guerrilla scene; in which case her days were numbered, because the CorpSeCorps were said to be bent on eliminating all such activists. They'd have the samples from her old HelthWyzer identity, and once you were in their system you never got out of it except by turning up as a corpse with dental work and DNA that matched their records.

Toby ordered the Total Aromatics for the Hammerhead, and an extra Deep Pore Relax. She looked as if she needed them.

There was one serious hazard at the AnooYoo: Lucerne was a regular customer. She came every month, toting a Compound senior-level wife's wardrobe. She always had the Luscious Polish, the Plum Skin Plumper, and the AnooYoo Fountain of Yooth Total Immersion. She looked more stylish than she'd been at the Gardeners – not difficult, thought Toby, because in a plastic bag you'd be more stylish than a Gardener – but she also looked older and more desiccated. Her once-lush lower lip had developed a downward sag, despite all the collagen and plant extracts Toby knew had been pumped into it, and her eyelids were getting the crinkly texture of poppy petals. These signs of decline were gratifying to Toby, though it dismayed her to be burdened with such a petty and jealous emotion. *Give it up*, she told herself. *Just because Lucerne's turning into an old puffball doesn't mean you're a hot babe.*

It would of course be catastrophic if Lucerne were suddenly to burst out from behind a shrub or a shower curtain and shout out Toby's real name. So Toby took evasive action. She'd review the advance bookings so she'd know exactly when Lucerne was going to show up. Then she'd assign her most vigorous operatives – Melody with her big shoulders, Symphony with her firm hands – and keep herself out of Lucerne's sightline. But as Lucerne was usually prone and covered with brown goop and eye pads, she was unlikely to spot Toby; and even if she did see her, she'd be sure to look right through her. To women like Lucerne, women like Tobiatha were faceless.

What if I crept up on her during the Fountain of Yooth Total Immersion and gunned the lasers? Toby wondered. Or shorted the heat lamp? She'd melt like a marshmallow. A nematode snack. The Earth would cheer.

Dear Eve Six, said Adam One's voice. Such fantasies are unworthy of you. What would Pilar think?

One afternoon there was a knock at Toby's office door. "Come in," she said. It was a large man in a groundsman's green denim overall. He was whistling – surely – a familiar tune.

"I'm here to prune the lumiroses," he said. Toby looked up, drew her breath in sharply. She knew better than to say anything: her office could be crawling with bugs.

Zeb glanced back along the hallway, then stepped in and shut the door. He sat down at her computer, then took a Sharpie and wrote on her desk pad: *Watch what I do.*

The Gardeners? Toby wrote. *Adam One?*

Schism, Zeb wrote. *Own group now.* "Having any trouble with the plantings?" he said out loud.

Shackleton and Crozier? Toby wrote. *With you?*

Manner of speaking, Zeb replied. *Oates. Katuro, Rebecca. New ones too.*

Amanda?

Got out. Higher education. Art. Smart.

He'd pulled up a site: EXTINCTATHON. Monitored by MaddAddam. *Adam named the living animals, MaddAddam names the dead ones. Do you want to play?*

MaddAddam? Toby wrote on her desk pad. *Your group? You're plural?* She was elated: Zeb was here, beside her, in the flesh. After she'd thought for so long that she'd never see him again.

I contain multitudes, wrote Zeb. *Pick a codename. Life form, extinct.*

Dodo, Toby wrote.

Last fifty years, Zeb wrote. Not much time. *Pruning team waiting. Ask about aphids.*

"There's aphids on the lumiroses," Toby said. She was riffling through the old Gardener lists in her head – animals, fish, birds, flowers, clams, lizards, recently extinct. *Inaccessible Rail,* she wrote. That bird had gone ten years ago. *Can they hack this site?*

"We can take care of that," Zeb said. "Though there's supposed to be a built-in insecticidal deterrent . . . I'll take some samples. There's more than one way to skin a cat." *No,* he wrote. *Made our own virtual private networks. Quadrupally encrypted. Sorry about the cat-skinning ref. Here's your number.*

He wrote her new codename and a pass number on the pad. Then he typed his own number and code into the log-in space provided. *Welcome, Spirit Bear. Do you want to play a general game or do you want to play a Grandmaster?* said the screen.

Zeb clicked on Grandmaster. *Good. Find your playroom. MaddAddam will meet you there.*

Watch, he wrote on her pad. He entered a site advertising Mo'Hair transplants, skipped through a pixel gateway on the eye of a magenta-haired sheep, entered the blue percolating stomach of an ad for a Helth-Wyzer antacid, which led to the avid open mouth of a SecretBurger customer caught in mid-chomp. Then a wide green landscape unfolded – trees in the distance, a lake in the foreground, a rhino and three lions drinking. A scene from the past.

A line of type unscrolled across it: *Welcome to MaddAddam's playroom, Spirit Bear. You have a message.*

Deliver message, Zeb clicked.

The liver is evil and must be punished.

I hear you, Red-necked Crake, Zeb typed. *All is well.*

Then he closed the site and stood up. "Call me if there are any aphid recurrences," he said. "If you'd check our work from time to time and keep me informed, that would be good." He wrote on her pad: *The hair's great, babe. Love the slanty eyes.* Then he was gone.

Toby gathered up all the desk-pad pages. Luckily she had some matches to burn them with; she'd been hoarding matches for her Ararat, storing them in a container labelled Lemon Meringue Facial.

After Zeb's visit she felt less isolated. She'd log in to Extinctathon at irregular intervals and trace the path to the MaddAddam Grandmaster chatroom. Codenames and messages flitted across the screen: *Black Rhino to Spirit Bear: Newbies coming. Ivory Bill to Swift Fox: Fear no weevil. White Sedge and Lotis Blue: Micesplice a ten. Red-necked Crake to MaddAddam: Marshmallow hiways nice one!* She had no idea what most of these messages meant, but at least she felt included.

Sometimes there were e-bulletins that appeared to be CorpSeCorps classified information. Many of these were about strange outbreaks of new diseases, or peculiar infestations – the splice porcubeaver that was attacking the fan belts in cars, the bean weevil that was decimating Happicuppa coffee plantations, the asphalt-eating microbe that was melting highways.

Then the Rarity restaurant chain was obliterated by a series of lethal bombings. She saw the regular news, where these events were blamed on unspecified eco-terrorists; but she also read a detailed analysis on MaddAddam. It was the Wolf Isaiahists who'd done the bombings, they said, because Rarity had introduced a new menu item – liobam, a sacred animal for the Wolf Isaiahists. MaddAddam had added a P.S.: *Warning all God's Gardeners: They'll pin this on you. Go to ground.*

Shortly after that, Muffy came to the Spa unexpectedly. She was her usual elegant self; her manner gave nothing away. "Let's walk on the lawn," she said. When they were out in the open and away from any hidden mikes, she whispered, "I'm not here for a treatment. I just needed to tell you that we're going away, I can't say where. Don't worry. It's only urgent on the inside."

"Will you be all right?" Toby asked.

"Time will tell," said Muffy. "Good luck, dear Toby. Dear Tobiatha. Put Light around me."

She and her husband were listed as fatalities in an airship accident a week later. The CorpSeCorps were good at arranging high-class mishaps for highly placed suspects, Zeb had told her – people whose disappearance without a trace would cause a stir, up there among the Corps anointed.

Toby didn't go near the MaddAddam chatroom for months after that. She waited for the knock on the door, the shattering of glass, the *zipzip* of a spraygun. But nothing happened. When she finally screwed up the courage to enter MaddAddam again, there was a message for her:

Inaccessible Rail from Spirit Bear: The Garden is destroyed. Adams and Eves gone dark. Watch and wait.

POLLINATION DAY

‖‖‖‖‖
‖‖‖‖‖
‖‖‖‖‖

 **POLLINATION DAY**

YEAR TWENTY-ONE.

OF THE TREES, AND OF THE FRUITS IN THEIR SEASONS.
SPOKEN BY ADAM ONE.

Dear Friends and Fellow Mammals:

Today is a Feast day, but sadly we have no feast. Our flight was rapid: our escape narrow. Now, true to their nature, our enemies have laid waste to our Rooftop. But surely one day we will return to Edencliff and restore that blissful site to its former glory. The CorpSeCorps may have destroyed our Garden, but they have not destroyed our Spirit. Eventually, we shall plant again.

Why did the Corps strike? Alas, we were becoming too powerful for their liking. Many rooftops were blossoming as the rose; many hearts and minds were bent towards an Earth restored to balance. But in success lay the seeds of ruin, for those in power could no longer dismiss us as ineffectual faddists: they feared us, as prophets of the age to come. In short, we threatened their profit margins.

In addition, they linked us to the bio-attacks made on their infrastructures by the schismatic and heretical group calling itself MaddAddam. Last week's bombing attacks on the Rarity restaurant chain – though perpetrated by the Wolf Isaiahists alone – gave them an excuse to unleash a sweeping crackdown on all who have sided with God's Created Earth.

May they prove as blind in material vision as they have long been in Spiritual vision! For though our days of calling carnivores to open repentance on the pleebland streets are over, the lessons of Animal Camouflage have not been lost on us. Disguised to blend with the background, we thrive under the noses of our enemies. We have shed our plain vestments and swathed ourselves in mallway purchases. The monogrammed golf shirt, the lime green tank top, the striped pastel knit ensemble sported so courageously by Nuala – such is our defensive armour.

Some of you have chosen to allay suspicion by courageously eating the flesh of our fellow Creatures; but do not attempt feats beyond your strength, dear Friends. To bite into a SecretBurger and then choke on it will attract unwelcome scrutiny. If in doubts as to your limits, confine yourselves to a SoYummie ice cream. Such quasi-foods may be swallowed without undue strain.

Let us give thanks to the Fernside Truffle cell, which has made this Street of Dreams refuge available to us. The sign on our door proclaims, GREEN GENES, which purports to be a firm of botanic splice designers. The second sign – the one that says, CLOSED FOR RENOVATIONS – is our protection. If asked, say we've been having trouble with the contractor. That is always a plausible explanation.

Today is Pollination Day, on which we remember the contributions to forest preservation of Saint Suryamani Bhagat of India, Saint Stephen King of the Pureora Forest in New Zealand, and Saint Odigha of Nigeria, among so many others. This Festival is devoted to the mysteries of Plant Reproduction, especially that of those wondrous trees, the Angiosperms, with special emphasis upon the Drupes and the Pomaceous Fruits.

Legends of such Fruits have come down to us from the Ancients – the Golden Apples of the Hesperides, the similarly golden Apple of Discord. Some say that the Fruit of the Tree of Knowledge of Good and Evil was a fig, others prefer a date, yet others a pomegranate. It would have made sense for this foodstuff to have been truly evil – a meat object, such as a beefsteak. Why then a Fruit? Because our Ancestors were fruitivores, without a doubt, and only a Fruit would have tempted them.

The Fruit remains a deeply meaningful symbol for us, embodying the notions of healthful harvest, of rich culmination, and of new beginning, for within every Fruit is a seed – a potential new life. The Fruit ripens and falls and returns to the soil; but the Seed takes root, and grows, and brings forth more Life. As the Human Words of God have said, "By their Fruits ye shall know them." Let us pray that our Fruits be Fruits of Good, and not Fruits of Evil.

But a word of caution: we honour the Pollinating Insects, and in especial the Bees, but we are now informed that, in addition to the virus-resistant strain introduced after the recent honeybee die-off, the Corps have now developed a hybrid bee. It is not a genetic splice, my Friends. No: it is a greater abomination! Bees are seized while still in larval form, and micro-mechanical systems are inserted into them. Tissue grows around the insert, and when the full adult or "imago" emerges, it is a bee cyborg spy controllable by a CorpSeCorps operator, equipped to transmit, and thus to betray.

The ethical problems raised are troubling: Should we have recourse to insecticides? Is such a mechanized slave bee *alive*? If so, is it a true Creature of God or something else entirely? We must ponder the deeper implications, my Friends, and pray for guidance.

Let us sing.

THE PEACH OR PLUM

The Peach or Plum that spreads its boughs
Is beauteous at time of flower,
And Birds and Bees and Bats rejoice,
And sip its nectar hour by hour.

And Pollination then takes place:
For every Nut or Seed or Fruit,
A tiny golden particle
Has winged its way, and taken root.

Then swells the oval on the stem,
And slowly ripens, week by week –
Within it stored the nourishment
That Birds and Beasts and Men do seek.

And in each Seed or Fruit or Nut
Is coiled a silver infant Tree
That will arise if planted right,
Unfurling flowers, a joy to see.

When next you eat a golden Peach
And lightly throw away the pit,
Consider how it shines with Life –
God dwelling in the midst of it.

From *The God's Gardeners Oral Hymnbook*

49

YEAR TWENTY-FIVE

Adam One used to say, If you can't stop the waves, go sailing. Or else, What can't be mended may still be tended. Or else, Without the light, no chance; without the dark, no dance. Which meant that even bad things did some good because they were a challenge and you didn't always know what good effects they might have. Not that the Gardeners ever did any dancing, as such.

So I decided to perform a Meditation, which would be one way of dealing with the fact that there was nothing to do inside the Sticky Zone. If nothing's the problem, work with nothing, Philo the Fog would say. Turn off your mind chatter. Open up your inner eye, your inner ear. See what you can see. Hear what you can hear. Back at the Gardeners, what I'd see would be the pigtails of the girl in front of me and what I'd hear would be the snoring of Philo, because when he was leading Meditation he always went to sleep.

I wasn't much more successful now. I could hear the thump, thump of the bass line coming from the Snakepit and the humming of the mini-fridge, I could see the lights of the street making blurry patterns through the glass bricks of the window, but none of this was spiritually enlightening. So I stopped doing the Meditation and turned on the news.

There was another minor epidemic, they were saying, but nothing to get alarmed about. Viruses and bacteria were always mutating, but I knew the Corporations could always invent treatments for them, and anyway whatever this bug was I didn't have it myself because I'd been in isolation with a double virus barrier protecting me. I was in the safest place I could be.

I switched back to the Snakepit. A fight had broken out. It must have been the Painballers – the three who'd come in first and the other one.

As I watched, the CorpSeCorps minders moved in. They got one of the Painballers down on the floor, used their tasers on him. The bouncers were fighting now too – one of them staggered backwards, clutching his eye; then another one hit the bar. It didn't usually take this long to get things under control. Savona and Crimson Petal were still up on the trapezes trying to carry on, but the pole girls were scurrying off the stage. Then they ran back onto it again: the exits behind must be blocked. Oh no, I thought. Then a bottle flew into the camera and smashed it.

I went to another camera, but my hands were shaking and I'd forgotten the key-in, and by the time I'd turned it on and got it focused the Snakepit was a lot emptier. The lights were still on and the music was playing, but the room was a shambles. The customers must have all run out. Savona was lying on the bar: I could tell it was her by the sparkly costume, even though it was half torn off. Her head was bent at a strange angle and there was blood all over her face. Crimson Petal was hanging from the trapeze; one of the ropes was around her neck, and between her legs was the glint of a bottle – someone must have shoved it up her. Her frills and ruffles were ripped to shreds. She looked like a limp bouquet.

Where was Mordis?

A dark flailing bundle tumbled across the screen: a shadow dance, a kinky ballet. There was the *bam!* of a door slammed back, and then something that sounded like hooting. Then sirens, in the distance. Feet running.

Then there was shouting in the hallway outside the Sticky Zone and the videoscreen from outside my door lit up, and on it was Mordis, close up, staring in at me with one eye. The other one was closed. His face looked chewed.

"Your name," he whispered.

Then an arm grabbed him around the throat, pulled his head back. One of the Painballers. I could see his hand, holding a slice of bottle: red and blue veins. "Open the fucking door, asshole," he said. "Bitch in heat! Time to share!"

Mordis was howling. What they wanted from him was the door code. "The numbers, the numbers," they were saying.

I saw Mordis for one more instant. There was a gurgling, and he was gone. In his place was the Painballer – a faceful of scars.

"Open up and we'll let your buddy live," he said. "We won't hurt you." But he was lying because Mordis was already dead.

Then there was more shouting, and then the CorpSeMen must have tasered him, because he howled in his turn and vanished from the screen, and there was a thudding sound like someone kicking a sack.

I went to the Snakepit camera: more CorpSeMen, in riot gear, a swarm of them. They were pushing and dragging the Painballers out the door – one dead one, three still alive. It would be back to Painball for them – they should never have been let out, not ever.

Then I realized what would happen. The Sticky Zone was a fortress. No one could get in without the door code, and nobody but Mordis knew that code. That's what he always said. And hadn't told it: he'd saved my life.

But now I was locked inside, with no one to let me out. *Oh please*, I thought. *I don't want to be dead.*

50

I told myself not to panic. SeksMart would send a cleaning crew, and they'd realize I was in there, and they'd get someone to work on the lock. They wouldn't leave me in there to starve and dry up like a mummy: when they reopened Scales they'd need me. It wouldn't be at all the same without Mordis – already I missed him – but at least I would have a function. I wasn't only a disposable, I was talent. That's what Mordis always said.

So it was just a matter of waiting it out.

I took a shower – I felt dirty, as if those Painballers really had got in, or as if I had the blood of Mordis all over me.

Then I did another Meditation, a real one. *Put Light around Mordis*, I prayed. *Let him go into the Universe. May his Spirit go in peace.* I pictured him flying up out of his demolished body in the form of a small, brown beady-eyed bird.

The next day, two bad things happened. First, I turned on the news. The minor epidemic they'd been talking about earlier wasn't behaving in the usual way – a local outbreak, one they could contain. Now it was an emergency. They showed a map of the world, with the hotspots lighting up in red – Brazil, Taiwan, Saudi Arabia, Bombay, Paris, Berlin – it was like watching the planet being spraygunned. It was an eruptive plague, they said, and the thing was spreading fast – no, not even spreading, breaking out at the same time in cities far apart, which wasn't the normal pattern. Ordinarily the Corps would have called for lies and cover-ups, and we'd hear something like the real story only in rumours, so the fact that all this was right out there on the news showed how serious it was – the Corps couldn't keep the lid on.

The news jockeys were trying to keep calm. The experts didn't know what the superbug was, but it was a pandemic for sure, and a lot of people were dying fast – just sort of melting. As soon as they said, "No need for panic," in that eerie calm tone with those glued-on smiles, I could tell it was really serious.

The second bad thing was that some guys in biosuits came into the Snakepit and stuffed the dead people into body bags and took them out. But they didn't check out the second floor, although I screamed and screamed. I guess they couldn't hear me because the Sticky Zone walls were thick and the Snakepit music was still going and it must have drowned me out. That was lucky for me, because if I'd left the Sticky Zone right then I'd have caught what everyone else was catching. So it wasn't really a bad thing, but it felt like it at the time.

The next day the news was even worse. The plague was spreading, and there was rioting and looting and killing going on, and the CorpSeCorps had just more or less vanished: they must've been dying too.

And a few days after that, there wasn't any more news.

Now I was really scared. But I told myself that although I couldn't get out, nobody else could get in, and I'd be okay as long as the solar didn't break down. It would keep the water flowing and the minifridge running, and the freezer, and the air filters. Air filtering was a plus, because it would soon be smelling very bad out there. And I would take one day at a time and see what came of it.

I knew I'd have to be practical, or I'd lose hope and slide into a Fallow state and maybe never come out of it. So I opened the minifridge and the freezer and counted all the stuff inside – the Joltbars and energy drinks and snacks, and the frozen ChickieNobs and the faux fish. If I ate only a third of every meal instead of half, and saved the rest instead of tossing it down the chute, I'd have enough for at least six weeks.

I'd been trying to call Amanda, but she hadn't answered. All I could do was leave text messages: CUM 2 SCLS. My hope was that she'd get the texts and realize something was wrong, and then she'd come to Scales and figure out how to unlock the door. I'd kept my cellphone turned on all the time in case she called, but now when I tried to phone or even text I got NO SERVICE. Once I did get a short message – IM OK – but the channels must have been jammed with frantic people trying to reach their families, because I didn't get anything more.

Then I guess the calling must have thinned out as people died, and I was able to get through. No picture, just her voice. "Where are you?" I said, and she said, "Nicked a solarcar. Ohio."

"Don't go into the cities," I said. "Don't let anyone touch you." I wanted to tell her what I'd been learning from the news, but she'd faded out. After that I couldn't even get a signal. The relay towers must have gone down.

You create your own reality, the horoscopes always said, and the Gardeners said that too. So I tried to create the reality of Amanda. Now she was in her khaki desert-girl outfit. Now she'd stopped to have a drink of water. Now she was digging up a root and eating it. Now she was walking again. She was coming towards me, hour by hour. She wouldn't get the sickness, and no one would kill her, because she was so smart and strong. She was smiling. Now she was singing. But I knew I was just making it up.

51

I hadn't seen Amanda except on the phone for such a long time, not since I'd started working at Scales. Before that, there had been a period when I hadn't even known where she was. I'd lost touch when Lucerne had thrown out my purple phone, back when I'd still been living inside the HelthWyzer Compound. At that time I thought I'd never see Amanda again – that she was gone out of my life forever.

That was what I still believed as I sat on the bullet train on my way to the Martha Graham Academy. I was feeling very alone and sorry for myself: I hadn't lost only Amanda, I'd lost everything in my life that had any meaning. The Adams and the Eves, or some of them, such as Toby and Zeb. Amanda. But most of all, Jimmy. I was over the worst of the hurt he'd caused me, but there was a dull ache. He'd been so sweet to me, then he'd shut me out as if I wasn't really there. That was a cold and miserable feeling. I was so depressed that I'd even given up the idea that I might get together with Jimmy again, at Martha Graham: it seemed like a far-fetched daydream.

By the time I was on that bullet train it had been a long time since I'd been in love with Jimmy. No: it had been a long time since Jimmy had been in love with me – when I was being honest and not only angry and sad, I knew that I was still in love with Jimmy. I'd slept with other boys, but I'd just been going through the motions. I was going to Martha Graham partly to get away from Lucerne, but also I had to do something so I might as well get an education. That's how they talked about it, as if an education was a thing that you got, like a dress. I didn't care what happened to me one way or the other, I just felt grey.

That was not at all the Gardener way of thinking. The Gardeners said the only real education was the education of the Spirit. But I'd forgotten what that meant.

Martha Graham was an artistic school named after a famous ancient dancer, so dance courses were featured at it. Since I had to take something I took Dance Calisthenics and Dramatic Expression – you didn't need any background or math for those. I figured I could get a job in one of the Corps, leading the in-corp noon-hour exercise programs that the better ones had. Tone to Music, Yoga for Middle Management – one of those.

The Martha Graham campus was like the Buenavista Condos – it had been classy once, but now it was falling apart, and had mould issues, and the ceilings leaked. I couldn't eat the stuff in the cafeteria because who knew what was in it – I still had a lot of trouble with animal protein, especially if it might be organs and noses. But I felt more at home there than I had in the HelthWyzer Compound, because at least Martha Graham wasn't so shiny and fake-looking and it didn't smell of chemical cleaning products. Or any cleaning products at all.

Every freshperson at Martha Graham had to share a suite. The roommate I was given was called Buddy the Third; I didn't see much of him. He was in Football, but the Martha Graham team always got pulverized and Buddy the Third was drunk or stoned a lot as a result. I'd lock the door on my side of our shared bathroom because the guys on the football team were known for date rape and I didn't think Buddy would even bother with the date part of it, but I could hear him in there throwing up in the mornings.

There was a Happicuppa franchise on campus, and I'd go there for breakfast because they had vegan muffins, I wouldn't have to listen to

Buddy puking, and I could use their washroom, which stank less than mine. One day I was walking up to the Happicuppa, and there was Bernice. I recognized her right away. I was really startled to see her. It was shocking – like a jolt of electricity. All the guilt I'd once felt about her but had more or less forgotten came flooding back.

She was wearing a green T-shirt with a big G on it and holding a sign that said, A HAPPICUPPA IS A CRAPPICUPPA. There were two other kids with the same T-shirt, but different signs: BREW OF EVIL, DON'T DRINK DEATH. I could see from the outfits and facial expressions that they were extreme fanatic ultra-greens, and they were picketing the place. This was the year when there were all the Happicuppa riots – I'd seen them onscreen.

Bernice wasn't any prettier than she used to be. If anything, she was chunkier, and her scowling was fiercer. She didn't spot me, so I had a choice: I could have gone right past her and into the Happicuppa, pretending I hadn't seen her, or I could have turned around and slid away. But I found myself going right back into Gardener mode, remembering all those teachings about taking responsibility and if you killed a thing you had to eat it. And I had killed Burt, in a way. Or I felt I had.

So I didn't dodge it. Instead I went right up to her and said, "Bernice! It's me – Ren!"

She jumped as if I'd kicked her. Then she focused on me. "So I see," she said in a sour voice.

"Let me buy you a coffee," I said. I must've been really nervous to say that because why would Bernice want a coffee from a place she was picketing?

She must have thought I was making fun of her because she said, "Piss off."

"Sorry," I said. "I didn't mean it that way. How about a water, then? We could drink it over there, by the statue." The statue of Martha Graham was a sort of mascot: it showed her being Judith, holding up the head of her enemy Holofernes, and the students had painted the head's neck stump red and stuck steel wool under Martha's armpits. There was a flat base right underneath the Holofernes head where you could sit.

She gave me another scowl. "You are so backslidden," she said. "Bottled water is evil. Don't you know anything?"

I could have called her a bitch and just walked away from everything. But this was my one chance to put things right, at least with myself. "Bernice," I said, "I want to make you an apology. So just tell me what you can drink, and I'll get some of it, and we'll go someplace and drink it."

She was still grumpy – no one could hold a grudge like her – but after I'd said we needed to put Light around it, which must've triggered off the better Gardener part of her, she said there was this organic mix in a recyclable carton made of pressed kudzu leaves, you could get it at the campus supermarkette, and she still had some picketing to do, but by the time I came back with the stuff she could take a break.

We sat underneath the head of Holofernes with the two boxes of liquid mulch I'd bought, and the taste brought back my early days at the Gardeners – how unhappy I'd been at first, and how Bernice had stuck up for me then. "Didn't you go to the West Coast?" I asked her. "After all that . . ."

"Yeah," she said. "Well, I'm back here now." She said that Veena had backslidden and joined an entirely different religion called the Known Fruits, who claimed it was a mark of God's favour to be rich because *By their fruits ye shall know them*, and *fruits* meant bank accounts. Veena had gone into a HelthWyzer vitamin-supplements franchise, and had quickly expanded to five outlets, and was doing very well. Bernice said the West Coast was perfect for that because although they all did stuff like yoga and said it was Spiritual, they were really just twisted, fish-crunching, materialistic body-worshippers out there, with facelifts and bimplants and genework and totally warped values.

Veena had wanted Bernice to take Business at college, but Bernice had stayed a Gardener by faith, so they'd fought about it; and Martha Graham was a compromise because it had courses in How to Profit from Holistic Healing. Which was what Bernice was taking.

I couldn't picture Bernice healing anything, because I couldn't picture her wanting to heal anything. Grinding dirt into your cut was more her style. But I said that was really interesting.

I told her what I was taking, but I saw she didn't care. So I told her about my roommate, Buddy the Third, and she said the entire Martha Graham Academy was filled with people like that – Exfernals frittering away their time on Earth without one serious thought in their heads except drinking and getting laid. She'd had a roommate like that at first, plus he'd been an animal-murderer because he'd worn leather sandals. Though they'd been fleather. But they'd looked like leather. So she'd burnt them. And thank God she didn't have to share a bathroom with him any more, because she could hear him doing sexual things with girls practically every night, like some degenerate bonobo/rabbit splice.

"Jimmy!" she said. "What a meat-breath!"

When I heard the name Jimmy I thought, It can't be the same one, but then I thought, Oh yes it can. While this was running through my head, Bernice said why didn't I move into the room adjoining hers since now that Jimmy had moved out it was empty.

I'd wanted to make it up with her but not that much. So I launched into what I needed to say. "I'm very sorry about Burt," I said. "Your dad. About him dying like that. I feel so responsible."

She looked at me as if I was crazy. "What're you talking about?" she said.

"That time I told you he was having sex with Nuala, and you told Veena, and she blew up and called the CorpSeCorps? Well, I don't think he was having sex with Nuala. Me and Amanda – we kind of made it up because we were being mean. I feel terrible about it, and I'm really sorry. I don't think he ever did anything worse than girls' armpits."

"At least Nuala was a grown-up," said Bernice. "But he didn't stop at the armpits. With the girls. He was a degenerate, just like my mother said. He used to tell me I was his favourite little girl, but not even that was true. So I told Veena. That's why she ratted him out. So you can stop feeling so self-important." I got the old glare, though this time with red watery eyes. "You're just lucky it was never you."

"Oh," I said. "Bernice, I'm really sorry."

"I don't want to talk about this any more," said Bernice. "I prefer to spend my time in more productive ways." She said would I come and stencil Happicuppa protest signs with her, and I said I'd already skipped one class that day, but maybe some other time. She gave me that slitty-eyed look that said she could tell I was wriggling out of something. Then I asked her what her old roommate Jimmy had actually looked like, and she said why was that any of my business?

She was right back into her bossy mode, and I knew that if I hung around with her much longer I'd be nine years old again, and she'd have the same hold on me, only more so because however awful things might be for me in my life they'd always be worse in hers, and she'd have a victim hammerlock on me. I said I really had to run, and she said, "Yeah, right," and then she said I hadn't changed at all, I was still just as much of a simpy lightweight as I'd ever been.

Years later – when I was already working at Scales and Tails – I saw onscreen that Bernice had been spraygunned in a raid on a Gardeners safe house. That was after the Gardeners had been outlawed. Though being outlawed wouldn't have stopped Bernice; she was a person with the courage of her convictions. I had to admire her for that – for the convictions, and also for the courage – because I never really felt I had either one.

There was a close-up of her dead face, looking more gentle and peaceful than I'd ever seen her look in life. Maybe that was the real Bernice, I thought – kind and innocent. Maybe she was truly like that inside, and all the fighting we used to do and all her sharp and unpleasant edges – that was her way of struggling to get out of the hard skin she'd grown all over herself like a beetle shell. But no matter how she hit out and raged, she'd been stuck in there. That thought made me feel so sorry for her that I cried.

52

Before that conversation with Bernice when she'd talked about her former roommate, I'd been half expecting to see Jimmy – in a classroom, at the Happicuppa, or just walking somewhere. But now I felt he must be very close by. He was right around the corner, or on the other side of a window; or I'd wake up one morning and there he would be, right beside me, holding my hand and looking at me the way he used to do when we first got together. It was like being haunted.

Maybe I've imprinted on Jimmy, I thought. Like a baby duck hatching out of an egg and the first thing it sees is a weasel, so that's what it follows around for the rest of its life. Which is likely to be short. Why did it have to be Jimmy who was the very first person I'd fallen in love with? Why couldn't it have been someone with a better character? Or at least a less fickle person. A more serious person, not so given to playing the fool.

The worst thing about it was that I couldn't get interested in anyone else. There was a hole in my heart that only Jimmy could fill. I know that's a country-and-western thing to say – I'd heard enough of that kind of worldly music on my Sea/H/Ear Candy by then – but it's the only way I can explain it. And it isn't that I wasn't aware of Jimmy's faults, because I was.

I did see Jimmy eventually, of course. The campus wasn't huge, so it was bound to happen sooner or later. I saw him in the distance, and he saw me, but he didn't come rushing over. He stayed in the distance. He didn't even wave, he looked away as if he hadn't seen me. So if I'd been waiting for the answer to the question I was always asking myself – Does Jimmy still love me? – I had it now.

Then I met a girl in Dance Calisthenics – Shayluba somebody – who'd been with Jimmy for a while. She said it was great at first, but he started saying how he was really bad for her, he was incapable of commitment because of the girlfriend he'd had in high school. They were too young, it ended badly, and he'd been an emotional dumpster ever since, but maybe he was destructive by nature since he messed up every girl he touched.

"Was her name Wakulla Price?" I asked.

"No, actually," said Shayluba. "It was you. He pointed you out."

Jimmy, what a fraud and bullshitting liar you are, I thought. But then I thought, What if it's true? What if I'd crapped up Jimmy's life just as much as he'd crapped up mine?

I tried to forget all about him. But somehow I couldn't. Beating myself up over Jimmy had become a bad habit with me, like biting your nails. Every once in a while I'd see him drifting past in the distance, which was like having just one cigarette when you're trying to quit – it starts you off again. Not that I was ever a smoker.

I'd been at Martha Graham for almost two years when I got some really terrible news. Lucerne called me and said that my biofather, Frank, had been kidnapped by a rival Corp somewhere to the east of Europe. The Corps over there were always trying to poach on our Corps – their undercover thugs were even more cut-throat than ours, and they had an advantage because they were better at languages and could pretend to be immigrants. We couldn't do that to them, because why would we immigrate there?

They'd bagged Frank right inside the Compound – in the men's room of his lab building, said Lucerne – and shipped him out in a Zizzy Froots delivery van; then they'd carted him across the Atlantic Ocean in an airship wrapped up in gauze bandages and disguised as a patient recovering from a facelift. Worse, they'd sent back a DVD of him in a drugged-looking state, confessing that HelthWyzer had been sticking a slow-acting but incurable gene-spliced disease germ inside their supplements so they could make a lot of money on the treatments. It was blackmail pure and simple, said Lucerne – they'd trade Frank for a couple of the formulas they wanted, most notably the ones for the slow-acting diseases; and, in addition, they wouldn't make the incriminating DVD public. But otherwise, they'd said, Frank's head would have to kiss his body goodbye.

HelthWyzer had done a cost-benefit analysis, said Lucerne, and they'd decided the disease germs and formulas were worth more to them than Frank was. As for the adverse publicity, they could squelch it at source, since the media Corps controlled what was news and what wasn't. And the Internet was such a jumble of false and true factoids that no one believed what was on it any more, or else they believed all of it, which amounted to the same thing. So HelthWyzer wasn't going to pay up. They said they regretted Lucerne's loss, but it wasn't their policy to give in to blackmail demands, as that would encourage more kidnappings, which were numerous enough as it was.

Therefore Lucerne had lost her top-wife position at HelthWyzer, and the house along with it, and under the circumstances, which were unfortunate, she'd decided to move to the CryoJeenyus Compound and take up housekeeping with a very nice man she'd met through the golf club, whose name was Todd. And she certainly hoped I wouldn't go overboard with grief about Frank the way I went overboard on all my other emotions.

CryoJeenyus. What a scam that place was. You paid to get your head frozen when you died in case someone in the future invented a way to regrow a body onto your neck, though the kids at HelthWyzer used to joke that they didn't freeze anything but head shells because they'd already scooped out the neurons and transplanted them into pigs. They made a lot of gruesome jokes like that at HelthWyzer High, though you never knew whether they were actually jokes.

The upshot was – Lucerne continued – that money was tight. Todd wasn't a senior vice-president, he was only an accounts manager and he had three young children of his own to support who would have to take priority over me, and she could hardly ask Todd to pay for me in addition to everything else he was paying for. So I would have to stop coasting along at college, and leave Martha Graham, and take responsibility for myself.

I was out of the nest in one swift kick. Not that I was ever in much of a nest: I'd always been on the edge of the ledge with Lucerne.

This is Irony, I thought. I'd learned about Irony in Dance Theatrics. There was Lucerne, who'd told a slanderous whopper about being kidnapped, and now poor Frank, my biofather, really had been kidnapped, and probably murdered as well. It was clear that Lucerne didn't feel much of anything about that. As for me, I didn't know what to feel.

Before the spring term exams the various Corps set up interview booths in the main hallway. Not the serious Corps, the science ones – they wouldn't bother recruiting at Martha Graham, they wanted numbers people – but the more frivolous ones. I wasn't eligible for these interviews because I wasn't graduating that year, but I decided to go anyway and take a chance. I wouldn't get any of the jobs on offer, but maybe they'd take me on as a floor scrubber. I'd done some floor scrubbing at the Gardeners, though naturally I couldn't say that or I'd get stamped as a fanatical greenie weirdo.

My Dance Calisthenics teacher said I should talk to Scales and Tails. I was a good enough dancer, and Scales was part of SeksMart now, which was a legitimate Corp with health benefits and a dental plan, so it wasn't like being a prostitute. A lot of girls went into it, and some of them met nice men that way and did very well in life afterwards. So I thought I might try for it. I wasn't likely to get anything better without a degree. Even a Martha Graham degree was a lot better than none. And I didn't want to end up as a meat barista at some place like SecretBurgers.

That day I managed to line up five interviews. I had butterflies in my stomach, but I sucked it up and smiled, and talked my way in, even though I wasn't on the graduating list. I could have done six – CryoJeenyus was looking for a Comfort Girl to sooth the relatives who were getting the heads of their loved ones and sometimes their dead pets frozen – but I couldn't work there because of Lucerne. I didn't ever want to see her again, not only because of what she'd done to me but also because of how she'd done it. Like firing the maid.

I saw the hiring teams from Happicuppa, and ChickieNobs, and Zizzy Froots, and Scales and Tails, and finally AnooYoo. The first three didn't want me, but I did get an offer from Scales and Tails. Each Corp had a team doing the interviewing, and Mordis was part of the Scales team – there were some SeksMart higher-ups there too, but he was the man on the ground so it was really his call. I did a routine from Dance Calisthenics, and Mordis said I was exactly what he was looking for, such talent, and if I came to Scales he'd make sure I wouldn't regret it. "You can be whoever you want," he said. "Act it out!" So I almost signed up.

But the AnooYoo booth was right next to Scales, and on that team there was a woman who reminded me a lot of Toby at the Gardeners, though she was darker and had different hair, her eyes were green, and her voice was huskier. She took me a little aside and asked me if I was in trouble, and I found myself explaining that for family reasons I had to leave college. I'd do any kind of a job, I said; I was willing to learn. When she asked me what family reasons I blurted out about my father being kidnapped and my mother not having any money. I could hear my voice going trembly: it wasn't all acting.

Then she asked me what my mother's name was. I told her, and she nodded: she'd take me on at the AnooYoo Spa as an apprentice, and I could live right on the premises, and they'd train me. I'd be working with women, not with men who'd be drunk and violent as they often were at Scales, even if it did have a dental plan; and I wouldn't have to wear a Biofilm Bodysuit and let strange men touch me. It would be a healing atmosphere, and I'd be helping people.

This woman really did look like Toby, and strangely enough, the name on her tag was Tobiatha. That was like a sign to me – that I'd be really safe there, and welcomed, and also wanted. So I said yes.

Mordis gave me his card anyway, and said that if I changed my mind he'd take me on at Scales, any time, no questions asked.

53

The AnooYoo Spa was located in the middle of the Heritage Park. I'd heard a lot about it because Adam One had been so against it – he'd said that many Creatures and also Trees had been destroyed to build a pavilion to vanity. Sometimes on Pollination Day he'd preach a whole sermon about it. But in spite of that, I felt happy there. They had roses that glowed in the dark, and big pink butterflies in the daytime and beautiful kudzu moths at night, and a swimming pool, although staff couldn't use it, and fountains, and their own organic vegetable garden. The air was better there than it was in the middle of the city so you didn't have to wear nose cones so much. It was like a comforting dream. They put me to work in the laundry room folding the sheets and towels, and I liked that because it was peaceful: everything was pink.

On my third day there, Tobiatha came across me as I was carrying a stack of clean towels to one of the rooms and said she'd like to talk to me. I thought maybe I'd done something wrong. We walked out onto the lawn, and she told me to keep my voice down. Then she said that she could tell I'd partly recognized her, and she had certainly recognized me. She'd hired me because I'd been a Gardener, and now that they'd been outlawed and the Garden destroyed we had a duty to look after one another. She could see I was in trouble, beyond not having any money. What was the matter?

I started to cry because I hadn't known about the Garden. It was a shock: I must have had it in my mind that I could go back there if things got really bad. She took me to sit down beside one of the fountains – so the rushing water would blot out our voices in case there were any directional microphones, she said – and I told her about HelthWyzer, and how I'd been in touch with the Gardeners through Amanda before I'd lost my cell, and I didn't know anything about the Garden after that. I didn't say anything about being in love with Jimmy and how he'd broken my heart, but I did tell about Martha Graham, and about Lucerne cutting me off in that abrupt way after my father had been kidnapped.

Then I said I had no direction in life, and I felt numb inside, like an orphan. She said all of that must be very disturbing; she'd had a difficult time too when she'd been my age, and something similar had happened to her, about her father.

This new version of Toby wasn't nearly as hardass as she'd been when she was Eve Six. She was mellower. Or maybe I was older.

She looked around and lowered her voice. Then she told me she'd had to leave the Edencliff Rooftop Garden in a hurry and get some alterations done on herself because she'd been in danger there, so I'd have to be very careful not to tell anyone who she was. She'd taken a risk with me, and she hoped she could trust me, and I said she could. Then she warned me that Lucerne came to the Spa sometimes, and I should be aware of that and try to keep out of her sightline.

Finally she said that if anything should happen – some crisis – and she wasn't around, I should know that she'd put together a dried-foods Gardener-style Ararat, right in the AnooYoo Spa supply room; she told me the door code in case I might ever need to get in. Though she hoped it would never be necessary.

I thanked her very much, and then I asked if she knew where Amanda was. I'd really like to see her again, I said. She was about my only real friend. Toby said she might be able to find out.

We didn't talk often after that – Toby said it would look suspicious, even though she didn't know who might be watching – but we'd exchange a few words and nods. I felt she was guarding me – protecting me with some space-alien type of force field. Though of course I was only making that up.

One day, after I'd been there for nearly a year, Toby said she'd located Amanda through mutual acquaintances on the Internet. What she told me was surprising, though not too surprising when I thought about it. Amanda had become a bioartist: she did art involving Creatures or parts of Creatures arranged outdoors on a giant scale. She was living near the western entrance of the Heritage Park, and if I wanted to see her, Toby could arrange a pass for me and get me driven there in one of the pink AnooYoo minivans.

I threw my arms around Toby and hugged her, but she said I should watch that – a laundry-room girl hugging the manager. Then she said I shouldn't get too involved with Amanda: Amanda had a tendency to go too far, she didn't know the limits of her own strength. I wanted to ask her what she meant, but she was walking away.

On the day of the visit, Toby told me that Amanda had been alerted that I was coming; but the two of us should wait until I was inside the door before hugging or shrieking or other demonstrations. She gave me a basket of AnooYoo products to deliver, as an excuse in case anyone stopped the van and asked where I was going. The driver would wait for me: I would have only an hour, because it would look odd for an AnooYoo girl to be wandering around in the Exfernal too long.

I said maybe I should go in disguise, and she said no, because the guards would ask questions. So I had to put on my pink AnooYoo top-to-toe over my work smock and cotton pants and go off with my pink basket, like Little Pink Riding Hood.

I got delivered to Amanda's falling-apart condo by the AnooYoo minivan, as planned. I did remember what Toby had said. I waited until I was inside the door, where Amanda was waiting, and then we both said, "I can't believe it!" and held on to each other. But not for long; Amanda had never been much of a hugger.

She was taller than when I'd last seen her in the flesh. She'd got a tan – even through the sunblock and hats – from doing so much outdoors art, she said. We went into her kitchen, which had a lot of her designs pinned up on the walls, and some bones here and there; and we had a beer each. I've never liked drinking alcohol that much, but this was special.

We started talking about the Gardeners – Adam One, and Nuala, and Mugi the Muscle and Philo the Fog, and Katuro, and Rebecca. And Zeb. And Toby, though I didn't say she was now Tobiatha and managing the AnooYoo Spa. Amanda told me why Toby had to leave the Gardeners. It was because Blanco from the Sewage Lagoon was after her. Blanco had the street rep of snuffing anyone who'd annoyed him, especially women.

"Why her?" I said. Amanda said she'd heard it was some old sexual thing; which was puzzling, she said, because sexual things and Toby had never fitted together, which was most likely why we kids had called her the Dry Witch. And I said maybe Toby had been wetter than we'd thought, and Amanda laughed, and said obviously I still believed in miracles. But now I knew why Toby was hiding out with a different identity.

"Remember how we used to say, *Knock knock, who's there*? You and me and Bernice?" I said. The beer was creeping up on me.

"Gang," said Amanda. "Gang who?"

"Gang grene," I said, and we both snorted with laughter, and some of the beer went up my nose. Then I told her about running into Bernice, and how she'd been as crabby as ever. We laughed about that too. But we didn't mention dead Burt.

I said, "What about the time you arranged that superweed treat for me with Shackie and Croze, and we all went into the holospinner booth, and I threw up?" So we laughed some more.

She told me she had two roommates, who were artists as well; and also, for the first time in her life, she had a live-in boyfriend. I asked if she was in love with him, and she said, "I'll try anything once."

I asked what he was like, and she said really sweet, though moody at times because he was still getting over some teen-lust girlfriend.

And I said what was his name, and she said, "Jimmy – maybe you knew him at HelthWyzer High, he must have been there about the same time you were."

I got a very cold feeling. She said, "That's him on the fridge, two pictures down, on the right." It was Jimmy all right, with his arm around Amanda, grinning like an electrocuted frog. I felt as if she'd stuck a nail right into my heart. But there was no point in spoiling things for Amanda by telling her that. She hadn't done it on purpose.

I said, "He looks really cute, and now I have to go because it's time for the driver." She asked if there was anything wrong, and I said no. She gave me her cellphone number and said next time I came to visit she'd make sure Jimmy was there, and we'd all have spaghetti.

It would be nice to believe that love should be dished out in a fair way so that everyone got some. But that wasn't how it was going to be for me.

I went back to the AnooYoo Spa feeling totally dumped out and hollow. Then, just after I got back, when I was carting the towels around to the rooms, I almost ran right into Lucerne. It was her time to have her face lifted again: Toby had warned me about it each time she came so I could lower my profile and evade her, but because of Amanda and Jimmy it had gone right out of my head.

I smiled at her in the neutral way we'd been trained. I think she recognized me, but she blew me off like I was a piece of lint. Although I hadn't ever wanted to see her or talk to her, it was a very bad feeling to know that she didn't want to see me or talk to me either. It was like being erased off the slate of the universe – to have your own mother act as if you'd never been born.

At that moment I understood that I couldn't stay at AnooYoo. I needed to be on my own, apart from Amanda, apart from Jimmy, apart from Lucerne, even apart from Toby. I wanted to be someone else entirely, I didn't want to owe anyone anything, or be owed anything either. I wanted no strings, no past, and no questions asked. I was tired of asking questions.

I found the card Mordis had given me, and left a note for Toby thanking her for everything, and saying that for personal reasons I couldn't work at the Spa any longer. I still had the day pass I'd used for Amanda, so I left right then. Everything was ruined and destroyed, and there was no safe place for me; and if I had to be in an unsafe place it might as well be an unsafe place where I was appreciated.

When I got to Scales, I had to talk my way past the bouncers because they didn't believe I was really looking for a job there. But finally they called Mordis, and he said oh yes, he remembered me – I was the little dancer. Brenda, wasn't it? I said yes, but he could call me Ren – I already felt that comfortable with him. He asked if I was really serious about the job, and I said I was; and he said there was a minimum undertaking because they didn't want to waste the training, so would I be willing to sign a contract?

I said maybe I was too sad for the job: didn't they want a more upbeat personality in their girls? But Mordis smiled with his shiny black-ant eyes and said, as if he was patting me: "Ren. Ren. Everyone's too sad for everything."

54

So I did go to work at Scales after all. In some ways it was a relief. I liked having Mordis for a boss because at least it was clear what pleased him. He made me feel safe, maybe because he was the closest thing to a father I was ever going to get: Zeb had vanished into thin air and my real father hadn't found me very interesting, and in addition he was dead.

But Mordis said I was really something special – I was the answer to every dream, wet ones included. It was so encouraging to be doing something I was good at. I didn't like the other parts of the job that much, but I did like the trapeze dancing, because nobody could touch you then. You were up in the air, like a butterfly. I used to picture Jimmy looking at me, and thinking that it was really me he'd loved all along, not Wakulla Price or LyndaLee or any of the others, or even Amanda, and that I was dancing just for him.

I do know how useless this was.

After going to Scales, I was only in touch with Amanda by phone. She was away a lot, doing her art projects; also I didn't want to see her in person. I'd feel uncomfortable because of Jimmy, and she'd pick up on that feeling and ask about it, and I'd either lie or tell her; and if I told her she'd be angry, or maybe just curious; or she'd think I was being stupid. There was a hard side to Amanda.

Jealousy is a very destructive emotion, Adam One used to say. It's part of the stubborn Australopithecine heritage we're stuck with. It eats away at you and deadens your Spiritual life, but also it leads you to hatred, and causes you to harm others. But Amanda was the last person I'd ever want to harm.

I tried to visualize my jealousy as a yellowy-brown cloud boiling around inside me, then going out through my nose like smoke and turning into a stone and falling down into the ground. That did work a little. But in my visualization a plant covered with poison berries would grow out of the stone, whether I wanted it to or not.

Then Amanda broke up with Jimmy. She let me know about it in a round-about way. She'd already told me about her outdoor art landscape installation series called The Living Word – how she was spelling words out in giant letters, using bioforms to make the words appear and then disappear, just like the words she used to do with ants and syrup when we were kids. Now she said, "I'm up to the four-letter words." And I said, "You mean the dirty ones, like *shit*?" And she laughed and said, "Worse ones than that." And I said, "You mean the c-word and the f-word?" and she said, "No. Like *love*."

And I said, "Oh. So Jimmy didn't work out." And she said, "Jimmy can't be serious." So I knew he must've cheated on her, or something like that.

"I'm sorry," I said. "Are you really pissed off at him?" I tried to keep the happiness out of my own voice. *Now I can forgive her*, I thought. But really there was nothing to forgive her for because she hadn't done anything hurtful to me on purpose.

"Pissed off?" she said. "You can't be pissed off with Jimmy." I wondered what she meant by that, because I was certainly pissed off with Jimmy. Though I still loved him.

Maybe that's what love is, I thought: it's being pissed off.

After a while, Glenn started coming to Scales – not every night, but often enough to get discounts. I hadn't seen him since HelthWyzer – he'd been with the brainiacs, doing science at the Watson-Crick Institute – but now he was a top guy at the Rejoov Corp. He wasn't shy about bragging, though with Glenn it was more like stating a fact, the way you'd say, "It's going to rain." What I picked up from listening in on his conversations with the Mr. Bigs and his funders was that he was in charge of a really important initiative called the Paradice Project. They'd built a special dome for it, with its own air supply and quadruple security. He'd assembled a team of the best brains available, and they were working night and day.

Glenn was vague about what they were working on. *Immortality* was a word he used – Rejoov had been interested in it for decades, something about changing your cells so they'd never die; people would pay a lot for immortality, he said. Every couple of months he'd claim they'd made a breakthrough, and the more breakthroughs he made, the more money he could raise for the Paradice Project.

Sometimes he'd say he was working on solutions to the biggest problem of all, which was human beings – their cruelty and suffering, their wars and poverty, their fear of death. "What would you pay for the design of a perfect human being?" he'd say. Then he'd hint that the Paradice Project was designing one, and they'd dump more money on him.

For the finales of these meetings he'd rent the feather-ceiling room and order up the drinks and the drugs and the Scalies – not for himself, but for the guys he'd bring with him. Sometimes he'd even entertain the top CorpSeMen. They were sinister, those guys. I never had to do the Painballers, but I had to do the CorpSeMen, and they were my least favourite clients. It was like they had machine parts in behind their eyes.

Occasionally Glenn would rent two or three Scalies for the whole evening, not for sex but for some very strange things. Once he wanted us to purr like cats so he could measure our vocal cords. Another time he wanted us to sing like birds so he could record us. Starlite complained to Mordis that this wasn't what we were paid for, but Mordis only said, "So, he's a loony. You've seen those before. But he's a rich loony and he's harmless, so just humour him."

I was part of the threesome the night he gave us a sort of quiz. What would make us happy? he wanted to know. Was happiness more like excitement, or more like contentment? Was happiness inside or outside? With trees, or without? Did it have running water nearby? Did too much of it get boring? Starlite and Crimson Petal tried to figure out what he wanted to hear so they could tell the right lies. "No," I said. I knew what Glenn was like. "He's a geek. He wants us to say what we honestly feel." Which confused them a lot.

He never asked us about sadness, though. Maybe he thought he knew enough about that.

Then he started bringing a woman – an Asian Fusion body type with a foreign accent. He said she wanted to familiarize herself with Scales because ReJoov had picked us as one of their prime test venues, and she'd be explaining a new product to us – the BlyssPluss pill, which would solve every known problem connected with sex. We had been awarded the privilege of introducing it to our clients. This woman had a ReJoov executive title – Senior VP Satisfaction Enhancement – though her real job was Glenn's main plank.

I could tell she'd been one of us: a girl for rent, of one kind or another. It was obvious if you knew the signs. She was acting all the time, giving nothing away about herself. I'd watch them onscreen: I was curious because Glenn was such a cold fish, but he could have sex all right, just like a human being. This girl had more moves than an octopus, and her plankwork was astonishing. Glenn acted like she was the first, last, and only girl on the planet. Mordis used to watch them too, and he said Scales would pay this girl top dollar. But I told him he couldn't afford her: she was way out of his price range.

The two of them had pet names for each other. She'd call him Crake, he'd call her Oryx. The other girls found it strange – the two of them being lovey-dovey – because it was so out of character for Glenn. But I thought it was kind of nice.

"That Russian or something?" Crimson Petal asked me. "Oryx and Crake?"

"I guess," I said. They were extinct animal names – every Gardener had to memorize a ton of those – but if I said it the girls would wonder why I knew.

The first time Glenn came to Scales I recognized him right away, but of course he didn't recognize me, in my Biofilm Bodysuit and with green sequins all over my face, and I didn't let on. Mordis told us not to forge personal bonds with the customers, because if they wanted a relationship they could get one elsewhere. He said that Scales customers didn't care about your life history, they just wanted epidermis and fantasy. They wanted to be carried away to Never-Never Land, where they could have sinful experiences they'd never, never be able to have at home. Dragon ladies winding around them, snake women slithering over them. So we should save our private emotional crap for people who actually cared about us, like the other Scalies.

One night Glenn arranged an evening of extra-special treatment – for an extra-special guest, he said. He ordered up the feather room with the green bedspread, plus the most powerful Scales and Tails martinis – "kicktails," they called them – plus two Scalies, me and Crimson Petal. Mordis picked us because Glenn said this extra-special guest preferred the slender body type.

"Does he want the schoolgirl sailor suit thing?" I asked; sometimes that's what "slender body type" meant. "Do I need to bring my skipping rope?" If so I'd have to change, because right then I was in full glitter.

"This guy's already so shitfaced he doesn't know what he wants," Mordis said. "Just give him your all, baby bunny. We want to see the high-number tips. Make those multiple zeroes shoot right out of his ears."

When we got to the room, the guy was lying on the green satin bedspread as if he'd been thrown from a plane, but happy about it, because he had a whole-body grin.

It was Jimmy. Sweet, ruinous Jimmy. Jimmy, who'd trashed my life.

My heart flipped over. Oh shit, I thought. I'm not up to this. I'm going to lose it and start crying. I knew he wouldn't know it was me: I was covered in glitz, and he was flying so high he was almost blind. So I just slid into the usual act and started in on his buttons and Velcro. We Scalies used to call it "peeling the shrimp." "Oh, nice abs," I whispered. "Honey, just lie back."

Did I hate this or love it? Why did it have to be one or the other? As Vilya always said about her boobs, *Take two, they're cheap.*

Now he was trying to pull the scales off my face, so I had to keep taking his hands and putting them elsewhere. "Are you a fish?" he was saying. He didn't seem to know.

Oh Jimmy, I thought. What's left of you?

SAINT DIAN, MARTYR

Dear Friends, dear Faithful Companions:

Our Edencliff Rooftop Garden blooms now only in our memories. On this Earthly plane it is now a desolation – a swamp or a desert, depending on rainfall. How changed is our situation from our former green and salad days! How shrunk, how dwindled are our numbers! We are driven from one refuge to another, we are hounded and pursued. Some former Friends have renounced our creeds, others have borne false witness against us. Yet others have tried extremism and violence, and have been murderously spraygunned in the course of raids carried out against them. We remember in this connection our dear former Child, Bernice. Let us put Light around her.

Some have been mutilated and tossed into vacant lots to sow panic among us. Yet others have disappeared, snatched from their places of refuge, to vanish into the prisons of the Exfernal Powers, denied trial, forbidden even to know the names of their accusers. Their minds may already have been destroyed by drugs and torture, their bodies melted into garboil. Because of unjust Laws, we cannot learn the whereabouts of these, our fellow Gardeners. We can only hope that they will die in unwavering Faith.

Today is Saint Dian's Day, consecrated to interspecies empathy. On this day we invoke Saint Jerome of Lions, and Saint Robert Burns of Mice, and Saint Christopher Smart of Cats; also Saint Farley Mowat of Wolves, and the Ikhwan al-Safa and their *Letter of the Animals*. But especially Saint Dian Fossey, who gave her life while defending the Gorillas from ruthless exploitation. She laboured for a Peaceable Kingdom, in which all

312 | MARGARET ATWOOD

Life would be respected; yet malignant forces combined to destroy both her and her gentle Primate companions. Her murder was horrific; and equally horrific were the malicious rumours spread about her, both during her lifetime and after it. For the Exfernal Powers kill both in deed and in word.

Saint Dian embodies an ideal we hold dear: loving care for all other Creatures. She believed that these deserve the same tenderness we would show to beloved friends and kinfolk, and in this she is a revered model for us. She is buried among her Gorilla Friends, on the mountain she tried to protect.

Like many martyrs, Saint Dian did not live to see the fulfilment of her labours. At least she has been spared the knowledge that the Species for which she gave her life is no more. Like so many others, it has been wiped from the face of God's Planet.

What is it about our own Species that leaves us so vulnerable to the impulse to violence? Why are we so addicted to the shedding of blood? Whenever we are tempted to become puffed up, and to see ourselves as superior to all other Animals, we should reflect on our own brutal history.

Take comfort in the thought that this history will soon be swept away by the Waterless Flood. Nothing will remain of the Exfernal World but decaying wood and rusting metal implements; and over these the Kudzu and other vines will climb; and Birds and Animals will nest in them, as we are told in the Human Words of God: "They shall be left together unto the Fowls of the mountains, and to the Beasts of the Earth; and the Fowls shall summer upon them, and all the Beasts of the Earth shall winter upon them." For all works of Man will be as words written on water.

As we crouch together in this dim cellar, speaking softly behind darkened windows, worried lest we have been infiltrated, or that listening devices or cyborg insects are nearby, or the vindictive functionaries of the CorpSeCorps may even now be speeding towards us, we have more need than ever of our resolve. We pray that the Spirit of Saint Dian may inspire us, and help us to stand firm in the moment of trial. Fear not, says that Spirit, even if the worst shall come: for we shelter in the wings of a yet greater Spirit.

An hour before dawn, we must move out of this hiding place, singly and in twos or threes. Be silent then, my Friends; be invisible; merge with your own shadows. And with Grace we will prevail.

We cannot sing, for fear of being overheard, but:

Let us whisper.

TODAY WE PRAISE OUR SAINT DIAN

Today we praise our Saint Dian,
Whose blood for bounteous Life was spilled –
Although she interposed her Faith,
One Species more was killed.

For all around the misty hills
She tracked the wild Gorilla bands,
Until they learned to trust her Love,
And take her by the hand.

The timid giants, huge and strong,
She held in her courageous arms;
She guarded them with anxious care,
Lest they should come to harm.

They knew her as their Friend and kin,
Around her they would feast and play –
And yet cruel Murderers came by night,
And slew her where she lay.

Too many violent hands and hearts!
Dian, too sadly few like you –
For when a Species dies from Earth,
We die a little too.

Among the green and misty hills,
Where once the shy Gorillas gathered,
Your kindly Spirit wanders still,
In watchfulness, forever.

From *The God's Gardeners Oral Hymnbook*

55

YEAR TWENTY-FIVE

You create your own world by your inner attitude, the Gardeners used to say. And I didn't want to create the world out there: the world of the dead and dying. So I sang some old Gardener hymns, especially the happy ones. Or I danced. Or I played the songs on my Sea/H/Ear Candy, though I couldn't help thinking that now there'd be no more new music.

Say the Names, Adam One would tell us. And we'd chant these lists of Creatures: Diplodocus, Pterosaurus, Octopus, and Brontosaurus; Trilobite, Nautilus, Ichthyosaurus, Platypus. Mastodon, Dodo, Great Auk, Komodo. I could see all the names, as clear as pages. Adam One said that saying the names was a way of keeping those animals alive. So I said them.

I said other names too. Adam One, Nuala, Zeb. Shackie, Croze, and Oates. And Glenn – I just couldn't picture anyone so smart being dead.

And Jimmy, despite what he'd done.

And Amanda.

I said those names over and over, in order to keep them alive.

Then I thought about what Mordis had whispered, at the end. *Your name*, he'd said. It must have been important.

I counted the food I had left. Four weeks' worth, three weeks, two. I marked off the time with my eyebrow pencil. If I ate less, I could make it last longer. But if Amanda didn't come soon, I'd be dead. I couldn't really imagine it.

316 | MARGARET ATWOOD

Glenn used to say the reason you can't really imagine yourself being dead was that as soon as you say, "I'll be dead," you've said the word *I*, and so you're still alive inside the sentence. And that's how people got the idea of the immortality of the soul – it was a consequence of grammar. And so was God, because as soon as there's a past tense, there has to be a past before the past, and you keep going back in time until you get to *I don't know*, and that's what God is. It's what you don't know – the dark, the hidden, the underside of the visible, and all because we have grammar, and grammar would be impossible without the FoxP2 gene; so God is a brain mutation, and that gene is the same one birds need for singing. So music is built in, Glenn said: it's knitted into us. It would be very hard to amputate it because it's an essential part of us, like water.

I said, in that case is God knitted in as well? And he said maybe so, but it hadn't done us any good.

His explanation of God was a lot different from the Gardeners' explanation. He said "God is a Spirit" was meaningless because you couldn't measure a Spirit. Also he'd say *Use your meat computer* when he meant *Use your mind*. I found that idea repulsive: I hated the idea of my head being full of meat.

I kept thinking I could hear people walking around in the building, but when I scanned the rooms I couldn't see anyone moving. At least the solar was still working.

I counted the food again. Five days left, and that was stretching it.

56

I first spotted Amanda as a shadow on the videoscreen. She came into the Snakepit carefully, hugging the wall: the lights were still on, so she wasn't groping in the dark. The music was still blaring and thumping, and once she'd looked around to make sure the place was empty she went over behind the stage and switched it off.

"Ren?" I heard her say.

Then she went offscreen. After a pause the videocam mike in the hallway picked up her soft footsteps, and then I could see her. And she could see me. I was crying so much with relief I couldn't speak.

"Hi," she said. "There's a dead guy right outside the door. He's gross. I'll be back." Mordis was who she meant – he'd never been taken away. She told me later that she got him onto a shower curtain and dragged him down the hall and bundled him into an elevator, what was left of him. The rats had been having a party, she said, not just at Scales but anywhere even close to urban. She'd put on the gloves of someone's Biofilm Bodysuit before touching him – even though she was daring, Amanda didn't take stupid risks.

After a while she was back on my screen. "So," she said. "Here I am. Stop crying, Ren."

"I thought you'd never get here," I managed to say.

"That's what I thought too," she said. "Now. How does the door open?"

"I don't have the code," I said. I explained about Mordis – how he was the only one who'd known the Sticky Zone numbers.

"He never told you?"

"He said why would we need to know the codes? He changed them every day – he didn't want them leaking out because crazies might get in. He just wanted to protect us." I was trying hard not to panic: there was Amanda, outside the door, but what if she couldn't do anything?

"Any clue?" she said.

"He did say something about my name," I said. "Just before he – before they – Maybe that's what he meant."

Amanda tried. "Nope," she said. "Well then. Maybe it's your birthday. Month and day? Year?"

I could hear her punching in numbers, swearing gently to herself. After what seemed a long time, I heard the clunk of the lock. The door swung open, and there she was, right in front of me.

"Oh, Amanda," I said. She was sunburned, tattered, and grimy, but she was real. I reached out my arms to her, but she stepped back and away.

"It was a simple A equals One code," she said. "It was your name, after all. Brenda, only backwards. Don't touch me, I might have germs. I need to shower."

While Amanda was taking her shower in my Sticky Zone bathroom I propped the door open with a chair because I didn't want it to swing shut and lock both of us inside. The air outside my room smelled awful compared with the filtered air I'd been breathing: rotting meat, and also smoke and burnt chemicals, because there'd been fires and nobody to put them out. It was lucky that Scales hadn't caught fire and burned down with me inside it.

After Amanda had taken a shower I took one too, so I'd be as clean as her. Then we put on the green Scales dressing gowns Mordis kept for his best girls and sat around eating Joltbars from the minifridge and microwaving ChickieNobs, and drinking some beers we'd found downstairs, and telling each other the stories of why it was that we were still alive.

57

YEAR TWENTY-FIVE

Toby wakes up suddenly, her blood rushing in her head: *katoush, katoush, katoush*. She knows at once that something in her space has changed. Someone's sharing her oxygen.

Breathe, she tells herself. Move as if swimming. Don't smell like fear.

She lifts the pink sheet off her damp body as slowly as she can, sits up, looks carefully around. Nothing large, not in this cubicle: there isn't room. Then she sees it. It's only a bee. A honeybee, walking along the sill.

A bee in the house means a visitor, said Pilar; and if the bee dies, the visit will not be good. I mustn't kill it, Toby thinks. She folds it carefully in a pink washcloth. "Send a message," she says to it. "Tell those in the Spirit world: 'Please send help soon.'" Superstition, she knows that; yet she feels oddly encouraged. Though maybe the bee is one of the transgenics they let loose after the virus wiped out the natural bees; or it may even be a cyborg spy, wandering around with no one left to control it. In which case it will make a very poor messenger.

She slips the washcloth into the pocket of her top-to-toe: she'll take the bee up to the roof, release it there, watch it set off on its errand to the dead. But in slinging the rifle over her shoulder by the strap she must have crushed the pocket, because when she unwraps the bee it looks less than alive. She shakes the cloth over the railing, hoping the bee will fly. It moves through the air, but more like a seed than an insect: the visit will not be a good one.

She walks to the garden side of the roof, looks over. Sure enough, the bad visit has already occurred: the pigs have been back. They've dug under the fence, then gone on a rampage. Surely it was less like a feeding frenzy than a deliberate act of revenge. The earth is furrowed and trampled: anything they haven't eaten they've bulldozed.

If she were a cryer, she'd cry. She lifts her binoculars, scans the meadow. At first she doesn't see them, but then she spots two pinkish-grey heads – no, three – no, five – lifting above the weedy flowers. Beady eyes, one per pig: they're looking at her sideways. They've been watching for her: it's as if they want to witness her dismay. Moreover, they're out of range: if she shoots at them she'll waste the bullets. She wouldn't put it past them to have figured that out.

"You fucking pigs!" she yells at them, "Fuck-pigs! Pig-faces!" Of course, for them none of these names would be insults.

What now? Her supply of dried greens is tiny, her goji berries and chia are almost gone, her plant protein is finished. She was counting on the garden for all of that. Worst of all, she's out of fats: she's already eaten the last of the Shea and Avocado Body Butter. There's fat in Joltbars – she still has some of those – but not enough to last for long. Without lipids your body eats your fat and then your muscles, and the brain is pure fat and the heart is a muscle. You become a feedback loop, and then you fall over.

She'll have to resort to foraging. Go out into the meadow, the forest: find protein and lipids. The boar will be putrid by now, she can't eat that. She could shoot a green rabbit, maybe; but no, it's a fellow mammal and she isn't up to that kind of slaughter. Ant larvae and eggs, or grubs of any kind, for starters.

Is that what the pigs want her to do? Go outside her defensive walls, into the open, so they can jump her, knock her down, then rip her open? Have a pig-style outdoor picnic. A pig-out. She has a fair idea of what that would look like. The Gardeners weren't squeamish about describing the eating habits of God's various Creatures: to flinch at these would be hypocritical. No one comes into the world clutching a knife and fork and a frying pan, Zeb was fond of saying. Or a table napkin. And if we eat pigs, why shouldn't pigs eat us? If they find us lying around.

No point in trying to repair the garden. The pigs would just wait until there was something worth destroying, and then destroy it. Maybe she should build a rooftop garden, like the old Gardener ones: then she'd never have to go outside the main building. But she'd have to haul the soil up all those stairs, in pails. Then there's the watering in the dry seasons and the drainage in the wet seasons: without the Gardeners' elaborate systems the thing would be impossible.

There are the pigs, peering at her above the daisies. They have a festive air. Are they snorting in derision? Certainly there's some grunting going on, and some juvenile squealing, as there used to be when the topless bars in the Sewage Lagoon closed at night.

"Assholes!" she screams at them. It makes her feel better to scream. At least she's talking to someone other than herself.

58

The worst, said Amanda, was the thunderstorms – she thought she was dead a couple of times, the lightning came so close. But then she'd lifted a rubber mat from a mallway hardware store to crouch on, and she'd felt safer after that.

She'd avoided people as much as possible. She abandoned the solarcar in upstate New York because the highway was too jammed with scrap metal. There'd been some spectacular crashes: the drivers must have started dissolving right inside their cars. "Blood hand lotion," she said. There'd been about a million vultures. Some people would have been freaked out by them, but not Amanda – she'd worked with them in her art. "That highway was the biggest Vulture Sculpture you could imagine," she said. She wished she'd had a camera.

After ditching the solarcar she'd walked for a while and then lifted another solar, a bike this time – easier to get through the metal snarls. When in doubt she'd kept to the urban fringes, or else the woods. She'd had a couple of close calls because other people must've had the same idea – she'd almost tripped over a few bodies. Good thing she hadn't actually touched them.

She'd seen some living people. A couple of them had seen her too, but by then everyone must have known this bug was ultra-catching, so they'd stayed far away from her. Some of them were in the last stages, wandering around like zombies; or they were already down, folded in on themselves like cloth.

She slept on top of garages whenever she could, or inside abandoned buildings, though never on the main floor. Otherwise, in trees: the ones with sturdy forks. Uncomfortable but you got used to it, and best to be above ground level because there'd been some strange animals around. Huge pigs, those lion/lamb splices, packs of wild dogs on the prowl – one pack had almost cornered her. Anyway you were safer from the zombie people, up in trees: you wouldn't want a clot on legs to fall on top of you in the darkness.

What she was telling was gruesome, but we laughed a lot that night. I guess we should have been mourning and wailing, but I'd already done that, and anyway what good would it be? Adam One said we should always look on the positive side, and the positive side was that we were still alive.

We didn't talk about anyone we knew.

I didn't want to sleep in my Sticky Zone room because I'd been there long enough, and we couldn't use my old room either because the husk of Starlite was still in it. Finally we chose one of the client facilities, the one with the giant bed and the green satin bedspread and the featherwork ceiling. That room looked elegant if you didn't think too much about what it had been used for.

The last time I'd seen Jimmy had been in that room. But having Amanda there was like an eraser: it smudged that earlier memory. It made me safer.

We slept in the next morning. Then we got up and put on our green dressing gowns and went into the Scales kitchen where they used to make the bar snacks. We microwaved some frozen soybread out of the main freezer and had that for breakfast, with instant Happicuppa.

"Didn't you think I must be dead?" I asked Amanda. "And so maybe you shouldn't bother coming here?"

"I knew you weren't dead," said Amanda. "You get a feeling when someone's dead. Someone you know really well. Don't you think?"

I wasn't sure about that. So I said, "Anyway, thanks." Whenever you thanked Amanda for something she pretended not to hear; or else she'd say, "You'll pay me back." That's what she said now. She wanted everything to be a trade, because giving things for nothing was too soft.

"What should we do now?" I said.

"Stay here," said Amanda. "Until the food's gone. Or if the solar shuts off and the stuff in the freezers begins to rot. That could get ugly."

"Then what?" I said.

"Then we'll go somewhere else."

"Like where?"

"We don't need to worry about that now," said Amanda.

Time got stretchy. We'd sleep as long as we wanted, then get up and have showers – we still had water because of the solar – and then eat something out of the freezers. Then we'd talk about things we'd done at the Gardeners – old stuff. We'd sleep some more when it got too hot. Later we'd go into the Sticky Zone rooms and turn on the air conditioning and watch DVDs of old movies. We didn't feel like going outside the building.

In the evenings we'd have a few drinks – there were still some unbroken bottles behind the bar – and raid the expensive tinned foods Mordis kept for the high-roller clients and also for his best girls. Loyalty Snacks, he called them; he'd dish them out when you'd gone the extra mile, though you never knew in advance what that extra mile would be. That's how I got to eat my first caviar. It was like salty bubbles.

There was no more caviar left at Scales for me and Amanda, though.

59

Here comes famine, thinks Toby. Saint Euell, pray for me and for all who starve in the midst of plenty. Help me to find that plenty. Send animal protein quickly.

In the meadow the dead boar is entering the afterlife. Gases are rising from it, fluids are seeping away. The vultures have been at it; the crows are hanging around on the perimeter like runts at a street fight, grabbing what they can. Whatever's going on out there, maggots are a part of it.

When in extreme need, Adam One used to say, begin at the bottom of the food chain. Those without central nervous systems must surely suffer less.

Toby gathers the necessary items – her pink top-to-toe, her sunhat, her sunglasses, a water bottle, a pair of surgical gloves. The binoculars, the rifle. Her mop-handle cane, for balance. She finds a plastic snap-top and punches some holes in the lid, adds a spoon, and stows everything in a plastic gift bag with the winky-eye AnooYoo Spa logo on it. A packsack would be better, it would leave her hands free. There used to be some packsacks around here – the ladies took them on strolls, with picnic sandwiches in them – but she can't remember where she put them.

There's still some AnooYoo All-Natural SolarNix in stock. It's stale-dated and smells rancid, but she spreads it on her face anyway, then sprays her ankles and wrists with SuperD in case of mosquitoes. She has a good long drink of water, then visits the violet biolet: if panic arises, at least she won't piss herself. Nothing worse than sprinting in a wet top-to-toe. She hangs the binoculars around her neck, then goes up to the roof for a last double-check. No ears in the meadow, no snouts. No furry golden tails.

"Quit stalling," she tells herself. She has to leave immediately so she can get back before the afternoon rainstorm. Stupid to get struck by lightning. Any death is stupid from the viewpoint of whoever is under-going it, Adam One used to say, because no matter how much you've been warned, Death always comes without knocking. Why now? is the cry. Why so soon? It's the cry of a child being called home at dusk, it's the universal protest against Time. Just remember, dear Friends: What am I living for and what am I dying for are the same question.

A question – Toby says to herself very firmly – that I will not ask myself just now.

She puts on the surgical gloves and slings the AnooYoo bag over her shoulder, and lets herself out. She goes first to the ruined garden, where she salvages one onion and two radishes, and spoons a layer of damp earth into the plastic snap-top. Then she crosses the parking lot and walks past the silent fountains.

It's been a long time since she's been this far away from the Spa buildings. Now she's in the meadow: it's a big space. The light is dazzling, even though she has the broad hat and the sunglasses on.

Don't panic, she tells herself. This is how mice feel when they venture onto the open floor, but you aren't a mouse. The weeds catch at her top-to-toe and tangle her feet as if to hold her back and keep her with them. There are little thorns in them somewhere, little claws and traps. It's like pushing through a giant piece of knitting: knitting done with barbed wire.

What's this? A shoe.

Not to think about shoes. Not to think about the mouldering handbag she's just glimpsed nearby. Stylish. Red fleather. A tatter of the past that hasn't yet been drawn down into the earth. She doesn't want to step on any of these remnants, but it's hard to see down through the nets and meshes of the ensnaring weeds.

She moves forward. Her legs are tingling, the way flesh does when it knows it's about to be touched. Does she really think a hand will come up from among the clover and sow thistles and grab her by the ankle?

"No," she says out loud. She stops to calm her heart, and to reconnoiter. The wide brim of the hat impedes her view: she swivels her whole body like an owl's head – to left, to right, behind, then to the front again. All around her is a sweet scent – the tall clover's in bloom, the Queen Anne's lace, the lavender and marjoram and lemon balm, self-seeded. The field hums with pollinators: bumblebees, shining wasps, iridescent beetles. The sound is lulling. Stay here. Sink down. Go to sleep.

Nature full strength is more than we can take, Adam One used to say. It's a potent hallucinogen, a soporific, for the untrained Soul. We're no longer at home in it. We need to dilute it. We can't drink it straight. And God is the same. Too much God and you overdose. God needs to be filtered.

Ahead of her in the middle distance is the line of dark trees that marks the edge of the forest. She feels it drawing her, luring her in, as the depths of the ocean and the mountain heights are said to lure people, higher and higher or deeper and deeper, until they vanish into a state of rapture that is not human.

See yourself as a predator sees you, Zeb once taught. She places herself behind the trees, looking out through the filigree of leaves and branches. There's an enormous wild savannah, and in the middle of it a small soft pink figure, like an embryo or an alien, with big dark eyes – alone, unprotected, vulnerable. Behind this figure is its dwelling, an absurd box made of straw that only looks like bricks. So easy to blow down.

The smell of fear comes to her, from herself.

She lifts the binoculars. The leaves are moving a little, but only in the breeze. Walk forward slowly, she tells herself. Remember what you came to do.

After what seems a long time she reaches the dead boar. A horde of glittering green and bronze flies dithers in the air above it. At her approach the vultures lift their red, featherless heads, their boiled-looking necks. She waves her mop handle at them and they scrabble away, hissing with indignation. Some of them spiral upwards, keeping an eye on her; others flap towards the trees and settle their dust-rag feathers, waiting.

There are fronds scattered about, on top of the boar's carcass and beside it. Fern fronds. Such ferns don't grow in the meadow. Some are old and dry and brown, some quite fresh. Also flowers. Are those rose petals, from the roses by the driveway? She'd heard of something like this; no, she read it as a child, in a kid's book about elephants. The elephants would stand around their dead ones, sombrely, as if meditating. Then they'd scatter branches and earth.

But pigs? Usually they'd just eat a dead pig, the same way they'd eat anything else. But they haven't been eating this one.

Could the pigs have been having a funeral? Could they be bringing memorial bouquets? She finds this idea truly frightening.

But why not? says the kindly voice of Adam One. We believe the Animals have Souls. Why then would they not have funerals?

"You're mad," she says out loud.

The smell of decaying flesh is rank: it's hard to keep from gagging. She lifts a fold of her top-to-toe, clamps it over her nose. With the other hand she pokes at the dead boar with her stick: maggots boil forth. They're like giant grey rice.

Just think of them as land shrimp, says the voice of Zeb. Same body plan. "You're up to this," she tells herself. She has to set down the rifle and the mop handle in order to do the next part. She scoops up the twirling white maggots with the spoon and transfers them to the plastic snap-on. She drops some; her hands are shaking. There's a buzzing in her head like tiny drills, or is it only the flies? She makes herself slow down.

Thunder in the distance.

She turns her back on the forest, heads back across the meadow. She doesn't run.

Surely the trees have moved closer.

60

One day we were drinking champagne and I said, "Let's do our nails, they're a wreck." I thought maybe it would cheer us up. Amanda laughed and said, "Nothing wrecks your nails like a lethal pandemic plague," but we did our nails anyway. Amanda's were an orangey-pink shade called Satsuma Parfait, mine were Slick Raspberry. We were like two kids with fingerpaints, having a party. I love the smell of nail polish. I know it's toxic, but it smells so clean. Crisp, like starched linen. It did make us feel better.

After that we had some more champagne, and I had another party idea, so I went upstairs. There was only one room with a person in it – Starlite, in our old bedroom. I felt terrible about her, but I'd stuffed sheets all around the door so no more smell could get out, and I hoped the microbes would get on with the job so she could be transformed into something else really fast. I took the Biofilm Bodysuits and costumes from Savona's empty room and Crimson Petal's, and brought them downstairs in a giant armful, and we started trying them on.

The Biofilms needed to be sprayed with water and lubricant skin-food – they were dried out – but once we'd done that they slid on as usual, and you could feel the pleasant suction as their layers of living cells bonded with your skin, and then the warm, tickly feeling as they started to breathe. Nothing in but oxygen, nothing out but your natural excretions, said the labels. The face unit even did your nostrils for you. A lot of the Scales customers would have preferred membrane and bristle work if it was completely safe, but at least with the Biofilms they could relax, because they knew they weren't planking a fester.

"This feels great," said Amanda. "It sort of gives you a massage."

"Recommended for the complexion," I said, and we laughed some more. Then Amanda put on a flamingo outfit with pink feathers and I put on a peagret one, and we turned on the music and the coloured spotlights and got up on the stage and danced. Amanda was still a great dancer, she could really shake those feathers. But I was better than her by then, because of all the training I'd had, and the trapeze work; and she knew it. And that pleased me.

That was stupid of us, the whole dancing event: we'd cranked the music up really loud, and it was going right out through the open door, and if there was anyone in the neighbourhood they'd be sure to hear it. But I wasn't thinking about that. "Ren, you're not the only person on the planet," Toby used to say when I was little. It was a way of telling us to have consideration. But now I really did think I was the only person on the planet. Or me and Amanda. So there we were in our flamingo-pink and peagret-blue costumes and our fresh nail polish, dancing on the Scales stage together with the music turned up, whump whump babadedump, bam bam kabam, singing along as if we didn't have a care in the world.

Then the number came to the end, and we heard clapping. We stood there as if frozen. I felt a chill shoot through me: I had a flash of Crimson Petal hanging from the trapeze rope with a bottle shoved up her, and I couldn't breathe.

Three guys had come in – they must have snuck in very carefully – and there they were. "Don't run," said Amanda to me in a quiet voice. Then she said, "You alive or dead?" She smiled. "Because if you're alive, maybe you'd like a drink?"

"Nice dancing," said the tallest one. "How come you didn't get this bug?"

"Maybe we did," said Amanda. "Maybe we're contagious and we just don't know it yet. Now I'm turning down the stage lights so we can see you."

"Anyone else here?" said the tallest one. "Like, any guys?"

"None that I know of," said Amanda. She'd dimmed the lights. "Take off your face," she said to me. She meant the green sequins, the Biofilm. She went down the steps from the stage. "There's some Scotch left, or we could make you a coffee." She was peeling off her own Biofilm headpiece, and I knew what she was thinking: Make direct eye contact, like Zeb taught us. Don't turn away, they're more likely to swarm you from behind. And the less we looked like sparkly birds rather than people, the less likely we'd be mangled.

Now I could see the three of them better. A tall one, a shorter one, another tall one. They were in camouflage suits, very dirty ones, and they looked as if they'd been out in the sun too much. The sun, the rain, the wind.

Then all of a sudden I knew. "Shackie?" I said. "Shackie! Amanda, it's Shackie and Croze!"

The tall one turned his face towards me. "Who the fuck are you?" he said. Not angry, just kind of stunned.

"It's Ren," I said. "Is that little Oates?" I started to cry.

All five of us moved towards each another like a slow-motion football huddle on TV, and then we were hugging each other. Just hugging and hugging, and holding on.

There was some orange-coloured juice in the freezer, so Amanda mixed up mimosas with the champagne that was left. We opened some salted soynuts, and microwaved a pack of faux fish, and all five of us sat at the bar. The three boys – I still thought of them as boys – practically inhaled the food. Amanda made them drink some water, but not too fast. They weren't starving – they'd been breaking into supermarkettes and even into houses, living off what they could glean, and they'd even snared a couple of rabbits and broiled the chunks, the way we'd done it back at the Gardeners in Saint Euell Week. Still, they were thin.

Then we told one another about where we'd all been when the Waterless Flood hit. I told about the Sticky Zone, and Amanda told about the cow bones in Wisconsin. Dumb luck for both of us, I said – that we hadn't been with other people when the thing got going. Though Adam One used to say no luck was dumb because luck was just another name for miracle.

Shackie and Croze and Oates nearly hadn't made it. They'd been shut up in the Painball Arena. Red Team, said Oates, showing me his thumb tattoo; he seemed proud of it. "They put us in there because of what we'd been doing," said Shackie. "With MaddAddam."

"Mad Adam?" I said. "Like Zeb, at the Gardeners?"

"More than Zeb. It was a bunch of us – him and us, and some others," said Shackie. "Top scientists – gene-splicers who'd bailed out of the Corps and gone underground because they hated what the Corps were doing. Rebecca and Katuro were in it – they helped distribute the product."

"We had a website," said Croze. "We could share our info that way, in the hidden chatroom."

"Product?" said Amanda. "You were pushing superweed? Cool!" She laughed.

"No way. We were doing bioform resistance," said Croze importantly. "The splicers put the bioforms together and Shackie and me and Rebecca and Katuro had top identities – insurance and real estate, stuff like that you could travel with. So we'd take the bioforms to the locations and let them loose."

"We'd plant them," said Oates. "Like, you know, time bombs."

"Some of those suckers were really cool," said Shackie. "The microbes that ate the asphalt, the mice that attacked cars . . ."

"Zeb figured if you could destroy the infrastructure," said Croze, "then the planet could repair itself. Before it was too late and everything went extinct."

"So this plague, was it a MaddAddam thing?" said Amanda.

"No way," said Shackie. "Zeb didn't believe in killing people, not as such. He just wanted them to stop wasting everything and fucking up."

"He wanted to make them think," said Oates. "Though some of those mice got out of control. They got confused. Attacked shoes. There were foot injuries."

"Where is he now?" I asked. It would be so comforting if Zeb was there: he'd know what we should do next.

Shackie said, "We only talked to him online. He flew solo."

"CorpSeCorps nabbed our MaddAddam splicers, though," said Croze. "Tracked us down. I figure some creep in our chatroom was a plant."

"They shot them?" Amanda asked. "The scientists?"

"Don't know," said Shackie, "but they didn't end up with us in Painball."

"We were only in there a couple of days," said Oates. "In Painball."

"Three of us, three of them. The Gold team – they were beyond vicious. One of them – remember Blanco, from the Sewage Lagoon? Rip off your head and eat it? Lost some weight, but it was him all right," said Croze.

"You're joking," said Amanda. She looked – not frightened exactly. But concerned.

"Tossed in for trashing Scales – killed some people, sounded proud of it. Said Painball was like home to him, he'd done it so much."

"Did he know who you were?" said Amanda.

"Definitely," said Shackie. "Yelled at us. Said it was payback time for that brawl on the Edencliff Rooftop – he'd slit us like fish."

"What brawl on the Edencliff Rooftop?" I said.

"You'd gone by then," said Amanda. "How did you get out?"

"Walked," said Shackie. "We were figuring out how to kill the other team before they killed us – they gave you three days to plan, before the Start gong – but all of a sudden there were no guards. They were just gone."

"I'm really tired," said Oates. "I need to sleep." He put his head down on the bar.

"Guards were still there, it turned out," said Shackie. "In the gate-house. Only they were kind of melted."

"So we went online," said Croze, "The news was still working. Big disaster coverage, so we figured we shouldn't go out and mingle. We locked ourselves into one of the guardhouses – they had some food in there."

"Problem was, the Golds were in the guardhouse on the other side of the gate. We kept thinking they'd whack us when we were sleeping."

"We took turns staying awake, but it was too much strain, just waiting. So we forced them out," said Croze. "Shackie went through a window at night and cut their water lines."

"Fuck!" said Amanda with admiration. "Really?"

"So they had to leave," said Oates. "No water."

"Then we ran out of food and we had to leave too," said Shackie. "We thought maybe they'd be waiting for us, but they weren't." He shrugged. "End of story."

"Why did you come here?" I said. "To Scales."

Shackie grinned. "This place had a reputation," he said.

"A legend," said Croze. "Even though we didn't think there'd be any girls still left in it. We could at least see it."

"Something to do before you die," said Oates. He yawned.

"Come on, Oatie," said Amanda. "Let's put you to bed."

We took them upstairs and ran each of them through a Sticky Zone shower, and they came out a lot cleaner than when they went in. We gave them towels and they dried off, and then we tucked them into beds, one in each room.

It was me who took care of Oates – gave him his towel and soap, and showed him the bed where he could sleep. I hadn't seen him for such a long time. When I left the Gardeners he was just a little kid. A little brat – always getting into trouble. That's how I remembered him. But cute, even then.

"You've grown a lot," I said. He was almost as tall as Shackie. His blond hair was all damp, like a dog that's been swimming.

"I always thought you were the best," he said. "I had a huge crush on you when I was eight."

"I didn't know," I said.

"Can I kiss you?" he said. "I don't mean in a sexy way."

"Okay," I said. And he did, he gave me the sweetest kiss, beside my nose.

"You're so pretty," he said. "Please keep your bird suit on." He touched my feathers, the ones on my bum. Then he gave this shy little grin. It reminded me of Jimmy, the way he was at first, and I could feel my heart lurch. But I tiptoed out of the room.

"We could lock them in," I whispered to Amanda out in the hallway.

"Why would we do that?" said Amanda.

"They've been in Painball."

"So?"

"So, all Painball guys are unhinged. You don't know what they'll do, they just go crazy. Plus, they might have the germ. The plague thing."

"We hugged them," said Amanda. "We've already got every germ they've got. Anyway, they're old Gardener."

"Which means?" I said.

"Which means they're our friends."

"They weren't exactly our friends back then. Not always."

"Relax," said Amanda. "Those guys and me did lots of stuff together. Why would they hurt us?"

"I don't want to be a time-share meat-hole," I said.

"That's pretty crude," said Amanda. "It's not them you should be afraid of, it's the three Painball guys who were in there with them. Blanco's not a joke. They must be out there somewhere. I'm putting my real clothes back on." She was already peeling off her flamingo suit, pulling on her khaki.

"We should lock the front door," I said.

"The lock's broken," said Amanda.

Then we heard voices coming along the street. They were singing and yelling, the way men did at Scales when they're more than drunk. Stinking drunk, smashing-up drunk. We heard the crash of glass.

We ran into the bedrooms and woke up our guys. They put on their clothes very fast, and we took them to the second-floor window that overlooked the street. Shackie listened, then peered cautiously out. "Oh shit," he said.

"Is there another door in this place?" Croze whispered. His face was white, despite his sunburn. "We need to get out. Right now."

We went down the back stairs and slipped out the trash door, into the yard where the garboil dumpsters were, and the bins for empty bottles. We could hear the Gold Teamers bashing around inside the Scales building, demolishing whatever hadn't been demolished already. There was a giant smash: they must have pulled down the shelving behind the bar.

We squeezed through the gap in the fence and ran across the vacant lot to the far corner and down the alleyway there. They couldn't possibly see us, yet I felt as if they could – as if their eyes could pierce through brick, like TV mutants.

Blocks away, we slowed to a walk. "Maybe they won't figure it out," I say. "That we were there."

"They'll know," said Amanda. "The dirty plates. The wet towels. The beds. You can tell when a bed's just been slept in."

"They'll come after us," said Croze. "No question."

61

We turned corners and went up alleyways to mix up our tracks. Tracks were a problem – there was a layer of ashy mud – but Shackie said the rain would wash away our marks, and anyway the Gold Team weren't dogs, they wouldn't be able to smell us.

It had to be them: the three Painballers who'd smashed up Scales, that first night of the Flood. The ones who'd killed Mordis. They'd seen me on the intercom. That's why they'd come back to Scales – to open up the Sticky Zone like an oyster in order to get at me. They would have found tools. It might have taken a while, but they'd have done it in the end.

That thought gave me a very cold feeling, but I didn't tell the others about it. They had enough to worry about anyway.

There was a lot of trash cluttering the streets – burnt things, broken things. Not only cars and trucks. Glass – a lot of that. Shackie said we had to be careful which buildings we went into: they'd been right near one when it collapsed. We should stay away from the tall ones because the fires could have eaten away at them, and if the glass windows fell on you, goodbye head. It would be safer in a forest than in a city now. Which was the reverse of what people used to think.

It was the small normal things that bothered me the most. Somebody's old diary, with the words melting off the pages. The hats. The shoes – they were worse than the hats, and it was worse if there were two shoes the same. The kids' toys. The strollers minus the babies.

THE YEAR OF THE FLOOD | 339

The whole place was like a doll's house that had been turned upside down and stepped on. Out of one shop there was a trail of bright T-shirts, like huge cloth footprints, going all along the sidewalk. Someone must have smashed in through the window and robbed the place, though why did they think a bundle of T-shirts was going to do them any good? There was a furniture store spewing chair arms and legs and leather cushions onto the sidewalk, and an eyeglasses place with high-fashion frames, gold and silver – nobody had bothered to take those. A pharmacy – they'd trashed it completely, looking for party drugs. There were a lot of empty BlyssPluss containers. I'd thought it was just at the testing stage, but that place must have been selling it black market.

There were bundles of rag and bone. "Ex-people," said Croze. They were dried out and picked over, but I didn't like the eyeholes. And the teeth – mouths look a lot worse without lips. And the hair was so stringy and detachable. Hair takes years to decay; we learned that in Composting, at the Gardeners.

We hadn't had any time to grab food from Scales, so we went into a supermarkette. There was junk all over the floor, but we found a couple of Zizzy Froots and some Joltbars, and in another place there was a solar-freezer that was still running. It had soybeans and berries – we ate those right away – and frozen SecretBurger patties, six to a box.

"How're we going to cook them?" asked Oates.

"Lighters," said Shackie. "See?" On the counter there was a rack of lighters in the shape of frogs. Shackie tried one: the flame shot out of its mouth, and it said Ribbit.

"Take a handful," said Amanda.

By this time we were near the Sinkhole, so we headed for the old Wellness Clinic because it was a place we knew. I hoped there'd be some Gardeners left inside it, but it was empty. We had a picnic in our old classroom: we made a fire out of broken desks, though not a big fire because we didn't want to send any smoke signals to the Gold Painballers, but we had to open the windows because we were coughing too much. We broiled the SecretBurgers and ate them, and half of the soybeans – we didn't bother cooking those – and drank the Zizzy Froots. Oates kept making the frog lighter say Ribbit until Amanda told him to stop because he was wasting fuel.

The adrenalin of running away had worn off by then. It was sad to be back in the place where we'd been children: even if we hadn't liked it all the time, I felt so homesick for it now.

I guess this is what the rest of my life will be like, I thought. Running away, scrounging for leftovers, crouching on floors, getting dirtier and dirtier. I wished I had some real clothes, because I was still in my peagret outfit. I wanted to go back to the T-shirt place to see if there was anything left inside the store that wasn't damp and mouldy, but Shackie said it was too dangerous.

I thought maybe we should have sex: it would have been a kind and generous thing to do. But everyone was too tired, and also we were shy with one another. It was the surroundings – though the Gardeners weren't there in their bodies, they were there in Spirit, and it was hard to do anything they'd have disapproved of if they'd seen us doing it when we were ten.

We went to sleep in a pile, on top of one another, like puppies.

The next morning when we woke up there was a huge pig standing in the doorway, staring in at us and sniffing the air with its wet, sluggy-looking nose. It must have come in the door and all the way down the hall. It turned and went away when it saw us looking at it. Maybe it smelled the burger patties being cooked, said Shackie. He said it was an enhanced splice – MaddAddam had known about those – and that it had human brain tissue in it.

"Oh yeah," said Amanda, "and it's doing advanced physics. You're bullshitting us."

"Truth," said Shackie, a little sulky.

"Too bad we don't have a spraygun," said Croze. "Long time since I had bacon."

"None of that language," I said in a Toby voice, and we all laughed.

Before we left the Wellness Clinic we went into the Vinegar Room, for a last look at it. The big barrels were still there, though someone had taken an axe to them. There was a smell of vinegar, and also a toilet smell: people had been using a corner of the room for that, and not long ago either. The little closet door where they used to keep the vinegar bottles was standing open. There weren't any bottles; but there were some shelves. They were at a strange angle, and Amanda went over and took an edge and pulled, and the shelves swung out.

"Look," she said. "There's a whole other room in here!"

We went in. There was a table that took up most of the room, and some chairs. But the most interesting thing was a futon, like our old Gardener ones, and a bunch of empty food containers – soydines, chickenpeas, dried gojiberries. Over in one corner was a dead laptop.

"Somebody else made it through," said Shackie.

"Not a Gardener," I said. "Not with a laptop."

"Zeb had a laptop," said Croze. "But he'd stopped being a Gardener."

We left the Wellness Clinic without any clear plan. It was me who said we should go to the AnooYoo Spa: there might be food in the Ararat that Toby put together in the storeroom; she'd told me the doorcode. Also there could still be something growing in the garden. I even wondered if maybe Toby was hiding out there, but I didn't want to get any hopes up, so I didn't say that.

We thought we were being really careful. We couldn't see anybody anywhere. We went into the Heritage Park and headed towards the Spa's west gatehouse, staying on the forest pathway, under the trees – we felt less visible that way.

We were going single file. Shackie was at the front of the line, then Croze, then Amanda, then me; Oates was at the very back. Then I had a cold feeling, and I looked behind me, and Oates wasn't there. I said, "Shackie!"

And then Amanda lurched sideways, right off the path.

Then there was a dark patch like going through brambles – everything painful and tangled. There were bodies on the ground, and one of them was mine, and that must have been when I got hit.

When I woke up again, Shackie and Croze and Oates weren't there. But Amanda was.

I don't want to think about what happened next.

It was worse for Amanda than for me.

PREDATOR DAY

YEAR TWENTY-FIVE.

OF GOD AS THE ALPHA PREDATOR.
SPOKEN BY ADAM ONE.

Dear Friends, dear Fellow Creatures, dear Fellow Mortals:

Long ago, we celebrated Predator Day on our lovely Edencliff Rooftop Garden. Our Children would don their faux-fur Predator ears and tails, and at sunset we'd light candles inside the Lions and Tigers and Bears fashioned from perforated tin cans, and the burning-bright eyes of these Predator images would sparkle upon our Predator Day feast.

But today our Festival must be held in the inner Gardens of our Minds. We are fortunate to have even these, for the Waterless Flood has now rolled over our city, and indeed over the entire Planet. Most were taken by surprise, but we relied on Spiritual guidance. Or, to put it in a materialistic way: we knew a global pandemic when we saw one.

Let us give thanks for this Ararat in which we have been sheltering over the past months. It is not perhaps the Ararat we would have chosen, situated as it is in the cellars of the Buenavista Condo Complex, which were dank even at the time of Pilar's mushroom beds, and are even danker now. But we are blessed that so many of our Rat relatives have donated their protein to us, thus enabling us to remain on this Earthly plane. It is also fortunate that Pilar had built an Ararat in this very cellar, hidden behind a concrete block marked with a tiny bee symbol. How providential that so many of her supplies retained their freshness! Though unhappily not all.

But these resources are now exhausted, and we must either move or starve. Let us pray that the outer world is Exfernal no more – that the Waterless Flood has cleansed as well as destroyed, and that all the world is now a new Eden. Or, if it is not a new Eden yet, that it will be one soon. Or so we trust.

On Predator Day we celebrate, not God the loving and gentle Father and Mother, but God the Tiger. Or God the Lion. Or God the Bear. Or God the Wild Boar. Or God the Wolf. Or even God the Shark. Whatever the symbol, Predator Day is devoted to the qualities of terrifying appearance and overwhelming strength, which, since they are at times desired by us, must also belong to God, as all good things belong to Him.

As Creator, God has put a little of Himself into each of His Creatures – how could it be otherwise? – and therefore the Tiger, the Lion, the Wolf, the Bear, the Boar, and the Shark – or, on the miniscale of things, the Water Shrew and the Praying Mantis – are in their way reflections of the Divine. Human societies through the ages have known this. On their flags and coats of arms, they have not placed prey Animals such as Rabbits and Mice, but Animals capable of inflicting death, and when they invoked God as defender, was it not these qualities upon which they called?

Thus on Predator Day we meditate on the Alpha Predator aspects of God. The suddenness and ferocity with which an apprehension of the Divine may appear to us; our smallness and fearfulness – may I say, our Mouselikeness – in the face of such Power; our feelings of individual annihilation in the brightness of that splendid Light. God walks in the tender dawn Gardens of the mind, but He also prowls in its night Forests. He is not a tame Being, my Friends: he is a wild Being, and cannot be summoned and controlled like a Dog.

Human Beings may well have killed the last Tiger and the last Lion, but their Names are cherished by us; and as we say those Names, we hear behind them the tremendous Voice of God at the moment of their Creation. God must have said to them: My Carnivores, I command you to fulfil your appointed task of culling your Prey Species, lest these multiply overmuch, and exhaust their food supply, and sicken, and die out. Go forth, therefore! Leap! Run! Roar! Lurk! Spring! For I delight in your dread hearts, and in the gold and green jewels of your eyes, and in your well-fashioned sinews, and in your scissor teeth and your scimitar claws, which I Myself have bestowed upon you. And I give you My Blessing, and pronounce you Good.

For they do seek their meat from God, as Psalm 104 so joyfully puts it.

As we prepare to leave our sheltering Ararat, let us ask ourselves: Which is more blessed, to eat or to be eaten? To flee or to chase? To give or to receive? For these are at heart the same question. Such a question may soon cease to be theoretical: we do not know what Alpha Predators may lurk without.

Let us pray that if we must sacrifice our own protein so it may circulate among our fellow Species, we will recognize the sacred nature of the transaction. We would not be Human if we did not prefer to be the devourers rather than the devoured, but either is a blessing. Should your life be required of you, rest assured that it is required by Life.

Let us sing.

THE WATER-SHREW THAT RENDS ITS PREY

The Water-Shrew that rends its Prey
Acts purely out of Nature's need;
It does not stop to plot its course,
But simply does the deed.

The Leopard pouncing in the night
Is kin to soft domestic Puss –
They love to hunt, and hunt to love,
Because God made them thus.

And who can say if joy or fear
Are each in other's lasting debt?
Does every Prey enjoy each breath
Because of constant threat?

But we are not as Animals –
We cherish other Creatures' lives;
And so we do not eat their flesh
Unless dread Famine drives.

And if dread Famine drives us on,
And if we yield to tempting Meat,
May God forgive our broken Vows,
And bless the Life we eat.

From *The God's Gardeners Oral Hymnbook*

62

A red sunrise, meaning rain later. But there's always rain later.

Mist rising.

Oodle-oodle-ooo. Oodle-oodle-oo. Chirrup, twareep. Aw aw aw. Ey ey ey. Hoom hoom baroom.

Mourning dove, robin, crow, bluejay, bullfrog. Toby says their names, but these names mean nothing to them. Soon her own language will be gone out of her head and this will be all that's left in there. Ooodle-oodle-oo, hoom hoom. The ceaseless repetition, the song with no beginning and no end. No questions, no answers, not in so many words. Not in any words at all. Or is it all one huge Word?

Where has this notion come from, out of nowhere and into her head? *Tobeee!*

So much like someone calling her. But it's only birdsong.

She's up on the roof, cooking her daily portion of land shrimp in the cool of the morning. Don't scorn the lowly table of Saint Euell, says the voice of Adam One. The Lord provides, and sometimes what He provides is land shrimp, says Zeb. Rich in lipids, a good source of protein. How do you think bears get so fat?

Best to cook outside, because of the smoke and heat. She's using her Saint Euell–inspired hobo stove, made of a bulk-sized body-butter can: hole in the bottom for dry sticks and the draft, hole on the side for smoke. The maximum heat for the minimum fuel. No more than needed. The land shrimp sizzle on the top.

Suddenly there's a racket of crows: they're excited about something. Not alarm calls, so not an owl. More like astonishment: *Aw Aw! Look! Look! Look at that!*

Toby scrapes the crispy land shrimp off the top of her tin can onto her plate – to waste food is to waste Life, says Adam One – then douses the fire with her pot of rainwater and hits the rooftop, flat on her belly. Lifts the binoculars. The crows are flying around above the treetops, a flock of them. Six or seven. *Aw! Aw! Look! Look! Look!*

Two men come out from among the trees. They aren't singing, and they aren't naked and blue: they have clothes on.

There are still people, Toby thinks. Alive. Maybe one of them is Zeb, come in search of her: he must have guessed she'd still be here, still be holed up, still holding out. She blinks: are these tears? She wants to rush downstairs and out into the open, hold out her arms in welcome, laugh with happiness. But caution restrains her, and she crouches down behind the air-conditioning exhaust unit and peers through the rooftop railings.

It could be a trick of the senses. Is she seeing things again?

The men are in camouflage gear. The one in front has a weapon of some kind – a spraygun, perhaps. Surely not Zeb: wrong shape. Neither of them is. There's another person with them – man or woman? Tall, in a khaki outfit. Head hanging down; hard to tell which. Hands held together in front, as if in prayer. One of the men has this person by the arm or elbow. Pushing or pulling.

Then another man emerges from the shadows. He's leading a huge bird on a leash – no, on a rope – a bird with blue-green iridescent plumes like a peagret. But this bird has the head of a woman.

I must be hallucinating again, thinks Toby. Because no matter what the gene splicers could do, they couldn't do this. The men and the bird-woman look real and solid enough, but then, hallucinations do.

One of them has a burden slung over his shoulder. At first she thinks it's a sack, but no, it's a haunch of something. It has fur. Golden fur. Is it a liobam? A shiver of horror runs through her: sacrilege! They've killed an Animal on the Peaceable Kingdom list!

Think clearly, Toby orders herself. First of all, since when are you a fanatical Peaceable Kingdom Isaiahist? Second, if these men are real and not just runoff from an addled brain, they've been killing things. Killing and butchering large Creatures, in which case they have lethal weapons and they've started at the top of the food chain. They're a menace, they'll stop at nothing, and I ought to shoot them before they get as far as me. Then I can free the large bird or whatever it is, before they kill it as well.

Anyway, if they aren't real, it won't matter if I shoot them. They'll just dissolve like smoke.

Then the one leading the bird-woman looks up. He must have seen Toby, because he begins to shout, waving his free arm. Light glints from a knife. The other two men look, and then they all start trotting towards the Spa. The bird creature has to keep up with them because of the rope, and now Toby can see that the feathers are a costume of some kind. It's a woman. No wings. A noose around her neck.

Not a hallucination, then. Real. Real evil.

She centres the knife man in her scope and shoots at him. He staggers backwards and yells and stumbles. But she isn't fast enough, so although she squeezes off a couple more, she misses the other two.

Now the wounded man's up again, limping, and all of them are running back to the trees. The bird woman's running with them. Not that she has a choice, because of the rope. Then she falls down and vanishes into the weeds.

Behind the others, the green tree-leaves open, swallow. Gone now. All of them. She can't spot the place where the woman tumbled: the weeds are too tall. Should she go out and look for her? No. It could be a decoy. There'd be three against her one.

She watches for a long time. The crows must be following them – the men, the one in khaki. *Aw aw aw aw.* A trail of sound, off into the distance.

Will they be back? They'll be back, thinks Toby. They know I'm in here, they'll guess I must have food in order to have stayed alive this long. Also I shot one of them: they'll want revenge, it's only human. They'll be vindictive, like the pigs. But they won't come soon, because they know I have a rifle. They'll have to plan.

63

YEAR TWENTY-FIVE

No men. No pigs either. No liobams.

No bird woman.

Maybe I lost my mind, thinks Toby. Not lost. Temporarily misplaced.

It's bath time; she's up on the roof. She pours rainwater from her collection of smaller bowls and pans into the largest bowl, soaps herself, hands and face only: she won't risk the vulnerability of a full bath, because who knows who may be peering? She's in the midst of sponging off the suds when she hears the crows making a commotion, close by. *Aw aw aw!* This time it sounds like laughing.

Toby! Toby! Help me!

Was that my name? thinks Toby. She looks over the railing, sees nothing. But the voice comes again, right close to the building.

Is it a trap? A woman calling out to her, a man's arm around her throat, a knife to the jugular?

Toby! It's me! Please!

She blots herself with a towel, slides into her top-to-toe, shoulders the rifle, makes her way down the stairs. Opens the door: no one. But the voice again, so near. *Oh please!*

Left corner: nobody. Right corner, nobody again. She's just outside the garden gate when a woman comes around the building. She's hobbling, she's thin and beat up; her long hair's across her face, matted with dirt and dried blood. She's wearing a spangled body suit, with damp, tattered blue feathers.

The bird woman. Some freak from a sex circus. She's bound to be infected, a walking plague. If she touches me, thinks Toby, I'm dead.

"Keep away from me!" she shouts. She backs up against the garden fence. "Fuck off out of here!"

The woman sways on her feet. She has a gash on her leg, and her bare arms are scratched and bleeding – she must have run through brambles. All Toby can think of is the fresh blood: boiling with microbes and viruses.

"Piss off! Get away!!"

"I'm not sick," says the woman. Tears are running down her face. But they'd all said that in their despair. They'd said it, pleading, holding up their hands for help, for comfort, and then they'd turned into pink porridge. Toby had watched them from the roof.

They'll be drowning. Don't let them clutch you. Don't let yourself be that last straw, my Friends, says Adam One.

The rifle. She fumbles with the strap: it's caught in the fabric of her top-to-toe. How to fend off this festering hotspot? Yelling's no good without a weapon. Maybe I could bang her on the head with a stone, thinks Toby. But she doesn't have a stone. A good kick in the solar plexus, then wash my feet.

You are an uncharitable person, says the voice of Nuala. You have scorned God's Creatures, for are not Human beings God's Creatures too?

From under the mat of hair the woman pleads: "Toby! It's me!" She crumples, falls to her knees. Then Toby sees it's Ren. Beneath all the dirt and mangled glitz, it's only little Ren.

64

Toby hauls Ren inside the Spa building and dumps her on the floor while she locks the door behind them. Ren is still crying hysterically, in great gulping sobs.

"Never you mind," says Toby. She takes Ren under the arms and pulls her upright, and they stumble down the hall into one of the treatment cubicles. Ren's a dead weight, but she's not very heavy, and Toby manages to hoist her onto a massage table. She smells of sweat and earth, and blood somewhere, and another smell: something's decaying.

"Stay here," says Toby unnecessarily: Ren isn't going anywhere. She's lying back on the pink pillow with her eyes closed. One of those eyes is black and blue. AnooYoo Soothing Aloe Eye Pads, thinks Toby. With Extra Arnica. She breaks open a packet and applies them, and adds a pink sheet, tucked in at the sides so Ren won't fall off the table. There's a cut on Ren's forehead, another on her cheek: nothing too serious, she'll deal with those later.

She goes into the kitchen, boils up some water in the Kelly kettle. Most likely Ren's dehydrated. She pours hot water into a cup, adds a little of her cherished honey, a pinch of salt. Some dried green onions from her dwindling stash. Carries the cup into Ren's cubicle, takes off the eye pads, sits her up.

Ren's eyes are huge in her thin, bruised face. "I'm not sick," she says, which is untrue: she's burning with fever. But there's more than one kind of sickness. Toby checks the symptoms: no blood oozing from the pores, no froth. Still, Ren could be a plague carrier, an incubator; in which case, Toby's already infected.

"Try to drink," says Toby.

"I can't," says Ren. But she does manage to get some of the water down. "Where's Amanda? I need to get dressed."

"It's okay," says Toby. "Amanda's nearby. Now try to sleep." She eases Ren back down. So Amanda's in this story somewhere, she thinks. That girl was always trouble.

"I can't see," says Ren. She's trembling all over.

Back in the kitchen, Toby pours the rest of the boiled water into a bowl: she needs to clean away those bedraggled feathers and sequins. She carries the bowl and a pair of scissors and a bar of soap and a stack of pink washcloths into Ren's cubicle, folds back the sheet, and cuts away the grubby outfit. It isn't cloth, it's some other substance, underneath the feathers. Stretchy. Almost like skin. She soaks the patches where it's stuck on so she can peel them off more easily. The crotch has been torn away. Cripes, thinks Toby, what a mess. Later she'll make a poultice.

There are abrasions around the neck – rope burns, no doubt. The gash on the left leg is what's festering. Toby's as gentle as she can be, but Ren winces and yelps. "That fucking hurts!" she says. Then she throws up the salt-and-sugar water.

After she's wiped away the filth, Toby starts washing the leg wound. "How did you get this?" she asks.

"I don't know." Ren is whispering. "I fell down."

Toby cleans out the gash and puts some honey on it. Antibiotics in it, Pilar used to say. There ought to be a first-aid kit, somewhere in the Spa. "Hold still. You don't want gangrene," she says to Ren.

Ren giggles. "Knock, knock," she says, "Gang grene."

The dirty covering's all stripped away, and Ren has been sponged. "I'll give you some Willow and Chamomile," Toby says. And Poppy, she thinks. "You need to sleep." Ren will be safer on the floor than on the table: she makes a nest of pink towels, eases her down onto it, adds extra padding because Ren can't make it to the bathroom, she's too weak. She's hot as an ember.

Toby brings the Willow mixture in a small glass. Ren swallows, her throat moving like a bird's. Nothing comes up.

There's no use trying the maggots yet. Ren needs to be coherent for that, able to obey instructions: no scratching, for instance. The first thing is to get the temperature down.

While Ren sleeps, Toby sorts through her store of dried mushrooms. She chooses the immune-system boosters: reishi, maitake, shitake, birch polypore, zhu ling, lion's mane, coryceps, ice man. She puts them in boiled water to soak. Then in the afternoon she prepares a mushroom elixir – the simmering, the straining, the cooling – and gives Ren thirty drops of it.

The cubicle stinks. Toby lifts Ren up, rolls her to the side, pulls out the soiled towels, wipes Ren off. She's put on rubber gloves for the purpose: if dysentery's going around she has no wish to catch it. She smoothes down clean towels, rolls Ren back. Her arms flop, her head wilts; she's muttering.

This is going to be a lot of work, thinks Toby. And when Ren recovers – if she recovers – there will be two people eating instead of one. So the food stash will be gone twice as quickly. What's left of it. Which isn't much.

Maybe the fever will get the better of Ren. Maybe she'll die in her sleep.

Toby considers the powdered Death Angels. It wouldn't take much. Just a little, in Ren's weakened condition. Put her out of her misery. Help her to fly away on white, white wings. Maybe it would be kinder. A blessing.

I am an unworthy person, Toby thinks. Merely to have such an idea. You've known this girl since she was a child, she's come to you for help, she has every right to trust you. Adam One would say that Ren is a precious gift that has been given to Toby so that Toby may demonstrate unselfishness and sharing and those higher qualities the Gardeners had been so eager to bring out in her. Toby can't quite see it that way, not at the moment. But she'll have to keep trying.

Ren sighs and groans and flails. She's having a bad dream.

When it's dark, Toby lights a candle and sits beside her, listening to her breathe. In out, in out. Pause. In. Then out. Raggedy. At intervals she feels Ren's forehead. Cooler? There must be a thermometer in the building; in the morning she'll look for it. She takes her pulse: rapid, irregular.

Then she nods off in her chair, and the next thing she knows she wakes up in the dark with a smell of singeing. She winds up her flashlight: the candle has fallen over, and a corner of Ren's pink sheet is smouldering. Luckily it's damp.

That was terminally stupid, Toby tells herself. No more candles unless I'm fully awake.

65

In the morning Ren feels cooler. Her pulse is stronger, and she can even hold the cup of warm water in her own two trembling hands. Toby's put mint in it this morning, as well as the honey and salt.

Once Ren has gone to sleep again, Toby hauls the dirty sheets and towels up to the roof to wash them. She's brought her binoculars, and while the sheets and towels are soaking she scans the Spa grounds.

Pigs far away, over in the southwest corner of the meadow. Two Mo'Hairs, a blue one and a silver one, grazing quietly together. No liobams. Dogs barking somewhere. Vultures flapping around the pig funeral site.

"Get away from there, you archeologists," says Toby. She's feeling light-headed, almost giddy – in the mood to tell herself jokes. Three huge pink butterflies circle her head, alight on the damp sheets. Maybe they think they've found the biggest pink butterfly of all. Maybe it's a love affair. Now they have their thin tongues unrolled, licking. Not love, then: salt.

Some will tell you Love is merely chemical, my Friends, said Adam One. Of course it is chemical: where would any of us be without chemistry? But Science is merely one way of describing the world. Another way of describing it would be to say: where would any of us be without Love?

Dear Adam One, thinks Toby. He must be dead. And Zeb – dead also, despite wishful thinking. Though maybe not; because if I'm alive – more to the point, if Ren's alive – then anyone at all could be alive too.

She stopped listening on her wind-up radio months ago because the silence was so discouraging. But just because she's heard no one doesn't mean no one's there. Which had been among Adam One's hypothetical proofs for the existence of God.

Toby washes Ren's infected leg, applies more honey. Ren eats a little, drinks a little. More mushroom elixir, more Willow. After much rummaging, Toby locates a Spa first-aid kit; there's a tube of antibiotic cream, but it's stale-dated. No thermometer. Who ordered this crap? she thinks. Oh yes. I did.

Anyway maggots are better.

In the afternoon she lifts the maggots from the plastic snap-top, rinses them in tepid water. Then she transfers them to a sheet of gauze from the first-aid kit, applies another sheet over the top, and tapes the maggot-filled envelope over the wound. It won't take long for the maggots to eat through the gauze: they know what they like.

"This will tickle," she tells Ren. "But they'll make you better. Try not to move your leg."

"What are they?" says Ren.

"They're your friends," says Toby. "But you don't need to look."

Her homicidal impulse of the night before is gone: she will not drag dead Ren out into the meadow for the pigs and vultures. Now she'd like to cure her, cherish her, for isn't it miraculous that Ren is here? That she's come through the Waterless Flood with only minor damage? Or fairly minor. Just to have a second person on the premises – even a feeble person, even a sick person who sleeps most of the time – just this makes the Spa seem like a cozy domestic dwelling rather than a haunted house.

I've been the ghost, thinks Toby.

66

TOBY. SAINT HENRI FABRE, SAINT ANNA ATKINS, SAINT TIM FLANNERY,
SAINT ICHIDA-SAN, SAINT DAVID SUZUKI, SAINT PETER MATTHIESSEN

YEAR TWENTY-FIVE

It takes the maggots three days to clean the wound. Toby watches them carefully: if they run out of dead tissue, they'll start in on living flesh.

By the second morning Ren's fever has gone, though Toby continues the mushroom drops just to make sure. Ren's eating more now. Toby helps her up the stairs to the roof and sits her down on the imitation-wood bench, in the early morning light. The maggots are photophobic: light drives them into the deepest corners of the wound, which is where they need to be.

No movement out there in the meadow. No sounds from the forest.

Toby tries asking Ren where she's been ever since the Flood hit, and how she escaped it, and how she got here, why she'd been dressed in those blue feathers; but she only tries once because Ren starts crying. All she'll say is, "I've lost Amanda!"

"Never mind," says Toby. "We'll find her."

On the fourth morning Toby removes the maggot plaster: the wound is clean, and healing. "Now to get your muscles back in shape," she tells Ren.

Ren starts walking, up and down the stairs, along the corridors. She's gained a little weight: Toby's been feeding her the last few jars of AnooYoo Lemon Meringue Facial, which has a lot of sugar in it and nothing toxic that Toby can think of. She leads Ren through some exercises from Zeb's old Urban Bloodshed Limitation classes – the *satsuma*, the *unagi*. Centred like a Fruit, sinuous like an Eel. She needs the refresher herself; she's out of practice.

After a few days Ren tells her story, or a little of her story. It comes out in short clumps of words punctuated by long periods of staring into space. She tells about being locked in at Scales, and how Amanda came all the way from the Wisconsin desert and figured out the door code. Then Shackie and Croze and Oates appeared from nowhere, just like magic, and she was so happy – they'd been saved by being in Painball when the plague broke out. But then three horrible men from the Painball Gold Team came to Scales, and she and Amanda and the boys ran away. She'd said they should come to AnooYoo because Toby might be there, and they'd almost made it – they were walking along through the trees, and then blackout. She can't get any farther than that.

"What did they look like?" says Toby. "Did they have any . . ." She wants to say "distinguishing marks," but Ren shakes her head, meaning that that subject is closed. "I have to find Amanda," she says, wiping away tears. "I really have to. They'll kill her."

"Here, blow your nose," says Toby, handing her a pink washcloth. "Amanda's very clever." It's best to talk as if Amanda is still alive. "She's very resourceful. She'll be all right." She's about to say that women are in short supply and therefore Amanda will surely be preserved and rationed, but she thinks better of it.

"You don't understand," says Ren, crying harder. "There's three of them, they're Painball – they're not really human. I have to find her."

"We'll look," Toby says, to be soothing. "But we don't know where they – where she's gone."

"Where would you go?" says Ren. "If you were them?"

"Maybe east," says Toby. "To the sea. Where they could fish."

"We can go there."

"When you're strong enough," says Toby. They have to move somewhere else anyway: the food supply's shrinking fast.

"I'm strong enough now," says Ren.

Toby scours the garden, unearths one more lone onion. She digs up three burdocks from the near edge of the meadow, and some Queen Anne's lace – the spindly white proto-carrot roots. "Do you think you could eat a rabbit?" she asks Ren. "If I cut it up very small and make it into soup?"

"I guess so," said Ren. "I'll try."

Toby's almost ready for the switch to full-blown carnivore herself. There's the sound of the rifle shot to worry about, but if there are still Painballers lurking in the forest they already know she has a gun. No harm in reminding them.

There are often green rabbits near the swimming pool. Toby shoots at one of them from the rooftop, but she can't seem to hit it. Is conscience twisting her aim? Maybe she needs a bigger target, a deer or a dog. She hasn't seen the pigs lately, or any of the sheep. Just as she was getting all set to eat them, they're gone.

She locates the packsacks on a laundry-room shelf. She hasn't been down there since the pumps stopped working, and the air's thick with mildew. Luckily the packsacks aren't cotton but impenetrable synthetic. She takes them up to the roof, sponges them off, leaves them in the hot sun to dry.

She lays out her available supplies on the kitchen counter. Don't carry so much weight that you burn more calories than you can eat, says the voice of Zeb. Tools are more important than food. Your best tool is your brain.

The rifle, of course. Ammunition. Trowel, for digging roots. Matches. Barbecue lighter, which won't last long but it might as well be used up. Pocket knife with scissors and tweezers. Rope. Two sheets of plastic, handy in rain. Windup flashlight. Gauze bandages. Duct tape. Plastic snap-top containers. Cloth bags for wild edibles. Cooking pot. The Kelly kettle. Toilet paper – a luxury item, but she can't resist. Two medium-sized Zizzy Froots from a Spa minibar, raspberry flavour: junk food, but food, since it has calories in it. The bottles can be used later, for water.

Spoons, metal, two; cups, plastic, two. The remaining sunblock. The last SuperD bug spray. Binoculars: heavy but necessary. The mop handle. Sugar. Salt. The last of the honey. The last Joltbars. The last soybits.

The syrup of Poppy. The dried mushrooms. The Death Angels.

The day before they leave, she cuts her hair short. It's a shorn look – it reminds her of Joan of Arc on a bad day – but she doesn't want a hair handle growing out of her head, all the better to grab you by and slash your throat. She cuts Ren's hair as well. They'll be cooler that way, she tells her.

"We should bury the hair," says Ren. She wants it out of sight for some reason Toby can't fathom.

"Why don't we put it on the roof?" says Toby. "That way the birds can make nests out of it." She doesn't intend to waste her body's calories digging a hair burial site.

"Oh. Okay," says Ren. This idea seems to please her.

67

YEAR TWENTY-FIVE

They leave the Spa building just before dawn. They're dressed in pink cotton exercise outfits, the loose pants and the T-shirt top with the kissy mouth and the winky eye on the front. Pink canvas sport shoes, of the kind the ladies wore to do their rope skipping and weight training. Broad pink hats. They smell of SuperD, and of rancid SolarNix. In their pack-sacks are their pink top-to-toes, for when the sun gets too high. If only everything weren't so pink, thinks Toby – like baby clothes or girly birth-day parties. Not an adventurous colour. Terrible choice for camouflage.

She knows the situation is grave, as the news used to say – of course it is. But nonetheless she feels cheerful, almost giggly. As if she's a little drunk. As if they're just going on a picnic. It must be a surge of adrenalin.

The eastern horizon is brightening; mist rises from the trees. Dew shimmers on the lumirose bushes, mirroring the faint eerie light of their flowers. The sweetness of the damp meadow breathes all around them. The birds are beginning to stir and chirp; the vultures on the bare branches are spreading their wings to dry. A peagret flaps towards them from the south, sails over the meadow, then swoops in for a landing on the edge of the green-scummed swimming pool.

It occurs to Toby that she may never see this vista again. Amazing how the heart clutches at anything familiar, whimpering, *Mine! Mine!* Did she enjoy her enforced stay in the AnooYoo Spa? No. But it's her home territory now: she's left her skin flakes all over it. A mouse would understand: it's her nest. *Farewell* is the song Time sings, Adam One used to say.

Somewhere dogs are barking. She's heard them at intervals over the past months, but today they sound closer. She doesn't much like this. With nobody to feed them, any dogs left by now are sure to have turned wild.

She'd climbed up to the rooftop before they left, scanned the fields. No pigs, no Mo'Hairs, no liobams. Or none in plain view. How little I've ever been able to see, she thinks. The meadow, the driveway, the swimming pool, the garden. The edge of the forest. She'd like to avoid going in there, among the trees. Nature may be dumb as a sack of hammers, Zeb used to say, but it's smarter than you.

Look, she thinks at the forest, with its hidden pigs and liobams. And Painballers too, for all she knows. Don't push me. I may be pink, but I've got a rifle. Bullets too. Longer range than a spraygun. So back off, assholes.

The Spa grounds and its woodland perimeter are separated from the surrounding Heritage Park by a chain-link fence topped with electrified barbed wire, though the electricity won't be functional now. Four gates, east, west, north, and south, with winding driveways connecting them. It's Toby's plan to spend the night at the eastern gatehouse. That's not too far for Ren to walk: she's still not strong enough for heroic trekking. The next morning they can begin to make their way gradually towards the sea.

Ren still believes they'll find Amanda. They'll find her, and Toby will shoot the Gold Painballers with her rifle, and then Shackleton and Crozier and Oates will reappear from wherever they've been hiding. Ren's not yet free of the effects of her illness. She wants Toby to fix and cure everything, as if she herself were still a child; as if Toby were still Eve Six, with magic adult powers.

They pass the crashed pink minivan and, around a curve in the road, two other vehicles – a solarcar, a jeep-sized garboil guzzler. Judging from the blackened wreckage, both must have burned. There's a rusty, sweetish odour mixed in with the charred smell.

"Don't look inside," Toby tells Ren as they walk past.

"It's okay," Ren says. "I saw a lot of stuff like that in the pleebs, when we were coming here from Scales."

Farther along there's a dog – a spaniel, recently dead. Something's torn it open; there's a scribble of entrails, a buzzing of flies, but no vultures yet. Whatever it was will surely return to its kill: predators don't waste. Toby eyes the roadside bushes: the vines are growing almost audibly, shutting out sight. What a lot of kudzu. "We should walk faster," she says.

But Ren can't walk faster. She's tired, her packsack's too heavy. "I think I'm getting a blister," she says. They stop under a tree for a drink of Zizzy Froot. Toby can't shake the feeling that something's crouched up in the branches, waiting to leap on them. Can liobams climb? She forces herself to slow down, to breathe deeply, to take her time.

"Let's see your blister," she says to Ren. It's not a blister yet. She tears a strip off her top-to-toe, winds it around Ren's foot. The sun's at ten. They put on their top-to-toes and Toby smears their faces with more SolarNix, then sprays them again with SuperD.

Ren begins to limp before they've reached the next curve in the road.

"We'll cut across the meadow," says Toby. "It's shorter that way."

SAINT RACHEL AND ALL BIRDS

OF THE GIFTS OF SAINT RACHEL; AND OF THE FREEDOM OF THE SPIRIT.
SPOKEN BY ADAM ONE.

Dear Friends, dear Fellow Creatures and Fellow Mortals:

What a cause for rejoicing is this rearranged world in which we find ourselves! True, there is a certain – let us not say *disappointment*. The debris left by the Waterless Flood, like that left by any receding flood, is not attractive. It will take time for our longed-for Eden to appear, my Friends.

But how privileged we are to witness these first precious moments of Rebirth! How much clearer the air is, now that man-made pollution has ceased! This freshly cleansed air is to our lungs as the air up there in the clouds is to the lungs of Birds. How light, how ethereal they must feel as they soar above the trees! For many ages, Birds have been linked to the freedom of the Spirit, as opposed to the heavy burden of Matter. Does not the Dove symbolize Grace, the all-forgiving, the all-accepting?

It is in the spirit of that Spirit of grace that we welcome among us three fellow Mortal companions on our journey – Melissa, Darren, and Quill. They have miraculously escaped the Waterless Flood by having been providentially sequestered: Melissa in a hilltop yoga and weight-loss establishment, Darren in a hospital isolation ward, and Quill in a place of solitary incarceration. We rejoice that these three appear not to have been exposed to viral contamination. Although not of our Faith – or not still of our Faith in the case of Quill and Melissa – they are our fellow Creatures; and we are happy to aid them at this common time of trial.

We are grateful also for this temporary abode, which, though it is a former Happicuppa franchise, has sheltered us from the grilling sun and the gruelling storm. Thanks to the skills of Stuart – in especial, his acquaintance with chisels – we have gained entrance to the storeroom, thereby procuring access to much Happicuppa product: the dried milk substitute, the vanilla-flavoured syrup, the moccachino mix, and the single-serving packets of sugar, both raw and white. You all know my view of refined sugar products, but there are times when the rules must bend. Thank you to Nuala, our indomitable Eve Nine, for the skill with which she has whipped up a sustaining brew for our refreshment.

We remember on this Day that the Happicuppa Corp was in direct contravention to the Spirit of Saint Rachel. Its sun-grown, pesticide-sprayed, rainforest-habitat-destroying coffee products were the biggest threat to God's feathered Creatures in our times, just as DDT was the biggest threat to them in the times of Saint Rachel Carson. It was in the Spirit of Saint Rachel that some of our more radical former members joined the militant campaign against Happicuppa. Other groups were protesting its treatment of indigenous workers, but those ex-Gardeners were protesting its anti-Bird policies. Although we could not condone the violent methods, we did endorse the intention.

Saint Rachel dedicated her life to the Feathered Ones, and thus to the welfare of the entire Planet – for as the Birds sickened and died out, did this not indicate the growing illness of Life itself? Imagine God's sorrow as he viewed the distress of His most exquisite and tuneful feathered Creations!

Saint Rachel was attacked by the powerful chemical corps of her day, and scorned and pilloried for her truth-telling, but her campaign did at last prevail. Sadly, the anti-Happicuppa campaign did not meet with equal success, but that problem has now been solved by a greater power: Happicuppa has not survived the Waterless Flood. As the Human Words of God put it, in Isaiah 34, "From generation to generation it shall lie waste. . . . But the Cormorant and the Bittern shall possess it. . . . There shall the great Owl make her nest, and lay, and hatch, and gather under her shadow; there shall the Vultures also be gathered, every one with her mate."

And so it has come to pass. Even now, my Friends, the rainforest must be regenerating!

Let us sing.

WHEN GOD SHALL HIS BRIGHT WINGS UNFOLD

When God shall His bright wings unfold
And fly from Heaven's blue,
He first will as a Dove appear
Of pure and sparkling hue.

Then next the Raven's form He'll take,
To show there's beauty too
In any Bird that He did make,
The oldest and the new.

He'll sail with Swans, with Hawks He'll glide,
With Cockatoo and Owl,
The chorus of the dawn He'll sing,
He'll dive with Waterfowl.

As Vulture He will next appear,
The Holy Bird of yore,
Who Death does eat, corruption too,
And thus does Life restore.

Under His wings we'll sheltered be:
From fowler's nets He'll save;
His Eye will note the Sparrow's fall,
And mark the Eagle's grave.

For those who Avian blood do shed
In idle sport and play
Are murderers of God's Holy Peace
That blessed the Seventh Day.

From *The God's Gardeners Oral Hymnbook*

68

YEAR TWENTY-FIVE

We walk through the shimmering meadow. There's a humming like a thousand tiny vibrators; huge pink butterflies float all around. The clover scent is very strong. Toby probes in front of her with her mop handle. I try to pay attention to where I'm putting my feet, but the ground is lumpy and I trip, and when I look down it's a boot. Beetles scurry out.

There's some animals up ahead. They weren't there a minute ago. I wonder if they were lying down in the grass and then stood up. I hang back, but Toby says, "It's okay, they're just Mo'Hairs."

I've never seen a live one before, only online. They stand there looking at us with their jaws moving sideways. "Would they let me pat them?" I say. They're blue and pink and silver and purple; they look like candy, or sunny-day clouds. So cheerful and peaceful.

"I doubt it," says Toby. "We need to walk faster."

"They're not afraid of us," I say.

"They should be," says Toby. "Come on. Let's go."

The Mo'Hairs watch us. When we're closer to them, they turn in a group and move slowly away.

At first Toby says we're going to the eastern gatehouse. Then after we walk for a while on the paved road, she says it's farther than she thought. I start to feel dizzy because it's so hot, especially inside the top-to-toe, so Toby says we'll head for the trees at the far side of the meadow because it will be cooler in there. I don't like the trees, it's too dark in there, but I know we can't stay out in the meadow.

It is shadier under the trees, but not cooler. It's dank, and there's no breeze, and the air is thick, as if it has more air stuffed into it than other air does. But at least we're out of the sun, so we take off our top-to-toes and walk along the pathway. There's that rich deep smell of rotting wood, the mushroomy smell I remember from the Gardeners, when we'd go to the Park for Saint Euell's. The vines have been moving in over the gravel, but a lot of the branches are broken back and stepped on, and Toby says that someone else has come this way; not today though, because the leaves have wilted.

There's crows up ahead, making a racket.

We come to a stream, with a little bridge. The water's rippling over stones, and I can see minnows in it. On the far bank there are signs of digging. Toby stands still, turns her head to listen. Then she crosses the bridge and looks at the hole that's been dug. "Gardeners," she says, "or someone smart."

The Gardeners taught that you should never drink right from a stream, especially one near a city: you should make a hole beside it, so the water would be filtered at least a little. Toby has an empty bottle, the one we've been drinking from. She fills it from the water hole so only the top layer of water runs into the bottle: she doesn't want any drowned worms.

Up ahead, off in a small clearing, there's a patch of mushrooms. Toby says they're Sweet Tooth – hydnum repandum – and they used to be a fall variety, when we still had fall. We pick them, and Toby puts them into one of the cloth bags she's brought, and hangs the bag outside her pack so the mushrooms won't get squashed. Then we continue on.

We smell the thing before we see it. "Don't scream," says Toby.

This is what the crows have been cawing about. "Oh no," I whisper.

It's Oates. He's hanging from a tree, twisting slowly. The rope is passed under his arms and knotted at the back. He doesn't have any clothes on except for his socks and shoes. This makes it worse, because he's less like a statue that way. His head is thrown back, too far because his throat has been cut; crows flap around his head, scrabbling for footholds. His blond hair's all matted. There's a gaping wound in his back, like those on the bodies they used to dump in vacant lots after a kidney theft. But these kidneys wouldn't have been stolen for transplants.

"Somebody has a very sharp knife," says Toby.

I'm crying now. "They killed little Oatie," I say. "I feel sick." I crumple down onto the ground. Right now I don't care if I die here: I don't want to be in a world where they'd do this to Oates. It's so unfair. I'm gulping air in huge gasps, crying so hard I can barely see.

Toby takes hold of my shoulders, and pulls me up, and shakes me. "Stop that," she says. "We don't have time for it. Now come on." She pushes me ahead of her along the path.

"Can't we at least cut him down?" I manage to say. "And bury him?"

"We'll do that later," says Toby. "But he's not in his body any more. He's in Spirit now. Shhh, it's okay." She stops and puts her arms around me and rocks me to and fro, then pushes me gently forward again. We need to reach the gatehouse before the afternoon thunderstorm, she says, and the clouds are moving in fast from the south and west.

69

Toby feels bludgeoned – that was brutal, it was horrifying – but she can't show her feelings to Ren. The Gardeners would have encouraged mourning – within limits – as part of the healing process, but there isn't the space for it now. The storm clouds are yellowy green, the lightning's ferocious: she suspects a twister. "Hurry," she says to Ren. "Unless you want to be blown away." For the last fifty metres they hold hands and run, heads down, into the wind.

The gatehouse is retro Tex-Mex, with rounded lines and pink adobe-style solarskin: all it lacks is a chapel tower and some bells. Already there's kudzu clambering up the walls. The wrought-iron gate is standing open. In the ornamental garden with its ring of whitewashed stones – WELCOME TO ANOOYOO spelled out in petunias, but now invaded by purslane and sow thistles – something has been rooting. The pigs, most likely.

"There's some legs," says Ren. "Over there by the gate." Her teeth are chattering: she's still in shock.

"Legs?" says Toby. She feels affronted: how many demi-bodies does she have to encounter in one day? She goes over to the gate to look. The legs aren't human, they're Mo'Hair legs – a complete set of four; just the lower legs, the skinny parts. A little hair still on them, lavender in colour. There's a head as well, though not a Mo'Hair head: it's the head of a liobam, the golden fur scruffy, the eye sockets empty and crusted. The tongue's gone, as well. Liobam tongue, once an expensive gourmet feature at Rarity.

Toby walks back to where Ren stands quivering, hands to her mouth.

"They're Mo'Hair," she says. "I'll make them into soup. With our nice mushrooms."

"Oh, I can't eat anything," says Ren in a doleful voice. "He was just a – he was a boy. I used to carry him around." The tears are rolling down her cheeks. "Why did they do that?"

"You have to eat," says Toby. "It's your duty." Duty to what? she wonders. Your body is a gift from God and you must honour that gift, said Adam One. But right now she feels no such conviction.

The gatehouse door is open. She looks through the window into the reception area – nobody – and propels Ren inside: the storm's coming fast. She flicks a light switch: no power. There's the usual bulletproof check-in window, a blank-faced document scanner, the fingerscan and iris cameras. You'd stand there knowing that you had five wall-mounted sprayguns pointed at your back and controlled from the inside room where the guards used to slouch.

She shines her flashlight through the counter window into the darkness of the inner space. Desks, filing cabinets, trash. Over in the corner, a shape: large enough to be someone. Someone dead, someone asleep, or – worst case – someone who's heard them coming and is pretending to be a garbage bag. Then, once they're at ease, there'd be some sneaking up and baring of canines, some slashing and rending.

The door to the inner room's ajar: she sniffs the air. Mildew, of course. What else? Excrement. Decaying meat. Other noxious undertones. She wishes she had the nose of a dog, to sort one smell from another.

She pulls the door closed. Then she goes outside despite the rain and wind and hauls in the biggest stone from the ornamental flower-garden border. Not enough to stop a strong person, but it might slow down someone weak, or ill. She doesn't wish to be leapt on from behind by a carnivorous mound of tatters.

"Why are you doing that?" says Ren.

"Just in case," says Toby. She doesn't elaborate. Ren is shaky enough as it is: one more horror and she could collapse.

The full force of the storm hits. A thicker darkness howls around them; thunder hollows out the air. In the lightning, Ren's face comes and goes, her eyes closed, her mouth a frightened O. She clutches Toby's arm as if about to topple from a cliff.

After what seems like a long time, the thunder trundles away. Toby goes outside to inspect the Mo'Hair legs. Her skin's prickling: those legs didn't walk there by themselves, and they're still quite fresh. No sign of a fire: whoever killed the animal didn't cook the rest here. She notes the cut marks: Mister Sharp Knife has passed this way. How close might he be?

She looks both ways along the road, strewn now with ripped-off leaves. No movement. The sun's back now. Steam rises. Crows in the distance.

She uses her own knife to scrape much of the hairy skin from one of the Mo'Hair legs. If she had a large cleaver she could hack it into pieces small enough for her cooking pot. Finally she places one end on the top of the step leading up to the gatehouse and the other on the pavement and hits it with a rock. Now there's the problem of a fire. She could spend a long time rummaging among the trees for dry wood and still come up empty-handed. "I need to go through that door," she says to Ren.

"Why?" says Ren weakly. She's huddled in the empty front room.

"There's stuff we can burn," says Toby. "To make a fire. Now listen. There might be someone in there."

"A dead person?"

"I don't know," says Toby.

"I don't want any more dead people," says Ren fretfully. There may not be much choice about that, thinks Toby.

"Here's the rifle," she says. "This is the trigger. I want you to stand right here. If anyone but me comes out that door, shoot. Don't hit me by mistake. Okay?" If she herself gets whacked in there, at least Ren will have a weapon.

"Okay," says Ren. She takes the rifle awkwardly. "But I don't like it."

This is crazy, Toby thinks. She's jumpy enough to shoot me in the back if I sneeze. But if I don't check that room out, no sleep tonight and maybe a slit throat in the morning. And no fire.

She goes in with her flashlight and her mop handle. Papers litter the floor, smashed lamps. There's broken glass, crunching underfoot. The smell is stronger now. Flies buzzing. The hairs on her arms lift, the blood rushes in her head.

The bundle on the floor is definitely human, covered with some sort of gruesome blanket. Now she can see the dome of a bald head, some wisps of hair. She pokes at the blanket with the mop handle, keeping the beam of light on the bundle. A moan. She pokes again, harder: there's a feeble twitching of cloth. Now there are the slits of eyes, and a mouth, lips crusted and blistered.

"Fuckin' hell," says the mouth. "Who in fuck are you?"

"Are you sick?" says Toby.

"Asshole shot me," says the man. His eyes are blinking in the light. "Turn that fuckin' thing off." No sign of blood leaking out of his nose or mouth or eyes: with any luck, he doesn't have the plague.

"Shot you where?" says Toby. The bullet must have been hers, from that time in the meadow. A hand scrabbles forth: red and blue veins. Although he's shrivelled and filthy, his eyes sunken with fever, this is Blanco, no doubt of it. She ought to know, she's had the close-up view.

"Leg," he says. "Went bad on me. Fuckers dumped me here."

"Two of them?" says Toby. "Did they have a woman with them?" She makes her voice level.

"Gimme some water," says Blanco. There's an empty bottle in the corner, near his head. Two bottles, three. Gnawed ribs: the lavender Mo'Hair? "Who else is out there?" he rasps. His breath's coming hard. "More bitches. I heard more."

"Let me see your leg," says Toby. "I may be able to help." He won't be the first person ever to have shammed injury.

"I'm fuckin' dying," says Blanco. "Turn off that light!" Toby sees various courses of action rippling across his forehead in waves of little frowns. Does he know who she is? Will he try to jump her?

"Take the blanket off," says Toby, "and I'll get you some water."

"Take it off yourself," croaks Blanco.

"No," says Toby. "If you don't want help I'll just lock you in."

"Lock's broken," he says. "Asshole skinny bitch! Gimme some water!"

Toby pinpoints the other smell: whatever else is wrong with him, he's decaying. "I've got a Zizzy Froot," she says. "You'll like that better." She backs out through the door and closes it behind her, but not before Ren's had a look.

"It's him," she whispers. "The third one, the worst one!"

"Take a deep breath," says Toby. "You're perfectly safe. You've got the rifle, he doesn't. Just keep it pointed at that door."

She digs into her packsack, finds the remaining Zizzy Froot, drinks a quarter of the warm, sugary, fizzy liquid: *Waste not.* Then she fills the bottle up with Poppy and adds a generous dollop of powdered amanitas for good measure. The white Death Angel, granter of dark wishes. If there's two bad choices take the lesser evil, Zeb would say.

She pushes the door open with her mop handle and shines the flashlight in. Sure enough Blanco is shoving himself across the floor, grinning with the effort. In one hand is his knife: most likely he was hoping to get near enough so he could grab her by the ankles when she went in. Take her down with him, or use her as a bargaining chip to get hold of Ren.

Mad dogs bite. What else is there to know?

"Here you are," she says. She rolls the bottle towards him. His knife falls with a clink as he grabs for the bottle, unscrews it with shaking hands, guzzles. Toby waits to make sure it all goes down. "Now you'll feel better," she says gently. She closes the door.

"He'll get out!" says Ren. She's ashen.

"If he gets out, we'll shoot him," says Toby. "I've given him some painkillers to calm him down." Silently she says the words of apology and release, the same as she would for a beetle.

She waits until the Poppy has taken hold, then re-enters the room. Blanco's snoring heavily: if the Poppy doesn't finish him, the Death

Angels will. She lifts the blanket: his left thigh is a mess – decaying cloth and decaying flesh all simmering together. It takes a lot of self-restraint for her not to throw up.

Then she sorts through the room for flammables, gathering what she can – paper, some remnants of a smashed chair, a stack of CDs. There's a second floor, but Blanco's blocking the door to what must be the stairway and she's not ready to get that close to him yet. She searches under the trees for dead branches: with the barbecue lighter and the paper and the CDs, they catch eventually. She makes bone soup with the Mo'Hair leg, adding the mushrooms and some purslane from the flower bed; they eat it sitting in the smoke of the fire, because of the mosquitoes.

They sleep on the flat roof, using a tree to climb up. Toby drags the packsacks up too, and the other three Mo'Hair legs, so nothing can steal them during the night. The rooftop's pebbly, and wet as well: they lie on the two sheets of plastic. The stars are brighter than bright; the moon's invisible. Just before they go to sleep, Ren whispers, "What if he wakes up?"

"He'll never wake up," says Toby.

"Oh," says Ren in a tiny voice. Is that admiration of Toby, or simply awe in the face of death? He wouldn't have lived, Toby tells herself, not with a leg as bad as that. Attempting to treat it would have been a waste of maggots. Still, she's just committed a murder. Or an act of mercy: at least he didn't die thirsty.

Don't kid yourself, babe, says the voice of Zeb in her head. You had vengeance in mind.

"May his Spirit go in peace," she says out loud. Such as it is, the fuck-pig.

70

TOBY. SAINT RACHEL AND ALL BIRDS

YEAR TWENTY-FIVE

Toby wakes just before dawn. In the distance there's a liobam, its odd plaintive roar. Dogs barking. She moves her arms, then her legs: she's stiff as a slab of cement. The dampness of the mist goes right into the marrow.

Here comes the sun, a hot rose lifting out of peach-coloured clouds. The leaves on the overhanging trees are covered with tiny droplets that shine in the strengthening pink light. Everything looks so fresh, as if newly created: the stones on the rooftop, the trees, the spiderwebbing slung from branch to branch. Sleeping Ren seems luminous, as if silvered all over. With the pink top-to-toe tucked around her oval face and the mist beading her long eyelashes, she's frail and otherworldly, as if made of snow.

The light hits Ren directly, and her eyes open. "Oh shit, oh shit," she says. "I'm late! What time is it?"

"You're not late for anything," says Toby, and for some reason both of them laugh.

Toby scouts with the binoculars. To the east, where they'll be going, there's no movement, but to the west there's a group of pigs, the biggest gathering of them she's seen to date – six adults, two young. They're strung out along the roadside like round flesh pearls on a necklace; they have their snouts down, snuffling along as if they're tracking.

Tracking us, thinks Toby. Maybe they're the same pigs: the grudge-bearing pigs, the funeral-holding pigs. She stands up, waves the rifle in the air, shouts at them: "Go away! Piss off!" At first they just stare, but when she brings the rifle down and aims it at them they lollop off into the trees.

"It's almost like they know what a rifle is," says Ren. She's a lot steadier this morning. Stronger.

"Oh, they know," says Toby.

They clamber down the tree, and Toby lights the Kelly kettle. Although there's no sign of anyone around, she doesn't want to risk making a bigger fire. She's worried about the smoke – will anyone smell it? Zeb's rule was: Animals shun fire, humans are drawn to it.

Once the water has boiled she makes tea. Then she parboils more of the purslane. That will warm them up enough for their early walking. Later they can have more Mo'Hair soup, from the three legs remaining.

Before they leave, Toby checks the gatehouse room. Blanco's cold; he smells even worse, if that's possible. She rolls him onto the blanket and drags him out to the rooted-up earth of the flower bed. Then she finds his knife on the floor where he dropped it. It's sharp as a razor; with it she slits his filthy shirt up the front. Hairy fishbelly. If she was being thorough, she'd open him up – the vultures would thank her – but she remembers the sickening reek of innards from the dead boar. The pigs will take care of it. Maybe they'll view Blanco as an atonement offering to them and forgive her for shooting their fellow pig. She leaves the knife among the flowers. Good tool, but bad karma.

She heaves the wrought-iron gate shut behind them; the electronic lock's non-functional, so she uses some of her rope to tie it shut. If the pigs decide to follow, the gate won't deter them for long – they can dig under – but it may give them pause.

Now she and Ren are outside the AnooYoo grounds, walking along the weed-bordered road that leads through the Heritage Park. They come to some picnic-table clearings; the kudzu is crawling over the trash barrels and barbecues, the tables and benches. In the sunlight, which is hotter by the minute, butterflies waft and spiral.

Toby takes her bearings: downhill, to the east, must be the shore and then the sea. To the southwest, the Arboretum, with the creek where the Gardener children used to launch their miniature Arks. The road leading to the SolarSpace entrance ought to join in somewhere around here. Nearby is where they'd buried Pilar: sure enough, there's her Elderberry, quite tall now, and in flower. Bees buzz around it.

Dear Pilar, thinks Toby. If you were here today you'd have something wise to tell us. What would it be?

Up ahead they hear bleating, and five – no, nine – no, fourteen Mo'Hairs scramble up the bank and out onto the road. Silver, blue, purple, black, a red one with its hair in many braids – and now there's a man. A man in a white bedsheet, belted around the waist. It's a biblical getup: he even has a long staff, for sheep-prodding no doubt. When he sees them he stops and turns, watching them quietly. He's got sunglasses on; he's also got a spraygun. He holds it casually by his side, but lets it be clearly seen. The sun's behind him.

Toby stands still, her scalp and arms tingling. Is this one of the Painballers? He'd turn her into a sieve before she could even get the rifle aimed: the sun's in his favour.

"It's Croze!" says Ren. She runs towards him with her arms outstretched, and Toby certainly hopes she's right. But she must be, because the man lets her throw her arms around him. He drops his spraygun and his staff on the ground and clutches Ren tightly, while the Mo'Hairs amble about munching flowers.

71

"Croze!" I say. "I can't believe it! I thought you were dead!" I'm talking into his bedsheet because we're holding on so tight I'm smushed up against him. He doesn't say anything – maybe he's crying – so I say, "I bet you thought I was dead too," and I feel him nod.

I let go and we look at each other. He tries a grin. "Where'd you get the bedsheet?" I say.

"There's a lot of beds around," he says. "These things are better than pants, you don't get so hot. Did you see Oates?" He sounds worried.

I don't know what to say. I don't want to spoil this time by telling him about something so unhappy. Poor Oates, hanging in a tree with his throat cut and his kidneys missing. But then I look at his face and realize I've misunderstood: it's me he's worried about, because he already knows about Oates. He and Shackie were up ahead of us on the path. They'd have heard me shout, they'd have hidden. Then they would have heard the screaming, all sorts of screaming. Then, later – because of course they would have come back to check – they would have heard the crows.

If I say no, he'll most likely pretend that Oates is still alive, so as not to upset me. "Yes," I say. "We did see him. I'm sorry."

He looks at the ground. I think of how I can change the subject. The Mo'Hairs have been nibbling all around us – they want to stay close to Croze – so I say, "Are those your sheep?"

"We've started herding them," he says. "We've got them kind of tamed. But they keep getting out." Who is *we*, I'd like to ask; but Toby comes up, so I say, "This is Toby, remember?" and Croze says, "No shit! From the Gardeners?"

Toby gives him one of her dry little nods and says, "Crozier. You've certainly grown," as if it's a school reunion. It's hard to throw her off balance. She sticks out her hand and Croze shakes it. It's so strange – Croze in a bedsheet, looking like Jesus though his beard isn't exactly flowing, and Toby and me in our pink outfits with the winking eyes and lipstick mouths; and Toby with three purple Mo'Hair legs sticking up out of her packsack.

"Where's Amanda?" he says.

"She's not dead," I say too quickly. "I just know she isn't." He and Toby trade a look over my head, as if they don't want to tell me my pet bunny got run over. "What about Shackleton?" I say, and Croze says, "He's okay. Let's go back to the place."

"What place?" says Toby, and he says, "The cobb house. Where we used to have the Tree of Life Exchange. Remember?" he says to me. "It's not too far."

The sheep are heading that way anyway. They seem to know where they're going. We follow along behind them.

The sun's so hot by now that it's boiling inside our top-to-toes. Croze has part of his bedsheet draped over his head; he looks a lot cooler than me.

It's noon when we reach the old Tree of Life parkette. The plastic swings are gone, but the cobb house is the same – even the spraypainted pleeb tags are there – except they've been building onto it. There's a fence made of poles and planks and wire and a lot of duct tape. Croze opens the gate, and the sheep go in and file towards a pen in the yard.

"I got the sheep," Croze calls, and a man with a spraygun comes out through the house door, and then two more men. Then four women – two young, one a bit older, and an older one, maybe as old as Toby. Their clothes aren't Gardener clothes, but they aren't new and they aren't pretty. Two of the men are wearing bedsheets, the third has cut-offs and a shirt. The women have long cover-ups, like top-to-toes.

They stare at us. Not friendly: anxious. Croze says our names. "You sure they're not infected?" says the first man, the one with the spraygun.

"No way," says Croze. "They were isolated the whole time." He looks at us for confirmation, and Toby nods. "Friends of Zeb," Croze adds. "Toby and Ren." Then he tells us, "This is MaddAddam."

"What's left of us," says the shortest man. He says their names: his is Beluga, and the other three are Ivory Bill, Manatee, and Zunzuncito. The women are Lotis Blue, Swift Fox, White Sedge, and Tamaraw. We don't shake hands: they're still nervous about us and our germs.

"MaddAddam," says Toby. "Good to meet you. I followed some of your work online."

"How'd you get in?" Ivory Bill says to Toby. "To the playroom?" He's eyeing her antique rifle as if it's made of gold.

"I was Inaccessible Rail," says Toby.

They look at one another. "You," says Lotis Blue. "You were Inaccessible! The secret lady!" She laughs. "Zeb would never tell us who you were. We thought you were some hot bimbo he had." Toby gives her a thin little smile.

"He said you were solid, though," says Tamaraw. "He insisted on that."

"Zeb?" says Toby, as if she's talking to herself. I know she wants to ask if he's still alive, but she's afraid to.

"MaddAddam was a great caper," says Beluga. "Until we got snatched."

"So-called drafted by fucking ReJoov," says White Sedge, the youngest woman. "Crake, that little bastard." She's brown-skinned but she has kind of an English accent, so it comes out *bahstahd*. They're a lot friendlier now that Toby's told them she was really somebody else.

I'm confused. I look up at Croze, and he says, "It was that thing we were doing, the bioresistance thing. Why they put us in Painball. These are the scientists they scooped. Remember I told you? At Scales?"

"Oh," I say. But I'm still not clear. Why did ReJoov scoop them? Was it a brain kidnapping, like what happened to my father?

"We had visitors," Ivory Bill says to Croze. "After you went for the sheep. Two guys, with a woman and a spraygun and a dead rakunk."

"Really," says Croze. "That's major."

"Said they were Painball, like we should respect that," says Beluga. "They wanted to trade the woman for spraygun cells and Mo'Hair meat – the woman and the rakunk."

"I bet it was them got our purple Mo'Hair," says Croze. "Toby found the legs."

"Rakunk! Why would we trade for that?" says White Sedge indignantly. "We're not stahving!"

"We should've shot them," says Manatee. "But they were holding the woman in front."

"What was she wearing?" I say, but they ignore me.

"We said no trade," says Ivory Bill. "Tough for the girl. But they're desperate for cells, which means they're running out. So we'll deal with them later."

"It's Amanda," I say. They could have saved her. Though I don't blame them for not trading: you can't give spraycells to guys who'll use them to kill you. "What about Amanda?" I say. "Shouldn't we go and get her?"

"Yeah – we need to get everyone together now that the Flood's over," says Croze. "Like we've said." He's backing me up.

"Then we can, you know, rebuild the human race," I say. I know it sounds stupid, but it's the only thing I can think of. "Amanda could really help us – she's so good at everything." But they just smile at me sadly as if they know it's hopeless.

Croze takes my hand and walks me away from them. "You mean that?" he says. "About the human race?" He smiles. "You'll have to have babies."

"Maybe not just yet," I say.

"Come on," he says. "I'll show you the garden."

They have a cookhouse, and some violet porta-biolets over in one corner, and some solar they're fixing up. There's no shortage of parts for just about everything back in the pleebs, though you have to look out for falling buildings.

Their vegetable garden is in behind: they don't have a lot of stuff planted yet. "We get pig attacks," he says. "They dig under the fence. We shot one of them, so maybe the others got the point. Zeb says they're superpigs, because they're spliced with human brain tissue."

"Zeb?" I say. "Is Zeb alive?" I feel dizzy all of a sudden. All of these dead people, coming alive again – it's overwhelming.

"Sure," says Croze. "Are you all right?" He puts his arm around me, to keep me from falling down.

72

TOBY. SAINT RACHEL AND ALL BIRDS

YEAR TWENTY-FIVE

Ren and Crozier have wandered off behind the cobb house. No harm, thinks Toby. Young love, no doubt. She's telling Ivory Bill about the third man – the dead one. Blanco. He listens carefully. "Plague?" he asks. An infected bullet wound, she says. She doesn't add the Poppy and the Death Angels.

While they're talking, another woman comes around from behind the house. "Hey, Toby," she says. It's Rebecca. Older, less plump, but still Rebecca. Solid. She takes hold of Toby's shoulders. "You're too thin, sweetheart," she says. "Never mind. We've got bacon. Fatten you up for sure."

Bacon is not a concept that Toby can grasp right now. "Rebecca," she says. She wants to add, "Why are you alive?" but this is – increasingly – a meaningless question. Why are any of them alive? So she merely says, "Wonderful."

"Zeb said you'd make it. He always said that. Hey. Gimme a smile!"

Toby doesn't like the past tense. It has a deathbed smell. "When did he say it?" she asks.

"Heck, he says it most days. Now come on in the kitchen, eat something. Tell me where you've been."

Zeb's alive then, thinks Toby. Now that it's true she feels she's always known it. She also doubts it – it won't really be true until she sees him. Touches him.

They have coffee – dandelion roots, roasted, Rebecca says proudly – and some baked burdock root with herbs, and a slice of – could

392 | MARGARET ATWOOD

it be cold pork? "Those pigs are a nuisance," says Rebecca. "Too smart by half." She eyes Toby challengingly. "Needs must when the devil drives," she says. "Anyways, at least we know what's in it – not like at SecretBurgers."

"It's delicious," Toby says truthfully.

After their snack, Toby hands over the three remaining Mo'Hair legs, not that fresh but Rebecca says they'll be fine for stock. Then they plunge right into history. Toby runs through her time in the AnooYoo Spa, and tells about the arrival of Ren; Rebecca describes her fake identity selling life insurance in gated communities out west while planting MaddAddam's inventive bioforms, and how she got the last bullet train east – a risk, lot of folks coughing but she wore a nose cone and gloves – and then holed up in the Wellness Clinic, along with Zeb and Katuro. "In our old meeting room, remember?" she says. "Our Ararat supplies were still there."

"And Katuro?" says Toby.

"Doing fine. Had a germ of some kind, but not the bad one; he's over it now. He's off with Zeb and Shackleton, and Black Rhino. They're looking for Adam One and the rest of them. Zeb says if anyone could get through, they could."

"Really? There's a chance?" says Toby. *Did he look for me?* she wants to ask. Probably not. He'd have thought she'd do fine on her own. And she had, hadn't she?

"We've been listening on the windup shortwave, 24/7, and sending too. Couple of days ago we finally got an answer," says Rebecca.

"It was him?" Toby's prepared to believe anything now. "Adam One?"

"We just heard the one voice. All it said was, 'I'm here, I'm here.'"

"Let's hope," says Toby. And she does hope; or she tries to.

There's the barking of dogs outside, and a confusion of shouting. "Shit. Dog attack," says Rebecca. "Bring that gun."

The MaddAddams with sprayguns are already at the fence. Big dogs and small ones, maybe fifteen, bounding towards them wagging their tails. The spraygunners begin shooting. Before Toby can fire, seven of the dogs are dead and the rest have run away.

"Watson-Crick splices," says Ivory Bill. "They're not really dogs, they only look like it. They'll tear out your throat. Used them in prison moats and such – you couldn't hack them, not like an alarm system code – but they got loose during the Flood."

"Are they breeding?" says Toby. Will they have to fight off wave after wave of these non-dogs, or are they few in number?

"Lord knows," says Ivory Bill.

Lotis Blue and White Sedge go out to make sure the dogs are dead. Then Tamaraw and Swift Fox and Rebecca and Toby join them, and they skin and butcher, with the spraygunners standing guard in case the other dogs come back. Toby's hands remember how to do this from long ago. The smell is the same too. A childhood smell.

The dog skins are laid aside, the meat's cut up and put into a pot. Toby feels a little sick. But she also feels hungry.

73

I ask Croze if I should be helping to skin the dogs, but Croze says there's enough people doing it and I look tired, so why don't I lie down on his bed, inside the cobb house? The room is cool and smells the cobb-house way I remember, so I feel safe. Croze's bed is just a platform, but it has a silver Mo'Hair fleece on it with a sheet, and Croze says, Sleep tight and then goes away, and I take off my AnooYoo top and pants because it's getting too hot, and the Mo'Hair is soft and silky, and I go to sleep.

When the afternoon thunderstorm wakes me up, Croze is curled around behind me, and I can tell he's worried and sad; so I turn around and then we're hugging each other, and he wants to have sex. But all of a sudden I don't want to have sex without loving the person, and I haven't really loved anybody in that way since Jimmy; certainly not at Scales, where it was just acting, with other people's kinky scripts.

Also there's a dark place in me, like ink spilled into my brain – I can't think about sex, in that place. It has brambles in it, and something about Amanda, and I don't want to be there. So I say, "Not yet." And even though Croze used to be kind of crude he seems to understand, so we just hold on to each other and talk.

He's full of plans. They'll build this, they'll build that; they'll get rid of the pigs, or else tame them. After the two Painballers are dead – he personally will take care of that – he'll take me, and Amanda and Shackie too, and we'll all go down to the beach and do some fishing. As for the MaddAddam group – Bill and Sedge and Tamaraw and Rhino, all them – they're really smart, so they'll have the communications going in no time.

"Who are we going to communicate with?" I ask, and Croze says there must be others out there. Then he tells me about the MaddAddams – how they were working with Zeb, but then the CorpSeCorps tracked them down through a MaddAddam codenamed Crake, and they ended up as brain slaves in a place called the Paradice Project dome. It was a choice between that and being spraygunned, so they took the jobs. Then when the Flood came and the guards vanished, they deactivated the security and walked out, but that wasn't too hard for them because they're all brainiacs.

He's told me some of this before, but he hasn't said *Paradice Project* or *Crake*. "Just a minute," I say. "That's what they were working on inside the dome? Immortality?"

Yes, Croze says: they were all helping Crake with his big experiment: some kind of perfectly beautiful human gene splice that could live forever. They were the ones who'd done the heavy lifting on the BlyssPluss pill too, but they weren't allowed to take it themselves. Not that they were tempted: it gave you the best sex ever, but it had serious side effects, such as death.

"That's how the pandemic plague got started," Croze says. "They said Crake ordered them to put it in the supersex pill." I felt lucky all over again that I'd been in the Sticky Zone because I might've gulped down the BlyssPluss pill secretly even though Mordis said no drugs for Scalies. It sounded so great, like a whole other reality.

"Who'd do a thing like that?" I say. "A poison sex pill?" It was Glenn, it must have been. That's the sort of stuff he was telling the ReJoov Mr. Bigs, at Scales. He didn't tell about the poison part, of course. I remembered those nicknames, Oryx and Crake. I'd thought it was just sex talk, with Glenn and his main plank: a lot of people used animal names at such times. Panther and Tiger and Wolverine, Pussycat and Doggie-wog. So, not sex talk: codenames. Or maybe both.

For one split second I think about saying all this to Croze – how I know quite a lot about this Crake from a former life. But then I'd have to tell about what I used to do at Scales – not just the trapeze dancing or even Glenn making us purr and sing like birds, but the other things, the feather-ceiling room things. Croze wouldn't want to hear about that: guys hate to picture other guys doing sex things with you that they want to do themselves.

So instead I ask, "What about the splice people? The perfect ones? Did they actually make them?" Glenn always wanted everything to be more perfect.

"Yeah, they made them," says Croze, as if it's an everyday thing, making people.

"I guess those people died along with everyone else," I say.

"Nope," says Croze. "They're living down by the shore. They don't need clothes, they eat leaves, they purr like cats. Not my idea of perfect." He laughs. "Perfect is more like you!"

I let that go by. "You're making this up," I say.

"No, I swear," says Croze. "They get these huge – their dicks turn blue. Then they have group sex with these blue-assed women. It's wicked!"

"It's a joke, right?" I say.

"Seen them myself," says Croze. "We aren't supposed to go near them in case we mess them up. But Zeb says we can look at them from a distance, like the zoo. He says they're not dangerous – it's us that's dangerous to them."

"When can I see them?"

"Once we take care of those Painballers," says Croze. "I'd have to go with you, though. There's another guy down there – sleeps in a tree, talks to himself, crazy as a bag of snakes, no offence to snakes. We leave him alone – figure he might be infected. I wouldn't want him bothering you."

"Thanks," I say. "This Crake, in the Paradice Project dome. What did he look like?"

"Never saw him," says Croze. "Nobody said."

"Did he have a friend?" I asked. "Inside the dome thing?" When Glenn brought Jimmy to Scales that time, they were definitely into something together.

"Rhino says he wasn't much on friends. But he did have some pal of his in there, plus his girlfriend – the two of them were supposed to be planning the marketing. Rhino says the guy was a waste of time. Told a lot of stupid jokes, drank too much."

That would be Jimmy all right, I thought. "Did he make it out?" I say. "Out of the dome? With the blue people?"

"How would I know? Anyway, who gives a shit?" says Croze.

I do. I don't want Jimmy to be dead. "That's kind of harsh," I say.

"Hey, be cool," says Croze. He puts his arm around me, lets his hand fall onto my breast, as if by accident. I take it off. "Okay," he says in a disappointed voice. He kisses my ear.

The next thing I know Croze is waking me up. "They're back," he says. He hurries out and I put my clothes on, and when I go outside Zeb is there in the yard, and Toby's got her arms around him. Katuro's there; and the man they call Black Rhino, who's even kind of black. Shackie's there too, grinning over at me. He hasn't heard yet about the two Painballers and Amanda. Croze will have to tell him. If I do he'll ask me questions, and I only have bad answers.

I go slowly over to Zeb – I'm feeling shy – and Toby lets go of him. She's smiling – not a thin smile, a real one – and I think, *She can still be pretty sometimes.* "Little Ren. You grew up," Zeb says to me. He's greyer than the last time I saw him. He smiles, and squeezes my shoulder briefly. I remember him singing in our shower, back at the Gardeners; I remember the times he was nice to me. I'd like him to be proud of me for making it through, even though that part was mostly luck. I'd like him to be more surprised and happy that I'm alive. But he must have a lot on his mind.

Zeb and Shackie and Black Rhino have sprayguns and packsacks, and now they start opening up the packsacks and taking things out. Tins of soydines, a couple of bottles – looks like booze – a handful of Joltbars. Three cellpacks, for the sprayguns.

"From Compounds," Katuro says. "Gates open on a lot of them. Looters have been through."

"CryoJeenyus was locked up tight," says Zeb. "Guess they thought they could tough it out inside."

"Them and all the frozen heads they had in there," says Shackie.

"I doubt anyone got out," says Black Rhino. I'm sorry to hear that, because Lucerne must have been inside that Compound, and despite how she acted later, she was my mother once, and I used to love her. I look over at Zeb, because maybe he did too.

"You find Adam One?" says Ivory Bill.

Zeb shakes his head. "We looked in the Buenavista," Zeb says. "They must've been there for some time – them, or someone. There were all the signs. Then we tried a few more Ararats, but nothing. They must have moved on."

"Did you tell him someone was living in the Wellness Clinic?" I say to Croze. "In that little room in behind the vinegar barrels? With the laptop?"

"Yeah, I did," says Croze. "It was him. And Rebecca and Katuro."

"We did see that crazy guy, limping along and talking to himself," says Shackie. "The one who sleeps in a tree, down by the shore. He didn't see us, though."

"You didn't shoot him?" says Ivory Bill. "In case he's catching?"

"Why waste the ammo?" says Black Rhino. "He won't last long."

When the sun's low we make a fire outside in the yard and have nettle soup with chunks of meat in it – I'm not sure what kind – and burdock, and some Mo'Hair-milk cheese. I'm expecting them to begin the meal with "Dear Friends, we are the only people left on Earth, let us give thanks" or some Gardener thing like that, but they don't; we just have the dinner.

After we've finished, they talk about what to do next. Zeb says they have to find Adam One and the Gardeners before anything or anyone else gets to them. He'll go to the Sinkhole tomorrow to check out the Edencliff Rooftop and some of the Truffle safe houses, and other places they might've gone. Shackie says he'll go with him, and Black Rhino and Katuro say the same. The others need to stay and defend the cobb house against the dogs and pigs, and also the two Painballers in case they come back.

Then Ivory Bill tells Zeb about Toby and how Blanco's dead now, and Zeb looks at Toby and says, "Well done, babe." It's kind of shocking to hear Toby called a babe: sort of like calling God a studmuffin.

I work up my courage and say we need to find Amanda and get her away from the Painballers. Shackie says he'll vote for that, and I think he means it. Zeb says he's very sorry, but we have to understand that it's an either/or choice. Amanda's just one person and Adam One and the Gardeners are many; and if it was Amanda, she'd decide the same thing. Then I say, "Okay, I'll go alone then," and Zeb says, "Don't be silly," as if I'm still eleven.

Then Croze says he'll go with me, and I squeeze his hand for thank you. But Zeb says he's needed at the cobb house, they can't do without him. If I wait until he and Shackie and Rhino and Katuro get back, he says, they'll send three guys with me, with sprayguns, which will give us a much better chance.

But I say there isn't enough time, because if those Painballers want to trade Amanda, it means they're tired of her and they could kill her at any minute. I know how it works, I say. It's like Scales, with the temporaries – she's a disposable – so I really have to find her right now, and I know it's dangerous, but I don't care. Then I start crying.

Nobody says anything. Then Toby says she'll go with me. She'll take her own rifle – she's not a bad shot, she says. Maybe the Painballers have used up their last spraygun cell, which would lengthen the odds.

Zeb says, "That's not such a good idea." Toby pauses, then says it's the best idea she can come up with because she can't let me wander off into the woods by myself: it would be like murder. And Zeb nods and says, "Be very careful." So it's settled.

The MaddAddams hang up some duct-tape hammocks in the main room for Toby and me. Toby's still talking with Zeb and the rest of them, so I go to bed first. With a Mo'Hair rug the hammock's quite comfortable; and though I'm worrying a lot about how to find Amanda and what will happen then, I finally manage to sleep.

When we get up the next morning, Zeb and Shackie and Katuro and Black Rhino have already left, but Rebecca tells Toby that Zeb's drawn a map for her in the sand of the old kids' sandbox, with the cobb house and the shore marked on it, so she'll know the directions. Toby studies it for a long time with an odd expression on her face – a sad kind of smile. But maybe she's just memorizing it. Then she wipes it away.

After breakfast Rebecca gives us some dried meat, and Ivory Bill gets two lighter hammocks for us because it's not safe to sleep on the ground, and we refill our water bottles from the well they've dug. Toby leaves a bunch of stuff behind – her bottles of Poppy, her mushrooms, her maggot container, all the medical stuff – but she takes her cooking pot and her knife and the matches and some rope, because we don't know how long we'll be gone. Rebecca hugs her and says, "Watch your back, sweetheart," and then we set out.

We walk and walk; at noon we stop to eat. Toby's listening all the time: too many birdcalls of the wrong kind, such as crows – or else no bird calls at all – means *Look out*, she says. But all we're hearing is background cheeping and chirping. "Bird wallpaper," says Toby.

We keep walking, and eat again, and walk some more. There are so many leaves; they steal the air. Also they make me nervous because of the last time we walked in a forest and found Oates hanging.

When it gets dark, we choose some big-enough trees and string up the hammocks and climb in. But it's hard for me to sleep. Then I hear singing. It's beautiful, but it's not like normal singing – it's clear, like glass, but with layers. It's like bells.

The singing fades away, and I think maybe I was imagining things. And then I think, it must have been the blue people: that must be how they sing. I picture Amanda among them: they're feeding her, taking care of her, purring to heal her and comfort her.

It's make-believe. Wishful thinking, I know I shouldn't do it: I should face reality. But reality has too much darkness in it. Too many crows.

The Adams and the Eves used to say, *We are what we eat*, but I prefer to say, *We are what we wish*. Because if you can't wish, why bother?

SAINT TERRY
AND ALL WAYFARERS

SAINT TERRY AND ALL WAYFARERS

YEAR TWENTY-FIVE.

OF THE WANDERING STATE.
SPOKEN BY ADAM ONE.

Dear Friends, dear Fellow Creatures, Fellow Sojourners on this dangerous road that is now our pathway through life:

How long it has been since our last Saint Terry's Day on our
beloved Edencliff Rooftop Garden! We did not realize then how much
better those times were, compared with the dark days we are living
through now. Then, we enjoyed the prospect from our peaceful Garden,
and though that prospect was one of slums and crime, yet we viewed it
from a space of restoration and renewal, flourishing with innocent Plants
and industrious Bees. We raised our voices in song, sure that we would
prevail, for our aims were worthy and our methods without malice. So
we believed, in our innocence. Many woeful things have happened since,
but the Spirit that moved us then is present still.

Saint Terry's Day is dedicated to all Wayfarers – prime among them Saint
Terry Fox, who ran so far with one mortal and one metallic leg; who set
a shining example of courage in the face of overwhelming odds; who
showed what the human body can do in the way of locomotion without
fossil fuels; who raced against Mortality, and in the end outran his own
Death, and lives on in Memory.

On this day we remember, too, Saint Sojourner Truth, guide of
escaping slaves two centuries ago, who walked so many miles with only
the stars to guide her; and Saints Shackleton and Crozier, of Antarctic
and Arctic fame; and Saint Laurence "Titus" Oates of the Scott
Expedition, who hiked where no man had ever hiked before, and who
sacrificed himself during a blizzard for the welfare of his companions. Let

his immortal last words be an inspiration to us on our journey: "I am just going outside and may be some time."

The Saints of this day are all Wayfarers. They knew so well that it is better to journey than to arrive, as long as we journey in firm faith and for selfless ends. Let us hold that thought in our hearts, my Friends and fellow Voyagers.

It is fitting that we remember those whom we have lost so far on our journey. Darren and Quill have succumbed to an illness, the early symptoms of which are cause for grave apprehension. At their own request we have left them behind us. We thank them for showing such praiseworthy concern for those of us who remain healthy.

Philo has entered a Fallow state, and is at peace on top of a parking garage, a location that reminds him perhaps of our own dear Rooftop.

We should not have allowed Melissa to lag so far behind us. Via the conduit of a wild dog pack, she has now made the ultimate Gift to her fellow Creatures, and has become part of God's great dance of proteins.

Put Light around her in your hearts.

Let us sing.

THE LONGEST MILE

The last mile is the longest mile –
'Tis then we weaken;
We lose the strength to run the race,
We doubt Hope's beacon.

Shall we turn back from this dark Road,
Footsore and weary,
When deep Despair has drained our Faith,
And all seems dreary?

Shall we give up the narrow path,
The plodding byway –
Choose swift transport and false delight:
Destruction's highway?

Shall Enemies erase our Life,
Our Message bury?
And shall they quench in war and strife
The Torch we carry?

Take heart, oh dusty Travellers:
Though you may falter,
Though you be felled along the way,
You'll reach the Altar.

Race on, race on, though eyes grow dim,
And faint the Chorus;
God gives us Nature's green applause –
Such will restore us.

For in the effort is the Goal,
'Tis thus we're treasured:

He knows us by our Pilgrim Soul –
'Tis thus we're measured.

From *The God's Gardeners Oral Hymnbook*

74

When I wake up, Toby's already sitting in her hammock doing some arm stretches. She smiles at me: she's smiling more lately. Maybe she does it now to encourage me. "What day is today?" she says.

I think for a moment. "Saint Terry, Saint Sojourner," I say. "All Wayfarers."

Toby nods. "We should do a short Meditation," she says. "The path our feet will travel on today will be a dangerous one; we'll need inner peace."

When any of the Adams or the Eves tells you to do a Meditation, you don't say no. Toby climbs out of her hammock, and I stand watch in case of surprises while she goes into the Lotus: she's quite flexible for someone her age. But when it's my turn, although I bend myself into the shape just like rubber, I can't do the Meditation properly. I can't manage the first three parts: the Apology, the Gratitude, the Forgiveness – and especially not the Forgiveness, because I don't know who I need to forgive. Adam One would say I'm too fearful and angry.

So I think about Amanda, and everything she did for me, and how I never did anything for her. Instead I allowed myself to feel jealous of her about Jimmy, though Jimmy was in no way her fault. Which wasn't fair. I have to find her, and get her away from whatever may be happening to her. Though maybe she's already hanging in a tree with parts of her cut out, like Oates.

But I don't want to picture that, so instead I imagine myself walking towards her because that's what I'll have to do.

It is not only the body that travels, Adam One used to say, it is also the Soul. And the end of one journey is the beginning of another.

"I'm ready now," I say to Toby.

We eat some of the dried Mo'Hair meat and drink some water, and cache the hammocks under a bush so we won't have to carry them. We should take the packsacks, though, says Toby, with the food and stuff. Then we look around to make sure we haven't left any obvious traces of ourselves. Toby checks the rifle. "I'll only need two bullets," she says.

"If you don't miss," I say. One for each Painballer: I picture the bullets moving through the air, straight into – what? An eye? A heart? It makes me flinch.

"I can't afford to miss," she says. "They've got a spraygun."

Then we rejoin the pathway and continue on in the direction of the sea, towards where I heard the voices coming from in the night.

After a while we hear those voices, but they aren't singing, just talking. There's the smell of smoke – a wood fire – and children laughing. It's Glenn's made-on-purpose people. It has to be.

"Walk slowly," she says in a low voice. "The same rules as for animals. Stay very calm. If we have to leave, back away. Don't turn and run."

I don't know what I'm expecting, but it isn't what I see. There's a clearing, and in the clearing there's a fire, and around the fire there are people, maybe thirty of them. They're all different colours – black, brown, yellow, and white – but not one of them is old. And not one of them has any clothes on.

A nudist camp, I think. But that's only a joke I make to myself. They're too good-looking – way too perfect. They look like ads for the AnooYoo Spas. Bimplants and totally waxed – no body hair at all. Resurfaced. Airbrushed.

Sometimes you can't believe in a thing until you actually see it, and these people are like that. I didn't quite believe that Glenn had really done it; I didn't believe what Croze told me, even though he'd actually seen these people. But now here they are, right in front of me. It's like seeing unicorns. I want to hear them purr.

When they spot us – first one of the children, then a woman, then all of them – they stop whatever they're doing and turn to stare at us, all together. They don't look frightened or threatening: they look interested but placid. It's like being stared at by the Mo'Hairs, and they're chewing like the Mo'Hairs as well. Whatever they're eating is green: a couple of the kids are amazed enough by us that they keep their mouths open.

"Hello," says Toby. To me she says, "Stay here." She steps forward. One of the men stands up – he'd been squatting beside the fire – and moves out in front of the rest.

"Greetings," he says. "Are you a friend of Snowman?"

I can hear Toby pondering her choices: Who is Snowman? If she answers yes, will they think she's an enemy? What if she answers no?

"Is Snowman good?" says Toby.

"Yes," the man says. He's taller than the others, and seems to be their spokesman. "Snowman is very good. He is our friend." The rest nod, still chewing.

"Then we are his friends too," says Toby. "And we are your friends as well."

"You are like him," says the man. "You have an extra skin, like his. But you have no feathers. Do you live in a tree?"

"Feathers?" says Toby. "On his extra skin?"

"No, on his face," says the man. "Another came, like Snowman. With feathers. And one with him, who had short feathers. And a woman who smelled blue but did not act blue. Perhaps the woman with you is like that?"

Toby nods as if she understands all of this. Maybe she does. I can't ever tell exactly what she understands.

"She smells blue," says another man. "That woman with you."

All the men are now sniffing in my direction, as if I'm a flower or maybe a cheese. A number of them have sprouted huge blue erections. Croze warned me about this, but I've never seen anything like it, even at Scales, where some of the clients went in for body paint and extenders. Several of these men are giving out a strange humming sound, like the kind you make by rubbing your finger around the rim of a crystal glass.

"But the other woman that came was frightened when we sang to her and offered her flowers, and signalled to her with our penises," says the chief one.

"Yes. The two men were frightened also. They ran away."

"How tall was she?" says Toby. "The woman. Taller than this one?" She points to me.

"Yes. Taller. She was not well. Also she was sad. We would have purred over her and made her better. Then we could have mated with her."

It must be Amanda, I think. So she's still alive, they haven't killed her yet. *Hurry up!* I want to shout. But Toby's not going anywhere yet.

"We wished her to choose which four of us she would copulate with," says the main one. "Perhaps the woman with you will choose. She smells very blue!" At this, the men all smile – they have brilliantly white teeth – and their penises point at me and wag from side to side like the tails of happy dogs.

Four? All at once? I don't want Toby to shoot any of these men – they seem so gentle, and they're very good-looking – but also I don't want those bright-blue penises anywhere near me.

"My friend isn't really blue," says Toby. "It's just her extra skin. It was given to her by a blue person. That's why she smells blue. Where did they go? These two men and the woman?"

"They went along the shore," says the main one. "And then, this morning, Snowman went to find them."

"We could look under her extra skin and see how blue she is."

"Snowman has a hurt foot. We purred over it, but it needs more purring."

"If Snowman was here, he would find out about the blue. He would tell us how we should act."

"Blue should not be wasted. It is a gift from Crake."

"We wanted to go with him. But he told us to stay here."

"Snowman knows," says one of the women. So far the women have been taking no part in the conversation, but now they all nod and smile.

"We must go now and help Snowman," says Toby. "He is our friend."

"We will come with you," says another man – a shorter one, yellow in tone, with green eyes. "We will help Snowman too." Now that I notice, they all have green eyes. They smell like citrus fruits.

"Snowman often needs our help," says the tall man. "His smell is weak. It has no power. And this time he is sick. He is sick in his foot. He is limping."

"If Snowman told you to stay here, you must stay here," says Toby. They look at one another: something's worrying them.

"We will stay here," says the tall man. "But you must come back soon."

"And bring Snowman," says one of the women. "So we can help him. Then he can live in his tree again."

"And give him a fish. A fish makes him happy."

"He eats it," says one of the children, making a face. "He chews it up. He swallows it. Crake said he has to."

"Crake lives in the sky. He loves us," says a short woman. They seem to think this Crake is God. Glenn as God, in a black T-shirt – that's pretty funny, considering what he was really like. But I don't laugh.

"We could give you a fish too," says the woman. "Would you like a fish?"

"Yes. Bring Snowman," says the tall man. "Then we will catch two fish. Three. One for you, one for Snowman, one for the woman who smells blue."

"We'll do our best," says Toby.

This seems to puzzle them. "What is 'best'?" says the man.

We step out from under the trees, into the open sunlight and the sound of the waves, and walk over the soft dry sand, down to the hard wet strip above the water's edge. The water slides up, then falls back with a gentle hiss, like a big snake breathing. Bright junk litters the shore: shards of plastic, empty cans, broken glass.

"I thought they were going to jump me," I say.

"They smelled you," says Toby. "They smelled the estrogen. They thought you were in season. They only mate when they turn blue. It's like baboons."

"How do you know all that?" I say. Croze told me about the blue penises but not about the estrogen.

"From Ivory Bill," says Toby. "The MaddAddams helped to design that feature. It was supposed to make life simpler. Facilitate mate selection. Eliminate romantic pain. Now we should keep very quiet."

Romantic pain, I think. I wonder what Toby knows about that?

There's a line of deserted high-rises standing in the offshore water: I remember them from our Gardener trips to the Heritage Park beach. It was dry land out there before the sea levels rose so much, and all the hurricanes: we'd learned that in school. Gulls are soaring and settling on the flat roofs.

We can get eggs there, I think. And fish. Jacklight, Zeb taught us, if you're desperate. Make a torch, the fish will swim to the light. There's a few crab holes in the sand, small ones. Nettles growing farther up the beach. You can eat seaweed too. All those Saint Euell things.

I'm wishing again: planning lunch, when in the back of my head is just plain fear. We can never do it. We'll never get Amanda back. We'll be killed.

Toby's found some tracks in the wet sand – several people with shoes or boots, and the place where they took the shoes off, maybe to wash their feet, and then where they put the shoes back on and headed up towards the trees.

They could be in among those trees right now, looking out. They could be watching us. They could be aiming.

On top of those tracks is another set. Barefoot. "Someone limping," whispers Toby, and I think, It must be Snowman. The crazy man who lives in a tree.

We slip our packsacks off and leave them where the sand ends and the grass and weeds begin, under the first trees. Toby says we don't need them weighing us down: we need our arms free.

75

So, God, thinks Toby. What's Your view? Supposing You exist. Tell me now, please, because this may be the end of it: once we tangle with the Painballers, we don't have a cat's chance in a bonfire, the way I see it.

Are the new people Your idea of an improved model? Is this what the first Adam was supposed to be? Will they replace us? Or do You intend to shrug your shoulders and carry on with the present human race? If so, you've chosen some odd marbles: a clutch of one-time scientists, a handful of renegade Gardeners, two psychotics on the loose with a nearly dead woman. It's hardly the survival of the fittest, except for Zeb; but even Zeb's tired.

Then there's Ren. Couldn't you have picked someone less fragile? Less innocent? A little tougher? If she were an animal, what would she be? Mouse? Thrush? Deer in the headlights? She'll fall apart at the crucial moment: I should have left her back there on the beach. But that would prolong the inevitable, because if I go down, so will she. Even if she runs, it's too far back to the cobb house: she'll never make it, and even if she outruns them she'll get lost. And who's going to protect her from the dogs and pigs, in the wild woods? Not the blue folks back there. Not if the Painballers have a spraygun that works. Much worse for her if she doesn't die immediately.

The Human moral keyboard is limited, Adam One used to say: there's nothing you can play on it that hasn't been played before. And, my dear Friends, I am sorry to say this, but it has its lower notes.

She stops, checks the rifle. Safety off.

Left foot, right foot, quietly along. The faint sounds of her feet on the fallen leaves hit her ears like shouts. How visible, how audible I am, she thinks. Everything in the forest is watching. They're waiting for blood, they can smell it, they can hear it running through my veins, *katoush*. Above her head, clustering in the treetops, the crows are treacherous: *Hawhawhaw!* They want her eyes, those crows.

Yet each flower, each twig, each pebble, shines as though illuminated from within, as once before, on her first day in the Garden. It's the stress, it's the adrenalin, it's a chemical effect: she knows this well enough. But why is it built in? she thinks. Why are we designed to see the world as supremely beautiful just as we're about to be snuffed? Do rabbits feel the same as the fox teeth bite down on their necks? Is it mercy?

She pauses, turns, smiles at Ren. Do I look reassuring? she wonders. Calm and in control? Do I look as if I know what the hell I'm doing? I'm not up to this. I'm not fast enough, I'm too old, I'm rusty, I don't have the whiplash reflexes, I'm weighed down with scruples. Forgive me, Ren. I'm leading you to doom. I pray that if I miss we both die quickly. No bees to save us this time.

What Saint should I call upon? Who has the resolution and the skill? The ruthlessness. The judgment. The accuracy.

Dear Leopard, dear Wolf, dear Liobam: lend me your Spirits now.

76

As soon as we hear voices we go forward very silently. Heel on the ground, said Toby, then roll forward on the foot, other heel on the ground. That way nothing dry snaps.

The voices are men. We can smell the smoke from their fire, and another smell: charred meat. I realize how hungry I am: I can feel myself drooling. I try to think about this hunger instead of being scared.

We peer through the leaves. It's them all right: the one with the longer dark beard, the one with the light stubbly beard and the shaved head that's growing in. I remember everything about them, and I feel like throwing up. It's hate and fear grabbing at my stomach and sending tendrils through my whole body.

But now I see Amanda, and I feel so light all of a sudden. As if I could fly.

Her hands are free, but there's a rope around her neck, with the other end tied to the leg of the dark-bearded guy. She's still wearing her khaki desert-girl outfit, though it's filthier than ever. Her face is smudged with dirt, her hair is dull and stringy. She has a purple bruise under one eye, and there are other bruises on the bare parts of her arms. She still has some of the orange nail polish on her fingers from Scales. Seeing it makes me want to cry.

She's only skin and bones. But the two of them don't look so fat themselves.

I feel myself breathing fast. Toby takes hold of my arm and gives it a squeeze. That means *Keep calm.* She turns her brown face towards me and smiles a shrunken-head smile; the edges of her teeth glint through her lips, the muscles of her jaws tighten, and all of a sudden I feel sorry for those two men. Then she lets go of my arm and lifts the rifle, very slowly.

The two men are sitting cross-legged, broiling chunks of meat on sticks over the coals. Rakunk meat. The black-and-white-striped tail is on the ground, over to the side. There's a spraygun on the ground too. Toby must have seen it. I can hear her thinking: If I shoot one of them, will I have time to shoot the other one before he can shoot me?

"Maybe it's some fuckin' savages thing," the dark-bearded one is saying. "Blue paint."

"Nah. Tattoos," says the shorthair.

"Who'd get their dick tattooed?" says the bearded one.

"Savages will tattoo anything," says the other. "It's some cannibal thing."

"You been watching too many dumb movies."

"Bet they'd human-sacrifice her in about two minutes," says the bearded one. "After they all had sex with her." They look over at Amanda, but she's staring at the ground. The bearded one jerks the rope. "We're talkin' to you, bitch," he says. Amanda raises her head.

"A sex toy you can eat," says the shorthair, and the two of them laugh. "You see the bimplants on those bitches, though?"

"Not bimplants, they were real. Way to find out, cut them open. The fake ones've got, like, some kind of gel in them. Maybe we could go back there, do a trade," says the bearded one. "With the savages. They get this one, they seem to want her so much, stick their blue dicks into her, and we get some of those hot babes of theirs. Fuckin' good deal!"

I see Amanda as they see her: used up, worn out. Worthless.

"Why trade?" says the shorthair. "Why not just go back and shoot the fuckers?"

"Not enough juice in this thing to shoot all of them. Cellpack's really low. They'd figure that out, they'd rush us. Tear us apart and eat us."

"We got to get farther away," says the shorthair, alarmed now. "Thirty of them, two of us. What if they sneak up on us in the dark?"

There's a pause while they think about this. My skin is crawling all over, I hate them so much. I wonder why Toby's waiting. Why doesn't she just kill them? Then I think, she's old Gardener – she can't do it, not in cold blood. It's against her religion.

"Not too bad," says the bearded one, lifting a skewer from the coals. "We can bag another one of these tasty little suckers tomorrow."

"We gonna feed her?" says the shorthair. He's licking his fingers.

"Give her some of yours," says the bearded one. "She's no use to us dead."

"No use to *me* dead," says the shorthair. "You're such a pervert you'd plank a fuckin' corpse."

"Speaking of which, your turn first. Get the pump primed. I hate a dry fuck."

"It was me first yesterday."

"So, we arm-wrestle?"

Then suddenly there's a fourth person in the clearing – a naked man, but not one of the green-eyed beautiful ones. This one is emaciated and scabby. He has a long scraggly beard, and he looks very crazy. But I know him. Or I think I know him. Is it Jimmy?

He's carrying a spraygun, and he has it aimed it at the two men. He's going to shoot them. He has that kind of maniac focus.

But he'll shoot Amanda too, because the dark-bearded guy sees him and scrambles up onto his knees and pulls Amanda in front of him, one arm around her neck. The shorthair ducks in behind them. Jimmy hesitates, but he doesn't lower the spraygun.

"Jimmy!" I scream from inside the shrubbery. "Don't! That's Amanda!"

He must think the bushes are talking to him. His face turns. I come out from behind the leaves.

"Great! The other bimbo," says the bearded one. "Now we'll have one each!" He's grinning. The shorthair crouches forward, reaches for their spraygun.

Toby steps into the clearing. She has the rifle up and aimed. "Don't touch that," she says to the shorthair. Her voice is strong and clear but dead flat even. She must sound scary to him, and look it too – skinny, tattered, teeth bared. Like a TV banshee, like a walking skeleton; like someone with nothing to lose.

The shorthair freezes. The one holding Amanda doesn't know which way to turn: Jimmy's in front of him, but Toby's off to the side. "Back off! I'll break her neck," he says to all of us. His voice is very loud: that means he's afraid.

"I might care about that, but he doesn't," Toby says, meaning Jimmy. To me: "Get that spraygun. Don't let him grab you." To the shorthair: "Lie down." To me: "Watch your ankles." To the bearded one: "Let go of her."

This is very fast, but at the same time slowed down. The voices are coming from far away; the sun's so bright it hurts me; the light crackles on our faces; we glare and sparkle, as if electricity's running all over us like water. I can almost see into the bodies – everyone's bodies. The veins, the tendons, the blood flowing. I can hear their hearts, like thunder coming nearer.

I think I might faint. But I can't, because I need to help Toby. I don't know how, but I run over. So close I can smell them. Rancid sweat, oily hair. Snatch up their spraygun.

"Around behind him," Toby tells me. To the Painballer: "Hands behind your head." To me: "Shoot him in the back if you don't see those hands quick." She's talking as if I know how to work this thing. To Jimmy, she says, "Easy now," as if he's a big frightened animal.

All this time Amanda has kept still, but when the dark-bearded one lets go of her she moves like a snake. She pulls the rope noose up and over her head and whips the guy across the face with it. Then she kicks him in the nuts. I can tell she doesn't have a lot of strength left, but she uses all she has, and when he doubles over on the ground she kicks the other one. Then she grabs a stone and whacks each of them over the head, and there's blood. Then she drops the stone and hobbles over to me. She's crying, big gulping sobs, and I know it must have been very terrible, those

days when I wasn't there, because it takes more than a lot to make
Amanda cry.

"Oh, Amanda," I say to her. "I'm so sorry."

Jimmy's swaying on his feet. "Are you real?" he says to Toby. He
looks so bewildered. He rubs his eyes.

"As real as you," says Toby. "You'd better tie them up," she says
to me. "Do a good job. When they come out of it they're going to be
very angry."

Amanda wipes her face on her sleeve. Then we start knotting the
two of them together, the hands behind the backs, a loop around each
neck. We could use more rope, but it will do for now.

"Is it you?" says Jimmy. "I think I've seen you before."

I walk towards him, slowly and carefully because he still has his
gun. "Jimmy," I say. "It's Ren. Remember me? You can put that down.
It's okay now." It's how you'd say it to a child.

He lowers the spraygun and I wrap my arms around him and give
him a long hug. He's shivering, but his skin's burning hot.

"Ren?" he says. "Are you dead?"

"No, Jimmy. I'm alive, and so are you." I smooth back his hair.

"I'm such a mess," he says. "Sometimes I think everyone's dead."

SAINT JULIAN AND ALL SOULS

■■■■■
■■■■■
■■■■■

YEAR TWENTY-FIVE.

OF THE FRAGILITY OF THE UNIVERSE.
SPOKEN BY ADAM ONE.

My dear Friends, those few that now remain:

Only a little time is left to us. We have used some of that time to make our way up here, to the site of our once-flourishing Edencliff Rooftop Garden, where in a more hopeful era we spent such happy days together.

Let us take this opportunity to dwell, for one final moment, on the Light.

For the new moon is rising, signalling the beginning of Saint Julian and All Souls. All Souls is not restricted to Human Souls: among us, it encompasses the Souls of all the living Creatures that have passed through Life, and have undergone the Great Transformation, and have entered that state sometimes called Death, but more rightly known as Renewed Life. For in this our World, and in the eye of God, not a single atom that has ever existed is truly lost.

Dear Diplodocus, dear Pterosaur, dear Trilobite; dear Mastodon, dear Dodo, dear Great Auk, dear Passenger Pigeon; dear Panda, dear Whooping Crane; and all you countless others who have played in this our shared Garden in your day: be with us at this time of trial, and strengthen our resolve. Like you, we have enjoyed the air and the sunlight and the moonlight on the water; like you, we have heard the call of the seasons and have answered them. Like you, we have replenished the Earth. And like you, we must now witness the end of our Species, and pass from Earthly view.

As always on this day, the words of Saint Julian of Norwich, that compassionate fourteenth-century Saint, remind us of the fragility of our Cosmos – a fragility affirmed anew by the physicists of the twentieth century, when Science discovered the vast spaces of emptiness that lie, not only within the atoms, but between the stars. What is our Cosmos but a snowflake? What is it but a piece of lace? As our dear Saint Julian so beautifully said, in words of tenderness that have echoed down through the centuries:

> . . . He showed me a little thing, the quantity of a hazel nut, lying in the palm of my hand . . . as round as any ball. I looked at it and thought, What may this be, and I was answered generally thus: It is all that is made. I marvelled how it might last. For I thought it might fall suddenly to nothing, for little cause; and I was answered in my understanding: It lasts and ever shall, for God loves it. And so has everything its being, through the love of God.

Do we deserve this Love by which God maintains our Cosmos? Do we deserve it as a Species? We have taken the World given to us and carelessly destroyed its fabric and its Creatures. Other religions have taught that this World is to be rolled up like a scroll and burnt to nothingness, and that a new Heaven and a new Earth will then appear. But why would God give us another Earth when we have mistreated this one so badly?

No, my Friends. It is not this Earth that is to be demolished: it is the Human Species. Perhaps God will create another, more compassionate race to take our place.

For the Waterless Flood has swept over us – not as a vast hurricane, not as a barrage of comets, not as a cloud of poisonous gasses. No: as we suspected for so long, it is a plague – a plague that infects no Species but our own, and that will leave all other Creatures untouched. Our cities are darkened, our lines of communication are no more. The blight and ruin of our Garden is now mirrored by the blight and ruin that have emptied the streets below. We need not fear discovery now: our old enemies cannot pursue us, occupied as they must be by the hideous torments of their own bodily dissolution, if they are not already dead.

We should not – indeed we cannot – rejoice at that. For yesterday the plague took three of us. Already I sense within myself those changes that I see reflected in your own eyes. We know only too well what awaits us.

But let our going out be brave and joyous! Let us end with a prayer for All Souls. Among these are the Souls of those who have persecuted us; those who have murdered God's Creatures, and extinguished His Species; those who have tortured in the name of Law; who have worshipped nothing but riches; and who, to gain wealth and worldly power, have inflicted pain and death.

Let us forgive the killers of the Elephant, and the exterminators of the Tiger; and those who slaughtered the Bear for its gall bladder, and the Shark for its cartilage, and the Rhinoceros for its horn. May we forgive them freely, as we may hope to be forgiven by God, who holds our frail Cosmos in His hand, and keeps it safe through His endless Love.

This Forgiveness is the hardest task we shall ever be called upon to perform. Give us the strength for it.

I would like us all to join hands now.

Let us sing.

THE EARTH FORGIVES

The Earth forgives the Miner's blast
That rends her crust and burns her skin;
The centuries bring Trees again,
And water, and the Fish therein.

The Deer at length forgives the Wolf
That tears his throat and drinks his blood;
His bones return to soil, and feed
The trees that flower and fruit and seed.

And underneath those shady trees
The Wolf will spend her restful days;
And then the Wolf in turn will pass,
And turn to grass the Deer will graze.

All Creatures know that some must die
That all the rest may take and eat;
Sooner or later, all transform
Their blood to wine, their flesh to meat.

But Man alone seeks Vengefulness,
And writes his abstract Laws on stone;
For this false Justice he has made,
He tortures limb and crushes bone.

Is this the image of a god?
My tooth for yours, your eye for mine?
Oh, if Revenge did move the stars
Instead of Love, they would not shine.

We dangle by a flimsy thread,
Our little lives are grains of sand:
The Cosmos is a tiny sphere
Held in the hollow of God's hand.

Give up your anger and your spite,
And imitate the Deer, the Tree;
In sweet Forgiveness find your joy,
For it alone can set you free.

From *The God's Gardeners Oral Hymnbook*

77

The new moon's rising now, out over the sea: Saint Julian and All Souls has begun.

I loved Saint Julian's when I was little. Each of us kids would make our own Cosmos, out of stuff we'd gleaned. Then we'd stick glittery things onto it and hang it on a string. The Feast that night was round foods, like radishes and pumpkins, and the whole Garden would be decorated with our shining worlds. One year we made the Cosmos balls out of wire and put candle ends inside them: that was really pretty. Another year we tried to make Divine Hands for holding the Cosmos balls, but the yellow plastic housework gloves we came up with looked very strange, like zombie hands. Anyway you don't picture God as wearing gloves.

We're sitting around the fire – Toby and Amanda and me. And Jimmy. And the two Gold Team Painballers, I have to include them. The light flickers on all of us and makes us look softer and more beautiful than we really are. But sometimes it makes us darker and scarier too, when the faces go into shadow and you can't see the eyes, only the eye sockets. Deep pools of blackness welling out of our heads.

My body hurts all over, but at the same time I feel so joyful. We're lucky, I think. To be here. All of us, even the Painballers.

After the mid-day heat and the thunderstorm I went back to the beach for our packsacks and brought them to the clearing, along with some wild mustard greens I'd found along the way. Toby took out her cooking

THE YEAR OF THE FLOOD | 429

pot, and the cups, and her knife, and her big spoon. Then she made soup with the leftovers from the rakunk and the rest of Rebecca's meat, some of her dried botanicals. When she put the bones of the rakunk into the water she spoke the words of apology and asked for its pardon.

"But you didn't kill it," I said to her.

"I know," she said. "But I wouldn't feel right unless somebody did this."

The Painballers are tied to a nearby tree with the rope and also some braided strips torn from Toby's once-pink top-to-toe. I did the braiding: if there's one thing the Gardeners taught you, it was craft uses for recycled materials.

The Painballers aren't saying much. They can't be feeling great, not after being pounded by Amanda. They must also be feeling stupid. I would be if I were them. Dumb as a box of hair – as Zeb would say – for letting us creep up on them like that.

Amanda must be still in shock. She's crying gently, off and on, and twisting the raggedy ends of her hair. The first thing Toby did – once the Painballers were safely roped up – was to give her a cup of warm water with honey, for dehydration, with some of her lamb's-quarters powder stirred in.

"Don't drink it all at once," she said. "Just little sips." Once Amanda's electrolyte levels were back up, said Toby, she could start to deal with whatever else about Amanda needed fixing. The cuts and bruises, to begin with.

Jimmy's in bad shape. He has a high fever, and a festering sore on his foot. Toby says that if only we can get him back to the cobb house, she can use maggots – those might work in the long run. But Jimmy may not have the long run.

Earlier she spread some honey on his foot, and fed him a spoonful of it, as well. She can't give him any Willow or Poppy, because she left those back at the cobb house. We wrapped him up in Toby's top-to-toe, but he keeps unwrapping himself. "We need to find him a bedsheet or some-thing," Toby says. "For tomorrow. And figure some way of keeping it on him or he'll broil to death in the sun."

Jimmy doesn't recognize me at all, or Amanda either. He keeps talking to some other woman, who appears to be standing by the fire. "Owl music. Don't fly away," he says to her. There's such longing in his voice. I feel jealous, but how can I be jealous of some woman who isn't there?

"Who are you talking to?" I ask him.

"There's an owl," he says. "Calling. Right up there." But I don't hear any owl.

"Look at me, Jimmy," I say.

"The music's built in," he says. "No matter what." He's gazing up into the trees.

Oh Jimmy, I think. Where have you gone?

The moon's moved westward. Toby says the bone soup has boiled enough. She adds the mustard greens I collected, waits a minute, then ladles out. We've got only two cups – we'll have to take turns, she says.

"Not them too?" said Amanda. She won't look at the Painballers.

"Yes," said Toby. "Them too. This is Saint Julian and All Souls."

"What happens to them?" says Amanda. "Tomorrow?" At least she's taking an interest in something.

"You can't just let them loose," I say. "They'll kill us. They murdered Oates. And look what they did to Amanda!"

"I'll consider that problem," says Toby, "later. Tonight is a Feast night." She dips the soup into the cups, then looks around the firelight circle. "Some feast," she says in her dry-witch voice. She laughs a little. "But we're not finished yet! Are we?" She says this last thing to Amanda.

"Kaputt," says Amanda. Her voice is so small.

"Don't think about it," I say, but she begins to cry again, softly: she's in a Fallow state. I put my arms around her. "I'm here, you're here, it's okay," I whisper.

"What is the point?" says Amanda, not to me but to Toby.

"This is not the time," says Toby in her old Eve voice, "for dwelling on ultimate purposes. I would like us all to forget the past, the worst parts of it. Let us be grateful for this food that has been given to us. Amanda. Ren. Jimmy. You, too, if you can manage it." This to the two Painballers.

One of them mutters something like *Fuck off*, but he doesn't say it very loudly. He wants some of the soup.

Toby continues on as if she hasn't heard. "And I would like us to remember those who are gone, throughout the world but most especially our absent friends. Dear Adams, dear Eves, dear Fellow Mammals and Fellow Creatures, all those now in Spirit – keep us in your view and lend us your strength, because we are surely going to need it."

Then she takes a sip from the cup and passes it to Amanda. The other cup she gives to Jimmy, but he can't hold it right and he spills half of the soup into the sand. I crouch down beside him to help him drink. Maybe he's dying, I think. Maybe in the morning he'll be dead.

"I knew you'd come back," he says, this time to me. "I knew it. Don't turn into an owl."

"I'm not an owl," I say. "You're out of your mind. I'm Ren – remember? I just want you to know that you broke my heart; but anyway, I'm happy you're still alive." Now that I've said it, something heavy and smothering lifts away from me, and I truly do feel happy.

He smiles at me, or at whoever he thinks I am. A blistery little grin. "Here we go again," he says to his sick foot. "Listen to the music." He tilts his head to the side; his expression is rapturous. "You can't kill the music," he says. "You can't!"

"What music?" I say, because I don't hear anything.

"Quiet," says Toby.

We listen. Jimmy's right, there is music. It's faint and far away, but moving closer. It's the sound of many people singing. Now we can see the flickering of their torches, winding towards us through the darkness of the trees.

ACKNOWLEDGMENTS

The Year of the Flood is fiction, but the general tendencies and many of the details in it are alarmingly close to fact. The God's Gardeners cult appeared in the novel *Oryx and Crake*, as did Amanda Payne, Brenda (Ren), Bernice, Jimmy the Snowman, Glenn (alias Crake), and the MaddAddam group. The Gardeners themselves are not modelled on any extant religion, though some of their theology and practices are not without precedent. Their saints have been chosen for their contributions to those areas of life dear to the hearts of the Gardeners; they have many more saints, as well, but they are not in this book. The clearest influence on Gardener hymn lyrics is William Blake, with an assist from John Bunyan and also from *The Hymn Book of the Anglican Church of Canada and the United Church of Canada*. Like all hymn collections, those of the Gardeners have moments that may not be fully comprehensible to non-believers.

The music for the hymns came about by fortunate coincidence. Singer and musician Orville Stoeber of Venice, California, began composing the music to several of these hymns to see what might happen, and then got swept away. The extraordinary results can be heard on the CD, *Hymns of the God's Gardeners*. Anyone who wishes to use any of these hymns for amateur devotional or environmental purposes is more than welcome to do so. Visit them at www.yearoftheflood.com, www.yearoftheflood.co.uk, or www.yearoftheflood.ca.

The name Amanda Payne originally appeared as that of a character in *Oryx and Crake*, courtesy of an auction for the Medical Foundation for the Care of Victims of Torture (U.K.). Saint Allan Sparrow of Clean Air was sponsored by an auction run by CAIR (CommunityAIR, Toronto). The name Rebecca Eckler appears thanks to a benefit auction for *The Walrus* magazine (Canada). My thanks to all name donors.

My gratitude as always to my enthusiastic and loyal but hard-pressed editors, Ellen Seligman of McClelland & Stewart (Canada), Nan Talese of Doubleday (U.S.A.), and Alexandra Pringle and Liz Calder of Bloomsbury (U.K.), as well as Louise Dennys of Vintage/Knopf Canada, LuAnn Walther of Anchor (U.S.A.), Lennie Goodings of Virago (U.K.), and Maya Mavjee of Doubleday Canada. Also to my agents, Phoebe Larmore (North America) and Vivienne Schuster and Betsy Robbins of Curtis Brown (U.K.); and to Ron Bernstein; and to all my other agents and publishers around the world. Thanks also to Heather Sangster for her heroic job of copy-editing; and to my exceptional office support staff, Sarah Webster, Anne Joldersma, Laura Stenberg, and Penny Kavanaugh; and to Shannon Shields, who helped as well. Also to Joel Rubinovitch and Sheldon Shoib; and to Michael Bradley and Sarah Cooper. Also to Coleen Quinn and Xiaolan Zhang, for keeping my writing arm moving.

Special thanks to the dauntless early readers of this book: Jess Atwood Gibson, Eleanor and Ramsay Cook, Rosalie Abella, Valerie Martin, John Cullen, and Xandra Bingley. You are highly valued.

And finally, my special thanks to Graeme Gibson, with whom I've celebrated so many April Fish, Serpent Wisdom, and All Wayfarers' Feasts. It's been a fine long journey.

Oryx and Crake

MARGARET ATWOOD

Oryx and Crake

Margaret Atwood is the author of more than forty books—novels, short stories, poetry, literary criticism, social history, and books for children.

Atwood's work is acclaimed internationally and has been published around the world. Her novels include *The Handmaid's Tale*; *Cat's Eye*; *The Robber Bride*, winner of the Trillium Book Award; *Alias Grace*, winner of the Giller Prize in Canada and the Premio Mondello in Italy; *The Blind Assassin*, winner of the Booker Prize; and *Oryx and Crake*, the first novel in the MaddAddam Trilogy. Recent books include *The Penelopiad*, *The Tent*, *Moral Disorder*, and *Payback*. Her latest novel, *The Year of the Flood* (2009), is the second book in the MaddAddam Trilogy.

Atwood lives in Toronto with writer Graeme Gibson.

by Margaret Atwood

FICTION

The Edible Woman (1969)
Surfacing (1972)
Lady Oracle (1976)
Dancing Girls (1977)
Life Before Man (1979)
Bodily Harm (1981)
Murder in the Dark (1983)
Bluebeard's Egg (1983)
The Handmaid's Tale (1985)
Cat's Eye (1988)
Wilderness Tips (1991)
Good Bones (1992)
The Robber Bride (1993)
Alias Grace (1996)
The Blind Assassin (2000)
Good Bones and Simple Murders (2001)
Oryx and Crake (2003)
The Penelopiad (2005)
The Tent (2006)
The Year of the Flood (2009)

FOR CHILDREN

Up in the Tree (1978)
Anna's Pet [with Joyce Barkhouse] (1980)
For the Birds (1990)
Princess Prunella and the Purple Peanut (1995)
Rude Ramsay and the Roaring Radishes (2003)
Bashful Bob and Doleful Dorinda (2004)

NONFICTION

Survival: A Thematic Guide to Canadian Literature (1972)
Days of the Rebels 1815–1840 (1977)
Second Words (1982)
Strange Things: The Malevolent North in Canadian Literature (1996)
Two Solicitudes: Conversations [with Victor-Lévy Beaulieu] (1998)
Negotiating with the Dead: A Writer on Writing (2002)
Moving Targets: Writing with Intent 1982–2004 (2004)
Payback: Debt and the Shadow Side of Wealth (2008)

POETRY

Double Persephone (1961)
The Circle Game (1966)
The Animals in That Country (1968)
The Journals of Susanna Moodie (1970)
Procedures for Underground (1970)
Power Politics (1971)
You Are Happy (1974)
Selected Poems (1976)
Two-Headed Poems (1978)
True Stories (1981)
Interlunar (1984)
Selected Poems II: Poems Selected and New 1976–1986 (1986)
Morning in the Burned House (1995)
The Door (2008)

Oryx and Crake

ORYX
and
CRAKE a novel

margaret atwood

ANCHOR BOOKS

A Division of Random House, Inc. • New York

FIRST ANCHOR BOOKS EDITION, MAY 2004

Copyright © 2003 by O. W. Toad, Ltd.

All rights reserved under International and Pan-American Copyright
Conventions. Published in the United States by Anchor Books, a division
of Random House, Inc., New York. Originally published in hardcover in
the United States by Nan A. Talese, an imprint of Doubleday,
a division of Random House, Inc., New York, in 2003.

Anchor Books and colophon are registered trademarks of Random House, Inc.

The Library of Congress has cataloged the Nan A. Talese/Doubleday
edition as follows:
Atwood, Margaret Eleanor, 1939–
Oryx and Crake / Margaret Atwood.—1st ed.
p. cm.
1. Triangles (Interpersonal relations)—Fiction.
2. Genetic engineering—Fiction. 3. New York (State)—Fiction.
4. Male friendship—Fiction. I. Title.
PR9199.3.A8 O7 2003
813'.54—dc21
2002073290

Anchor ISBN: 0-385-72167-6

www.anchorbooks.com

Printed in the United States of America
40 39 38 37 36 35 34 33 32 31

For my family

I could perhaps like others have astonished you
with strange improbable tales; but I rather chose
to relate plain matter of fact in the simplest
manner and style; because my principal design
was to inform you, and not to amuse you.

Jonathan Swift,
Gulliver's Travels

Was there no safety? No learning by heart of the ways of the world? No guide, no shelter, but all was miracle and leaping from the pinnacle of a tower into the air?

Virginia Woolf,
To the Lighthouse

Contents

1

2

3

4

5

6

7

8

Oryx and Crake

Mango

~

Snowman wakes before dawn. He lies unmoving, listening to the tide coming in, wave after wave sloshing over the various barricades, wish-wash, wish-wash, the rhythm of heartbeat. He would so like to believe he is still asleep.

On the eastern horizon there's a greyish haze, lit now with a rosy, deadly glow. Strange how that colour still seems tender. The offshore towers stand out in dark silhouette against it, rising improbably out of the pink and pale blue of the lagoon. The shrieks of the birds that nest out there and the distant ocean grinding against the ersatz reefs of rusted car parts and jumbled bricks and assorted rubble sound almost like holiday traffic.

Out of habit he looks at his watch — stainless-steel case, burnished aluminum band, still shiny although it no longer works. He wears it now as his only talisman. A blank face is what it shows him: zero hour. It causes a jolt of terror to run through him, this absence of official time. Nobody nowhere knows what time it is.

"Calm down," he tells himself. He takes a few deep breaths, then scratches his bug bites, around but not on the itchiest places, taking care not to knock off any scabs: blood poisoning is the last thing he needs. Then he scans the ground below for wildlife: all quiet, no scales and tails. Left hand, right foot, right hand, left foot, he makes his way down from the tree. After brushing off the twigs and bark, he winds his dirty bedsheet around himself like a toga. He's hung his authentic-replica Red Sox baseball cap on a branch overnight for safekeeping; he checks inside it, flicks out a spider, puts it on.

He walks a couple of yards to the left, pisses into the bushes. "Heads up," he says to the grasshoppers that whir away at the impact. Then he goes to the other side of the tree, well away from his customary urinal, and rummages around in the cache he's improvised from a few slabs of concrete, lining it with wire mesh to keep out the rats and mice. He's stashed some mangoes there, knotted in a plastic bag, and a can of Sveltana No-Meat Cocktail Sausages, and a precious half-bottle of Scotch — no, more like a third — and a chocolate-flavoured energy bar scrounged from a trailer park, limp and sticky inside its foil. He can't bring himself to eat it yet: it might be the last one he'll ever find. He keeps a can opener there too, and for no particular reason an ice pick; and six empty beer bottles, for sentimental reasons and for storing fresh water. Also his sunglasses; he puts them on. One lens is missing but they're better than nothing.

He undoes the plastic bag: there's only a single mango left. Funny, he remembered more. The ants have got in, even though he tied the bag as tightly as he could. Already they're running up his arms, the black kind and the vicious little yellow kind. Surprising what a sharp sting they can give, especially the yellow ones. He rubs them away.

"It is the strict adherence to daily routine that tends towards the maintenance of good morale and the preservation of sanity," he says out loud. He has the feeling he's quoting from a book, some obsolete, ponderous directive written in aid of European colonials running plantations of one kind or another. He can't recall ever having read such a thing, but that means nothing. There are a lot of blank spaces in his stub of a brain, where memory used to be. Rubber plantations, coffee plantations, jute plantations. (What was jute?) They would have been told to wear solar topis, dress for dinner, refrain from raping the natives. It wouldn't have said *raping*. Refrain from fraternizing with the female inhabitants. Or, put some other way . . .

He bets they didn't refrain, though. Nine times out of ten.

"In view of the mitigating," he says. He finds himself standing with his mouth open, trying to remember the rest of the sentence. He sits down on the ground and begins to eat the mango.

Flotsam

~

On the white beach, ground-up coral and broken bones, a group of the children are walking. They must have been swimming, they're still wet and glistening. They should be more careful: who knows what may infest the lagoon? But they're unwary; unlike Snowman, who won't dip a toe in there even at night, when the sun can't get at him. Revision: especially at night.

He watches them with envy, or is it nostalgia? It can't be that: he never swam in the sea as a child, never ran around on a beach without any clothes on. The children scan the terrain, stoop, pick up flotsam; then they deliberate among themselves, keeping some items, discarding others; their treasures go into a torn sack. Sooner or later — he can count on it — they'll seek him out where he sits wrapped in his decaying sheet, hugging his shins and sucking on his mango, in under the shade of the trees because of the punishing sun. For the children — thick-skinned, resistant to ultraviolet — he's a creature of dimness, of the dusk.

Here they come now. "Snowman, oh Snowman," they chant in their singsong way. They never stand too close to him. Is that from respect, as he'd like to think, or because he stinks?

(He does stink, he knows that well enough. He's rank, he's gamy, he reeks like a walrus — oily, salty, fishy — not that he's ever smelled such a beast. But he's seen pictures.)

Opening up their sack, the children chorus, "Oh Snowman, what have we found?" They lift out the objects, hold them up as if offering them for sale: a hubcap, a piano key, a chunk of pale-green pop bottle smoothed by the ocean. A plastic BlyssPluss container, empty; a ChickieNobs Bucket O'Nubbins, ditto. A computer mouse, or the busted remains of one, with a long wiry tail.

Snowman feels like weeping. What can he tell them? There's no way of explaining to them what these curious items are, or were. But surely they've guessed what he'll say, because it's always the same.

"These are things from before." He keeps his voice kindly but remote. A cross between pedagogue, soothsayer, and benevolent uncle — that should be his tone.

"Will they hurt us?" Sometimes they find tins of motor oil, caustic solvents, plastic bottles of bleach. Booby traps from the past. He's considered to be an expert on potential accidents: scalding liquids, sickening fumes, poison dust. Pain of odd kinds.

"These, no," he says. "These are safe." At this they lose interest, let the sack dangle. But they don't go away: they stand, they stare. Their beachcombing is an excuse. Mostly they want to look at him, because he's so unlike them. Every so often they ask him to take off his sunglasses and put them on again: they want to see whether he has two eyes really, or three.

"Snowman, oh Snowman," they're singing, less to him than to one another. To them his name is just two syllables. They don't know what a snowman is, they've never seen snow.

It was one of Crake's rules that no name could be chosen for which a physical equivalent — even stuffed, even skeletal — could not be demonstrated. No unicorns, no griffins, no manticores or basilisks. But those rules no longer apply, and it's given Snowman a bitter pleasure to adopt this dubious label. The Abominable Snowman — existing and not existing, flickering at the edges of blizzards, apelike man or manlike ape, stealthy, elusive, known only through rumours and through its backward-pointing footprints. Mountain tribes were said to have chased it down and killed it when they had the chance. They were said to have boiled it, roasted it, held special feasts; all the more exciting, he supposes, for bordering on cannibalism.

For present purposes he's shortened the name. He's only Snowman. He's kept the *abominable* to himself, his own secret hair shirt.

After a few moments of hesitation the children squat down in a half-circle, boys and girls together. A couple of the younger ones are still munching on their breakfasts, the green juice running down their chins. It's discouraging how grubby everyone gets without mirrors. Still, they're amazingly attractive, these children – each one naked, each one perfect, each one a different skin colour – chocolate, rose, tea, butter, cream, honey – but each with green eyes. Crake's aesthetic.

They're gazing at Snowman expectantly. They must be hoping he'll talk to them, but he isn't in the mood for it today. At the very most he might let them see his sunglasses, up close, or his shiny, dysfunctional watch, or his baseball cap. They like the cap, but don't understand his need for such a thing – removable hair that isn't hair – and he hasn't yet invented a fiction for it.

They're quiet for a bit, staring, ruminating, but then the oldest one starts up. "Oh Snowman, please tell us – what is that moss growing out of your face?" The others chime in. "Please tell us, please tell us!" No nudging, no giggling: the question is serious.

"Feathers," he says.

They ask this question at least once a week. He gives the same answer. Even over such a short time – two months, three? He's lost count – they've accumulated a stock of lore, of conjecture about him: *Snowman was once a bird but he's forgotten how to fly and the rest of his feathers fell out, and so he is cold and he needs a second skin, and he has to wrap himself up. No: he's cold because he eats fish, and fish are cold. No: he wraps himself up because he's missing his man thing, and he doesn't want us to see. That's why he won't go swimming. Snowman has wrinkles because he once lived underwater and it wrinkled up his skin. Snowman is sad because the others like him flew away over the sea, and now he is all alone.*

"I want feathers too," says the youngest. A vain hope: no beards on the men, among the Children of Crake. Crake himself had found beards irrational; also he'd been irritated by the task of shaving, so he'd abolished the need for it. Though not of course for Snowman: too late for him.

Now they all begin at once. "Oh Snowman, oh Snowman, can we have feathers too, please?"

"No," he says.

"Why not, why not?" sing the two smallest ones.

"Just a minute, I'll ask Crake." He holds his watch up to the sky, turns it around on his wrist, then puts it to his ear as if listening to it. They follow each motion, enthralled. "No," he says. "Crake says you can't. No feathers for you. Now piss off."

"Piss off? Piss off?" They look at one another, then at him. He's made a mistake, he's said a new thing, one that's impossible to explain. Piss isn't something they'd find insulting. "What is *piss off*?"

"Go away!" He flaps his sheet at them and they scatter, running along the beach. They're still not sure whether to be afraid of him, or how afraid. He hasn't been known to harm a child, but his nature is not fully understood. There's no telling what he might do.

Voice

~

"Now I'm alone," he says out loud. "All, all alone. Alone on a wide, wide sea." One more scrap from the burning scrapbook in his head.

Revision: seashore.

He feels the need to hear a human voice — a fully human voice, like his own. Sometimes he laughs like a hyena or roars like a lion — his idea of a hyena, his idea of a lion. He used to watch old DVDs of such creatures when he was a child: those animal-behaviour programs featuring copulation and growling and innards, and mothers licking their young. Why had he found them so reassuring?

Or he grunts and squeals like a pigoon, or howls like a wolvog: *Aroo! Aroo!* Sometimes in the dusk he runs up and down on the sand, flinging stones at the ocean and screaming, *Shit, shit, shit, shit, shit!* He feels better afterwards.

He stands up and raises his arms to stretch, and his sheet falls off. He looks down at his body with dismay: the grimy, bug-bitten skin, the salt-and-pepper tufts of hair, the thickening yellow toenails. Naked as the day he was born, not that he can remember a thing about that. So many crucial events take place behind people's backs, when they aren't in a position to watch: birth and death, for instance. And the temporary oblivion of sex.

"Don't even think about it," he tells himself. Sex is like drink, it's bad to start brooding about it too early in the day.

He used to take good care of himself; he used to run, work out at the gym. Now he can see his own ribs: he's wasting away. Not enough animal protein. A woman's voice says caressingly in his ear, *Nice buns!* It isn't Oryx, it's some other woman. Oryx is no longer very talkative.

"Say anything," he implores her. She can hear him, he needs to believe that, but she's giving him the silent treatment. "What can I do?" he asks her. "You know I . . ."

Oh, nice abs! comes the whisper, interrupting him. *Honey, just lie back.* Who is it? Some tart he once bought. Revision, professional sex-skills expert. A trapeze artist, rubber spine, spangles glued onto her like the scales of a fish. He hates these echoes. Saints used to hear them, crazed lice-infested hermits in their caves and deserts. Pretty soon he'll be seeing beautiful demons, beckoning to him, licking their lips, with red-hot nipples and flickering pink tongues. Mermaids will rise from the waves, out there beyond the crumbling towers, and he'll hear their lovely singing and swim out to them and be eaten by sharks. Creatures with the heads and breasts of women and the talons of eagles will swoop down on him, and he'll open his arms to them, and that will be the end. Brainfrizz.

Or worse, some girl he knows, or knew, will come walking towards him through the trees, and she'll be happy to see him but she'll be made of air. He'd welcome even that, for the company.

He scans the horizon, using his one sunglassed eye: nothing. The sea is hot metal, the sky a bleached blue, except for the hole burnt in it by the sun. Everything is so empty. Water, sand, sky, trees, fragments of past time. Nobody to hear him.

"Crake!" he yells. "Asshole! Shit-for-brains!"

He listens. The salt water is running down his face again. He never knows when that will happen and he can never stop it. His

breath is coming in gasps, as if a giant hand is clenching around
his chest — clench, release, clench. Senseless panic.

"You did this!" he screams at the ocean.

No answer, which isn't surprising. Only the waves, wish-wash,
wish-wash. He wipes his fist across his face, across the grime and
tears and snot and the derelict's whiskers and sticky mango juice.
"Snowman, Snowman," he says. "Get a life."

2

Bonfire

~

Once upon a time, Snowman wasn't Snowman. Instead he was Jimmy. He'd been a good boy then.

Jimmy's earliest complete memory was of a huge bonfire. He must have been five, maybe six. He was wearing red rubber boots with a smiling duck's face on each toe; he remembers that, because after seeing the bonfire he had to walk through a pan of disinfectant in those boots. They'd said the disinfectant was poisonous and he shouldn't splash, and then he was worried that the poison would get into the eyes of the ducks and hurt them. He'd been told the ducks were only like pictures, they weren't real and had no feelings, but he didn't quite believe it.

So let's say five and a half, thinks Snowman. That's about right.

The month could have been October, or else November; the leaves still turned colour then, and they were orange and red. It was muddy underfoot – he must have been standing in a field – and it was drizzling. The bonfire was an enormous pile of cows and sheep and pigs. Their legs stuck out stiff and straight; gasoline had been poured onto them; the flames shot up and out, yellow and white and red and orange, and a smell of charred flesh filled the air. It was like the barbecue in the backyard when his father cooked things but a lot stronger, and mixed in with it was a gas-station smell, and the odour of burning hair.

Jimmy knew what burning hair smelled like because he'd cut off some of his own hair with the manicure scissors and set fire to it with his mother's cigarette lighter. The hair had frizzled up, squiggling like a clutch of tiny black worms, so he'd cut off some more and done it again. By the time he was caught, his hair was ragged all along the front. When accused he'd said it was an experiment.

His father had laughed then, but his mother hadn't. At least (his father said) Jimmy'd had the good sense to cut the hair off before torching it. His mother said it was lucky he hadn't burnt the house down. Then they'd had an argument about the cigarette lighter, which wouldn't have been there (said his father) if his mother didn't smoke. His mother said that all children were arsonists at heart, and if not for the lighter he'd have used matches.

Once the fight got going Jimmy felt relieved, because he'd known then that he wouldn't be punished. All he had to do was say nothing and pretty soon they'd forget why they'd started arguing in the first place. But he also felt guilty, because look what he'd made them do. He knew it would end with a door being slammed. He scrunched down lower and lower in his chair with the words whizzing back and forth over his head, and finally there was the bang of the door – his mother this time – and the wind that came with it. There was always a wind when the door got slammed, a small puff – whuff! – right in his ears.

"Never mind, old buddy," said his father. "Women always get hot under the collar. She'll cool down. Let's have some ice cream." So that's what they did, they had Raspberry Ripple in the cereal bowls with the blue and red birds on them that were handmade in Mexico so you shouldn't put them in the dishwasher, and Jimmy ate his all up to show his father that everything was okay.

Women, and what went on under their collars. Hotness and coldness, coming and going in the strange musky flowery variable-weather country inside their clothes — mysterious, important, uncontrollable. That was his father's take on things. But men's body temperatures were never dealt with; they were never even mentioned, not when he was little, except when his dad said, "Chill out." Why weren't they? Why nothing about the hot collars of men? Those smooth, sharp-edged collars with their dark, sulphurous, bristling undersides. He could have used a few theories on that.

The next day his father took him to a haircut place where there was a picture of a pretty girl in the window with pouty lips and a black T-shirt pulled down off one shoulder, glaring out through smudgy charcoal eyes with a mean stare and her hair standing up stiff like quills. Inside, there was hair all over the tiled floor, in clumps and wisps; they were sweeping it up with a push broom. First Jimmy had a black cape put on him, only it was more like a bib, and Jimmy didn't want that, because it was babyish. The haircut man laughed and said it wasn't a bib, because who ever heard of a baby with a black bib on? So it was okay; and then Jimmy got a short all-over cut to even out the ragged places, which maybe was what he'd wanted in the first place — shorter hair. Then he had stuff out of a jar put on to make it spiky. It smelled like orange peels. He smiled at himself in the mirror, then scowled, thrusting down his eyebrows.

"Tough guy," said the haircut man, nodding at Jimmy's father. "What a tiger." He whisked Jimmy's cut-off hair onto the floor with all the other hair, then removed the black cape with a flourish and lifted Jimmy down.

~   ~   ~

At the bonfire Jimmy was anxious about the animals, because they were being burned and surely that would hurt them. No, his father told him. The animals were dead. They were like steaks and sausages, only they still had their skins on.

And their heads, thought Jimmy. Steaks didn't have heads. The heads made a difference: he thought he could see the animals looking at him reproachfully out of their burning eyes. In some way all of this — the bonfire, the charred smell, but most of all the lit-up, suffering animals — was his fault, because he'd done nothing to rescue them. At the same time he found the bonfire a beautiful sight — luminous, like a Christmas tree, but a Christmas tree on fire. He hoped there might be an explosion, as on television.

Jimmy's father was beside him, holding on to his hand. "Lift me up," said Jimmy. His father assumed he wanted to be comforted, which he did, and picked him up and hugged him. But also Jimmy wanted to see better.

"This is where it ends up," said Jimmy's father, not to Jimmy but to a man standing with them. "Once things get going." Jimmy's father sounded angry; so did the man when he answered.

"They say it was brought in on purpose."

"I wouldn't be surprised," said Jimmy's father.

"Can I have one of the cow horns?" said Jimmy. He didn't see why they should be wasted. He wanted to ask for two but that might be pushing it.

"No," said his father. "Not this time, old buddy." He patted Jimmy's leg.

"Drive up the prices," said the man. "Make a killing on their own stuff, that way."

"It's a killing all right," said Jimmy's father in a disgusted tone. "But it could've been just a nutbar. Some cult thing, you never know."

"Why not?" said Jimmy. Nobody else wanted the horns. But this time his father ignored him.

"The question is, how did they do it?" he said. "I thought our people had us sealed up tight as a drum."

"I thought they did too. We fork out enough. What were the guys doing? They're not paid to sleep."

"It could've been bribery," said Jimmy's father. "They'll check out the bank transfers, though you'd have to be pretty dumb to stick that kind of money into a bank. Anyway, heads will roll."

"Fine-tooth comb, and I wouldn't want to be them," said the man. "Who comes in from outside?"

"Guys who repair things. Delivery vans."

"They should bring all that in-house."

"I hear that's the plan," said his father. "This bug is something new though. We've got the bioprint."

"Two can play at that game," said the man.

"Any number can play," said Jimmy's father.

"Why were the cows and sheep on fire?" Jimmy asked his father the next day. They were having breakfast, all three of them together, so it must have been a Sunday. That was the day when his mother and his father were both there at breakfast.

Jimmy's father was on his second cup of coffee. While he drank it, he was making notes on a page covered with numbers. "They had to be burned," he said, "to keep it from spreading." He didn't look up; he was fooling with his pocket calculator, jotting with his pencil.

"What from spreading?"

"The disease."

"What's a disease?"

"A disease is like when you have a cough," said his mother.

"If I have a cough, will I be burned up?"

"Most likely," said his father, turning over the page.

Jimmy was frightened by this because he'd had a cough the week before. He might get another one at any moment: already there was something sticking in his throat. He could see his hair on fire, not just a strand or two on a saucer, but all of it, still attached to his head. He didn't want to be put in a heap with the cows and pigs. He began to cry.

"How many times do I have to tell you?" said his mother. "He's too young."

"Daddy's a monster once again," said Jimmy's father. "It was a joke, pal. You know — joke. Ha ha."

"He doesn't understand those kinds of jokes."

"Sure he does. Don't you, Jimmy?"

"Yes," said Jimmy, sniffling.

"Leave Daddy alone," said his mother. "Daddy is thinking. That's what they pay him for. He doesn't have time for you right now."

His father threw down the pencil. "Cripes, can't you give it a rest?"

His mother stuck her cigarette into her half-empty coffee cup. "Come on, Jimmy, let's go for a walk." She hauled Jimmy up by one wrist, closed the back door with exaggerated care behind them. She didn't even put their coats on. No coats, no hats. She was in her dressing gown and slippers.

The sky was grey, the wind chilly; she walked head down, her hair blowing. Around the house they went, over the soggy lawn at a double-quick pace, hand in hand. Jimmy felt he was being dragged through deep water by something with an iron claw. He felt buffeted, as if everything was about to be wrenched apart and whirled away. At the same time he felt exhilarated. He watched his mother's slippers: already they were stained with damp earth. He'd get in big trouble if he did that to his own slippers.

They slowed down, then stopped. Then his mother was talking to him in the quiet, nice-lady TV-teacher voice that meant she was furious. A disease, she said, was invisible, because it was so small. It could fly through the air or hide in the water, or on little boys' dirty fingers, which was why you shouldn't stick your fingers up your nose and then put them into your mouth, and why you should always wash your hands after you went to the bathroom, and why you shouldn't wipe . . .

"I know," said Jimmy. "Can I go inside? I'm cold."

His mother acted as if she hadn't heard him. A disease, she continued in that calm, stretched voice, a disease got into you and changed things inside you. It rearranged you, cell by cell, and that made the cells sick. And since you were all made up of tiny cells, working together to make sure you stayed alive, and if enough of the cells got sick, then you . . .

"I could get a cough," said Jimmy. "I could get a cough, right now!" He made a coughing sound.

"Oh, never mind," said his mother. She often tried to explain things to him; then she got discouraged. These were the worst moments, for both of them. He resisted her, he pretended he didn't understand even when he did, he acted stupid, but he didn't want her to give up on him. He wanted her to be brave, to try her best with him, to hammer away at the wall he'd put up against her, to keep on going.

"I want to hear about the tiny cells," he said, whining as much as he dared. "I want to!"

"Not today," she said. "Let's just go in."

OrganInc Farms

~

Jimmy's father worked for OrganInc Farms. He was a genographer, one of the best in the field. He'd done some of the key studies on mapping the proteonome when he was still a post-grad, and then he'd helped engineer the Methuselah Mouse as part of Operation Immortality. After that, at OrganInc Farms, he'd been one of the foremost architects of the pigoon project, along with a team of transplant experts and the microbiologists who were splicing against infections. *Pigoon* was only a nickname: the official name was *sus multiorganifer*. But pigoon was what everyone said. Sometimes they said Organ-Oink Farms, but not as often. It wasn't really a farm anyway, not like the farms in pictures.

The goal of the pigoon project was to grow an assortment of foolproof human-tissue organs in a transgenic knockout pig host – organs that would transplant smoothly and avoid rejection, but would also be able to fend off attacks by opportunistic microbes and viruses, of which there were more strains every year. A rapid-maturity gene was spliced in so the pigoon kidneys and livers and hearts would be ready sooner, and now they were perfecting a pigoon that could grow five or six kidneys at a time. Such a host animal could be reaped of its extra kidneys; then, rather than being destroyed, it could keep on living and grow more organs, much as a lobster could grow another claw to replace a missing one. That would be less wasteful, as it took a lot of food and care to grow a pigoon. A great deal of investment money had gone into OrganInc Farms.

All of this was explained to Jimmy when he was old enough.

Old enough, Snowman thinks as he scratches himself, around but not on top of the insect bites. Such a dumb concept. Old enough for what? To drink, to fuck, to know better? What fathead was in charge of making those decisions? For example, Snowman himself isn't old enough for this, this – what can it be called? This situation. He'll never be old enough, no sane human being could ever . . .

Each one of us must tread the path laid out before him, or her, says the voice in his head, a man's this time, the style bogus guru, *and each path is unique. It is not the nature of the path itself that should concern the seeker, but the grace and strength and patience with which each and every one of us follows the sometimes challenging* . . .

"Stuff it," says Snowman. Some cheap do-it-yourself enlightenment handbook, Nirvana for halfwits. Though he has the nagging feeling that he may well have written this gem himself.

In happier days, naturally. Oh, so much happier.

The pigoon organs could be customized, using cells from individual human donors, and the organs were frozen until needed. It was much cheaper than getting yourself cloned for spare parts – a few wrinkles left to be ironed out there, as Jimmy's dad used to say – or keeping a for-harvest child or two stashed away in some illegal baby orchard. In the OrganInc brochures and promotional materials, glossy and discreetly worded, stress was laid on the efficacy and comparative health benefits of the pigoon procedure. Also, to set the queasy at ease, it was claimed that none of the defunct pigoons ended up as bacon and sausages: no one would want to eat an animal whose cells might be identical with at least some of their own.

Still, as time went on and the coastal aquifers turned salty and the northern permafrost melted and the vast tundra bubbled with methane, and the drought in the midcontinental plains regions went on and on, and the Asian steppes turned to sand dunes, and meat became harder to come by, some people had their doubts. Within OrganInc Farms itself it was noticeable how often back bacon and ham sandwiches and pork pies turned up on the staff café menu. André's Bistro was the official name of the café, but the regulars called it Grunts. When Jimmy had lunch there with his father, as he did when his mother was feeling harried, the men and women at nearby tables would make jokes in bad taste.

"Pigoon pie again," they would say. "Pigoon pancakes, pigoon popcorn. Come on, Jimmy, eat up!" This would upset Jimmy; he was confused about who should be allowed to eat what. He didn't want to eat a pigoon, because he thought of the pigoons as creatures much like himself. Neither he nor they had a lot of say in what was going on.

"Don't pay any attention to them, sweetheart," said Ramona. "They're only teasing, you know?" Ramona was one of his dad's lab technicians. She often ate lunch with the two of them, him and his dad. She was young, younger than his father and even his mother; she looked something like the picture of the girl in the haircut man's window, she had the same sort of puffed-out mouth, and big eyes like that, big and smudgy. But she smiled a lot, and she didn't have her hair in quills. Her hair was soft and dark. Jimmy's mother's hair was what she herself called *dirty blonde*. ("Not dirty enough," said his father. "Hey! Joke. Joke. Don't kill me!")

Ramona would always have a salad. "How's Sharon doing?" she would say to Jimmy's father, looking at him with her eyes wide and solemn. Sharon was Jimmy's mother.

"Not so hot," Jimmy's father would say.

"Oh, that's too bad."

"It's a problem. I'm getting worried."

Jimmy watched Ramona eat. She took very small bites, and managed to chew up the lettuce without crunching. The raw carrots too. That was amazing, as if she could liquefy those hard, crisp foods and suck them into herself, like an alien mosquito creature on DVD.

"Maybe she should, I don't know, see someone?" Ramona's eyebrows lifted in concern. She had mauve powder on her eyelids, a little too much; it made them crinkly. "They can do all sorts of things, there's so many new pills . . ." Ramona was supposed to be a tech genius but she talked like a shower-gel babe in an ad. She wasn't stupid, said Jimmy's dad, she just didn't want to put her neuron power into long sentences. There were a lot of people like that at OrganInc, and not all of them were women. It was because they were numbers people, not word people, said Jimmy's father. Jimmy already knew that he himself was not a numbers person.

"Don't think I haven't suggested it, I asked around, found the top guy, made the appointment, but she wouldn't go," said Jimmy's father, looking down at the table. "She's got her own ideas."

"It's such a shame, a waste. I mean, she was so smart!"

"Oh, she's still smart enough," said Jimmy's father. "She's got *smart* coming out of her ears."

"But she used to be so, you know . . ."

Ramona's fork would slide out of her fingers, and the two of them would stare at each other as if searching for the perfect adjective to describe what Jimmy's mother used to be. Then they'd notice Jimmy listening, and beam their attention down on him like extraterrestrial rays. Way too bright.

"So, Jimmy sweetheart, how's it going at school?"

"Eat up, old buddy, eat the crusts, put some hair on your chest!"

"Can I go look at the pigoons?" Jimmy would say.

The pigoons were much bigger and fatter than ordinary pigs, to leave room for all of the extra organs. They were kept in special buildings, heavily secured: the kidnapping of a pigoon and its finely honed genetic material by a rival outfit would have been a disaster. When Jimmy went in to visit the pigoons he had to put on a biosuit that was too big for him, and wear a face mask, and wash his hands first with disinfectant soap. He especially liked the small pigoons, twelve to a sow and lined up in a row, guzzling milk. Pigoonlets. They were cute. But the adults were slightly frightening, with their runny noses and tiny, white-lashed pink eyes. They glanced up at him as if they saw him, really saw him, and might have plans for him later.

"Pigoon, balloon, pigoon, balloon," he would chant to pacify them, hanging over the edge of the pen. Right after the pens had been washed out they didn't smell too bad. He was glad he didn't live in a pen, where he'd have to lie around in poop and pee. The pigoons had no toilets and did it anywhere; this caused him a vague sensation of shame. But he hadn't wet his bed for a long time, or he didn't think he had.

"Don't fall in," said his father. "They'll eat you up in a minute."

"No they won't," said Jimmy. Because I'm their friend, he thought. Because I sing to them. He wished he had a long stick, so he could poke them – not to hurt them, just to make them run around. They spent far too much time doing nothing.

When Jimmy was really little they'd lived in a Cape Cod–style frame house in one of the Modules – there were pictures of him, in a carry-cot on the porch, with dates and everything, stuck into a photo album at some time when his mother was still bothering – but now they lived in a large Georgian centre-plan with an indoor swimming pool and a small gym. The furniture in it was called *reproduction*. Jimmy was quite old before he realized what this word meant – that for each reproduction item, there was supposed to be an original somewhere. Or there had been once. Or something.

The house, the pool, the furniture – all belonged to the OrganInc Compound, where the top people lived. Increasingly, the middle-range execs and the junior scientists lived there too. Jimmy's father said it was better that way, because nobody had to commute to work from the Modules. Despite the sterile transport corridors and the high-speed bullet trains, there was always a risk when you went through the city.

Jimmy had never been to the city. He'd only seen it on TV — endless billboards and neon signs and stretches of buildings, tall and short; endless dingy-looking streets, countless vehicles of all kinds, some of them with clouds of smoke coming out the back; thousands of people, hurrying, cheering, rioting. There were other cities too, near and far; some had better neighbourhoods in them, said his father, almost like the Compounds, with high walls around the houses, but those didn't get on TV much.

Compound people didn't go to the cities unless they had to, and then never alone. They called the cities *the pleeblands*. Despite the fingerprint identity cards now carried by everyone, public security in the pleeblands was leaky: there were people cruising around in those places who could forge anything and who might be anybody, not to mention the loose change — the addicts, the muggers, the paupers, the crazies. So it was best for everyone at OrganInc Farms to live all in one place, with foolproof procedures.

Outside the OrganInc walls and gates and searchlights, things were unpredictable. Inside, they were the way it used to be when Jimmy's father was a kid, before things got so serious, or that's what Jimmy's father said. Jimmy's mother said it was all artificial, it was just a theme park and you could never bring the old ways back, but Jimmy's father said why knock it? You could walk around without fear, couldn't you? Go for a bike ride, sit at a sidewalk café, buy an ice-cream cone? Jimmy knew his father was right, because he himself had done all of these things.

Still, the CorpSeCorps men — the ones Jimmy's father called *our people* — these men had to be on constant alert. When there was so much at stake, there was no telling what the other side might resort to. The other side, or the other sides: it wasn't just one other side you had to watch out for. Other companies, other countries, various factions and plotters. There was too much hardware around, said Jimmy's father. Too much hardware, too much software, too many hostile bioforms, too many weapons of every kind. And too much envy and fanaticism and bad faith.

Long ago, in the days of knights and dragons, the kings and dukes had lived in castles, with high walls and drawbridges and slots on the ramparts so you could pour hot pitch on your enemies, said Jimmy's father, and the Compounds were the same idea. Castles were for keeping you and your buddies nice and safe inside, and for keeping everybody else outside.

"So are we the kings and dukes?" asked Jimmy.

"Oh, absolutely," said his father, laughing.

Lunch

~

At one time Jimmy's mother had worked for OrganInc Farms. That was how his mother had met his father: they'd both worked at the same Compound, on the same project. His mother was a microbiologist: it had been her job to study the proteins of the bioforms unhealthy to pigoons, and to modify their receptors in such a way that they could not bond with the receptors on pigoon cells, or else to develop drugs that would act as blockers.

"It's very simple," she said to Jimmy in one of her explaining moods. "The bad microbes and viruses want to get in through the cell doors and eat up the pigoons from the inside. Mummy's job was to make locks for the doors." On her computer screen she showed Jimmy pictures of the cells, pictures of the microbes, pictures of the microbes getting into the cells and infecting them and bursting them open, close-up pictures of the proteins, pictures of the drugs she had once tested. The pictures looked like the candy bins at the supermarket: a clear plastic bin of round candies, a clear plastic bin of jelly beans, a clear plastic bin of long licorice twizzles. The cells were like the clear plastic bins, with the lids you could lift up.

"Why aren't you making the locks for the doors any more?" said Jimmy.

"Because I wanted to stay home with you," she said, looking over the top of Jimmy's head and puffing on her cigarette.

"What about the pigoons?" said Jimmy, alarmed. "The microbes will get into them!" He didn't want his animal pals to burst open like the infected cells.

"Other people are in charge of that now," said his mother. She didn't seem to care at all. She let Jimmy play with the pictures on her computer, and once he learned how to run the programs, he could play war games with them — cells versus microbes. She said it was all right if he lost stuff off the computer, because all that material was out of date anyway. Though on some days — days when she appeared brisk and purposeful, and aimed, and steady — she would want to fool around on the computer herself. He liked it when she did that — when she seemed to be enjoying herself. She was friendly then, too. She was like a real mother and he was like a real child. But those moods of hers didn't last long.

When had she stopped working at the lab? When Jimmy started at the OrganInc School full-time, in the first grade. Which didn't make sense, because if she'd wanted to stay home with Jimmy, why had she started doing that when Jimmy stopped being at home? Jimmy could never figure out the reasons, and when he'd first heard this explanation he'd been too young to even think about them. All he'd known was that Dolores, the live-in from the Philippines, had been sent away, and he'd missed her a lot. She'd called him Jim-Jim and had smiled and laughed and cooked his egg just the way he liked it, and had sung songs and indulged him. But Dolores had to go, because now Jimmy's real mummy would be there all the time — this was held out to him like a treat — and nobody needed two mummies, did they?

Oh yes they did, thinks Snowman. Oh yes, they really did.

~   ~   ~

Snowman has a clear image of his mother – of Jimmy's mother – sitting at the kitchen table, still in her bathrobe when he came home from school for his lunch. She would have a cup of coffee in front of her, untouched; she would be looking out the window and smoking. The bathrobe was magenta, a colour that still makes him anxious whenever he sees it. As a rule there would be no lunch ready for him and he would have to make it himself, his mother's only participation being to issue directions in a flat voice. ("The milk's in the fridge. To the right. No, the *right*. Don't you know which is your right hand?") She sounded so tired; maybe she was tired of him. Or maybe she was sick.

"Are you infected?" he asked her one day.

"What do you mean, Jimmy?"

"Like the cells."

"Oh. I see. No, I'm not," she said. Then, after a moment, "Maybe I am." But when his face crumpled, she took it back.

More than anything, Jimmy had wanted to make her laugh – to make her happy, as he seemed to remember her being once. He would tell her funny things that had happened at school, or things he tried to make funny, or things he simply invented. ("Carrie Johnston went poo on the floor.") He would caper around the room, crossing his eyes and cheeping like a monkey, a trick that worked with several of the little girls in his class and almost all of the boys. He would put peanut butter on his nose and try to lick it off with his tongue. Most of the time these activities just irritated his mother: "That is not amusing, that is disgusting." "Stop it, Jimmy, you're giving me a headache." But then he might get a smile out of her, or more. He never knew what would work.

Once in a while there would be a real lunch waiting for him, a lunch that was so arranged and extravagant it frightened him, for what was the occasion? Place setting, paper napkin – *coloured* paper napkin, like parties – the sandwich peanut butter and jelly, his preferred combo; only it would be open-face and round, a peanut butter head with a jelly smile-face. His mother would be carefully dressed, her lipstick smile an echo of the jelly smile on the sandwich, and she would be all sparkling attention, for him and his silly stories, looking at him directly, her eyes bluer than blue. What she reminded him of at such times was a porcelain sink: clean, shining, hard.

He knew he was expected to appreciate all the effort she had put into this lunch, and so he too made an effort. "Oh boy, my favourite!" he would say, rolling his eyes, rubbing his stomach in a caricature of hunger, overdoing it. But he'd get what he wanted, because then she would laugh.

As he grew older and more devious, he found that on the days when he couldn't grab some approval, he could at least get a reaction. Anything was better than the flat voice, the blank eyes, the tired staring out of the window.

"Can I have a cat?" he would begin.

"No, Jimmy, you cannot have a cat. We've been over this before. Cats might carry diseases that would be bad for the pigoons."

"But you don't care." This in a sly voice.

A sigh, a puff of smoke. "Other people care."

"Can I have a dog then?"

"No. No dogs either. Can't you find something to do in your room?"

"Can I have a parrot?"

"No. Now stop it." She wouldn't really be listening.

"Can I have nothing?"

"No."

"Oh good," he would crow. "I can't have nothing! So I get to have something! What do I get to have?"

"Jimmy, sometimes you are a pain in the ass, do you know that?"

"Can I have a baby sister?"

"No!"

"A baby brother then? Please?"

"No means no! Didn't you hear me? I said no!"

"Why not?"

That was the key, that would do it. She might start crying and jump up and run out of the room, banging the door behind her, whuff. Or else she might start crying and hugging him. Or she might throw the coffee cup across the room and start yelling, "It's all shit, it's total shit, it's hopeless!" She might even slap him, and then cry and hug him. It could be any combination of those things.

Or it would just be the crying, with her head down on her arms. She would shake all over, gasp for breath, choking and sobbing. He wouldn't know what to do then. He loved her so much when he made her unhappy, or else when she made him unhappy: at these moments he scarcely knew which was which. He would pat her, standing well back as with strange dogs, stretching out his hand, saying, "I'm sorry, I'm sorry." And he was sorry, but there was more to it: he was also gloating, congratulating himself, because he'd managed to create such an effect.

He was frightened, as well. There was always that knife-edge: had he gone too far? And if he had, what came next?

3
~

Nooners

~

Noon is the worst, with its glare and humidity. At about eleven o'clock Snowman retreats back into the forest, out of sight of the sea altogether, because the evil rays bounce off the water and get at him even if he's protected from the sky, and then he reddens and blisters. What he could really use is a tube of heavy-duty sunblock, supposing he could ever find one.

In the first week, when he'd had more energy, he'd made himself a lean-to, using fallen branches and a roll of duct tape and a plastic tarp he'd found in the trunk of a smashed-up car. At that time he'd had a knife, but he lost it a week later, or was it two weeks? He must keep better track of such things as weeks. The knife was one of those pocket items with two blades, an awl, a tiny saw, a nail file, and a corkscrew. Also a little pair of scissors, which he'd used to cut his toenails and the duct tape as well. He regrets the loss of the scissors.

He was given a knife like that for his ninth birthday, by his father. His father was always giving him tools, trying to make him more practical. In his father's opinion Jimmy couldn't screw in a light bulb. *So who wants to screw in a light bulb?* says the voice in Snowman's head, a stand-up comic this time. *I'd rather do it in bed.*

"Shut up," says Snowman.

"Did you give him a dollar?" Oryx had asked him when he told her about the knife.

"No. Why?"

"You need to give money when someone gives you a knife. So the bad luck won't cut you. I wouldn't like it for you to be cut by the bad luck, Jimmy."

"Who told you that?"

"Oh, someone," said Oryx. *Someone* played a big part in her life.

"Someone who?" Jimmy hated him, this someone – faceless, eyeless, mocking, all hands and dick, now singular, now double, now a multitude – but Oryx had her mouth right next to his ear and was whispering, *Oh, oh, some, one,* and laughing at the same time, so how could he concentrate on his stupid old hate?

In the short period of the lean-to he'd slept on a fold-up cot he'd dragged from a bungalow half a mile away, a metal frame with a foam mattress on top of a grillwork of springs. The first night he'd been attacked by ants, and so he'd filled four tin cans with water and stuck the cot legs into them. That put a stop to the ants. But the build-up of hot, damp air under the tarp was too uncomfortable: at night, at ground level, with no breeze, the humidity felt like a hundred per cent: his breath fogged the plastic.

Also the rakunks were a nuisance, scuffling through the leaves and sniffing at his toes, nosing around him as if he were already garbage; and one morning he'd woken to find three pigoons gazing in at him through the plastic. One was a male; he thought he could see the gleaming point of a white tusk. Pigoons were supposed to be tusk-free, but maybe they were reverting to type now they'd gone feral, a fast-forward process considering their rapid-maturity genes. He'd shouted at them and waved his arms and they'd run off, but who could tell what they might do the next time they came around? Them, or the wolvogs: it wouldn't take them forever to figure out that he no longer had a spraygun. He'd thrown it away when he'd run out of virtual bullets for it. Dumb not to have swiped a recharger for it: a mistake, like setting up his sleeping quarters at ground level.

So he'd moved to the tree. No pigoons or wolvogs up there, and few rakunks: they preferred the undergrowth. He'd constructed a rough platform in the main branches out of scrap wood and duct tape. It's not a bad job: he's always been handier at putting things together than his father gave him credit for. At first he'd taken the foam mattress up there, but he had to toss it when it began to mildew, and to smell tantalizingly of tomato soup.

The plastic tarp on the lean-to was torn away during an unusually violent storm. The bed frame remains, however; he can still use it at noon. He's found that if he stretches out on it flat on his back, with his arms spread wide and his sheet off, like a saint arranged ready for frying, it's better than lying on the ground: at least he can get some air on all the surfaces of his body.

From nowhere, a word appears: *Mesozoic*. He can see the word, he can hear the word, but he can't reach the word. He can't attach anything to it. This is happening too much lately, this dissolution of meaning, the entries on his cherished wordlists drifting off into space.

"It's only the heat," he tells himself. "I'll be fine once it rains." He's sweating so hard he can almost hear it; trickles of sweat crawl down him, except that sometimes the trickles are insects. He appears to be attractive to beetles. Beetles, flies, bees, as if he's dead meat, or one of the nastier flowers.

The best thing about the noon hours is that at least he doesn't get hungry: even the thought of food makes him queasy, like chocolate cake in a steam bath. He wishes he could cool himself by hanging out his tongue.

Now the sun is at full glare; the zenith, it used to be called. Snowman lies splayed out on the grillwork of the bed, in the liquid shade, giving himself up to the heat. *Let's pretend this is a vacation!* A schoolteacher's voice this time, perky, condescending.

Ms. Stratton Call-Me-Sally, with the big butt. *Let's pretend this, let's pretend that.* They spent the first three years of school getting you to pretend stuff and then the rest of it marking you down if you did the same thing. *Let's pretend I'm here with you, big butt and all, getting ready to suck your brains right out your dick.*

Is there a faint stirring? He looks down at himself: no action. Sally Stratton vanishes, and just as well. He has to find more and better ways of occupying his time. *His time*, what a bankrupt idea, as if he's been given a box of time belonging to him alone, stuffed to the brim with hours and minutes that he can spend like money. Trouble is, the box has holes in it and the time is running out, no matter what he does with it.

He might whittle, for instance. Make a chess set, play games with himself. He used to play chess with Crake but they'd played by computer, not with actual chessmen. Crake won mostly. There must be another knife somewhere; if he sets his mind to it, goes foraging, scrapes around in the leftovers, he'd be sure to find one. Now that he's thought of it he's surprised he hasn't thought of it before.

He lets himself drift back to those after-school times with Crake. It was harmless enough at first. They might play Extinctathon, or one of the others. Three-Dimensional Waco, Barbarian Stomp, Kwiktime Osama. They all used parallel strategies: you had to see where you were headed before you got there, but also where the other guy was headed. Crake was good at those games because he was a master of the sideways leap. Jimmy could sometimes win at Kwiktime Osama though, as long as Crake played the Infidel side.

No hope of whittling that kind of game, however. It would have to be chess.

Or he could keep a diary. Set down his impressions. There must be lots of paper lying around, in unburned interior spaces that are still leak-free, and pens and pencils; he's seen them on his scavenging forays but he's never bothered taking any. He could emulate the captains of ships, in olden times – the ship going down in a storm, the captain in his cabin, doomed but intrepid, filling in the logbook. There were movies like that. Or castaways on desert islands, keeping their journals day by tedious day. Lists of supplies, notations on the weather, small actions performed — the sewing on of a button, the devouring of a clam.

He too is a castaway of sorts. He could make lists. It could give his life some structure.

But even a castaway assumes a future reader, someone who'll come along later and find his bones and his ledger, and learn his fate. Snowman can make no such assumptions: he'll have no future reader, because the Crakers can't read. Any reader he can possibly imagine is in the past.

A caterpillar is letting itself down on a thread, twirling slowly like a rope artist, spiralling towards his chest. It's a luscious, unreal green, like a gumdrop, and covered with tiny bright hairs. Watching it, he feels a sudden, inexplicable surge of tenderness and joy. Unique, he thinks. There will never be another caterpillar just like this one. There will never be another such moment of time, another such conjunction.

These things sneak up on him for no reason, these flashes of irrational happiness. It's probably a vitamin deficiency.

The caterpillar pauses, feeling around in the air with its blunt head. Its huge opaque eyes look like the front end of a riot-gear helmet. Maybe it's smelling him, picking up on his chemical aura. "We are not here to play, to dream, to drift," he says to it. "We have hard work to do, and loads to lift."

Now, what atrophying neural cistern in his brain did that come from? The Life Skills class, in junior high. The teacher had been a shambling neo-con reject from the heady days of the legendary dot.com bubble, back in prehistory. He'd had a stringy ponytail stuck to the back of his balding head, and a faux-leather jacket; he'd worn a gold stud in his bumpy, porous old nose, and had pushed self-reliance and individualism and risk-taking in a hopeless tone, as if even he no longer believed in them. Once in a while he'd come out with some hoary maxim, served up with a wry irony that did nothing to reduce the boredom quotient; or else he'd say, "I coulda been a contender," then glare meaningfully at the class as if there was some deeper-than-deep point they were all supposed to get.

Double-entry on-screen bookkeeping, banking by fingertip, using a microwave without nuking your egg, filling out housing applications for this or that Module and job applications for this or that Compound, family heredity research, negotiating your own marriage-and-divorce contracts, wise genetic match-mating, the proper use of condoms to avoid sexually transmitted bioforms: those had been the Life Skills. None of the kids had paid much attention. They either knew it already or didn't want to. They'd treated the class as a rest hour. *We are not here to play, to dream, to drift. We are here to practise Life Skills.*

"Whatever," says Snowman.

Or, instead of chess or a journal, he could focus on his living conditions. There's room for improvement in that department, a lot of room. More food sources, for one thing. Why didn't he ever bone up on roots and berries and pointed-stick traps for skewering small game, and how to eat snakes? Why had he wasted his time?

Oh honey, don't beat yourself up! breathes a female voice, regretfully, in his ear.

If only he could find a cave, a nice cave with a high ceiling and good ventilation and maybe some running water, he'd be better off. True, there's a stream with fresh water a quarter of a mile away; at one place it widens into a pool. Initially he'd gone there to cool off, but the Crakers might be splashing around in it or resting on the banks, and the kids would pester him to go swimming, and he didn't like being seen by them without his sheet. Compared to them he is just too weird; they make him feel deformed. If not people, there might well be animals: wolvogs, pigoons, bobkittens. Watering holes attract carnivores. They lie in wait. They slaver. They pounce. Not very cozy.

The clouds are building, the sky darkening. He can't see much through the trees but he senses the change in light. He slides off into half-sleep and dreams of Oryx, floating on her back in a swimming pool, wearing an outfit that appears to be made of delicate white tissue-paper petals. They spread out around her, expanding and contracting like the valves of a jellyfish. The pool is painted a vibrant pink. She smiles up at him and moves her arms gently to keep afloat, and he knows they are both in great danger. Then there's a hollow booming sound, like the door of a great vault shutting.

Downpour

~

He awakes to thunder and a sudden wind: the afternoon storm is upon him. He scrambles to his feet, grabs his sheet. Those howlers can come on very fast, and a metal bed frame in a thunderstorm is no place to be. He's built himself an island of car tires back in the woods; it's simply a matter of crouching on them, keeping their insulation between himself and the ground until the storm is over. Sometimes there are hailstones as big as golf balls, but the forest canopy slows their fall.

He reaches the pile of tires just as the storm breaks. Today it's only rain, the usual deluge, so heavy the impact turns the air to mist. Water sluices down onto him as the lightning sizzles. Branches thrash around overhead, rivulets amble along the ground. Already it's cooling down; the scent of freshly washed leaves and wet earth fills the air.

Once the rain has slowed to a drizzle and the rumbles of thunder have receded, he slogs back to his cement-slab cache to collect the empty beer bottles. Then he makes his way to a jagged concrete overhang that was once part of a bridge. Beneath it there's a triangular orange sign with the black silhouette of a man shovelling. Men at Work, that used to mean. Strange to think of the endless labour, the digging, the hammering, the carving, the lifting, the drilling, day by day, year by year, century by century; and now the endless crumbling that must be going on everywhere. Sandcastles in the wind.

Runoff is pouring through a hole in the side of the concrete. He stands under it with his mouth open, gulping water full of grit and twigs and other things he doesn't want to think about — the water must have found a channel through derelict houses and pungent cellars and clotted-up ditches and who knows what else. Then he rinses himself off, wrings out his sheet. He doesn't get himself very clean this way, but at least he can shed the surface layer of grime and scum. It would be useful to have a bar of soap: he keeps forgetting to pick one up during his pilfering excursions.

Lastly he fills up the beer bottles. He should get himself a better vessel, a Thermos or a pail — something that would hold more. Also the bottles are awkward: they're slippery and hard to position. He keeps imagining he can still smell beer inside them, though it's only wishful thinking. *Let's pretend this is beer.*

He shouldn't have brought that up. He shouldn't torture himself. He shouldn't dangle impossibilities in front of himself, as if he were some caged, wired-up lab animal, trapped into performing futile and perverse experiments on his own brain.

Get me out! he hears himself thinking. But he isn't locked up, he's not in prison. What could be more *out* than where he is?

"I didn't do it on purpose," he says, in the snivelling child's voice he reverts to in this mood. "Things happened, I had no idea, it was out of my control! What could I have done? Just someone, anyone, listen to me please!"

What a bad performance. Even he isn't convinced by it. But now he's weeping again.

It is important, says the book in his head, *to ignore minor irritants, to avoid pointless repinings, and to turn one's mental energies to immediate realities and to the tasks at hand.* He must have read that somewhere. Surely his own mind would never have come up with *pointless repinings*, not all by itself.

He wipes his face on a corner of the sheet. "Pointless repinings," he says out loud. As often, he feels he has a listener: someone unseen, hidden behind the screen of leaves, watching him slyly.

4
~

Rakunk

~

He does have a listener: it's a rakunk, a young one. He can see it now, its bright eyes peering out at him from under a bush.

"Here girl, here girl," he says to it coaxingly. It backs away into the underbrush. If he worked at it, if he really tried, he could probably tame one of those, and then he'd have someone to talk to. Someone to talk to was nice, Oryx used to tell him. "You should try it sometime, Jimmy," she'd say, kissing him on the ear.

"But I talk to you," he'd protest.

Another kiss. "Do you?"

When Jimmy was ten he'd been given a pet rakunk, by his father.

What did his father look like? Snowman can't get a fix on it. Jimmy's mother persists as a clear image, full colour, with a glossy white paper frame around her like a Polaroid, but he can recall his father only in details: the Adam's apple going up and down when he swallowed, the ears backlit against the kitchen window, the left hand lying on the table, cut off by the shirt cuff. His father is a sort of pastiche. Maybe Jimmy could never get far enough away from him to see all the parts at once.

The occasion for the gift of the rakunk must have been his birthday. He's repressed his birthdays: they weren't a matter for general celebration, not after Dolores the live-in Philippina left. When she was there, she'd always remember his birthday; she'd make a cake, or maybe she'd buy one, but anyway there it would be, a genuine cake, with icing and candles — isn't that true? He clutches on to the reality of those cakes; he closes his eyes, conjures them up, hovering all in a row, their candles alight, giving off their sweet, comforting scent of vanilla, like Dolores herself.

His mother on the other hand could never seem to recall how old Jimmy was or what day he was born. He'd have to remind her, at breakfast; then she'd snap out of her trance and buy him some mortifying present — pyjamas for little kids with kangaroos or bears on them, a disk nobody under forty would ever listen to, underwear ornamented with whales — and tape it up in tissue paper and dump it on him at the dinner table, smiling her increasingly weird smile, as if someone had yelled *Smile!* and goosed her with a fork.

Then his father would put them all through an awkward excuse about why this really, really special and important date had somehow just slid out of his head, and ask Jimmy if everything was okay, and send him an e-birthday card — the OrganInc standard design with five winged pigoons doing a conga line and *Happy Birthday, Jimmy, May All Your Dreams Come True* — and come up with a gift for him the day after, a gift that would not be a gift but some tool or intelligence-enhancing game or other hidden demand that he measure up. But measure up to what? There was never any standard; or there was one, but it was so cloudy and immense that nobody could see it, especially not Jimmy. Nothing he could achieve would ever be the right idea, or enough. By OrganInc's math-and-chem-and-applied-bio yardstick he must have seemed dull normal: maybe that was why his father stopped telling him he could do much better if he'd only try, and switched to doling out secretly disappointed praise, as if Jimmy had a brain injury.

So Snowman has forgotten everything else about Jimmy's tenth birthday except the rakunk, brought home by his father in a carry-cage. It was a tiny one, smallest of the litter born from the second generation of rakunks, the offspring of the first pair that had been spliced. The rest of the litter had been snapped up immediately. Jimmy's father made out that he'd had to spend a great deal of his time and throw his weight around and pull a lot of strings to get hold of this one, but all the effort had been worth it for this really, really special day, which had just happened as usual to fall on the day before.

The rakunks had begun as an after-hours hobby on the part of one of the OrganInc biolab hotshots. There'd been a lot of fooling around in those days: create-an-animal was so much fun, said the guys doing it; it made you feel like God. A number of the experiments were destroyed because they were too dangerous to have around – who needed a cane toad with a prehensile tail like a chameleon's that might climb in through the bathroom window and blind you while you were brushing your teeth? Then there was the snat, an unfortunate blend of snake and rat: they'd had to get rid of those. But the rakunks caught on as pets, inside OrganInc. They hadn't come in from the outside world – the world outside the Compound – so they had no foreign microbes and were safe for the pigoons. In addition to which they were cute.

The little rakunk let Jimmy pick it up. It was black and white – black mask, white stripe down its back, black and white rings around its fluffy tail. It licked Jimmy's fingers, and he fell in love with it.

"No smell to it, not like a skunk," said Jimmy's father. "It's a clean animal, with a nice disposition. Placid. Racoons never made good pets once they were grown up, they got crabby, they'd tear your house to pieces. This thing is supposed to be calmer. We'll see how the little guy does. Right, Jimmy?"

Jimmy's father had been apologetic towards him lately, as if he'd punished Jimmy for something Jimmy hadn't done and was sorry about it. He was saying *Right, Jimmy?* a bit too much.

Jimmy didn't like that – he didn't like being the one handing out the good marks. There were a few other moves of his father's he could do without as well – the sucker punches, the ruffling of the hair, the way of pronouncing the word *son*, in a slightly deeper voice. This hearty way of talking was getting worse, as if his father were auditioning for the role of Dad, but without much hope. Jimmy had done enough faking himself so he could spot it in others, most of the time. He stroked the little rakunk and didn't answer.

"Who's going to feed it and empty the litter box?" said Jimmy's mother. "Because it won't be me." She didn't say this angrily, but in a detached, matter-of-fact voice, as if she was a bystander, someone on the sidelines; as if Jimmy and the chore of taking care of him, and his unsatisfactory father, and the scufflings between her and him, and the increasingly heavy baggage of all their lives, had nothing to do with her. She didn't seem to get angry any more, she didn't go charging out of the house in her slippers. She had become slowed-down and deliberate.

"Jimmy hasn't asked you to. He'll do it himself. Right, Jimmy?" said his father.

"What are you going to call it?" said his mother. She didn't really want to know, she was getting at Jimmy in some way. She didn't like it when he warmed up to anything his father gave him. "Bandit, I suppose."

That was exactly the name Jimmy had been thinking of, because of the black mask. "No," he said. "That's boring. I'm calling him Killer."

"Good choice, son," said his father.

"Well, if Killer wets on the floor, be sure you clean it up," said his mother.

Jimmy took Killer up to his room, where it made a nest in his pillow. It did have a faint smell, strange but not unpleasant, leathery and sharp, like a bar of designer soap for men. He slept with his arm crooked around it, his nose next to its own small nose.

~   ~   ~

It must have been a month or two after he got the rakunk that Jimmy's father changed jobs. He was headhunted by NooSkins and hired at the second-in-command level — the Vice level, Jimmy's mother called it. Ramona the lab tech from OrganInc made the move with him; she was part of the deal because she was an invaluable asset, said Jimmy's father; she was his right-hand man. ("Joke," he would say to Jimmy, to show that he knew Ramona wasn't really a man. But Jimmy knew that anyway.) Jimmy was more or less glad he might still be seeing Ramona at lunch — at least she was someone familiar — even though his lunches with his father had become few in number and far between.

NooSkins was a subsidiary of HelthWyzer, and so they moved into the HelthWyzer Compound. Their house this time was in the style of the Italian Renaissance, with an arched portico and a lot of glazed earth-tone tiles, and the indoor pool was bigger. Jimmy's mother called it "this barn." She complained about the tight security at the HelthWyzer gates — the guards were ruder, they were suspicious of everyone, they liked to strip search people, women especially. They got a kick out of it, she said.

Jimmy's father said she was making a big deal about nothing. Anyway, he said, there'd been an incident only a few weeks before they'd moved in — some fanatic, a woman, with a hostile bioform concealed in a hairspray bottle. Some vicious Ebola or Marburg splice, one of the fortified hemorrhagics. She'd nuked a guard who'd unwisely had his face mask off, contrary to orders but because of the heat. The woman had been spraygunned at once and neutralized in a vat of bleach, and the poor guard had been whisked into HotBioform and stuck into an isolation room, where he'd dissolved into a puddle of goo. No greater damage done, but naturally the guards were jumpy.

Jimmy's mother said that didn't change the fact that she felt like a prisoner. Jimmy's father said she didn't understand the reality of the situation. Didn't she want to be safe, didn't she want her son to be safe?

"So it's for my own good?" she said. She was cutting a piece of French toast into even-sided cubes, taking her time.

"For *our* own good. For us."

"Well, I happen to disagree."

"No news there," said Jimmy's father.

According to Jimmy's mother their phones and e-mail were bugged, and the sturdy, laconic HelthWyzer housecleaners that came twice a week – always in pairs – were spies. Jimmy's father said she was getting paranoid, and anyway they had nothing to hide, so why worry about it?

The HelthWyzer Compound was not only newer than the OrganInc layout, it was bigger. It had two shopping malls instead of one, a better hospital, three dance clubs, even its own golf course. Jimmy went to the HelthWyzer Public School, where at first he didn't know anyone. Despite his initial loneliness, that wasn't too bad. Actually it was good, because he could recycle his old routines and jokes: the kids at OrganInc had become used to his antics. He'd moved on from the chimpanzee act and was into fake vomiting and choking to death – both popular – and a thing where he drew a bare-naked girl on his stomach with her crotch right where his navel was, and made her wiggle.

He no longer came home for lunch. He got picked up by the school's combo ethanol-solarvan in the morning and returned by it at night. There was a bright and cheerful school cafeteria with balanced meals, ethnic choices – perogies, felafels – and a kosher option, and soy products for the vegetarians. Jimmy was so pleased to be able to eat lunch with neither one of his parents present that he felt light-headed. He even put on some weight, and stopped being the skinniest kid in class. If there was any lunchtime left over and nothing else going on, he could go to the library and watch old instructional CD-ROMs. Alex the parrot was his favourite, from *Classics in Animal Behaviour Studies*. He liked the part where Alex invented a new word – *cork-nut*, for almond – and, best of all, the part where Alex got fed up with the blue-triangle and yellow-square exercise and said, *I'm going away now. No, Alex, you come back here! Which is the blue triangle – no, the blue triangle?* But Alex was out the door. Five stars for Alex.

One day Jimmy was allowed to bring Killer to school, where she — it was now officially a she — made a big hit. "Oh Jimmy, you are so lucky," said Wakulla Price, the first girl he'd ever had a crush on. She stroked Killer's fur, brown hand, pink nails, and Jimmy felt shivery, as if her fingers were running over his own body.

Jimmy's father spent more and more time at his work, but talked about it less and less. There were pigoons at NooSkins, just as at OrganInc Farms, but these were smaller and were being used to develop skin-related biotechnologies. The main idea was to find a method of replacing the older epidermis with a fresh one, not a laser-thinned or dermabraded short-term resurfacing but a genuine start-over skin that would be wrinkle- and blemish-free. For that, it would be useful to grow a young, plump skin cell that would eat up the worn cells in the skins of those on whom it was planted and replace them with replicas of itself, like algae growing on a pond.

The rewards in the case of success would be enormous, Jimmy's father explained, doing the straight-talking man-to-man act he had recently adopted with Jimmy. What well-to-do and once-young, once-beautiful woman or man, cranked up on hormonal supplements and shot full of vitamins but hampered by the unforgiving mirror, wouldn't sell their house, their gated retirement villa, their kids, and their soul to get a second kick at the sexual can? NooSkins for Olds, said the snappy logo. Not that a totally effective method had been found yet: the dozen or so ravaged hopefuls who had volunteered themselves as subjects, paying no fees but signing away their rights to sue, had come out looking like the Mould Creature from Outer Space — uneven in tone, greenish brown, and peeling in ragged strips.

But there were other projects at NooSkins as well. One evening Jimmy's father came home late and a little drunk, with a bottle of champagne. Jimmy took one look at this and got himself out of the way. He'd hidden a tiny mike behind the picture of the seashore in the living room and another one behind the kitchen wall clock − the one that gave a different irritating bird call for every hour − so he could listen in on stuff that was none of his business. He'd put the mikes together in the Neotechnology class at school; he'd used standard components out of the mini-mikes for wireless computer dictating, which, with a few adjustments, worked fine for eavesdropping.

"What's that for?" said the voice of Jimmy's mother. She meant the champagne.

"We've done it," said Jimmy's father's voice. "I think a little celebration is in order." A scuffle: maybe he'd tried to kiss her.

"Done what?"

Pop of the champagne cork. "Come on, it won't bite you." A pause: he must be pouring it out. Yes: the clink of glasses. "Here's to us."

"Done what? I need to know what I'm drinking to."

Another pause: Jimmy pictured his father swallowing, his Adam's apple going up and down, bobbity-bobble. "It's the neuro-regeneration project. We now have genuine human neo-cortex tissue growing in a pigoon. Finally, after all those duds! Think of the possibilities, for stroke victims, and . . ."

"That's all we need," said Jimmy's mother. "More people with the brains of pigs. Don't we have enough of those already?"

"Can't you be positive, just for once? All this negative stuff, *this is no good, that's no good,* nothing's ever good enough, according to you!"

"Positive about what? That you've thought up yet another way to rip off a bunch of desperate people?" said Jimmy's mother in that new slow, anger-free voice.

"God, you're cynical!"

"No, you are. You and your smart partners. Your colleagues. It's wrong, the whole organization is wrong, it's a moral cesspool and you know it."

"We can give people hope. Hope isn't ripping off!"

"At NooSkins' prices it is. You hype your wares and take all their money and then they run out of cash, and it's no more treatments for them. They can rot as far as you and your pals are concerned. Don't you remember the way we used to talk, everything we wanted to do? Making life better for people — not just people with money. You used to be so . . . you had ideals, then."

"Sure," said Jimmy's father in a tired voice. "I've still got them. I just can't afford them."

A pause. Jimmy's mother must've been mulling that over. "Be that as it may," she said — a sign that she wasn't going to give in. "Be that as it may, there's research and there's research. What you're doing — this pig brain thing. You're interfering with the building blocks of life. It's immoral. It's . . . sacrilegious."

Bang, on the table. Not his hand. The bottle? "I don't believe I'm hearing this! Who've you been listening to? You're an educated person, you did this stuff yourself! It's just proteins, you know that! There's nothing sacred about cells and tissue, it's just . . ."

"I'm familiar with the theory."

"Anyway it's been paying for your room and board, it's been putting the food on your table. You're hardly in a position to take the high ground."

"I know," said Jimmy's mother's voice. "Believe me, that is one thing I really do know. Why can't you get a job doing something honest? Something basic."

"Like what and like where? You want me to dig ditches?"

"At least your conscience would be clean."

"No, *yours* would. You're the one with the neurotic guilt. Why don't you dig a few ditches yourself, at least it would get you off your butt. Then maybe you'd quit smoking — you're a one-woman emphysema factory, plus you're single-handedly supporting the tobacco companies. Think about that if you're so ethical. They're the folks who get six-year-olds hooked for life by passing out free samples."

"I know all that." A pause. "I smoke because I'm depressed. The tobacco companies depress me, *you* depress me, Jimmy depresses me, he's turning into a . . ."

"Take some pills if you're so fucking depressed!"

"There's no need for swearing."

"I think maybe there is!" Jimmy's father yelling wasn't a complete novelty, but combined with the swearing it got Jimmy's full attention. Maybe there would be action, broken glass. He felt afraid — that cold lump in his stomach was back again — but he also felt compelled to listen. If there was going to be a catastrophe, some final collapse, he needed to witness it.

Nothing happened though, there was just the sound of footsteps going out of the room. Which one of them? Whoever it was would now come upstairs and check to make sure Jimmy was asleep and hadn't heard. Then they could tick off that item on the Terrific Parenting checklist they both carted around inside their heads. It wasn't the bad stuff they did that made Jimmy so angry, it was the good stuff. The stuff that was supposed to be good, or good enough for him. The stuff they patted themselves on the backs for. They knew nothing about him, what he liked, what he hated, what he longed for. They thought he was only what they could see. A nice boy but a bit of a goof, a bit of a show-off. Not the brightest star in the universe, not a numbers person, but you couldn't have everything you wanted and at least he wasn't a total washout. At least he wasn't a drunk or an addict like a lot of boys his age, so touch wood. He'd actually heard his dad say that: *touch wood*, as if Jimmy was bound to fuck up, wander off the tracks, but he just hadn't got around to it yet. About the different, secret person living inside him they knew nothing at all.

He turned off his computer and unplugged the earphones and doused the lights and got into bed, quietly and also carefully, because Killer was in there already. She was down at the bottom, she liked it there; she'd taken to licking his feet to get the salt off. It was ticklish; head under the covers, he shook with silent laughter.

Hammer
~

Several years passed. They must have passed, thinks Snowman: he can't actually remember much about them except that his voice cracked and he began to sprout body hair. Not a big thrill at the time except that it would have been worse not to. He got some muscles too. He started having sexy dreams and suffering from lassitude. He thought about girls a lot in the abstract, as it were — girls without heads — and about Wakulla Price with her head on, though she wouldn't hang out with him. Did he have zits, was that it? He can't remember having any; though, as he recalls, the faces of his rivals were covered in them.

Cork-nut, he'd say to anyone who pissed him off. Anyone who wasn't a girl. No one but him and Alex the parrot knew exactly what cork-nut meant, so it was pretty demolishing. It became a fad, among the kids at the HelthWyzer Compound, so Jimmy was considered medium-cool. *Hey, cork-nut!*

His secret best friend was Killer. Pathetic, that the only person he could really talk to was a rakunk. He avoided his parents as much as possible. His dad was a cork-nut and his mother was a drone. He was no longer frightened by their negative electrical field, he simply found them tedious, or so he told himself.

At school, he enacted a major piece of treachery against them. He'd draw eyes on each of his index-finger knuckles and tuck his thumbs inside his fists. Then, by moving the thumbs up and down to show the mouths opening and closing, he could make these two hand-puppets argue together. His right hand was Evil Dad, his left hand was Righteous Mom. Evil Dad blustered and theorized and dished out pompous bullshit, Righteous Mom complained and accused. In Righteous Mom's cosmology, Evil Dad was the sole source of hemorrhoids, kleptomania, global conflict, bad breath, tectonic-plate fault lines, and clogged drains, as well as every migraine headache and menstrual cramp Righteous Mom had ever suffered. This lunchroom show of his was a hit; a crowd would collect, with requests. *Jimmy, Jimmy – do Evil Dad!* The other kids had lots of variations and routines to suggest, filched from the private lives of their own parental units. Some of them tried drawing eyes on their own knuckles, but they weren't as good at the dialogue.

Jimmy felt guilty sometimes, afterwards, when he'd gone too far. He shouldn't have had Righteous Mom weeping in the kitchen because her ovaries had burst; he shouldn't have done that sex scene with the Monday Special Fish Finger, 20% Real Fish – Evil Dad falling upon it and tearing it apart with lust because Righteous Mom was sulking inside an empty Twinkies package and wouldn't come out. Those skits were undignified, though that alone wouldn't have stopped him. They were also too close to an uncomfortable truth Jimmy didn't want to examine. But the other kids egged him on, and he couldn't resist the applause.

"Was that out of line, Killer?" he would ask. "Was that too vile?" *Vile* was a word he'd recently discovered: Righteous Mom was using it a lot these days.

Killer would lick his nose. She always forgave him.

One day Jimmy came home from school and there was a note on the kitchen table. It was from his mother. He knew as soon as he saw the writing on the outside – *For Jimmy*, underlined twice in black – what sort of note it would be.

Dear Jimmy, it said. *Blah blah blah, suffered with conscience long enough, blah blah, no longer participate in a lifestyle that is not only meaningless in itself but blah blah.* She knew that when Jimmy was old enough to consider the implications of *blah blah*, he would agree with her and understand. She would be in contact with him later, if there was any possibility. *Blah blah* search will be conducted, inevitably; thus necessary to go into hiding. A decision not taken without much soul-searching and thought and anguish, but *blah.* She would always love him very much.

Maybe she had loved Jimmy, thinks Snowman. In her own manner. Though he hadn't believed it at the time. Maybe, on the other hand, she hadn't loved him. She must have had some sort of positive emotion about him though. Wasn't there supposed to be a maternal bond?

P.S., she'd said. *I have taken Killer with me to liberate her, as I know she will be happier living a wild, free life in the forest.*

Jimmy hadn't believed that either. He was enraged by it. How dare she? Killer was his! And Killer was a tame animal, she'd be helpless on her own, she wouldn't know how to fend for herself, everything hungry would tear her into furry black and white pieces. But Jimmy's mother and her ilk must have been right, thinks Snowman, and Killer and the other liberated rakunks must have been able to cope just fine, or how else to account for the annoyingly large population of them now infesting this neck of the woods?

Jimmy had mourned for weeks. No, for months. Which one of them was he mourning the most? His mother, or an altered skunk?

His mother had left another note. Not a note – a wordless message. She'd trashed Jimmy's father's home computer, and not only the contents: she'd taken the hammer to it. Actually she'd employed just about every single tool in Jimmy's father's neatly arranged and seldom-used Mr. Home Handyman tool box, but the hammer seemed to have been her main weapon of choice. She'd done her own computer too, if anything more thoroughly. Thus neither Jimmy's father nor the CorpSeCorps men who were soon all over the place had any idea of what coded messages she might have been sending, what information she may or may not have downloaded and taken out with her.

As for how she'd got through the checkpoints and the gates, she'd said she was going for a root canal procedure, to a dentist in one of the Modules. She'd had the paperwork, all the necessary clearances, and the backstory was real: the root canal specialist at the HelthWyzer dental clinic had toppled over with a heart attack and his replacement hadn't arrived, so they were contracting out. She'd even made a genuine appointment with the Module dentist, who'd billed Jimmy's dad for the time when she hadn't shown up. (Jimmy's dad refused to pay, because it wasn't his missed appointment; he and the dentist had a shouting match about it later, over the phone.) She hadn't packed any luggage, she'd been smarter than that. She'd booked a CorpSeCorps man as protection in the taxi ride from the sealed bullet-train station through the short stretch of pleebland that had to be crossed before reaching the perimeter wall of the Module, which was the usual thing to do. No one questioned her, she was a familiar sight and she had the requisition and the pass and everything. No one at the Compound gate had looked inside her mouth, though there wouldn't have been much to see: nerve pain wouldn't have shown.

The CorpSeCorps man must have been in cahoots with her, or else he'd been done away with; in any case he didn't come back and he was never found. Or so it was said. That really stirred things up. It meant there had been others involved. But what others, and what were their goals? It was urgent that these matters be clarified, said the Corps guys who grilled Jimmy. Had Jimmy's mother ever said anything to him, the Corpsmen asked?

Like, what did they mean by *anything*? said Jimmy. There
were the conversations he'd overheard on his mini-mikes, but he
didn't want to talk about those. There were the things his mother
rambled on about sometimes, about how everything was being
ruined and would never be the same again, like the beach house
her family had owned when she was little, the one that got washed
away with the rest of the beaches and quite a few of the eastern
coastal cities when the sea-level rose so quickly, and then there was
that huge tidal wave, from the Canary Islands volcano. (They'd
taken it in school, in the Geolonomics unit. Jimmy had found the
video simulation pretty exciting.) And she used to snivel about her
grandfather's Florida grapefruit orchard that had dried up like a
giant raisin when the rains had stopped coming, the same year
Lake Okeechobee had shrunk to a reeking mud puddle and the
Everglades had burned for three weeks straight.

But everyone's parents moaned on about stuff like that.
*Remember when you could drive anywhere? Remember when every-
one lived in the pleeblands? Remember when you could fly anywhere
in the world, without fear? Remember hamburger chains, always real
beef, remember hot-dog stands? Remember before New York was
New New York? Remember when voting mattered?* It was all standard lunchtime hand-puppet stuff. *Oh it was all so great once.
Boohoo. Now I'm going into the Twinkies package. No sex tonight!*

His mother was just a mother, Jimmy told the CorpSeCorps
man. She did what mothers did. She smoked a lot.

"She belong to any, like, organizations? Any strange folk come
to the house? She spend a lot of time on the cellphone?"

"Anything you could help us out with, we'd appreciate it,
son," said the other Corpsman. It was the *son* that clinched
it. Jimmy said he didn't think so.

Jimmy's mother had left some new clothes for him, in the
sizes she said he would soon grow into. They were sucky, like
the clothes she always bought. Also they were too small. He put
them away in a drawer.

~   ~   ~

His father was rattled, you could tell; he was scared. His wife had broken every rule in the book, she must've had a whole other life and he'd had no idea. That sort of thing reflected badly on a man. He said he hadn't kept any crucial information on the home computer she'd wrecked, but of course he would have said that, and there was no way of proving otherwise. Then he'd been debriefed, elsewhere, for quite a long time. Maybe he was being tortured, as in old movies or on some of the nastier Web sites, with electrodes and truncheons and red-hot nails, and Jimmy worried about that and felt bad. Why hadn't he seen it all coming and headed it off, instead of playing at mean ventriloquism?

Two cast-iron CorpSeCorps women had stayed in the house while Jimmy's father was away, looking after Jimmy, or so it was called. A smiling one and a flat-faced one. They made a lot of phone calls on their ether cells; they went through the photo albums and Jimmy's mother's closets, and tried to get Jimmy to talk. *She looks really pretty. You think she had a boyfriend? Did she go to the pleeblands much?* Why would she go there, said Jimmy, and they said some people liked to. Why, said Jimmy again, and the flat-faced one said some people were twisted, and the smiling one laughed and blushed, and said you could get things out there you couldn't get in here. What sorts of things, Jimmy wanted to ask, but he didn't because the answer might entangle him in more questions, about what his mother liked or might want to get. He'd done all of his betrayal of her in the HelthWyzer High lunchroom, he wasn't going to do any more.

The two of them cooked terrible leathery omelettes in an attempt to throw Jimmy off guard by feeding him. After that didn't work, they microwaved frozen dinners and ordered in pizza. *So, your mother go to the mall a lot? Did she go dancing? I bet she did.* Jimmy wanted to slug them. If he'd been a girl he could have burst into tears and got them to feel sorry for him, and shut them up that way.

~   ~   ~

After Jimmy's dad came back from wherever he'd been taken, he'd had counselling. He looked like he needed it, his face was green and his eyes were red and puffy. Jimmy had counselling too, but it was a waste of time.

You must be unhappy that your mother's gone.

Yeah, right.

You mustn't blame yourself, son. It's not your fault she left.

How do you mean?

It's okay, you can express your emotions.

Which ones would you like me to express?

No need to be hostile, Jimmy, I know how you feel.

So, if you already know how I feel, why are you asking me, and so on.

Jimmy's dad told Jimmy that they two fellows would just have to forge ahead the best way they could. So they did forge ahead. They forged and they forged, they poured out their own orange juice in the morning and put the dishes in the dishwasher when they remembered, and after a few weeks of forging Jimmy's dad lost his greenish tint and started playing golf again.

Underneath you could tell he wasn't feeling too shabby, now that the worst was over. He began whistling while he shaved. He shaved more. After a decent interval Ramona moved in. Life took on a different pattern, which involved bouts of giggly, growly sex going on behind doors that were closed but not soundproof, while Jimmy turned his music up high and tried not to listen. He could have put a bug in their room, taken in the whole show, but he had a strong aversion to that. Truth to tell, he found it embarrassing. Once there was a difficult encounter in the upstairs hall, Jimmy's father in a bath towel, ears standing out from the sides of his head, jowls flushed with the energy of his latest erotic tussle, Jimmy red with shame and pretending not to notice. The two hormone-sodden love bunnies might have had the decency to do it in the garage, instead of rubbing Jimmy's nose in it all the time. They made him feel invisible. Not that he wanted to feel anything else.

How long had they been going at it? Snowman wonders now. Had the two of them been having it off behind the pigoon pens in their biosuits and germ-filtering face masks? He doesn't think so: his father was a nerd, not a shit. Of course you could be both: a nerdy shit, a shitty nerd. But his father (or so he believes) was too awkward and bad at lying to have become involved in full-fledged treachery and betrayal without Jimmy's mother noticing.

Though maybe she had noticed. Maybe that was why she'd fled, or part of the reason. You don't take a hammer – not to mention an electric screwdriver and a pipe wrench – to a guy's computer without being quite angry.

Not that she hadn't been angry in general: her anger had gone way beyond any one motive.

The more Snowman thinks about it, the more he's convinced that Ramona and his father had refrained. They'd waited till Jimmy's mother had buggered off in a splatter of pixels before toppling into each other's arms. Otherwise they wouldn't have done so much earnest, blameless gazing at each other in André's Bistro at OrganInc. If they'd been having a thing already they'd have been brusque and businesslike in public, they'd have avoided each other if anything; they'd have had quick and dirty trysts in grungy corners, weltering around in their own popped buttons and stuck zippers on the office carpet, chewing each other's ears in car parks. They wouldn't have bothered with those antiseptic lunches, with his father staring at the tabletop while Ramona liquefied the raw carrots. They wouldn't have salivated on each other over the greenery and pork pies while using young Jimmy as a human shield.

Not that Snowman passes judgment. He knows how these

things go, or used to go. He's a grown-up now, with much worse things on his conscience. So who is he to blame them?

(He blames them.)

Ramona sat Jimmy down and gazed at him with her big black-fringed smudgy sincere eyes, and told him that she knew this was very hard on him and it was a trauma for them all, it was hard on her too, though maybe he, you know, might not think so, and she was aware that she couldn't replace his real mother but she hoped, maybe they could be buddies? Jimmy said, *Sure, why not*, because apart from her connection with his father he liked her well enough and wanted to please her.

She did try. She laughed at his jokes, a little late sometimes — she was not a word person, he reminded himself — and some-times when Jimmy's father was away she microwaved dinner for just herself and Jimmy; lasagna and Caesar salad were her staples. Sometimes she would watch DVD movies with him, sitting beside him on the couch, making them a bowl of popcorn first, pouring melted butter substitute onto it, dipping into it with greasy fingers she'd lick during the scary parts while Jimmy tried not to look at her breasts. She asked him if there was anything he wanted to ask her about, like, you know. Her and his dad, and what had hap-pened to the marriage. He said there wasn't.

In secret, in the night, he yearned for Killer. Also — in some corner of himself he could not quite acknowledge — for his real, strange, insufficient, miserable mother. Where had she gone, what danger was she in? That she was in danger of some sort was a given. They'd be looking for her, he knew that, and if he were her he wouldn't want to be found.

But she'd said she would contact him, so why wasn't she doing it? After a while he did get a couple of postcards, with stamps from England, then Argentina. They were signed *Aunt Monica*, but he knew they were from her. *Hope you're well*, was all they said. She must have known they'd be read by about a hundred snoops before ever getting to Jimmy, and that was right, because along came the Corpsmen after each one, asking who Aunt Monica was. Jimmy said he didn't know. He didn't think his mother was in any of the countries the stamps were from, because she was way smarter than that. She must have got other people to mail them for her.

Didn't she trust him? Evidently not. He felt he'd disappointed her, he'd failed her in some crucial way. He'd never understood what was required of him. If only he could have one more chance to make her happy.

"I am not my childhood," Snowman says out loud. He hates these replays. He can't turn them off, he can't change the subject, he can't leave the room. What he needs is more inner discipline, or a mystic syllable he could repeat over and over to tune himself out. What were those things called? Mantras. They'd had that in grade school. Religion of the Week. *All right, class, now quiet as mice, that means you, Jimmy. Today we're going to pretend we live in India, and we're going to do a mantra. Won't that be fun? Now let's all choose a word, a different word, so we can each have our own special mantra.*

"Hang on to the words," he tells himself. The odd words, the old words, the rare ones. *Valance. Norn. Serendipity. Pibroch. Lubricious.* When they're gone out of his head, these words, they'll be gone, everywhere, forever. As if they had never been.

Crake
~

A few months before Jimmy's mother vanished, Crake appeared. The two things happened in the same year. What was the connection? There wasn't one, except that the two of them seemed to get on well together. Crake was among the scant handful of Jimmy's friends that his mother liked. Mostly she'd found his male pals juvenile, his female ones airheaded or sluttish. She'd never used those words but you could tell.

Crake though, Crake was different. More like an adult, she'd said; in fact, more adult than a lot of adults. You could have an objective conversation with him, a conversation in which events and hypotheses were followed through to their logical conclusions. Not that Jimmy ever witnessed the two of them having such a conversation, but they must have done or else she wouldn't have said that. When and how did these logical, adult conversations take place? He's often wondered.

"Your friend is intellectually honourable," Jimmy's mother would say. "He doesn't lie to himself." Then she'd gaze at Jimmy with that blue-eyed, wounded-by-him look he knew so well. If only *he* could be like that — intellectually honourable. Another baffling item on the cryptic report card his mother toted around in some mental pocket, the report card on which he was always just barely passing. *Jimmy would do better at intellectual honourableness if only he would try harder.* Plus, if he had any fucking clues about what the fuck it meant.

"I don't need supper," he'd tell her yet again. "I'll just grab a snack." If she wanted to do that wounded thing she could do it for the kitchen clock. He'd fixed it so the robin said *hoot* and the owl said *caw caw*. Let her be disappointed with them for a change.

He had his doubts about Crake's honourableness, intellectual or otherwise. He knew a bit more about Crake than his mother did.

When Jimmy's mother took off like that, after the rampage with the hammer, Crake didn't say much. He didn't seem surprised or shocked. All he said was that some people needed to change, and to change they needed to be elsewhere. He said a person could be in your life and then not in it any more. He said Jimmy should read up on the Stoics. That last part was mildly aggravating: Crake could be a little too instructive sometimes, and a little too free with the *should*s. But Jimmy appreciated his calmness and lack of nosiness.

Of course Crake wasn't Crake yet, at that time: his name was Glenn. Why did it have two n's instead of the usual spelling? "My dad liked music," was Crake's explanation, once Jimmy got around to asking him about it, which had taken a while. "He named me after a dead pianist, some boy genius with two n's."

"So did he make you take music lessons?"

"No," said Crake. "He never made me do much of anything."

"Then what was the point?

"Of what?"

"Of your name. The two n's."

"Jimmy, Jimmy," said Crake. "Not everything has a point."

Snowman has trouble thinking of Crake as Glenn, so thoroughly has Crake's later persona blotted out his earlier one. The

Crake side of him must have been there from the beginning, thinks Snowman: there was never any real Glenn, *Glenn* was only a disguise. So in Snowman's reruns of the story, Crake is never Glenn, and never *Glenn-alias-Crake* or *Crake/Glenn*, or *Glenn, later Crake*. He is always just Crake, pure and simple.

Anyway *Crake* saves time, thinks Snowman. Why hyphenate, why parenthesize, unless absolutely necessary?

Crake turned up at HelthWyzer High in September or October, one of those months that used to be called *autumn*. It was a bright warm sunny day, otherwise undistinguished. He was a transfer, the result of some headhunt involving a parental unit: these were frequent among the Compounds. Kids came and went, desks filled and emptied, friendship was always contingent.

Jimmy wasn't paying much attention when Crake was introduced to the class by Melons Riley, their Hoodroom and Ultratexts teacher. Her name wasn't Melons — that was a nickname used among the boys in the class — but Snowman can't remember her real name. She shouldn't have bent down so closely over his Read-A-Screen, her large round breasts almost touching his shoulder. She shouldn't have worn her NooSkins T-shirt tucked so tightly into her zipleg shorts: it was too distracting. So that when Melons announced that Jimmy would be showing their new classmate Glenn around the school, there was a pause while Jimmy scrambled to decipher what it was she'd just said.

"Jimmy, I made a request," said Melons.

"Sure, anything," said Jimmy, rolling his eyes and leering, but not taking it too far. There was some class laughter; even Ms. Riley gave him a remote, unwilling smile. He could usually get round her with his boyish-charm act. He liked to imagine that if he hadn't been a minor, and she his teacher and subject to abuse charges, she'd have been gnawing her way through his bedroom walls to sink her avid fingers into his youthful flesh.

Jimmy had been full of himself back then, thinks Snowman with indulgence and a little envy. He'd been unhappy too, of course. It went without saying, his unhappiness. He'd put a lot of energy into it.

When Jimmy got around to focusing on Crake, he wasn't too cheered. Crake was taller than Jimmy, about two inches; thinner too. Straight brown-black hair, tanned skin, green eyes, a half-smile, a cool gaze. His clothes were dark in tone, devoid of logos and visuals and written commentary – a no-name look. He was possibly older than the rest of them, or trying to act it. Jimmy wondered what kinds of sports he played. Not football, nothing too brawny. Not tall enough for basketball. He didn't strike Jimmy as a team player, or one who would stupidly court injury. Tennis, maybe. (Jimmy himself played tennis.)

At lunch hour Jimmy collected Crake and the two of them grabbed some food – Crake put down two giant soy-sausage dogs and a big slab of coconut-style layer cake, so maybe he was trying to bulk up – and then they trudged up and down the halls and in and out of the classrooms and labs, with Jimmy giving the running commentary. *Here's the gym, here's the library, those are the readers, you have to sign up for them before noon, in there's the girls' shower room, there's supposed to be a hole drilled through the wall but I've never found it. If you want to smoke dope don't use the can, they've got it bugged; there's a microlens for Security in that air vent, don't stare at it or they'll know you know.*

Crake looked at everything, said nothing. He volunteered no information about himself. The only comment he made was that the Chemlab was a dump.

Well stuff it, Jimmy thought. If he wants to be an asshole it's a free country. Millions before him have made the same life choice. He was annoyed with himself for jabbering and capering, while Crake gave him brief, indifferent glances, and that one-sided demi-smile. Nevertheless there was something about Crake. That kind of cool slouchiness always impressed Jimmy, coming from another guy: it was the sense of energies being held back, held in reserve for something more important than present company.

Jimmy found himself wishing to make a dent in Crake, get a reaction; it was one of his weaknesses, to care what other people thought of him. So after school he asked Crake if he'd like to go to one of the malls, hang out, see the sights, maybe there would be some girls there, and Crake said why not. There wasn't much else to do after school in the HelthWyzer Compound, or in any of the Compounds, not for kids their age, not in any sort of group way. It wasn't like the pleeblands. There, it was rumoured, the kids ran in packs, in hordes. They'd wait until some parent was away, then get right down to business – they'd swarm the place, waste themselves with loud music and toking and boozing, fuck everything including the family cat, trash the furniture, shoot up, overdose. Glamorous, thought Jimmy. But in the Compounds the lid was screwed down tight. Night patrols, curfews for growing minds, sniffer dogs after hard drugs. Once, they'd loosened up, let in a real band – The Pleebland Dirtballs, it had been – but there'd been a quasi-riot, so no repeats. No need to apologize to Crake, though. He was a Compound brat himself, he'd know the score.

Jimmy was hoping he might catch a glimpse of Wakulla Price, at the mall; he was still sort of in love with her, but after the I-value-you-as-my-friend speech she'd ruined him with, he'd tried one girl and then another, ending up – currently – with blonde LyndaLee. LyndaLee was on the rowing team and had muscular thighs and impressive pecs, and had smuggled him up to her bedroom on more than one occasion. She had a foul mouth and more experience than Jimmy, and every time he went with her he felt as if he'd been sucked into a Pachinko machine, all flashing lights and random tumbling and cascades of ball bearings. He didn't like her much, but he needed to keep up with her, make sure he was still on her list. Maybe he could get Crake into the queue – do him a favour, build up some gratitude equity. He wondered what kind of girls Crake preferred. So far there'd been zero signals.

At the mall there was no Wakulla to be seen, and no Lynda-Lee. Jimmy tried calling LyndaLee, but her cellphone was off. So Jimmy and Crake played a few games of Three-Dimensional Waco in the arcade and had a couple of SoyOBoyburgers – no beef that month, said the chalkboard menu – and an iced Happicuppuchino, and half a Joltbar each to top up their energy and mainline a few steroids. Then they ambled down the enclosed hallway with its fountains and plastic ferns, through the warm-bathwater music they always played in there. Crake was not exactly voluble, and Jimmy was about to say he had to go do his homework, when up ahead there was a noteworthy sight: it was Melons Riley with a man, heading towards one of the adults-only dance clubs. She'd changed out of her school clothes and had on a loose red jacket over a tight black dress, and the man had his arm around her waist, inside the jacket.

Jimmy nudged Crake. "You think he's got his hand on her ass?" he said.

"That's a geometrical problem," said Crake. "You'd have to work it out."

"What?" said Jimmy. Then, "How?"

"Use your neurons," said Crake. "Step one: calculate length of man's arm, using single visible arm as arm standard. Assumption: that both arms are approximately the same length. Step two: calculate angle of bend at elbow. Step three: calculate curvature of ass. Approximation of this may be necessary, in absence of verifiable numbers. Step four: calculate size of hand, using visible hand, as above."

"I'm not a numbers person," said Jimmy, laughing, but Crake kept on: "All potential hand positions must now be considered. Waist, ruled out. Upper right cheek, ruled out. Lower right cheek or upper thigh would seem by deduction to be the most likely. Hand between both upper thighs a possibility, but this position would impede walking on the part of the subject, and no limping or stumbling is detectable." He was doing a pretty good imitation of their Chemlab teacher – the use-your-neurons line, and that clipped, stiff delivery, sort of like a bark. More than pretty good, good.

Already Jimmy liked Crake better. They might have something in common after all, at least the guy had a sense of humour.

But he was also a little threatened. He himself was a good imitator, he could do just about all the teachers. What if Crake turned out to be better at it? He could feel it within himself to hate Crake, as well as liking him.

But in the days that followed, Crake gave no public performances.

Crake had had a thing about him even then, thinks Snowman. Not that he was popular, exactly, but people felt flattered by his regard. Not just the kids, the teachers too. He'd look at them as if he was listening, as if what they were talking about was worthy of his full attention, though he would never say so exactly. He generated awe — not an overwhelming amount of it, but enough. He exuded potential, but potential for what? Nobody knew, and so people were wary of him. All of this in his dark laconic clothing.

Brainfrizz

~

Wakulla Price had been Jimmy's lab partner in Nanotech Biochem, but her father was headhunted by a Compound on the other side of the continent, and she'd taken the high-speed sealed bullet train and was never seen again. After she'd gone Jimmy moped for a week, and not even LyndaLee's dirty-mouthed convulsions could console him.

Wakulla's vacant place at the lab table was filled by Crake, who was moved up from his solitary latecomer's position at the back of the room. Crake was very smart — even in the world of HelthWyzer High, with its overstock of borderline geniuses and polymaths, he had no trouble floating at the top of the list. He turned out to be excellent at Nanotech Biochem, and together he and Jimmy worked on their single-molecular-layer splicing project, managing to produce the required purple nematode — using the colour-coder from a primitive seaweed — before schedule, and with no alarming variations.

Jimmy and Crake took to hanging out together at lunch hour, and then — not every day, they weren't gay or anything, but at least twice a week — after school. At first they'd play tennis, on the clay court behind Crake's place, but Crake combined method with lateral thinking and hated to lose, and Jimmy was impetuous and lacked finesse, so that wasn't too productive and they dropped it. Or, under pretence of doing their homework, which sometimes they really would do, they would shut themselves up in Crake's room, where they would play computer chess or Three-Dimensionals, or Kwiktime Osama, tossing to see who got Infidels. Crake had two computers, so they could sit with their backs to each other, one at each.

"Why don't we use a real set?" Jimmy asked one day when they were doing some chess. "The old kind. With plastic men." It did seem weird to have the two of them in the same room, back to back, playing on computers.

"Why?" said Crake. "Anyway, this *is* a real set."

"No it's not."

"Okay, granted, but neither is plastic men."

"What?"

"The real set is in your head."

"Bogus!" Jimmy yelled. It was a good word, he'd got it off an old DVD; they'd taken to using it to tear each other down for being pompous. "Way too bogus!"

Crake laughed.

Crake would get fixated on a game, and would want to play it and play it and perfect his attack until he was sure he could win, nine times out of ten anyway. For a whole month they'd had to play Barbarian Stomp (See If You Can Change History!). One side had the cities and the riches and the other side had the hordes, and – usually but not always – the most viciousness. Either the barbarians stomped the cities or else they got stomped, but you had to start out with the historical disposition of energies and go on from there. Rome versus the Visigoths, Ancient Egypt versus the Hyksos, Aztecs versus the Spaniards. That was a cute one, because it was the Aztecs who represented civilization, while the Spaniards were the barbarian hordes. You could customize the game as long as you used real societies and tribes, and for a while Crake and Jimmy vied with each other to see who could come up with the most obscure pairing.

"Petchenegs versus Byzantium," said Jimmy, one memorable day.

"Who the fuck are the Petchenegs? You made that up," said Crake.

But Jimmy had found it in the *Encyclopedia Britannica*, 1957 edition, which was stored on CD-ROM — for some forgotten reason — in the school library. He had chapter and verse. "'Matthew of Edessa referred to them as wicked blood-drinking beasts,'" he was able to say with authority. "'They were totally ruthless and had no redeeming features.'" So they tossed for sides, and Jimmy got Petchenegs, and won. The Byzantines were slaughtered, because that was what Petchenegs did, Jimmy explained. They always slaughtered everyone immediately. Or they slaughtered the men, at least. Then they slaughtered the women after a while.

Crake took the loss of all of his players badly, and sulked a little. After that he'd switched his loyalty to Blood and Roses. It was more cosmic, said Crake: the field of battle was larger, both in time and space.

Blood and Roses was a trading game, along the lines of Monopoly. The Blood side played with human atrocities for the counters, atrocities on a large scale: individual rapes and murders didn't count, there had to have been a large number of people wiped out. Massacres, genocides, that sort of thing. The Roses side played with human achievements. Artworks, scientific breakthroughs, stellar works of architecture, helpful inventions. *Monuments to the soul's magnificence*, they were called in the game. There were sidebar buttons, so that if you didn't know what *Crime and Punishment* was, or the Theory of Relativity, or the Trail of Tears, or *Madame Bovary*, or the Hundred Years' War, or *The Flight into Egypt*, you could double-click and get an illustrated rundown, in two choices: R for children, PON for

Profanity, Obscenity, and Nudity. That was the thing about history, said Crake: it had lots of all three.

You rolled the virtual dice and either a Rose or a Blood item would pop up. If it was a Blood item, the Rose player had a chance to stop the atrocity from happening, but he had to put up a Rose item in exchange. The atrocity would then vanish from history, or at least the history recorded on the screen. The Blood player could acquire a Rose item, but only by handing over an atrocity, thus leaving himself with less ammunition and the Rose player with more. If he was a skilful player he could attack the Rose side by means of the atrocities in his possession, loot the human achievement, and transfer it to his side of the board. The player who managed to retain the most human achievements by Time's Up was the winner. With points off, naturally, for achievements destroyed through his own error and folly and cretinous play.

The exchange rates – one *Mona Lisa* equalled Bergen-Belsen, one Armenian genocide equalled the *Ninth Symphony* plus three Great Pyramids – were suggested, but there was room for haggling. To do this you needed to know the numbers – the total number of corpses for the atrocities, the latest open-market price for the artworks; or, if the artworks had been stolen, the amount paid out by the insurance policy. It was a wicked game.

"Homer," says Snowman, making his way through the dripping-wet vegetation. "*The Divine Comedy*. Greek statuary. Aqueducts. *Paradise Lost*. Mozart's music. Shakespeare, complete works. The Brontës. Tolstoy. The Pearl Mosque. Chartres Cathedral. Bach. Rembrandt. Verdi. Joyce. Penicillin. Keats. Turner. Heart transplants. Polio vaccine. Berlioz. Baudelaire. Bartok. Yeats. Woolf."

There must have been more. There were more.

The sack of Troy, says a voice in his ear. *The destruction of Carthage. The Vikings. The Crusades. Ghenghis Khan. Attila the Hun. The massacre of the Cathars. The witch burnings. The destruction of the Aztec. Ditto the Maya. Ditto the Inca. The*

Inquisition. Vlad the Impaler. The massacre of the Huguenots. Cromwell in Ireland. The French Revolution. The Napoleonic Wars. The Irish Famine. Slavery in the American South. King Leopold in the Congo. The Russian Revolution. Stalin. Hitler. Hiroshima. Mao. Pol Pot. Idi Amin. Sri Lanka. East Timor. Saddam Hussein.

"Stop it," says Snowman.

Sorry, honey. Only trying to help.

That was the trouble with Blood and Roses: it was easier to remember the Blood stuff. The other trouble was that the Blood player usually won, but winning meant you inherited a wasteland. This was the point of the game, said Crake, when Jimmy complained. Jimmy said if that was the point, it was pretty pointless. He didn't want to tell Crake that he was having some severe nightmares: the one where the Parthenon was decorated with cut-off heads was, for some reason, the worst.

By unspoken consent they'd given up on Blood and Roses, which was fine with Crake because he was into something new – Extinctathon, an interactive biofreak masterlore game he'd found on the Web. *EXTINCTATHON, Monitored by MaddAddam. Adam named the living animals, MaddAddam names the dead ones. Do you want to play?* That was what came up when you logged on. You then had to click Yes, enter your codename, and pick one of the two chat rooms – Kingdom Animal, Kingdom Vegetable. Then some challenger would come on-line, using his own codename – Komodo, Rhino, Manatee, Hippocampus Ramulosus – and propose a contest. *Begins with, number of legs, what is it?* The *it* would be some bioform that had kakked out within the past fifty years – no T-Rex, no roc, no dodo, and points off for getting the time frame wrong. Then you'd narrow it down, Phylum Class Order Family Genus Species, then the habitat and when last seen, and what had snuffed it. (Pollution, habitat destruction, credulous morons who thought that eating its horn would give them a boner.) The longer the challenger held out, the more points he got, but you could win big bonuses for speed. It helped to have the MaddAddam printout of every extinct species, but that gave you only the Latin names, and anyway it was a couple of hundred pages of fine print and filled with obscure bugs, weeds, and frogs nobody had ever heard of. Nobody except, it seemed, the Extinctathon Grandmasters, who had brains like search engines.

You always knew when you were playing one of those because a little Coelacanth symbol would come up on the screen. *Coelacanth. Prehistoric deep-sea fish, long supposed extinct until specimens found in mid-twentieth. Present status unknown.* Extinctathon was nothing if not informative. It was like some tedious pedant you got trapped beside on the school van, in Jimmy's view. It wouldn't shut up.

"Why do you like this so much?" said Jimmy one day, to Crake's hunched-over back.

"Because I'm good at it," said Crake. Jimmy suspected him of wanting to make Grandmaster, not because it meant anything but just because it was there.

Crake had picked their codenames. Jimmy's was Thickney, after a defunct Australian double-jointed bird that used to hang around in cemeteries, and – Jimmy suspected – because Crake liked the sound of it as applied to Jimmy. Crake's codename was Crake, after the Red-necked Crake, another Australian bird – never, said Crake, very numerous. For a while they called each other Crake and Thickney, as an in-joke. After Crake had realized Jimmy was not wholeheartedly participating and they'd stopped playing Extinctathon, Thickney as a name had faded away. But Crake had stuck.

When they weren't playing games they'd surf the Net – drop in on old favourites, see what was new. They'd watch open-heart surgery in live time, or else the Noodie News, which was good for a few minutes because the people on it tried to pretend there was nothing unusual going on and studiously avoided looking at one another's jujubes.

Or they'd watch animal snuff sites, Felicia's Frog Squash and the like, though these quickly grew repetitious: one stomped frog, one cat being torn apart by hand, was much like another. Or they'd watch dirtysockpuppets.com, a current-affairs show about world political leaders. Crake said that with digital genalteration you couldn't tell whether any of these generals and whatnot existed any more, and if they did, whether they'd actually said what you'd heard. Anyway they were toppled and replaced with such rapidity that it hardly mattered.

Or they might watch hedsoff.com, which played live coverage of executions in Asia. There they could see enemies of the people being topped with swords in someplace that looked like China, while thousands of spectators cheered. Or they could watch alibooboo.com, with various supposed thieves having their hands cut off and adulterers and lipstick-wearers being stoned to death by howling crowds, in dusty enclaves that purported to be in fundamentalist countries in the Middle East. The coverage was usually poor on that site: filming was said to be prohibited, so it was just some desperate pauper with a hidden minivideocam, risking his life for filthy Western currency. You saw mostly the backs and heads of the spectators, so it was like being trapped inside a huge clothes rack unless the guy with the camera got caught, and then there would be a flurry of hands and cloth before the picture went black. Crake said these bloodfests were probably taking place on a back lot somewhere in California, with a bunch of extras rounded up off the streets.

Better than these were the American sites, with their sports-event commentary – "Here he comes now! Yes! It's Joe 'The Ratchet Set' Ricardo, voted tops by you viewers!" Then a rundown of the crimes, with grisly pictures of the victims. These sites would have spot commercials, for things like car batteries and tranquil-izers, and logos painted in bright yellow on the background walls. At least the Americans put some style into it, said Crake.

Shortcircuit.com, brainfrizz.com, and deathrowlive.com were the best; they showed electrocutions and lethal injections. Once they'd made real-time coverage legal, the guys being executed had started hamming it up for the cameras. They were mostly guys, with the occasional woman, but Jimmy didn't like to watch those: a woman being croaked was a solemn, weepy affair, and people tended to stand around with lighted candles and pictures of the kids, or show up with poems they'd written themselves. But the guys could be a riot. You could watch them making faces, giving the guards the finger, cracking jokes, and occasionally breaking free and being chased around the room, trailing restraint straps and shouting foul abuse.

Crake said these incidents were bogus. He said the men were paid to do it, or their families were. The sponsors required them to put on a good show because otherwise people would get bored and turn off. The viewers wanted to see the executions, yes, but after a while these could get monotonous, so one last fighting chance had to be added in, or else an element of surprise. Two to one it was all rehearsed.

Jimmy said this was an awesome theory. *Awesome* was another old word, like *bogus*, that he'd dredged out of the DVD archives. "Do you think they're really being executed?" he said. "A lot of them look like simulations."

"You never know," said Crake.

"You never know what?"

"What is *reality*?"

"Bogus!"

There was an assisted-suicide site too – nitee-nite.com, it was called – which had a this-was-your-life component: family albums, interviews with relatives, brave parties of friends standing by while the deed was taking place to background organ music. After the sad-eyed doctor had declared that life was extinct, there were taped testimonials from the participants themselves, stating why they'd chosen to depart. The assisted-suicide statistics shot way up after this show got going. There was said to be a long lineup of people willing to pay big bucks for a chance to appear on it and snuff themselves in glory, and lotteries were held to choose the participants.

Crake grinned a lot while watching this site. For some reason he found it hilarious, whereas Jimmy did not. He couldn't imagine doing such a thing himself, unlike Crake, who said it showed flair to know when you'd had enough. But did Jimmy's reluctance mean he was a coward, or was it just that the organ music sucked?

These planned departures made him uneasy: they reminded him of Alex the parrot saying *I'm going away now*. There was too fine a line between Alex the parrot and the assisted suicides and his mother and the note she'd left for him. All three gave notice of their intentions; then all vanished.

Or they would watch At Home With Anna K. Anna K. was a self-styled installation artist with big boobs who'd wired up her apartment so that every moment of her life was sent out live to millions of voyeurs. "This is Anna K., thinking always about my happiness and my unhappiness," was what you'd get as you joined her. Then you might watch her tweezing her eyebrows, waxing her bikini line, washing her underwear. Sometimes she'd read scenes from old plays out loud, taking all the parts, while sitting on the can with her retro-look bell-bottom jeans around her ankles. This was how Jimmy first encountered Shakespeare – through Anna K.'s rendition of *Macbeth*.

> Tomorrow, and tomorrow, and tomorrow.
> Creeps in this petty pace from day to day,
> To the last syllable of recorded time;
> And all our yesterdays have lighted fools
> The way to dusty death,

read Anna K. She was a terrible ham, but Snowman has always been grateful to her because she'd been a doorway of sorts. Think

what he might not have known if it hadn't been for her. Think of
the words. *Sere*, for instance. *Incarnadine*.

"What is this shit?" said Crake. "Channel change!"

"No, wait, wait," said Jimmy, who had been seized by – what?
Something he wanted to hear. And Crake waited, because he did
humour Jimmy sometimes.

Or they would watch the Queek Geek Show, which had contests featuring the eating of live animals and birds, timed by
stopwatches, with prizes of hard-to-come-by foods. It was amazing
what people would do for a couple of lamb chops or a chunk of
genuine brie.

Or they would watch porn shows. There were a lot of those.

When did the body first set out on its own adventures? Snowman
thinks; after having ditched its old travelling companions, the
mind and the soul, for whom it had once been considered a mere
corrupt vessel or else a puppet acting out their dramas for them,
or else bad company, leading the other two astray. It must have
got tired of the soul's constant nagging and whining and the
anxiety-driven intellectual web-spinning of the mind, distracting
it whenever it was getting its teeth into something juicy or its
fingers into something good. It had dumped the other two back
there somewhere, leaving them stranded in some damp sanctu-
ary or stuffy lecture hall while it made a beeline for the topless
bars, and it had dumped culture along with them: music and
painting and poetry and plays. Sublimation, all of it; nothing but
sublimation, according to the body. Why not cut to the chase?

But the body had its own cultural forms. It had its own art.
Executions were its tragedies, pornography was its romance.

To access the more disgusting and forbidden sites – those for
which you had to be over eighteen, and for which you needed a
special password – Crake used his Uncle Pete's private code, via

a complicated method he called a lily-pad labyrinth. He'd construct a winding pathway through the Web, hacking in at random through some easy-access commercial enterprise, then skipping from lily pad to lily pad, erasing his footprints as he went. That way when Uncle Pete got the bill he couldn't find out who'd run it up.

Crake had also located Uncle Pete's stash of high-grade Vancouver skunkweed, kept in orange-juice cans in the freezer; he'd take out about a quarter of the can, then mix in some of the low-octane carpet sweepings you could buy at the school tuck shop for fifty bucks a baggie. He said Uncle Pete would never know because he never smoked except when he wanted to have sex with Crake's mother, which – judging from the number of orange-juice cans and the rate at which they were getting used up – wasn't often. Crake said Uncle Pete got his real kicks at the office, bossing people around, whipping the wage slaves. He used to be a scientist, but now he was a large managerial ultra-cheese at HelthWyzer, on the financial end of things.

So they'd roll a few joints and smoke them while watching the executions and the porn – the body parts moving around on the screen in slow motion, an underwater ballet of flesh and blood under stress, hard and soft joining and separating, groans and screams, close-ups of clenched eyes and clenched teeth, spurts of this or that. If you switched back and forth fast, it all came to look like the same event. Sometimes they'd have both things on at once, each on a different screen.

These sessions would take place for the most part in silence, except for the sound effects coming from the machines. It would be Crake who'd decide what to watch and when to stop watching it. Fair enough, they were his computers. He might say, "Finished with that?" before changing. He didn't seem to be affected by anything he saw, one way or the other, except when he thought it was funny. He never seemed to get high, either. Jimmy suspected he didn't really inhale.

Jimmy on the other hand would wobble homewards, still fuzzy from the dope and feeling as if he'd been to an orgy, one at which he'd had no control at all over what had happened to him. What had been done to him. He also felt very light, as if he were made of air; thin, dizzying air, at the top of some garbage-strewn Mount Everest. Back at home base, his parental units – supposing they were there, and downstairs – never seemed to notice a thing.

"Getting enough to eat?" Ramona might say to him. She'd interpret his mumble as a yes.

HottTotts

~

Late afternoons were the best time for doing these things at Crake's place. Nobody interrupted them. Crake's mother was out a lot, or in a hurry; she worked as a diagnostician at the hospital complex. She was an intense, square-jawed, dark-haired woman with not much of a chest. On the rare occasions when Jimmy had been there at the same time as Crake's mother, she hadn't said much. She'd dug around in the kitchen cupboards for something that would pass as a snack for "you boys," as she called the two of them. Sometimes she would stop in the middle of her preparations – the dumping of stale crackers onto a plate, the sawing up of chewy orange-and-white-marbled hunks of cheesefood – and stand stock-still, as if she could see someone else in the room. Jimmy had the impression she couldn't remember his name; not only that, she couldn't remember Crake's name either. Sometimes she would ask Crake if his room was tidy, though she never went in there herself.

"She believes in respecting a child's privacy," said Crake, straight-faced.

"I bet it's your mouldy socks," said Jimmy. "All the perfumes of Arabia will not sweeten these little socks." He'd recently discovered the joys of quotation.

"For that we've got room spray," said Crake.

As for Uncle Pete, he was rarely home before seven. HelthWyzer was expanding like helium, and therefore he had a lot of new responsibilities. He wasn't Crake's real uncle, he was just Crake's mother's second husband. He'd taken on that status when Crake had been twelve, a couple of years too old for the "uncle" tag to have been viewed by him as anything but totally rancid. Yet Crake had accepted the status quo, or so it appeared. He'd smile, he'd say *Sure, Uncle Pete* and *That's right, Uncle Pete* when the man was around, even though Jimmy knew Crake disliked him.

One afternoon in – what? March, it must have been, because it was already hot as hell outside – the two of them were watching porn in Crake's room. Already it felt like old time's sake, already it felt like nostalgia – something they were too grown-up for, like middle-aged guys cruising the pleebland teeny clubs. Still, they dutifully lit up a joint, hacked into Uncle Pete's digital charge card via a new labyrinth, and started surfing. They checked into Tart of the Day, which featured elaborate confectionery in the usual orifices, then went to Superswallowers; then to a Russian site that employed ex-acrobats, ballerinas, and contortionists.

"Whoever said a guy can't suck his own?" was Crake's comment. The high-wire act with the six flaming torches was pretty good, but they'd seen things like that before.

Then they went to HottTotts, a global sex-trotting site. "The next best thing to being there," was how it was advertised. It claimed to show real sex tourists, filmed while doing things they'd be put in jail for back in their home countries. Their faces weren't visible, their names weren't used, but the possibilities for blackmail, Snowman realizes now, must have been extensive. The locations were supposed to be countries where life was

cheap and kids were plentiful, and where you could buy anything you wanted.

This was how the two of them first saw Oryx. She was only
about eight, or she looked eight. They could never find out for
certain how old she'd been then. Her name wasn't Oryx, she
didn't have a name. She was just another little girl on a porno site.

None of those little girls had ever seemed real to Jimmy —
they'd always struck him as digital clones — but for some reason
Oryx was three-dimensional from the start. She was small-boned
and exquisite, and naked like the rest of them, with nothing on
her but a garland of flowers and a pink hair ribbon, frequent
props on the sex-kiddie sites. She was on her knees, with another
little girl on either side of her, positioned in front of the standard
gargantuan Gulliver-in-Lilliput male torso — a life-sized man
shipwrecked on an island of delicious midgets, or stolen away and
entranced, forced to experience agonizing pleasures by a trio of
soulless pixies. The guy's distinguishing features were concealed
— bag with eyeholes over the head, surgical tape over the tattoos
and scars: few of these types wanted to be spotted by the folks
back home, though the possibility of detection must have been
part of the thrill.

The act involved whipped cream and a lot of licking. The
effect was both innocent and obscene: the three of them were
going over the guy with their kittenish tongues and their tiny
fingers, giving him a thorough workout to the sound of moans
and giggles. The giggles must have been recorded, because they
weren't coming from the three girls: they all looked frightened,
and one of them was crying.

Jimmy knew the drill. They were supposed to look like that,
he thought; if they stopped the action, a walking stick would
come in from offside and prod them. This was a feature of the
site. There were at least three layers of contradictory make-
believe, one on top of the other. *I want to, I want to not, I want to.*

Oryx paused in her activities. She smiled a hard little smile
that made her appear much older, and wiped the whipped cream

from her mouth. Then she looked over her shoulder and right into the eyes of the viewer – right into Jimmy's eyes, into the secret person inside him. *I see you*, that look said. *I see you watching. I know you. I know what you want.*

Crake pushed the reverse, then the freeze, then the download. Every so often he froze frames; by now he had a small archive of them. Sometimes he'd print them out and give a copy to Jimmy. It could be dangerous – it could leave a footprint for anyone who might manage to trace a way through the labyrinth – but Crake did it anyway. So now he saved that one moment, the moment when Oryx looked.

Jimmy felt burned by this look – eaten into, as if by acid. She'd been so contemptuous of him. The joint he'd been smoking must have had nothing in it but lawn mowings: if it had been stronger he might have been able to bypass guilt. But for the first time he'd felt that what they'd been doing was wrong. Before, it had always been entertainment, or else far beyond his control, but now he felt culpable. At the same time he felt hooked through the gills: if he'd been offered instant teleportation to wherever Oryx was he'd have taken it, no question. He'd have begged to go there. It was all too complicated.

"This a keeper?" Crake said. "You want it?"

"Yeah," said Jimmy. He could barely get the word out. He hoped he sounded normal.

So Crake had printed it, the picture of Oryx looking, and Snowman had saved it and saved it. He'd shown it to Oryx many years later.

"I don't think this is me," was what she'd said at first.

"It has to be!" said Jimmy. "Look! It's your eyes!"

"A lot of girls have eyes," she said. "A lot of girls did these things. Very many." Then, seeing his disappointment, she said, "It might be me. Maybe it is. Would that make you happy, Jimmy?"

"No," said Jimmy. Was that a lie?

"Why did you keep it?"

"What were you thinking?" Jimmy said instead of answering.

Another woman in her place would have crumpled up the picture, cried, denounced him as a criminal, told him he understood nothing about her life, made a general scene. Instead she smoothed out the paper, running her fingers gently over the soft, scornful child's face that had — surely — once been hers.

"You think I was thinking?" she said. "Oh Jimmy! You always think everyone is thinking. Maybe I wasn't thinking anything."

"I know you were," he said.

"You want me to pretend? You want me to make something up?"

"No. Just tell me."

"Why?"

Jimmy had to think about that. He remembered himself watching. How could he have done that to her? And yet it hadn't hurt her, had it? "Because I need you to." Not much of a reason, but it was all he could come up with.

She sighed. "I was thinking," she said, tracing a little circle on his skin with her fingernail, "that if I ever got the chance, it would not be me down on my knees."

"It would be someone else?" said Jimmy. "Who? What someone?"

"You want to know everything," said Oryx.

5

Toast

~

Snowman in his tattered sheet sits hunched at the edge of the trees, where grass and vetch and sea grapes merge into sand. Now that it's cooler he feels less dejected. Also he's hungry. There's something to be said for hunger: at least it lets you know you're still alive.

A breeze riffles the leaves overhead; insects rasp and trill; red light from the setting sun hits the tower blocks in the water, illuminating an unbroken pane here and there, as if a scattering of lamps has been turned on. Several of the buildings once held roof gardens, and now they're top-heavy with overgrown shrubbery. Hundreds of birds are streaming across the sky towards them, roostward bound. Ibis? Herons? The black ones are cormorants, he knows that for sure. They settle down into the darkening foliage, croaking and squabbling. If he ever needs guano he'll know where to find it.

Across the clearing to the south comes a rabbit, hopping, listening, pausing to nibble at the grass with its gigantic teeth. It glows in the dusk, a greenish glow filched from the iridicytes of a deep-sea jellyfish in some long-ago experiment. In the half-light the rabbit looks soft and almost translucent, like a piece of

Turkish delight; as if you could suck off its fur like sugar. Even in Snowman's boyhood there were luminous green rabbits, though they weren't this big and they hadn't yet slipped their cages and bred with the wild population, and become a nuisance.

This one has no fear of him, though it fills him with carnivorous desires: he longs to whack it with a rock, tear it apart with his bare hands, then cram it into his mouth, fur and all. But rabbits belong to the Children of Oryx and are sacred to Oryx herself, and it would be a bad idea to offend the women.

It's his own fault. He must have been stupefied with drink when he was laying down the laws. He should have made rabbits edible, by himself at any rate, but he can't change that now. He can almost hear Oryx, laughing at him with indulgent, faintly malicious delight.

The Children of Oryx, the Children of Crake. He'd had to think of something. Get your story straight, keep it simple, don't falter: this used to be the expert advice given by lawyers to criminals in the dock. *Crake made the bones of the Children of Crake out of the coral on the beach, and then he made their flesh out of a mango. But the Children of Oryx hatched out of an egg, a giant egg laid by Oryx herself. Actually she laid two eggs: one full of animals and birds and fish, and the other one full of words. But the egg full of words hatched first, and the Children of Crake had already been created by then, and they'd eaten up all the words because they were hungry, and so there were no words left over when the second egg hatched out. And that is why the animals can't talk.*

Internal consistency is best. Snowman learned this earlier in his life, when lying had posed more of a challenge for him. Now even when he's caught in a minor contradiction he can make it stick, because these people trust him. He's the only one left who'd known Crake face to face, so he can lay claim to the inside track. Above his head flies the invisible banner of Crakedom, of Crakiness, of Crakehood, hallowing all he does.

The first star appears. "Star light, star bright," he says. Some grade-school teacher. Big-bum Sally. *Now close your eyes right up tight. Tighter! Really tight! There! See the wishing star? Now we will all wish for the thing we want the very, very most of all in the whole wide world. But shhh – don't tell anyone, or the wish won't come true!*

Snowman screws his eyes shut, pushes his fists into them, clenches his entire face. There's the wishing star all right: it's blue. "I wish I may, I wish I might," he says. "Have the wish I wish tonight."

Fat chance.

"Oh Snowman, why are you talking to no one?" says a voice. Snowman opens his eyes: three of the older children are standing just out of reach, regarding him with interest. They must have crept up on him in the dusk.

"I'm talking to Crake," he says.

"But you talk to Crake through your shiny thing! Is it broken?"

Snowman lifts his left arm, holds out his watch. "This is for *listening* to Crake. *Talking* to him is different."

"Why are you talking to him about stars? What are you telling to Crake, oh Snowman?"

What, indeed? thinks Snowman. *When dealing with indigenous peoples*, says the book in his head – a more modern book this time, late twentieth century, the voice a confident female's – *you must attempt to respect their traditions and confine your explanations to simple concepts that can be understood within the contexts of their belief systems.* Some earnest aid worker in a khaki jungle outfit, with netting under the arms and a hundred pockets. Condescending self-righteous cow, thinks she's got all the answers. He'd known girls like that at college. If she were here she'd need a whole new take on *indigenous*.

"I was telling him," says Snowman, "that you ask too many questions." He holds his watch to his ear. "And he's telling me that if you don't stop doing that, you'll be toast."

"Please, oh Snowman, what is toast?"

Another error, Snowman thinks. He should avoid arcane metaphors. "Toast," he says, "is something very, very bad. It's so bad I can't even describe it. Now it's your bedtime. Go away."

"What is toast?" says Snowman to himself, once they've run off. *Toast is when you take a piece of bread – What is bread? Bread is when you take some flour – What is flour? We'll skip that part, it's too complicated. Bread is something you can eat, made from a ground-up plant and shaped like a stone. You cook it . . . Please, why do you cook it? Why don't you just eat the plant? Never mind that part – Pay attention. You cook it, and then you cut it into slices, and you put a slice into a toaster, which is a metal box that heats up with electricity – What is electricity? Don't worry about that. While the slice is in the toaster, you get out the butter – butter is a yellow grease, made from the mammary glands of – skip the butter. So, the toaster turns the slice of bread black on both sides with smoke coming out, and then this "toaster" shoots the slice up into the air, and it falls onto the floor . . .*

"Forget it," says Snowman. "Let's try again." *Toast was a pointless invention from the Dark Ages. Toast was an implement of torture that caused all those subjected to it to regurgitate in verbal form the sins and crimes of their past lives. Toast was a ritual item devoured by fetishists in the belief that it would enhance their kinetic and sexual powers. Toast cannot be explained by any rational means.*

Toast is me.

I am toast.

Fish

~

The sky darkens from ultramarine to indigo. God bless the namers of oil paints and high-class women's underwear, Snowman thinks. Rose-Petal Pink, Crimson Lake, Sheer Mist, Burnt Umber, Ripe Plum, Indigo, Ultramarine — they're fantasies in themselves, such words and phrases. It's comforting to remember that *Homo sapiens sapiens* was once so ingenious with language, and not only with language. Ingenious in every direction at once.

Monkey brains, had been Crake's opinion. Monkey paws, monkey curiosity, the desire to take apart, turn inside out, smell, fondle, measure, improve, trash, discard — all hooked up to monkey brains, an advanced model of monkey brains but monkey brains all the same. Crake had no very high opinion of human ingenuity, despite the large amount of it he himself possessed.

There's a murmuring of voices from the direction of the village, or from what would be a village if it had any houses. Right on schedule, here come the men, carrying their torches, and behind them the women.

Every time the women appear, Snowman is astonished all over again. They're every known colour from deepest black to whitest white, they're various heights, but each one of them is admirably proportioned. Each is sound of tooth, smooth of skin. No ripples of fat around their waists, no bulges, no dimpled orange-skin cellulite on their thighs. No body hair, no bushiness. They look like retouched fashion photos, or ads for a high-priced workout program.

Maybe this is the reason that these women arouse in Snowman not even the faintest stirrings of lust. It was the thumbprints of human imperfection that used to move him, the flaws in the design: the lopsided smile, the wart next to the navel, the mole, the bruise. These were the places he'd single out, putting his mouth on them. Was it consolation he'd had in mind, kissing the wound to make it better? There was always an element of melancholy involved in sex. After his indiscriminate adolescence he'd preferred sad women, delicate and breakable, women who'd been messed up and who needed him. He'd liked to comfort them, stroke them gently at first, reassure them. Make them happier, if only for a moment. Himself too, of course; that was the payoff. A grateful woman would go the extra mile.

But these new women are neither lopsided nor sad: they're placid, like animated statues. They leave him chilled.

The women are carrying his weekly fish, grilled the way he's taught them and wrapped in leaves. He can smell it, he's starting to drool. They bring the fish forward, put it on the ground in front of him. It will be a shore fish, a species too paltry and tasteless to have been coveted and sold and exterminated, or else a bottom-feeder pimply with toxins, but Snowman couldn't care less, he'll eat anything.

"Here is your fish, oh Snowman," says one of the men, the one called Abraham. Abraham as in Lincoln: it had amused Crake to name his Crakers after eminent historical figures. It had all seemed innocent enough, at the time.

"This is the one fish chosen for you tonight," says the woman holding it; the Empress Josephine, or else Madame Curie or Sojourner Truth, she's in the shade so he can't tell which. "This is the fish Oryx gives you."

Oh good, thinks Snowman. Catch of the Day.

Every week, according to the phases of the moon — dark, first quarter, full, second quarter — the women stand in the tidal pools and call the unlucky fish by name — only *fish*, nothing more specific. Then they point it out, and the men kill it with rocks and sticks. That way the unpleasantness is shared among them and no single person is guilty of shedding the fish's blood.

If things had gone as Crake wanted, there would be no more such killing — no more human predation — but he'd reckoned without Snowman and his beastly appetites. Snowman can't live on clover. The people would never eat a fish themselves, but they have to bring him one a week because he's told them Crake has decreed it. They've accepted Snowman's monstrousness, they've known from the beginning he was a separate order of being, so they weren't surprised by this.

Idiot, he thinks. I should have made it three a day. He unwraps the warm fish from its leaves, trying to keep his hands from trembling. He shouldn't get too carried away. But he always does.

The people keep their distance and avert their eyes while he crams handfuls of fishiness into his mouth and sucks out the eyes and cheeks, groaning with pleasure. Perhaps it's like hearing a lion gorge itself, at the zoo, back when there were zoos, back when there were lions — a rending and crunching, a horrible gobbling and gulping — and, like those long-gone zoo visitors, the Crakers can't help peeking. The spectacle of depravity is of interest even to them, it seems, purified by chlorophyll though they are.

When Snowman has finished he licks his fingers and wipes them on his sheet, and places the bones back in their leaf wrappings, ready to be returned to the sea. He's told them Oryx wants that — she needs the bones of her children so she can make other children out of them. They've accepted this without question, like everything he says about Oryx. In reality it's one of his smarter ploys: no sense leaving the scraps around on land, to attract rakunks and wolvogs and pigoons and other scavengers.

The people move closer, men and women both, gathering around, their green eyes luminescent in the semi-darkness, just like the rabbit: same jellyfish gene. Sitting all together like this, they smell like a crateful of citrus fruit — an added feature on the part of Crake, who'd thought those chemicals would ward off mosquitoes. Maybe he was right, because all the mosquitoes for miles around appear to be biting Snowman. He resists the urge to swat: his fresh blood only excites them. He shifts to the left so he's more in the smoke of the torches.

"Snowman, tell us please about the deeds of Crake."

A story is what they want, in exchange for every slaughtered fish. Well, I owe them, Snowman thinks. God of Bullshit, fail me not.

"What part would you like to hear tonight?" he says.

"In the beginning," prompts a voice. They're fond of repetition, they learn things by heart.

"In the beginning, there was chaos," he says.

"Show us chaos, please, oh Snowman!"

"Show us a picture of chaos!"

They'd struggled with pictures, at first — flowers on beach-trash lotion bottles, fruits on juice cans. *Is it real? No, it is not real. What is this not real? Not real can tell us about real.* And so forth. But now they appear to have grasped the concept.

"Yes! Yes! A picture of chaos!" they urge.

Snowman has known this request would be made — all the stories begin with chaos — and so he's ready for it. From behind his concrete-slab cache he brings out one of his finds — an orange plastic pail, faded to pink but otherwise undamaged. He tries not to imagine what has happened to the child who must once have owned it. "Bring some water," he says, holding out the pail. There's a scramble around the ring of torches: hands reach out, feet scamper off into the darkness.

"In the chaos, everything was mixed together," he says. "There were too many people, and so the people were all mixed up with the dirt." The pail comes back, sloshing, and is set down in the circle of light. He adds a handful of earth, stirs it with a stick. "There," he says. "Chaos. You can't drink it . . ."

"No!" A chorus.

"You can't eat it . . ."

"No, you can't eat it!" Laughter.

"You can't swim in it, you can't stand on it . . ."

"No! No!" They love this bit.

"The people in the chaos were full of chaos themselves, and the chaos made them do bad things. They were killing other people all the time. And they were eating up all the Children of Oryx, against the wishes of Oryx and Crake. Every day they were eating them up. They were killing them and killing them, and eating them and eating them. They ate them even when they weren't hungry."

Gasping here, widened eyes: it's always a dramatic moment. Such wickedness! He continues: "And Oryx had only one desire – she wanted the people to be happy, and to be at peace, and to stop eating up her children. But the people couldn't be happy, because of the chaos. And then Oryx said to Crake, *Let us get rid of the chaos.* And so Crake took the chaos, and he poured it away." Snowman demonstrates, sloshing the water off to the side, then turns the pail upside down. "There. Empty. And this is how Crake did the Great Rearrangement and made the Great Emptiness. He cleared away the dirt, he cleared room . . ."

"For his children! For the Children of Crake!"

"Right. And for . . ."

"And for the Children of Oryx, as well!"

"Right," says Snowman. Is there no end to his shameless inventions? He feels like crying.

"Crake made the Great Emptiness . . . ," say the men.

"For us! For us!" say the women. It's becoming a liturgy. "Oh, good, kind Crake!"

Their adulation of Crake enrages Snowman, though this adulation has been his own doing. The Crake they're praising is his fabrication, a fabrication not unmixed with spite: Crake was against the notion of God, or of gods of any kind, and would surely be disgusted by the spectacle of his own gradual deification.

If he were here. But he's not here, and it's galling for Snowman to listen to all this misplaced sucking up. Why don't they glorify Snowman instead? Good, kind Snowman, who deserves glorification more — much more — because who got them out, who got them here, who's been watching over them all this time? Well, sort of watching. It sure as hell wasn't Crake. Why can't Snowman revise the mythology? *Thank me, not him! Lick my ego instead!*

But for now his bitterness must be swallowed. "Yes," he says. "Good, kind Crake." He twists his mouth into what he hopes is a gracious and benevolent smile.

At first he'd improvised, but now they're demanding dogma: he would deviate from orthodoxy at his peril. He might not lose his life — these people aren't violent or given to bloodthirsty acts of retribution, or not so far — but he'd lose his audience. They'd turn their backs on him, they'd wander away. He is Crake's prophet now, whether he likes it or not; and the prophet of Oryx as well. That, or nothing. And he couldn't stand to be nothing, to know himself to be nothing. He needs to be listened to, he needs to be heard. He needs at least the illusion of being understood.

"Oh Snowman, tell us about when Crake was born," says one of the women. This is a new request. He isn't ready for it, though he should have expected it: children are of great interest to these women. Careful, he tells himself. Once he provides a mother and a birth scene and an infant Crake for them, they'll want the details. They'll want to know when Crake cut his first tooth and spoke his first word and ate his first root, and other such banalities.

"Crake was never born," says Snowman. "He came down out of the sky, like thunder. Now go away please, I'm tired." He'll add to this fable later. Maybe he'll endow Crake with horns, and wings of fire, and allow him a tail for good measure.

Bottle
~

After the Children of Crake have filed away, taking their torches with them, Snowman clambers up his tree and tries to sleep. All around him are noises: the slurping of the waves, insect chirpings and whirrings, bird whistles, amphibious croaks, the rustling of leaves. His ears deceive him: he thinks he can hear a jazz horn, and under that a rhythmic drumming, as if from a muffled nightclub. From somewhere farther along the shore comes a booming, bellowing sound: now what? He can't think of any animal that makes such a noise. Perhaps it's a crocodile, escaped from a defunct Cuban handbag farm and working its way north along the shore. That would be bad news for the kids in swimming. He listens again, but the sound doesn't recur.

There's a distant, peaceful murmur from the village: human voices. If you can call them human. As long as they don't start singing. Their singing is unlike anything he ever heard in his vanished life: it's beyond the human level, or below it. As if crystals are singing; but not that, either. More like ferns unscrolling – something old, carboniferous, but at the same time newborn, fragrant, verdant. It reduces him, forces too many unwanted emotions upon him. He feels excluded, as if from a party to which he will never be invited. All he'd have to do is step forward into the firelight and there'd be a ring of suddenly blank faces turned towards him. Silence would fall, as in tragic plays of long ago when the doomed protagonist made an entrance, enveloped in his cloak of contagious bad news. On some non-conscious level Snowman must serve as a reminder to these people, and not a pleasant one: he's what they may have been once. *I'm your past*, he might intone. *I'm your ancestor, come from the land of the dead. Now I'm lost, I can't get back, I'm stranded here, I'm all alone. Let me in!*

Oh Snowman, how may we be of help to you? The mild smiles, the polite surprise, the puzzled goodwill.

Forget it, he would say. There's no way they can help him, not really.

There's a chilly breeze blowing; the sheet is damp; he shivers. If only this place had a thermostat. Maybe he could figure out some way of building a little fire, up here in his tree.

"Go to sleep," he orders himself. With no result. After a long session of tossing, turning, and scratching, he climbs back down to seek out the Scotch bottle in his cache. There's enough starlight so he can get his bearings, more or less. He's made this trip many times in the past: for the first month and a half, after he was fairly sure it was safe to relax his vigilance, he got pissed out of his mind every night. This was not a wise or mature thing for him to have done, granted, but of what use are wisdom and maturity to him now?

So every night had been party night, party of one. Or every night he'd had the makings, whenever he'd been able to locate another stash of alcohol in the abandoned pleebland buildings within reach. He'd scoured the nearby bars first, then the restaurants, then the houses and trailers. He'd done cough medicine, shaving lotion, rubbing alcohol; out behind the tree he's accumulated an impressive dump of empty bottles. Once in a while he'd come across a stash of weed and he'd done that too, though often enough it was mouldy; still, he might manage to get a buzz out of it. Or he might find some pills. No coke or crack or heroin — that would have been used up early, stuffed into veins and noses in one last burst of *carpe diem*; anything for a vacation from reality, under the circumstances. There'd been empty BlyssPluss containers everywhere, all you'd need for a non-stop orgy. The revellers hadn't managed to get through all the booze, though often enough on his hunting and gathering trips he's discovered that others had been there before him and there was nothing left but broken glass. There must have been riotous behaviour of all sorts imaginable, until finally there had been no one left to keep it up.

At ground level it's dark as an armpit. A flashlight would come in handy, one of the windup kind. He should keep an eye out. He gropes and stumbles in the right direction, scanning the ground for a glimmer of the vicious white land crabs that come out of their burrows and scuttle around after dark — those things can give you quite a nip — and after a short detour into a clump of bushes, he locates his cement hidey-hole by stubbing his toe on it. He refrains from swearing: no way of telling what else might be prowling around in the night. He slides open the cache, fumbles blindly within it, retrieves the third of Scotch.

He's been saving it up, resisting the urge to binge, keeping it as a sort of charm — as long as he's known it was still there it's been easier to get through time. This might be the last of it. He's certain he has explored every likely site within a day's out-and-back radius of his tree. But he's feeling reckless. Why hoard the stuff? Why wait? What's his life worth anyway, and who cares? Out, out, brief candle. He's served his evolutionary purpose, as fucking Crake knew he would. He's saved the children.

"*Fucking* Crake!" he can't help yelling.

Clutching the bottle with one hand, feeling his way with the other, he reaches his tree again. He needs both hands for climbing, so he knots the bottle securely into his sheet. Once up, he sits on his platform, gulping down the Scotch and howling at the stars – *Aroo! Aroo!* – until he's startled by a chorus of replies from right near the tree.

Is that the gleam of eyes? He can hear panting.

"Hello, my furry pals," he calls down. "Who wants to be man's best friend?" In answer there's a supplicating whine. That's the worst thing about wolvogs: they still look like dogs, still behave like dogs, pricking up their ears, making playful puppy leaps and bounces, wagging their tails. They'll sucker you in, then go for you. It hasn't taken much to reverse fifty thousand years of man-canid interaction. As for the real dogs, they never stood a chance: the wolvogs have simply killed and eaten all those who'd shown signs of vestigial domesticated status. He's seen a wolvog advance to a yapping Pekinese in a friendly manner, sniff its bum, then lunge for its throat, shake it like a mop, and canter off with the limp body.

For a while there were still a few woebegone house pets scrounging around, skinny and limping, their fur matted and dull, begging with bewildered eyes to be taken in by some human, any human. The Children of Crake hadn't fit their bill – they must have smelled weird to a dog, sort of like walking fruits, especially at dusk when the citrus-oil insect repellant kicked in – and in any case they'd shown no interest in puppy-dogs as a concept, so the strays had concentrated on Snowman. He'd almost given in a couple of times, he'd found it hard to resist their ingratiating wriggles, their pitiful whining, but he couldn't afford to feed them; anyway they were useless to him. "It's sink or swim," he'd told them. "Sorry, old buddy." He'd driven them away with stones, feeling like a complete shit, and there haven't been any more lately.

What a fool he'd been. He'd let them go to waste. He should have eaten them. Or taken one in, trained it to catch rabbits. Or to defend him. Or something.

Wolvogs can't climb trees, which is one good thing. If they get numerous enough and too persistent, he'll have to start swinging from vine to vine, like Tarzan. That's a funny idea, so he laughs.

"All you want is my body!" he yells at them. Then he drains the bottle and throws it down. There's a yelp, a scuttling: they still respect missiles. But how long can that last? They're smart; very soon they'll sense his vulnerability, start hunting him. Once they begin he'll never be able to go anywhere, or anywhere without trees. All they'll have to do is get him out in the open, encircle him, close in for the kill. There's only so much you can do with stones and pointed sticks. He really needs to find another spraygun.

After the wolvogs have gone he lies on his back on the platform, gazing up at the stars through the gently moving leaves. They seem close, the stars, but they're far away. Their light is millions, billions of years out of date. Messages with no sender.

Time passes. He wants to sing a song but can't think of one. Old music rises up in him, fades; all he can hear is the percussion. Maybe he could whittle a flute, out of some branch or stem or something, if only he could find a knife.

"Star light, star bright," he says. What comes next? It's gone right out of his head.

No moon, tonight is the dark of the moon, although the moon is there nevertheless and must be rising now, a huge invisible ball of stone, a giant lump of gravity, dead but powerful, drawing the sea towards itself. Drawing all fluids. *The human body is ninety-eight per cent water*, says the book in his head. This time it's a man's voice, an encyclopedia voice; no one he knows, or knew. *The other two per cent is made up of minerals, most importantly the iron in the blood and the calcium of which the skeletal frame and the teeth are comprised.*

"Who gives a rat's ass?" says Snowman. He doesn't care about the iron in his blood or the calcium in his skeletal frame; he's tired of being himself, he wants to be someone else. Turn over all his cells, get a chromosome transplant, trade in his head for some other head, one with better things in it. Fingers moving over him, for instance, little fingers with oval nails, painted ripe plum or crimson lake or rose-petal pink. *I wish I may, I wish I might, Have the wish I wish tonight.* Fingers, a mouth. A dull heavy ache begins, at the base of his spine.

"Oryx," he says. "I know you're there." He repeats the name. It's not even her real name, which he'd never known anyway; it's only a word. It's a mantra.

Sometimes he can conjure her up. At first she's pale and shadowy, but if he can say her name over and over, then maybe she'll glide into his body and be present with him in his flesh, and his hand on himself will become her hand. But she's always been evasive, you can never pin her down. Tonight she fails to materialize and he is left alone, whimpering ridiculously, jerking off all by himself in the dark.

6

Oryx
~

Snowman wakes up suddenly. Has someone touched him? But there's nobody there, nothing.

It's totally dark, no stars. Clouds must have come in.

He turns over, pulls his sheet around him. He's shivering: it's the night breeze. Most likely he's still drunk; sometimes it's hard to tell. He stares up into the darkness, wondering how soon it will be morning, hoping he'll be able to go back to sleep.

There's an owl hooting somewhere. That fierce vibration, up close and far away at once, like the lowest note on a Peruvian flute. Maybe it's hunting. Hunting what?

Now he can feel Oryx floating towards him through the air, as if on soft feathery wings. She's landing now, settling; she's very close to him, stretched out on her side just a skin's distance away. Miraculously she can fit onto the platform beside him, although it isn't a large platform. If he had a candle or a flashlight he'd be able to see her, the slender outline of her, a pale glow against the darkness. If he put out his hand he could touch her; but that would make her vanish.

"It wasn't the sex," he says to her. She doesn't answer, but he can feel her disbelief. He's making her sad because he's taking

away some of her knowledge, her power. "It wasn't just the sex."
A dark smile from her: that's better. "You know I love you. You're
the only one." She isn't the first woman he's ever said that to. He
shouldn't have used it up so much earlier in his life, he shouldn't
have treated it like a tool, a wedge, a key to open women. By the
time he got around to meaning it, the words had sounded fraudulent to him and he'd been ashamed to pronounce them. "No,
really," he says to Oryx.

No answer, no response. She was never very forthcoming at
the best of times.

"Tell me just one thing," he'd say, back when he was still Jimmy.

"Ask me a question," she'd reply.

. So he would ask, and then she might say, "I don't know. I've
forgotten." Or, "I don't want to tell you that." Or, "Jimmy, you are
so bad, it's not your business." Once she'd said, "You have a lot of
pictures in your head, Jimmy. Where did you get them? Why do
you think they are pictures of me?"

He thought he understood her vagueness, her evasiveness.
"It's all right," he'd told her, stroking her hair. "None of it was
your fault."

"None of what, Jimmy?"

How long had it taken him to piece her together from the slivers
of her he'd gathered and hoarded so carefully? There was Crake's
story about her, and Jimmy's story about her as well, a more
romantic version; and then there was her own story about herself,
which was different from both, and not very romantic at all.
Snowman riffles through these three stories in his head. There
must once have been other versions of her: her mother's story, the
story of the man who'd bought her, the story of the man who'd
bought her after that, and the third man's story – the worst man
of them all, the one in San Francisco, a pious bullshit artist; but
Jimmy had never heard those.

Oryx was so delicate. Filigree, he would think, picturing her bones inside her small body. She had a triangular face – big eyes, a small jaw – a Hymenoptera face, a mantid face, the face of a Siamese cat. Skin of the palest yellow, smooth and translucent, like old, expensive porcelain. Looking at her, you knew that a woman of such beauty, slightness, and one-time poverty must have led a difficult life, but that this life would not have consisted in scrubbing floors.

"Did you ever scrub floors?" Jimmy asked her once.

"Floors?" She thought a minute. "We didn't have floors. When I got as far as the floors, it wasn't me scrubbing them." One thing about that early time, she said, the time without floors: the pounded-earth surfaces were swept clean every day. They were used for sitting on while eating, and for sleeping on, so that was important. Nobody wanted to get old food on themselves. Nobody wanted fleas.

When Jimmy was seven or eight or nine, Oryx was born. Where, exactly? Hard to tell. Some distant, foreign place.

It was a village though, said Oryx. A village with trees all around and fields nearby, or possibly rice paddies. The huts had thatch of some kind on the roofs – palm fronds? – although the best huts had roofs of tin. A village in Indonesia, or else Myanmar? Not those, said Oryx, though she couldn't be sure. It wasn't India though. Vietnam? Jimmy guessed. Cambodia? Oryx looked down at her hands, examining her nails. It didn't matter.

She couldn't remember the language she'd spoken as a child. She'd been too young to retain it, that earliest language: the words had all been scoured out of her head. But it wasn't the same as the language of the city to which she'd first been taken, or not the same dialect, because she'd had to learn a different way of speaking. She did remember that: the clumsiness of the words in her mouth, the feeling of being struck dumb.

This village was a place where everyone was poor and there were many children, said Oryx. She herself was quite little when she was sold. Her mother had a number of children, among them two older sons who would soon be able to work in the fields, which was a good thing because the father was sick. He coughed and coughed; this coughing punctuated her earliest memories.

Something wrong with the lungs, Jimmy had guessed. Of course they all probably smoked like maniacs when they could get the cigarettes: smoking dulled the edge. (He'd congratulated himself on this insight.) The villagers set the father's illness down to bad water, bad fate, bad spirits. Illness had an element of shame to it; no one wanted to be contaminated by the illness of another. So the father of Oryx was pitied, but also blamed and shunned. His wife tended him with silent resentment.

Bells were rung, however. Prayers were said. Small images were burned in the fire. But all of this was useless, because the father died. Everyone in the village knew what would happen next, because if there was no man to work in the fields or in the rice paddies, then the raw materials of life had to come from somewhere else.

Oryx had been a younger child, often pushed to the side, but suddenly she was made much of and given better food than usual, and a special blue jacket, because the other village women were helping out and they wanted her to look pretty and healthy. Children who were ugly or deformed, or who were not bright or couldn't talk very well – such children went for less, or might not be sold at all. The village women might need to sell their own children one day, and if they helped out they would be able to count on such help in return.

In the village it was not called "selling," this transaction. The talk about it implied apprenticeship. The children were being trained to earn their living in the wide world: this was the gloss put on it. Besides, if they stayed where they were, what was there for them to do? Especially the girls, said Oryx. They would only get married and make more children, who would then have to be sold in their turn. Sold, or thrown into the river, to float away to the sea; because there was only so much food to go around.

One day a man came to the village. It was the same man who always came. Usually he arrived in a car, bumping over the dirt track, but this time there had been a lot of rain and the road was too muddy. Each village had its own such man, who would make the dangerous journey from the city at irregular intervals, although it was always known ahead of time that he was on his way.

"What city?" asked Jimmy.

But Oryx only smiled. Talking about this made her hungry, she said. Why didn't sweet Jimmy phone out for some pizza? Mushrooms, artichoke hearts, anchovies, no pepperoni. "You want some too?" she said.

"No," said Jimmy. "Why won't you tell me?"

"Why do you care?" said Oryx. "I don't care. I never think about it. It's long ago now."

This man — said Oryx, contemplating the pizza as if it were a jigsaw puzzle, then picking off the mushrooms, which she liked to eat first — would have two other men with him, who were his servants and who carried rifles to fend off the bandits. He wore expensive clothes, and except for the mud and dust — everyone got muddy and dusty on the way to the village — he was clean and well-kempt. He had a watch, a shiny gold-coloured watch he consulted often, pulling up his sleeve to display it; this watch was reassuring, a badge of quality. Maybe the watch was real gold. There were some who said it was.

This man wasn't regarded as a criminal of any sort, but as an honourable businessman who didn't cheat, or not much, and who paid in cash. Therefore he was treated with respect and shown hospitality, because no one in the village wanted to get on his bad side. What if he ceased to visit? What if a family needed to sell a child and he would not buy it because he'd been offended on a previous visit? He was the villagers' bank, their insurance policy, their kind rich uncle, their only charm against bad luck. And he had been needed more and more often, because the weather had become so strange and could no longer be predicted – too much rain or not enough, too much wind, too much heat – and the crops were suffering.

The man smiled a lot, greeted many of the village men by name. He always gave a little speech, the same one every time. He wanted everyone to be happy, he would say. He wanted satisfaction on both sides. He didn't want any hard feelings. Hadn't he bent over backwards for them, taking children that were plain and stupid and a burden on his hands, just to oblige them? If they had any criticism of the way he conducted affairs, they should tell him. But there was never any criticism, though there was grumbling behind his back: he never paid any more than he had to, it was said. He was admired for this, however: it showed he was good at his trade, and the children would be in competent hands.

Each time the gold-wristwatch man came to the village he would take several children away with him, to sell flowers to tourists on the city streets. The work was easy and the children would be well treated, he assured the mothers: he wasn't a low-down thug or a liar, he wasn't a pimp. They would be well fed and given a safe place to sleep, they would be carefully guarded, and they would be paid a sum of money, which they could send home to their families, or not, whatever they chose. This sum would be a percentage of their earnings minus the expense of their room and board. (No money was ever sent to the village. Everyone knew it would not be.) In exchange for the child apprentice, he would give the fathers, or else the widowed mothers, a good price, or what he said was a good price; and it was a decent-enough price, considering what people were used to. With this money, the mothers who sold their children would be able to give the remaining children a better chance in life. So they told one another.

Jimmy was outraged by this the first time he heard about it. That was in the days of his outrage. Also in the days of his making a fool of himself over anything concerning Oryx.

"You don't understand," said Oryx. She was still eating the pizza in bed; with that she was having a Coke, and a side of fries. She'd finished with the mushrooms and now she was eating the artichoke hearts. She never ate the crust. She said it made her feel very rich to throw away food. "Many people did it. It was the custom."

"An asshole custom," said Jimmy. He was sitting on a chair beside the bed, watching her pink cat's tongue as she licked her fingers.

"Jimmy, you are bad, don't swear. You want a pepperoni? You didn't order them but they put them on anyway. I guess they heard you wrong."

"*Asshole* isn't swearing, it's only graphic description."

"Well, I don't think you should say it." She was eating the anchovies now: she always saved them till last.

"I'd like to kill this guy."

"What guy? You want this Coke? I can't finish it."

"The guy you just told me about."

"Oh Jimmy, you would like it better maybe if we all starved to death?" said Oryx, with her small rippling laugh. This was the laugh he feared most from her, because it disguised amused contempt. It chilled him: a cold breeze on a moonlit lake.

Of course he'd marched his outrage off to Crake. He'd whammed the furniture: those were his furniture-whamming days. What Crake had to say was this: "Jimmy, look at it realistically. You can't couple a minimum access to food with an expanding population indefinitely. *Homo sapiens* doesn't seem able to cut himself off at the supply end. He's one of the few species that doesn't limit reproduction in the face of dwindling resources. In other words — and up to a point, of course — the less we eat, the more we fuck."

"How do you account for that?" said Jimmy.

"Imagination," said Crake. "Men can imagine their own deaths, they can see them coming, and the mere thought of impending death acts like an aphrodisiac. A dog or a rabbit doesn't behave like that. Take birds — in a lean season they cut down on the eggs, or they won't mate at all. They put their energy into staying alive themselves until times get better. But human beings hope they can stick their souls into someone else, some new version of themselves, and live on forever."

"As a species we're doomed by hope, then?"

"You could call it hope. That, or desperation."

"But we're doomed without hope, as well," said Jimmy.

"Only as individuals," said Crake cheerfully.

"Well, it sucks."

"Jimmy, grow up."

Crake wasn't the first person who'd ever said that to Jimmy.

The wristwatch man would stay overnight in the village with his two servants and their guns, and would eat and then drink with the men. He would hand out cigarettes, entire packs of them, in gold and silver paper boxes with the cellophane still on. In the morning he would look over the children on offer and ask some questions about them — had they been sick, were they obedient? And he'd check their teeth. They had to have good teeth, he said, because they would need to smile a lot. Then he would make his selections, and the money would change hands, and he'd say his farewells, and there would be polite nods and bows all round. He would take three or four children with him, never more; that was the number he could manage. This meant he could pick the best of the crop. He did the same in the other villages in his territory. He was known for his taste and judgment.

Oryx said it must have been too bad for a child not to be chosen. Things would be worse for it in the village then, it would lose value, it would be given less to eat. She herself had been chosen first of all.

Sometimes the mothers would cry, and also the children, but the mothers would tell the children that what they were doing was good, they were helping their families, and they should go with the man and do everything he told them. The mothers said that after the children had worked in the city for a while and things were better, then they could come back to the village. (No children ever came back.)

All of this was understood, and if not condoned, at least pardoned. Still, after the man had left, the mothers who had sold their children felt empty and sad. They felt as if this act, done freely by themselves (no one had forced them, no one had threatened them) had not been performed willingly. They felt cheated as well, as if the price had been too low. Why hadn't they demanded more? And yet, the mothers told themselves, they'd had no choice.

The mother of Oryx sold two of her children at the same time, not only because she was hard up. She thought the two might keep each other company, look out for each other. The other child was a boy, a year older than Oryx. Fewer boys were sold than girls, but they were not therefore more valued.

(Oryx took this double sale as evidence that her mother had loved her. She had no images of this love. She could offer no anecdotes. It was a belief rather than a memory.)

The man said he was doing Oryx's mother a special favour, as boys were more trouble and did not obey, and ran away more often, and who would pay him for his trouble then? Also this boy did not have a right attitude, that much was clear at a glance, and he had a blackened front tooth that gave him a criminal expression. But as he knew she needed the money he would be generous, and would take the boy off her hands.

Birdcall
~

Oryx said she couldn't remember the trip from the village to the city, but she could remember some of the things that had happened. It was like pictures hanging on a wall, with around them the blank plaster. It was like looking through other people's windows. It was like dreams.

The man with the watch said his name was Uncle En, and they must call him that or there would be very big trouble.

"Was that En as in a name, or N as in an initial?" Jimmy asked.

"I don't know," said Oryx.

"Did you ever see it written?"

"Nobody in our village could read," said Oryx. "Here, Jimmy. Open your mouth. I give you the last piece."

Remembering this, Snowman can almost taste it. The pizza, then Oryx's fingers in his mouth.

Then the Coke can rolling onto the floor. Then joy, crushing his whole body in its boa-constrictor grip.

Oh stolen secret picnics. Oh sweet delight. Oh clear memory, oh pure pain. Oh endless night.

~   ~   ~

This man – Oryx continued, later that night, or on some other night – this man said he was their uncle from now on. Now that they were out of sight of the village he wasn't smiling so much. They must walk very quickly, he said, because the forest around them was full of wild animals with red eyes and long sharp teeth, and if they ran in among the trees or walked too slowly, these animals would come and tear them to pieces. Oryx was frightened and wanted to hold hands with her brother, but that wasn't possible.

"Were there tigers?" Jimmy asked.

Oryx shook her head for no. No tigers.

"What were these animals then?" Jimmy wanted to know. He thought he might get some clues that way, as to the location. He could look at the list of habitats, that might help.

"They didn't have names," said Oryx, "but I knew what they were."

At first they went single file along the muddy road, walking on the side where it was higher, watching out for snakes. A gun-carrying man was at the front, then Uncle En, then the brother, then the two other children who had also been sold – both girls, both older – and then Oryx. At the end came the other gun man. They stopped for a noon meal – cold rice, it was, packed for them by the villagers – and then they walked some more. When they came to a river one of the men with the guns carried Oryx across. He said she was so heavy he would have to drop her into the water and then the fish would eat her, but that was a joke. He smelled of sweaty cloth and smoke, and some sort of perfume or grease that was in his hair. The water came up to his knees.

After that the sun was on a slant and got into her eyes – they must have been going west then, thought Jimmy – and she was very tired.

As the sun got lower and lower the birds began singing and calling, unseen, hidden in the branches and vines of the forest: raucous croaks and whistles, and four clear sounds in a row, like a bell. These were the same birds that always called like this as dusk approached, and at dawn just before the sun came up, and Oryx was consoled by their sounds. The birdcalls were familiar, they were part of what she knew. She imagined that one of them – the one like a bell – was her mother's spirit, sent out in the shape of a bird to keep watch over her, and that it was saying *You will come back.*

In that village, she told him, some of the people could send their spirits out like that even before they were dead. It was well known. You could learn how to do it, the old women could teach you, and that way you could fly everywhere, you could see what was coming in the future, and send messages, and appear in other people's dreams.

The bird called and called and then fell silent. Then the sun went down abruptly and it was dark. That night they slept in a shed. Possibly it was a shed for livestock; it had that smell. They had to pee in the bushes, all together in a row, with one of the gun men standing guard. The men made a fire outside and laughed and talked, and smoke came in, but Oryx didn't care because she went to sleep. Did they sleep on the ground, or in hammocks, or on cots, asked Jimmy, but she said it wasn't important. Her brother was there beside her. He'd never paid very much attention to her before, but now he wanted to be close to her.

The next morning they walked some more and came to the place where Uncle En's car had been left, under the protection of several men in a small village: smaller than their own village, and dirtier. Women and children peered at them from the doorways but did not smile. One woman made a sign against evil.

Uncle En checked to make sure nothing was missing from the car and then he paid the men, and the children were told to get in. Oryx had never been inside a car before and she didn't like the smell. It wasn't a solarcar, it was the gasoline kind, and not new. One of the men drove, Uncle En beside him; the other man sat in the back with all four children jammed in beside him. Uncle En was in a bad temper and told the children not to ask any questions. The road was bumpy and it was hot inside the car. Oryx felt sick and thought she would vomit, but then she dozed off.

They must have driven for a long time; they stopped when it was night again. Uncle En and the man in front went into a low building, some sort of inn perhaps; the other man stretched out on the front seat and soon began to snore. The children slept in the back of the car, as best they could. The back doors were locked: they couldn't get out of the car without climbing over the man, and they were afraid to do that because he would think they were trying to run away. Somebody wet their pants during the night, Oryx could smell it, but it wasn't her. In the morning they were all herded around to the back of the building where there was an open latrine. A pig on the other side of it watched them while they squatted.

After more hours of bumpy driving they stopped where there was a gate across the road, with two soldiers. Uncle En told the soldiers that the children were his nieces and his nephew: their mother had died and he was taking them to live in his own house, with his own family. He was smiling again.

"You have a lot of nieces and nephews," said one of the soldiers, grinning.

"That is my misfortune," said Uncle En.

"And all their mothers die."

"This is the sad truth."

"We aren't sure we should believe you," said the other soldier, also grinning.

"Here," said Uncle En. He pulled Oryx out of the car. "What's my name?" he said to her, putting his smiling face down close.

"Uncle En," she said. The two soldiers laughed and Uncle En laughed also. He patted Oryx on the shoulder and told her to get back into the car, and shook hands with the soldiers, putting his hand into his pocket first, and then the soldiers swung the gate open. Once the car was going along the road again Uncle En gave Oryx a hard candy, in the shape of a tiny lemon. She sucked it for a while and then took it out to keep. She had no pocket so she held it in her sticky fingers. That night she comforted herself by licking her own hand.

The children cried at night, not loudly. They cried to themselves. They were frightened: they didn't know where they were going, and they had been taken away from what they knew. Also, said Oryx, they had no more love, supposing they'd had some in the first place. But they had a money value: they represented a cash profit to others. They must have sensed that – sensed they were worth something.

Of course (said Oryx), having a money value was no substitute for love. Every child should have love, every person should have it. She herself would rather have had her mother's love – the love she still continued to believe in, the love that had followed her through the jungle in the form of a bird so she would not be too frightened or lonely – but love was undependable, it came and then it went, so it was good to have a money value, because then at least those who wanted to make a profit from you would make sure you were fed enough and not damaged too much. Also there were many who had neither love nor a money value, and having one of these things was better than having nothing.

Roses

~

The city was a chaos, filled with people and cars and noise and bad smells and a language that was hard to understand. The four new children were shocked by it at first, as if they'd been plunged into a cauldron of hot water – as if the city was physically hurtful to them. Uncle En had experience, however: he treated the new children as if they were cats, he gave them time to get used to things. He put them into a small room in a three-storey building, on the third floor, with a barred window they could look out but not climb out, and then he led them outside gradually, a short distance at first and an hour at a time. There were already five children staying in the room, so it was crowded; but there was enough space for a thin mattress for each child, laid down at night so the entire floor was covered with mattresses and children, then rolled up during the day. These mattresses were worn and stained, and smelled of urine; but rolling them up neatly was the first thing the new children had to learn.

From the other, more seasoned children they learned more things. The first was that Uncle En would always be watching them, even when it appeared they had been left in the city on their own. He would always know where they were: all he had to do was hold his shiny watch up to his ear and it would tell him, because there was a little voice inside it that knew everything. This was reassuring, as nobody else would be allowed to harm them. On the other hand, Uncle En would see if you didn't work hard enough or tried to run away, or if you kept for yourself any of the money you got from the tourists. Then you would be punished. Uncle En's men would beat you and then you would have bruises. They might burn you as well. Some of the children claimed to have endured these punishments, and were proud of it: they had scars. If you tried these forbidden things often enough – laziness, theft, running away – you would be sold, to someone much worse – it was said – than Uncle En. Or else you would be killed and tossed on a rubbish heap, and nobody would care because nobody would know who you were.

Oryx said that Uncle En really knew his business, because children would believe other children about punishments more readily than they would believe adults. Adults threatened to do things they never did, but children told what would happen. Or what they were afraid would happen. Or what had happened already, to them or to other children they'd known.

The week after Oryx and her brother arrived in the mattress room, three of the older children were taken away. They were going to another country, said Uncle En. This country was called San Francisco. Was it because they'd been bad? No, said Uncle En, it was a reward for being good. All who were obedient and diligent might go there some day. There was nowhere Oryx wanted to go except home, but "home" was becoming hazy in her mind. She could still hear her mother's spirit calling *You will come back*, but that voice was becoming fainter and more indistinct. It was no longer like a bell, it was like a whisper. It was a question now, rather than a statement; a question with no answer.

Oryx and her brother and the other two newcomers were taken to watch the more experienced children selling flowers. The flowers were roses, red and white and pink; they were collected at the flower market early in the morning. The thorns had been removed from the stems so the roses could be passed from hand to hand without pricking anyone. You had to loiter around the entranceways to the best hotels – the banks where foreign money could be changed and the expensive shops were good locations too – and you had to keep an eye out for policemen. If a policeman came near or stared hard at you, you should walk the other way quickly. Selling flowers to the tourists was not allowed unless you had an official permit, and such permits were too expensive. But there was nothing to worry about, said Uncle En: the police knew all about it, only they had to appear as if they didn't know.

When you saw a foreigner, especially one with a foreign woman beside him, you should approach and hold up the roses, and you should smile. You should not stare or laugh at their strange foreign hair and water-coloured eyes. If they took a flower and asked how much, you should smile even more and hold out your hand. If they spoke to you, asking questions, you should look as if you didn't understand. That part was easy enough. They would always give you more – sometimes much more – than the flower was worth.

The money had to be put into a little bag hanging inside your clothes; that was to protect against pickpockets and random snatching from street urchins, those unlucky ones without an Uncle En to look after them. If anyone – especially any man – tried to take you by the hand and lead you off somewhere, you should pull your hand away. If they held on too tight you should sit down. That would be a signal, and one of Uncle En's men would come, or Uncle En himself. You should never get into a car or go into a hotel. If a man asked you to do that, you should tell Uncle En as soon as possible.

Oryx had been given a new name by Uncle En. All the children got new names from him. They were told to forget their old names, and soon they did. Oryx was now SuSu. She was good at selling roses. She was so small and fragile, her features so clear and pure. She was given a dress that was too big for her, and in it she looked like an angelic doll. The other children petted her, because she was the littlest one. They took turns sleeping beside her at night; she was passed from one set of arms to another.

Who could resist her? Not many of the foreigners. Her smile was perfect — not cocky or aggressive, but hesitant, shy, taking nothing for granted. It was a smile with no ill will in it: it contained no resentment, no envy, only the promise of heartfelt gratitude. "Adorable," the foreign ladies would murmur, and the men with them would buy a rose and hand it to the lady, and that way the men would become adorable too; and Oryx would slip the coins into the bag down the front of her dress and feel safe for one more day, because she had sold her quota.

Not so her brother. He had no luck. He didn't want to sell flowers like a girl, and he hated smiling; and when he did smile, the effect was not good because of his blackened tooth. So Oryx would take some of his leftover roses and try to sell them for him. Uncle En didn't mind at first — money was money — but then he said Oryx shouldn't be seen too much in the same locations because it wouldn't do for people to become tired of her.

Something else would have to be found for the brother — some other occupation. He would have to be sold elsewhere. The older children in the room shook their heads: the brother would be sold to a pimp, they said; a pimp for hairy white foreign men or bearded brown men or fat yellow men, any kind of men who liked little boys. They described in detail what these men would do; they laughed about it. He would be a melon-bum boy, they said: that's what boys like him were called. Firm and round on the outside, soft and sweet on the inside; a nice melon bum, for anyone who paid. Either that or he would be put to work as a messenger, sent from street to street, doing errands for gamblers, and that was hard work and very dangerous, because the rival gamblers would kill you. Or he could be a messenger and a melon boy, both. That was the most likely thing.

Oryx saw her brother's face darken and grow hard, and she wasn't surprised when he ran away; and whether he was ever caught and punished Oryx never knew. Nor did she ask, because asking – she had now found out – would do no good.

One day a man did take Oryx by the hand and say she should come into the hotel with him. She gave him her shy smile, and looked up sideways and said nothing, and pulled her hand away and told Uncle En afterwards. Then Uncle En said a surprising thing. If the man asked again, he said, she was to go into the hotel with him. He would want to take her up to his room, and she must go with him. She should do whatever the man asked, but she shouldn't worry, because Uncle En would be watching and would come to get her. Nothing bad would happen to her.

"Will I be a melon?" she asked. "A melon-bum girl?" and Uncle En laughed and said where did she pick up that word. But no, he said. That was not what would happen.

Next day the man appeared and asked Oryx if she would like some money, a lot more money than she could make by selling roses. He was a long white hairy man with a thick accent, but she could make out the words. This time Oryx went with him. He held her hand and they went up in an elevator – this was the frightening part, a tiny room with doors that shut, and when the doors opened you were in a different place, and Uncle En hadn't explained about that. She could feel her heart thumping. "Don't be afraid," said the man, thinking she was afraid of him. But it was the other way around, he was afraid of her, because his hand had a tremor. He unlocked a door with a key and they went in, and he locked the door behind them, and they were in a mauve-and-gold-coloured room with a giant bed in it, a bed for giants, and the man asked Oryx to take off her dress.

Oryx was obedient and did as she was told. She had a general idea of what else the man might want – the other children already knew about such things and discussed them freely, and laughed about them. People paid a lot of money for the kinds of things this man wanted, and there were special places in the city for men like him to go; but some wouldn't go there because it was too public and they were ashamed, and they foolishly wanted to arrange things for themselves, and this man was one of that kind. So Oryx knew the man would now take off his own clothes, or some of them, and he did, and seemed pleased when she stared at his penis, which was long and hairy like himself, with a bend in it like a little elbow. Then he kneeled down so he was on her level, with his face right next to hers.

What did this face look like? Oryx couldn't remember. She could remember the singularity of his penis but not the singularity of his face. "It was like no face," she said. "It was all soft, like a dumpling. There was a big nose on it, a carrot nose. A long white penis nose." She laughed, holding her two hands over her mouth. "Not like your nose, Jimmy," she added in case he felt self-conscious. "Your nose is beautiful. It is a sweet nose, believe me."

"I won't hurt you," said the man. His accent was so ridiculous that Oryx wanted to giggle, but she knew that would be wrong. She smiled her shy smile, and the man took hold of one of her hands and placed it on himself. He did this gently enough, but at the same time he seemed angry. Angry, and in a hurry.

That was when Uncle En plunged suddenly into the room — how? He must have had a key, he must have been given a key by someone at the hotel. He picked Oryx up and hugged her and called her his little treasure, and yelled at the man, who seemed very frightened and tried to scramble into his clothes. He got caught in his trousers and hopped around on one foot while trying to explain something with his bad accent, and Oryx felt bad for him. Then the man gave money to Uncle En, a lot of money, all the money in his wallet, and Uncle En went out of the room carrying Oryx like a precious vase and still muttering and scowling. But out on the street he laughed, and made jokes about the man hopping around in his snarled-up trousers, and told Oryx she was a good girl and wouldn't she like to play this game again?

So that became her game. She felt a little sorry for the men: although Uncle En said they deserved what happened to them and they were lucky he never called the police, she somewhat regretted her part. But at the same time she enjoyed it. It made her feel strong to know that the men thought she was helpless but she was not. It was they who were helpless, they who would soon have to stammer apologies in their silly accents and hop around on one foot in their luxurious hotel rooms, trapped in their own pant legs with their bums sticking out, smooth bums and hairy bums, bums of different sizes and colours, while Uncle En berated them. From time to time they would cry. As for the money, they emptied their pockets, they threw all the money they had at Uncle En, they thanked him for taking it. They didn't want to spend any time in jail, not in that city, where the jails were not hotels and it took a very long time for charges to be laid and for trials to be held. They wanted to get into taxis, as soon as they could, and climb onto big airplanes, and fly away through the sky.

"Little SuSu," Uncle En would say, as he set Oryx down on the street outside the hotel. "You are a smart girl! I wish I could marry you. Would you like that?"

This was as close to love as Oryx could get right then, so she felt happy. But what was the right answer, yes or no? She knew it was not a serious question but a joke: she was only five, or six, or seven, so she couldn't get married. Anyway the other children said that Uncle En had a grown-up wife who lived in a house elsewhere, and he had other children as well. His real children. They went to school.

"Can I listen to your watch?" said Oryx with her shy smile. *Instead of*, was what she meant. *Instead of marrying you, instead of answering your question, instead of being your real child.* And he laughed some more, and he did let her listen to his watch, but she didn't hear any little voice inside.

Pixieland Jazz

~

One day a different man came, one they'd never seen before – a tall thin man, taller than Uncle En, with ill-fitting clothes and a pock-marked face – and said that all of them would have to come with him. Uncle En had sold his flower business, this man said; the flowers, and the flower-sellers, and everything else. He'd gone away, he'd moved to a different city. So this tall man was the boss now.

A year or so later, Oryx was told – by a girl who'd been with her the first weeks in the room with the mattresses, and had turned up again in her new life, her life of movie-making – that this wasn't the real story. The real story was that Uncle En had been found floating in one of the city's canals with his throat cut.

This girl had seen him. No, that was wrong – she hadn't seen him, but she knew somebody who had. There was no doubt about who it was. His stomach was puffed up like a pillow, his face was bloated, but it was Uncle En all right. He had no clothes on – someone must have taken them. Maybe someone else, not the one who'd cut his throat, or maybe the same one, because what use did a corpse have for good clothes like his? No watch on him either.

"No money," the girl had said, and she'd laughed. "No pockets, so no money!"

"There were canals in this city?" Jimmy asked. He thought maybe that would give him a clue as to which city it had been. In those days he'd wanted to know whatever it was possible to know, about Oryx, about anywhere she'd been. He'd wanted to track down and personally injure anyone who had ever done harm to her or made her unhappy. He'd tortured himself with painful knowledge: every white-hot factoid he could collect he'd shove up under his fingernails. The more it hurt, the more – he was convinced – he loved her.

"Oh yes, there were canals," Oryx said. "The farmers used them, and the flower-growers, to get to the markets. They tied up their boats and sold what they had right there, right at the quays. That was a pretty sight, from a distance. So many flowers." She looked at him: she could often tell what he was thinking. "But a lot of cities have canals," she said. "And rivers. The rivers are so useful, for the garbage and the dead people and the babies that get thrown away, and the shit." Although she didn't like it when he swore, she sometimes liked to say what she called *bad words* herself, because it shocked him. She had a large supply of bad words once she got going. "Don't worry so much, Jimmy," she added more gently. "It was a long time ago." More often than not she acted as if she wanted to protect him, from the image of herself – herself in the past. She liked to keep only the bright side of herself turned towards him. She liked to shine.

So Uncle En had ended up in the canal. He'd been unlucky. He hadn't paid off the right people, or he hadn't paid them off enough. Or maybe they'd tried to buy his business and the price was too low and he wouldn't do it. Or his own men had sold him out. There were many things that could have happened to him. Or maybe it was nothing planned – just an accident, a random killing, just a thief. Uncle En had been careless, he'd gone out walking by himself. Though he wasn't a careless man.

"I cried when I heard about it," said Oryx. "Poor Uncle En."

"Why are you defending him?" Jimmy asked. "He was vermin, he was a cockroach!"

"He liked me."

"He liked the money!"

"Of course, Jimmy," said Oryx. "Everyone likes that. But he could have done much worse things to me, and he didn't do them. I cried when I heard he was dead. I cried and cried."

"What worse things? What much worse?"

"Jimmy, you worry too much."

The children were herded out of the room with the grey mattresses, and Oryx never saw it again. She never saw most of the other children again. They were divided up, and one went this way and one that. Oryx was sold to a man who made movies. She was the only one of them that went with the movie man. He told her she was a pretty little girl and asked how old she was, but she didn't know the answer to that. He asked her wouldn't she like to be in a movie. She'd never seen a movie so she didn't know whether she would like it or not; but it sounded like an offer of a treat, so she said yes. By this time she was good at knowing when *yes* was the expected answer.

The man drove her in a car with some other girls, three or four, girls she didn't know. They stayed overnight at a house, a big house. It was a house for rich people; it had a high wall around it with broken glass and barbed wire on the top, and they went in through a gate. Inside, it had a rich smell.

"What do you mean, a rich smell?" Jimmy asked, but Oryx couldn't say. *Rich* was just a thing you learned to tell. The house smelled like the better hotels she'd been in: many different foods cooking, wooden furniture, polishes and soap, all those smells mixed in. There must have been flowers, flowering trees or bushes nearby, because that was some of the smell. There were carpets on the floor but the children didn't walk on them; the carpets were in a big room, and they went past the open door and looked in and saw them. They were blue and pink and red, such beauty.

The room they were put in was next to the kitchen. Perhaps it was a storeroom, or it had been one: there was the smell of rice and of the bags it was packed in, though no rice was in that room then. They were fed — better food than usual, said Oryx, there was chicken in it — and told not to make any noise. Then they were locked in. There were dogs at that house; you could hear them outside in the yard, barking.

The next day some of them went in a truck, in the back of a truck. There were two other children, both girls, both of them small like Oryx. One of them had just come from a village and missed her people there, and cried a lot, silently, hiding her face. They were lifted up into the back of the truck and locked in, and it was dark and hot and they got thirsty, and when they had to pee they had to do it in the truck because there was no stopping. There was a little window though, up high, so some air got in.

It was only a couple of hours, but it seemed like more because of the heat and the darkness. When they got to where they were going they were handed over to another man, a different one, and the truck drove off.

"Was there any writing on it? The truck?" asked Jimmy, sleuthing.

"Yes. It was red writing."

"What did it say?"

"How would I know?" said Oryx reproachfully.

Jimmy felt foolish. "Was there a picture, then?"

"Yes. There was a picture," said Oryx after a moment.

"A picture of what?"

Oryx thought. "It was a parrot. A red parrot."

"Flying, or standing?"

"Jimmy, you are too strange!"

Jimmy held on to it, this red parrot. He kept it in mind. Sometimes it would appear to him in reveries, charged with mystery and hidden significance, a symbol free of all contexts. It must have been a brand name, a logo. He searched the Internet for Parrot, Parrot Brand, Parrot Inc., Redparrot. He found Alex the cork-nut parrot who'd said *I'm going away now*, but that was no help to him because Alex was the wrong colour. He wanted the red parrot to be a link between the story Oryx had told him and the so-called real world. He wanted to be walking along a street or trolling through the Web, and eureka, there it would be, the red parrot, the code, the password, and then many things would become clear.

The building where the movies were made was in a different city, or it might have been in a different part of the same city, because the city was very big, said Oryx. The room she stayed in with the other girls was in that building too. They almost never went outside, except up onto the flat roof sometimes when the movie was to be made up there. Some of the men who came to the building wanted to be outside while the movie was being filmed. They wanted to be seen, and at the same time they wanted to be hidden: the roof had a wall around it. "Maybe they wanted God to see them," said Oryx. "What do you think, Jimmy? They were showing off to God? I think so."

These men all had ideas about what should be in their movie. They wanted things in the background, chairs or trees, or they wanted ropes or screaming, or shoes. Sometimes they would say, *Just do it, I'm paying for it*, or things like that, because everything in these movies had a price. Every hair bow, every flower, every object, every gesture. If the men thought up something new, there would have to be a discussion about how much that new thing ought to cost.

"So I learned about life," said Oryx.

"Learned what?" said Jimmy. He shouldn't have had the pizza, and the weed they'd smoked on top of that. He was feeling a little sick.

"That everything has a price."

"Not everything. That can't be true. You can't buy time. You can't buy . . ." He wanted to say *love*, but hesitated. It was too soppy.

"You can't buy it, but it has a price," said Oryx. "Everything has a price."

"Not me," said Jimmy, trying to joke. "I don't have a price."

Wrong, as usual.

Being in a movie, said Oryx, was doing what you were told. If they wanted you to smile then you had to smile, if they wanted you to cry you had to do that too. Whatever it was, you had to do it, and you did it because you were afraid not to. You did what they told you to do to the men who came, and then sometimes those men did things to you. That was movies.

"What sort of things?" said Jimmy.

"You know," said Oryx. "You saw. You have the picture of it."

"I only saw that one," said Jimmy. "Only the one, with you in."

"I bet you saw more with me in. You don't remember. I could look different, I could wear different clothes and wigs, I could be someone else, do other things."

"Like what else? What else did they make you do?"

"They were all the same, those movies," said Oryx. She'd washed her hands, she was painting her nails now, her delicate oval nails, so perfectly shaped. Peach-coloured, to match the flowered wrapper she was wearing. Not a smudge on her. Later on she would do her toes.

It was less boring for the children to make the movies than to do what they did the rest of the time, which was nothing much.

They watched cartoons on the old DVD in one of the rooms, mice and birds being chased around by other animals that could never catch them; or they brushed and braided one another's hair, or they ate and slept. Sometimes other people came to use the space, to make different kinds of movies. Grown-up women came, women with breasts, and grown-up men − actors. The children could watch them making those movies if they didn't get in the way. Though sometimes the actors objected because the little girls would giggle at their penises − so big, and then sometimes, all of a sudden, so small − and then the children had to go back into their room.

They washed a lot − that was important. They took showers with a bucket. They were supposed to be pure-looking. On a bad day when there was no business they would get tired and restless, and then they would argue and fight. Sometimes they'd be given a toke or a drink to calm them down − beer, maybe − but no hard drugs, those would shrivel them up; and they weren't allowed to smoke. The man in charge − the big man, not the man with the camera − said they shouldn't smoke because it would make their teeth brown. They did smoke sometimes anyway, because the man with the camera might give them a cigarette to share.

The man with the camera was white, and his name was Jack. He was the one they mostly saw. He had hair like frayed rope and he smelled too strong, because he was a meat-eater. He ate so much meat! He didn't like fish. He didn't like rice either, but he liked noodles. Noodles with lots of meat.

Jack said that where he came from the movies were bigger and better, the best in the world. He kept saying he wanted to go home. He said it was only pure dumb chance he wasn't dead − that this fucking country hadn't killed him with its lousy food. He said he'd almost died from some disease he'd got from the water and the only thing that had saved him was getting really, really pissed, because alcohol killed germs. Then he had to explain to them about germs. The little girls laughed about the germs, because they didn't believe in them; but they believed about the disease, because they'd seen that happen. Spirits caused it, everyone knew that. Spirits and bad luck. Jack had not said the right prayers.

Jack said he would get sick more often from the rotten food and water, only he had a really strong stomach. He said you needed a strong stomach in this business. He said the videocam was antique-roadshow junk and the lights were poor so no wonder everything looked like cheap shit. He said he wished he had a million dollars but he'd pissed all his money away. He said he couldn't hold on to money, it slid off him like water off a greased whore. "Don't be like me when you grow up," he would say. And the girls would laugh, because whatever else happened to them they would never be like him, a rope-haired clownish giant with a cock like a wrinkly old carrot.

Oryx said she had many chances to see that old carrot up close, because Jack wanted to do movie things with her when there were no movies. Then he would be sad and tell her he was sorry. That was puzzling.

"You did it for nothing?" said Jimmy. "I thought you said everything has a price." He didn't feel he'd won the argument about money, he wanted another turn.

Oryx paused, lifting the nail-polish brush. She looked at her hand. "I traded him," she said.

"Traded him for what?" said Jimmy. "What did that pathetic prick of a loser have to offer?"

"Why do you think he is bad?" said Oryx. "He never did anything with me that you don't do. Not nearly so many things!"

"I don't do them against your will," said Jimmy. "Anyway you're grown up now."

Oryx laughed. "What is my will?" she said. Then she must have seen his pained look, so she stopped laughing. "He taught me to read," she said quietly. "To speak English, and to read English words. Talking first, then reading, not so good at first, and I still don't talk so good but you always have to start somewhere, don't you think so, Jimmy?"

"You talk perfectly," said Jimmy.

"You don't need to tell lies to me. So that is how. It took a long time, but he was very patient. He had one book, I don't know where he got it but it was a book for children. It had a girl in it with long braids, and stockings — that was a hard word, *stockings* — who jumped around and did whatever she liked. So this is what we read. It was a good trade, because, Jimmy, if I hadn't done it I couldn't be talking to you, no?"

"Done what?" said Jimmy. He couldn't stand it. If he had this Jack, this piece of garbage, in the room right now he'd wring his neck like a wormy old sock. "What did you do for him? You sucked him off?"

"Crake is right," said Oryx coldly. "You do not have an elegant mind."

Elegant mind was just mathtalk, that patronizing jargon the math nerds used, but it hurt Jimmy anyway. No. What hurt was the thought of Oryx and Crake discussing him that way, behind his back.

"I'm sorry," he said. He ought to know better than to speak so bluntly to her.

"Now maybe I wouldn't do it, but I was a child then," said Oryx more softly. "Why are you so angry?"

"I don't buy it," said Jimmy. Where was her rage, how far down was it buried, what did he have to do to dig it up?

"You don't buy what?"

"Your whole fucking story. All this sweetness and acceptance and crap."

"If you don't want to buy that, Jimmy," said Oryx, looking at him tenderly, "what is it that you would like to buy instead?"

Jack had a name for the building where the movies went on. He called it Pixieland. None of the children knew what that meant — *Pixieland* — because it was an English word and an English idea, and Jack couldn't explain it. "All right, pixies, rise and shine," he'd say. "Candy time!" He brought candies for them as a treat, sometimes. "Want a candy, candy?" he'd say. That also was a joke, but they didn't know what it meant either.

He let them see the movies of themselves if he felt like it, or if he'd just been doing drugs. They could tell when he'd been shooting or snorting, because he was happier then. He liked to play pop music while they were working, something with a bounce. Upbeat, he called it. Elvis Presley, things like that. He said he liked the golden oldies, from back when songs had words. "Call me sentimental," he said, causing puzzlement. He liked Frank Sinatra too, and Doris Day: Oryx knew all the words to "Love Me or Leave Me" before she had any idea what they meant. "Sing us some pixieland jazz," Jack would say, and so that was what Oryx would sing. He was always pleased.

"What was this guy's name?" said Jimmy. What a jerk, this Jack. Jack the jerk, the jerkoff. Name-calling helped, thought Jimmy. He'd like to twist the guy's head off.

"His name was Jack. I told you. He told us a poem about it, in English. *Jack be nimble, Jack be quick, Jack has got a big candlestick.*"

"I mean his other name."

"He didn't have another name."

Working was what Jack called what they did. *Working girls*, he called them. He used to say, *Whistle while you work.* He used to say, *Work harder.* He used to say, *Put some jazz into it.* He used to say, *Act like you mean it, or you want to get hurt?* He used to say, *Come on, sex midgets, you can do better.* He used to say, *You're only young once.*

"That's all," said Oryx.

"What do you mean, that's all?"

"That's all there was," she said. "That's all there was to it."

"What about, did they ever . . ."

"Did they ever what?"

"They didn't. Not when you were that young. They couldn't have."

"Please, Jimmy, tell me what you are asking." Oh, very cool. He wanted to shake her.

"Did they rape you?" He could barely squeeze it out. What answer was he expecting, what did he want?

"Why do you want to talk about ugly things?" she said. Her voice was silvery, like a music box. She waved one hand in the air to dry the nails. "We should think only beautiful things, as much as we can. There is so much beautiful in the world if you look around. You are looking only at the dirt under your feet, Jimmy. It's not good for you."

She would never tell him. Why did this drive him so crazy? "It wasn't real sex, was it?" he asked. "In the movies. It was only acting. Wasn't it?"

"But Jimmy, you should know. All sex is real."

Sveltana
~

Snowman opens his eyes, shuts them, opens them, keeps them open. He's had a terrible night. He doesn't know which is worse, a past he can't regain or a present that will destroy him if he looks at it too clearly. Then there's the future. Sheer vertigo.

The sun is above the horizon, lifting steadily as if on a pulley; flattish clouds, pink and purple on top and golden underneath, stand still in the sky around it. The waves are waving, up down up down. The thought of them makes him queasy. He's violently thirsty, and he has a headache and a hollow cottony space between his ears. It takes him some moments to register the fact that he has a hangover.

"It's your own fault," he tells himself. He behaved foolishly the night before: he guzzled, he yelled, he gibbered, he indulged in pointless repinings. Once he wouldn't have had a hangover after so little booze, but he's out of practice now, and out of shape.

At least he didn't fall out of the tree. "Tomorrow is another day," he declaims to the pink and purple clouds. But if tomorrow is another day, what's today? The same day as it always is, except that he feels as if he has tongue fur all over his body.

~   ~   ~

A long scrawl of birds unwinds from the empty towers – gulls, egrets, herons, heading off to fish along the shore. A mile or so to the south, a salt marsh is forming on a one-time landfill dotted with semi-flooded townhouses. That's where all the birds are going: minnow city. He watches them with resentment: everything is fine with them, not a care in the world. Eat, fuck, poop, screech, that's all they do. In a former life he might have snuck up on them, studied them through binoculars, wondering at their grace. No, he never would have done that, it hadn't been his style. Some grade-school teacher, a nature snoop – Sally Whatshername? – herding them along on what she called field trips. The Compound golf course and lily ponds had been their hunting grounds. *Look! See the nice ducks? Those are called mallards!* Snowman had found birds tedious even then, but he wouldn't have wished to harm them. Whereas right now he yearns for a big slingshot.

He climbs down from the tree, more carefully than usual: he's still a bit dizzy. He checks his baseball cap, dumps out a butterfly – attracted by the salt, no doubt – and pisses on the grasshoppers, as usual. I have a daily routine, he thinks. Routines are good. His entire head is becoming one big stash of obsolete fridge magnets.

Then he opens up his cement-block cache, puts on his one-eyed sunglasses, drinks water from a stored beer bottle. If only he had a real beer, or an aspirin, or more Scotch.

"Hair of the dog," he says to the beer bottle. He mustn't drink too much water at a time, he'll throw up. He pours the rest of the water over his head, gets himself a second bottle, and sits down with his back against the tree, waiting for his stomach to settle. He wishes he had something to read. To read, to view, to hear, to study, to compile. Rag ends of language are floating in his head: *mephitic, metronome, mastitis, metatarsal, maudlin.*

"I used to be erudite," he says out loud. *Erudite.* A hopeless word. What are all those things he once thought he knew, and where have they gone?

~   ~   ~

After a while he finds he's hungry. What's in the cache, foodwise? Shouldn't there be a mango? No, that was yesterday. All that's left of it is a sticky ant-covered plastic bag. There's the chocolate energy Joltbar, but he doesn't feel up to that, so he opens the can of Sveltana No-Meat Cocktail Sausages with his rusty can opener. He could use a better one of those. The sausages are a diet brand, beige and unpleasantly soft − babies' turds, he thinks − but he manages to get them down. Sveltanas are always better if you don't look.

They're protein, but they're not enough for him. Not enough calories. He drinks the warm, bland sausage juice, which − he tells himself − must surely be full of vitamins. Or minerals, at least. Or something. He used to know. What's happening to his mind? He has a vision of the top of his neck, opening up into his head like a bathroom drain. Fragments of words are swirling down it, in a grey liquid he realizes is his dissolving brain.

Time to face reality. Crudely put, he's slowly starving to death. A fish a week is all he can depend on, and the people take that literally: it can be a decent-sized fish or a very small one, all spikes and bones. He knows that if he doesn't balance out the protein with starches and that other stuff − carbohydrates, or are those the same as starches? − he'll start dissolving his own fat, what's left of it, and after that his own muscles. The heart is a muscle. He pictures his heart, shrivelling up until it's no bigger than a walnut.

At first he'd been able to get fruit, not only from the cans of it he'd been able to scrounge, but also from the deserted arboretum an hour's walk to the north. He'd known how to find it, he'd had a map then, but it's long gone, blown away in a thunderstorm. Fruits of the World was the section he'd headed for. There'd been some bananas ripening in the Tropicals area, and several other things, round, green, and knobbly, that he hadn't wanted to eat because they might have been poisonous. There'd been some grapes too, on a trellis, in the Temperate zone. The solar air conditioning was still functioning, inside the greenhouse, though one of the panes was broken. There'd been some apricots as well, espaliered against a wall; though only a few, browning where the wasps had eaten into them and beginning to rot. He'd devoured them anyway; also some lemons. They'd been very sour, but he'd forced himself to drink the juice: he was familiar with scurvy from old seafaring movies. Bleeding gums, teeth coming out in handfuls. That hasn't happened to him yet.

Fruits of the World is cleaned out now. How long till more fruits of the world appear and ripen? He has no clue. There ought to be some wild berries. He'll ask the kids about that, the next time they come poking around: they'll know about berries. But though he can hear them farther down the beach, laughing and calling to one another, they don't seem to be coming his way this morning. Maybe they're getting bored with him, tired of pestering him for answers he won't give or that make no sense to them. Maybe he's old hat, an outworn novelty, a mangy toy. Maybe he's lost his charisma, like some shoddy, balding pop star of yesteryear. He ought to welcome the possibility of being left alone, but he finds the thought dispiriting.

If he had a boat he might row out to the tower blocks, climb up, rob nests, steal some eggs, if he had a ladder. No, bad idea: the towers are too unstable, even in the months he's been here several of them have come crashing down. He could walk to the area of the bungalows and trailers, hunt for rats, barbecue them over the glowing coals. It's something to consider. Or he could try going as far as the closest Module, better pickings than the trailers because the goodies there had been thicker on the ground. Or one of the retirement colonies, the gated communities, something like that. But he has no maps any more and he can't risk getting lost, wandering around at dusk with no cover and no suitable tree. The wolvogs would be after him for sure.

He could trap a pigoon, bludgeon it to death, butcher it in secret. He'd have to hide the mess: he has a notion that the sight of full frontal blood and guts might take him over the threshold as far as the Children of Crake are concerned. But a pigoon feast would do him a world of good. Pigoons are fat, and fat is a carbohydrate. Or is it? He searches his mind for some lesson or long-lost chart that would tell him: he knew that stuff once, but it's no use, the file folders are empty.

"Bring home the bacon," he says. He can almost smell it, that bacon, frying in a pan, with an egg, to be served up with toast and a cup of coffee . . . *Cream with that?* whispers a woman's voice. Some naughty, nameless waitress, out of a white-aprons-and-feather-dusters porno farce. He finds himself salivating.

Fat isn't a carbohydrate. Fat is a fat. He whacks his own forehead, lifts his shoulders, spreads his hands. "So, wise guy," he says. "Next question?"

Do not overlook a plentiful source of nutrition that may be no farther away than your feet, says another voice, in an annoying, instructive tone he recognizes from a survival manual he once leafed through in someone else's bathroom. When jumping off a bridge, clench your bum so the water won't rush up your anus. When drowning in quicksand, take a ski pole. Great advice! This is the same guy who said you could catch an alligator with a pointed stick. Worms and grubs were what he recommended for a snack food. You could toast them if you wanted.

Snowman can see himself turning over logs, but not just yet. There's something else he'll try first: he'll retrace his steps, go back to the RejoovenEsense Compound. It's a long hike, longer than any he's taken yet, but worth it if he can get there. He's sure there will still be a lot left, back there: not only canned goods, booze as well. Once they'd figured out what was going on, the Compound inhabitants had dropped everything and fled. They wouldn't have stayed long enough to clean out the supermarkets.

What he really needs is a spraygun, though − with one of those, he could shoot pigoons, hold off the wolvogs − and, Idea! Light bulb over head! − he knows exactly where to find one. Crake's bubble-dome contains a whole arsenal, which ought to be right where he left it. *Paradice*, was what they'd named the place. He'd been one of the angels guarding the gate, in a manner of speaking, so he knows where everything is, he'll be able to lay his hands on the necessary items. A quick in and out, a snatch and grab. Then he'll be equipped for anything.

But you don't want to go back there, do you? a soft voice whispers.

"Not particularly."

Because?

"Because nothing."

Go on, say it.

"I forget."

No, you don't. You've forgotten nothing.

"I'm a sick man," he pleads. "I'm dying of scurvy! Go away!"

What he needs to do is concentrate. Prioritize. Whittle things down to essentials. The essentials are: *Unless you eat, you die.* You can't get any more essential than that.

The Rejoov Compound is too far away for a casual day trip: it's more like an expedition. He'll have to stay out overnight. He doesn't welcome that thought – where will he sleep? – but if he's careful he should be okay.

With the can of Sveltana sausages inside him and a goal in sight, Snowman's beginning to feel almost normal. He has a mission: he's even looking forward to it. He might unearth all sorts of things. Cherries preserved in brandy; dry-roasted peanuts; a precious can of imitation Spam, if serendipity strikes. A truckload of booze. The Compounds hadn't stinted themselves, you could find the full range of goods and services there when there were shortages everywhere else.

He gets to his feet, stretches, scratches around the old scabs on his back – they feel like misplaced toenails – then walks back along the path behind his tree, picking up the empty Scotch bottle he threw down at the wolvogs the night before. He gives it a wistful sniff, then tosses it and the Sveltana can onto his midden-heap of empty containers, where a whole crowd of debauched flies is making merry. Sometimes at night he can hear the rakunks pawing through this private dump of his, searching for a free meal among the leavings of catastrophe, as he himself has often done, and is about to do again.

Then he sets about making his preparations. He reties his sheet, arranging it over his shoulders and pulling the extra up through his legs and tucking it in through the belt effect at the front, and knotting his last chocolate energy bar into a corner. He finds himself a stick, long and fairly straight. He decides to take only one bottle of water: most likely there'll be water along the way. If not, he can always catch the runoff from the afternoon storm.

He'll have to tell the Children of Crake he's going. He doesn't want them to discover he's missing and set out looking for him. They could run into dangers, or get lost. Despite their irritating qualities — among which he counts their naive optimism, their open friendliness, their calmness, and their limited vocabularies — he feels protective towards them. Intentionally or not, they've been left in his care, and they simply have no idea. No idea, for instance, of how inadequate his care really is.

Stick in hand, rehearsing the story he'll tell them, he goes along the path to their encampment. They call this path the Snowman Fish Path, because they carry his fish along it every week. It skirts the edge of the beach while keeping to the shade; nevertheless he finds it too bright, and tilts his baseball cap down to keep out the rays. He whistles as he approaches them, as he always does to let them know he's coming. He doesn't want to startle them, strain their politeness, cross their boundaries without being invited — loom up on them suddenly out of the shrubbery, like some grotesque flasher exposing himself to schoolkids.

His whistle is like a leper's bell: all those bothered by cripples can get out of his way. Not that he's infectious: what he's got they'll never catch. They're immune from him.

Purring

~

The men are performing their morning ritual, standing six feet apart in a long line curving off into the trees at either side. They're facing outward as in pictures of muskoxen, pissing along the invisible line that marks their territory. Their expressions are grave, as befits the seriousness of their task. They remind Snowman of his father heading out the door in the morning, briefcase in hand, an earnest aiming-for-the-target frown between his eyes.

The men do this twice a day, as they've been taught: it's necessary to keep the volume constant, the odour renewed. Crake's model had been the canids and the mustelids, and a couple of other families and species as well. Scent-marking was a wide-ranging mammalian leitmotif, he'd said, nor was it confined to the mammals. Certain reptiles, various lizards . . .

"Never mind about the lizards," said Jimmy.

According to Crake — and Snowman has seen nothing since to disprove it — the chemicals programmed into the men's urine are effective against wolvogs and rakunks, and to a lesser extent against bobkittens and pigoons. The wolvogs and bobkittens are reacting to the scent of their own kind and must imagine a huge wolvog or bobkitten, from which they would be wise to keep their distance. The rakunks and pigoons imagine large predators. Or this was the theory.

Crake allotted the special piss to men only; he said they'd need something important to do, something that didn't involve child-bearing, so they wouldn't feel left out. Woodworking, hunting, high finance, war, and golf would no longer be options, he'd joked.

There are some disadvantages to this plan, in action – the ring-of-pee boundary line smells like a rarely cleaned zoo – but the circle is large enough so that there's ample smell-free room inside it. Anyway Snowman is used to it by now.

He waits politely for the men to finish. They don't ask him to join them: they already know his piss is useless. Also it's their habit to say nothing while performing their task: they need to concentrate, to make sure their urine lands in exactly the right place. Each has his own three feet of borderland, his own area of responsibility. It's quite a sight: like the women, these men – smooth-skinned, well-muscled – look like statues, and grouped like this they resemble an entire Baroque fountain. A few mermaids and dolphins and cherubs and the scene would be complete. Into Snowman's head comes the image of a circle of naked car mechanics, each holding a wrench. A whole squad of Mr. Fix-its. A gay magazine centre-fold. Witnessing their synchronized routine, he almost expects them to break into some campy chorus line from one of the seedier nightclubs.

The men shake off, break their circle, look over at Snowman with their uniformly green eyes, smile. They're always so god-damn affable.

"Welcome, oh Snowman," says the one called Abraham Lincoln. "Will you join us inside our home?" He's getting to be a bit of a leader, that one. *Watch out for the leaders*, Crake used to say. *First the leaders and the led, then the tyrants and the slaves, then the massacres. That's how it's always gone.*

Snowman steps over the wet line on the ground, ambles along with the men. He'd just had a brilliant idea: what if he were to take some of the saturated earth with him on his journey, as a protective device? It might ward off the wolvogs. But on second thought, the men would find the gap dug in their defences and would know he'd done it. Such an act could be misinterpreted: he wouldn't want to be suspected of weakening their fortress, exposing their young to danger.

He'll have to cook up a new directive from Crake, present it to them later. *Crake has told me you must collect an offering of your scent.* Get them all to piss in a tin can. Sprinkle it around his tree. Make a fairy ring. Draw his own line in the sand.

They reach the open space at the centre of the territorial circle. Off to one side, three of the women and one man are tending to a little boy, who appears to be hurt in some way. These people are not immune from wounds – the children fall down or bash their heads on trees, the women burn their fingers tending the fires, there are cuts and scrapes – but so far the injuries have been minor, and easily cured by purring.

Crake had worked for years on the purring. Once he'd discovered that the cat family purred at the same frequency as the ultrasound used on bone fractures and skin lesions and were thus equipped with their own self-healing mechanism, he'd turned himself inside out in the attempt to install that feature. The trick was to get the hyoid apparatus modified and the voluntary nerve pathways connected and the neocortex control systems adapted without hampering the speech abilities. There'd been quite a few botched experiments, as Snowman recalled. One of the trial batch of kids had manifested a tendency to sprout long whiskers and scramble up the curtains; a couple of the others had vocal-expression impediments; one of them had been limited to nouns, verbs, and roaring.

Crake did it though, thinks Snowman. He pulled it off. Just look at the four of them now, heads down close to the child, purring away like car engines.

"What happened to him?" he asks.

"He was bitten," says Abraham. "One of the Children of Oryx bit him."

This is something new. "What kind?"

"A bobkitten. For no reason."

"It was outside our circle, it was in the forest," says one of the women – Eleanor Roosevelt? Empress Josephine? – Snowman can't always remember their names.

"We were forced to hit it with rocks, to make it go away," says Leonardo da Vinci, the man in the purring quartet.

So the bobkittens are hunting kiddies now, thinks Snowman. Maybe they're getting hungry – as hungry as he is himself. But they have lots of rabbits to choose from, so it can't be simple hunger. Maybe they see the Children of Crake, the little ones anyway, as just another kind of rabbit, though easier to catch.

"Tonight we will apologize to Oryx," says one of the women – Sacajawea? – "for the rocks. And we will request her to tell her children not to bite us."

He's never seen the women do this – this communion with Oryx – although they refer to it frequently. What form does it take? They must perform some kind of prayer or invocation, since they can hardly believe that Oryx appears to them in person. Maybe they go into trances. Crake thought he'd done away with all that, eliminated what he called the G-spot in the brain. *God is a cluster of neurons*, he'd maintained. It had been a difficult problem, though: take out too much in that area and you got a zombie or a psychopath. But these people are neither.

They're up to something though, something Crake didn't anticipate: they're conversing with the invisible, they've developed reverence. Good for them, thinks Snowman. He likes it when Crake is proved wrong. He hasn't caught them making any graven images yet, however.

"Will the child be all right?" he asks.

"Yes," says the woman calmly. "Already the tooth holes are closing. See?"

~   ~   ~

The rest of the women are doing the things they usually do in the morning. Some are tending the central fire; others squat around it, warming themselves. Their body thermostats are set for tropical conditions, so they sometimes find it cold before the sun is high. The fire is fed with dead twigs and branches, but primarily with dung, made into patties the size and shape of hamburgers and dried in the noonday sun. Since the Children of Crake are vegetarians and eat mostly grass and leaves and roots, this material burns well enough. As far as Snowman can tell, fire-tending is about the only thing the women do that might be classified as work. Apart from helping to catch his weekly fish, that is. And cooking it for him. On their own behalf they do no cooking.

"Greetings, oh Snowman," says the next woman he comes to. Her mouth is green from the breakfast she's been chewing. She's breastfeeding a year-old boy, who looks up at Snowman, lets the nipple pop out of his mouth, and begins to cry. "It's only Snowman!" she says. "He won't hurt you."

Snowman still hasn't got used to it, the growth rate of these kids. The yearling looks like a five-year-old. By the age of four he'll be an adolescent. Far too much time was wasted in child-rearing, Crake used to say. Childrearing, and being a child. No other species used up sixteen years that way.

Some of the older children have spotted him; they come closer, chanting, "Snowman, Snowman!" So he hasn't yet lost his allure. Now all the people are gazing at him curiously, wondering what he's doing here. He never arrives without a reason. On his first visits they'd thought − judging from his appearance − that he must be hungry, and they'd offered him food − a couple of handfuls of choice leaves and roots and grass, and several caeco-trophs they'd kept especially for him − and he'd had to explain carefully that their food was not his food.

He finds the caecotrophs revolting, consisting as they do of semi-digested herbage, discharged through the anus and re-swallowed two or three times a week. This had been another boy-genius concept on the part of Crake. He'd used the vermiform appendix as the base on which to construct the necessary organ, reasoning that at an earlier evolutionary stage, when the ancestral diet had been higher in roughage, the appendix must have fulfilled some such function. But he'd stolen the specific idea from the *Leporidae*, the hares and rabbits, which depend on caecotrophs rather than on several stomachs like the ruminants. Maybe this is why bobkittens have started hunting the young Crakers, Snowman thinks: beneath the citrus overlay, they can smell the rabbity aroma of the caecotrophs.

Jimmy had argued with Crake over this feature. However you look at it, he'd said, what it boiled down to was eating your own shit. But Crake had merely smiled. For animals with a diet consisting largely of unrefined plant materials, he'd pointed out, such a mechanism was necessary to break down the cellulose, and without it the people would die. Also, as in the *Leporidae*, the caecotrophs were enriched with Vitamin B1, and with other vitamins and minerals as well, at four or five times the level of ordinary waste material. Caecotrophs were simply a part of alimentation and digestion, a way of making maximum use of the nutrients at hand. Any objections to the process were purely aesthetic.

That was the point, Jimmy had said.

Crake had said that if so it was a bad one.

Snowman is now surrounded by an attentive circle. "Greetings, Children of Crake," he says. "I have come to tell you that I'm going on a journey." The adults must have deduced this already, from his long stick and the way he's tied his sheet: he's gone on journeys before, or that's what he's called his looting forays into the trailer parks and adjacent pleeblands.

"Are you going to see Crake?" asks one of the children.

"Yes," says Snowman. "I'll try to see him. I'll see him if he's there."

"Why?" says one of the older children.

"There are some things I need to ask him," says Snowman cautiously.

"You must tell him about the bobkitten," says Empress Josephine. "The one that bit."

"That is a matter for Oryx," says Madame Curie. "Not for Crake." The other women nod.

"We want to see Crake too," the children begin. "We too, we too! We want to see Crake too!" It's one of their favourite ideas, going to see Crake. Snowman blames himself: he shouldn't have told them such exciting lies at the beginning. He'd made Crake sound like Santa Claus.

"Don't bother Snowman," says Eleanor Roosevelt gently. "Surely he is making this journey to help us. We must thank him."

"Crake is not for children," says Snowman, looking as stern as he can manage.

"Let us come too! We want to see Crake!"

"Only Snowman can ever see Crake," Abraham Lincoln says mildly. That seems to settle it.

"This will be a longer journey," Snowman says. "Longer than the other journeys. Maybe I won't come back for two days." He holds up two fingers. "Or three," he adds. "So you shouldn't worry. But while I'm away, be sure to stay here in your home, and do everything the way Crake and Oryx have taught you."

A chorus of yesses, much nodding of heads. Snowman doesn't mention the possibility of danger to himself. Perhaps it isn't a thing they ever consider, nor is it a subject he brings up — the more invulnerable they think he is, the better.

"We will come with you," says Abraham Lincoln. Several of the other men look at him, then nod.

"No!" says Snowman, taken aback. "I mean, you can't see Crake, it isn't allowed." He doesn't want them tagging along, absolutely not! He doesn't want them witnessing any weaknesses or failures on his part. Also, some of the sights along the way might be bad for their state of mind. Inevitably they would shower him with questions. In addition to all of which, a day in their company would bore the pants off him.

But you don't have any pants, says a voice in his head – a small voice this time, a sad little child's voice. *Joke! Joke! Don't kill me!*

Please, not now, thinks Snowman. Not in company. In company, he can't answer back.

"We would come with you to protect you," says Benjamin Franklin, looking at Snowman's long stick. "From the bobkittens that bite, from the wolvogs."

"Your smell is not very strong," adds Napoleon.

Snowman finds this offensively smug. Also it's too euphemistic by half: as they all know, his smell is strong enough, it just isn't the right kind. "I'll be fine," he says. "You stay here."

The men look dubious, but he thinks they'll do as he says. To reinforce his authority he holds his watch up to his ear. "Crake says he'll be watching over you," he says. "To keep you safe." *Watch, watching over*, says the small child's voice. *It's a pun, you cork-nut.*

"Crake watches over us in the daytime, and Oryx watches over us at night," Abraham Lincoln says dutifully. He doesn't sound too convinced.

"Crake always watches over us," says Simone de Beauvoir serenely. She's a yellow-brown woman who reminds Snowman of Dolores, his long-lost Philippina nanny; he sometimes has to resist the urge to drop to his knees and throw his arms around her waist.

"He takes good care of us," says Madame Curie. "You must tell him that we are grateful."

Snowman goes back along the Snowman Fish Path. He feels mushy: nothing breaks him up like the generosity of these people, their willingness to be of help. Also their gratitude towards Crake. It's so touching, and so misplaced.

"Crake, you dickhead," he says. He feels like weeping. Then he hears a voice – his own! – saying *boohoo*; he sees it, as if it's a printed word in a comic-strip balloon. Water leaks down his face.

"Not this again," he says. What's the sensation? It isn't anger exactly; it's vexation. An old word but serviceable. *Vexation* takes in more than Crake, and indeed why blame Crake alone?

Maybe he's merely envious. Envious yet again. He too would like to be invisible and adored. He too would like to be elsewhere. No hope for that: he's up to his neck in the here and now.

He slows to a shamble, then to a halt. *Oh, boohoo!* Why can't he control himself? On the other hand, why bother, since nobody's watching? Still, the noise he's making seems to him like the exaggerated howling of a clown – like misery performed for applause.

Stop snivelling, son, says his father's voice. *Pull yourself together. You're the man around here.*

"Right!" Snowman yells. "What exactly would you suggest? You were such a great example!"

But irony is lost on the trees. He wipes his nose with his stick-free hand and keeps walking.

Blue

~

It's nine in the morning, sun clock, by the time Snowman leaves the Fish Path to turn inland. As soon as he's out of the sea breeze the humidity shoots up, and he attracts a coterie of small green biting flies. He's barefoot — his shoes disintegrated some time ago, and in any case they were too hot and damp — but he doesn't need them now because the soles of his feet are hard as old rubber. Nevertheless he walks cautiously: there might be broken glass, torn metal. Or there might be snakes, or other things that could give him a nasty bite, and he has no weapon apart from the stick.

At first he's walking under trees, formerly parkland. Some distance away he hears the barking cough of a bobkitten. That's the sound they make as a warning: perhaps it's a male, and it's met another male bobkitten. There'll be a fight, with the winner taking all — all the females in the territory — and dispatching their kittens, if he can get away with it, to make room for his own genetic package.

Those things were introduced as a control, once the big green rabbits had become such a prolific and resistant pest. Smaller than bobcats, less aggressive — that was the official story about the bobkittens. They were supposed to eliminate feral cats, thus improving the almost non-existent songbird population. The bobkittens wouldn't bother much about birds, as they would lack the lightness and agility necessary to catch them. Thus went the theory.

All of which came true, except that the bobkittens soon got out of control in their turn. Small dogs went missing from back-yards, babies from prams; short joggers were mauled. Not in the Compounds, of course, and rarely in the Modules, but there'd been a lot of grousing from the pleeblanders. He should keep a lookout for tracks, and be careful of overhanging branches: he doesn't like the thought of one of those things landing on his head.

There are always the wolvogs to worry about. But wolvogs are nocturnal hunters: in the heat of the day they tend to sleep, like most things with fur.

Every so often there's a more open space — the remains of a drive-in campsite, with a picnic table and one of those outdoor-barbecue fireplaces, though nobody used them very much once it got so warm and began to rain every afternoon. He comes upon one now, fungi sprouting from the decaying table, the barbecue covered in bindweed.

Off to the side, from what is probably a glade where the tents and trailers used to be set up, he can hear laughter and singing, and shouts of admiration and encouragement. There must be a mating going on, a rare-enough occasion among the people: Crake had worked out the numbers, and had decreed that once every three years per female was more than enough.

There'll be the standard quintuplet, four men and the woman in heat. Her condition will be obvious to all from the bright-blue colour of her buttocks and abdomen — a trick of variable pig-mentation filched from the baboons, with a contribution from the expandable chromosphores of the octopus. As Crake used to say, *Think of an adaptation, any adaptation, and some animal somewhere will have thought of it first.*

Since it's only the blue tissue and the pheromones released by it that stimulate the males, there's no more unrequited love these days, no more thwarted lust; no more shadow between the desire and the act. Courtship begins at the first whiff, the first faint blush of azure, with the males presenting flowers to the females — just as male penguins present round stones, said Crake, or as the male silverfish presents a sperm packet. At the same time they indulge in musical outbursts, like songbirds. Their penises turn bright blue to match the blue abdomens of the females, and they do a sort of blue-dick dance number, erect members waving to and fro in unison, in time to the foot movements and the singing: a feature suggested to Crake by the sexual semaphoring of crabs. From amongst the floral tributes the female chooses four flowers, and the sexual ardour of the unsuccessful candidates dissipates immediately, with no hard feelings left. Then, when the blue of her abdomen has reached its deepest shade, the female and her quartet find a secluded spot and go at it until the woman becomes pregnant and her blue colouring fades. And that is that.

No more *No means yes*, anyway, thinks Snowman. No more prostitution, no sexual abuse of children, no haggling over the price, no pimps, no sex slaves. No more rape. The five of them will roister for hours, three of the men standing guard and doing the singing and shouting while the fourth one copulates, turn and turn about. Crake has equipped these women with ultra-strong vulvas — extra skin layers, extra muscles — so they can sustain these marathons. It no longer matters who the father of the inevitable child may be, since there's no more property to inherit, no father-son loyalty required for war. Sex is no longer a mysterious rite, viewed with ambivalence or downright loathing, conducted in the dark and inspiring suicides and murders. Now it's more like an athletic demonstration, a free-spirited romp.

Maybe Crake was right, thinks Snowman. Under the old dispensation, sexual competition had been relentless and cruel: for every pair of happy lovers there was a dejected onlooker, the one excluded. Love was its own transparent bubble-dome: you could see the two inside it, but you couldn't get in there yourself.

That had been the milder form: the single man at the window, drinking himself into oblivion to the mournful strains of the tango. But such things could escalate into violence. Extreme emotions could be lethal. *If I can't have you nobody will*, and so forth. Death could set in.

"How much misery," Crake said one lunchtime – this must have been when they were in their early twenties and Crake was already at the Watson-Crick Institute – "how much needless despair has been caused by a series of biological mismatches, a misalignment of the hormones and pheromones? Resulting in the fact that the one you love so passionately won't or can't love you. As a species we're pathetic in that way: imperfectly monogamous. If we could only pair-bond for life, like gibbons, or else opt for total guilt-free promiscuity, there'd be no more sexual torment. Better plan – make it cyclical and also inevitable, as in the other mammals. You'd never want someone you couldn't have."

"True enough," Jimmy replied. Or Jim, as he was now insisting, without results: everyone still called him Jimmy. "But think what we'd be giving up."

"Such as?"

"Courtship behaviour. In your plan we'd just be a bunch of hormone robots." Jimmy thought he should put things in Crake's terms, which was why he said *courtship behaviour*. What he meant was the challenge, the excitement, the chase. "There'd be no free choice."

"There's courtship behaviour in my plan," said Crake, "except that it would always succeed. And we're hormone robots anyway, only we're faulty ones."

"Well, what about art?" said Jimmy, a little desperately. He was, after all, a student at the Martha Graham Academy, so he felt some need to defend the art-and-creativity turf.

"What about it?" said Crake, smiling his calm smile.

"All that mismatching you talk about. It's been an inspiration, or that's what they say. Think of all the poetry – think Petrarch, think John Donne, think the *Vita Nuova*, think . . ."

"Art," said Crake. "I guess they still do a lot of jabbering about that, over where you are. What is it Byron said? Who'd write if they could do otherwise? Something like that."

"That's what I mean," said Jimmy. He was alarmed by the reference to Byron. What right had Crake to poach on his own shoddy, threadbare territory? Crake should stick to science and leave poor Byron to Jimmy.

"What *do* you mean?" said Crake, as if coaching a stutterer.

"I mean, when you can't get the *otherwise*, then . . ."

"Wouldn't you rather be fucking?" said Crake. He wasn't including himself in this question: his tone was one of detached but not very strong interest, as if he were conducting a survey of people's less attractive personal habits, such as nose-picking.

Jimmy found that his face got redder and his voice got squeakier the more outrageous Crake became. He hated that. "When any civilization is dust and ashes," he said, "art is all that's left over. Images, words, music. Imaginative structures. Meaning – human meaning, that is – is defined by them. You have to admit that."

"That's not quite all that's left over," said Crake. "The archeologists are just as interested in gnawed bones and old bricks and ossified shit these days. Sometimes more interested. They think human meaning is defined by those things too."

Jimmy would like to have said *Why are you always putting me down?* but he was afraid of the possible answers, *because it's so easy* being one of them. So instead he said, "What have you got against it?"

"Against what? Ossified shit?"

"Art."

"Nothing," said Crake lazily. "People can amuse themselves any way they like. If they want to play with themselves in public, whack off over doodling, scribbling, and fiddling, it's fine with me. Anyway it serves a biological purpose."

"Such as?" Jimmy knew that everything depended on keeping his cool. These arguments had to be played through like a game: if he lost his temper, Crake won.

"The male frog, in mating season," said Crake, "makes as much noise as it can. The females are attracted to the male frog with the biggest, deepest voice because it suggests a more power-ful frog, one with superior genes. Small male frogs — it's been documented — discover that if they position themselves in empty drainpipes, the pipe acts as a voice amplifier, and the small frog appears much larger than it really is."

"So?"

"So that's what art is, for the artist," said Crake. "An empty drainpipe. An amplifier. A stab at getting laid."

"Your analogy falls down when it comes to female artists," said Jimmy. "They're not in it to get laid. They'd gain no biolog-ical advantage from amplifying themselves, since potential mates would be deterred rather than attracted by that sort of amplifi-cation. Men aren't frogs, they don't want women who are ten times bigger than them."

"Female artists are biologically confused," said Crake. "You must have discovered that by now." This was a snide dig at Jimmy's current snarled romance, with a brunette poet who'd renamed herself Morgana and refused to tell him what her given name had been, and who was currently on a twenty-eight-day sex fast in honour of the Great Moon-Goddess Oestre, patroness of soybeans and bunnies. Martha Graham attracted those kinds of girls. An error, though, to have confided this affair to Crake.

Poor Morgana, thinks Snowman. I wonder what happened to her. She'll never know how useful she's been to me, her and her claptrap. He feels a little paltry for having pawned Morgana's drivel off on the Crakers as cosmogony. But it seems to make them happy enough.

Snowman leans against a tree, listening to the noises off. My love is like a blue, blue rose. Moon on, harvest shine. So now Crake's had his way, he thinks. Hooray for him. There's no more jealousy, no more wife-butchers, no more husband-poisoners. It's all admirably good-natured: no pushing and shoving, more like the gods cavorting with willing nymphs on some golden-age Grecian frieze.

Why then does he feel so dejected, so bereft? Because he doesn't understand this kind of behaviour? Because it's beyond him? Because he can't jump in?

And what would happen if he tried? If he burst out of the bushes in his filthy tattered sheet, reeking, hairy, tumescent, leering like a goat-balled, cloven-hoofed satyr or a patch-eyed buccaneer from some ancient pirate film – *Aarr, me hearties!* – and attempted to join the amorous, blue-bottomed tussle? He can imagine the dismay – as if an orang-utang had crashed a formal waltzfest and started groping some sparkly pastel princess. He can imagine his own dismay too. What right does he have to foist his pustulant, cankered self and soul upon these innocent creatures?

"Crake!" he whimpers. "Why am I on this earth? How come I'm alone? Where's my Bride of Frankenstein?"

He needs to ditch this morbid tape-loop, flee the discouraging scene. *Oh honey*, a woman's voice whispers, *Cheer up! Look on the bright side! You've got to think positive!*

He hikes doggedly onward, muttering to himself. The forest blots up his voice, the words coming out of him in a string of colourless and soundless bubbles, like air from the mouths of the drowning. The laughter and singing dwindle behind him. Soon he can't hear them at all.

8

~

SoYummie

~

Jimmy and Crake graduated from HelthWyzer High on a warm humid day in early February. The ceremony used to take place in June; the weather then used to be sunny and moderate. But June was now the wet season all the way up the east coast, and you couldn't have held an outdoor event then, what with the thunderstorms. Even early February was pushing it: they'd ducked a twister by only one day.

HelthWyzer High liked to do things in the old style, with marquees and awnings and the mothers in flowered hats and the fathers in panamas, and fruit-flavoured punch, with or without alcohol, and Happicuppa coffee, and little plastic tubs of SoYummie Ice Cream, a HelthWyzer Own Brand, in chocolate soy, mango soy, and roasted-dandelion green-tea soy. It was a festive scene.

Crake was top of the class. The bidding for him by the rival EduCompounds at the Student Auction was brisk, and he was snatched up at a high price by the Watson-Crick Institute. Once a student there and your future was assured. It was like going to Harvard had been, back before it got drowned.

Jimmy on the other hand was a mid-range student, high on

his word scores but a poor average in the numbers columns. Even those underwhelming math marks had been achieved with the help of Crake, who'd coached Jimmy weekends, taking time away from his own preparations. Not that he himself needed any extra cramming, he was some sort of mutant, he could crank out the differential equations in his sleep.

"Why are you doing this?" Jimmy asked in the middle of one exasperating session. (*You need to look at it differently. You have to get the beauty of it. It's like chess. Here — try this. See? See the pattern? Now it all comes clear.* But Jimmy did not see, and it did not all come clear.) "Why help me out?"

"Because I'm a sadist," Crake said. "I like to watch you suffer."

"Anyway, I appreciate it," said Jimmy. He did appreciate it, for several reasons, the best being that because Crake was known to be tutoring him Jimmy's dad had no grounds for nagging.

If Jimmy had been from a Module school, or — better — from one of those dump bins they still called "the public system," he'd have shone like a diamond in a drain. But the Compound schools were awash in brilliant genes, none of which he'd inherited from his geeky, kak-hearted parents, so his talents shrank by comparison. Nor had he been given any extra points for being funny. He was less funny now, anyway: he'd lost interest in the general audience.

After a humiliating wait while the brainiacs were tussled over by the best EduCompounds and the transcripts of the mediocre were fingered and skimmed and had coffee spilled on them and got dropped on the floor by mistake, Jimmy was knocked down at last to the Martha Graham Academy; and even that only after a long spell of lacklustre bidding. Not to mention some arm-twisting — Jimmy suspected — on the part of his dad, who'd known the Martha Graham president from their long-defunct mutual summer camp and probably had the dirt on him. Shagging smaller boys, dabbling in black-market pharmaceuticals. Or this was Jimmy's suspicion, in view of the ill grace and excessive force with which his hand was shaken.

"Welcome to Martha Graham, son," said the president with a smile fake as a vitamin-supplement salesman's.

When can I stop being a son? thought Jimmy.

Not yet. Oh, not yet. "Attaboy, Jimmy," said his father at the garden party afterwards, giving him the arm punch. He had chocolate soy goo on his dweeby tie, which had a pattern of pigs with wings. Just don't hug me, Jimmy prayed.

"Honey, we're so proud of you," said Ramona, who'd come decked out like a whore's lampshade in an outfit with a low neckline and pink frills. Jimmy'd seen something like that on HottTotts once, only it was worn by an eight-year-old. Ramona's push-up-bra breast tops were freckled from too much sun, not that Jimmy was much interested in those any more. He was familiar with the tectonics of cantilevered mammary-gland support devices by now, and anyway he found Ramona's new matronly air repellent. She was getting little creases on either side of her mouth, despite the collagen injections; her biological clock was ticking, as she was fond of pointing out. Pretty soon it would be the NooSkins BeauToxique Treatment for her — Wrinkles Paralyzed Forever, Employees Half-Price — plus, in say five years, the Fountain of Yooth Total Plunge, which rasped off your entire epidermis. She kissed him beside the nose, leaving a smooch of cerise lipstick; he could feel it resting on his cheek like bicycle grease.

She was allowed to say *we* and to kiss him, because she was now officially his stepmother. His real mother had been divorced from his father *in absentia*, for "desertion," and the bogus wedding of his father had been celebrated, if that was the word for it, soon after. Not that his real mother would have given a wombat's anus, thought Jimmy. She wouldn't have cared. She was off having cutting-edge adventures on her own, far from the dolorous festivities. He hadn't had a postcard from her in months; the last one had shown a Komodo dragon and had borne a Malaysian stamp, and had prompted another visit from the CorpSeCorps.

At the wedding Jimmy got as drunk as it took. He propped himself against a wall, grinning stupidly as the happy couple cut the sugary cake, All Real Ingredients, as Ramona had made known. Lots of cackling over the fresh eggs. Any minute now Ramona would be planning a baby, a more satisfactory baby than Jimmy had ever been to anybody.

"Who cares, who cares," he'd whispered to himself. He didn't want to have a father anyway, or be a father, or have a son or be one. He wanted to be himself, alone, unique, self-created and self-sufficient. From now on he was going to be fancy-free, doing whatever he liked, picking globes of ripe life off the life trees, taking a bite or two, sucking out the juice, throwing away the rinds.

It was Crake who'd got him back to his room. By that time Jimmy had been morose, and barely ambulatory. "Sleep it off," said Crake in his genial fashion. "I'll call you in the morning."

Now here was Crake at the graduation garden party, looming up out of the crowd, shining with achievement. No, he wasn't, Snowman amends. Give him credit for that at least. He was never a triumphalist.

"Congratulations," Jimmy made himself say. It was easier because he was the only one at this gathering who'd known Crake well for any length of time. Uncle Pete was in attendance, but he didn't count. Also, he was staying as far away from Crake as possible. Maybe he'd finally figured out who'd been running up his Internet bill. As for Crake's mother, she'd died the month before.

It was an accident, or so went the story. (Nobody liked to say the word *sabotage*, which was notoriously bad for business.) She must have cut herself at the hospital – although, said Crake, her job didn't involve scalpels – or scratched herself, or maybe she'd been careless and had taken her latex gloves off and had been touched on a raw spot by some patient who was a carrier. It was possible: she was a nail-biter, she might have had what they called an integumental entry point. In any case she'd picked up a hot bioform that had chewed through her like a solar mower. It was a transgenetic staph, said some labcoat, mixed with a clever gene from the slime-mould family; but by the time they'd pinned it down and started what they hoped would be effective treatment, she was in Isolation and losing shape rapidly. Crake couldn't go in to see her, of course — nobody could, everything in there was done with robotic arms, as in nuclear-materials procedures — but he could watch her through the observation window.

"It was impressive," Crake told Jimmy. "Froth was coming out."

"Froth?"

"Ever put salt on a slug?"

Jimmy said he hadn't.

"Okay. So, like when you brush your teeth."

His mother was supposed to be able to speak her last words to him via the mike system, said Crake, but there was a digital failure; so though he could see her lips moving, he couldn't hear what she was saying. "Otherwise put, just like daily life," said Crake. He said anyway he hadn't missed much, because by that stage she'd been incoherent.

Jimmy didn't understand how he could be so nil about it — it was horrible, the thought of Crake watching his own mother dissolve like that. He himself wouldn't have been able to do it. But probably it was just an act. It was Crake preserving his dignity, because the alternative would have been losing it.

Happicuppa

~

For the vacation following graduation, Jimmy was invited to the Moosonee HelthWyzer Gated Vacation Community on the western shore of Hudson's Bay, where the top brass of HelthWyzer went to beat the heat. Uncle Pete had a nice place there, "nice place" being his term. Actually it was like a combination mausoleum and dirty-weekend hideaway — a lot of stonework, king-sized magic-finger beds, bidets in every bathroom — though it was hard to imagine Uncle Pete getting up to anything of much interest in there. Jimmy had been invited, he was pretty sure, so that Uncle Pete wouldn't have to be alone with Crake. Uncle Pete spent most of his time on the golf course and the rest of it in the hot tub, and Jimmy and Crake were free to do whatever they liked.

They probably would have gone back to interactives and state-sponsored snuff, and porn, as relaxation after their final exams, but that was the summer the gen-mod coffee wars got underway, so they watched those instead. The wars were over the new Happicuppa bean, developed by a HelthWyzer subsidiary. Until then the individual coffee beans on each bush had ripened at different times and had needed to be handpicked and processed and shipped in small quantities, but the Happicuppa coffee bush was designed so that all of its beans would ripen simultaneously, and coffee could be grown on huge plantations and harvested with machines. This threw the small growers out of business and reduced both them and their labourers to starvation-level poverty.

The resistance movement was global. Riots broke out, crops were burned, Happicuppa cafés were looted, Happicuppa personnel were car-bombed or kidnapped or shot by snipers or beaten to death by mobs; and, on the other side, peasants were massacred by the army. Or by the armies, various armies; a number of countries were involved. But the soldiers and dead peasants all looked much the same wherever they were. They looked dusty. It was amazing how much dust got stirred up in the course of such events.

"Those guys should be whacked," said Crake.

"Which ones? The peasants? Or the guys killing them?"

"The latter. Not because of the dead peasants, there's always been dead peasants. But they're nuking the cloud forests to plant this stuff."

"The peasants would do that too if they had half a chance," said Jimmy.

"Sure, but they don't have half a chance."

"You're taking sides?"

"There aren't any sides, as such."

Nothing much to be said to that. Jimmy thought about shouting *bogus*, decided it might not apply. Anyway they'd used up that word. "Let's change channels," he said.

But there was Happicuppa coverage, it seemed, wherever you turned. There were protests and demonstrations, with tear gas and shooting and bludgeoning; then more protests, more demonstrations, more tear gas, more shooting, more bludgeoning. This went on day after day. There hadn't been anything like it since the first decade of the century. Crake said it was history in the making.

Don't Drink Death! said the posters. Union dockworkers in Australia, where they still had unions, refused to unload Happicuppa cargoes; in the United States, a Boston Coffee Party sprang up. There was a staged media event, boring because there was no violence – only balding guys with retro tattoos or white patches where they'd been taken off, and severe-looking baggy-boobed women, and quite a few overweight or spindly members of marginal, earnest religious groups, in T-shirts with smiley-faced angels flying with birds or Jesus holding hands with a peasant or God Is Green on the front. They were filmed dumping Happicuppa products into the harbour, but none of the boxes sank. So there was the Happicuppa logo, lots of copies of it, bobbing around on the screen. It could have been a commercial.

"Makes me thirsty," said Jimmy.

"Shit for brains," said Crake. "They forgot to add rocks."

As a rule they watched the unfolding of events on the Noodie News, via the Net, but for a change they sometimes watched fully clothed newscasters on the wall-sized plasma screen in Uncle Pete's leatherette-upholstered TV room. The suits and shirts and ties seemed bizarre to Jimmy, especially if he was mildly stoned. It was weird to imagine what all those serious-faced talking heads would look like minus their fashion items, full frontal on the Noodie News.

Uncle Pete sometimes watched too, in the evenings, when he was back from the golf course. He'd pour himself a drink, then provide a running commentary. "The usual uproar," he said. "They'll get tired of it, they'll settle down. Everybody wants a cheaper cup of coffee – you can't fight that."

"No, you can't," Crake would say agreeably. Uncle Pete had a chunk of Happicuppa stock in his portfolio, and not just a little chunk. "What a mort," Crake would say as he scanned Uncle Pete's holdings on his computer.

"You could trade his stuff," said Jimmy. "Sell the Happicuppa, buy something he really hates. Buy windpower.

No, better – buy a croaker. Get him some South American cattle futures."

"Nah," said Crake. "I can't risk that with a labyrinth. He'd notice. He'd find out I've been getting in."

Things escalated after a cell of crazed anti-Happicuppa fanatics bombed the Lincoln Memorial, killing five visiting Japanese schoolkids that were part of a Tour of Democracy. *Stop the Hipocrissy*, read the note left at a safe distance.

"That's pathetic," said Jimmy. "They can't even spell."

"They made their point though," said Crake.

"I hope they fry," said Uncle Pete.

Jimmy didn't answer, because now they were looking at the blockade of the Happicuppa head-office compound in Maryland. There in the shouting crowd, clutching a sign that read A Happicup Is a Crappi Cup, with a green bandanna over her nose and mouth, was – wasn't it? – his vanished mother. For a moment the bandanna slipped down and Jimmy saw her clearly – her frowning eyebrows, her candid blue eyes, her determined mouth. Love jolted through him, abrupt and painful, followed by anger. It was like being kicked: he must have let out a gasp. Then there was a CorpSeCorps charge and a cloud of tear gas and a smattering of what sounded like gunfire, and when Jimmy looked again his mother had disappeared.

"Freeze the frame!" he said. "Turn back!" He wanted to be sure. How could she be taking such a risk? If they got hold of her she'd really disappear, this time forever. But after a brief glance at him Crake had already switched to another channel.

I shouldn't have said anything, thought Jimmy. I shouldn't have called attention. He was cold with fear now. What if Uncle Pete made the connection and phoned the Corpsmen? They'd be right on her trail, she'd be roadkill.

But Uncle Pete didn't seem to have noticed. He was pouring himself another Scotch. "They should spraygun the whole bunch of them," he said. "Once they've smashed those cameras. Who took that footage anyway? Sometimes you wonder who's running this show."

"So what was that about?" said Crake when they were alone.

"Nothing," said Jimmy.

"I did freeze it," said Crake. "I got the whole sequence."

"I think you better erase it," said Jimmy. He was past being frightened, he'd entered full-blown dejection. Surely at this very moment Uncle Pete was turning on his cellphone and punching in the numbers; hours from now it would be the CorpSeCorps interrogation all over again. His mother this, his mother that. He would just have to go through it.

"It's okay," said Crake, which Jimmy took to mean: *You can trust me.* Then he said, "Let me guess. Phylum Chordata, Class Vertebrata, Order Mammalia, Family Primates, Genus *Homo*, Species *sapiens sapiens*, subspecies your mother."

"Big points," said Jimmy listlessly.

"Not a stretch," said Crake. "I spotted her right away, those blue eyes. It was either her or a clone."

If Crake had recognized her, who else might have done so? Everyone in the HelthWyzer Compound had doubtless been shown pictures: *You seen this woman?* The story of his deviant mother had followed Jimmy around like an unwanted dog, and was probably half responsible for his poor showing at the Student Auction. He wasn't dependable, he was a security risk, he had a taint.

"My dad was the same," said Crake. "He buggered off too."

"I thought he died," said Jimmy. That's all he'd ever got out of Crake before: dad died, full stop, change the subject. It wasn't anything Crake would talk about.

"That's what I mean. He went off a pleebland overpass. It was rush hour, so by the time they got to him he was cat food."

"Did he jump, or what?" said Jimmy. Crake didn't seem too worked up about it, so he felt it was okay to ask that.

"It was the general opinion," said Crake. "He was a top researcher over at HelthWyzer West, so he got a really nice funeral. The tact was amazing. Nobody used the word *suicide*. They said 'your father's accident.'"

"Sorry about that," said Jimmy.

"Uncle Pete was over at our place all the time. My mother said he was really *supportive*." Crake said *supportive* like a quote. "She said, besides being my dad's boss and best friend, he was turning out to be a really good friend of the family, not that I'd ever seen him around much before. He wanted things to be *resolved* for us, he said he was anxious about that. He kept trying to have these heart-to-heart talks with me – tell me all about how my father had *problems*."

"Meaning your dad was a nutbar," said Jimmy.

Crake looked at Jimmy out of his slanty green eyes. "Yeah. But he wasn't. He was acting worried lately, but he didn't have *problems*. He had nothing like that on his mind. Nothing like jumping. I'd have known."

"You think he maybe fell off?"

"Fell off?"

"Off the overpass." Jimmy wanted to ask what he'd been doing on a pleebland overpass in the first place, but it didn't seem like the right time. "Was there a railing?"

"He was kind of uncoordinated," said Crake, smiling in an odd way. "He didn't always watch where he was going. He was head in the clouds. He believed in contributing to the improvement of the human lot."

"You get along with him?"

Crake paused. "He taught me to play chess. Before it happened."

"Well, I guess not *after*," said Jimmy, trying to lighten things up, because by this time he was feeling sorry for Crake, and he didn't like that at all.

~   ~   ~

How could I have missed it? Snowman thinks. What he was telling me. How could I have been so stupid?

No, not stupid. He can't describe himself, the way he'd been. Not unmarked – events had marked him, he'd had his own scars, his dark emotions. Ignorant, perhaps. Unformed, inchoate.

There had been something willed about it though, his ignorance. Or not willed, exactly: structured. He'd grown up in walled spaces, and then he had become one. He had shut things out.

Applied Rhetoric

~

At the end of that vacation, Crake went off to Watson-Crick and Jimmy to Martha Graham. They shook hands at the bullet-train station.

"See you around," said Jimmy.

"We'll e-mail," said Crake. Then, noticing Jimmy's dejection, he said, "Come on, you did okay, the place is famous."

"Was famous," said Jimmy.

"It won't be that bad."

Crake was wrong, for once. Martha Graham was falling apart. It was surrounded – Jimmy observed as the train pulled in – by the tackiest kind of pleeblands: vacant warehouses, burnt-out tenements, empty parking lots. Here and there were sheds and huts put together from scavenged materials – sheets of tin, slabs of plywood – and inhabited no doubt by squatters. How did such people exist? Jimmy had no idea. Yet there they were, on the other side of the razor wire. A couple of them raised their middle fingers at the train, shouted something that the bulletproof glass shut out.

The security at the Martha Graham gateway was a joke. The guards were half asleep, the walls – scrawled all over with faded graffiti – could have been scaled by a one-legged dwarf. Inside them, the Bilbao-ripoff cast-concrete buildings leaked, the lawns were mud, either baked or liquid depending on the season, and there were no recreational facilities apart from a swimming pool that looked and smelled like a giant sardine can. Half the time the air conditioning in the dorms didn't work; there was a brownout problem with the electrical supply; the food in the cafeteria was mostly beige and looked like rakunk shit. There were arthropods in the bedrooms, families and genera various, but half of them were cockroaches. Jimmy found the place depressing, as did – it seemed – everyone there with any more neural capacity than a tulip. But this was the hand life had dealt him, as his dad had said during their awkward goodbye, and now Jimmy would just have to play it as well as he could.

Right, Dad, Jimmy had thought. I've always known I could count on you for really, really sage advice.

The Martha Graham Academy was named after some gory old dance goddess of the twentieth century who'd apparently mowed quite a swath in her day. There was a gruesome statue of her in front of the administration building, in her role – said the bronze plaque – as Judith, cutting off the head of a guy in a historical robe outfit called Holofernes. Retro feminist shit, was the general student opinion. Every once in a while the statue got its tits decorated or steel wool glued onto its pubic region – Jimmy himself had done some of this glueing – and so comatose was the management that the ornaments often stayed up there for months before they were noticed. Parents were always objecting to this statue – poor role model, they'd say, too aggressive, too blood-thirsty, blah blah – whereupon the students would rally to its defence. Old Martha was their mascot, they'd say, the scowl, the dripping head and all. She represented life, or art, or something. Hands off Martha. Leave her alone.

The Academy had been set up by a clutch of now-dead rich liberal bleeding hearts from Old New York as an Arts-and-Humanities college at some time in the last third of the twentieth century, with special emphasis on the Performing Arts – acting, singing, dancing, and so forth. To that had been added Film-making in the 1980s, and Video Arts after that. These things were still taught at Martha Graham – they still put on plays, and it was there Jimmy saw *Macbeth* in the flesh and reflected that Anna K. and her Web site for peeping Toms had done a more convincing job of Lady Macbeth while sitting on her toilet.

The students of song and dance continued to sing and dance, though the energy had gone out of these activities and the classes were small. Live performance had suffered in the sabotage panics of the early twenty-first century – no one during those decades had wanted to form part of a large group at a public event in a dark, easily destructible walled space, or no one with any cool or status. Theatrical events had dwindled into versions of the singalong or the tomato bombardment or the wet T-shirt contest. And though various older forms had dragged on – the TV sitcom, the rock video – their audience was ancient and their appeal mostly nostalgic.

So a lot of what went on at Martha Graham was like studying Latin, or book-binding: pleasant to contemplate in its way, but no longer central to anything, though every once in a while the college president would subject them to some yawner about the vital arts and their irresistible reserved seat in the big red-velvet amphitheatre of the beating human heart.

As for Film-making and Video Arts, who needed them? Anyone with a computer could splice together whatever they wanted, or digitally alter old material, or create new animation. You could download one of the standard core plots and add whatever faces you chose, and whatever bodies too. Jimmy himself had put together a naked *Pride and Prejudice* and a naked *To the Lighthouse*, just for laughs, and in sophomore VizArts at HelthWyzer he'd done *The Maltese Falcon*, with costumes by Kate Greenaway and depth-and-shadow styling by Rembrandt. That one had been good. A dark tonality, great chiaroscuro.

With this kind of attrition going on – this erosion of its former intellectual territory – Martha Graham had found itself without a very convincing package to offer. As the initial funders had died off and the enthusiasm of the dedicated artsy money had waned and endowment had been sought in more down-to-earth quarters, the curricular emphasis had switched to other arenas. *Contemporary* arenas, they were called. Webgame Dynamics, for instance; money could still be made from that. Or Image Presentation, listed in the calendar as a sub-branch of Pictorial and Plastic Arts. With a degree in PicPlarts, as the students called it, you could go into advertising, no sweat.

Or Problematics. Problematics was for word people, so that was what Jimmy took. Spin and Grin was its nickname among the students. Like everything at Martha Graham it had utilitarian aims. Our Students Graduate With Employable Skills, ran the motto underneath the original Latin motto, which was *Ars Longa Vita Brevis*.

Jimmy had few illusions. He knew what sort of thing would be open to him when he came out the other end of Problematics with his risible degree. Window-dressing was what he'd be doing, at best – decorating the cold, hard, numerical real world in flossy 2-D verbiage. Depending on how well he did in his Problematics courses – Applied Logic, Applied Rhetoric, Medical Ethics and Terminology, Applied Semantics, Relativistics and Advanced Mischaracterization, Comparative Cultural Psychology, and the rest – he'd have a choice between well-paid window-dressing for a big Corp or flimsy cut-rate stuff for a borderline one. The prospect of his future life stretched before him like a sentence; not a prison sentence, but a long-winded sentence with a lot of unnecessary subordinate clauses, as he was soon in the habit of quipping during Happy Hour pickup time at the local campus bars and pubs. He couldn't say he was looking forward to it, this rest-of-his-life.

Nevertheless, he dug himself in at Martha Graham as if into a trench, and hunkered down for the duration. He shared a dorm suite – one cramped room either side, silverfish-ridden bathroom in the middle – with a fundamentalist vegan called Bernice, who had stringy hair held back with a wooden clip in the shape of a toucan and wore a succession of God's Gardeners T-shirts, which — due to her aversion to chemical compounds such as underarm deodorants — stank even when freshly laundered.

Bernice let him know how much she disapproved of his carnivorous ways by kidnapping his leather sandals and incinerating them on the lawn. When he protested that they hadn't been real leather, she said they'd been posing as it, and as such deserved their fate. After he'd had a few girls up to his room — none of Bernice's business, and they'd been quiet enough, apart from some pharmaceutically induced giggling and a lot of understandable moans — she'd manifested her views on consensual sex by making a bonfire of all Jimmy's jockey shorts.

He'd complained about that to Student Services, and after a few tries — Student Services at Martha Graham was notoriously grumpy, staffed as it was by burnt-out TV-series actors who could not forgive the world for their plunge from marginal fame — he got himself moved to a single room. (*First my sandals, then my underwear. Next it'll be me. The woman is a pyromaniac, let me rephrase that, she is reality-challenged in a major way. You wish to see the concrete evidence of her crotchwear auto-da-fé? Look into this tiny envelope. If you see me next in an urn, gritty ashes, couple of teeth, you want the responsibility? Hey, I'm the Student here and you're the Service. Here it is, right on the letterhead, see? I've e-mailed this to the president.*)

(This is not what he actually said, of course. He knew better than that. He smiled, he presented himself as a reasonable human being, he enlisted their sympathy.)

After that, after he got his new room, things were a little better. At least he was free to pursue his social life unhampered. He'd discovered that he projected a form of melancholy attractive to a certain kind of woman, the semi-artistic, wise-wound kind in large supply at Martha Graham. Generous, caring, idealistic women, Snowman thinks of them now. They had a few scars of their own, they were working on healing. At first Jimmy would rush to their aid: he was tender-hearted, he'd been told, and nothing if not chivalrous. He'd draw out of them their stories of hurt, he'd apply himself to them like a poultice. But soon the process would reverse, and Jimmy would switch from bandager to bandagee. These women would begin to see how fractured he was, they'd want to help him gain perspective on life and access the positive aspects of his own spirituality. They saw him as a creative project: the raw material, Jimmy in his present gloomy form; the end product, a happy Jimmy.

Jimmy let them labour away on him. It cheered them up, it made them feel useful. It was touching, the lengths to which they would go. Would this make him happy? Would this? Well then, how about *this*? But he took care never to get any less melancholy on a permanent basis. If he were to do that they'd expect a reward of some sort, or a result at least; they'd demand a next step, and then a pledge. But why would he be stupid enough to give up his grey rainy-day allure — the crepuscular essence, the foggy aureole, that had attracted them to him in the first place?

"I'm a lost cause," he would tell them. "I'm emotionally dyslexic." He would also tell them they were beautiful and they turned him on. True enough, no falsehood there, he always meant it. He would also say that any major investment on their part would be wasted on him, he was an emotional landfill site, and they should just enjoy the here and now.

Sooner or later they'd complain that he refused to take things seriously. This, after having begun by saying he needed to lighten up. When their energy flagged at last and the weeping began, he'd tell them he loved them. He took care to do this in a hopeless voice: being loved by him was a poison pill, it was spiritually toxic, it would drag them down to the murky depths where he himself was imprisoned, and it was because he loved them so much that he wanted them out of harm's way, i.e., out of his ruinous life. Some of them saw through it — *Grow up, Jimmy!* — but on the whole, how potent that was.

He was always sad when they decamped. He disliked the part where they'd get mad at him, he was upset by any woman's anger, but once they'd lost their tempers with him he'd know it was over. He hated being dumped, even though he himself had manoeuvred the event into place. But another woman with intriguing vulnerabilities would happen along shortly. It was a time of simple abundance.

He wasn't lying though, not all the time. He really did love these women, sort of. He really did want to make them feel better. It was just that he had a short attention span.

"You scoundrel," says Snowman out loud. It's a fine word, *scoundrel*; one of the golden oldies.

They knew about his scandalous mother, of course, these women. Ill winds blow far and find a ready welcome. Snowman is ashamed to remember how he'd used that story – a hint here, a hesitation there. Soon the women would be consoling him, and he'd roll around in their sympathy, soak in it, massage himself with it. It was a whole spa experience in itself.

By then his mother had attained the status of a mythical being, something that transcended the human, with dark wings and eyes that burned like Justice, and a sword. When he got to the part where she'd stolen Killer the rakunk away from him he could usually wring out a tear or two, not from himself but from his auditors.

What did you do? (Eyes wide, single pat of hand on arm, sympathetic gaze.)

Oh, you know. (Shrug, look away, change subject.)

It wasn't all acting.

Only Oryx had not been impressed by this dire, feathered mother of his. *So Jimmy, your mother went somewhere else? Too bad. Maybe she had some good reasons. You thought of that?* Oryx had neither pity for him nor self-pity. She was not unfeeling: on the contrary. But she refused to feel what he wanted her to feel. Was that the hook – that he could never get from her what the others had given him so freely? Was that her secret?

Asperger's U.

~

Crake and Jimmy kept in touch by e-mail. Jimmy whined about Martha Graham in what he hoped was an entertaining way, applying unusual and disparaging adjectives to his professors and fellow students. He described the diet of recycled botulism and salmonella, sent lists of the different multi-legged creatures he'd found in his room, moaned about the inferior quality of the mood-altering substances for sale in the dismal student mall. Out of self-protection, he concealed the intricacies of his sex life except for what he considered the minimum of hints. (*These babes may not be able to count to ten, but hey, who needs numeracy in the sack? Just so long as they think it's ten, haha, joke, ☺.*)

He couldn't help boasting a little, because this seemed to be – from any indications he'd had so far – the one field of endeavour in which he had the edge over Crake. At HelthWyzer, Crake hadn't been what you'd call sexually active. Girls had found him intimidating. True, he'd attracted a couple of obsessives who'd thought he could walk on water, and who'd followed him around and sent him slushy, fervent e-mails and threatened to slit their wrists on his behalf. Perhaps he'd even slept with them on occasion; but he'd never gone out of his way. Falling in love, although it resulted in altered body chemistry and was therefore real, was a hormonally induced delusional state, according to him. In addition it was humiliating, because it put you at a disadvantage, it gave the love object too much power. As for sex per se, it lacked both challenge and novelty, and was on the whole a deeply imperfect solution to the problem of intergenerational genetic transfer.

The girls Jimmy accumulated had found Crake more than a little creepy, and it had made Jimmy feel superior to come to his defence. "He's okay, he's just on another planet," was what he used to say.

But how to know about Crake's present circumstances? Crake divulged few factoids about himself. Did he have a roommate, a girlfriend? He never mentioned either, but that meant nothing. His e-mail descriptions were of the campus facilities, which were awesome – an Aladdin's treasure-trove of bio-research gizmos – and of, well, what else? What *did* Crake have to say in his terse initial communications from the Watson-Crick Institute? Snowman can't remember.

They'd played long drawn-out games of chess though, two moves a day. Jimmy was better at chess by now; it was easier without Crake's distracting presence, and the way he had of drumming his fingers and humming to himself, as if he already saw thirty moves ahead and was patiently waiting for Jimmy's tortoiselike mind to trundle up to the next rook sacrifice. Also, Jimmy could look up grandmasters and famous games of the past on various Net programs, in between moves. Not that Crake wasn't doing the same thing.

After five or six months Crake loosened up a bit. He was having to work harder than at HelthWyzer High, he wrote, because there was a lot more competition. Watson-Crick was known to the students there as Asperger's U. because of the high percentage of brilliant weirdos that strolled and hopped and lurched through its corridors. Demi-autistic, genetically speaking; single-track tunnel-vision minds, a marked degree of social ineptitude –

these were not your sharp dressers − and luckily for everyone there, a high tolerance for mildly deviant public behaviour.

More than at HelthWyzer? asked Jimmy.

Compared to this place, HelthWyzer was a pleebland, Crake replied. *It was wall-to-wall* NTs.

NTs?

Neurotypicals.

Meaning?

Minus the genius gene.

So, are you a neurotypical? Jimmy asked the next week, having had some time to think this over. Also to worry about whether he himself was a neurotypical, and if so, was that now bad, in the gestalt of Crake? He suspected he was, and that it was.

But Crake never answered that one. This was his way: when there was a question he didn't want to address, he acted as if it hadn't been asked.

You should come and see this joint, he told Jimmy in late October of their sophomore year. *Give yourself a lifetime experience. I'll pretend you're my dull-normal cousin. Come for Thanksgiving Week.*

The alternative for Jimmy was turkey with the parental-unit turkeys, *joke, haha,* ☺, said Jimmy, and he wasn't up for that; so it would be his pleasure to accept. He told himself he was being a pal and doing Crake a favour, for who did lone Crake have to visit with on his holidays, aside from his boring old australopithecine not-really-an-uncle Uncle Pete? But also he found he was missing Crake. He hadn't seen him now for more than a year. He wondered if Crake had changed.

Jimmy had a couple of term papers to finish before the holidays. He could have bought them off the Net, of course − Martha Graham was notoriously lax about scorekeeping, and plagiarism was a cottage industry there − but he'd taken a position on that. He'd write his own papers, eccentric though it seemed; a line that played well with the Martha Graham type of woman. They liked a dash of originality and risk-taking and intellectual rigour.

For the same reason he'd taken to spending hours in the more obscure regions of the library stacks, ferreting out arcane lore. Better libraries, at institutions with more money, had long ago burned their actual books and kept everything on CD-ROM, but Martha Graham was behind the times in that, as in everything. Wearing a nose-cone filter to protect against the mildew, Jimmy grazed among the shelves of mouldering paper, dipping in at random.

Part of what impelled him was stubbornness; resentment, even. The system had filed him among the rejects, and what he was studying was considered – at the decision-making levels, the levels of real power – an archaic waste of time. Well then, he would pursue the superfluous as an end in itself. He would be its champion, its defender and preserver. Who was it who'd said that all art was completely useless? Jimmy couldn't recall, but hooray for him, whoever he was. The more obsolete a book was, the more eagerly Jimmy would add it to his inner collection.

He compiled lists of old words too – words of a precision and suggestiveness that no longer had a meaningful application in today's world, or *toady's world*, as Jimmy sometimes deliberately misspelled it on his term papers. (*Typo*, the profs would note, which showed how alert they were.) He memorized these hoary locutions, tossed them left-handed into conversation: *wheelwright, lodestone, saturnine, adamant*. He'd developed a strangely tender feeling towards such words, as if they were children abandoned in the woods and it was his duty to rescue them.

One of his term papers – for his Applied Rhetoric course – was titled "Self-Help Books of the Twentieth Century: Exploiting Hope and Fear," and it supplied him with a great stand-up routine for use in the student pubs. He'd quote snatches of this and that – *Improve Your Self-Image*; *The Twelve-Step Plan for Assisted Suicide*; *How to Make Friends and Influence People*; *Flat Abs in Five Weeks*; *You Can Have It All*; *Entertaining*

Without a Maid; Grief Management for Dummies – and the circle around him would crack up.

He now had a circle around him again: he'd rediscovered that pleasure. *Oh Jimmy, do* Cosmetic Surgery for Everyone! *Do* Access Your Inner Child! *Do* Total Womanhood! *Do* Raising Nutria for Fun and Profit! *Do* The Survival Handbook of Dating and Sex! And Jimmy, the ever-ready song-and-dance man, would oblige. Sometimes he'd make up books that didn't exist – *Healing Diverticulitis Through Chanting and Prayer* was one of his best creations – and nobody would spot the imposture.

He'd turned that paper topic into his senior dissertation, later. He'd got an A.

There was a bullet-train connection between Martha Graham and Watson-Crick, with only one change. Jimmy spent a lot of the three-hour trip looking out the window at the pleeblands they were passing through. Rows of dingy houses; apartment buildings with tiny balconies, laundry strung on the railings; factories with smoke coming out of the chimneys; gravel pits. A huge pile of garbage, next to what he supposed was a high-heat incinerator. A shopping mall like the ones at HelthWyzer, only there were cars in the parking lots instead of electric golf carts. A neon strip, with bars and girlie joints and what looked like an archeological-grade movie theatre. He glimpsed a couple of trailer parks, and wondered what it was like to live in one of them: just thinking about it made him slightly dizzy, as he imagined a desert might, or the sea. Everything in the pleeblands seemed so boundless, so porous, so penetrable, so wide-open. So subject to chance.

Accepted wisdom in the Compounds said that nothing of interest went on in the pleeblands, apart from buying and selling: there was no life of the mind. Buying and selling, plus a lot of criminal activity; but to Jimmy it looked mysterious and exciting, over there on the other side of the safety barriers. Also dangerous. He wouldn't know the ways to do things there, he wouldn't know how to behave. He wouldn't even know how to pick up girls.

They'd turn him upside down in no time, they'd shake his head loose. They'd laugh at him. He'd be fodder.

The security going into Watson-Crick was very thorough, unlike the sloppy charade that took place at Martha Graham: the fear must have been that some fanatic would sneak in and blow up the best minds of the generation, thus dealing a crippling blow to something or other. There were dozens of CorpSeCorps men, complete with sprayguns and rubber clubs; they had Watson-Crick insignia, but you could tell who they really were. They took Jimmy's iris imprint and ran it through the system, and then two surly weightlifters pulled him aside for questioning. As soon as it happened he guessed why.

"You seen your runaway mother lately?"

"No," he said truthfully.

"Heard from her? Had a phone call, another postcard?" So they were still tracking his snail mail. All of the postcards must be stored on their computers; plus his present whereabouts, which was why they hadn't asked where he'd come from.

No again, he said. They had him hooked up to the neural-impulse monitor so they knew he wasn't lying; they must also have known that the question distressed him. He was on the verge of saying *And if I had I wouldn't tell you, apeface*, but he was old enough by then to realize that nothing would be served by that, and it was likely to land him on the next bullet train back to Martha Graham, or worse.

"Know what she's been doing? Who she's hanging out with?"

Jimmy didn't, but he had a feeling they themselves might have some idea. They didn't mention the Happicuppa demonstration in Maryland though, so maybe they were less informed than he feared.

"Why are you here, son?" Now they were bored. The important part was over.

"I'm visiting an old friend for Thanksgiving Week," said Jimmy. "A friend from HelthWyzer High. He's a student here.

I've been invited." He gave the name, and the visitor authorization number supplied to him by Crake.

"What sort of a student? What's he taking?"

Transgenics, Jimmy told them.

They pulled up the file to check, frowned at it, looked moderately impressed. Then they made a cellcall, as if they hadn't quite believed him. What was a serf like him doing visiting the nobility? their manner implied. But finally they let him through, and there was Crake in his no-name dark clothing, looking older and thinner and also smarter than ever, leaning on the exit barrier and grinning.

"Hi there, cork-nut," said Crake, and nostalgia swept through Jimmy like sudden hunger. He was so pleased to see Crake he almost wept.

Wolvogs
~

Compared with Martha Graham, Watson-Crick was a palace. At the entranceway was a bronzed statue of the Institute's mascot, the spoat/gider — one of the first successful splices, done in Montreal at the turn of the century, goat crossed with spider to produce high-tensile spider silk filaments in the milk. The main application nowadays was bulletproof vests. The CorpSeCorps swore by the stuff.

The extensive grounds inside the security wall were beautifully laid out: the work, said Crake, of the JigScape Faculty. The students in Botanical Transgenics (Ornamental Division) had created a whole array of drought-and-flood-resistant tropical blends, with flowers or leaves in lurid shades of chrome yellow and brilliant flame red and phosphorescent blue and neon purple. The pathways, unlike the crumbling cement walks at Martha Graham, were smooth and wide. Students and faculty were beetling along them in their electric golf carts.

Huge fake rocks, made from a combo-matrix of recycled plastic bottles and plant material from giant tree cacti and various lithops — the living-stone members of the Mesembryanthemaceae — were dotted here and there. It was a patented process, said

Crake, originally developed at Watson-Crick and now a nice little money-spinner. The fake rocks looked like real rocks but weighed less; not only that, they absorbed water during periods of humidity and released it in times of drought, so they acted like natural lawn regulators. Rockulators, was the brand name. You had to avoid them during heavy rainfalls, though, as they'd been known to explode.

But most of the bugs had now been ironed out, said Crake, and new varieties were appearing every month. The student team was thinking of developing something called the Moses Model, for dependable supplies of fresh drinking water in times of crisis. Just Hit It With a Rod, was the proposed slogan.

"How do those things work?" asked Jimmy, trying not to sound impressed.

"Search me," said Crake. "I'm not in NeoGeologicals."

"So, are the butterflies – are they recent?" Jimmy asked after a while. The ones he was looking at had wings the size of pancakes and were shocking pink, and were clustering all over one of the purple shrubs.

"You mean, did they occur in nature or were they created by the hand of man? In other words, are they real or fake?"

"Mm," said Jimmy. He didn't want to get into the *what is real* thing with Crake.

"You know when people get their hair dyed or their teeth done? Or women get their tits enlarged?"

"Yeah?"

"After it happens, that's what they look like in real time. The process is no longer important."

"No way fake tits feel like real tits," said Jimmy, who thought he knew a thing or two about that.

"If you could tell they were fake," said Crake, "it was a bad job. These butterflies fly, they mate, they lay eggs, caterpillars come out."

"Mm," said Jimmy again.

~   ~   ~

Crake didn't have a roommate. Instead he had a suite, accented in wood tones, with push-button venetians and air conditioning that really worked. It consisted of a large bedroom, an enclosed bath and shower unit with steam function, a main living-dining room with a pullout couch – that was where Jimmy would camp out, said Crake – and a study with a built-in sound system and a full array of compu-gizmos. It had maid service too, and they picked up and delivered your laundry. (Jimmy was depressed by this news, as he had to do his own laundry at Martha Graham, using the clanking, wheezy washers and the dryers that fried your clothes. You had to slot plastic tokens into them because the machines had been jimmied regularly when they'd taken coins.)

Crake also had a cheery kitchenette. "Not that I microwave much," said Crake. "Except for snack food. Most of us eat at our dining halls. There's one for each faculty."

"How's the food?" Jimmy asked. He was feeling more and more like a troglodyte. Living in a cave, fighting off the body parasites, gnawing the odd bone.

"It's food," said Crake indifferently.

On day one they toured some of the wonders of Watson-Crick. Crake was interested in everything – all the projects that were going on. He kept saying "Wave of the future," which got irritating after the third time.

First they went to Décor Botanicals, where a team of five seniors was developing Smart Wallpaper that would change colour on the walls of your room to complement your mood. This wallpaper – they told Jimmy – had a modified form of Kirlian-energy-sensing algae embedded in it, along with a sublayer of algae nutrients, but there were still some glitches to be fixed. The wallpaper was short-lived in humid weather because it ate up all the nutrients and then went grey; also it could not tell the difference between drooling lust and murderous rage, and was likely to turn your wallpaper an erotic pink when what you really needed was a murky, capillary-bursting greenish red.

That team was also working on a line of bathroom towels that would behave in much the same way, but they hadn't yet solved the marine-life fundamentals: when algae got wet it swelled up and began to grow, and the test subjects so far had not liked the sight of their towels from the night before puffing up like rectangular marshmallows and inching across the bathroom floor.

"Wave of the future," said Crake.

Next they went to NeoAgriculturals. AgriCouture was its nickname among the students. They had to put on biosuits before they entered the facility, and scrub their hands and wear nose-cone filters, because what they were about to see hadn't been bioform-proofed, or not completely. A woman with a laugh like Woody Woodpecker led them through the corridors.

"This is the latest," said Crake.

What they were looking at was a large bulblike object that seemed to be covered with stippled whitish-yellow skin. Out of it came twenty thick fleshy tubes, and at the end of each tube another bulb was growing.

"What the hell is it?" said Jimmy.

"Those are chickens," said Crake. "Chicken parts. Just the breasts, on this one. They've got ones that specialize in drumsticks too, twelve to a growth unit."

"But there aren't any heads," said Jimmy. He grasped the concept — he'd grown up with *sus multiorganifer*, after all — but this thing was going too far. At least the pigoons of his childhood hadn't lacked heads.

"That's the head in the middle," said the woman. "There's a mouth opening at the top, they dump the nutrients in there. No eyes or beak or anything, they don't need those."

"This is horrible," said Jimmy. The thing was a nightmare. It was like an animal-protein tuber.

"Picture the sea-anemone body plan," said Crake. "That helps."

"But what's it thinking?" said Jimmy.

The woman gave her jocular woodpecker yodel, and explained that they'd removed all the brain functions that had nothing to do with digestion, assimilation, and growth.

"It's sort of like a chicken hookworm," said Crake.

"No need for added growth hormones," said the woman, "the high growth rate's built in. You get chicken breasts in two weeks – that's a three-week improvement on the most efficient low-light, high-density chicken farming operation so far devised. And the animal-welfare freaks won't be able to say a word, because this thing feels no pain."

"Those kids are going to clean up," said Crake after they'd left. The students at Watson-Crick got half the royalties from anything they invented there. Crake said it was a fierce incentive. "ChickieNobs, they're thinking of calling the stuff."

"Are they on the market yet?" asked Jimmy weakly. He couldn't see eating a ChickieNob. It would be like eating a large wart. But as with the tit implants – the good ones – maybe he wouldn't be able to tell the difference.

"They've already got the takeout franchise operation in place," said Crake. "Investors are lining up around the block. They can undercut the price of everyone else."

Jimmy was becoming annoyed by Crake's way of introducing him – "This is Jimmy, the neurotypical" – but he knew better than to show it. Still, it seemed to be like calling him a Cro-Magnon or something. Next step they'd be putting him in a cage, feeding him bananas, and poking him with electroprods.

Nor did he think much of the Watson-Crick women on offer. Maybe they weren't even on offer: they seemed to have other things on their minds. Jimmy's few attempts at flirtation got him some surprised stares – surprised and not at all pleased, as if he'd widdled on these women's carpets.

Considering their slovenliness, their casual approach to personal hygiene and adornment, they ought to have fainted at the attention. Plaid shirts were their formal wear, hairstyles not their strong suit: a lot of them looked as if they'd had a close encounter with the kitchen shears. As a group, they reminded him of Bernice, the God's Gardeners pyromaniac vegan. The Bernice model was an exception at Martha Graham, where the girls tried to give the impression they were, or had been once, or could well be, dancers or actresses or singers or performance artists or conceptual photographers or something else artistic. Willowy was their aim, style was their game, whether they played it well or not. But here the Bernice look was the rule, except that there were few religious T-shirts. More usual were ones with complex mathematical equations on them that caused snickers among those who could decode them.

"What's the T-shirt say?" asked Jimmy, when he'd had one too many of these experiences – high-fives among the others, himself standing with the foolish look of someone who's just had his pocket picked.

"That girl's a physicist," said Crake, as if this explained everything.

"So?"

"So, her T-shirt's about the eleventh dimension."

"What's the joke?"

"It's complicated," said Crake.

"Try me."

"You have to know about the dimensions and how they're supposed to be all curled up inside the dimensions we know about."

"And?"

"It's sort of like, I can take you out of this world, but the route to it is just a few nanoseconds long, and the way of measuring those nanoseconds doesn't exist in our space-frame."

"All that in symbols and numbers?"

"Not in so many words."

"Oh."

"I didn't say it was *funny*," said Crake. "These are physicists. It's only funny to them. But you asked."

"So it's sort of like she's saying they could make it together if he only had the right kind of dick, which he doesn't?" said Jimmy, who'd been thinking hard.

"Jimmy, you're a genius," said Crake.

"This is BioDefences," said Crake. "Last stop, I promise." He could tell Jimmy was flagging. The truth was that all this was too reminiscent. The labs, the peculiar bioforms, the socially spastic scientists — they were too much like his former life, his life as a child. Which was the last place he wanted to go back to. Even Martha Graham was preferable.

They were standing in front of a series of cages. Each contained a dog. There were many different breeds and sizes, but all were gazing at Jimmy with eyes of love, all were wagging their tails.

"It's a dog pound," said Jimmy.

"Not quite," said Crake. "Don't go beyond the guardrail, don't stick your hand in."

"They look friendly enough," said Jimmy. His old longing for a pet came over him. "Are they for sale?"

"They aren't dogs, they just look like dogs. They're wolvogs — they're bred to deceive. Reach out to pat them, they'll take your hand off. There's a large pit-bull component."

"Why make a dog like that?" said Jimmy, taking a step back. "Who'd want one?"

"It's a CorpSeCorps thing," said Crake. "Commission work. A lot of funding. They want to put them in moats, or something."

"Moats?"

"Yeah. Better than an alarm system — no way of disarming these guys. And no way of making pals with them, not like real dogs."

"What if they get out? Go on the rampage? Start breeding, then the population spirals out of control — like those big green rabbits?"

"That would be a problem," said Crake. "But they won't get out. Nature is to zoos as God is to churches."

"Meaning what?" said Jimmy. He wasn't paying close attention, he was worrying about the ChickieNobs and the wolvogs. Why is it he feels some line has been crossed, some boundary transgressed? How much is too much, how far is too far?

"Those walls and bars are there for a reason," said Crake. "Not to keep us out, but to keep them in. Mankind needs barriers in both cases."

"Them?"

"Nature and God."

"I thought you didn't believe in God," said Jimmy.

"I don't believe in Nature either," said Crake. "Or not with a capital N."

Hypothetical

~

"So, you got a girlfriend?" said Jimmy on the fourth day. He'd been saving this question for the right time. "I mean, there's quite an array of babes to choose from." He meant this to be ironic. He couldn't picture himself with the Woody Woodpecker–laugh girl or the ones with numbers all over their chests, but he couldn't picture Crake with one of them either. Crake was too suave for that.

"Not as such," said Crake shortly.

"What do you mean, *not as such*? You've got a girl, but she's not a human being?"

"Pair-bonding at this stage is not encouraged," said Crake, sounding like a guidebook. "We're supposed to be focusing on our work."

"Bad for your health," said Jimmy. "You should get yourself fixed up."

"Easy for you to say," said Crake. "You're the grasshopper, I'm the ant. I can't waste time in unproductive random scanning."

For the first time in their lives, Jimmy wondered — could it be? — whether Crake might be jealous of him. Though maybe

Crake was just being a pompous tightass; maybe Watson-Crick was having a bad effect on him. *So what's the super-cerebellum-triathlon ultralife mission?* Jimmy felt like saying. *Deign to divulge?* "I wouldn't call it a waste," he said instead, trying to lighten Crake up, "unless you fail to score."

"If you really need to, you can arrange that kind of thing through Student Services," Crake said, rather stiffly. "They deduct the price from your scholarship, same as room and board. The workers come in from the pleeblands, they're trained professionals. Naturally they're inspected for disease."

"Student Services? In your dreams! They do *what?*"

"It makes sense," said Crake. "As a system, it avoids the diversion of energies into unproductive channels, and short-circuits malaise. The female students have equal access, of course. You can get any colour, any age – well, almost. Any body type. They provide everything. If you're gay or some kind of a fetishist, they'll fix that too."

At first Jimmy thought Crake might be joking, but he wasn't. Jimmy longed to ask him what he'd tried – had he done a double amputee, for instance? But all of a sudden such a question seemed intrusive. Also it might be mistaken for mockery.

The food in Crake's faculty dining hall was fantastic – real shrimps instead of the CrustaeSoy they got at Martha Graham, and real chicken, Jimmy suspected, though he avoided that because he couldn't forget the ChickieNobs he'd seen; and something a lot like real cheese, though Crake said it came from a vegetable, a new species of zucchini they were trying out.

The desserts were heavy on the chocolate, real chocolate. The coffee was heavy on the coffee. No burnt grain products, no molasses mixed in. It was Happicuppa, but who cared? And real beer. For sure the beer was real.

So all of that was a welcome change from Martha Graham, though Crake's fellow students tended to forget about cutlery and eat with their hands, and wipe their mouths on their sleeves. Jimmy wasn't picky, but this verged on gross. Also they talked all the time, whether anyone was listening or not, always about the ideas they were developing. Once they found Jimmy wasn't working on a *space* – was attending, in fact, an institution they clearly regarded as a mud puddle – they lost any interest in him. They referred to other students in their own faculties as their conspecifics, and to all other human beings as nonspecifics. It was a running joke.

So Jimmy had no yen to mingle after hours. He was happy enough to hang out at Crake's, letting Crake beat him at chess or Three-Dimensional Waco, or trying to decode Crake's fridge magnets, the ones that didn't have numbers and symbols. Watson-Crick was a fridge-magnet culture: people bought them, traded them, made their own.

> No Brain, No Pain (with a green hologram of a brain).
> Siliconsciousness.
> I wander from Space to Space.
> Wanna Meet a Meat Machine?
> Take Your Time, Leave Mine Alone.
> Little spoat/gider, who made thee?
> Life experiments like a rakunk at play.
> I think, therefore I spam.
> The proper study of Mankind is Everything.

Sometimes they'd watch TV or Web stuff, as in the old days. The Noodie News, brainfrizz, alibooboo, comfort eyefood like that. They'd microwave popcorn, smoke some of the enhanced weed the Botanical Transgenic students were raising in one of the greenhouses; then Jimmy could pass out on the couch. After he got used to his status in this brainpound, which was equivalent to that of a house plant, it wasn't too bad. You just had to relax and breathe into the stretch, as in workouts. He'd be out of here in a few days. Meanwhile it was always interesting to listen to

Crake, when Crake was alone, and when he was in the mood to say anything.

On the second to last evening, Crake said, "Let me walk you through a hypothetical scenario."

"I'm game," said Jimmy. Actually he was sleepy – he'd had too much popcorn and beer – but he sat up and put on his paying-attention look, the one he'd perfected in high school. Hypothetical scenarios were a favourite thing of Crake's.

"Axiom: that illness isn't productive. In itself, it generates no commodities and therefore no money. Although it's an excuse for a lot of activity, all it really does moneywise is cause wealth to flow from the sick to the well. From patients to doctors, from clients to cure-peddlers. Money osmosis, you might call it."

"Granted," said Jimmy.

"Now, suppose you're an outfit called HelthWyzer. Suppose you make your money out of drugs and procedures that cure sick people, or else – better – that make it impossible for them to get sick in the first place."

"Yeah?" said Jimmy. Nothing hypothetical here: that was what HelthWyzer actually did.

"So, what are you going to need, sooner or later?"

"More cures?"

"After that."

"What do you mean, after that?"

"After you've cured everything going."

Jimmy made a pretence of thinking. No point doing any actual thought: it was a foregone conclusion that Crake would have some lateral-jump solution to his own question.

"Remember the plight of the dentists, after that new mouth-wash came in? The one that replaced plaque bacteria with friendly ones that filled the same ecological niche, namely your mouth? No one ever needed a filling again, and a lot of dentists went bust."

"So?"

"So, you'd need more sick people. Or else – and it might be the same thing – more diseases. New and different ones. Right?"

"Stands to reason," said Jimmy after a moment. It did, too. "But don't they keep discovering new diseases?"

"Not discovering," said Crake. "They're *creating* them."

"Who is?" said Jimmy. Saboteurs, terrorists, is that what Crake meant? It was well known they went in for that kind of thing, or tried to. So far they hadn't had a lot of successes: their puny little diseases had been simple-minded, in Compound terms, and fairly easy to contain.

"HelthWyzer," said Crake. "They've been doing it for years. There's a whole secret unit working on nothing else. Then there's the distribution end. Listen, this is brilliant. They put the hostile bioforms into their vitamin pills – their HelthWyzer over-the-counter premium brand, you know? They have a really elegant delivery system – they embed a virus inside a carrier bacterium, E. coli splice, doesn't get digested, bursts in the pylorus, and bingo! Random insertion, of course, and they don't have to keep on doing it – if they did they'd get caught, because even in the pleeblands they've got guys who could figure it out. But once you've got a hostile bioform started in the pleeb population, the way people slosh around out there it more or less runs itself. Naturally they develop the antidotes at the same time as they're customizing the bugs, but they hold those in reserve, they practise the economics of scarcity, so they're guaranteed high profits."

"Are you making this up?" said Jimmy.

"The best diseases, from a business point of view," said Crake, "would be those that cause lingering illnesses. Ideally – that is, for maximum profit – the patient should either get well or die just before all of his or her money runs out. It's a fine calculation."

"This would be really evil," said Jimmy.

"That's what my father thought," said Crake.

"He *knew*?" Jimmy really was paying attention now.

"He found out. That's how come they pushed him off a bridge."

"Who did?" said Jimmy.

"Into oncoming traffic."

"Are you going paranoid, or what?"

"Not in the least," said Crake. "This is the bare-naked truth. I hacked into my dad's e-mails before they deep-cleansed his computer. The evidence he'd been collecting was all there. The tests he'd been running on the vitamin pills. Everything."

Jimmy felt a chill up his spine. "Who knows that you know?"

"Guess who else he told?" said Crake. "My mother and Uncle Pete. He was going to do some whistle-blowing through a rogue Web site — those things have a wide viewership, it would have wrecked the pleebland sales of every single HelthWyzer vitamin supplement, plus it would have torched the entire scheme. It would have caused financial havoc. Think of the job losses. He wanted to warn them first." Crake paused. "He thought Uncle Pete didn't know."

"Wow," said Jimmy. "So one or the other of them . . ."

"Could have been both," said Crake. "Uncle Pete wouldn't have wanted the bottom line threatened. My mother may just have been scared, felt that if my dad went down, she could go too. Or it could have been the CorpSeCorps. Maybe he'd been acting funny at work. Maybe they were checking up. He encrypted everything, but if I could hack in, so could they."

"That is so weird," said Jimmy. "So they murdered your father?"

"Executed," said Crake. "That's what they'd have called it. They'd have said he was about to destroy an elegant concept. They'd have said they were acting for the general good."

The two of them sat there. Crake was looking up at the ceiling, almost as if he admired it. Jimmy didn't know what else to say. Words of comfort would be superfluous.

Finally Crake said, "How come your mother took off the way she did?"

"I don't know," said Jimmy. "A lot of reasons. I don't want to talk about it."

"I bet your dad was in on something like that. Some scam like the HelthWyzer one. I bet she found out."

"Oh, I don't think so," said Jimmy. "I think she got involved with some God's Gardeners–type outfit. Some bunch of wackos. Anyway, my dad wouldn't have . . ."

"I bet she knew they were starting to know she knew."

"I'm really tired," said Jimmy. He yawned, and suddenly it was true. "I think I'll turn in."

Extinctathon

~

On the last evening, Crake said, "Want to play Extinctathon?"

"Extinctathon?" said Jimmy. It took him a moment, but then he remembered it: the boring Web interactive with all those defunct animals and plants. "When was it we used to play that? It can't still be going."

"It's never stopped," said Crake. Jimmy took in the implications: Crake had never stopped. He must've been playing it by himself, all these years. Well, he was a compulsive, no news there.

"So, how's your cumulative score?" he asked, to be polite.

"Once you rack up three thousand," said Crake, "you get to be a Grandmaster." Which meant Crake was one, because he wouldn't have mentioned it otherwise.

"Oh good," said Jimmy. "So do you get a prize? The tail and both ears?"

"Let me show you something," said Crake. He went onto the Web, found the site, pulled it up. There was the familiar gateway: *EXTINCTATHON, Monitored by MaddAddam. Adam named the living animals, MaddAddam names the dead ones. Do you want to play?*

Crake clicked Yes, and entered his codename: *Rednecked Crake*. The little coelacanth symbol appeared over his name, meaning Grandmaster. Then something new came up, a message Jimmy had never seen before: *Welcome Grandmaster Rednecked Crake. Do you want to play a general game or do you want to play another Grandmaster?*

Crake clicked the second. *Good. Find your playroom. MaddAddam will meet you there.*

"MaddAddam is a person?" asked Jimmy.

"It's a group," said Crake. "Or groups."

"So what do they do, this MaddAddam?" Jimmy was feeling silly. It was like watching some corny old spy DVD, James Bond or something. "Besides counting the skulls and pelts, I mean."

"Watch this." Crake left Extinctathon, then hacked into a local pleeb bank, and from there skipped to what looked to be a manufacturer of solarcar parts. He went into the image of a hubcap, which opened into a folder — HottTotts Pinups, it was titled. The files were dated, not named; he chose one of them, transferred it into one of his lily pads, used that to skip to another, erased his footprints, opened the file there, loaded an image.

It was the picture of Oryx, seven or eight years old, naked except for her ribbons, her flowers. It was the picture of the look she'd given him, the direct, contemptuous, knowing look that had dealt him such a blow when he was — what? Fourteen? He still had the paper printout, folded up, hidden deep. It was a private thing, this picture. His own private thing: his own guilt, his own shame, his own desire. Why had Crake kept it? *Stolen* it.

Jimmy felt ambushed. *What's she doing here?* he wanted to yell. *That's mine! Give it back!* He was in a lineup; fingers pointed at him, faces scowled, while some rabid Bernice clone set fire to his undershorts. Retribution was at hand, but for what? What had he done? Nothing. He'd only looked.

Crake moved to the girl's left eye, clicked on the iris. It was a gateway: the playroom opened up.

Hello, Grandmaster Crake. Enter passnumber now.

Crake did so. A new sentence popped up: *Adam named the animals. MaddAddam customizes them.*

Then there was a string of e-bulletins, with places and dates — CorpSeCorps issue, by the look of them, marked For Secure Addresses Only.

A tiny parasitic wasp had invaded several ChickieNobs installations, carrying a modified form of chicken pox, specific to the ChickieNob and fatal to it. The installations had had to be incinerated before the epidemic could be brought under control.

A new form of the common house mouse addicted to the insulation on electric wiring had overrun Cleveland, causing an unprecedented number of house fires. Control measures were still being tested.

Happicuppa coffee bean crops were menaced by a new bean weevil found to be resistant to all known pesticides.

A miniature rodent containing elements of both porcupine and beaver had appeared in the northwest, creeping under the hoods of parked vehicles and devastating their fan belts and transmission systems.

A microbe that ate the tar in asphalt had turned several interstate highways to sand. All interstates were on alert, and a quarantine belt was now in place.

"What's going on?" said Jimmy. "Who's putting this stuff out there?"

The bulletins vanished, and a fresh entry appeared. *MaddAddam needs fresh initiatives. Got a bright idea? Share with us.*

Crake typed, *Sorry, interruption. Must go.*

Right, Grandmaster Rednecked Crake. We'll talk later. Crake closed down.

Jimmy had a cold feeling, a feeling that reminded him of the time his mother had left home: the same sense of the forbidden, of a door swinging open that ought to be kept locked, of a stream of secret lives, running underground, in the darkness just beneath his feet. "What was all that about?" he said. It might not be about anything, he told himself. It might be about Crake showing off. It might be an elaborate setup, an invention of Crake's, a practical joke to frighten him.

"I'm not sure," said Crake. "I thought at first they were just another crazy Animal Liberation org. But there's more to it than that. I think they're after the machinery. They're after the whole system, they want to shut it down. So far they haven't done any people numbers, but it's obvious they could."

"You shouldn't be messing around!" said Jimmy. "You don't want to be connected! Someone could think you're part of it. What if you get caught? You'll end up on brainfrizz!" He was frightened now.

"I won't get caught," said Crake. "I'm just cruising. But do me a favour and don't mention this when you e-mail."

"Sure," said Jimmy. "But why even take the chance?"

"I'm curious, that's all," said Crake. "They've let me into the waiting room, but not any further. They've got to be Compound, or Compound-trained. These are sophisticated bioforms they're putting together; I don't think a pleeblander would be able to make anything like that." He gave Jimmy his green-eyed side-ways look – a look (Snowman thinks now) that meant trust. Crake trusted him. Otherwise he wouldn't have shown him the hidden playroom.

"It could be a CorpSeCorps flytrap," said Jimmy. The Corpsmen were in the habit of setting up schemes of that sort, to capture subversives in the making. Weeding the pea patch, he'd heard it called. The Compounds were said to be mined with such potentially lethal tunnels. "You need to watch your step."

"Sure," said Crake.

What Jimmy really wanted to know was: *Out of all the possibilities you had, out of all the gateways, why did you choose her?*

He couldn't ask, though. He couldn't give himself away.

Something else happened during that visit; something important, though Jimmy hadn't realized it at the time.

The first night, as he was sleeping on Crake's pullout sofa bed, he'd heard shouting. He'd thought it was coming from outside — at Martha Graham it would have been student pranksters — but in fact it was coming from Crake's room. It was coming from Crake.

More than shouting: screaming. There were no words. It happened every night he was there.

"That was some dream you were having," said Jimmy the next morning, after the first time it happened.

"I never dream," said Crake. His mouth was full and he was looking out the window. For such a thin man he ate a lot. It was the speed, the high metabolic rate: Crake burned things up.

"Everyone dreams," Jimmy said. "Remember the REM-sleep study at HelthWyzer High?"

"The one where we tortured cats?"

"Virtual cats, yeah. And the cats that couldn't dream went crazy."

"I never remember my dreams," said Crake. "Have some more toast."

"But you must have them anyway."

"Okay, point taken, wrong words. I didn't mean *I never dream.* I'm not crazy, therefore I must dream. Hypothesis, demonstration, conclusion, if A then not B. Good enough?" Crake smiled, poured himself some coffee.

So Crake never remembered his dreams. It's Snowman that remembers them instead. Worse than remembers: he's immersed in them, he'd wading through them, he's stuck in them. Every moment he's lived in the past few months was dreamed first by Crake. No wonder Crake screamed so much.

9
~

Hike

~

After an hour of walking, Snowman comes out from the former park. He picks his way farther inland, heading along the trashed pleebland boulevards and avenues and roads and streets. Wrecked solarcars are plentiful, some piled up in multi-vehicle crashes, some burnt out, some standing intact as if temporarily parked. There are trucks and vans, fuel-cell models and also the old gas or diesel kind, and ATVs. A few bicycles, a few motorcycles – not a bad choice considering the traffic mayhem that must have lasted for days. On a two-wheeled item you'd have been able to weave in and out among the larger vehicles until someone shot you or ran into you, or you fell off.

This was once a semi-residential sector – shops on the ground floor, gutted now; small dim apartments above. Most of the signs are still in place despite the bullet holes in them. People had hoarded the lead bullets from the time before sprayguns, despite the ban on the pleebs having any kind of gun at all. Snowman's been unable to find any bullets; not that he'd had a rusty old firearm that would have taken them.

The buildings that didn't burn or explode are still standing, though the botany is thrusting itself through every crack. Given time it will fissure the asphalt, topple the walls, push aside the roofs. Some kind of vine is growing everywhere, draping the windowsills, climbing in through the broken windows and up the bars and grillwork. Soon this district will be a thick tangle of vegetation. If he'd postponed the trip much longer the way back would have become impassable. It won't be long before all visible traces of human habitation will be gone.

But suppose — just suppose, thinks Snowman — that he's not the last of his kind. Suppose there are others. He wills them into being, these possible remnants who might have survived in isolated pockets, cut off by the shutdown of the communications networks, keeping themselves alive somehow. Monks in desert hideaways, far from contagion; mountain goatherders who'd never mixed with the valley people; lost tribes in the jungles. Survivalists who'd tuned in early, shot all comers, sealed themselves into their underground bunkers. Hillbillies, recluses; wandering lunatics, swathed in protective hallucinations. Bands of nomads, following their ancient ways.

How did this happen? their descendants will ask, stumbling upon the evidence, the ruins. The ruinous evidence. *Who made these things? Who lived in them? Who destroyed them?* The Taj Mahal, the Louvre, the Pyramids, the Empire State Building — stuff he's seen on TV, in old books, on postcards, on Blood and Roses. Imagine coming upon them, 3-D, life-sized, with no preparation — you'd be freaked, you'd run away, and after that you'd need an explanation. At first they'll say giants or gods, but sooner or later they'll want to know the truth. Like him, they'll have the curious monkey brain.

Perhaps they'll say, *These things are not real. They are phantasmagoria. They were made by dreams, and now that no one is dreaming them any longer they are crumbling away.*

~   ~   ~

"Let's suppose for the sake of argument," said Crake one evening, "that civilization as we know it gets destroyed. Want some popcorn?"

"Is that real butter?" said Jimmy.

"Nothing but the best at Watson-Crick," said Crake. "Once it's flattened, it could never be rebuilt."

"Because why? Got any salt?"

"Because all the available surface metals have already been mined," said Crake. "Without which, no iron age, no bronze age, no age of steel, and all the rest of it. There's metals farther down, but the advanced technology we need for extracting those would have been obliterated."

"It could be put back together," said Jimmy, chewing. It was so long since he'd tasted popcorn this good. "They'd still have the instructions."

"Actually not," said Crake. "It's not like the wheel, it's too complex now. Suppose the instructions survived, suppose there were any people left with the knowledge to read them. Those people would be few and far between, and they wouldn't have the tools. Remember, no electricity. Then once those people died, that would be it. They'd have no apprentices, they'd have no successors. Want a beer?"

"Is it cold?"

"All it takes," said Crake, "is the elimination of one generation. One generation of anything. Beetles, trees, microbes, scientists, speakers of French, whatever. Break the link in time between one generation and the next, and it's game over forever."

"Speaking of games," said Jimmy, "it's your move."

The walking has become an obstacle course for Snowman: in several places he's needed to make detours. Now he's in a narrow sidestreet, choked with vines; they've festooned themselves across the street, from roof to roof. Through the clefts in the overhead greenery he can see a handful of vultures, circling idly in the sky. They can see him too, they have eyesight like ten magnifying glasses, those things can count the change in your pocket. He knows a thing or two about vultures. "Not yet," he calls up at them.

But why disappoint them? If he were to stumble and fall, cut himself open, knock himself out, then be set upon by wolvogs or pigoons, what difference would it make to anyone but himself? The Crakers are doing fine, they don't need him any more. For a while they'll wonder where he's gone, but he's already provided an answer to that: he's gone to be with Crake. He'll become a secondary player in their mythology, such as it is – a sort of backup demiurge. He'll be falsely remembered. He won't be mourned.

The sun is climbing higher, intensifying its rays. He feels light-headed. A thick tendril slithers away, flickering its tongue, as his foot comes down beside it. He needs to pay more attention. Are any of the snakes venomous? Did that long tail he almost stepped on have a small furry body at the front? He didn't see it clearly. He certainly hopes not. The claim was that all the snats had been destroyed, but it would take only one pair of them. One pair, the Adam and Eve of snats, and some weirdo with a grudge, bidding them go forth and multiply, relishing the idea of those things twirling up the drainpipes. Rats with long green scaly tails and rattlesnake fangs. He decides not to think about that.

Instead he begins to hum, to cheer himself up. What's the song? "Winter Wonderland." They used to recycle that in the malls every Christmas, long after the last time it snowed. Some tune about playing pranks on a snowman, before it got mushed.

Maybe he's not the Abominable Snowman after all. Maybe he's the other kind of snowman, the grinning dope set up as a joke and pushed down as an entertainment, his pebble smile and carrot nose an invitation to mockery and abuse. Maybe that's the real him, the last *Homo sapiens* – a white illusion of a man, here today, gone tomorrow, so easily shoved over, left to melt in the sun, getting thinner and thinner until he liquefies and trickles away altogether. As Snowman is doing now. He pauses, wipes the sweat off his face, drinks half of his bottle of water. He hopes there will be more somewhere, soon.

Up ahead, the houses thin out and vanish. There's an interval of parking lots and warehouses, then barbed wire strung between cement posts, an elaborate gate off its hinges. End of urban sprawl and pleeb city limits, beginning of Compound turfdom. Here's the last station of the sealed-tunnel bullet train, with its plastic jungle-gym colours. *No risks here*, the colours are saying. *Just kiddie fun.*

But this is the dangerous part. Up to here he's always had something he could climb or scramble up or dodge around in case of a flank attack, but now comes an open space with no shelter and few verticals. He pulls the sheet up over his baseball cap to protect himself from the sun's glare, shrouding himself like an Arab, and plods on, picking up the pace as much as he can. He knows he'll burn some even through the sheet if he stays out here long enough: his best hope is speed. He'll need to get to shelter before noon, when the asphalt will be too hot to walk on.

Now he's reached the Compounds. He passes the turnoff to CryoJeenyus, one of the smaller outfits: he'd like to have been a fly on the wall when the lights went out and two thousand frozen millionaires' heads awaiting resurrection began to melt in the dark. Next comes Genie-Gnomes, with the elfin mascot popping its pointy-eared head in and out of a test tube. The neon was on, he noted: the solar hookup must still be functioning, though not perfectly. Those signs were supposed to go on only at night.

And, finally, RejoovenEsense. Where he'd made so many mistakes, misunderstood so much, gone on his last joyride. Bigger than OrganInc Farms, bigger than HelthWyzer. The biggest of them all.

He passes the first barricade with its crapped-out scopers and busted searchlights, then the checkpoint booth. A guard is lying half in, half out. Snowman isn't too surprised by the absence of a head: in times of crisis emotions run high. He checks to see if the guy still has his spraygun, but no dice.

Next comes a tract kept free of buildings. No Man's Land, Crake used to call it. No trees here: they'd mowed down anything you could hide behind, divided the territory into squares with lines of heat-and-motion sensors. The eerie chessboard effect is already gone; weeds are poking up like whiskers all over the flat surface. Snowman takes a few minutes to scan the field, but apart from a cluster of dark birds squabbling over some object on the ground, nothing's moving. Then he goes forward.

Now he's on the approach proper. Along the road is a trail of objects people must have dropped in flight, like a treasure hunt in reverse. A suitcase, a knapsack spilling out clothes and trinkets; an overnight bag, broken open, beside it a forlorn pink toothbrush. A bracelet; a woman's hair ornament in the shape of a butterfly; a notebook, its pages soaked, the handwriting illegible.

The fugitives must have had hope, to begin with. They must have thought they'd have a use for these things later. Then they'd changed their minds and let go.

RejoovenEsense
~

He's out of breath and sweating too much by the time he reaches
the RejoovenEsense Compound curtain wall, still twelve feet high
but no longer electrified, its iron spikes rusting. He goes through
the outer gate, which looks as if someone blew it apart, pausing
in its shadow to eat the chocolate energy bar and drink the rest of
his water. Then he continues on, across the moat, past the sentry
boxes where the CorpSeCorps armed guards once stood and the
glassed-in cubicles where they'd monitored the surveillance
equipment, then past the rampart watchtower with the steel door
— standing forever open, now — where he'd once have been ordered
to present his thumbprint and the iris of his eye.

Beyond is the vista he remembers so well: the residences laid
out like a garden suburb with large houses in fake Georgian and
fake Tudor and fake French provincial, the meandering streets
leading to the employees' golf course and their restaurants and
nightclubs and medical clinics and shopping malls and indoor
tennis courts, and their hospitals. To the right are the off-bounds
hot-bioform isolation facilities, bright orange, and the black
cube-shaped shatterproof-glass fortresses that were the business
end of things. In the distance is his destination — the central park,

with the top of Crake's charmed dome visible above the trees, round and white and glaring, like a bubble of ice. Looking at it, he shivers.

But no time for pointless repining. He hikes rapidly along the main street, stepping around the huddles of cloth and gnawed human carcasses. Not much left except the bones: the scavengers have done their work. At the time he walked out of here this place looked like a riot scene and stank like an abattoir, but now all is quiet and the stench is mostly gone. The pigoons have rooted up the lawns; their hoofmarks are everywhere, though luckily not too fresh.

His first object is food. It would make sense to go all the way along the road to where the malls are – more chance of a square meal there – but he's too hungry for that. Also he needs to get out of the sun, right now.

So he takes the second left, into one of the residential sections. Already the weeds are thick along the curbs. The street is circular; in the island in the middle, a clutch of shrubs, unpruned and scraggly, flares with red and purple flowers. Some exotic splice: in a few years they'll be overwhelmed. Or else they'll spread, make inroads, choke out the native plants. Who can tell which? The whole world is now one vast uncontrolled experiment – the way it always was, Crake would have said – and the doctrine of unintended consequences is in full spate.

The house he chooses is medium-sized, a Queen Anne. The front door's locked, but a diamond-paned window has been smashed: some doomed looter must have been there before him. Snowman wonders what the poor guy was looking for: food, useless money, or just a place to sleep? Whatever it was, it wouldn't have done him much good.

He drinks a few handfuls of water from a stone birdbath, ornamented with witless-looking frogs and still mostly full from yesterday's downpour, and not too muddied with bird droppings. What disease do birds carry, and is it in their shit? He'll have to chance it. After splashing his face and neck he refills his bottle. Then he studies the house for signs, for movements. He can't rid himself of the notion that someone — someone like him — is lying in wait, around some corner, behind some half-opened door.

He takes off his sunglasses, knots them into his sheet. Then he climbs in through the broken window, one leg and then the other, throwing his stick in first. Now he's in the dimness. The hair on his arms prickles: claustrophobia and bad energy are already pressing him down. The air is thick, as if panic has condensed in here and hasn't yet had time to dissipate. It smells like a thousand bad drains.

"Hello!" he calls. "Anybody home?" He can't help it: any house speaks to him of potential inhabitants. He feels like turning back; nausea simmers in his throat. But he holds a corner of his rancid sheet over his nose — at least it's his own smell — and makes his away across the mouldering broadloom, past the dim shapes of the plump reproduction furniture. There's a squeaking, a scurrying: the rats have taken over. He picks his steps with care. He knows what he looks like to rats: carrion on the hoof. They sound like real rats though, not snats. Snats don't squeak, they hiss.

Did squeak, *did* hiss, he corrects himself. They were liquidated, they're extinct, he must insist on that.

First things first. He locates the liquor cabinet in the dining room and goes through it quickly. A half-bottle of bourbon; nothing else, only a bunch of empties. No cigarettes. It must have been a non-smoking household, or else the looter before him pinched them. "Fuck you," he says to the fumed oak sideboard.

Then he tiptoes up the carpeted stairs to the second floor. Why so quietly, as if he's a real burglar? He can't help it. Surely there are people here, asleep. Surely they will hear him and wake up. But he knows that's foolish.

There's a man in the bathroom, sprawled on the earth-tone tiles, wearing — what's left of him — a pair of blue-and-maroon-striped pyjamas. Strange, thinks Snowman, how in an emergency a lot of people would head for the bathroom. Bathrooms were the closest things to sanctuaries in these houses, places where you could be alone to meditate. Also to puke, to bleed from the eyes, to shit your guts out, to grope desperately in the medicine cabinet for some pill that would save you.

It's a nice bathroom. A Jacuzzi, ceramic Mexican mermaids on the walls, their heads crowned with flowers, their blonde hair waving down, their painted nipples bright pink on breasts that are small but rounded. He wouldn't mind a shower – this place probably has a gravity-flow rainwater backup tank – but there's some form of hardened guck in the tub. He takes a bar of soap, for later, and checks the cabinet for sunblock, without success. A BlyssPluss container, half full; a bottle of aspirin, which he snags. He thinks about adding a toothbrush, but he has an aversion to sticking a dead person's toothbrush into his mouth, so he takes only the toothpaste. For a Whiter Smile, he reads. Fine with him, he needs a whiter smile, though he can't at the moment think what for.

The mirror on the front of the cabinet has been smashed: some last act of ineffectual rage, of cosmic protest – *Why this? Why me?* He can understand that, he'd have done the same. Broken something; turned his last glimpse of himself into fragments. Most of the glass is in the sink, but he's careful where he places his feet: like a horse, his life now depends on them. If he can't walk, he's rat food.

He continues along the hall. The lady of the house is in the bedroom, tucked under the king-sized pink and gold duvet, one arm and shoulder blade outside the covers, bones and tendons in a leopard-skin-print nightie. Her face is turned away from him, which is just as well, but her hair is intact, all of a piece, as if it's a wig: dark roots, frosted wisps, a sort of pixie look. On the right woman that could be attractive.

At one time in his life he used to go through other people's bureau drawers given half the chance, but in this room he doesn't want to. Anyway it would be the same sort of thing. Underwear, sex aids, costume jewellery, mixed in with pencil stubs, spare change, and safety pins, and a diary if he got lucky. When he was still in high school he'd liked reading girls' diaries, with their capital letters and multiple exclamation marks and extreme phrasing — *love love love, hate hate hate* — and their coloured underlining, like the crank letters he used to get, later, at work. He'd wait till the girl was in the shower, do a lightning-swift rummage. Of course it was his own name he'd be searching for, though he hadn't always liked what he'd found.

Once he'd read, *Jimmy you nosy brat I know your reading this, I* hate *it just because I fucked you doesn't mean I like you so* STAY OUT!!! Two red lines under *hate*, three under *stay out*. Her name had been Brenda. Cute, a gum-chewer, sat in front of him in Life Skills class. She'd had a solar-battery robodog on her dresser that barked, fetched a plastic bone, and lifted its leg to pee yellow water. It's always struck him how the toughest and most bitchy girls had the schmaltziest, squishiest doodads in their bedrooms.

The vanity table holds the standard collection of firming creams, hormone treatments, ampoules and injections, cosmetics, colognes. In the half-light that comes through the slatted blinds these things gleam darkly, like a still life muted with varnish. He sprays himself with the stuff in one of the bottles, a musky scent he hopes might cut the other smells in here. Crack Cocaine, its label says in raised gold lettering. He thinks briefly about drinking it, but remembers he has the bourbon.

Then he bends down to take stock of himself in the oval mirror. He can't resist the mirrors in the places he breaks into, he sneaks a peek at himself every chance he has. Increasingly it's a shock. A stranger stares back at him, bleary-eyed, hollow-cheeked, pocked with bug-bite scabs. He looks twenty years older than he is. He winks, grins at himself, sticks out his tongue: the effect is truly sinister. Behind him in the glass the husk of the woman in the bed seems almost like a real woman; as if at any moment she might turn towards him, open her arms, whisper to him to come and get her. Her and her pixie hair.

Oryx had a wig like that. She liked to dress up, change her appearance, pretend to be different women. She'd strut around the room, do a little strip, wiggle and pose. She said men liked variety.

"Who told you that?" Jimmy asked her.

"Oh, someone." Then she laughed. That was right before he scooped her up and her wig fell off . . . *Jimmee!* But he can't afford to think about Oryx right now.

He finds himself standing in the middle of the room, hands dangling, mouth open. "I have been unintelligent," he says out loud.

Next door there's a child's room, with a computer in gay red plastic, a shelf of teddy bears, a wallpaper frieze of giraffes, and a stash of CDs containing – judging from the pictures on them – some extremely violent computer games. But there's no child, no child's body. Maybe it died and was cremated in those first few days when cremations were still taking place; or maybe it was frightened when its parents keeled over and began gurgling blood, and it ran away somewhere else. Maybe it was one of the cloth and bone bundles he passed on the streets outside. Some of them were quite small.

He locates the linen closet in the hall and exchanges his filthy sheet for a fresh one, this time not plain but patterned with scrolls and flowers. That will make an impression among the Craker kids. "Look," they'll say. "Snowman is growing leaves!" They wouldn't put it past him. There's a whole stack of clean sheets in the closet, neatly folded, but he takes only the one. He doesn't want to weight himself down with stuff he doesn't really need. If he has to he can always come back for more.

He hears his mother's voice telling him to put the discarded sheet into the laundry hamper – old neurological pathways die hard – but he drops it onto the floor instead and goes back downstairs, into the kitchen. He hopes he'll find some canned food there, soy stew or beans and fake wieners, anything with protein in it – even some vegetables would be nice, ersatz or not, he'll take anything – but whoever smashed the window also cleaned out the cupboard. There's a handful of dry cereal in a plastic snap-top container, so he eats that; it's unadulterated junk-gene cardboard and he has to chew it a lot and drink some water to get it down. He finds three packets of cashew nuts, snac-pacs from the bullet train, and gobbles one of them immediately; it isn't too stale. There's also a tin of SoyOBoy sardines. Otherwise there's only a half-empty bottle of ketchup, dark brown and fermenting.

He knows better than to open the refrigerator. Some of the smell in the kitchen is coming from there.

In one of the drawers under the counter there's a flashlight that works. He takes that, and a couple of candle ends, and some matches. He finds a plastic garbage bag, right where it should be, and puts everything into it, including the sardines and the other two packs of cashews, and the bourbon and the soap and aspirin. There are some knives, not very sharp; he chooses two, and a small cooking pot. That will come in handy if he can find something to cook.

Down the hallway, tucked in between the kitchen and the utility room, there's a small home office. A desk with a dead computer, a fax, a printer; also a container with plastic pens, a shelf with reference books – a dictionary, a thesaurus, a Bartlett's, the *Norton Anthology of Modern Poetry*. The striped-pyjamas guy upstairs must have been a word person, then: a RejoovenEsense speechwriter, an ideological plumber, a spin doctor, a hairsplitter for hire. Poor bugger, thinks Snowman.

Beside a vase of withered flowers and a framed father-and-son snapshot – the child was a boy then, seven or eight – there's a telephone scratch pad. Scrawled across the top page are the words GET LAWN MOWED. Then, in smaller, fainter letters, *Call clinic* . . . The ballpoint pen is still on the paper, as if dropped from a slackening hand: it must have come suddenly, right then, the sickness and the realization of it both. Snowman can picture the guy figuring it out as he looked down at his own moving hand. He must have been an early case, or he wouldn't still have been worrying about his lawn.

The back of his neck prickles again. Why does he have the feeling that it's his own house he's broken into? His own house from twenty-five years ago, himself the missing child.

Twister

~

Snowman makes his way through the curtained demi-light of the living room to the front of the house, plotting his future course. He'll have to try for a house richer in canned goods, or even a mall. He could camp out there overnight, up on one of the top shelving racks; that way he could take his time, bag only the best. Who knows? There may still be some chocolate bars. Then, when he knows he's covered the nutrition angle, he can head for the bubble-dome, pilfer the arsenal. Once he's got a functional spraygun in his hands again he'll feel a lot safer.

He throws his stick out through the broken window, then climbs out himself, taking care not to rip his new flowered sheet or cut himself or tear his plastic bag on the jagged glass. Directly across from him on the overgrown lawn, cutting off access to the street, there's a quintuplet of pigoons, rooting around in a small heap of trash he hopes is only clothing. A boar, two sows, two young. When they hear him they stop feeding and lift their heads: they see him, all right. He raises his stick, shakes it at them. Usually they bolt if he does that – pigoons have long memories, and sticks look like electroprods – but this time they stand their ground. They're sniffing in his direction, as if puzzled;

maybe they smell the perfume he sprayed on himself. The stuff could have analogue mammalian sex pheromones in it, which would be just his luck. Trampled to death by lustful pigoons. What a moronic finish.

What can he do if they charge? Only one option: scramble back through the window. Does he have time for that? Despite the stubby legs carrying their enormous bulk, the damn things can run very fast. The kitchen knives are in his garbage bag; in any case they're too short and flimsy to do much damage to a full-sized pigoon. It would be like trying to stick a paring knife into a truck tire.

The boar lowers its head, hunching its massive neck and shoulders and swaying uneasily back and forth, making up its mind. But the others have already begun moving away, so the boar thinks better of it and follows them, marking its contempt and defiance by dropping a pile of dung as it goes. Snowman stands still until they're all out of sight, then proceeds with caution, looking frequently behind him. There are too many pigoon tracks around here. Those beasts are clever enough to fake a retreat, then lurk around the next corner. They'd bowl him over, trample him, then rip him open, munch up the organs first. He knows their tastes. A brainy and omnivorous animal, the pigoon. Some of them may even have human neocortex tissue growing in their crafty, wicked heads.

Yes: there they are, up ahead. They're coming out from behind a bush, all five of them; no, all seven. They're staring in his direction. It would be a mistake to turn his back, or to run. He raises the stick, and walks sideways, back in the direction from which he's come. If necessary he can take refuge inside the checkpoint gatehouse and stay there till they go away. Then he'll have to find a roundabout route to the bubble-dome, keeping to the side streets, where evasion is possible.

But in the time it takes him to cover the distance, slip-stepping as if in some grotesque dance with the pigoons still staring, dark clouds have come boiling up from the south, blotting out the sun. This isn't the usual afternoon storm: it's too early, and the sky has an ominous greenish-yellow tinge. It's a twister, a big one. The pigoons have vanished now, gone to seek shelter.

He stands outside the checkpoint cubicle watching the storm roll forward. It's a grand spectacle. He once saw an amateur documentary-maker with a camcorder sucked right up into one of those. He wonders how Crake's Children are getting along, back at the shore. Too bad for Crake if the living results of all his theories are whirled away into the sky or swept out to sea on a big wave. But that won't happen: in case of high seas, the break-waters formed by fallen rubble will protect them. As for the twister, they've weathered one of those before. They'll retreat into the central cavern in the jumble of concrete blocks they call their thunder home and wait it out.

The advance winds hit, stirring up debris on the open field. Lightning zips between the clouds. He can see the thin dark cone, zigzagging downwards; then darkness descends. Luckily the checkpoint is built into the security building beside it, and those things are like bunkers, thick and solid. He ducks inside as the first rain strikes.

There's a shrieking of wind, a crashing of thunder, a vibrating sound as everything still nailed down hums like a gear in a giant engine. A large object hits the outer wall. He moves inward, through one doorway and then another, scrabbling in his garbage bag for the flashlight. He's got it out and is fumbling with it when there's another gigantic crash, and the overhead lights blink on. Some previously fried solar circuit must have been refried.

He almost wishes the lights hadn't gone on: there's a couple of biosuits off in the corner, with whatever's left inside them in a bad state of repair. Filing cabinets pulled open, paper scattered everywhere. Looks as if the guards were overwhelmed. Maybe they were trying to stop people from getting out through the gates; there was an attempt to enforce a quarantine, as he recalls. But the antisocial elements, which would have included just about everyone by then, must have broken in and trashed the secret files. How optimistic of them to have believed that any of the paperwork and storage disks might still have been of use to anyone.

He forces himself to go over to the suits; he prods them with his stick, turns them over. Not as bad as he thought, not too smelly, only a few beetles; anything soft is mostly gone. But he can't find any weapons. The antisocials must have made off with those, as he would have done. As he did do.

He leaves the inmost room, goes back to the receptionist's area, the part with the counter and the desk. All at once he's very tired. He sits down in the ergonomic chair. It's been a long time since he sat in a chair, and it feels strange. He decides to set out his matches and candle ends, in case the lights go out again; while he's at it he has a drink of birdbath water and the second package of cashews. From outside comes the howling of the wind, an unearthly noise like a huge animal unchained and raging. Gusts are coming in, past the doors he's closed, stirring up the dust; everything rattles. His hands are shaking. This is getting to him, more than he's allowed himself to admit.

What if there are rats in here? There must be rats. What if it starts to flood? They'll run up his legs! He pulls his legs up onto the chair, folds them over one of the ergonomic arms, tucks the floral sheet around them. No hope of hearing any telltale squeaking, the racket of the storm is too loud.

A great man must rise to meet the challenges in his life, says a voice. Who is it this time? A motivational lecturer from RejoovTV, some fatuous drone in a suit. A gabbler for hire. *This is surely the lesson taught to us by history. The higher the hurdle the greater the jump. Having to face a crisis causes you to grow as a person.*

"I haven't grown as a person, you cretin," Snowman shouts. "Look at me! I've shrunk! My brain is the size of a grape!"

But he doesn't know which it is, bigger or smaller, because there's nobody to measure himself by. He's lost in the fog. No benchmarks.

The lights go out. Now he's alone in the dark.

"So what?" he tells himself. "You were alone in the light. No big difference." But there is.

He's ready though. He gets a grip. He stands the flashlight on end, strikes a match in its feeble beam, manages to light a candle. It wavers in the drafty air but it burns, casting a small glowing circle of soft yellow on the desk, turning the room around him into an ancient cave, dark but protective.

He rummages in his plastic bag, finds the third pack of cashews, rips it open, eats the contents. He takes out the bottle of bourbon, thinks about it, then unscrews the top and drinks. *Gluk gluk gluk*, goes the cartoon writing in his head. *Firewater*.

Oh sweetie, a woman's voice says from the corner of the room. *You're doing really well.*

"No I'm not," he says.

A puff of air — whuff! — hits his ears, blows out the candle. He can't be bothered relighting it, because the bourbon is taking over. He'd rather stay in the dark. He can sense Oryx drifting towards him on her soft feathery wings. Any moment now she'll be with him. He sits crouched in the chair with his head down on the desk and his eyes closed, in a state of misery and peace.

10

Vulturizing

~

After four deranged years Jimmy graduated from Martha Graham with his dingy little degree in Problematics. He didn't expect to get a job right away, and in this he was not deceived. For weeks he'd parcel up his meagre credentials, send them out, then get them back too quickly, sometimes with grease spots and fingerprints from whatever sub-basement-level cog had been flipping through them while eating lunch. Then he'd replace the dirty pages and send the package out again.

He'd snared a summer job at the Martha Graham library, going through old books and earmarking them for destruction while deciding which should remain on earth in digital form, but he lost this post halfway through its term because he couldn't bear to throw anything out. After that he shacked up with his girlfriend of the moment, a conceptual artist and long-haired brunette named Amanda Payne. This name was an invention, like much about her: her real name was Barb Jones. She'd had to reinvent herself, she told Jimmy, the original Barb having been so bulldozed by her abusive, white-trash, sugar-overdosed family that she'd been nothing but a yard-sale reject, like a wind chime made of bent forks or a three-legged chair.

This had been her appeal for Jimmy, for whom "yard sale" was in itself an exotic concept: he'd wanted to mend her, do the repairs, freshen up the paint. Make her like new. "You have a good heart," she'd told him, the first time she'd let him inside her defences. Revision: overalls.

Amanda had a rundown condo in one of the Modules, shared with two other artists, both men. The three of them were all from the pleeblands, they'd gone to Martha Graham on scholarship, and they considered themselves superior to the privileged, weak-spined, degenerate offspring of the Compounds, such as Jimmy. They'd had to be tough, take it on the chin, battle their way. They claimed a clarity of vision that could only have come from being honed on the grindstone of reality. One of the men had tried suicide, which conferred on him − he implied − a special vantage. The other one had shot a lot of heroin and dealt it too, before taking up art instead, or possibly in addition. After the first few weeks, during which he'd found them charismatic, Jimmy had decided these two were bullshit technicians, in addition to which they were puffed-up snots.

The two who were not Amanda tolerated Jimmy, but just marginally. In order to ingratiate himself with them he took a turn in the kitchen now and then − all three of the artists sneered at microwaves and were into boiling their own spaghetti − but he wasn't a very good cook. He made the mistake of bringing home a ChickieNobs Bucket O'Nubbins one night − a franchise had opened around the corner, and the stuff wasn't that bad if you could forget everything you knew about the provenance − and after that the two of them who were not Amanda barely spoke to him.

That didn't stop them from speaking to each other. They had lots to say about all kinds of junk they claimed to know something about, and would drone on in an instigated way, delivering themselves of harangues and oblique sermons that were in fact − Jimmy felt − aimed at himself. According to them it had been game over once agriculture was invented, six or seven thousand years ago. After that, the human experiment was doomed, first to gigantism due to a maxed-out food supply, and then to extinction, once all the available nutrients had been hoovered up.

"You've got the answers?" said Jimmy. He'd come to enjoy needling them, because who were they to judge? The artists, who were not sensitized to irony, said that correct analysis was one thing but correct solutions were another, and the lack of the latter did not invalidate the former.

Anyway, maybe there weren't any solutions. Human society, they claimed, was a sort of monster, its main by-products being corpses and rubble. It never learned, it made the same cretinous mistakes over and over, trading short-term gain for long-term pain. It was like a giant slug eating its way relentlessly through all the other bioforms on the planet, grinding up life on earth and shitting it out the backside in the form of pieces of manufactured and soon-to-be-obsolete plastic junk.

"Like your computers?" murmured Jimmy. "The ones you do your art on?"

Soon, said the artists, ignoring him, there would be nothing left but a series of long subterranean tubes covering the surface of the planet. The air and light inside them would be artificial, the ozone and oxygen layers of Planet Earth having been totally destroyed. People would creep along through this tubing, single file, stark naked, their only view the asshole of the one before them in the line, their urine and excrement flowing down through vents in the floor, until they were randomly selected by a digitalized mechanism, at which point they would be sucked into a side tunnel, ground up, and fed to the others through a series of nipple-shaped appendages on the inside of the tube. The system would be self-sustaining and perpetual, and would serve everybody right.

"So, I guess that would do away with war," said Jimmy, "and we'd all have very thick kneecaps. But what about sex? Not so easy, packed into a tube like that." Amanda shot him a dirty look. Dirty, but complicit: you could tell the same question had occurred to her.

~   ~   ~

Amanda herself wasn't very talkative. She was an image person, not a word person, she said: she claimed to think in pictures. That was fine with Jimmy, because a bit of synesthesia never went amiss.

"So what do you see when I do this?" he'd ask her, in their earliest, most ardent days.

"Flowers," she'd say. "Two or three. Pink."

"How about this? What do you see?"

"Red flowers. Red and purple. Five or six."

"How about this? Oh baby I love you!"

"Neon!" Afterwards she would sigh, and tell him, "That was the whole bouquet."

He was susceptible to those invisible flowers of hers: they were after all a tribute to his talents. She had a very fine ass too, and the tits were real, but — and he'd noticed this early — she was a little flinty around the eyes.

Amanda was from Texas, originally; she claimed to be able to remember the place before it dried up and blew away, in which case, thought Jimmy, she was about ten years older than she made out. She'd been working for some time on a project called Vulture Sculptures. The idea was to take a truckload of large dead-animal parts to vacant fields or the parking lots of abandoned factories and arrange them in the shapes of words, wait until the vultures had descended and were tearing them apart, then photograph the whole scene from a helicopter. She'd attracted a lot of publicity at first, as well as a few sacks of hate mail and death threats from the God's Gardeners, and from isolated crazies. One of the letters was from Jimmy's old dorm roommate, Bernice, who'd cranked her rhetorical volume up considerably.

Then some wrinkly, corrupt old patron who'd made a couple of fortunes out of a string of heart-parts farms had given her a hefty grant, under the illusion that what she was doing was razor-sharp cutting-edge. This was good, said Amanda, because without that chunk of change she would have had to abandon her artwork: helicopters cost a lot of money, and then of course there was the security clearance. The Corpsmen were really anal about airspace, she said; they suspected everyone of wanting to nuke stuff from above, and you practically had to let them climb into your underpants before they'd let you fly anywhere in a hired copter, unless you were some graft-ridden prince from a Compound, that is.

The words she vulturized – her term – had to have four letters. She gave a great deal of thought to them: each letter of the alphabet had a vibe, a plus or minus charge, so the words had to be selected with care. Vulturizing brought them to life, was her concept, and then it killed them. It was a powerful process – "Like watching God thinking," she'd said on a Net Q&A. So far she'd done PAIN – a pun on her last name, as she'd pointed out in chat-room interviews – and WHOM, and then GUTS. She was having a hard time during the summer of Jimmy because she was blocked on the next word.

Finally, when Jimmy didn't think he could stand any more boiled spaghetti, and the sight of Amanda staring into space while chewing on a strand of her hair no longer brought on an attack of lust and rapture, he landed a job. It was with an outfit called AnooYoo, a minor Compound situated so close to one of the more dilapidated pleeblands that it might as well have been in it. Not too many people would work there if they'd had other choices, was what he felt on the day he went for the interview; which might have accounted for the slightly abject manner of the interviewers. He could bet they'd been rejected by a dozen or two job-hunters before him. Well, he beamed at them telepathically, I may not be what you had in mind, but at least I'm cheap.

What had impressed them, said the interviewers – there were two of them, a woman and a man – was his senior dissertation on self-help books of the twentieth century. One of their core products, they told him, was the improvement items – not books any more, of course, but the DVDs, the CD-ROMs, the Web sites, and so forth. It wasn't these instructionals as such that generated the cash surplus, they explained: it was the equipment and the alternative medicines you needed in order to get the optimum effect. Mind and body went hand in hand, and Jimmy's job would be to work on the mind end of things. In other words, the promotionals.

"What people want is perfection," said the man. "In themselves."

"But they need the steps to it to be pointed out," said the woman.

"In a simple order," said the man.

"With encouragement," said the woman. "And a positive attitude."

"They like to hear about the before and the after," said the man. "It's the art of the possible. But with no guarantees, of course."

"You showed great insight into the process," the woman said. "In your dissertation. We found it very mature."

"If you know one century, you know them all," said the man.

"But the adjectives change," said Jimmy. "Nothing's worse than last year's adjectives."

"Exactly!" said the man, as if Jimmy had just solved the riddle of the universe in one blinding flashbulb of light. He got a finger-cracking handshake from the man; from the woman he got a warm but vulnerable smile, which left him wondering whether or not she was married. The pay at AnooYoo wasn't that great, but there might be other advantages.

That evening he told Amanda Payne about his good fortune. She'd been carping about money lately – or not carping, but she'd inserted a few pointed remarks about pulling your own weight into the prolonged and intent silences that were her specialty – so he thought she'd be pleased. Things hadn't been that good in the sack lately, ever since his ChickieNobs blunder, in fact. Maybe they'd pick up now, in time for a heartfelt, plangent, and action-filled finale. Already he was rehearsing his exit lines: *I'm not what you need, you deserve better, I'll ruin your life*, and so forth. But it was best to work up to these things, so he elaborated on his new job.

"Now I'll be able to bring home the bacon," he concluded in what he hoped was a winsome but responsible tone.

Amanda wasn't impressed. "You're going to work where?" was her comment; point being, as it unfolded, that AnooYoo was a collection of cesspool denizens who existed for no other reason than to prey on the phobias and void the bank accounts of the anxious and the gullible. It seemed that Amanda, until recently, had had a friend who'd signed up for an AnooYoo five-month plan, touted as being able to cure depression, wrinkles, and insomnia all at the same time, and who'd pushed herself over the edge — actually, over the windowsill of her ten-storey-up apartment — on some kind of South American tree bark.

"I could always turn them down," said Jimmy, when this tale had been told. "I could join the ranks of the permanently unemployed. Or, hey, I could go on being a kept man, like now. Joke! Joke! Don't kill me!"

Amanda was more silent than ever for the next few days. Then she told him she'd unblocked herself artistically: the next key word for the Vulture Sculpture had come to her.

"And what's that?" said Jimmy, trying to sound interested.

She looked at him speculatively. "Love," she said.

AnooYoo

~

Jimmy moved into the junior apartment provided for him in the AnooYoo Compound: bedroom in an alcove, cramped kitchenette, reproduction 1950s furniture. As a dwelling place it was only a small step up from his dorm room at Martha Graham, but at least there was less insect life. He discovered quite soon that, corporately speaking, he was a drudge and a helot. He was to cudgel his brains and spend ten-hour days wandering the labyrinths of the thesaurus and cranking out the verbiage. Then those above would grade his offerings, hand them back for revision, hand them back again. *What we want is more . . . is less . . . that's not quite it.* But with time he improved, whatever that meant.

Cosmetic creams, workout equipment, Joltbars to build your muscle-scape into a breathtaking marvel of sculpted granite. Pills to make you fatter, thinner, hairier, balder, whiter, browner, blacker, yellower, sexier, and happier. It was his task to describe and extol, to present the vision of what − oh, so easily! − could come to be. Hope and fear, desire and revulsion, these were his stocks-in-trade, on these he rang his changes. Once in a while he'd make up a word − *tensicity, fibracionous, pheromonimal* − but he never once got caught out. His proprietors liked those kinds of words in the small print on packages because they sounded scientific and had a convincing effect.

He should have been pleased by his success with these verbal fabrications, but instead he was depressed by it. The memos that came from above telling him he'd done a good job meant nothing to him because they'd been dictated by semi-literates; all they proved was that no one at AnooYoo was capable of appreciating how clever he had been. He came to understand why serial killers sent helpful clues to the police.

His social life was – for the first time in many years – a zero: he hadn't been stranded in such a sexual desert since he was eight. Amanda Payne shimmered in the past like a lost lagoon, its crocodiles for the moment forgotten. Why had he abandoned her so casually? Because he'd been looking forward to the next in the series. But the woman interviewer from AnooYoo about whom he'd had such hopes was never seen again, and the other women he encountered, at the office or in the AnooYoo bars, were either mean-minded eye-the-target sharks or so emotionally starved even Jimmy avoided them as if they were quagmires. He was reduced to flirting with waitpersons, and even they turned a cold shoulder. They'd seen fast-talking youngsters like him before, they knew he had no status.

In the company café he was a new boy, alone once more, starting over. He took to eating SoyOBoy burgers in the Compound mall, or taking out a greasy box of ChickieNobs Nubbins to munch on while working overtime at his computer terminal. Every week there was a Compound social barbecue, a comprehensive ratfuck that all employees were expected to attend. These were dire occasions for Jimmy. He lacked the energy to work the crowd, he was fresh out of innocuous drivel; he loitered on the edges gnawing on a burned soydog and silently ripping apart everyone within eyesight. *Saggy boobs*, ran the thought balloon in his head. *Bunfaced tofubrain. Thumbsucking posterboy. Fridgewoman. Sell his granny. Wobble-bummed bovine. Bladderheaded jerk.*

He got the occasional e-mail from his father; an e-birthday card perhaps, a few days later than his real birthday, something with dancing pigoons on it, as if he were still eleven. *Happy Birthday, Jimmy, May All Your Dreams Come True.* Ramona would write him chatty, dutiful messages: no baby brother for him yet, she'd say, but they were still "working on it." He did not wish to visualize the hormone-sodden, potion-ridden, gel-slathered details of such work. If nothing "natural" happened soon, she said, they'd try "something else" from one of the agencies – Infantade, Foetility, Perfectababe, one of those. Things had changed a lot in the field since Jimmy came along! (*Came along*, as if he hadn't actually been born, but had just sort of dropped by for a visit.) She was doing her "research," because of course they wanted the best for their money.

Terrific, thought Jimmy. They'd have a few trial runs, and if the kids from those didn't measure up they'd recycle them for the parts, until at last they got something that fit all their specs – perfect in every way, not only a math whiz but beautiful as the dawn. Then they'd load this hypothetical wonderkid up with their bloated expectations until the poor tyke burst under the strain. Jimmy didn't envy him.

(He envied him.)

Ramona invited Jimmy for the holidays, but he had no wish to go, so he pleaded overwork. Which was the truth, in a way, as he'd come to see his job as a challenge: how outrageous could he get, in the realm of fatuous neologism, and still achieve praise?

After a while he was granted a promotion. Then he could buy new toys. He got himself a better DVD player, a gym suit that cleaned itself overnight due to sweat-eating bacteria, a shirt that displayed e-mail on its sleeve while giving him a little nudge every time he had a message, shoes that changed colour to match his outfits, a talking toaster. Well, it was company. *Jimmy, your toast is done.* He upgraded to a better apartment.

Now that he was climbing up the ladder he found a woman, and then another one, and another one after that. He no longer thought of these women as girlfriends: now they were lovers.

They were all married or the equivalent, looking for a chance to sneak around on their husbands or partners, to prove they were still young or else to get even. Or else they were wounded and wanted consolation. Or they simply felt ignored.

There was no reason he couldn't have several of them at once, as long as he was conscientious about his scheduling. At first he enjoyed the rushed impromptu visits, the secrecy, the sound of Velcro ripped open in haste, the slow tumbling onto the floor; though he figured out pretty soon that he was an extra for these lovers – not to be taken seriously, but instead to be treasured like some child's free gift dug out of a box of cereal, colourful and delightful but useless: the joker among the twos and threes they'd been dealt in their real lives. He was merely a pastime for them, as they were for him, though for them there was more at stake: a divorce, or a spate of non-routine violence; at the least, a dollop of verbal uproar if they got caught.

One good thing, they never told him to grow up. He suspected they kind of liked it that he hadn't.

None of them wanted to leave their husbands and settle down with him, or to run away to the pleeblands with him, not that this was very possible any more. The pleeblands were said to have become ultra-hazardous for those who didn't know their way around out there, and the CorpSeCorps security at the Compound gates was tighter than ever.

Garage

~

So this was the rest of his life. It felt like a party to which he'd been invited, but at an address he couldn't actually locate. Someone must be having fun at it, this life of his; only, right at the moment, it wasn't him.

His body had always been easy to maintain, but now he had to work at it. If he skipped the gym he'd develop flab overnight, where none was before. His energy level was sinking, and he had to watch his Joltbar intake: too many steroids could shrink your dick, and though it said on the package that this problem had been fixed due to the addition of some unpronounceable patented compound, he'd written enough package copy not to believe this. His hair was getting sparser around the temples, despite the six-week AnooYoo follicle-regrowth course he'd done. He ought to have known it was a scam – he'd put together the ads for it – but they were such good ads he'd convinced even himself. He found himself wondering what shape Crake's hairline was in.

Crake had graduated early, done post-grad work, then written his own ticket. He was at RejoovenEsense now – one of the most powerful Compounds of them all – and climbing fast. At first the two of them had continued to keep in touch by e-mail. Crake spoke vaguely of a special project he was doing, something white-hot. He'd been given carte blanche, he said; the sun shone out of his bum as far as the top brass were concerned. Jimmy should come and visit sometime and he'd show him around. What was it that Jimmy was doing, again?

Jimmy countered with a suggestion that they play chess.

Crake's next news was that Uncle Pete had died suddenly. Some virus. Whatever it was had gone through him like shit through a goose. It was like watching pink sorbet on a barbecue – instant meltdown. Sabotage was suspected, but nothing had been proved.

Were you there? asked Jimmy.

In a manner of speaking, said Crake.

Jimmy pondered this; then he asked if anyone else had caught the virus. Crake said no.

As time went by, the intervals between their messages became longer and longer, the thread connecting them stretched thinner. What did they have to say to each other? Jimmy's wordserf job was surely one that Crake would despise, though affably, and Crake's pursuits might not be something Jimmy could understand any more. He realized he was thinking of Crake as someone he used to know.

Increasingly he was restless. Even sex was no longer what it had once been, though he was still as addicted to it as ever. He felt jerked around by his own dick, as if the rest of him was merely an inconsequential knob that happened to be attached to one end of it. Maybe the thing would be happier if left to roam around on its own.

On the evenings when none of his lovers had managed to lie to their husbands or equivalents well enough to spend time with him, he might go to a movie at the mall, just to convince himself he was part of a group of other people. Or he'd watch the news: more plagues, more famines, more floods, more insect or microbe or small-mammal outbreaks, more droughts, more chickenshit boy-soldier wars in distant countries. Why was everything so much like itself?

There were the usual political assassinations out there in the pleebs, the usual strange accidents, the unexplained disappearances. Or there were sex scandals: sex scandals always got the newscasters excited. For a while it was sports coaches and little boys; then there was a wave of adolescent girls found locked in garages. These girls were said – by those who had done the locking – to be working as maids, and to have been brought from their squalid countries-of-origin for their own good. Being locked in the garage was for the protection of these girls, said the men – respectable men, accountants, lawyers, merchants dealing in patio furniture – who were dragged into court to defend themselves. Frequently their wives backed them up. These girls, said the wives, had been practically adopted, and were treated almost like one of the family. Jimmy loved those two words: *practically, almost.*

The girls themselves told other stories, not all of them credible. They'd been drugged, said some. They'd been made to perform obscene contortions in unlikely venues, such as pet shops. They'd been rowed across the Pacific Ocean on rubber rafts, they'd been smuggled in container ships, hidden in mounds of soy products. They'd been made to commit sacrilegious acts involving reptiles. On the other hand, some of these girls seemed content with their situations. The garages were nice, they said, better than what they'd had at home. The meals were regular. The work wasn't too hard. It was true they weren't paid and they couldn't go out anywhere, but there was nothing different or surprising to them about that.

One of these girls – found locked in a garage in San Francisco, at the home of a prosperous pharmacist – said she used to be in movies, but was glad she'd been sold to her Mister, who had seen her on the Net and had felt sorry for her, and had come in person to fetch her and had paid a lot of cash to rescue her, and had flown with her on a plane across the ocean, and had promised to send her to school once her English was good enough. She refused to say anything negative about the man; she appeared to be simple, truthful, and sincere. When asked why the garage was locked, she said it was so nobody bad could get in. When asked what she did in there, she said she studied English and watched TV. When asked how she felt about her captor, she said she would always be grateful to him. The prosecution failed to shake her testimony, and the guy got off scot-free, although he was ordered to send her to school immediately. She said she wanted to study child psychology.

There was a close-up of her, of her beautiful cat's face, her delicate smile. Jimmy thought he recognized her. He froze her image, then unpacked his old printout, the one from when he was fourteen – he'd kept it with him through all his moves, almost like a family photo, out of sight but never discarded, tucked in among his Martha Graham Academy transcripts. He compared the faces, but a lot of time had gone by since then. That girl, the eight-year-old in the printout, must be seventeen, eighteen, nineteen by now, and the one from the news broadcast seemed a lot younger. But the look was the same: the same blend of innocence and contempt and understanding. It made him feel light-headed, precariously balanced, as if he were standing on a cliff-edge above a rock-filled gorge, and it would be dangerous for him to look down.

Gripless

~

The CorpSeCorps had never lost sight of Jimmy. During his time at Martha Graham they'd hauled him in regularly, four times a year, for what they called *little talks*. They'd ask him the same questions they'd already asked a dozen times, just to see if they got the same answers. *I don't know* was the safest thing Jimmy could think of to say, which most of the time was accurate enough.

After a while they'd taken to showing him pictures – stills from buttonhole snoop cameras, or black-and-whites that looked as if they'd been pulled off the security videocams at pleebland bank ATMs, or news-channel footage of this or that: demonstrations, riots, executions. The game was to see if he recognized any of the faces. They'd have him wired up, so even if he pretended ignorance they'd catch the spikes of neural electricity he wouldn't be able to control. He'd kept waiting for the Happicuppa caper in Maryland to turn up, the one with his mother in it – he dreaded that – but it never showed.

He hadn't received any foreign postcards for a long time.

~ ~ ~

After he'd gone to work at AnooYoo, the Corpsmen appeared to have forgotten about him. But no, they were just paying out the rope — seeing if he, or else the other side, meaning his mother, would use his new position, his dollop of extra freedom, to try to make contact again. After a year or so, there was the familiar knocking on the door. He always knew it was them because they never used the intercom first, they must have had some kind of bypass, not to mention the door code. *Hello, Jimmy, how ya doing, we just need to ask you a few questions, see if you can help us out a little here.*

Sure, be glad to.

Attaboy.

And so it went.

In — what? — his fifth year at AnooYoo, they finally hit pay dirt. He'd been looking at their pictures for a couple of hours by then. Shots of a boondocks war in some arid mountain range across the ocean, with close-ups of dead mercenaries, male and female; a bunch of aid workers getting mauled by the starving in one of those dusty famines far away; a row of heads on poles — that was in the ex-Argentine, said the CorpSeCorps, though they didn't say whose heads they were or how they'd got onto the poles. Several women going through a supermarket checkout, all in sunglasses. A dozen bodies sprawled on the floor after a raid on a God's Gardeners safe house — that outfit was outlawed now — and one of them sure looked a lot like his old roomie, the incendiary Bernice. He said so, being a good boy, and got a pat on the back, but obviously they'd known that already because they weren't interested. He felt bad about Bernice: she'd been a nut and a nuisance, but she hadn't deserved to die like that.

A lineup of mug shots from a Sacramento prison. The driver's licence photo from a suicide car-bomber. (But if the car had blown up, how had they come by the licence?) Three pantiless waitresses from a pleebland no-touching nookie bar — they threw that in for fun, and it did cause a waver on the neural monitor, unnatural if it hadn't, and smiles and chuckles all round. A riot scene Jimmy recognized from a movie remake of

Frankenstein. They always put in a few tricks like that to keep him on his toes.

Then more mug shots. *Nope*, said Jimmy. *Nope, nope, nothing.*

Then came what looked like a routine execution. No horse-play, no prisoners breaking free, no foul language: by this Jimmy knew before he saw her that it was a woman they were erasing. Then came the figure in the loose grey prison clothing shuffling along, hair tied back, wrists handcuffed, the female guard to either side, the blindfold. Shooting by spraygun, it was going to be. No need for a firing squad, one spraygun would have done, but they kept the old custom, five in a row, so no single execu-tioner need lose sleep over whose virtual bullet had killed first.

Shooting was only for treason. Otherwise it was gas, or hanging, or the big brainfrizz.

A man's voice, words coming from outside the shot: the Corpsmen had the sound turned down because they wanted Jimmy to concentrate on the visuals, but it must have been an order because now the guards were taking off the blindfold. Pan to close-up: the woman was looking right at him, right out of the frame: a blue-eyed look, direct, defiant, patient, wounded. But no tears. Then the sound came suddenly up. *Goodbye. Remember Killer. I love you. Don't let me down.*

No question, it was his mother. Jimmy was shocked by how old she'd become: her skin was lined, her mouth withered. Was it the hard living she'd been doing on the run, or was it bad treat-ment? How long had she been in prison, in their grip? What had they been doing to her?

Wait, he wanted to yell, but that was that, pullback shot, eyes covered again, zap zap zap. Bad aim, red spurts, they almost took her head off. Long shot of her crumpling to the ground.

"Anything there, Jimmy?"

"Nope. Sorry. Nothing." How could she have foreseen he'd be looking?

They must have picked up the heartbeat, the surge of energy. After a few neutral questions – "Want a coffee? Need a leak?" – one of them said, "So, who was this killer?"

"Killer," Jimmy said. He began to laugh. "Killer was a skunk." There, he'd done it. Another betrayal. He couldn't help himself.

"Not a nice guy, eh? Some sort of biker?"

"No," said Jimmy, laughing more. "You don't get it. A skunk. A rakunk. An animal." He put his head down on his two fists, weeping with laughter. Why did she have to drag Killer into it? So he'd know it was really her, that's why. So he'd believe her. But what did she mean about letting her down?

"Sorry about that, son," said the older of the two Corpsmen. "We just had to be sure."

It didn't occur to Jimmy to ask when the execution had taken place. Afterwards, he realized it might have been years ago. What if the whole thing was a fake? It could even have been digital, at least the shots, the spurts of blood, the falling down. Maybe his mother was still alive, maybe she was even still at large. If so, what had he given away?

The next few weeks were the worst he could remember. Too many things were coming back to him, too much of what he'd lost, or – sadder – had never had in the first place. All that wasted time, and he didn't even know who'd wasted it.

He was angry most days. At first he sought out his various lovers, but he was moody with them, he failed to be entertaining, and worse, he'd lost interest in the sex. He stopped answering their e-messages – *Is anything wrong, was it something I did, how can I help* – and didn't return their calls: explaining wasn't worth it. In earlier days he would have made his mother's death into a psychodrama, harvested some sympathy, but that wasn't what he wanted now.

What did he want?

He went to the Compound singles bar; no joy there, he already knew most of those women, he didn't need their neediness. He went back to Internet porn, found it had lost its bloom: it was repetitive, mechanical, devoid of its earlier allure. He searched the Web for the HottTotts site, hoping that something familiar would help him to feel less isolated, but it was defunct.

He was drinking alone now, at night, a bad sign. He shouldn't be doing that, it only depressed him, but he had to dull the pain. The pain of what? The pain of the raw torn places, the damaged membranes where he'd whanged up against the Great Indifference of the Universe. One big shark's mouth, the universe. Row after row of razor-sharp teeth.

He knew he was faltering, trying to keep his footing. Everything in his life was temporary, ungrounded. Language itself had lost its solidity; it had become thin, contingent, slippery, a viscid film on which he was sliding around like an eyeball on a plate. An eyeball that could still see, however. That was the trouble.

He remembered himself as carefree, earlier, in his youth. Carefree, thick-skinned, skipping light-footed over the surfaces, whistling in the dark, able to get through anything. Turning a blind eye. Now he found himself wincing away. The smallest setbacks were major – a lost sock, a jammed electric toothbrush. Even the sunrise was blinding. He was being rubbed all over with sandpaper. "Get a grip," he told himself. "Get a handle on it. Put it behind you. Move forward. Make a new you."

Such positive slogans. Such bland inspirational promotions vomit. What he really wanted was revenge. But against whom, and for what? Even if he had the energy for it, even if he could focus and aim, such a thing would be less than useless.

On the worst nights he'd call up Alex the parrot, long dead by then but still walking and talking on the Net, and watch him go through his paces. Handler: *What colour is the round ball, Alex? The round* ball? Alex, head on side, thinking: *Blue.* Handler: *Good boy!* Alex: *Cork-nut, cork-nut!* Handler: *There you are!* Then Alex would be given a cob of baby corn, which wasn't what he'd asked for, he'd asked for an almond. Seeing this would bring tears to Jimmy's eyes.

Then he'd stay up too late, and once in bed he'd stare at the ceiling, telling over his lists of obsolete words for the comfort that was in them. *Dibble. Aphasia. Breast plough. Enigma. Gat.* If Alex the parrot were his, they'd be friends, they'd be brothers. He'd teach him more words. *Knell. Kern. Alack.*

But there was no longer any comfort in the words. There was nothing in them. It no longer delighted Jimmy to possess these small collections of letters that other people had forgotten about. It was like having his own baby teeth in a box.

At the edge of sleep a procession would appear behind his eyes, moving out of the shadows to the left, crossing his field of vision. Young slender girls with small hands, ribbons in their hair, bearing garlands of many-coloured flowers. The field would be green, but it wasn't a pastoral scene: these were girls in danger, in need of rescue. There was something – a threatening presence – behind the trees.

Or perhaps the danger was in him. Perhaps he was the danger, a fanged animal gazing out from the shadowy cave of the space inside his own skull.

Or it might be the girls themselves that were dangerous. There was always that possibility. They could be a bait, a trap. He knew they were much older than they appeared to be, and much more powerful as well. Unlike himself they had a ruthless wisdom.

The girls were calm, they were grave and ceremonious. They'd look at him, they'd look into him, they would recognize and accept him, accept his darknesses. Then they would smile.

Oh honey, I know you. I see you. I know what you want.

Pigoons
~

Jimmy's in the kitchen of the house they lived in when he was five, sitting at the table. It's lunchtime. In front of him on a plate is a round of bread — a flat peanut butter head with a gleaming jelly smile, raisins for teeth. This thing fills him with dread. Any minute now his mother will come into the room. But no, she won't: her chair is empty. She must have made his lunch and left it for him. But where has she gone, where is she?

There's a scraping sound; it's coming from the wall. There's someone on the other side, digging a hole through, breaking in. He looks at that part of the wall, below the clock with the different birds marking the hours. *Hoot hoot hoot*, says the robin. He'd done that, he'd altered the clock — the owl says *caw caw*, the crow says *cheerup, cheerup*. But that clock wasn't there when he was five, they'd got it later. Something's wrong, the time's wrong, he can't tell what it is, he's paralyzed with fright. The plaster begins to crumble, and he wakes up.

He hates these dreams. The present's bad enough without the past getting mixed into it. *Live in the moment.* He'd put that on a giveaway calendar once, some fraudulent sex-enhancement product for women. Why chain your body to the clock, you can break the shackles of time, and so on and so forth. The picture was of a woman with wings, taking flight from a pile of dirty old wrinkled cloth, or possibly skin.

So here it is then, the moment, this one, the one he's supposed to be living in. His head's on a hard surface, his body's crammed into a chair, he's one big spasm. He stretches, yelps with pain.

It takes him a minute to place himself. Oh yes – the tornado, the gatehouse. All is quiet, no puffs of wind, no howling. Is it the same afternoon, or the night, or the next morning? There's light in the room, daylight; it's coming in through the window over the counter, the bulletproof window with the intercom, where once upon a time, long long ago, you'd had to state your business. The slot for your micro-coded documents, the twenty-four-hour video-cam, the talking smiley-faced box that would put you through the Q&A – the whole mechanism is literally shot to hell. Grenades, possibly. There's a lot of fallen rubble.

The scraping continues: there's something in the corner of the room. He can't make it out at first: it looks like a skull. Then he sees it's a land crab, a rounded white-yellow shell as big as a shrunken head, with one giant pincer. It's enlarging a hole in the rubble. "What the shit are you doing in here?" he asks it. "You're supposed to be outside, ruining the gardens." He throws the empty bourbon bottle at it, misses; the bottle shatters. That was a stupid thing to do, now there's broken glass. The land crab whips around to face him, big pincer up, then backs into its half-dug hole, where it sits watching him. It must have come in here to escape the twister, just as he did, and now it can't find its way out.

He unwinds himself from the chair, looking first for snakes and rats and any other thing he might not wish to step on. Then he drops the candle end and the matches into his plastic bag and walks carefully over to the doorway leading into the front reception area. He pulls the door shut behind him: he doesn't want any crab attacks from the back.

At the outer doorway he pauses to reconnoitre. No animals about, apart from a trio of crows perched on the rampart. They exchange a few caws, of which he is probably the subject. The sky is the pearly grey-pink of early morning, hardly a cloud in it. The landscape has been rearranged since yesterday: more pieces of detached metal sheeting than before, more uprooted trees. Leaves and torn fronds litter the muddy ground.

If he sets out now he'll have a good chance of making it to the central mall before mid-morning. Although his stomach is growling, he'll have to wait till he gets there to have breakfast. He wishes he had some cashews left, but there's only the SoyOBoy sardines, which he's saving as a last resort.

The air is cool and fresh, the scent of crushed leaves luxurious after the dank, decaying smell of the gatehouse. He inhales with pleasure, then sets off in the direction of the mall. Three blocks along he stops: seven pigoons have materialized from nowhere. They're staring at him, ears forward. Are they the same as yesterday's? As he watches, they begin to amble in his direction.

They have something in mind, all right. He turns, heads back towards the gatehouse, quickens his pace. They're far enough away so he can run if he has to. He looks over his shoulder: they're trotting now. He speeds up, breaks into a jog. Then he spots another group through the gateway up ahead, eight or nine of them, coming towards him across No Man's Land. They're almost at the main gate, cutting him off in that direction. It's as if they've had it planned, between the two groups; as if they've known for some time that he was in the gatehouse and have been waiting for him to come out, far enough out so they can surround him.

He reaches the gatehouse, goes through the doorway, pulls the door shut. It doesn't latch. The electronic lock is nonfunctional, of course.

"Of course!" he shouts. They'll be able to lever it open, pry with their trotters or snouts. They were always escape artists, the pigoons: if they'd had fingers they'd have ruled the world. He runs through the next doorway into the reception area, slams the door behind him. That lock's kaput as well, oh naturally. He shoves the desk he's just slept on up against the door, looks out through the bulletproof window: here they come. They've nosed the door open, they're in the first room now, twenty or thirty of them, boars and sows but the boars foremost, crowding in, grunting eagerly, snuffling at his footprints. Now one of them spots him through the window. More grunting: now they're all looking up at him. What they see is his head, attached to what they know is a delicious meat pie just waiting to be opened up. The two biggest ones, two boars, with – yes – sharp tusks, move side by side to the door, bumping it with their shoulders. Team players, the pigoons. There's a lot of muscle out there.

If they can't push through the door they'll wait him out. They'll take it in relays, some grazing outside, others watching. They can keep it up forever, they'll starve him out. They can smell him in there, smell his flesh.

Now he remembers to check for the land crab, but it's gone. It must have backed all the way into its burrow. That's what he needs, a burrow of his own. A burrow, a shell, some pincers.

"So," he says out loud. "What next?"

Honey, you're fucked.

Radio

~

After an interval of blankness during which nothing at all occurs to him, Snowman gets up out of the chair. He can't remember having sat down in it but he must have done. His guts are cramping, he must be really scared, though he doesn't feel it; he's quite calm. The door is moving in time to the pushing and thumping from the other side; it won't be long before the pigoons break through. He takes the flashlight out of his plastic bag, turns it on, goes back to the inner room where the two guys in the biosuits are lying on the floor. He shines all around. There are three closed doors; he must have seen them last night, but last night he wasn't trying to get out.

Two of the doors don't move when he tries them; they must be locked somehow, or blocked on the other side. The third one opens easily. There, like sudden hope, is a flight of stairs. Steep stairs. Pigoons, it occurs to him, have short legs and fat stomachs. The opposite of himself.

He scrambles up the stairs so fast he trips on his flowered sheet. From behind him comes an excited grunting and squealing, and then a crash as the desk topples over.

He emerges into a bright oblong space. What is it? The watchtower. Of course. He ought to have known that. There's a watchtower on either side of the main gate, and other towers all the way around the rampart wall. Inside the towers are the searchlights, the monitor videocams, the loudspeakers, the controls for locking the gates, the tear-gas nozzles, the long-range sprayguns. Yes, here are the screens, here are the controls: find the target, zero in on it, push the button. You never needed to see the actual results, the splatter and fizzle, not in the flesh. During the period of chaos the guards probably fired on the crowd from up here while they still could, and while there was still a crowd.

None of this high-tech stuff is working now, of course. He looks for manually operated backups — it would be fine to be able to mow down the pigoons from above — but no, there's nothing.

Beside the wall of dead screens there's a little window: from it he has a bird's-eye view of the pigoons, the group of them that's posted outside the checkpoint cubicle door. They look at ease. If they were guys, they'd be having a smoke and shooting the shit. Alert, though; on the lookout. He pulls back: he doesn't want them to see him, see that he's up here.

Not that they don't know already. They must have figured out by now that he went up the stairs. But do they also know they've got him trapped? Because there's no way out of here that he can see.

He's in no immediate danger — they can't climb the stairs or they'd have done it by now. There's time to explore and regroup. *Regroup*, what an idea. There's only one of him.

The guards must have taken catnaps up here, turn and turn about: there's a couple of standard-issue cots in a side room. Nobody in them, no bodies. Maybe the guards tried to get out of RejoovenEsense, just like everyone else. Maybe they too had hoped they could outrun contagion.

One of the beds is made, the other not. A digital voice-operated alarm clock is still flashing beside the unmade bed. "What's the time?" he asks it, but he gets no answer. He'll have to reprogram the thing, set it to his own voice.

The guys were well equipped: twin entertainment centres, with the screens, the players, the headphones attached. Clothes hanging on hooks, the standard off-duty tropicals; a used towel on the floor, ditto a sock. A dozen downloaded printouts on one of the night tables. A skinny girl wearing nothing but high-heeled sandals and standing on her head; a blonde dangling from a hook in the ceiling in some kind of black-leather multiple-fracture truss, blindfolded but with her mouth sagging open in a hit-me-again drool; a big woman with huge breast implants and wet red lipstick, bending over and sticking out her pierced tongue. Same old stuff.

The guys must have left in a hurry. Maybe it's them downstairs, the ones in the biosuits. That would make sense. Nobody seems to have come up here though, after the two of them left; or if they did, there'd been nothing they'd wanted to take.

In one of the night-table drawers there's a pack of cigarettes, only a couple gone. Snowman taps one out – damp, but right now he'd smoke pocket fluff – and looks around for a way to light it. He has matches in his garbage bag, but where is it? He must've dropped it on the stairs in his rush to get up here. He goes back to the stairwell, looks down. There's the bag all right, four stairs from the bottom. He starts cautiously downward. As he's stretching out his hand, something lunges. He jumps up out of reach, watches while the pigoon slithers back down, then launches itself again. Its eyes gleam in the half-light; he has the impression it's grinning.

They were waiting for him, using the garbage bag as bait. They must have been able to tell there was something in it he'd want, that he'd come down to get. Cunning, so cunning. His legs are shaking by the time he reaches the top level again.

Off the nap room is a small bathroom, with a real toilet in it. Just in time: fear has homogenized his bowels. He takes a dump – there's paper, a small mercy, no need for leaves – and is about to flush when he reasons that the tank at the back must be full of water, and it's water he may need. He lifts the tank top: sure enough, it's full, a mini-oasis. The water is a reddish colour but it smells okay, so he sticks his head down and drinks like a dog. After all that adrenalin, he's parched.

Now he feels better. No need to panic, no need to panic yet. In the kitchenette he finds matches and lights the cigarette. After a couple of drags he feels dizzy, but still it's wonderful.

"If you were ninety and you had the chance for one last fuck but you knew it would kill you, would you still do it?" Crake asked him once.

"You bet," said Jimmy.

"Addict," said Crake.

Snowman finds himself humming as he goes through the kitchen cupboards. Chocolate in squares, real chocolate. A jar of instant coffee, ditto coffee whitener, ditto sugar. Shrimp paste for spreading on crackers, ersatz but edible. Cheese food in a tube, ditto mayo. Noodle soup with vegetables, chicken flavour. Crackers in a plastic snap-top. A stash of Joltbars. What a bonanza.

He braces himself, then opens the refrigerator, betting on the fact that these guys wouldn't have kept too much real food in there, so the stench won't be too repulsive. Frozen meat gone bad in a melted freezer unit is the worst; he came across quite a lot of that in the early days of rummaging through the pleeblands.

There's nothing too smelly; just a shrivelled apple, an orange covered with grey fur. Two bottles of beer, unopened – real beer! The bottles are brown, with thin retro necks.

He opens a beer, downs half of it. Warm, but who cares? Then he sits down at the table and eats the shrimp paste, the crackers, the cheese food and the mayo, finishing off with a spoonful of coffee powder mixed with whitener and sugar. He saves the noodle soup and the chocolate and the Joltbars for later.

In one of the cupboards there's a windup radio. He can remember when those things started being doled out, in case of tornadoes or floods or anything else that might disrupt the electronics. His parents had one when they were still his parents; he used to play with it on the sly. It had a handle that turned to recharge the batteries, it would run for half an hour.

This one looks undamaged, so he cranks the thing up. He doesn't expect to hear anything, but expectation isn't the same as desire.

White noise, more white noise, more white noise. He tries the AM bands, then the FM. Nothing. Just that sound, like the sound of starlight scratching its way through outer space: *kkkkkkk*. Then he tries the short-wave. He moves the dial slowly and carefully. Maybe there are other countries, distant countries, where the people may have escaped – New Zealand, Madagascar, Patagonia – places like that.

They wouldn't have escaped though. Or most of them wouldn't. Once it got started, the thing was airborne. Desire and fear were universal, between them they'd been the gravediggers.

Kkkkk. Kkkkk. Kkkkk.

Oh, talk to me, he prays. Say something. Say anything.

Suddenly there's an answer. It's a voice, a human voice. Unfortunately it's speaking some language that sounds like Russian.

Snowman can't believe his ears. He's not the only one then – someone else has made it through, someone of his own species. Someone who knows how to work a short-wave transmitter. And if one, then likely others. But this one isn't much use to Snowman, he's too far away.

Dickhead! He's forgotten about the CB function. That was what they'd been told to use, in emergencies. If there's anyone close by, the CB is what they'd be doing.

He turns the dial. *Receive*, is what he'll try.

Kkkkkk.

Then, faintly, a man's voice: "Is anyone reading me? Anyone out there? Do you read me? Over."

Snowman fumbles with the buttons. How to send? He's forgotten. Where is the fucker?

"I'm here! I'm here!" he shouts.

Back to *Receive*. Nothing.

Already he's having second thoughts. Was that too hasty of him? How does he know who's at the other end? Quite possibly no one he'd care to have lunch with. Still, he feels buoyant, elated almost. There are more possibilities now.

Rampart
~

Snowman's been so entranced — by the excitement, the food, the voices on the radio — that he's forgotten about the cut on his foot. Now it's reminding him: there's a jabbing sensation, like a thorn. He sits down at the kitchen table, pulls the foot up as high as he can to examine it. Looks like there's a sliver of bourbon-bottle glass still in there. He picks and squeezes and wishes he had some tweezers, or longer fingernails. Finally he gets a grip on the tiny shard, then pulls. There's pain but not much blood.

Once he's got the glass piece out he washes the cut with a little of the beer, then hobbles into the bathroom and rummages in the medicine cabinet. Nothing of use, apart from a tube of sunblock — no good for cuts — some out-of-date antibiotic ointment, which he smears on the wound, and the dregs of a bottle of shaving lotion that smells like fake lemons. He pours that on too, because there must be alcohol in it. Maybe he should hunt for some drain cleaner or something, but he doesn't want to go too far, fry the entire foot sole. He'll just have to cross his fingers, wish for luck: an infected foot would slow him right down. He shouldn't have neglected the cut for so long, the floor downstairs must be percolating with germs.

In the evening he watches the sunset, through the narrow slit of the tower window. How glorious it must have been when all ten of the videocam screens were on and you could get the full panoramic view, turn up the colour brightness, enhance the red tones. Toke up, sit back, drift on cloud nine. As it is the screens turn their blind eyes towards him, so he has to make do with the real thing, just a slice of it, tangerine, then flamingo, then watered-down blood, then strawberry ice cream, off to the side of where the sun must be.

In the fading pink light the pigoons waiting for him down below look like miniature plastic figurines, bucolic replicas from a child's playbox. They have the rosy tint of innocence, as many things do at a distance. It's hard to imagine that they wish him ill.

Night falls. He lies down on one of the cots in the bedroom, the bed that's made. Where I'm lying now, a dead man used to sleep, he thinks. He never saw it coming. He had no clue. Unlike Jimmy, who'd had clues, who ought to have seen but didn't. If I'd killed Crake earlier, thinks Snowman, would it have made any difference?

The place is too hot and stuffy, though he's managed to pry the emergency air vents open. He can't get to sleep right away, so he lights one of the candles — it's in a tin container with a lid, survival supplies, you're supposed to be able to boil soup on those things — and smokes another cigarette. This time it doesn't make him so dizzy. Every habit he's ever had is still there in his body, lying dormant like flowers in the desert. Given the right conditions, all his old addictions would burst into full and luxuriant bloom.

He thumbs through the sex-site printouts. The women aren't his type — too bulgy, too altered, too obvious. Too much leer and mascara, too much cowlike tongue. Dismay is what he feels, not lust.

Revision: dismayed lust.

"How could you," he murmurs to himself, not for the first time, as he couples in his head with a rent-a-slut decked out in a red Chinese silk halter and six-inch heels, a dragon tattooed on her bum.

Oh sweetie.

In the small hot room he dreams; again, it's his mother. No, he never dreams about his mother, only about her absence. He's in the kitchen. Whuff, goes the wind in his ear, a door closing. On a hook her dressing gown is hanging, magenta, empty, frightening.

He wakes with his heart pounding. He remembers now that after she'd left he'd put it on, that dressing gown. It still smelled of her, of the jasmine-based perfume she used to wear. He'd looked at himself in the mirror, his boy's head with its cool practised fish-eye stare topping a neck that led down into that swaddling of female-coloured fabric. How much he'd hated her at that moment. He could hardly breathe, he'd been suffocating with hatred, tears of hatred had been rolling down his cheeks. But he'd hugged his arms around himself all the same.

Her arms.

He's set the alarm on the voice-operated digital clock for an hour before dawn, guessing when that must be. "Rise and shine," the clock says in a seductive female voice. "Rise and shine. Rise and shine."

"Stop," he says, and it stops.

"Do you want music?"

"No," he says, because although he's tempted to lie in bed and interact with the woman in the clock — it would be almost like a conversation — he has to get a move on today. How long has he been away from the shore, from the Crakers? He counts on his fingers: day one, the hike to RejoovenEsense, the twister; day two, trapped by the pigoons. This must be the third day then.

Outside the window there's a mouse-grey light. He pisses into the kitchen sink, splashes water onto his face from the toilet tank. He shouldn't have drunk that stuff yesterday without boiling it. He boils up a potful now — there's still gas for the propane burner — and washes his foot, a little red around the cut but nothing to freak about, and makes himself a cup of instant coffee with lots of sugar and whitener. He chews up a Three-Fruit Joltbar, savouring the familiar taste of banana oil and sweetened varnish, and feels the energy surge.

Somewhere in all the running around yesterday he lost his water bottle, just as well considering what was in it. Bird dung, mosquito wrigglers, nematodes. He fills up an empty beer bottle with boiled water, then snaffles a standard-issue micro-fibre laundry bag from the bedroom, into which he packs the water, all the sugar he can find, and the half-dozen Joltbars. He rubs on sunblock and bags the rest of the tube, and puts on a lightweight khaki shirt. There's a pair of sunglasses too, so he discards his old single-eyed ones. He deliberates over a pair of shorts, but they're too big around the waist and wouldn't protect the backs of his legs, so he hangs on to his flowered sheet, doubling it over, knotting it like a sarong. On second thought he takes it off and packs it into the laundry bag: it might snag on something while he's in transit, he can put it back on later. He replaces his lost aspirin and candles, and throws in six small boxes of matches and a paring knife, and his authentic-replica Red Sox baseball cap. He wouldn't want to have that fall off during the great escape.

There. Not too heavy. Now to break out.

He tries smashing the kitchen window — he could lower himself down onto the Compound rampart with the bedsheet he's torn into strips and twisted — but no luck: the glass is attack-proof. The narrow window overlooking the gateway is out of the question, as even if he could get through it there'd be a sheer drop into a herd of slavering pigoons. There's a small window in the bathroom, high up, but it too is on the pigoon side.

After three hours of painstaking labour and with the aid of — initially — a kitchen stepstool, a corkscrew, and a table knife, and — ultimately — a hammer and a battery-operated screwdriver he found at the back of the utility closet, he manages to disassemble the emergency air vent and dislodge the mechanism inside it. The vent leads up like a chimney, then there's a bend to the side. He thinks he's skinny enough to fit through — semi-starvation has its advantages — though if he gets stuck he'll die an agonizing and also ludicrous death. Cooked in an air vent, very funny. He ties one end of his improvised rope to a leg of the kitchen table — happily it's bolted to the floor — and winds the rest around his waist. He attaches his bag of supplies to the end of a second rope. Holding his breath, he squeezes in, torques his body, wriggles. Lucky he's not a woman, the wide butt would foil him. No room to spare, but now his head's in the outside air, then — with a twist — his shoulders. It's an eight-foot drop to the rampart. He'll have to go head first, hope the improvised rope will hold.

A last push, a wrench as he's pulled up short, and he's dangling askew. He grabs the rope, rights himself, unties the end around his waist, lowers himself hand over hand. Then he pulls the supply bag through. Nothing to it.

Damn and shit. He's forgotten to bring the windup radio. Well, no going back.

The rampart is six feet wide, with a wall on either side. Every ten feet there's a pair of slits, not opposite each other but staggered, meant for observation but useful too for the emplacement of last-ditch weaponry. The rampart is twenty feet high, twenty-seven counting the walls. It runs all the way around the Compound, punctuated at intervals by a watchtower like the one he's just left.

The Compound is shaped like an oblong, and there are five other gates. He knows the plan, having studied it thoroughly during his days at Paradice, which is where he's going now. He can see the dome, rising up through the trees, shining like half a moon. His plan is to get what he needs out of there, then circle around via the rampart – or, if conditions are right, he can cut across the Compound space on level ground – and make his way out by a side gate.

The sun is well up. He'd better hurry, or he'll fry. He'd like to show himself to the pigoons, jeer at them, but he resists this impulse: they'd follow along beside the rampart, keep him from descending. So every time he reaches an observation slit he crouches, holding himself below the sightline.

At the third watchtower along he pauses. Over the top of the rampart wall he can see something white – greyish white and cloudlike – but it's too low down to be a cloud. Also it's the wrong shape. It's thin, like a wavering pillar. It must be near the seashore, a few miles north of the Craker encampment. At first he thinks it's mist, but mist doesn't rise in an isolated stem like that, it doesn't puff. No question now, it's smoke.

The Crakers often have a fire going, but it's never a large one, it wouldn't make smoke like this. It could be a result of yesterday's storm, a lightning-strike fire that was dampened by the rain and has begun smouldering again. Or it might be that the Crakers have disobeyed orders and have come looking for him, and have built a signal fire to guide him home. That's unlikely – it isn't how they think – but if so, they're way off course.

He eats half a Joltbar, downs some water, continues along the rampart. He's limping a little now, conscious of his foot, but he can't stop and tend to it, he has to go as fast as he can. He needs that spraygun, and not just because of the wolvogs and the pigoons. From time to time he looks over his shoulder. The smoke is still there, just the one column of it. It hasn't spread. It keeps on rising.

12

Pleebcrawl
~

Snowman limps along the rampart, towards the glassy white swell of the bubble-dome, which is receding from him like a mirage. Because of his foot he's making poor time, and around eleven o'clock the concrete gets too hot for him to walk on. He's got the sheet over his head, draped himself as much as possible, over his baseball cap and over the tropical shirt, but he could still burn, despite the sunblock and the two layers of cloth. He's grateful for his new two-eyed sunglasses.

He hunches down in the shade of the next watchtower to wait out the noon, sucks water from a bottle. After the worst of the glare and heat is past, after the daily thunderstorm has come and gone, he'll have maybe three hours to go. All things being equal, he can get there before nightfall.

Heat pours down, bounces up off the concrete. He relaxes into it, breathes it in, feels the sweat trickling down, like millipedes walking on him. His eyes waver shut, the old films whir and crackle through his head. "What the fuck did he need me for?" he says. "Why didn't he leave me alone?"

No point thinking about it, not in this heat, with his brain turning to melted cheese. Not melted cheese: better to avoid food images. To putty, to glue, to hair product, in creme form, in a tube. He once used that. He can picture its exact position on the shelf, lined up next to his razor: he'd liked neatness, in a shelf. He has a sudden clear image of himself, freshly showered, running the creme hair product through his damp hair with his hands. In Paradice, waiting for Oryx.

He'd meant well, or at least he hadn't meant ill. He'd never wanted to hurt anyone, not seriously, not in real space-time. Fantasies didn't count.

It was a Saturday. Jimmy was lying in bed. He was finding it hard to get up these days; he'd been late for work a couple of times in the past week, and added to the times before that and the times before that, it was going to be trouble for him soon. Not that he'd been out carousing: the reverse. He'd been avoiding human contact. The AnooYoo higher-ups hadn't chewed him out yet; probably they knew about his mother and her traitor's death. Well, of course they did, though it was the kind of deep dark open secret that was never mentioned in the Compounds – bad luck, evil eye, might be catching, best to act dumb and so forth. Probably they were cutting him some slack.

There was one good thing anyway: maybe now that they'd finally scratched his mother off their list, the Corpsmen would leave him alone.

"Get it up, get it up, get it up," said his voice clock. It was pink, phallus-shaped: a Cock Clock, given to him as a joke by one of his lovers. He'd thought it was funny at the time, but this morning he found it insulting. That's all he was to her, to all of them: a mechanical joke. Nobody wanted to be sexless, but nobody wanted to be nothing but sex, Crake said once. Oh yes siree, thought Jimmy. Another human conundrum.

"What's the time?" he said to the clock. It dipped its head, sproinged upright again.

"It's noon. It's noon, it's noon, it's . . ."

"Shut up," said Jimmy. The clock wilted. It was programmed to respond to harsh tones.

Jimmy considered getting out of bed, going to the kitchenette, opening a beer. That was quite a good idea. He'd had a late night. One of his lovers, the woman who'd given him the clock in fact, had made her way through his wall of silence. She'd turned up around ten with some takeout – Nubbins and fries, she knew what he liked – and a bottle of Scotch.

"I've been concerned about you," she'd said. What she'd really wanted was a quick furtive jab, so he'd done his best and she'd had a fine time, but his heart wasn't in it and that must have been obvious. Then they'd had to go through *What's the matter, Are you bored with me, I really care about you*, and so forth and blah blah.

"Leave your husband," Jimmy had said, to cut her short. "Let's run away to the pleeblands and live in a trailer park."

"Oh, I don't think . . . You don't mean that."

"What if I did?"

"You know I care about you. But I care about him too, and . . ."

"From the waist down."

"Pardon?" She was a genteel woman, she said *Pardon?* instead of *What?*

"I said, from the waist down. That's how you really care about me. Want me to spell it out for you?"

"I don't know what's got into you, you've been so mean lately."

"No fun at all."

"Well, actually, no."

"Then piss off."

After that they'd had a fight, and she'd cried, which strangely enough had made Jimmy feel better. After that they'd finished the Scotch. After that they'd had more sex, and this time Jimmy had enjoyed himself but his lover hadn't, because he'd been too rough and fast and had not said anything flattering to her the way he usually did. *Great ass*, and so on and so forth.

He shouldn't have been so crabby. She was a fine woman with real tits and problems of her own. He wondered whether he'd ever see her again. Most likely he would, because she'd had that *I can cure you* look in her eyes when she'd left.

After Jimmy had taken a leak and was getting the beer out of the fridge, his intercom buzzed. There she was, right on cue. Immediately he felt surly again. He went over to the speakerphone. "Go away," he said.

"It's Crake. I'm downstairs."

"I don't believe it," said Jimmy. He punched in the numbers for the videocam in the lobby: it was Crake, all right, giving him the finger and the grin.

"Let me in," said Crake, and Jimmy did, because right then Crake was about the only person he wanted to see.

Crake was much the same. He had the same dark clothing. He wasn't even balder.

"What the fuck are you doing here?" said Jimmy. After the initial surge of pleasure he felt embarrassed that he wasn't dressed yet, and that his apartment was knee-deep in dust bunnies and cigarette butts and dirty glassware and empty Nubbins containers, but Crake didn't seem to notice.

"Nice to feel I'm welcome," said Crake.

"Sorry. Things haven't been too good lately," said Jimmy.

"Yeah. I saw that. Your mother. I e-mailed, but you didn't answer."

"I haven't been picking up my e-mails," said Jimmy.

"Understandable. It was on brainfrizz: inciting to violence, membership in a banned organization, hampering the dissemination of commercial products, treasonable crimes against society. I guess that last was the demos she was in. Throwing bricks or something. Too bad, she was a nice lady."

Neither *nice* nor *lady* was applicable in Jimmy's view, but he wasn't up to debating this, not so early in the day. "Want a beer?" he said.

"No thanks," said Crake. "I just came to see you. See if you were all right."

"I'm all right," said Jimmy.

Crake looked at him. "Let's go to the pleeblands," he said. "Troll a few bars."

"This is a joke, right?" said Jimmy.

"No, really. I've got the passes. My regular one, and one for you."

By which Jimmy knew that Crake really must be somebody. He was impressed. But much more than that, he was touched that Crake would experience concern for him, would come all this way to seek him out. Even though they hadn't been in close touch lately – Jimmy's fault – Crake was still his friend.

Five hours later they were strolling through the pleeblands north of New New York. It had taken only a couple of hours to get there – bullet train to the nearest Compound, then an official Corps car with an armed driver, laid on by whoever was doing Crake's bidding. The car had taken them into the heart of what Crake called the action, and dropped them off there. They'd be shadowed though, said Crake. They'd be protected. So no harm would come to them.

Before setting out, Crake had stuck a needle in Jimmy's arm – an all-purpose, short-term vaccine he'd cooked himself. The pleeblands, he said, were a giant Petri dish: a lot of guck and contagious plasm got spread around there. If you grew up surrounded by it you were more or less immune, unless a new bioform came raging through; but if you were from the Compounds and you set foot in the pleebs, you were a feast. It was like having a big sign on your forehead that said, Eat Me.

Crake had nose cones for them too, the latest model, not just to filter microbes but also to skim out particulate. The air was worse in the pleeblands, he said. More junk blowing in the wind, fewer whirlpool purifying towers dotted around.

Jimmy had never been to the pleeblands before, he'd only looked over the wall. He was excited to finally be there, though he wasn't prepared for so many people so close to one another, walking, talking, hurrying somewhere. Spitting on the sidewalk was a feature he personally could skip. Rich pleeblanders in luxury cars, poor ones on solarbikes, hookers in fluorescent Spandex, or in short shorts, or − more athletically, showing off their firm thighs − on scooters, weaving in and out of traffic. All skin colours, all sizes. Not all prices though, said Crake: this was the low end. So Jimmy could window-shop, but he shouldn't purchase. He should save that for later.

The pleebland inhabitants didn't look like the mental deficients the Compounders were fond of depicting, or most of them didn't. After a while Jimmy began to relax, enjoy the experience. There was so much to see − so much being hawked, so much being offered. Neon slogans, billboards, ads everywhere. And there were real tramps, real beggar women, just as in old DVD musicals: Jimmy kept expecting them to kick up their battered bootsoles, break into song. Real musicians on the street corners, real bands of street urchins. Asymmetries, deformities: the faces here were a far cry from the regularity of the Compounds. There were even bad teeth. He was gawking.

"Watch your wallet," said Crake. "Not that you'll need cash."

"Why not?"

"My treat," said Crake.

"I can't let you do that."

"Your turn next time."

"Fair enough," said Jimmy.

"Here we are − this is what they call the Street of Dreams."

The shops here were mid-to-high end, the displays elaborate. Blue Genes Day? Jimmy read. Try SnipNFix! Herediseases Removed. Why Be Short? Go Goliath! Dreamkidlets. Heal Your Helix. Cribfillers Ltd. Weenie Weenie? Longfellow's the Fellow!

"So this is where our stuff turns to gold," said Crake.

"Our stuff?"

"What we're turning out at Rejoov. Us, and the other body-oriented Compounds."

"Does all of it work?" Jimmy was impressed, not so much by

the promises as by the slogans: minds like his had passed this way. His dank mood of that morning had vanished, he was feeling quite cheerful. There was so much coming at him, so much information; it took up all of his headroom.

"Quite a lot of it," said Crake. "Of course, nothing's perfect. But the competition's ferocious, especially what the Russians are doing, and the Japanese, and the Germans, of course. And the Swedes. We're holding our own though, we have a reputation for dependable product. People come here from all over the world — they shop around. Gender, sexual orientation, height, colour of skin and eyes — it's all on order, it can all be done or redone. You have no idea how much money changes hands on this one street alone."

"Let's get a drink," said Jimmy. He was thinking about his hypothetical brother, the one that wasn't born yet. Was this where his father and Ramona had gone shopping?

They had a drink, then something to eat — real oysters, said Crake, real Japanese beef, rare as diamonds. It must have cost a fortune. Then they went to a couple of other places and ended up in a bar featuring oral sex on trapezes, and Jimmy drank something orange that glowed in the dark, and then a couple more of the same. Then he was telling Crake the story of his life — no, the story of his mother's life — in one long garbled sentence, like a string of chewing gum that just kept coming out of his mouth. Then they were somewhere else, on an endless green satin bed, being worked over by two girls covered from head to toe in sequins that were glued onto their skin and shimmered like the scales of a virtual fish. Jimmy had never known a girl who could twist and twine to such advantage.

Was it there, or at one of the bars, earlier, that the subject of the job had come up? The next morning he couldn't remember. Crake had said, *Job, You, Rejoov*, and Jimmy had said, *Doing what, cleaning the toilets*, and Crake had laughed and said, *Better than that*. Jimmy couldn't remember saying yes, but he must have. He would have taken any job, no matter what it was. He wanted to move, move on. He was ready for a whole new chapter.

BlyssPluss

~

On the Monday morning after his weekend with Crake, Jimmy turned up at AnooYoo for another day of word-mongering. He felt pretty wasted, but hoped it didn't show. Though it encouraged all kinds of chemical experiments by its paying clientele, AnooYoo frowned upon anything similar amongst the hired help. It figured, Jimmy thought: in the olden days, bootleggers had seldom been drunks. Or so he'd read.

Before going to his desk he visited the Men's, checked himself in the mirror: he looked like a regurgitated pizza. Plus he was late, but for once nobody noticed. All of a sudden there was his boss, and some other functionaries so elevated that Jimmy had never seen them before. Jimmy's hand was being shaken, his back gently slapped, a glass of champagne look-alike pressed into his hand. *Oh good! Hair of the dog! Glug-glug-glug*, went Jimmy's voice balloon, but he took care to merely sip.

Then he was being told what a pleasure it had been to have him with AnooYoo, and what an asset he'd proved to be, and how many warm wishes would accompany him where he was going, and by the way, many, many congratulations! His severance package would be deposited immediately to his Corpsbank account. It would be a generous one, more generous than his length of service warranted, because, let's be frank, his friends at AnooYoo wanted Jimmy to remember them in a positive manner, in his terrific new position.

Whatever that may be, thought Jimmy, as he sat in the sealed bullet train. The train had been arranged for him, and so had the move – a team would arrive, they'd pack up everything, they were professionals, never fear. He barely had time to contact his various lovers, and when he did he discovered that each one of them had already been discreetly informed by Crake personally, who – it appeared – had long tentacles. How had he known about them? Maybe he'd been hacking into Jimmy's e-mail, easy for him. But why bother?

I'll miss you Jimmy, said an e-message from one.

Oh Jimmy, you were so funny, said another.

Were was a creep-out. It wasn't as if he'd died or anything.

Jimmy spent his first night in RejoovenEsense at the VIP guest hotel. He poured himself a drink from the mini-bar, straight Scotch, as real as it came, then spent a while looking out the picture window at the view, not that he could make out very much except lights. He could see the Paradice dome, an immense half-circle in the distance, floodlit from below, but he didn't yet know what it was. He thought it was a skating rink.

Next morning Crake took him for a preliminary tour of the RejoovenEsense Compound in his souped-up electric golf cart. It was, Jimmy had to admit, spectacular in all ways. Everything was sparkling clean, landscaped, ecologically pristine, and very expensive. The air was particulate-free, due to the many solar whirlpool purifying towers, discreetly placed and disguised as modern art. Rockulators took care of the microclimate, butter-flies as big as plates drifted among the vividly coloured shrubs. It made all the other Compounds Jimmy had ever been in, Watson-Crick included, look shabby and retro.

"What pays for all this?" he asked Crake, as they passed the state-of-the-art Luxuries Mall — marble everywhere, colonnades, cafés, ferns, takeout booths, roller-skating path, juice bars, a self-energizing gym where running on the treadmill kept the light bulbs going, Roman-look fountains with nymphs and sea-gods.

"Grief in the face of inevitable death," said Crake. "The wish to stop time. The human condition."

Which was not very informative, said Jimmy.

"You'll see," said Crake.

They had lunch at one of the five-star Rejoov restaurants, on an air-conditioned pseudobalcony overlooking the main Compound organic-botanics greenhouse. Crake had the kanga-lamb, a new Australian splice that combined the placid character and high-protein yield of the sheep with the kangaroo's resistance to disease and absence of methane-producing, ozone-destroying flatulence. Jimmy ordered the raisin-stuffed capon — real free-range capon, real sun-dried raisins, Crake assured him. Jimmy was so used to ChickieNobs by now, to their bland tofulike consistency and their inoffensive flavour, that the capon tasted quite wild.

"My unit's called Paradice," said Crake, over the soy-banana flambé. "What we're working on is immortality."

"So is everyone else," said Jimmy. "They've kind of done it in rats."

"*Kind of* is crucial," said Crake.

"What about the cryogenics guys?" said Jimmy. "Freeze your head, get your body reconstituted once they've figured out how? They're doing a brisk business, their stock's high."

"Sure, and a couple of years later they toss you out the back door and tell your relatives there was a power failure. Anyway, we're cutting out the deep-freeze."

"How do you mean?"

"With us," said Crake, "you wouldn't have to die first."

"You've really done it?"

"Not yet," said Crake. "But think of the R&D budget."

"Millions?"

"Mega-millions," said Crake.

"Can I have another drink?" said Jimmy. This was a lot to take in.

"No. I need you to listen."

"I can listen and drink too."

"Not very well."

"Try me," said Jimmy.

Within Paradice, said Crake — and they'd visit the facility after lunch — there were two major initiatives going forward. The first — the BlyssPluss Pill — was prophylactic in nature, and the logic behind it was simple: eliminate the external causes of death and you were halfway there.

"External causes?" said Jimmy.

"War, which is to say misplaced sexual energy, which we consider to be a larger factor than the economic, racial, and religious causes often cited. Contagious diseases, especially sexually transmitted ones. Overpopulation, leading — as we've seen in spades — to environmental degradation and poor nutrition."

Jimmy said it sounded like a tall order: so much had been tried in those areas, so much had failed. Crake smiled. "If at first you don't succeed, read the instructions," he said.

"Meaning?"

"The proper study of Mankind is Man."

"Meaning?"

"You've got to work with what's on the table."

The BlyssPluss Pill was designed to take a set of givens, namely the nature of human nature, and steer these givens in a more beneficial direction than the ones hitherto taken. It was based on studies of the now unfortunately extinct pygmy or bonobo chimpanzee, a close relative of *Homo sapiens sapiens*. Unlike the latter species, the bonobo had not been partially monogamous with polygamous and polyandrous tendencies. Instead it had been indiscriminately promiscuous, had not pair-bonded, and had spent most of its waking life, when it wasn't eating, engaged in copulation. Its intraspecific aggression factor had been very low.

Which had led to the concept of BlyssPluss. The aim was to produce a single pill, that, at one and the same time:

a) would protect the user against all known sexually transmitted diseases, fatal, inconvenient, or merely unsightly;

b) would provide an unlimited supply of libido and sexual prowess, coupled with a generalized sense of energy and well-being, thus reducing the frustration and blocked testosterone that led to jealousy and violence, and eliminating feelings of low self-worth;

c) would prolong youth.

These three capabilities would be the selling points, said Crake; but there would be a fourth, which would not be advertised. The BlyssPluss Pill would also act as a sure-fire one-time-does-it-all birth-control pill, for male and female alike, thus automatically lowering the population level. This effect could be made reversible, though not in individual subjects, by altering the components of the pill as needed, i.e., if the populations of any one area got too low.

"So basically you're going to sterilize people without them knowing it under the guise of giving them the ultra in orgies?"

"That's a crude way of putting it," said Crake.

Such a pill, he said, would confer large-scale benefits, not only on individual users – although it had to appeal to these or it would be a failure in the marketplace – but on society as a whole; and not only on society, but on the planet. The investors were very keen on it, it was going to be global. It was all upside. There was no downside at all. He, Crake, was very excited about it.

"I didn't know you were so altruistic," said Jimmy. Since when had Crake been a cheerleader for the human race?

"It's not altruism exactly," said Crake. "More like sink or swim. I've seen the latest confidential Corps demographic reports.

As a species we're in deep trouble, worse than anyone's saying. They're afraid to release the stats because people might just give up, but take it from me, we're running out of space-time. Demand for resources has exceeded supply for decades in marginal geo-political areas, hence the famines and droughts; but very soon, demand is going to exceed supply *for everyone*. With the BlyssPluss Pill the human race will have a better chance of swimming."

"How do you figure?" Maybe Jimmy shouldn't have had that extra drink. He was getting a bit confused.

"Fewer people, therefore more to go around."

"What if the fewer people are very greedy and wasteful?" said Jimmy. "That's not out of the question."

"They won't be," said Crake.

"You've got this thing now?" said Jimmy. He was beginning to see the possibilities. Endless high-grade sex, no consequences. Come to think of it, his own libido could use a little toning up. "Does it make your hair grow back?" He almost said *Where can I get some*, but stopped himself in time.

It was an elegant concept, said Crake, though it still needed some tweaking. They hadn't got it to work seamlessly yet, not on all fronts; it was still at the clinical trial stage. A couple of the test subjects had literally fucked themselves to death, several had assaulted old ladies and household pets, and there had been a few unfortunate cases of priapism and split dicks. Also, at first, the sexually transmitted disease protection mechanism had failed in a spectacular manner. One subject had grown a big genital wart all over her epidermis, distressing to observe, but they'd taken care of that with lasers and exfoliation, at least temporarily. In short, there had been errors, false directions taken, but they were getting very close to a solution.

Needless to say, Crake continued, the thing would become a huge money-spinner. It would be the must-have pill, in every country, in every society in the world. Of course the crank religions wouldn't like it, in view of the fact that their raison d'être was based on misery, indefinitely deferred gratification, and sexual frustration, but they wouldn't be able to hold out long. The tide of human desire, the desire for more and better, would overwhelm them. It would take control and drive events, as it had in every large change throughout history.

Jimmy said the thing sounded very interesting. Provided its shortcomings could be remedied, that is. Good name, too — BlyssPluss. A whispering, seductive sound. He liked it. He had no further wish to try it out himself, however: he had enough problems without his penis bursting.

"Where do you get the subjects?" he said. "For the clinical trials?"

Crake grinned. "From the poorer countries. Pay them a few dollars, they don't even know what they're taking. Sex clinics, of course — they're happy to help. Whorehouses. Prisons. And from the ranks of the desperate, as usual."

"Where do I fit in?"

"You'll do the ad campaign," said Crake.

MaddAddam

~

After lunch they went to Paradice.

The dome complex was at the far right side of the Rejoov Compound. It had its own park around it, a dense climate-controlling plantation of mixed tropical splices above which it rose like a blind eyeball. There was a security installation around the park, very tight, said Crake; even the Corpsmen were not allowed inside. Paradice had been his concept, and he'd made that a condition when he'd agreed to actualize it: he didn't want a lot of heavy-handed ignoramuses poking into things they couldn't understand.

Crake's pass was good for both of them, of course. They rolled in through the first gate and along the roadway through the trees. Then there was another checkpoint, with guards – Paradice uniforms, Crake explained, not Corps – that seemed to materialize from the bushes. Then more trees. Then the curved wall of the bubble-dome itself. It might look delicate, said Crake, but it was made of a new mussel-adhesive/silicon/dendrite-formation alloy, ultra-resistant. You'd have to have some very advanced tools to cut through it, as it would reconform itself after pressure and automatically repair any gashes. Moreover, it had the capacity to both filter and breathe, like an eggshell, though it required a solar-generated current to do so.

They turned the golf cart over to one of the guards and were coded through the outer door, which closed with a whuff behind them.

"Why did it make that sound?" said Jimmy nervously.

"It's an airlock," said Crake. "As in spaceships."

"What for?"

"In case this place ever has to be sealed off," said Crake. "Hostile bioforms, toxin attacks, fanatics. The usual."

By this time Jimmy was feeling a little strange. Crake hadn't really told him what went on in here, not in specific detail. "Wait and see," was all he'd said.

Once they were through the inner door they were in a familiar-enough complex. Halls, doors, staff with digital clipboards, others hunched in front of screens; it was like OrganInc Farms, it was like HelthWyzer, it was like Watson-Crick, only newer. But physical plants were just a shell, said Crake: what really counted in a research facility was the quality of the brains.

"These are top-of-the-line," he said, nodding left and right. In return there was a lot of deferential smiling, and – this wasn't faked – a lot of awe. Jimmy had never been clear about Crake's exact position, but whatever his nominal title – he'd been vague about that – he was obviously the biggest ant in the anthill.

Each of the staff had a name tag with block lettering – one or two words only. BLACK RHINO. WHITE SEDGE. IVORY-BILLED WOODPECKER. POLAR BEAR. INDIAN TIGER. LOTIS BLUE. SWIFT FOX.

"The names," he said to Crake. "You raided Extinctathon!"

"It's more than the names," said Crake. "These people *are* Extinctathon. They're all Grandmasters. What you're looking at is MaddAddam, the cream of the crop."

"You're joking! How come they're here?" said Jimmy.

"They're the splice geniuses," said Crake. "The ones that were pulling those capers, the asphalt-eating microbes, the outbreak of neon-coloured herpes simplex on the west coast, the ChickieNob wasps and so on."

"Neon herpes? I didn't hear about that," said Jimmy. Pretty funny. "How did you track them down?"

"I wasn't the only person after them. They were making themselves very unpopular in some quarters. I just got to them ahead of the Corps, that's all. Or I got to most of them, anyway."

Jimmy was going to ask *What happened to the others*, but he thought better of it.

"So you kidnapped them, or what?" That wouldn't have surprised Jimmy, brain-snatching being a customary practice; though usually the brains were snatched between countries, not within them.

"I merely persuaded them they'd be a lot happier and safer in here than out there."

"Safer? In Corps territory?"

"I got them secure papers. Most of them agreed with me, especially when I offered to destroy their so-called real identities and all records of their previous existences."

"I thought those guys were anti-Compound," said Jimmy. "The stuff MaddAddam was doing was pretty hostile, from what you showed me."

"They were anti-Compound. Still are, probably. But after the Second World War in the twentieth century, the Allies invited a lot of German rocket scientists to come and work with them, and I can't recall anyone saying no. When your main game's over, you can always move your chessboard elsewhere."

"What if they try sabotage, or . . ."

"Escape? Yeah," said Crake. "A couple were like that at the beginning. Not team players. Thought they'd take what they'd done here, cart it offshore. Go underground, or set up elsewhere."

"What did you do?"

"They fell off pleebland overpasses," said Crake.

"Is that a joke?"

"In a manner of speaking. You'll need another name," Crake said, "a MaddAddam name, so you'll fit in. I thought, since I'm Crake here, you could go back to being Thickney, the way you were when we were – how old?"

"Fourteen."

"Those were definitive times," said Crake.

Jimmy wanted to linger, but Crake was already hurrying him along. He'd have liked to talk with some of these people, hear their stories – had any of them known his mother, for instance? – but maybe he could do that later. On the other hand, maybe not: he'd been seen with Crake, the alpha wolf, the silverback gorilla, the head lion. Nobody would want to get too cozy with him. They'd see his as the jackal position.

Paradice
~

They dropped in at Crake's office, so Jimmy could get a little oriented, said Crake. It was a large space with many gizmos in it, as Jimmy would have expected. There was a painting on the wall: an eggplant on an orange plate. It was the first picture Jimmy ever remembered seeing in a place of Crake's. He thought of asking if that was Crake's girlfriend, but thought better of it.

He zeroed in on the mini-bar. "Anything in that?"

"Later," said Crake.

Crake still had a collection of fridge magnets, but they were different ones. No more science quips.

> Where God is, Man is not.
> There are two moons, the one you can see and
>   the one you can't.
> Du musz dein Leben andern.
> We understand more than we know.
> I think, therefore.
> To stay human is to break a limitation.
> Dream steals from its lair towards its prey.

"What are you really up to here?" said Jimmy.

Crake grinned. "What is *really*?"

"Bogus," said Jimmy. But he was thrown off balance.

Now, said Crake, it was time to get serious. He was going to show Jimmy the other thing they were doing – the main thing, here at Paradice. What Jimmy was about to see was . . . well, it couldn't be described. It was, quite simply, Crake's life's work.

Jimmy put on a suitably solemn face. What next? Some gruesome new food substance, no doubt. A liver tree, a sausage vine. Or some sort of zucchini that grew wool. He braced himself.

Crake led Jimmy along and around; then they were standing in front of a large picture window. No: a one-way mirror. Jimmy looked in. There was a large central space filled with trees and plants, above them a blue sky. (Not really a blue sky, only the curved ceiling of the bubble-dome, with a clever projection device that simulated dawn, sunlight, evening, night. There was a fake moon that went through its phases, he discovered later. There was fake rain.)

That was his first view of the Crakers. They were naked, but not like the Noodie News: there was no self-consciousness, none at all. At first he couldn't believe them, they were so beautiful. Black, yellow, white, brown, all available skin colours. Each individual was exquisite. "Are they robots, or what?" he said.

"You know how they've got floor models, in furniture stores?" said Crake.

"Yeah?"

"These are the floor models."

It was the result of a logical chain of progression, said Crake that evening, over drinks in the Paradice Lounge (fake palm trees, canned music, real Campari, real soda). Once the proteonome had been fully analyzed and interspecies gene and part-gene splicing were thoroughly underway, the Paradice Project or something like it had been only a matter of time. What Jimmy had seen was the next-to-end result of seven years of intensive trial-and-error research.

"At first," said Crake, "we had to alter ordinary human embryos, which we got from – never mind where we got them. But these people are *sui generis*. They're reproducing themselves, now."

"They look more than seven years old," said Jimmy.

Crake explained about the rapid-growth factors he'd incorporated. "Also," he said, "they're programmed to drop dead at age thirty – suddenly, without getting sick. No old age, none of those anxieties. They'll just keel over. Not that they know it; none of them has died yet."

"I thought you were working on immortality."

"Immortality," said Crake, "is a concept. If you take 'mortality' as being, not death, but the foreknowledge of it and the fear of it, then 'immortality' is the absence of such fear. Babies are immortal. Edit out the fear, and you'll be . . ."

"Sounds like Applied Rhetoric 101," said Jimmy.

"What?"

"Never mind. Martha Graham stuff."

"Oh. Right."

Other Compounds in other countries were following similar lines of reasoning, said Crake, they were developing their own prototypes, so the population in the bubble-dome was ultra-secret. Vow of silence, closed-circuit internal e-mailing only unless you had special permission, living quarters inside the security zone but outside the airlock. This would reduce the chances of infection in case any of the staff got sick; the Paradice models had enhanced immune-system functions, so the probability of contagious diseases spreading among them was low.

Nobody was allowed out of the complex. Or almost nobody. Crake could go out, of course. He was the liaison between Paradice and the Rejoov top brass, though he hadn't let them in yet, he was making them wait. They were a greedy bunch, nervous about their investment; they'd want to jump the gun, start marketing too soon.

Also they'd talk too much, tip off the competition. They were all boasters, those guys.

"So, now that I'm in here I can never get out?" said Jimmy. "You didn't tell me that."

"You'll be an exception," said Crake. "Nobody's going to kidnap you for what's inside your skull. You're just doing the ads, remember?" But the rest of the team, he said – the MaddAddamite contingent – was confined to base for the duration.

"The duration?"

"Until we go public," said Crake. Very soon, RejoovenEsense hoped to hit the market with the various blends on offer. They'd be able to create totally chosen babies that would incorporate any feature, physical or mental or spiritual, that the buyer might wish to select. The present methods on offer were very hit-or-miss, said Crake: certain hereditary diseases could be screened out, true, but apart from that there was a lot of spoilage, a lot of waste. The customers never knew whether they'd get exactly what they'd paid for; in addition to which, there were too many unintended consequences.

But with the Paradice method, there would be ninety-nine per cent accuracy. Whole populations could be created that would have pre-selected characteristics. Beauty, of course; that would be in high demand. And docility: several world leaders had expressed interest in that. Paradice had already developed a UV-resistant skin, a built-in insect repellant, an unprecedented ability to digest unrefined plant material. As for immunity from microbes, what had until now been done with drugs would soon be innate.

Compared to the Paradice Project, even the BlyssPluss Pill was a crude tool, although it would be a lucrative interim solution. In the long run, however, the benefits for the future human race of the two in combination would be stupendous. They were inextricably linked – the Pill and the Project. The Pill would put a stop to haphazard reproduction, the Project would replace it with a superior method. They were two stages of a single plan, you might say.

It was amazing – said Crake – what once-unimaginable things had been accomplished by the team here. What had been altered was nothing less than the ancient primate brain. Gone were its destructive features, the features responsible for the world's current illnesses. For instance, racism – or, as they referred to it in Paradice, pseudospeciation – had been eliminated in the model group, merely by switching the bonding mechanism: the Paradice people simply did not register skin colour. Hierarchy could not exist among them, because they lacked the neural complexes that would have created it. Since they were neither hunters nor agriculturalists hungry for land, there was no territoriality: the king-of-the-castle hard-wiring that had plagued humanity had, in them, been unwired. They ate nothing but leaves and grass and roots and a berry or two; thus their foods were plentiful and always available. Their sexuality was not a constant torment to them, not a cloud of turbulent hormones: they came into heat at regular intervals, as did most mammals other than man.

In fact, as there would never be anything for these people to inherit, there would be no family trees, no marriages, and no divorces. They were perfectly adjusted to their habitat, so they would never have to create houses or tools or weapons, or, for that matter, clothing. They would have no need to invent any harmful symbolisms, such as kingdoms, icons, gods, or money. Best of all, they recycled their own excrement. By means of a brilliant splice, incorporating genetic material from . . .

"Excuse me," said Jimmy. "But a lot of this stuff isn't what the average parent is looking for in a baby. Didn't you get a bit carried away?"

"I told you," said Crake patiently. "These are the floor models. They represent the art of the possible. We can list the individual features for prospective buyers, then we can customize. Not everyone will want all the bells and whistles, we know that. Though you'd be surprised how many people would like a very beautiful, smart baby that eats nothing but grass. The vegans are highly interested in that little item. We've done our market research."

Oh good, thought Jimmy. Your baby can double as a lawn mower.

"Can they speak?" he asked.

"Of course they can speak," said Crake. "When they have something they want to say."

"Do they make jokes?"

"Not as such," said Crake. "For jokes you need a certain edge, a little malice. It took a lot of trial and error and we're still testing, but I think we've managed to do away with jokes." He raised his glass, grinned at Jimmy. "Glad you're here, cork-nut," he said. "I needed somebody I could talk to."

Jimmy was given his own suite inside the Paradice dome. His belongings were there before him, each one tidied away just where it ought to be — underwear in the underwear drawer, shirts neatly stacked, electric toothbrush plugged in and recharged — except that there were more of these belongings than he remembered possessing. More shirts, more underwear, more electric toothbrushes. The air conditioning was set at the temperature he liked it, and a tasty snack (melon, prosciutto, a French brie with a label that appeared authentic) was set out on the dining-room table. The dining-room table! He'd never had a dining-room table before.

Crake in Love

~

The lightning sizzles, the thunder booms, the rain's pouring down, so heavy the air is white, white all around, a solid mist; it's like glass in motion. Snowman — goon, buffoon, poltroon — crouches on the rampart, arms over his head, pelted from above like an object of general derision. He's humanoid, he's hominid, he's an aberration, he's abominable; he'd be legendary, if there were anyone left to relate legends.

If only he had an auditor besides himself, what yarns he could spin, what whines he could whine. The lover's complaint to his mistress, or something along those lines. Lots to choose from there.

Because now he's come to the crux in his head, to the place in the tragic play where it would say: *Enter Oryx.* Fatal moment. But which fatal moment? *Enter Oryx as a young girl on a kiddie-porn site, flowers in her hair, whipped cream on her chin;* or, *Enter Oryx as a teenage news item, sprung from a pervert's garage;* or, *Enter Oryx, stark naked and pedagogical in the Crakers' inner sanctum;* or, *Enter Oryx, towel around her hair, emerging from the shower;* or, *Enter Oryx, in a pewter-grey silk pantsuit and demure half-high heels, carrying a briefcase, the image of a professional*

Compound globewise saleswoman? Which of these will it be, and how can he ever be sure there's a line connecting the first to the last? Was there only one Oryx, or was she legion?

But any would do, thinks Snowman as the rain runs down his face. They are all time present, because they are all here with me now.

Oh Jimmy, this is so positive. It makes me happy when you grasp this. Paradise is lost, but you have a Paradice within you, happier far. Then that silvery laugh, right in his ear.

Jimmy hadn't spotted Oryx right away, though he must have seen her that first afternoon when he was peering through the one-way mirror. Like the Crakers she had no clothes on, and like the Crakers she was beautiful, so from a distance she didn't stand out. She wore her long dark hair without ornament, her back was turned, she was surrounded by a group of other people; just part of the scene.

A few days later, when Crake was showing him how to work the monitor screens that picked up images from the hidden minicams among the trees, Jimmy saw her face. She turned into the camera and there it was again, that look, that stare, the stare that went right into him and saw him as he truly was. The only thing that was different about her was her eyes, which were the same luminescent green as the eyes of the Crakers.

Gazing into those eyes, Jimmy had a moment of pure bliss, pure terror, because now she was no longer a picture – no longer merely an image, residing in secrecy and darkness in the flat printout currently stashed between his mattress and the third cross-slat of his new Rejoov-suite bed. Suddenly she was real, three-dimensional. He felt he'd dreamed her. How could a person be caught that way, in an instant, by a glance, the lift of an eyebrow, the curve of an arm? But he was.

"Who's that?" he asked Crake. She was carrying a young rakunk, holding out the small animal to those around; the others were touching it gently. "She's not one of them. What's she doing in there?"

"She's their teacher," said Crake. "We needed a go-between, someone who could communicate on their level. Simple concepts, no metaphysics."

"What's she teaching?" Jimmy said this indifferently: bad plan for him to show too much interest in any woman, in the presence of Crake: oblique mockery would follow.

"Botany and zoology," said Crake with a grin. "In other words, what not to eat and what could bite. And what not to hurt," he added.

"For that she has to be naked?"

"They've never seen clothes. Clothes would only confuse them."

The lessons Oryx taught were short: one thing at a time was best, said Crake. The Paradice models weren't stupid, but they were starting more or less from scratch, so they liked repetition. Another staff member, some specialist in the field, would go over the day's item with Oryx – the leaf, insect, mammal, or reptile she was about to explain. Then she'd spray herself with a citrus-derived chemical compound to disguise her human pheromones – unless she did that there could be trouble, as the men would smell her and think it was time to mate. When she was ready, she'd slip through a reconforming doorway concealed behind dense foliage. That way she could appear and disappear in the homeland of the Crakers without raising awkward questions in their minds.

"They trust her," said Crake. "She has a great manner."

Jimmy's heart sank. Crake was in love, for the first time ever. It wasn't just the praise, rare enough. It was the tone of voice.

"Where'd you find her?" he asked.

"I've known her for a while. Ever since post-grad at Watson-Crick."

"She was studying there?" If so, thought Jimmy, what?

"Not exactly," said Crake. "I encountered her through Student Services."

"You were the student, she was the service?" said Jimmy, trying to keep it light.

"Exactly. I told them what I was looking for − you could be very specific there, take them a picture or a video stimulation, stuff like that, and they'd do their best to match you up. What I wanted was something that looked like − do you remember that Web show? . . ."

"What Web show?"

"I gave you a printout. From HottTotts − you know."

"Rings no bells," said Jimmy.

"That show we used to watch. Remember?"

"I guess," said Jimmy. "Sort of."

"I used the girl for my Extinctathon gateway. That one."

"Oh, right," said Jimmy. "Each to his own. You wanted the sex-kiddie look?"

"Not that she was underage, the one they came up with."

"Of course not."

"Then I made private arrangements. You weren't supposed to, but we all bent the rules a little."

"Rules are there to be bent," said Jimmy. He was feeling worse and worse.

"Then, when I came here to head up this place, I was able to offer her a more official position. She was delighted to accept. It was triple the pay she'd been getting, with a lot of perks; but also she said the work intrigued her. I have to say she's a devoted employee." Crake gave a smug little smile, an alpha smile, and Jimmy wanted to smash him.

"Great," he said. Knives were going through him. No sooner found than lost again. Crake was his best friend. Revision: his only friend. He wouldn't be able to lay a finger on her. How could he?

They waited for Oryx to come out of the shower room, where she was removing her protective spray, and, Crake added, her luminous-green gel contact lenses: the Crakers would have found her brown eyes off-putting. She emerged finally, her hair braided now and still damp, and was introduced, and shook Jimmy's hand with her own small hand. (I touched her, thought Jimmy like a ten-year-old. I actually touched her!)

She had clothes on now, she was wearing the standard-issue lab outfit, the jacket and trousers. On her it looked like lounge pyjamas. Clipped to the pocket was her name tag: ORYX BEISA. She'd chosen it herself from the list provided by Crake. She liked the idea of being a gentle water-conserving East African herbivore, but had been less pleased when told the animal she'd picked was extinct. Crake had needed to explain that this was the way things were done in Paradice.

The three of them had coffee in the Paradice staff cafeteria. The talk was of the Crakers – this is what Oryx called them – and of how they were doing. It was the same every day, said Oryx. They were always quietly content. They knew how to make fire now. They'd liked the rakunk. She found them very relaxing to spend time with.

"Do they ever ask where they came from?" said Jimmy. "What they're doing here?" At that moment he couldn't have cared less, but he wanted to join the conversation so he could look at Oryx without being obvious.

"You don't get it," said Crake, in his you-are-a-moron voice. "That stuff's been edited out."

"Well, actually, they did ask," said Oryx. "Today they asked who made them."

"And?"

"And I told them the truth. I said it was Crake." An admiring smile at Crake: Jimmy could have done without that. "I told them he was very clever and good."

"Did they ask who this Crake was?" said Crake. "Did they want to see him?"

"They didn't seem interested."

Night and day Jimmy was in torment. He wanted to touch Oryx, worship her, open her up like a beautifully wrapped package, even though he suspected that there was something – some harmful snake or homemade bomb or lethal powder – concealed within. Not within her, of course. Within the situation. She was off limits, he told himself, again and again.

He behaved as honourably as he could: he showed no interest in her, or he tried to show none. He took to visiting the pleeblands, paying for girls in bars. Girls with frills, with spangles, with lace, whatever was on offer. He'd shoot himself up with Crake's quicktime vaccine, and he had his own Corps bodyguard now, so it was quite safe. The first couple of times it was a thrill; then it was a distraction; then it was merely a habit. None of it was an antidote to Oryx.

He fiddled around at his job: not much of a challenge there. The BlyssPluss Pill would sell itself, it didn't need help from him. But the official launch was looming closer, so he had his staff turn out some visuals, a few catchy slogans: Throw Away Your Condoms! BlyssPluss, for the Total Body Experience! Don't Live a Little, Live a Lot! Simulations of a man and a woman, ripping off their clothes, grinning like maniacs. Then a man and a man. Then a woman and a woman, though for that one they didn't use the condom line. Then a threesome. He could churn out this crap in his sleep.

Supposing, that is, he could manage to sleep. At night he'd lie awake, berating himself, bemoaning his fate. *Berating, bemoaning*, useful words. *Doldrums. Lovelorn. Leman. Forsaken. Queynt.*

But then Oryx seduced him. What else to call it? She came to his suite on purpose, she marched right in, she had him out of his shell in two minutes flat. It made him feel about twelve. She was clearly a practised hand at this, and so casual on that first occasion it took his breath away.

"I didn't want to see you so unhappy, Jimmy," was her explanation. "Not about me."

"How could you tell I was unhappy?"

"Oh, I always know."

"What about Crake?" he said, after she'd hooked him that first time, landed him, left him gasping.

"You are Crake's friend. He wouldn't want you to be unhappy."

Jimmy wasn't so sure about that, but he said, "I don't feel easy about this."

"What are you saying, Jimmy?"

"Aren't you – isn't he . . ." What a dolt!

"Crake lives in a higher world, Jimmy," she said. "He lives in a world of ideas. He is doing important things. He has no time to play. Anyway, Crake is my boss. You are for fun."

"Yes, but . . ."

"Crake won't know."

And it seemed to be true, Crake didn't know. Maybe he was too mesmerized by her to notice anything; or maybe, thought Jimmy, love really was blind. Or blinding. And Crake loved Oryx, no doubt there; he was almost abject about it. He'd touch her in public, even. Crake had never been a toucher, he'd been physically remote, but now he liked to have a hand on Oryx: on her shoulder, her arm, her small waist, her perfect butt. *Mine, mine,* that hand was saying.

Moreover, he appeared to trust her, more perhaps than he trusted Jimmy. She was an expert businesswoman, he said. He'd given her a slice of the BlyssPluss trials: she had useful contacts in the pleeblands, through her old pals who'd worked with her at Student Services. For that reason she had to make a lot of trips, here and there around the world. Sex clinics, said Crake. Whorehouses, said Oryx: who better to do the testing?

"Just as long as you don't do any testing on yourself," said Jimmy.

"Oh no, Jimmy. Crake said not to."

"You always do what Crake tells you?"

"He is my boss."

"He tell you to do this?"

Big eyes. "Do what, Jimmy?"

"What you're doing right now."

"Oh Jimmy. You always make jokes."

The times when she was away were hard for Jimmy. He worried about her, he longed for her, he resented her for not being there. When she'd get back from one of her trips, she'd materialize in his room in the middle of the night: she managed to do that no matter what might be on Crake's agenda. First she'd brief Crake, provide him with an account of her activities and their success — how many BlyssPluss Pills, where she'd placed them, any results so far: an exact account, because he was so obsessive. Then she'd take care of what she called the personal area.

Crake's sexual needs were direct and simple, according to Oryx; not intriguing, like sex with Jimmy. Not fun, just work — although she respected Crake, she really did, because he was a brilliant genius. But if Crake wanted her to stay longer on any given night, do it again maybe, she'd make some excuse — jet lag, a headache, something plausible. Her inventions were seamless, she was the best poker-faced liar in the world, so there would be a kiss goodbye for stupid Crake, a smile, a wave, a closed door, and the next minute there she would be, with Jimmy.

How potent was that word. *With.*

He could never get used to her, she was fresh every time, she was a casketful of secrets. Any moment now she would open herself up, reveal to him the essential thing, the hidden thing at the core of life, or of her life, or of his life — the thing he was longing to know. The thing he'd always wanted. What would it be?

"What went on in that garage, anyway?" said Jimmy. He couldn't leave her alone about her earlier life, he was driven to find out. No detail was too small for him in those days, no painful splinter of her past too tiny. Perhaps he was digging for her anger, but he never found it. Either it was buried too deeply, or it wasn't there at all. But he couldn't believe that. She wasn't a masochist, she was no saint.

They were in Jimmy's bedroom, lying on the bed together with the digital TV on, hooked into his computer, some copulation Web site with an animal component, a couple of well-trained German shepherds and a double-jointed ultra-shaved albino tattooed all over with lizards. The sound was off, it was just the pictures: erotic wallpaper.

They were eating Nubbins from one of the takeout joints in the nearest mall, with the soyafries and the salad. Some of the salad leaves were spinach, from the Rejoov greenhouses: no pesticides, or none that were admitted to. The other leaves were a cabbage splice – giant cabbage trees, continuous producers, very productive. The stuff had a whiff of sewage to it, but the special dressing drowned that out.

"What garage, Jimmy?" said Oryx. She wasn't paying attention. She liked to eat with her fingers, she hated cutlery. Why put a big chunk of sharp-edged metal into your mouth? She said it made the food taste like tin.

"You know what garage," he said. "The one in San Francisco. That creep. That geek who bought you, flew you over, got his wife to say you were the maid."

"Jimmy, why do you dream up such things? I was never in a garage." She licked her fingers, tore a Nubbin into bite-sized bits, fed one of the bits to Jimmy. Then she let him lick her fingers for her. He ran his tongue around the small ovals of her nails. This was the closest she could get to him without becoming food: she was in him, or part of her was in part of him. Sex was the other way around: while that was going on, he was in her. *I'll make you mine*, lovers said in old books. They never said, *I'll make you me*.

"I know it was you," Jimmy said. "I saw the pictures."

"What pictures?"

"The so-called maid scandal. In San Francisco. Did that creepy old geezer make you have sex?"

"Oh Jimmy." A sigh. "So that is what you have in mind. I saw that, on TV. Why do you worry about a man like that? He was so old he was almost dead."

"No, but did he?"

"No one made me have sex in a garage. I told you."

"Okay, revision: no one made you, but did you have it anyway?"

"You don't understand me, Jimmy."

"But I want to."

"Do you?" A pause. "These are such good soyafries. Just imagine, Jimmy – millions of people in the world never ate fries like this! We are so lucky!"

"Tell me." It must have been her. "I won't get mad."

A sigh. "He was a kind man," said Oryx, in a storytelling voice. Sometimes he suspected her of improvising, just to humour him; sometimes he felt that her entire past – everything she'd told him – was his own invention. "He was rescuing young girls. He paid for my plane ticket, just like it said. If it wasn't for him, I wouldn't be here. You should like him!"

"Why should I like such a hypocritical sanctimonious bastard? You didn't answer my question."

"Yes, I did, Jimmy. Now leave it alone."

"How long did he keep you locked in the garage?"

"It was more like an apartment," said Oryx. "They didn't have room in their house. I wasn't the only girl they took in."

"They?"

"Him and his wife. They were trying to be helpful."

"And she hated sex, is that it? Is that why she put up with you? You were getting the old goat off her back?"

Oryx sighed. "You always think the worst of people, Jimmy. She was a very spiritual person."

"Like fuck she was."

"Don't swear, Jimmy. I want to enjoy being with you. I don't have very much time, I have to go soon, I need to do some business. Why do you care about things that happened so long ago?" She leaned over him, kissed him with her Nubbin-smeared mouth.

Unguent, unctuous, sumptuous, voluptuous, salacious, lubricious, delicious, went the inside of Jimmy's head. He sank down into the words, into the feelings.

After a while he said, "Where are you going?"

"Oh, someplace. I'll call you when I get there." She never would tell him.

Takeout

~

Now comes the part that Snowman has replayed in his head time after time. *If only* haunts him. But *if only* what? What could he have said or done differently? What change would have altered the course of events? In the big picture, nothing. In the small picture, so much.

Don't go. Stay here. At least that way they would have been together. She might even have survived — why not? In which case she'd be right here with him, right now.

I just want some takeout. I'm just going to the mall. I need some air. I need a walk.

Let me come with you. It's not safe.

Don't be silly! There's guards everywhere. They all know who I am. Who's safer than me?

I have a gut feeling.

But Jimmy'd had no gut feeling. He'd been happy that evening, happy and lazy. She'd arrived at his door an hour earlier. She'd just come from being with the Crakers, teaching them a few more leaves and grasses, so she was damp from the shower. She was wearing some sort of kimono covered with red and orange butterflies; her dark hair was braided with pink ribbon, coiled up and pinned loosely. The first thing he'd done when she'd arrived at his door, hurrying, breathless, brimming with joyous excitement or a very good imitation of it, was to unpin her hair. The braid went three times around his hand.

"Where's Crake?" he whispered. She smelled of lemons, of crushed herbs.

"Don't worry, Jimmy."

"But where?"

"He's outside Paradice, he went out. He had a meeting. He doesn't want to see me when he comes back, he said he would be thinking tonight. He never wants sex when he's thinking."

"Do you love me?"

That laugh of hers. What had it meant? *Stupid question. Why ask? You talk too much.* Or else: *What is love?* Or possibly: *In your dreams.*

Then time passed. Then she was pinning her hair up again, then slipping on her kimono, then tying it with the sash. He stood behind her, watching in the mirror. He wanted to put his arms around her, take off the covering she'd just put back on, start all over again.

"Don't go yet," he said, but it was never any use saying *don't go yet* to her. When she'd decided a thing, she was on her way. Sometimes he felt he was merely a house call on a secret itinerary of hers – that she had a whole list of others to be dealt with before the night was over. Unworthy thoughts, but not out of the question. He never knew what she was doing when she wasn't with him.

"I'm coming back right away," she said, slipping her feet into her little pink and red sandals. "I'll bring pizza. You want any extras, Jimmy?"

"Why don't we dump all this crap, go away somewhere?" he said on impulse.

"Away from here? From Paradice? Why?"

"We could be together."

"Jimmy, you're funny! We're together now!"

"We could get away from Crake," said Jimmy. "We wouldn't have to sneak around like this, we could . . ."

"But Jimmy." Wide eyes. "Crake needs us!"

"I think he knows," said Jimmy. "About us." He didn't believe this; or he believed it and not, both at the same time. Surely they'd been more and more reckless lately. How could Crake have missed it? Was it possible for a man that intelligent in so many ways to be acutely brain-damaged in others? Or did Crake have a deviousness that outdid Jimmy's own? If so, there were no signs.

Jimmy had taken to sweeping his room for bugs: the hidden mini-mikes, the micro-cams. He'd known what to look for, or so he thought. But there'd been nothing.

There were signs, Snowman thinks. There were signs and I missed them.

For instance, Crake said once, "Would you kill someone you loved to spare them pain?"

"You mean, commit euthanasia?" said Jimmy. "Like putting down your pet turtle?"

"Just tell me," said Crake.

"I don't know. What kind of love, what kind of pain?"

Crake changed the subject.

Then, one lunchtime, he said, "If anything happens to me, I'm depending on you to look after the Paradice Project. Any time I'm away from here I want you to take charge. I've made it a standing order."

"What do you mean, anything?" said Jimmy. "What could happen?"

"You know."

Jimmy thought he meant kidnapping, or being whacked by the opposition: that was a constant hazard, for the Compound brainiacs. "Sure," he said, "but one, your security's the best, and two, there's people in here much better equipped than I am. I couldn't head up a thing like this, I don't have the science."

"These people are specialists," said Crake. "They wouldn't have the empathy to deal with the Paradice models, they wouldn't be any good at it, they'd get impatient. Even I couldn't do it. I couldn't begin to get onto their wavelength. But you're more of a generalist."

"Meaning?"

"You have a great ability to sit around not doing much of anything. Just like them."

"Thanks," said Jimmy.

"No, I'm serious. I want — I'd want it to be you."

"What about Oryx?" said Jimmy. "She knows the Crakers a lot better than I do." Jimmy and Oryx said *Crakers*, but Crake never did.

"If I'm not around, Oryx won't be either," said Crake.

"She'll commit suttee? No shit! Immolate herself on your funeral pyre?"

"Something like that," said Crake, grinning. Which at the time Jimmy had taken both as a joke and also as a symptom of Crake's truly colossal ego.

"I think Crake's been snooping on us," said Jimmy that last night. As soon as it was out he saw it could be true, though maybe he was just saying it to frighten Oryx. Stampede her, perhaps; though he had no concrete plans. Suppose they ran, where would they live, how would they keep Crake from finding them, what would they use for money? Would Jimmy have to turn pimp, live off the avails? Because he certainly had no marketable skills, nothing he could use in the pleeblands, not if they went underground. As they would have to do. "I think he's jealous."

"Oh Jimmy. Why would Crake be jealous? He doesn't approve of jealousy. He thinks it's wrong."

"He's human," said Jimmy. "What he approves of is beside the point."

"Jimmy, I think it's you that's jealous." Oryx smiled, stood on tiptoe, kissed his nose. "You're a good boy. But I would never leave Crake. I believe in Crake, I believe in his" — she groped for the word — "his vision. He wants to make the world a better place. This is what he's always telling me. I think that is so fine, don't you, Jimmy?"

"I don't believe that," said Jimmy. "I know it's what he says, but I've never bought it. He never gave a piss about anything like that. His interests were strictly . . ."

"Oh, you are wrong, Jimmy. He has found the problems, I think he is right. There are too many people and that makes the people bad. I know this from my own life, Jimmy. Crake is a very smart man!"

Jimmy should have known better than to bad-mouth Crake. Crake was her hero, in a way. An important way. As he, Jimmy, was not.

"Okay. Point taken." At least he hadn't completely blown it: she wasn't angry with him. That was the main thing.

What a mushball I was, thinks Snowman. How entranced. How possessed. Not *was*, *am*.

"Jimmy, I want you to promise me something."

"Sure, what?"

"If Crake isn't here, if he goes away somewhere, and if I'm not here either, I want you to take care of the Crakers."

"Not here? Why wouldn't you be here?" Anxiety again, suspicion: were they planning to go off together, leaving him behind? Was that it? Had he only been some sort of toy-boy for Oryx, a court jester for Crake? "You're going on a honeymoon, or what?"

"Don't be silly, Jimmy. They are like children, they need someone. You have to be kind with them."

"You're looking at the wrong man," said Jimmy. "If I had to spend more than five minutes with them they'd drive me nuts."

"I know you could do it. I'm serious, Jimmy. Say you'll do it, don't let me down. Promise?" She was stroking him, running a row of kisses up his arm.

"Okay then. Cross my heart and hope to die. Happy now?" It didn't cost him anything, it was all purely theoretical.

"Yes, now I'm happy. I'll be very quick, Jimmy, then we can eat. You want anchovies?"

What did she have in mind? Snowman wonders, for the millionth time. How much did she guess?

Airlock

~

He'd waited for her, at first with impatience, then with anxiety, then panic. It shouldn't take them that long to make a couple of pizzas.

The first bulletin came in at nine forty-five. Because Crake was off-site and Jimmy was second-in-command, they sent a staff member from the video monitor room to get him.

At first Jimmy thought it was routine, another minor epidemic or splotch of bioterrorism, just another news item. The boys and girls with the HotBiosuits and the flame-throwers and the isolation tents and the crates of bleach and the lime pits would take care of it as usual. Anyway, it was in Brazil. Far enough away. But Crake's standing order was to report any outbreaks, of anything, anywhere, so Jimmy went to look.

Then the next one hit, and the next, the next, the next, rapid-fire. Taiwan, Bangkok, Saudi Arabia, Bombay, Paris, Berlin. The pleeblands west of Chicago. The maps on the monitor screens lit up, spackled with red as if someone had flicked a loaded paintbrush at them. This was more than a few isolated plague spots. This was major.

Jimmy tried phoning Crake on his cell, but he got no reply. He told the monitor crew to go to the news channels. It was a rogue hemorrhagic, said the commentators. The symptoms were high fever, bleeding from the eyes and skin, convulsions, then breakdown of the inner organs, followed by death. The time from visible onset to final moment was amazingly short. The bug appeared to be airborne, but there might be a water factor as well.

Jimmy's cellphone rang. It was Oryx. "Where are you?" he shouted. "Get back here. Have you seen . . ."

Oryx was crying. This was so unusual Jimmy was rattled by it. "Oh Jimmy," she said. "I am so sorry. I did not know."

"It's all right," he said, to soothe her. Then, "What do you mean?"

"It was in the pills. It was in those pills I was giving away, the ones I was selling. It's all the same cities, I went there. Those pills were supposed to help people! Crake said . . ."

The connection was broken. He tried dialback: *ring ring ring*. Then a click. Then nothing.

What if the thing was already inside Rejoov? What if she'd been exposed? When she turned up at the door he couldn't lock her out. He couldn't bear to do that, even if she was bleeding from every pore.

By midnight the hits were coming almost simultaneously. Dallas. Seattle. New New York. The thing didn't appear to be spreading from city to city: it was breaking out in a number of them simultaneously.

There were three staff in the room now: Rhino, Beluga, White Sedge. One was humming, one whistling; the third — White Sedge — was crying. *This is the biggie.* Two of them had already said that.

"What's our fallback?"

"What should we do?"

"Nothing," said Jimmy, trying not to panic. "We're safe enough here. We can wait it out. There's enough supplies in the storeroom." He looked around at the three nervous faces. "We have to protect the Paradice models. We don't know the incubation period, we don't know who could be a carrier. We can't let anybody in."

This reassured them a little. He went out of the monitor room, reset the codes of the inmost door, and also those on the door leading into the airlock. While he was doing this his videocell beeped. It was Crake. His face on the tiny screen looked much as usual; he appeared to be in a bar.

"Where are you?" Jimmy yelled. "Don't you know what's going on?"

"Not to worry," said Crake. "Everything's under control." He sounded drunk, a rare thing for him.

"What fucking *everything*? It's a worldwide plague! It's the Red Death! What's this about it being in the BlyssPluss Pills?"

"Who told you that?" said Crake. "A little bird?" He was drunk for sure; drunk, or on some pharmaceutical.

"Never mind. It's true, isn't it?"

"I'm in the mall, at the pizza place. I'll be there right away," said Crake. "Hold the fort."

Crake hung up. Maybe he's found Oryx, Jimmy thought. Maybe he'll get her back safely. Then he thought, You halfwit.

He went to check up on the Paradice Project. The night-sky simulation was on, the faux moon was shining, the Crakers − as far as he could tell − were peacefully asleep. "Sweet dreams," he whispered to them through the glass. "Sleep tight. You're the only ones now who can."

What happened then was a slow-motion sequence. It was porn with the sound muted, it was brainfrizz without the ads. It was melodrama so overdone that he and Crake would have laughed their heads off at it, if they'd been fourteen and watching it on DVD.

First came the waiting. He sat in a chair in his office, told himself to calm down. The old wordlists were whipping through his head: *fungible, pullulate, pistic, cerements, trull.* After a while he stood up. *Prattlement, opsimath.* He turned on his computer, went through the news sites. There was a lot of dismay out there, and not nearly enough ambulances. The keep-calm politico speeches were already underway, the stay-in-your-house megaphone vehicles were prowling the streets. Prayer had broken out. *Concatenation. Subfusc. Grutch.*

He went to the emergency storeroom, picked up a spraygun, strapped it on, put a loose tropical jacket over top. He went back to the monitor room and told the three staff that he'd talked with CorpSeCorps Security for the Compound – a lie – and they were in no immediate danger here; also a lie, he suspected. He added that he'd heard from Crake, whose orders were that they should all go back to their rooms and get some sleep, because they would need their energy in the days to come. They seemed relieved, and happy to comply.

Jimmy accompanied them to the airlock and coded them into the corridor that led to their sleeping quarters. He watched their backs as they walked in front of him; he saw them as already dead. He was sorry about that, but he couldn't take chances. They were three to his one: if they became hysterical, if they tried to break out of the complex or let their friends into it, he wouldn't be able to control them. Once they were out of sight he locked them out, and himself in. Nobody in the inner bubble now but himself and the Crakers.

He watched the news some more, drinking Scotch to fortify himself, but spacing his intake. *Windlestraw. Laryngeal. Banshee. Woad.* He was waiting for Oryx, but without hope. Something must have happened to her. Otherwise she'd be here.

Towards dawn the door monitor beeped. Someone was punching in the numbers for the airlock. It wouldn't work, of course, because Jimmy had changed the code.

The video intercom jangled. "What are you doing?" said Crake. He looked and sounded annoyed. "Open up."

"I'm following Plan B," said Jimmy. "In the event of a bio attack, don't let anybody in. Your orders. I've sealed the airlock."

"*Anybody* didn't mean me," said Crake. "Don't be a cork-nut."

"How do I know you're not a carrier?" said Jimmy.

"I'm not."

"How do I know that?"

"Let's just suppose," said Crake wearily, "that I anticipated this event and took precautions. Anyway, you're immune to this."

"Why would I be?" said Jimmy. His brain was slow on logic tonight. There was something wrong with what Crake had just said, but he couldn't pinpoint it.

"The antibody serum was in the pleeb vaccine. Remember all those times you shot up with that stuff? Every time you went to the pleebs to wallow in the mud and drown your lovesick sorrows."

"How did you know?" said Jimmy. "How did you know where I, what I wanted?" His heart was racing; he wasn't being precise.

"Don't be a moron. Let me in."

Jimmy coded open the door into the airlock. Now Crake was at the inmost door. Jimmy turned on the airlock video monitor: Crake's head floated life-sized, right in front of his eyes. He looked wrecked. There was something – blood? – on his shirt collar.

"Where were you?' said Jimmy. "Have you been in a fight?"

"You have no idea," said Crake. "Now let me in."

"Where's Oryx?"

"She's right here with me. She's had a hard time."

"What happened to her? What's going on out there? Let me talk to her!"

"She can't talk right now. I can't lift her up. I've had a few injuries. Now quit fucking the dog and let us in."

Jimmy took out his spraygun. Then he punched in the code. He stood back and to the side. All the hairs on his arms were standing up. *We understand more than we know.*

The door swung open.

Crake's beige tropicals were splattered with redbrown. In his right hand was an ordinary storeroom jackknife, the kind with the two blades and the nail file and the corkscrew and the little scissors. He had his other arm around Oryx, who seemed to be asleep; her face was against Crake's chest, her long pink-ribboned braid hung down her back.

As Jimmy watched, frozen with disbelief, Crake let Oryx fall backwards, over his left arm. He looked at Jimmy, a direct look, unsmiling.

"I'm counting on you," he said. Then he slit her throat.

Jimmy shot him.

13

Bubble

~

In the aftermath of the storm the air is cooler. Mist rises from the distant trees, the sun declines, the birds are beginning their evening racket. Three crows are flying overhead, their wings black flames, their words almost audible. *Crake! Crake!* they're saying. The crickets are saying *Oryx*. I'm hallucinating, thinks Snowman.

He progresses along the rampart, step by wrenching step. His foot feels like a gigantic boiled wiener stuffed with hot, masticated flesh, boneless and about to burst. Whatever bug is fermenting inside it is evidently resistant to the antibiotics in the watch-tower ointment. Maybe in Paradice, in the jumble of Crake's ransacked emergency storeroom — he knows how ransacked it is, he did the ransacking himself — he'll be able to find something more effective.

Crake's emergency storeroom. Crake's wonderful plan. Crake's cutting-edge ideas. Crake, King of the Crakery, because Crake is still there, still in possession, still the ruler of his own domain, however dark that bubble of light has now become. Darker than dark, and some of that darkness is Snowman's. He helped with it.

"Let's not go there," says Snowman.

Sweetie, you're already there. You've never left.

At the eighth watchtower, the one overlooking the park surrounding Paradice, he checks to see if either of the doors leading
to the upper room are unlocked — he'd prefer to descend by a
stairway, if possible — but they aren't. Cautiously he surveys the
ground below through one of the observation slits: no large or
medium-sized life forms visible down there, though there's a
scuttering in the underbrush he hopes is only a squirrel. He
unpacks his twisted sheet, ties it to a ventilation pipe — flimsy, but
the only possibility — and lowers the free end over the edge of the
rampart. It's about seven feet short, but he can stand the drop, as
long as he doesn't land on his bad foot. Over he goes, hand over
hand down the ersatz rope. He hangs at the end of it like a spider,
hesitates — isn't there a technique for doing this? What has he
read about parachutes? Something about bending your knees.
Then he lets go.

He lands two-footed. The pain is intense, but after rolling
around on the muddy ground for a time and making speared-
animal noises, he hauls himself whimpering to his feet. Revision:
to his foot. Nothing seems to be broken. He looks around for a
stick to use as a crutch, finds one. Good thing about sticks, they
grow on trees.

Now he's thirsty.

Through the verdure and upspringing weeds he goes, hoppity
hoppity hop, gritting his teeth. On the way he steps on a huge
banana slug, almost falls. He hates that feeling: cold, viscous, like
a peeled, refrigerated muscle. Creeping snot. If he were a Craker
he'd have to apologize to it — *I'm sorry I stepped on you, Child of
Oryx, please forgive my clumsiness.*

He tries it out: "I'm sorry."

Did he hear something? An answer?

When the slugs begin to talk there's no time to lose.

He reaches the bubble-dome, circles around the white, hot, icy swell of it to the front. The airlock door is open, as he remembers it. A deep breath, and in he goes.

Here are Crake and Oryx, what's left of them. They've been vulturized, they're scattered here and there, small and large bones mingled and in disarray, like a giant jigsaw puzzle.

Here's Snowman, thick as a brick, dunderhead, frivol, and dupe, water running down his face, giant fist clenching his heart, staring down at his one true love and his best friend in all the world. Crake's empty eye sockets look up at Snowman, as his empty eyes, once before. He's grinning with all the teeth in his head. As for Oryx, she's face down, she's turned her head away from him as if in mourning. The ribbon in her hair is as pink as ever.

Oh, how to lament? He's a failure even at that.

Snowman goes through the inner doorway, past the security area, into the staff living quarters. Warm air, humid, unfresh. The first place he needs is the storeroom; he finds it without difficulty. Dark except for a few skylights, but he's got his flashlight. There's a smell of mildew and of rats or mice, but otherwise the place is untouched since he was last here.

He locates the medical-supply shelves, roots around. Tongue depressors, gauze pads, burn dressings. A box of rectal thermometers, but he doesn't need one of them stuffed up his anus to tell him he's burning up. Three or four kinds of antibiotics, pill form and therefore slow-acting, plus one last bottle of Crake's supergermicide short-term pleebland cocktail. *Gets you there and back, but don't stay until the clock strikes midnight or you'll turn into a pumpkin,* is what Crake used to say. He reads the label, Crake's precise notations, estimates the measurement. He's so weak now he can hardly lift the bottle; it takes him a while to get the top off.

Glug glug glug, says his voice balloon. *Down the hatch.*

But no, he shouldn't drink it. He finds a box of clean syringes, shoots himself up. "Bite the dust, foot germs," he says. Then he hobbles to his own suite, what used to be his own suite, and collapses onto the damp unmade bed, and goes brownout.

Alex the parrot comes to him in a dream. It flies in through the window, lands close to him on the pillow, bright green this time with purple wings and a yellow beak, glowing like a beacon, and Snowman is suffused with happiness and love. It cocks its head, looks at him first with one eye, then the other. "The blue triangle," it says. Then it begins to flush, to turn red, beginning with the eye. This change is frightening, as if it's a parrot-shaped light bulb filling up with blood. "I'm going away now," it says.

"No, wait," Snowman calls, or wants to call. His mouth won't move. "Don't go yet! Tell me . . ."

Then there's a rush of wind, whuff, and Alex is gone, and Snowman is sitting up in his former bed, in the dark, drenched in sweat.

Scribble
~

The next morning his foot is somewhat better. The swelling has gone down, the pain has decreased. When evening falls he'll give himself another shot of Crake's superdrug. He knows he can't overdo it, however: the stuff is very potent. Too much of it and his cells will pop like grapes.

Daylight filters through the insulating glass bricks facing the skylight window well. He roams around the space he once inhabited, feeling like a disembodied sensor. Here is his closet, here are the clothes once his, tropical-weight shirts and shorts, ranged neatly on hangers and beginning to moulder. Footwear too, but he can no longer stand the thought of footwear. It would be like adding hooves, plus his infected foot might not fit. Underpants in stacks on the shelves. Why did he used to wear such garments? They appear to him now as some sort of weird bondage gear.

In the storeroom he finds some packets and cans. For breakfast he has cold ravioli in tomato sauce and half a Joltbar, washed down with a warm Coke. No hard liquor or beer left, he'd gone through all of that during the weeks he'd been sealed in here. Just as well. His impulse would have been to drink it up as fast as possible, turn all memory to white noise.

No hope of that now. He's stuck in time past, the wet sand is rising. He's sinking down.

After he'd shot Crake, he'd recoded the inner door, sealed it shut. Crake and Oryx lay intertwined in the airlock; he couldn't bear to touch them, so he'd left them where they were. He'd had a fleeting romantic impulse — maybe he should cut off a piece of Oryx's dark braid — but he'd resisted it.

He went back to his room and drank some Scotch and then some more, as much as it took to conk himself out. What woke him up was the buzzer from the outer door: White Sedge and Black Rhino, trying to get back in. The others too, no doubt. Jimmy ignored them.

Some time the next day he made four slices of soytoast, forced himself to eat them. Drank a bottle of water. His entire body felt like a stubbed toe: numb but also painful.

During the day his cellphone rang. A high-ranking Corpsman, looking for Crake.

"Tell that fucker to get his big fat brain the fuck over here and help figure this thing out."

"He isn't here," said Jimmy.

"Who is this?"

"I can't tell you. Security protocol."

"Listen, whoever you are, I have an idea what sort of scam that creep's up to and when I lay my hands on him I'm going to break his neck. I bet he's got the vaccine for this and he's gonna hold us up for an arm and a leg."

"Really? Is that what you think?" said Jimmy.

"I know the bastard's there. I'm coming over and blow the door in."

"I wouldn't do that," said Jimmy. "We're seeing some very strange microbe activity here. Very unusual. The place is hotter than hell. I'm toughing it out in a biosuit, but I don't really know whether I'm contaminated or not. Something's really gone off the rails."

"Oh shit. Here? In Rejoov? I thought we were sealed off."

"Yeah, it's a bad break," said Jimmy. "My advice is, look in Bermuda. I think he went there with a lot of cash."

"So he sold us out, the little shit. Hawked it deliberately to the competition. That would figure. That would absolutely figure. Listen, thanks for the tip."

"Good luck," said Jimmy.

"Yeah, sure, same to you."

Nobody else buzzed the outer door, nobody tried to break in. The Rejoov folks must have got the message. As for the staff, once they'd realized the guards were gone they must have rushed outside and made a beeline for the outer gate. For what they'd confused with freedom.

Three times a day Jimmy checked on the Crakers, peering in at them like a voyeur. Scrap the simile: he was a voyeur. They seemed happy enough, or at least contented. They grazed, they slept, they sat for long hours doing what appeared to be nothing. The mothers nursed their babies, the young ones played. The men peed in a circle. One of the women came into her blue phase and the men performed their courtship dance, singing, flowers in hand, azure penises waving in time. Then there was a quintuplet fertility fest, off among the shrubbery.

Maybe I could do some social interaction, thought Jimmy. Help them invent the wheel. Leave a legacy of knowledge. Pass on all my words.

No, he couldn't. No hope there.

Sometimes they looked uneasy – they'd gather in groups, they'd murmur. The hidden mikes picked them up.

"Where is Oryx? When is she coming back?"

"She always comes back."

"She should be here, teaching us."

"She is always teaching us. She is teaching us now."

"Is she here?"

"Here and not here is the same thing, for Oryx. She said that."

"Yes. She said it."

"What does it mean?"

It was like some demented theology debate in the windier corners of chat-room limbo. Jimmy couldn't stand listening to it for very long.

The rest of the time he himself grazed, slept, sat for long hours doing nothing. For the first two weeks he followed world events on the Net, or else on the television news: the riots in the cities as transportation broke down and supermarkets were raided; the explosions as electrical systems failed, the fires no one came to extinguish. Crowds packed the churches, mosques, synagogues, and temples to pray and repent, then poured out of them as the worshippers woke up to their increased risk of exposure. There was an exodus to small towns and rural areas, whose inhabitants fought off the refugees as long as they could, with banned firearms or clubs and pitchforks.

At first the newscasters were thoroughly into it, filming the action from traffic helicopters, exclaiming as if at a football match: *Did you see that? Unbelievable! Brad, nobody can quite believe it. What we've just seen is a crazed mob of God's Gardeners, liberating a ChickieNobs production facility. Brad, this is hilarious, those ChickieNob things can't even walk! (Laughter.) Now, back to the studio.*

It must have been during the initial mayhem, thinks Snowman, that some genius let out the pigoons and the wolvogs. *Oh, thanks a bundle.*

Street preachers took to self-flagellation and ranting about the Apocalypse, though they seemed disappointed: where were the trumpets and angels, why hadn't the moon turned to blood? Pundits in suits appeared on the screen; medical experts, graphs showing infection rates, maps tracing the extent of the epidemic. They used dark pink for that, as for the British Empire once. Jimmy would have preferred some other colour.

There was no disguising the fear of the commentators. *Who's next, Brad? When are they going to have a vaccine? Well, Simon, they're working round the clock from what I hear, but nobody's claiming to have a handle on this thing yet. It's a biggie, Brad. Simon, you said a mouthful, but we've licked some biggies before.* Encouraging grin, thumbs-up sign, unfocused eyes, facial pallor.

Documentaries were hastily thrown together, with images of the virus – at least they'd isolated it, it looked like the usual melting gumdrop with spines – and commentary on its methods. *This appears to be a supervirulent splice. Whether it's a species-jumping mutation or a deliberate fabrication is anybody's guess.* Sage nods all round. They'd given the virus a name, to make it seem more manageable. Its name was JUVE, Jetspeed Ultra Virus Extraordinary. Possibly they now knew something, such as what Crake had really been up to, hidden safely in the deepest core of the RejoovenEsense Compound. Sitting in judgment on the world, thought Jimmy; but why had that been his right?

Conspiracy theories proliferated: it was a religious thing, it was God's Gardeners, it was a plot to gain world control. Boil-water and don't-travel advisories were issued in the first week, handshaking was discouraged. In the same week there was a run on latex gloves and nose-cone filters. About as effective, thought Jimmy, as oranges stuck with cloves during the Black Death.

This just in. The JUVE killer virus has broken out in Fiji, spared until now. CorpSeCorps chief declares New New York a disaster area. Major arteries sealed off.

Brad, this item is moving very fast. Simon, it's unbelievable.

"Change can be accommodated by any system depending on its rate," Crake used to say. "Touch your head to a wall, nothing happens, but if the same head hits the same wall at ninety miles an hour, it's red paint. We're in a speed tunnel, Jimmy. When the water's moving faster than the boat, you can't control a thing."

I listened, thought Jimmy, but I didn't hear.

In the second week, there was full mobilization. The hastily assembled epidemic managers called the shots – field clinics, isolation tents; whole towns, then whole cities quarantined. But these efforts soon broke down as the doctors and nurses caught the thing themselves, or panicked and fled.

England closes ports and airports.

All communication from India has ceased.

Hospitals are off limits until further notice. If you feel ill, drink plenty of water and call the following hotline number.

Do not, repeat do not, attempt to exit cities.

It wasn't Brad talking any more, or Simon. Brad and Simon were gone. It was other people, and then others.

Jimmy called the hotline number and got a recording saying it was out of service. Then he called his father, a thing he hadn't done in years. That line was out of service too.

He searched his e-mail. No recent messages. All he found was an old birthday card he'd failed to delete: *Happy Birthday, Jimmy, May All Your Dreams Come True.* Pigs with wings.

One of the privately run Web sites showed a map, with lit-up points on it for each place that was still communicating via satellite. Jimmy watched with fascination as the points of light blinked out.

He was in shock. That must have been why he couldn't take it in. The whole thing seemed like a movie. Yet there he was, and there were Oryx and Crake, dead, in the airlock. Any time he found himself thinking it was all an illusion, a practical joke of some kind, he went and looked at them. Through the bulletproof window, of course: he knew he shouldn't open the innermost door.

He lived off Crake's emergency stores, the frozen goods first:

if the bubble's solar system failed, the freezers and microwaves would no longer work, so he might as well eat his way through the ChickieNobs Gourmet Dinners while he had the chance. He smoked up Crake's stash of skunkweed in no time flat; he managed to miss about three days of horror that way. He rationed the booze at first, but soon he was getting through quite a pile of it. He needed to be fried just to face the news, he needed to be feeling not much.

"I don't believe it, I don't believe it," he'd say. He'd begun talking to himself out loud, a bad sign. "It isn't happening." How could he exist in this clean, dry, monotonous, ordinary room, gobbling caramel soycorn and zucchini cheese puffs and addling his brain on spirituous liquors and brooding on the total fiasco that was his personal life, while the entire human race was kakking out?

The worst of it was that those people out there – the fear, the suffering, the wholesale death – did not really touch him. Crake used to say that *Homo sapiens sapiens* was not hard-wired to individuate other people in numbers above two hundred, the size of the primal tribe, and Jimmy would reduce that number to two. Had Oryx loved him, had she loved him not, did Crake know about them, how much did he know, when did he know it, was he spying on them all along? Did he set up the grand finale as an assisted suicide, had he intended to have Jimmy shoot him because he knew what would happen next and he didn't deign to stick around to watch the results of what he'd done?

Or did he know he wouldn't be able to withhold the formula for the vaccine, once the CorpSeCorps got to work on him? How long had he been planning this? Could it be that Uncle Pete, and possibly even Crake's own mother, had been trial runs? With so much at stake, was he afraid of failure, of being just one more incompetent nihilist? Or was he tormented by jealousy, was he addled by love, was it revenge, did he just want Jimmy to put him out of his misery? Had he been a lunatic or an intellectually honourable man who'd thought things through to their logical conclusion? And was there any difference?

And so on and so forth, spinning the emotional wheels and sucking down the hootch until he could blank himself out.

Meanwhile, the end of a species was taking place before his very eyes. Kingdom, Phylum, Class, Order, Family, Genus, Species. How many legs does it have? *Homo sapiens sapiens*, joining the polar bear, the beluga whale, the onager, the burrowing owl, the long, long list. *Oh, big points, Grandmaster.*

Sometimes he'd turn off the sound, whisper words to himself. *Succulent. Morphology. Purblind. Quarto. Frass.* It had a calming effect.

Site after site, channel after channel went dead. A couple of the anchors, news jocks to the end, set the cameras to film their own deaths – the screams, the dissolving skins, the ruptured eyeballs and all. How theatrical, thought Jimmy. Nothing some people won't do to get on TV.

"You cynical shit," he told himself. Then he started to weep.

"Don't be so fucking sentimental," Crake used to tell him. But why not? Why shouldn't he be sentimental? It wasn't as if there was anyone around to question his taste.

Once in a while he considered killing himself – it seemed mandatory – but somehow he didn't have the required energy. Anyway, killing yourself was something you did for an audience, as on nitee-nite.com. Under the circumstances, the here and now, it was a gesture that lacked elegance. He could imagine Crake's amused contempt, and the disappointment of Oryx: *But Jimmy! Why do you give up? You have a job to do! You promised, remember?*

Perhaps he failed to take seriously his own despair.

Finally there was nothing more to watch, except old movies on DVD. He watched Humphrey Bogart and Edward G. Robinson in

Key Largo. He wants more, don't you, Rocco? Yeah, that's it, more! That's right, I want more. Will you ever get enough? Or else he watched Alfred Hitchcock's *The Birds. Flapflapflap, eek, screech.* You could see the strings where the avian superstars were tied to the roof. Or he watched *Night of the Living Dead. Lurch, aargh, gnaw, choke, gurgle.* Such minor paranoias were soothing to him.

Then he'd turn it off, sit in front of the empty screen. All the women he'd ever known would pass in front of his eyes in the semi-darkness. His mother too, in her magenta dressing gown, young again. Oryx came last, carrying white flowers. She looked at him, then walked slowly out of his field of vision, into the shadows where Crake was waiting.

These reveries were almost pleasurable. At least while they were going on everyone was still alive.

He knew this state of affairs couldn't continue much longer. Inside Paradice proper, the Crakers were munching up the leaves and grasses faster than they could regenerate, and one of these days the solar would fail, and the backup would fail too, and Jimmy had no idea about how to fix those things. Then the air circulation would stop and the doorlock would freeze, and both he and the Crakers would be trapped inside, and they'd all suffocate. He had to get them out while there was still time, but not too soon or there would still be some desperate people out there, and desperate would mean dangerous. What he didn't want was a bunch of disintegrating maniacs falling on their knees, clawing at him: *Cure us! Cure us!* He might be immune from the virus – unless, of course, Crake had been lying to him – but not from the rage and despair of its carriers.

Anyway, how could he have the heart to stand there and say: *Nothing can save you?*

In the half-light, in the dank, Snowman wanders from space to space. Here for instance is his office. His computer sits on the desk, turning a blank face to him like a discarded girlfriend encountered by chance at a party. Beside the computer are a few sheets of paper, which must have been the last he'd ever written. The last he'd ever write. He picks them up with curiosity. What is it that the Jimmy he'd once been had seen fit to communicate, or at least to record — to set down in black and white, with smudges — for the edification of a world that no longer existed?

To whom it may concern, Jimmy had written, in ballpoint rather than printout: his computer was fried by then, but he'd persevered, laboriously, by hand. He must still have had hope, he must still have believed that the situation could be turned around, that someone would show up here in the future, someone in authority; that his words would have a meaning then, a context. As Crake had once said, Jimmy was a romantic optimist.

I don't have much time, Jimmy had written.

Not a bad beginning, thinks Snowman.

I don't have much time, but I will try to set down what I believe to be the explanation for the recent ~~extraordinary events~~ catastrophe. I have gone through the computer of the man known here as Crake. He left it turned on — deliberately, I believe — and I am able to report that the JUVE virus was made here in the Paradice dome by splicers hand-selected by Crake ~~and subsequently eliminated~~, and was then encysted in the BlyssPluss product. There was a time-lapse factor built in to allow for wide distribution: the first batch of virus did not become active until all selected territories had been seeded, and the outbreak thus took the form of a series of rapidly overlapping waves. For the success of the plan, time was of the essence. Social disruption was maximized, and development of a vaccine effectively prevented. Crake himself had developed a vaccine concurrently with the virus, but he had destroyed it prior to his ~~assisted suicide~~ death.

Although various staff members of the BlyssPluss project contributed to JUVE on a piecework basis, it is my belief that none, with the exception of Crake, was cognizant of what that effect would be. As for Crake's motives, I can only speculate. Perhaps . . .

Here the handwriting stops. Whatever Jimmy's speculations might have been on the subject of Crake's motives, they had not been recorded.

Snowman crumples the sheets up, drops them onto the floor. It's the fate of these words to be eaten by beetles. He could have mentioned the change in Crake's fridge magnets. You could tell a lot about a person from their fridge magnets, not that he'd thought much about them at the time.

Remnant

~

On the second Friday of March — he'd been marking off the days on a calendar, god knows why — Jimmy showed himself to the Crakers for the first time. He didn't take his clothes off, he drew the line at that. He wore a set of standard-issue Rejoov khaki tropicals, with mesh underarms and a thousand pockets, and his favourite fake-leather sandals. The Crakers gathered around him, gazing at him with quiet wonder: they'd never seen textiles before. The children whispered and pointed.

"Who are you?" said the one Crake had christened Abraham Lincoln. A tall man, brown, thinnish. It was not said impolitely. From an ordinary man Jimmy would have found it brusque, even aggressive, but these people didn't go in for fancy language: they hadn't been taught evasion, euphemism, lily-gilding. In speech they were plain and blunt.

"My name is Snowman," said Jimmy, who had thought this over. He no longer wanted to be Jimmy, or even Jim, and especially not Thickney: his incarnation as Thickney hadn't worked out well. He needed to forget the past — the distant past, the immediate past, the past in any form. He needed to exist only in the present, without guilt, without expectation. As the Crakers did. Perhaps a different name would do that for him.

"Where have you come from, oh Snowman?"

"I come from the place of Oryx and Crake," he said. "Crake sent me." True, in a way. "And Oryx." He keeps the sentence structure simple, the message clear: he knows how to do this from watching Oryx through the mirror wall. And from listening to her, of course.

"Where has Oryx gone?"

"She had some things to do," said Snowman. That was all he could come up with: simply pronouncing her name had choked him up.

"Why have Crake and Oryx sent you to us?" asked the woman called Madame Curie.

"To take you to a new place."

"But this is our place. We are content where we are."

"Oryx and Crake wish you to have a better place than this," said Snowman. "Where there will be more to eat." There were nods, smiles. Oryx and Crake wished them well, as they'd always known. It seemed to be enough for them.

"Why is your skin so loose?" said one of the children.

"I was made in a different way from you," Snowman said. He was beginning to find this conversation of interest, like a game. These people were like blank pages, he could write whatever he wanted on them. "Crake made me with two kinds of skin. One comes off." He took off his tropical vest to show them. They stared with interest at the hair on his chest.

"What is that?"

"These are feathers. Little feathers. Oryx gave them to me, as a special favour. See? More feathers are growing out of my face." He lets the children touch the stubble. He'd been lax about shaving lately, there seemed little point to it, so his beard was sprouting.

"Yes. We see. But what are feathers?"

Oh, right. They'd never seen any. "Some of the Children of

Oryx have feathers on them," he said. "That kind are called birds. We'll go to where they are. Then you'll know about feathers."

Snowman marvelled at his own facility: he was dancing gracefully around the truth, light-footed, light-fingered. But it was almost too easy: they accepted, without question, everything he said. Much more of this – whole days, whole weeks of it – and he could see himself screaming with boredom. I could leave them behind, he thought. Just leave them. Let them fend for themselves. They aren't my business.

But he couldn't do that, because although the Crakers weren't his business, they were now his responsibility. Who else did they have?

Who else did he have, for that matter?

Snowman planned the route in advance: Crake's storeroom was well supplied with maps. He'd take the Children of Crake to the seashore, where he himself had never been. It was something to look forward to: at last he would see the ocean. He'd walk on a beach, as in stories told by the grown-ups when he was young. He might even go swimming. It wouldn't be too bad.

The Crakers could live in the park near the arboretum, coloured green on the map and marked with a tree symbol. They'd feel at home there, and certainly there would be lots of edible foliage. As for himself, there would surely be fish. He gathered together some supplies – not too much, not too heavy, he'd have to carry it all – and loaded up his spraygun with the full complement of virtual bullets.

The evening before the departure, he gave a talk. On the way to their new, better place, he would walk ahead – he said – with two of the men. He picked the tallest. Behind them would come the women and children, with a file of men to either side. The rest of the men would walk behind. They needed to do this because Crake had said that this was the proper way. (It was best to avoid mentioning the possible dangers: those would require too much exposition.) If the Crakers noticed anything moving – anything at all, in whatever shape or form – they were to tell him at once. Some of the things they might see would be puzzling, but they were not to be alarmed. If they told him in time, these things would not be able to hurt them.

"Why would they hurt us?" asked Sojourner Truth.

"They might hurt you by mistake," said Snowman. "As the ground hurts you when you fall on it."

"But it is not the ground's wish to hurt us."

"Oryx has told us that the ground is our friend."

"It grows our food for us."

"Yes," said Snowman. "But Crake made the ground hard. Otherwise we would not be able to walk on it."

It took them a minute to work this one through. Then there was much nodding of heads. Snowman's brain was spinning; the illogic of what he'd just said dazzled him. But it seemed to have done the trick.

In the dawn light he punched in the door code for the last time and opened up the bubble, and led the Crakers out of Paradice. They noticed the remains of Crake lying on the ground, but as they had never seen Crake when alive, they believed Snowman when he told them this was a thing of no importance – only a sort of husk, only a sort of pod. It would have been a shock to them to have witnessed their creator in his present state.

As for Oryx, she was face down and wrapped in silk. No one they'd recognize.

The trees surrounding the dome were lush and green, everything seemed pristine, but when they reached the RejoovenEsense Compound proper, the evidence of destruction and death lay all around. Overturned golf carts, sodden, illegible print-outs, computers with their guts ripped out. Rubble, fluttering cloth, gnawed carrion. Broken toys. The vultures were still at their business.

"Please, oh Snowman, what is that?"

It's a dead body, what do you think? "It's part of the chaos," said Snowman. "Crake and Oryx are clearing away the chaos, for you — because they love you — but they haven't quite finished yet." This answer seemed to content them.

"The chaos smells very bad," said one of the older children.

"Yes," said Snowman, with something he meant for a smile. "Chaos always smells bad."

Five blocks from the main Compound gate, a man staggered out of a side street towards them. He was in the penultimate stages of the disease: the sweat of blood was on his forehead. "Take me with you!" he shouted. The words were hardly audible. The sound was animal, an animal enraged.

"Stay where you are," Snowman yelled. The Crakers stood amazed, staring, but — it appeared — not frightened. The man came on, stumbled, fell. Snowman shot him. He was worried about contagion — could the Crakers get this thing, or was their genetic material too different? Surely Crake would have given them immunity. Wouldn't he?

When they reached the peripheral wall, there was another one, a woman. She lurched abruptly out of the gatehouse, weeping, and grabbed at a child.

"Help me!" she implored. "Don't leave me here!" Snowman shot her too.

During both incidents the Crakers looked on in wonder: they didn't connect the noise made by Snowman's little stick with the crumpling of these people.

"What is the thing that fell down, oh Snowman? Is it a man or a woman? It has extra skins, like you."

"It's nothing. It's a piece of a bad dream that Crake is dreaming."

They understood about dreaming, he knew that: they dreamed themselves. Crake hadn't been able to eliminate dreams. *We're hard-wired for dreams*, he'd said. He couldn't get rid of the singing either. *We're hard-wired for singing.* Singing and dreams were entwined.

"Why does Crake dream a bad dream like that?"

"He dreams it," said Snowman, "so you won't have to."

"It is sad that he suffers on our behalf."

"We are very sorry. We thank him."

"Will the bad dream be over soon?"

"Yes," said Snowman. "Very soon." The last one had been a close call, the woman was like a rabid dog. His hands were shaking now. He needed a drink.

"It will be over when Crake wakes up?"

"Yes. When he wakes up."

"We hope he will wake up very soon."

And so they walked together through No Man's Land, stopping here and there to graze or picking leaves and flowers as they went, the women and children hand in hand, several of them singing, in their crystal voices, their voices like fronds unrolling. Then they wound through the streets of the pleeblands, like a skewed parade or a fringe religious procession. During the afternoon storms they took shelter; easy to do, as doors and windows had ceased to have meaning. Then, in the freshened air, they continued their stroll.

Some of the buildings along the way were still smouldering. There were many questions, and much explaining to do. *What is that smoke? It is a thing of Crake's. Why is that child lying down, with no eyes? It was the will of Crake.* And so forth.

Snowman made it up as he went along. He knew what an improbable shepherd he was. To reassure them, he tried his best to appear dignified and reliable, wise and kindly. A lifetime of deviousness came to his aid.

Finally they reached the edge of the park. Snowman had to shoot only two more disintegrating people. He was doing them a favour, so he didn't feel too bad about it. He felt worse about other things.

Late in the evening, they came at last to the shore. The leaves of the trees were rustling, the water was gently waving, the setting sun was reflected on it, pink and red. The sands were white, the offshore towers overflowing with birds.

"It is so beautiful here."

"Oh look! Are those feathers?"

"What is this place called?"

"It is called *home*," said Snowman.

14

Idol
~

Snowman rifles the storeroom, packs what he can carry — the rest of the food, dried and in tins, flashlight and batteries, maps and matches and candles, ammunition packs, duct tape, two bottles of water, painkiller pills, antibiotic gel, a couple of sun-proof shirts, and one of those little knives with the scissors. And the spraygun, of course. He picks up his stick and heads out through the airlock doorway, avoiding Crake's gaze, Crake's grin; and Oryx, in her silk butterfly shroud.

Oh Jimmy. That's not me!

Birdsong's beginning. The predawn light is a feathery grey, the air misty; dew pearls the spiderwebs. If he were a child it would seem fresh and new, this ancient, magical effect. As it is, he knows it's an illusion: once the sun's up, all will vanish. Halfway across the grounds he stops, takes one last backward look at Paradice, swelling up out of the foliage like a lost balloon.

He has a map of the Compound, he's already studied it, charted his route. He cuts across a main artery to the golf course and crosses it without incident. His pack and the gun are beginning to weigh on him, so he stops for a drink. The sun's up now, the vultures are rising on their updrafts; they've spotted him, they'll note his limp, they'll be watching.

He makes his way through a residential section, then across a schoolground. He has to shoot one pigoon before he reaches the peripheral wall: it was just having a good stare, but he was certain it was a scout, it would have told the others. At the side gate he pauses. There's a watchtower here, and access to the rampart; he'd like to climb up, have a look around, check out that smoke he saw. But the door to the gatehouse is locked, so he goes on out.

Nothing in the moat.

He crosses No Man's Land, a nervous passage: he keeps seeing furry movement at the sides of his eyes, and worries that the clumps of weeds are changing shape. At last he's in the pleeblands; he wends his way through the narrow streets, alert for ambushes, but nothing hunts him. Only the vultures circle above, waiting for him to be meat.

An hour before noon he climbs a tree, conceals himself in the shade of the leaves. There he eats a tin of SoyOBoy wieners and finishes the first bottle of water. Once he stops walking, his foot asserts itself: there's a regular throbbing, it feels hot and tight, as if it's crammed into a tiny shoe. He rubs some antibiotic gel into the cut, but without much faith: the microbes infecting him have doubtless already mounted their resistance and are simmering away in there, turning his flesh to porridge.

He scans the horizon from his arboreal vantage point, but he can't see anything that looks like smoke. *Arboreal*, a fine word. *Our arboreal ancestors*, Crake used to say. *Used to shit on their enemies from above while perched in trees. All planes and rockets and bombs are simply elaborations on that primate instinct.*

What if I die up here, in this tree? he thinks. Will it serve me right? Why? Who will ever find me? And so what if they do? *Oh look, another dead man. Big fucking deal. Common as dirt. Yeah, but this one's in a tree. So, who cares?*

"I'm not just any dead man," he says out loud.

Of course not! Each one of us is unique! And every single dead person is dead in his or her very own special way! Now, who wants to share about being dead, in our own special words? Jimmy, you seem eager to talk, so why don't you begin?

Oh torture. Is this purgatory, and if it is, why is it so much like the first grade?

After a couple of hours of fitful rest he moves on, holing up from the afternoon storm in the remains of a pleebland condo. Nobody in it, dead or alive. Then he continues on, limpity-limp, picking up speed now, heading south and then east, towards the shore.

It's a relief when he hits the Snowman Fish Path. Instead of turning left towards his tree, he hobbles along towards the village. He's tired, he wants to sleep, but he'll have to reassure the Crakers — demonstrate his safe return, explain why he's been away so long, deliver his message from Crake.

He'll need to invent some lies about that. *What did Crake look like? I couldn't see him, he was in a bush.* A burning bush, why not? Best to be nonspecific about the facial features. *But he gave some orders: I get two fish a week — no, make it three — and roots and berries.* Maybe he should add seaweed to that. They'll know which kinds are good. And crabs too — not the land crabs, the other kinds. He'll order them up steamed, a dozen at a time. Surely that's not too much to ask.

After he's seen the Crakers, he'll stow away his new food and eat some of it, and then have a doze in his familiar tree. After that he'll be refreshed, and his brain will be working better, and he'll be able to think about what to do next.

What to do next about what? That's too difficult. But suppose there are other people around, people like himself — smoke-making people — he'll wish to be in some kind of shape to greet them. He'll wash up — this one time he can risk the bathing pool – then put on one of the clean sun-proof shirts he's brought, maybe hack off some of his beard with the little scissors on the knife.

Damn, he forgot to bring a pocket mirror. Brainfart!

As he approaches the village, he hears an unusual sound – an odd crooning, high voices and deep ones, men's and women's both – harmonious, two-noted. It isn't singing, it's more like chanting. Then a clang, a series of pings, a boom. What are they doing? Whatever it is, they've never done anything like it before.

Here's the line of demarcation, the stinky but invisible chemical wall of piss renewed by the men each day. He steps across it, moves cautiously forward, peers from behind a shrub. There they are. He does a quick head count – most of the young, all of the adults minus five – must be a fivesome off in the woods, mating. They're sitting in a semi-circle around a grotesque-looking figure, a scarecrowlike effigy. All their attention is focused on it: they don't at first see him as he steps out from behind the shrub and limps forward.

Ohhhh, croon the women.

Mun, the men intone.

Is that *Amen*? Surely not! Not after Crake's precautions, his insistence on keeping these people pure, free of all contamination of that kind. And they certainly didn't get that word from Snowman. It can't have happened.

Clank. Ping-ping-ping-ping. Boom. *Ohhh-mun*.

Now he can see the percussion group. The instruments are a hubcap and a metal rod – those create the clanks – and a series of empty bottles dangling from a tree branch and played with a serving spoon. The boom is from an oil drum, hit with what looks like a kitchen mallet. Where did they get these things? Off the beach, no doubt. He feels as if he's watching his day-care rhythm band of long ago, but with huge green-eyed children.

What's the thing – the statue, or scarecrow, or whatever it is? It has a head, and a ragged cloth body. It has a face of sorts – one pebble eye, one black one, a jar lid it looks like. It has an old string mop stuck onto the chin.

Now they've seen him. They scramble to their feet, hurry to greet him, surround him. All are smiling happily; the children jump up and down, laughing; some of the women clap their hands with excitement. This is more energy than they usually display about anything.

"Snowman! Snowman!" They touch him gently with their fingertips. "You are back with us!"

"We knew we could call you, and you would hear us and come back."

Not *Amen*, then. *Snowman*.

"We made a picture of you, to help us send out our voices to you."

Watch out for art, Crake used to say. *As soon as they start doing art, we're in trouble.* Symbolic thinking of any kind would signal downfall, in Crake's view. Next they'd be inventing idols, and funerals, and grave goods, and the afterlife, and sin, and Linear B, and kings, and then slavery and war. Snowman longs to question them – who first had the idea of making a reasonable facsimile of him, of Snowman, out of a jar lid and a mop? But that will have to wait.

"Look! Snowman has flowers on him!" (This from the children, who've noticed his new floral sarong.)

"Can we have flowers on us too?"

"Was it difficult, your journey into the sky?"

"Flowers too, flowers too!"

"What message does Crake send us?"

"Why do you think I've been into the sky?" Snowman asks, as neutrally as possible. He's clicking through the legend files in his head. When did he ever mention the sky? Did he relate some fable about where Crake had come from? Yes, now he remembers. He'd given Crake the attributes of thunder and lightning. Naturally they assume Crake must have gone back up to cloudland.

"We know Crake lives in the sky. And we saw the whirling wind – it went the way you went."

"Crake sent it for you – to help you rise from the ground."

"Now you have been to the sky, you are almost like Crake."

Best not to contradict them, but he can't let them continue in a belief that he can fly: sooner or later they might expect him to demonstrate. "The whirling wind was so Crake could come *down* out of the sky," he says. "He made the wind to blow him down from above. He decided not to stay up there, because the sun was too hot. So that isn't where I saw him."

"Where is he?"

"He's in the bubble," Snowman says, truthfully enough. "The place we came from. He's in Paradice."

"Let us go there and see him," says one of the older children. "We know how to get there. We remember."

"You can't see him," Snowman says, a little too sharply. "You wouldn't recognize him. He's turned himself into a plant." Now where did that come from? He's very tired, he's losing it.

"Why would Crake become food?" asks Abraham Lincoln.

"It's not a plant you can eat," says Snowman. "It's more like a tree."

Some puzzled looks. "He talks to you. How does he talk, if he is a tree?"

This is going to be hard to explain. He's made a narrative mistake. He has the sensation that he's lost his balance at the top of a flight of stairs.

He flails for a grip. "It's a tree with a mouth," he says.

"Trees don't have mouths," says one of the children.

"But look," says a woman – Madame Curie, Sacajawea? "Snowman has hurt his foot." The women can always sense his discomfort, they try to ease it by changing the subject. "We must help him."

"Let us get him a fish. Would you like a fish now, Snowman? We will ask Oryx to give us a fish, to die for you."

"That would be good," he says with relief.

"Oryx wants you to be well."

Soon he's lying on the ground and they're purring over him.

The pain lessens, but although they try very hard, the swelling will not go all the way down.

"It must have been a deep hurt."

"It will need more."

"We will try again later."

They bring the fish, cooked now and wrapped in leaves, and watch joyfully while he eats it. He's not that hungry — it's the fever — but he tries hard because he doesn't want to frighten them.

Already the children are destroying the image they made of him, reducing it to its component parts, which they plan to return to the beach. This is a teaching of Oryx, the women tell him: after a thing has been used, it must be given back to its place of origin. The picture of Snowman has done its work: now that the real Snowman is among them once more, there is no reason for the other, the less satisfactory one. Snowman finds it odd to see his erstwhile beard, his erstwhile head, travelling away piece-meal in the hands of the children. It's as if he himself has been torn apart and scattered.

Sermon
~

"Some others like you came here," says Abraham Lincoln, after Snowman has done his best with the fish. He's lying back against a tree trunk; his foot is gently tingling now, as if it's asleep; he feels drowsy.

Snowman jolts awake. "Others like me?"

"With those other skins, like you," says Napoleon. "And one of them had feathers on his face, like you."

"Another one had feathers too but not long feathers."

"We thought they were sent by Crake. Like you."

"One was a female."

"She must have been sent by Oryx."

"She smelled blue."

"We couldn't see the blue, because of her other skin."

"But she smelled very blue. The men began to sing to her."

"We offered her flowers and signalled to her with our penises, but she did not respond with joy."

"The men with the extra skins didn't look happy. They looked angry."

"We went towards them to greet them, but they ran away."

Snowman can imagine. The sight of these preternaturally calm, well-muscled men advancing *en masse*, singing their unusual music, green eyes glowing, blue penises waving in unison, both hands outstretched like extras in a zombie film, would have to have been alarming.

Snowman's heart is going very fast now, with excitement or fear, or a blend. "Were they carrying anything?"

"One of them had a noisy stick, like yours." Snowman's spray-gun is out of sight: they must remember the gun from before, from when they walked out of Paradice. "But they didn't make any noise with it." The Children of Crake are very nonchalant about all this, they don't realize the implications. It's as if they're discussing rabbits.

"When did they come here?"

"Oh, the day before, maybe."

Useless to try to pin them down about any past event: they don't count the days. "Where did they go?"

"They went there, along the beach. Why did they run away from us, oh Snowman?"

"Perhaps they heard Crake," says Sacajawea. "Perhaps he was calling to them. They had shiny things on their arms, like you. Things for listening to Crake."

"I'll ask them," says Snowman. "I'll go and talk with them. I'll do it tomorrow. Now I will go to sleep." He heaves himself upright, winces with pain. He still can't put much weight on that foot.

"We will come too," say several of the men.

"No," says Snowman. "I don't think that would be a very good idea."

"But you are not well enough yet," says the Empress Josephine. "You need more purring." She looks worried: a small frown has appeared between her eyes. Unusual to see such an expression on one of their perfect wrinkle-free faces.

Snowman submits, and a new purring team — three men this time, one woman, they must think he needs strong medicine — hovers over his leg. He tries to sense a responding vibration inside himself, wondering – not for the first time – whether this method is tailored to work only on them. Those who aren't purring watch the operation closely; some converse in low voices, and after half an hour or so a fresh team takes over.

He can't relax into the sound as he knows he should, because he's rehearsing the future, he can't help it. His mind is racing; behind his half-closed eyes possibilities flash and collide. Maybe all will be well, maybe this trio of strangers is good-hearted, sane, well-intentioned; maybe he'll succeed in presenting the Crakers to them in the proper light. On the other hand, these new arrivals could easily see the Children of Crake as freakish, or savage, or non-human and a threat.

Images from old history flip through his head, sidebars from Blood and Roses: Ghenghis Khan's skull pile, the heaps of shoes and eyeglasses from Dachau, the burning corpse-filled churches in Rwanda, the sack of Jerusalem by the Crusaders. The Arawak Indians, welcoming Christopher Columbus with garlands and gifts of fruit, smiling with delight, soon to be massacred, or tied up beneath the beds upon which their women were being raped.

But why imagine the worst? Maybe these people have been frightened off, maybe they'll have moved elsewhere. Maybe they're ill and dying.

Or maybe not.

Before he reconnoitres, before he sets out on what – he now sees – is a mission, he should make a speech of some kind to the Crakers. A sort of sermon. Lay down a few commandments, Crake's parting words to them. Except that they don't need commandments: no *thou shalt nots* would be any good to them, or even comprehensible, because it's all built in. No point in telling them not to lie, steal, commit adultery, or covet. They wouldn't grasp the concepts.

He should say something to them, though. Leave them with a few words to remember. Better, some practical advice. He should say he might not be coming back. He should say that the others, the ones with extra skins and feathers, are not from Crake. He should say their noisy stick should be taken away from them and thrown into the sea. He should say that if these people should become violent — *Oh Snowman, please, what is violent?* — or if they attempt to rape (*What is rape?*) the women, or molest (*What?*) the children, or if they try to force others to work for them . . .

Hopeless, hopeless. *What is work?* Work is when you build things — *What is build?* — or grow things — *What is grow?* — either because people would hit and kill you if you didn't, or else because they would give you money if you did.

What is money?

No, he can't say any of that. *Crake is watching over you*, he'll say. *Oryx loves you.*

Then his eyes close and he feels himself being lifted gently, carried, lifted again, carried again, held.

15

Footprint
~

Snowman wakes before dawn. He lies unmoving, listening to the tide coming in, wish-wash, wish-wash, the rhythm of heartbeat. He would so like to believe he is still asleep.

On the eastern horizon there's a greyish haze, lit now with a rosy, deadly glow. Strange how that colour still seems tender. He gazes at it with rapture; there is no other word for it. *Rapture.* The heart seized, carried away, as if by some large bird of prey. After everything that's happened, how can the world still be so beautiful? Because it is. From the offshore towers come the avian shrieks and cries that sound like nothing human.

He takes a few deep breaths, scans the ground below for wildlife, makes his way down from the tree, setting his good foot on the ground first. He checks the inside of his hat, flicks out an ant. Can a single ant be said to be alive, in any meaningful sense of the word, or does it only have relevance in terms of its anthill? An old conundrum of Crake's.

He hobbles across the beach to the water's edge, washes his foot, feels the sting of salt: there must have been a boil, the thing must have ruptured overnight, the wound feels huge now. The flies buzz around him, waiting for a chance to settle.

Then he limps back up to the treeline, takes off his flowered bedsheet, hangs it on a branch: he doesn't want to be impeded. He'll wear nothing but his baseball cap, to keep the glare out of his eyes. He'll dispense with the sunglasses: it's early enough so they won't be needed. He needs to catch every nuance of movement.

He pees on the grasshoppers, watches with nostalgia as they whir away. Already this routine of his is entering the past, like a lover seen from a train window, waving goodbye, pulled inexorably back, in space, in time, so quickly.

He goes to his cache, opens it, drinks some water. His foot hurts like shit, it's red around the wound again, his ankle's swollen: whatever's in there has overcome the cocktail from Paradice and the treatment of the Crakers as well. He rubs on some of the antibiotic gel, useless as mud. Luckily he's got aspirins; those will dull the pain. He swallows four, chews up half a Joltbar for the energy. Then he takes out his spraygun, checks the cellpack of virtual bullets.

He's not ready for this. He's not well. He's frightened.

He could choose to stay put, await developments.

Oh honey. You're my only hope.

He follows the beach northward, using his stick for balance, keeping to the shadow of the trees as much as possible. The sky's brightening, he needs to hurry. He can see the smoke now, rising in a thin column. It will take him an hour or more to get there. They don't know about him, those people; they know about the Crakers but not about him, they won't be expecting him. That's his best chance.

From tree to tree he limps, elusive, white, a rumour. In search of his own kind.

Here's a human footprint, in the sand. Then another one. They aren't sharp-edged, because the sand here is dry, but there's no mistaking them. And now here's a whole trail of them, leading down to the sea. Several different sizes. Where the sand turns damp he can see them better. What were these people doing? Swimming, fishing? Washing themselves?

They were wearing shoes, or sandals. Here's where they took them off, here's where they put them on again. He stamps his own good foot into the wet sand, beside the biggest footprint: a signature of a kind. As soon as he lifts his foot away the imprint fills with water.

He can smell the smoke, he can hear the voices now. Sneaking he goes, as if walking through an empty house in which there might yet be people. What if they should see him? A hairy naked maniac wearing nothing but a baseball cap and carrying a spraygun. What would they do? Scream and run? Attack? Open their arms to him with joy and brotherly love?

He peers out through the screen of leaves: there are only three of them, sitting around their fire. They've got a spraygun of their own, a CorpSeCorps daily special, but it's lying on the ground. They're thin, battered-looking. Two men, one brown, one white, a tea-coloured woman, the men in tropical khakis, standard issue but filthy, the woman in the remains of a uniform of some kind – nurse, guard? Must have been pretty once, before she lost all that weight; now she's stringy, her hair parched, broomstraw. All three of them look wasted.

They're roasting something – meat of some kind. A rakunk? Yes, there's the tail, over there on the ground. They must have shot it. The poor creature.

Snowman hasn't smelled roast meat for so long. Is that why his eyes are watering?

He's shivering now. He's feverish again.

What next? Advance with a strip of bedsheet tied to a stick, waving a white flag? *I come in peace.* But he doesn't have his bedsheet with him.

Or, *I can show you much treasure.* But no, he has nothing to trade with them, nor they with him. Nothing except themselves.

They could listen to him, they could hear his tale, he could hear theirs. They at least would understand something of what he's been through.

Or, *Get the hell off my turf before I blow you off*, as in some old-style Western film. *Hands up. Back away. Leave that spray-gun.* That wouldn't be the end of it though. There are three of them and only one of him. They'd do what he'd do in their place: they'd go away, but they'd lurk, they'd spy. They'd sneak up on him in the dark, conk him on the head with a rock. He'd never know when they might come.

He could finish it now, before they see him, while he still has the strength. While he can still stand up. His foot's like a shoeful of liquid fire. But they haven't done anything bad, not to him. Should he kill them in cold blood? Is he able to? And if he starts killing them and then stops, one of them will kill him first. Naturally.

"What do you want me to do?" he whispers to the empty air. It's hard to know.

Oh Jimmy, you were so funny.

Don't let me down.

From habit he lifts his watch; it shows him its blank face.

Zero hour, Snowman thinks. Time to go.

Acknowledgments

My thanks to the Society of Authors (England), as the literary representative of the estate of Virginia Woolf, for permission to quote from *To the Lighthouse*; to Anne Carson for permission to quote from *The Beauty of the Husband*; and to John Calder Publications and Grove Atlantic for permission to quote eight words from Samuel Beckett's novel, *Mercier and Camier*. A full list of the other quotations used or paraphrased on the fridge magnets in this book may be found at oryxandcrake.com. "Winter Wonderland," alluded to in Part 9, is by Felix Bernard and Richard B. Smith, and is copyrighted by Warner Bros.

The name "Amanda Payne" was graciously supplied by its auction-winning owner, thereby raising much-needed funds for the Medical Foundation for the Care of Victims of Torture (U.K.). Alex the parrot is a participant in the animal-intelligence work of Dr. Irene Pepperberg, and is the protagonist of many books, documentaries, and Web sites. He has given his name to the Alex Foundation. Thank you also to Tuco the parrot, who lives with Sharon Doobenen and Brian Brett, and to Ricki the parrot, who lives with Ruth Atwood and Ralph Siferd.

Deep background was inadvertently supplied by many magazines and newspapers and non-fiction science writers encountered over the years. A full list of these is available at oryxandcrake.com. Thanks also to Dr. Dave Mossop and Grace Mossop, and to Norman and Barbara Barichello, of Whitehorse, in the Yukon, Canada; to Max Davidson and team, of Davidson's Arnheimland Safaris, Australia; to my brother, neurophysiologist Dr. Harold Atwood (thank you for the study of sex hormones in unborn mice, and other arcana); to Lic. Gilberto Silva and Lic. Orlando Garrido, dedicated biologists, of Cuba; to Matthew Swan and team, of Adventure Canada, on one of whose Arctic voyages a portion of this book was written; to the boys at the lab, 1939–45; and to Philip and Sue Gregory of Cassowary House, Queensland, Australia, from whose balcony, in March 2002, the author observed that rare bird, the Red-necked Crake.

My gratitude as well to astute early readers Sarah Cooper, Matthew Poulakakis, Jess Atwood Gibson, Ron Bernstein, Maya Mavjee, Louise Dennys, Steve Rubin, Arnulf Conradi, and Rosalie Abella; to my agents, Phoebe Larmore, Vivienne Schuster, and Diana Mackay; to my editors, Ellen Seligman of McClelland & Stewart (Canada), Nan Talese of Doubleday (U.S.A.), and Liz Calder of Bloomsbury (U.K.); and to my dauntless copyeditor, Heather Sangster. Also to my hardworking assistant, Jennifer Osti, and to Surya Bhattacharya, the keeper of the ominous Brown Box of research clippings. Also to Arthur Gelgoot, Michael Bradley, and Pat Williams; and to Eileen Allen, Melinda Dabaay, and Rose Tornato. And finally, to Graeme Gibson, my partner of thirty years, dedicated nature-watcher, and enthusiastic participant in the Pelee Island Bird Race of Ontario, Canada, who understands the obsessiveness of the writer.

ALSO BY MARGARET ATWOOD

Other Books in the MaddAddam Trilogy

THE YEAR OF THE FLOOD
Book II of the MaddAddam Trilogy

Set in the visionary future of Atwood's acclaimed *Oryx and Crake*, *The Year of the Flood* is at once a moving tale of lasting friendship and a landmark work of speculative fiction. In this second book of the MaddAddam trilogy, the long-feared waterless flood has occurred, altering Earth as we know it and obliterating most human life. Among the survivors are Ren, a young trapeze dancer locked inside the high-end sex club Scales and Tails, and Toby, who is barricaded inside a luxurious spa. Amid shadowy, corrupt ruling powers and new, gene-spliced life forms, Ren and Toby will have to decide on their next move, but they can't stay locked away.

Fiction/Literature

MADDADDAM
Book III of the MaddAddam Trilogy

The final volume of the internationally celebrated MaddAddam trilogy opens with the end of civilization. The Waterless Flood pandemic has wiped out most of the population. Toby is part of a small band of survivors based in the MaddAddamite cobb house. With them are the Children of Crake: the gentle, bioengineered quasi-human species who, it seems, will inherit this new Earth. As Toby tries to explain the origin of their circumstances to the curious Crakers, her tales cohere into a luminous oral history that sets down humanity's past—and points toward its future. Blending action, humor, romance, and an imagination at once dazzlingly inventive and grounded in a recognizable world, *MaddAddam* is vintage Atwood—a moving and dramatic conclusion to her epic work of speculative fiction.

Fiction/Literature

Other Books by Margaret Atwood

THE BLIND ASSASSIN

This Booker Prize–winning novel opens with these simple words: "Ten days after the war ended, my sister Laura drove a car off a bridge." The inquest report proclaims the death accidental, but the truth is slowly revealed throughout the life of Laura's sister, Iris.

Fiction/Literature

ALIAS GRACE

Grace Marks has been convicted for her involvement in the vicious murders of her employer, Thomas Kinnear, and his mistress. Simon Jordan, an expert in mental illness, listens to her story while bringing her back to the murderous day she cannot remember.

Fiction/Literature

ALSO AVAILABLE

Bluebeard's Egg
Bodily Harm
Cat's Eye
Dancing Girls
The Edible Woman
The Handmaid's Tale
In Other Worlds
Lady Oracle
Life Before Man
Negotiating With the Dead
The Robber Bride
Surfacing
Wilderness Tips

ANCHOR BOOKS
Available wherever books are sold.
www.anchorbooks.com